Where Are You?

Dave Copson

Where Are You?
Copyright © 2023 Dave Copson

All rights reserved, including the right to reproduce this book, or portions thereof in any form. No part of this text may be reproduced, transmitted, downloaded, decompiled, reverse engineered, or stored, in any form or introduced into any information storage and retrieval system, in any form or by any means, whether electronic or mechanical without the express written permission of the author.

This is a work of fiction. Names and characters are the product of the author's imagination and any resemblance to actual persons, living or dead, is entirely coincidental.

The views expressed in this work are solely those of the author and do not necessarily reflect the views of the publisher, and the publisher hereby disclaims any responsibility for them.

ISBN: 978-1-916696-23-5

For Jo, Matt and Rick.

Reviews for *Syrup and Cyanide*

Jan H.
Really enjoyed this as it gripped me from the beginning and there was lots of twist and turns to keep me interested a really good story with fantastic story telling.

Catherine Brookes
Fantastic book. I loved this book from start to finish, was a really exciting read. Characters well written, every chapter was really interesting. Highly recommend read. Well done, even keeps you guessing until the end!

Chloe Firth
A fun and fast mystery. This was a cleverly written book that felt reminiscent of classic mystery novels. The large cast of characters were well written and made for a fun experience trying to piece everything together. There were twists and turns throughout that I didn't see coming, which made for a satisfying conclusion. Thoroughly enjoyed and can't wait for more in the future.

Sylvie Adler
This book was an absolute page-turner! Well-written and believable characters. The author obviously knows the area well - everything well described. Almost felt you were there... Highly recommended!!!!

Susan H.
Well done to the author. His first book. Look forward to the next one. Not a reader usually, but once I started I was intrigued and couldn't put it down. Great story and kept me guessing.

Stu S.
What a great book. Great story line with an unsuspected twist. Thoroughly enjoyed from start to finish. Looking forward to Dave's next book.

E M Midwinter
Absolutely gripping. Fantastic book. Devoured the whole thing in 3 days, I couldn't put it down. Beautifully written with an awesome plot twist.

S. Bell
Must read. An enjoyable read from start to finish and very difficult to put down. A great twist at the end when the pieces finally come together. A recommended read and I'm very much looking forward to the author's next work.

Eleanor
Loved it. Brilliant book, with a fantastic, fast-paced plot and interesting characters. A well written book full of twists and surprises.

Claire Green
Gripping new author's first thriller. One hell of a first book!...Was riveted from the beginning, and totally did not guess at the end game! A new author, and can't wait to get his next book please!

Lesley Packer
Absolutely loved it!!! Can't wait for the next one.

Bill Smith
Quality writing from an exciting new author. Brilliant, a very exciting read, can't wait for the next one.

It's twice the fun and twice the grins,
And double the trouble when you're gifted with twins.

PROLOGUE

*Minneapolis, Minnesota.
Ten years ago.*

It was Saturday, an hour after dawn.

The foreboding lure of daylight seemed to infiltrate the house with a dreaded sinister fog and the girls were already awake. Any quality sleep had been impossible. They lay in their beds whispering to each other as quietly as they could. At each sound in the hall, they fell silent and listened intently, calculating his exact position. Their father was pacing around downstairs and could be heard humming contently, as always. If they were quiet, maybe he would forget they were there. Maybe forever with any luck.

Their shared bedroom, one of four in the house, had a large window that looked out across the heart of the city. If she stood on tiptoes, Elizabeth could just see the white fabric domed roof of The Metrodome, the home of her beloved Minnesota Vikings. She adored watching the N.F.L. games on tv and had been to the see them play at 'The Dome' with a few of her college friends and their parents. She lived and breathed everything about them and despite her friends' efforts to catch her out, she was the font of all knowledge when it came to their history. Her best friend, Caterina, used to remark that Elizabeth had purple, gold and white blood, in reference to the colours worn by her heroes. Elizabeth would frown when people rumoured that they would be knocking down The Dome in a couple of years and replacing it with a new and fancy stadium. Not that she could do a lot about that. It was fairly uncommon for teenage girls to be so besotted with the Vikings, but this one was. Pretty much all of the extra bits and pieces that had been added to the bedroom were Elizabeth's. There was quite a selection of Minnesota Vikings merchandise; the rug beside her bed, the flag that draped over the door to the ensuite, the pictures of her most recent Vikings heartthrob, the quilt cover and far too many scarves, according to her father. None of which belonged to her sister. Not that Elizabeth would ever deny her sister anything or refuse to share. It was…well, prohibited.

They both lay quietly, staring up at the elegant Italian-style false ceiling with its numerous spotlights that were inset into a deep blue night sky. 'Don't leave the stars on all night', their mother would say. But not anymore. How they wished she would. It was their safe place, especially when it was just them and the stars.

His inevitable call up the stairs echoed into their room, 'Elizabeth,' not an ounce of softness in his command. He always called her name when he wanted both of them to come from their room. They were old enough by now to have separate rooms but had always preferred to share. Elisha had in particular, and Elizabeth didn't mind. She didn't need to respond and had gotten used to being the centre of his attention. Each morning it was the same, whether it be for breakfast or college or anything else. As teenagers they were anything but rebellious. The girls got dressed quickly. Elisha held her sister's hand as they tentatively made their way down the wide and lavish oak-stained staircase to the dining room; Elizabeth with her deep brown eyes, customary chestnut pigtails and almost Mediterranean skin and Elisha, blue eyed with her straight, bedraggled, mousy hair, shadowing close behind her sister. Elizabeth always considered Elisha to be the one who possessed something special. 'Men can resist beauty, but they can't resist charm' she would tell her. Once more they passed the grand old picture frames of relatives they never knew. 'Worth a fortune', they were often told and yet to them they were just *there*. Empty faces housed in gaudy frames. Of no interest to teenagers.

Francoise met them at the bottom of the staircase and looked at them both with a wrinkled smile and sad eyes. She was their live-in nanny, the third that the girls could remember, and affectionately called them Betty and Ellie. Father never had. In fact, he rarely called Elisha anything. From the moment their mother passed away, taken cruelly by pneumonia just two years ago, the house had grown cold and empty. Her warmth and her love, just a memory.

On Saturday mornings the girls shared the breakfast table with Francoise. Commonly, this was quite a relaxed affair and something that the girls and Francoise enjoyed, a change from the stricter routines of the weekdays. In the absence of a need to rush urgently out, it would give them a chance to speak freely and exchange some gossip. *Girl's talk*. Francoise loved to hear about what was happening at college and who was the centre of the latest speculative stories, however unlikely they might seem. They liked Francoise very much and relished the chance to absorb themselves in the feminine contact that had vanished from the house, far too abruptly. Most mornings were rather frantic and time to chat was short as the girls were always hurrying to get fed and leave the house in readiness for their walk to college. Today, however, the dining room was eerie and silent. Francoise tried to catch the eye of each of the girls, but they sat, head down and stared at the task in front of them, breakfast. Even the smiles that they always exchanged when Francoise spoke French to them were absent this morning. They only glanced occasionally sideways as their father wandered in and out of the room, busying himself in preparation for something that the girls were dreading.

The previous evening, after their college work had been completed and their essays had been checked for any 'unacceptable' grammatical errors, he and the girls had been outside in the garden. The evening was slightly chilled by a gentle breeze that drew in some threatening-looking clouds, a precursor to a predicted darker sky and a promise of a heavy shower before nightfall.

'Dig it here, near the shed', their father had insisted, as he jammed the spade into the ground.

Elizabeth pleaded with her father that they didn't have to do this tonight, that in another week or two everything might be ok again. The veterinary had said so. He had been ill, but he was going to be alright for a little while longer. Their father would hear none of it and besides Elisha had already began working the spade into the peaty soil, digging for all she was worth, with an uncharacteristic eagerness, out of obligation rather than desire.

'Four feet by two feet,' he ordered, 'no more, no less,' as he turned dismissively and walked back into the house. Elisha didn't seem to hear. Before much longer she was standing in a hole, energetically removing the soil, flinging it everywhere. Elizabeth helped as much as she could but there was only one spade and father had made it clear precisely who would be doing the digging. Elizabeth used her hands to scoop as much loose soil as possible and throw it to one side. It gathered under her fingernails and coated her palms. Elisha stared straight into the hole that she was creating and hardly paused for breath. Sweat, beaded on both of the girl's brows as they worked, dripped from their noses. Elizabeth looked up to see their father was at the sitting room window. He was watching, but he wasn't watching her. He was watching Elisha. As Elizabeth stared up at him, he caught her eye and simply nodded towards the hole by way of a prompt for her to keep going. He studied their progress and even when the rain began to fall, he didn't budge. The girls were getting wetter as the downpour increased in ferocity, but his glare was unaltered. It was only when the hole appeared to be to his liking that he stepped away from the window. It was almost as if it was a sign for them to stop.

Elizabeth was a grubby sight, with mud on her sneakers and on the knees of her jeans but in contrast, Elisha was filthy, having slipped and slithered in the muddy creation a number of times. Her clothes were covered in mud. Both girls carefully prised off their footwear, trying desperately not to leave any clods of mud on the hall floor. Elizabeth peeled her jeans off and gently lowered them into the wash basket that Francoise had left at the foot of the stairs for them both, and bound up the stairs, two at a time, to get to the shower first. Elisha knew that she would have to disrobe down to her underwear before she would be permitted to go anywhere. As she began to strip off, her father appeared at the sitting room door and leaned casually against the frame. Instinctively, without the need to turn her head, she knew he was watching. As she began to undress, she felt her skin crawl. Elisha slowly slid her sodden jeans off her. They were heavy with earth and rain. She held them in one hand by the waistband and carefully dropped them into the basket with a thud. Then she drew her sweater over her head. It seemed to resist as the rain-soaked garment clung to her face and dragged against her filthy hair only adding to the dirt on her face. Even her socks were wet from standing in the hole that had begun to fill with water, so she took them off and dropped them in the basket too. Elisha took a step onto the first of the polished stairs and felt her foot slip. Carefully she made her way up towards the bedroom, and as she climbed the stairs, she could feel his attention upon her. She could feel his eyes and imagine the crooked sinister smirk on his face. Elisha shared his distain. When she reached the top of the stairs, she turned to look back down towards the hall. He had gone.

Once the girls had eaten as much of their breakfast as their knotted stomachs would allow, they helped to wash and clear the dishes away. Having endured an uncomfortable breakfast, the girls left Francoise alone and made their way into the hallway. They donned their wax jackets and scarves, put on their boots and stood, waiting for their father, just as they had on so many Saturday mornings. Elisha tucked the scarf that had been loaned by Elizabeth, under her collar. It was the only part of the week that he spent any quality time with them. It had become a ritual, and they dare not upset their father's routine; either of them.

He had a passion for the crossbow. Bowhunting, he called it, and had painstakingly taught the girls how to shoot. They had dutifully and attentively followed his instructions, becoming proficient over time to the cost of numerous woodland creatures, and without question as to the principal morality. Rabbits, Hares, Foxes, Birds and Feral Cats; all had become victim to his insatiable sporting prowess. The girls, too, had claimed several kills, some with a sense of achievement and many others with no more than a sense of duty. This morning, however, they would not be required to ensure that the weapons were in perfect condition or count out the bolts and put them into the big old wooden box that their father liked to carry them in. They would not be clambering into the back seat of his treasured Dodge Ram Pick-up and driving into the local woods, close to their Minneapolis home. There was no anticipation of a kill, at least not one that they wanted to be witness to. Despite their very brief and feeble protests he was insistent that they should be outside with him today. *To watch. To learn. To admire.*

The sky's clear, pale orange canvas welcomed the morning as the spring sunshine marbled onto the precisely mown lawn which stretched down to a white picket fence near to the roadway. It was beautifully edged and cared for by old Harry Bones, a retired postal worker who lived nearby and welcomed the extra cash. He had been very fond of the girls' mother and even though in his twilight years, he often helped her with the planting of many spring bulbs. Harry was as reliable as time. Nowadays he carried out his tasks with an empty heart.

Rays of hope glinted through the tall Red Pines that surrounded the garden and much of the impressive house with its pretentious double story balcony that encompassed the brightly coloured wooden-slated building. It was by far the largest property in the street and, by some way, the most impressive. To the girls, it was home but to their father it was no more than a trophy to wave in front of the neighbours. For him it stood for prestige. It was a mark of his success and his hard-earned position at the largest bank in Minneapolis. As a safe and secure family home it was a poor second. The dewy grass revealed the spider web patterns left by the footprints of a night fox; one that had scurried around in the small hours in search of an unsuspecting meal. Snowdrops shone beneath the Red Pines in carefully placed clusters giving their equinox encouragement to the advancing Spring days. When a large patio door gave a slight creak, Hastings looked up from the farthest part of the garden, turning his interest from a rustling House Wren, and watched as the three of them walked out from the rear of the house. The girls and their father. The girls followed him closely until he held a hand up, stopping them in their tracks.

The Serpent, one of Darton's best-selling crossbows, had become his pride and joy. Advertised as an easy cocking bow, he had decided that it would be ideal for the girls too. As with so many products nowadays there were a number of accessories, and the cocking aid provided the girls with a little help when loading up. He had searched high and low for the appropriate style of bow he desired, immediately adoring it. Its weight and balance were perfect. And he never missed his target. The two bows he had purchased for the girls were of a slightly older vintage, but still good enough for their 'apprenticeship.' Today, however, only one bow counted. His.

'You must watch. You and her, you might learn something,' their father had said in a condescending fashion as he cocked and loaded the crossbow. Safety engaged.

Elizabeth, to her father's right, began to open her mouth to speak but knew it was pointless. All she could do was dig her fingernails into her palms in the hope that the pain would somehow divert her thoughts from the inexorable punishment unfolding in front of her eyes. Elisha stood motionless to her father's left, half-hidden under the canopy of the aged and rugged apple tree, close to the shed and the hole that she had sweated to create the previous evening. Her face now completely pale; blank and staring at the old, decrepit and weary family dog. The faces of the two girls grimaced, their lips tightened, and their eyes were already beginning to close to a squint as the first of the tears trickled out. Elizabeth took a pace back towards the sanctuary of the old house.

'Stand still, Elizabeth,' he said, 'You do not move when the crossbow is raised,' his expression serious, his voice unmistakably clear, as he shouldered the buttstock and disengaged the safety, 'Watch.'

Even though she had cupped her hands to cover her ears as she scampered, disobediently, back into the house, she still heard the sound of the weapon's action and the brief but pitifully sickening yelp from Hastings as the bolt hit him. Francoise held her tightly as she curled up on the stairs. The two of them comforted each other and buried their heads onto the other's shoulder. A few minutes later there was another bolt, as The Serpent delivered a further fatal missile. Elizabeth was trembling severely. They could both hear him speaking outside, but the words were not clear. The only comprehensible sound was when he shouted Elisha's name; just once, very loudly, and then silence. By the time she had reached her bedroom and thrown herself headlong onto the comforter that lay rucked and bedraggled on the top of her purple and gold Minnesota Vikings quilt cover, it was over.

Elizabeth lay there in a sort of stunned silence for what seemed like ages. She had lost all track of time. She didn't know whether she had been asleep or not. But she was awake now, her eyes still wet with tears. Unfortunately, it had not been a dream. She was gripping her bedclothes tightly in her hands. The sharp pains from where her nails had dug in reminded her again that this really was happening. She inspected the blood-stained crescents in her palms. As she drew her comforter over herself, she jumped with a start as the bedroom door opened suddenly and struck the wardrobe. Elisha stared ahead into the room, her eyes fixed and cold. Her jeans and boots were, once again, thick with mud, and her jacket was smeared red and covered in white dog hairs. Her hands dripped with blood which sat in spots on the polished floor. What the ghostly Elisha said without the slightest change in her expression, chilled Elizabeth to the bone.

'I'm a good girl, Daddy said I am.'

And then she saw it...

In Elisha's left hand was something white. A droplet of blood trickled down it and dripped onto the bedroom floor. Elizabeth swung a leg off the bed and had put one foot onto the rug beside it when she realised precisely what she was looking at. Hanging limp in Elisha's hand was the grotesque sight of Hastings' severed tail.

ONE

Now

Marc Sutton was already cursing the fact that the reduced number of buses available to him on yet another damp morning, meant that his journey into work would, undoubtedly, be filled with even more chaos than usual. Another trudge along the path that enabled him to cut through the park, past the High School, and onwards towards the main road wasn't what he was relishing right now as he gathered his rucksack and coat from the hallway. The sound of something soft and tranquil emanated from the radio in the bedroom where Grace was enjoying a lie in. No school today. Teacher training day didn't start until 11 and she was determined to make the most of the luxury of an extra couple of hours in bed, something to do with the caretaker not being able to open up as early as usual. But nobody minded. When the alarm had sounded at 6, Sutton had instinctively jumped out of bed and headed for the bathroom. All Grace did was request that he didn't bound around like a new puppy and ruin her treasured extended rest. He had looked back at her, resisting the temptation of joining her under the warm quilt, and plodded into the bathroom, courteously closing the door quietly and '*keeping the noise down*' as she had requested. After his shower he wandered back into the bedroom and thought about dropping his damp towel over Grace but decided that she might not find it funny. *Perhaps he should get in beside her after all,* he thought. He chose to get ready for work rather than end up late. Sitting downstairs he checked his messages but found very few of interest. The plan for the day would be exactly as it was for every day. See what happens. Once he was sure that he wasn't about to leave something important behind, he wandered down the Victorian hallway, turned at the bottom of the stairs and called to Grace.

'I'll see you later. Don't forget we're going to that Italian tonight. Don't go flying round to your Mum's and forget.'

'I won't forget, I'm not stupid, you know. Anyway, if anyone is going to forget it'll be you.'

'When has that ever happened?' he said, knowing full well what was coming next.

'Give me a couple of days and I'll draw up a list.'

'Sorry, can't wait that long. Have a good day at school. See you tonight. Love you.'

'Love you more, bye.'

It was just three days into the industrial action that had led to his, often quite relaxing trip, becoming grossly unpleasant. He'd done the maths and knew that less buses with the same number of people was a recipe for disaster. Once again, as he lined up at the bus stop, along with the regular crowd of school kids that were swinging bags and pushing and shoving for 'pole position', and ladies with their wheeled shopping trollies, like something out of *Chariots of Fire,* he regretted that he hadn't been able to use the car.

He could have done exactly that if he hadn't dropped the car into the local garage four days ago for what he believed was to be a quick repair, only to get the phone call later the same day and learn that the 'quick repair' had turned into a lengthy search for the correct part which, as ever with these things, would have to be ordered and ferried from heaven knows where. Tormented by the bad timing of his car being rendered out of action, and the recent London Transport dilemma, he refocused on the next challenge that was about to raise his blood pressure; that of holding his place in the queue that was beginning to lose its orderly shape and try to avoid the inevitable battle to find a seat on the approaching bus that would, very likely, already be at bursting point.

Turning right at the end of Willow Lane, Detective Chief Inspector Campbell Blackery strode purposefully onto Old Clapton Street. He hadn't needed the umbrella that was now tucked under his arm like a ceremonial baton, albeit the forecast suggested otherwise. His gleaming shoes beaded from the splash of the puddles, left by the overnight rain, as he walked towards the Police Station at the far end of the street. Once upon a time, the street had extended further along but following a large warehouse fire, the area had been closed to all traffic and eventually sealed off to all and sundry. The plan soon after the fire had been to turn the waste ground into a large recreational area with picnic benches and even a man-made lake with rowing boats, but the diminishing council budget had put that firmly on the back burner. Extra security, including numerous CCTV cameras were fitted, and plenty of razor wire, although unsightly, was erected to deter anyone foolish enough to try to find their way into the Police

Station from anywhere but the front entrance. The station itself had a huge footprint and an impressive feature. The turret that pointed skywards perched on one corner of the building. Its rounded brickwork and black tiled dome could be seen from several streets away. The local residents would have their children believe that that's where the worst of the criminals were kept. Locked in the tower with only barred windows to gaze at the outside world from. An unlikely story. Nowadays however, it was just an empty space and nothing more than a gothic-looking tower. As DCI Blackery stepped through the front doors of the old station his only concern was getting upstairs to his office and checking on whatever had been going on during the previous night. His laptop served as his diary which would give him an idea of how many tedious meetings he might have to attend. He already knew that a local councillor wanted desperately to speak with him about the current Youth Crime Prevention Programmes and to plague him about what the police were doing about the ever-increasing anti-social behaviour problems in and around one of the nearby estates. These issues were something that he often tried to shift onto someone else but on this occasion the councillor in question was an old friend and one that had been very generous in the past. He didn't like to disappoint, which in translation meant that he couldn't think of a feasible enough excuse with which to rid himself of the bother.

Marc Sutton sat next to an elderly lady on the bench seat towards the front of the 18C, waiting patiently for his stop to rescue him from the current claustrophobic crush inside the bus. *Can't imagine doing this every day,* he thought. He wondered once more just how long the part his car needed was going to take. Eagerly waiting for a call from the garage he looked down at his phone but there was no missed call, no hopeful text message, and no chance of getting into work any quicker. He looked out of the front window and gave a despondent sigh. As he sat, rocking gently with the bus's suspension as it reacted to the contours of the road, he gave some thought to what might be on his agenda when he finally got to work. There were a number of different people that he would like to be able to speak with. Some of whom he knew he never would. But there was always hope. Maybe one day the mysteries that always seemed to land on his desk would start to become clearer. He thought of Grace enjoying her lazy start to the day and wished he was beside her. She'd be up and ready by now though. She would be showered and dressed and planning her day. He could never quite make out how she always seemed to look so amazing. Even if she was dishevelled, she still radiated and glowed like a brand-new mother. *Maybe next time,* he reflected, sombrely. Teacher training day meant that there were not going to be any children getting under her feet for the whole day. He knew she was looking forward to that in particular, and yet he also knew it was all she really wanted.

As the bus drew to a halt, he and several other people raised from their seats and bustled their way along towards the exit. As he stepped down onto the street, he felt the cold shock of rainwater enter his shoe and chill his foot. *Damn it.* All he wanted to do now was get to his desk and end this infuriating journey. *Please fix my car soon.* He strode onward with a new determination and made short work of the rest of his walk. He could see the old turret now and knew he was almost out of the damp for a few hours before having to repeat his battle with the buses again later in the day. With less than 200 yards to go before he reached his destination; he felt his phone vibrate in his trouser pocket and could hear its faint message alert tone. *Might be the garage,* he thought. With one hand delving to retrieve it and trying not to slow his pace, he dug it out. The message from DCI Blackery simply read: *Get a move on. A girl's gone missing.*

TWO

*Malia, Crete.
One month ago.*

The hot, late afternoon sun reflected against the window opposite, causing him to raise a hand over his brow every so often to shield his eyes. He could still feel its burn on his skin as if he needed any reminding of its unyielding intensity. The dust that gathered daily on the busy main street gusted up from the guttering as a passing truck, its cloud following the old and barely roadworthy vehicle further along the main street towards the central church of Agios Nektarios, rumbled loudly past. He watched the single brake light briefly illuminate its intention to slow just enough for a group of youths that had chanced their luck, skipping between the truck and a taxi, at the intersection with Zachariadi or 'Beach Road,' as it was locally known, which joins further down to Dimokratias before ending the run of shops, clubs and bars at one end of Nissos Beach. The truck's horn blared out as it journeyed on across the junction that led out of Malia and onwards towards Crete's capital city, Heraklion, 21 miles further west. The ubiquitous swarm of scooters diced with cars and buses, slipping through tiny gaps that made him wince in anticipation of a collision; a fairly regular occurrence and something he had witnessed several times since he'd arrived here. Children and dogs perched perilously on the footplates between the knees of the riders. Shopping bags swung on the handlebars and travelled precariously between feet as they were ferried home. All part of the normal daily risks taken, seemingly unwittingly, by the locals. He dared to imagine what it must have been like before the Malia by-pass was finally opened.

His heavy, sun-dried hand clasped gratefully around a tall glass of cold water. His muscular tanned arms were crusted with sand as was most of his body. He wore a black and white t-shirt with a crazed pattern which made it look like a piece of shattered glass, a pair of old frayed denim shorts, and sandals. It was fast approaching shower time. He would look a lot smarter in an hour or two. His day at Siren's Beach Hotel, situated on the north coast of the island which sat in the southern half of the Aegean Sea, was done. Parasols and sun beds; he'd seen enough of them to last a lifetime. As the cold, refreshing water soothed his dry throat he looked up above the shops opposite. Telegraph poles had poorly tethered bunches of wires hanging within reach of the balconies and thick cables hung far too close to the passing coaches for his liking. Finches in birdcages battled in vain against the street noise from below. Ornate wrought iron balconies sat above the clothes shops that sported all the up-to-date football shirts. Those of the more popular Premiership teams blended in with those of Barcelona, Real Madrid and Bayern Munich, each of them dangling and blowing upon hangers above the shop entrance like the swaying crowds they excited. Eva was there at the doorway, almost wrapped in a colourful beach towel that had blown in the wind from the traffic and captured her in its grasp. She was doing her best to entice passers-by inside. Her mother sat on a white plastic chair and waved at the children. Holiday makers continued to bustle along the main street of the old coastal town, many of them young and either unaware, or too disinterested, in the municipality's Minoan archaeology. The '2 for 1 bars' and the locations of the nightclubs were much more familiar. He hauled himself off his comfortable chair and stepped inside the café to pay, but as had become a regular occurrence, he was waved away. '*Oxi*, Kevin.' Giannis returned his gratitude for the help he had received a month ago when Kevin had assisted him by loading and unloading numerous heavy boxes that had arrived unexpectedly. Giannis was stuck and he had offered his muscle power. When a rare gap in the traffic chaos appeared, he crossed the road and greeted Eva, 'Kalispera, Kevin,' she responded.

'Kalispera, Mama,' he said to the old lady who smiled and nodded her approval at his gesture. The bumbag that housed his wallet was in the grip of one hand as he plodded slowly along past a store with a plentiful supply of fruit and vegetables that spilled out onto the pavement. With all the people milling along and the scooters stopping announced anywhere they wanted to, there wasn't much room for anyone. Sometimes walking on the path could be almost as precarious as walking in the road, what with the crowds and the missing or broken paving. The tarmac on the road itself was smooth and could be slippery even when dry, which was the norm, but if it was wet it became even more treacherous. Turning left, past the hoard of taxis, with the impressive church in front of him, he ambled on past Alexis Taverna, noticing only that Georgios was not at his usual table at the front of the restaurant ready to exchange a hearty handshake and a warm 'Ti kanis'. The old town of Malia offered him some solitude as he wandered on past Avli Restaurant and up through the ever-narrowing streets towards its centre, dodging around seemingly abandoned scooters left close to the doorways of the dimly lit houses. As if a switch had turned off the drone of the vehicles, the comparative calmness of the old town soothed him and was always well received. Cats of all shapes and sizes and colours and ages were everywhere to be seen. Kittens could be seen peering out from derelict buildings with big, bright eyes. Most of them were out in the evening and regularly sat looking as angelic as possible close to the restaurant tables of their favourite haunts in the hope that, just maybe, something might be dropped down for them to eat. The finches could be heard again, and the elderly Greek folk sat on the shady side of the street, on more white plastic chairs and stools brought out from their houses. Turning left towards the old centre along Agiou Dimitriou, he passed a new shiny, almost anachronistic ATM, positioned on the wall of an ancient building where a group of girls were giggling as they wrestled with the instructions. Their pale skin suggested to him that they were probably recent arrivals.

'You have to select your language,' he said, glancing across and noticing a number of national flags that were presented on the screen.

'It should be in English,' a girl replied.

'You are in Greece, so why should it?' he said.

'Because we're English,' she responded, oblivious to how things really worked.

You don't say, he thought.

He'd heard enough and decided to let them fend for themselves, stifling the comment he wanted to make. He didn't really care whether they got their money out or not. After another 200 metres he walked past the shop where he would spend his evening. The Honeycomb was a relatively new shop. It faced out onto the square adjacent to Agios Dimitrios Church and across from Christina and Spiros Restaurant, a rather lovely building with several tables outside on the tiled area that sat before the tarmac. As the name suggested, The Honeycomb sold honey that had been collected in the mountains of eastern Crete. There was also plenty of olive oil along with the traditional Raki which many restaurants on the island served at the end of a splendid meal. It would sometimes be flavoured with honey or lemon or peach but, as far as he was concerned, there was only one thing that Raki should be mixed with and that was more Raki. He briefly wondered how the rather ignorant girl would cope with her first taste of *firewater,* as it was sometimes known. He was sure that the waiters enjoyed watching the tourists, especially if they knew they were first time visitors, as they downed their first Raki. He could imagine how they might allow themselves a sense of enjoyment as they watched it being drank down in one go, and then waited for the inevitable reaction as their all too eager customers swiftly found out about the afterburn. *Firewater.*

The Honeycomb had a few soft and welcoming chairs positioned outside the shop which provided customers with an opportunity for a relaxing coffee whilst they sat and absorbed the warm and peaceful atmosphere of the Old Town. Bougainvillea twisted and tangled amongst the overhead wires that fed the phonelines to a number of restaurants, delighting tourists with its pink and white and orange flowers. After turning right into Arkadiou and entering through the front door of the Old House the only thing on his mind was a shower, after which, he would reappear in a clean white shirt and smart black trousers and go along to one of his favourite restaurants in the old town of Malia; Petrino Inn with its full grape vines clinging to the beams that supported them and its soft Greek music. The scented waft of Jasmine acted like a therapy on him. A rather lovely old lemon tree, planted in one corner, was always a popular area to sit. The setting sun shone across a barren piece of ground to one side of the restaurant before finally conceding to the horizon. The candlelight took over from thereon and the comparative coolness of the evening aided those covered in moisturising cream. He had visited this particular restaurant many times and never tired of the genuine welcome that came from its hosts. Amelia and Thanasis were delightful. A different and more expensive pair of sandals would provide the comfortable footwear that his weary legs yearned for, having been on his feet for a lot of the day. But first, that shower. He stripped off and wasted no time getting under the steady flow of the soothing cool water. Sand gathered around his feet as he lathered his body. The shower was surprisingly powerful by Greek standards. He had experienced several others that were no more than a trickle. The much-needed shower invigorated him almost immediately, revitalising his muscular aches and pains. Stepping into the bedroom he looked at his reflection in the mirror. He had worked at his suntan and was looking very bronzed. He glanced down at the confirmation email that he'd left on the dressing table, displaying his flight information. His large holdall was mostly packed. Just one more shift to do at The Honeycomb. *I'll miss that place,* he thought. He had enjoyed the warmth of Crete and had made a number of good friends. He'll miss the mountains and the way they change colour as the sun drops from the skyline each evening. He'll miss the bustle of Malia and the solitude of the peaceful old town. He'll miss walking down to the local spring to fetch ice cold water and sitting outside on Christmas day in 25 degrees. Somewhat reluctantly, the time had come for him to return to England, and to leave his days in Crete as Kevin Marshall behind him for good.

THREE

Now

DI Marc Sutton's heart thumped an extra beat as he replaced his mobile phone into his trouser pocket. His mind's eye pictured another potentially gruesome scene as he made his way along Old Clapton Street towards the station. The antiquated Police lantern, sometimes referred to as a Tardis lamp, appeared proudly in his view. There used to be two of them, perched on either side of the main entrance but one had ironically been stolen, of all things! He bounded up the steps two at a time and shouldered the door which led him immediately into the rather grand vestibule. The décor had not been changed in this particular section of the building for many years and its Victorian ceiling with its intricately decorative plaster covings and elegant cornices did indeed make for an impressive entrance. A set of double doors opened automatically for him as he entered the modernised, main part of the ground floor. It was rarely quiet in Old Clapton Street Police Station at any time of the normal working day, and today was no exception. The noise hit him as soon as he began to make his way through the crowd that had gathered at the front desk. Voices were elevated to an unnecessary pitch and a number of the local people, some of which he recognised as residents from the nearby estate, began to jostle as he tried not to get drawn into whatever it was that they were unhappy about. Usually, it was a series of complaints that the Police had failed to attend to as quickly as they wanted or that there had been a house broken into, a car stolen, or a family feud which wasn't exactly unheard of in that area of the neighbourhood. The only words that struck him amongst the hullaballoo were 'missing since Saturday morning'.

Marc Sutton's office on the first floor was adjacent to that of DCI Campbell Blackery and as part of the Violent Crime Task Force it was rarely anything other than overloaded with any number of unsolved cases. As he reached to open the door, he heard the anything but dulcet tones of Blackery barking into the office telephone. Inside his little piece of sanctuary, Sutton took off his damp coat and prized off his right shoe in order that he could remove the offending wet sock. He wheeled his chair across to the radiator and draped the garment over it. As he did so, his office door opened.

'Took your bloody time, didn't you? I've had the world and her mother downstairs creating about some girl who hasn't come home for two days,' a very broad Scottish accent announced.

'I've had to take the bus. Car's in the garage. Do you fear it's an abduction then?' Sutton responded.

'Don't know yet but nothing would surprise me lately. The last one didn't end well though, if I remember rightly,' commented Blackery, as he peered sternly at Sutton.

The Detective Chief Inspector grew up on a farm that was run by his father, and hailed from Montrose, a town and former royal burgh in Angus, Scotland. He was a large, imposing man with a voice to match. His cheeks were always slightly reddened as if he was a little flushed. A nasty looking scar was visible on his balding, domed head and a slight dip in his skull was evident. The rumour that he had had his brain removed at some point was rife amongst everyone but him. His Policing career began 38 miles further north of Montrose, in Dundee. 20 years ago, Blackery moved from his beloved Scotland and relocated to London, working in the City, following what is believed to be a particularly toxic divorce. His reputation for being a philanderer soon began to follow him around like an unshakable shadow. The number of awkward occurrences he had entered into in Montrose was something of a lottery. Nobody knew for sure but that didn't stop the gossips having a field day. Blackery was also considered a bit of a bully and the bulk of the japes were confined to the locker room or to the pub after work. It was rumoured that he climbed the promotional ladder with a certain amount of force and intimidation. His posting as a Detective Inspector at Bishopsgate in the City of London suited him fine but was interrupted by another need to move on in an effort to avoid a certain attentive woman. It was expected that she probably needed to see the back of him rather than the other way around.

Sutton's sock was merrily steaming on the hot radiator, infusing a damp odour into the air, much to Blackery's annoyance.

'For fuck's sake man, put the bloody thing back on,' he insisted.

Sutton picked it off the radiator and wafted it around purely to be irritating. The desired effect was duly achieved with ease, as he knew it would be.

'Will you be useful and find out what's going on downstairs, and put that blessed thing back on your foot,' he droned.

The more agitated he got, the more 'Scottish' he became. The DCI hurried back to his own office and closed the door. *Mission accomplished,* thought Sutton, allowing himself a satisfying grin.

Rather than commit himself into the middle of the melee that had been taking place at the front desk, Sutton phoned a request for the details to be brought up to him as soon as they were available. Within the next 5 minutes DS Carrie Linton appeared at Sutton's door and gave a courteous tap on the frame as she came in and placed the paperwork with the full details he had requested on his desk. DS Linton was an old schoolfriend of Grace's, Sutton's wife. She had visited their home a number of times and had meals there too. She had also been on Blackery's list of potential casual acquaintances but was made of stronger stuff. Linton's 4th Dan in karate was enough to make him think twice, especially as she had made a point of telling him by way of a subtle, clear warning at an early stage in his arrival at Old Clapton Street. The stories that had travelled down the 'grapevine' ahead of him were all she needed to know.

Sutton thanked Carrie and turned his attention to the information in front of him and began to consider the details that related to the missing girl. Angelica Rowntree was 21 years old and still living at home on the local Lavender Road Estate, half a mile from the station. She was last seen around 10a.m. on Saturday morning. It was now Monday. *Teacher training day,* he thought. Briefly his mind turned to Grace as he wondered how she was. Coping admirably with herself wrapped around a cuppa, if he knows her. *Off to the Italian in Bazeley Street tonight. Must try to get away in time.*

The 6"x4" photo of Angelica Rowntree that had been provided by her parents looked up at him. Dark, perhaps auburn hair and brown eyes. A few freckles across the bridge of her nose and a smile that looked as though butter wouldn't melt. The attached notes reported that her parents considered her to be a sensible girl. She had worked at the nearby garage as a trainee mechanic since leaving college. *Good for her.* She went out of the house at approximately 10a.m and her parents thought that she was headed for the garage, as she sometimes did a shift on a Saturday morning, but they weren't clear as to whether she actually went there or not. Either way she hadn't returned by the late afternoon and wasn't responding to her phone. Something cramped in Sutton's stomach. He didn't like the sound of it even though she could have gone to see any one of her mates, but if she was as sensible as they had said then why didn't she make contact. The feeling he had lurking inside reminded him of the case of the missing girl from three years ago. She had lived in Church

Close, only a stone's throw away from the station. A search of the immediate area had proved fruitless, as had several further investigations into her whereabouts. Not a soul had seen her. It wasn't until one of the workmen who was carrying out some maintenance at the Bus Depot reported something odd at the rear of the premises, that she was eventually found. In the furthest reaches of the bus garage, behind the vehicle wash area and underneath a heap of discarded furniture which resembled the makings of a bonfire, lay the body of Haley Breen. She had been wrapped in a bedsheet which had absorbed some of her bodily fluid. Her hands and feet had been bound tightly with tape. None of her personal belongings were ever found. She wore only her bra on the top half of her body which had begun to reach the more advanced stages of decomposition. The pathologist at the time had established that she had received a single puncture wound to the right side of her neck which was recorded as the cause of death. Her hair had also been cut and a small wound on the back of her head had been recorded. She had been lying there for around 8-10 days, unnoticed except by the rats who had been regular visitors. Haley Breen was 18 and had gone missing following a night out with friends. Her walk home in the opposite direction to her friends had left her exposed and potentially at risk. They had left the pub as it closed and separated from there. Sutton reached into his filing cabinet and got out the folder that had Haley's name at the top of it. He didn't know why he felt the need to look again, but instinctively he pulled out the glossy A4 photos of Haley Breen's body. The case had greatly frustrated him and caused more than a few restless nights. On many occasions he had woken up in an armchair, having quietly left the bedroom so as not to disturb Grace. Whoever had been responsible for this heinous act had certainly gone to great lengths to ensure that there was nothing in the way of useful evidence left at or around the scene. There was no known motive for her disappearance and no answers as to why she had been murdered. Despite a thorough investigation, the case went cold. The bedsheet and the tape around her extremities led nowhere. CCTV had not existed at the Bus Depot. Sutton had been the one who was the most disillusioned about the outcome. He felt there was an answer just waiting for him to unearth, but nothing had ever come to light. Everything about Haley Breen's murder had followed an all-too-common pattern. A young, attractive girl, vulnerable, alone in the dark and eerie side streets of East London. Just another victim of an opportunist, or so it appeared. She was not sexually assaulted and had not been beaten or drugged. There was no estranged boyfriend or dysfunctional family. Whoever had taken her from the streets had kept her long enough to wrap her up and tie her. Maybe that was so she was easier to move around and dump. There was simply nothing to go on. Nothing except the one thing that plagued Marc Sutton. The one thing, and one thing alone, that focussed his attention. The *'tattoo'*. It wasn't a professional job and could hardly be called such. It had been scratched deeply onto her right shoulder, presumably by her killer. Going by the blood stain at the wound site, she had not been dead at the time it was done. Not quite anyway. Sutton grimaced at the cruelty of this act. No tattooists gun, no cleanliness or care had been taken. Just what appeared to be a sharp nail or maybe a sharpened screwdriver. Not the tools of the skilled tattooist but the gruesome work of a cruel, heartless killer who for some unknown reasons, needed to leave a signature.

FOUR

When the morning finally arrived, Kevin Marshall awoke and thumped his hand down onto the top of his alarm, frantically searching for the button that would return his cloudy world to a gentle silence and turned over in bed doubting for a brief moment as to whether he should even bother to show up but decided that it was too good to miss. *It's not every day you get to witness something like this,* he thought. Actually, you never should. His first glance out of the window of his rented room told him that it was not raining now. The mountains were shrouded in low cloud as the mist crawled its way over the tops of the trees. He wished that the weather was better for his *special day* but there was nothing he could do about that. The Crete sunshine was far away. He looked across the room at the holdall that he had packed the previous night and thought about the drive, deciding that it was not exactly enticing. The puddles confirmed that there had been a substantial downpour during the night; one that had woken him twice. The rain had run down the adjacent roof of the car paint sprayers and drained continually into the crooked guttering with its broken hopper, and dripped water onto a steel drum. Every annoying droplet bouncing with a frustrating regularity. He dragged himself away from the window and stood in the modest kitchen area leaving the light off, preferring to pull up a blind a few inches and fumble for the kettle in the half-light. His eyes weren't quite ready for a shock just yet. He reached for the toaster, that had been working when it felt like it lately and optimistically slotted in a couple of slices of bread. It accepted his offering on the fourth attempt. Maybe slamming the lever down with gradually increasing force wasn't the best of tactics. Still, he wouldn't be needing to replace it, he wouldn't be here long enough to worry about that. The previous evening, he had driven to the garage in North Keel, on the west side of the village, and had made sure that the car was fuelled up to the gunwales, ready for the journey. In three hours, he would need to be in position if he was going to make it on time. He would head off soon hoping that his trip would be trouble free as far as the traffic was concerned.

An hour later he was well clear of the village, enjoying the benefit of better roads and aiming straight and true in the direction of the motorway. His view was still restricted to the mountain roads and the flooded rivers and streams that combine to attract numerous walkers throughout the year, even when it snows. Just another 160 miles to go with an old, temperamental car radio for accompaniment. He'd got a fair amount of use out of the car in the recent weeks and couldn't really complain at that. As the day got closer, he often considered staying in the quiet, stone-walled village forever and never appearing outside of it again, but there were places to go and people to see. They wouldn't necessarily be seeing him though.

As he travelled on, the view of the mountains in his rear-view mirror diminished and familiar old place names came and went. Beside him on the front passenger seat was the mobile phone that he had infrequently used, and which would be discarded long before he reached his destination. There would be time to buy another, better version soon enough. He'd even thought to make himself a packed lunch before he left. It was likely to be a long day and he knew that if he could eat as he went along then he could keep moving. His recent life had revolved around good planning, and he knew he couldn't afford to take his mind from the job in hand now. This was a momentous day in a long and painful process, the success of which would depend upon care and concentration. He was just a few hours away from being in the very situation that people generally spent all their lives avoiding. For him, it simply had to be done.

Journey done, he pondered the scene about to befall him and sat silently in the car that he had parked an hour ago behind an old disused tractor shed that was once part of a busy farm in the quiet village of Cobbe's Chapel. Nowadays it was used for storage of some sort. The sign for Grady's Farm remained above the main entrance. The cattle sheds had been converted into substantial outbuildings and the old original rickety gates had been replaced by a more substantial, solid sliding door with exposed spikes pointing skywards on the top. The concrete drive into the old farm showed evidence of the amount it had been put to good use by local farmers and the people that shared the use of the large barns and outbuildings. Straw, blown around by the exposed site, littered the hardstanding. Well-rusted, disused farm equipment sat in full view like exhibits in a rural graveyard. Sections of the corrugated roof of one of the barns pointed to the heavens, looking like they could easily become completely dislodged. Victims of another harsh storm.

The spot he had chosen was away from the road, away from people. He had been here a few times before in the past and had driven onwards but today was different. Today was an important day. Not supposed to be special for him but in one, significant way, it was. When he had seen enough, he would drive the back way, straight out of the village and away towards the motorway once more and back into his world of secrets to a new location and to plan his next move. Greedily, he scoffed at a sandwich in an effort to satisfy his rumbling stomach. It was good. He checked his watch that confirmed to him that he had about another 10 minutes before he had to move. His position was elevated sufficiently that he could see the road that he would be taking after the main event had been and gone. From there it would be a matter of finding another place to lie low until he could assemble his thoughts and make sense of his past and then decide upon the order in which he was going to play out the next phase.

All too quickly, the time had arrived for him to leave the car and make his way around to the secluded rear of the old church about 50 metres from his chosen spot. He stepped cautiously out of the driver's seat ensuring that he had the hood of his coat over his head. The muddy track was drying, and the clods of earth were firm. He wore sturdy Hunters Wellington boots that he had changed into whilst he sat waiting, jeans and a thick Parka coat which, from a distance, ensured he would easily pass for anyone except himself. The largest of the old sheds was ideal cover and provided a number of decent views through the twisted iron and missing windows. Stealthily, he crept quietly into position. Happy with his view, he made himself as comfortable as possible as he leaned against a stone wall and gathered his coat around him. Now all he had to do was wait. But he didn't have to wait for long. From his vantage point he could see a couple of cars that were slowing in readiness to turn into the driveway that led to the car park at the front of the church. He didn't recognise them, but he could have a damned good guess at who might be travelling inside. The two vehicles parked side by side, but nobody got out. He could see the figures inside moving about. He zipped his Parka a little more and wished that they would hurry up. Standing around for too long out in the bleak countryside would soon have him chilled to the bone and desperate for the warmth of the car heater. Another three cars signalled and turned into the driveway 5 minutes behind the first arrivals and promptly parked up. At that moment he was immediately distracted by a large HGV that had appeared to his right and began turning into the old farm. The sound of the heavy vehicle's hissing brakes was unmistakably indicative of the driver's intention to slow before turning into the driveway. He allowed himself a slight glance around the hood of his coat, hoping that the truck would keep rolling gently in. He could see it was a very pale blue vehicle and recognised it as a similar one to that that he had seen on a previous visit. The sounds made by the tyres rolling over the stony ground, the steady increased rumble of the engine and the creaking of the bodywork under the weight of its load, was all he needed to be sure that nobody was going to start asking any questions and become a nuisance now that the show was about to begin.

When he looked back towards the cars, he could see that a few people had alighted from their vehicles and gathered in a sort of huddle, no doubt to exchange pleasantries. Probably fifteen of them. He smirked when he caught sight of some of them carrying small bouquets. *Really? How touching.* He began to spot one or two familiar faces. Faces that would not be seeing him today. He was far enough away from the proceedings not to be noticed and yet just close enough to see what was going on. He'd subconsciously hoped for more people to show but then it'd been a while. *Here today, gone tomorrow,* he thought. He had considered using binoculars but realised that he would look rather conspicuous and more than a little suspicious, so that idea was shelved. When he spotted a couple of particularly familiar faces, he couldn't control another cynical smirk. *Well, well.* Hand in hand with a man braver than he, was Betty Nelson. He expected her to be here but did wonder whether her companion was a significant other or not. When he had lived with Betty, Matt Richards had been a friend and neighbour to them both. Maybe that was all he was even now, but why should he care? It was nothing more than water under the bridge. *Good luck if you're committed to that one.* As the group started to move towards the entrance, and into the church for the memorial service, he found himself scanning all the faces, looking for another *significant other*, but he couldn't identify all of them. Just Betty and Matt and a few old mates from the days of old. The rest, he guessed, were likely to be her friends or friends of friends, perhaps. Support for her but not necessarily for the poor departed. He didn't suppose that they would be terribly welcome, but then it was probably all about her. Briefly, the scene served to remind him of his parents' funerals following the tragic road accident on the autobahn on the outskirts of Munich, thirteen years ago. His father had met his mother in Germany when on a business trip, a trip that ultimately led to him moving to Germany where they eventually married. As their only son, he was born in Bonn, about 50 miles from Dusseldorf and just south of the city of

Cologne with its twin-spired cathedral and it's sweeping river views. He was schooled there but didn't stay beyond his early adult life, moving to England and living with an aunt until she too, passed away. As the group filed inside and he lost sight of them, another car rolled down the driveway towards the church. The black BMW held his attention, as if, subconsciously, he *needed* to watch it approaching. He was getting colder by the minute now and his fingers were stiffening but he couldn't take his eyes off the gleaming car. Almost silently, it parked at the rear of the parking area. He considered that he could sit in the car and begin to defrost a little, but his feet were glued to the spot and his inquisitiveness was in full control. And then she stepped out. The guest he had not been able to forget. He couldn't mistake her, it was the way that she walked in a sexy, slinky way that confirmed it for him. *Another kind gesture of closure for a lost soul?* A sort of send-off for a missing person…presumed dead. The final nail in the coffin, so to speak.

The memorial service for Karter Swann was both necessary and timely, not because he was dead, but because he needed to be. As Kevin Marshall, he could continue his life, albeit secretly.

FIVE

Bazeley Street was within walking distance of Sutton's house so there was no need to make any arrangements for a taxi to ferry Marc and Grace Sutton to and from their favourite Trattoria. The informal atmosphere was the thing that they liked the most. That and the fabulous food. It wasn't pretentious and they would occasionally bump into neighbours that also chose to frequent the popular Italian restaurant. They always liked to sit downstairs, at least Grace did so that she could watch people coming and going. Grace was a pasta freak, absolutely loved the stuff. Marc couldn't see why but then he always thought she was a bit weird, but in a nice way. 'That's why you love me,' she'd say. He'd love her whatever she did. Grace was sometimes a bit of a loose cannon. Unpredictable and spontaneous. When he first met her, 12 years ago, she had been teaching at a primary school in a nearby borough. Sutton had attended the school as part of a local community safety project. The 'nice policeman' had come to see the little children and talk about not talking to strangers, that sort of thing. Unarguably, very worthwhile. He was good at it too. They children all sat agog; she had never seen them so attentive. Grace sat agog too. She was sure that she had blushed a little once or twice when he caught sight of her staring at him. Her efforts to hide it amused him and long before the end of the session he had decided that he was going to try to get her alone, if possible, and chat with the prettiest member of staff at the school. Sutton knew he had played it well. His timing was perfect. Grace didn't want him to leave without saying goodbye and Sutton had no intention of doing any such thing. Sutton's ability to connect with the children and the clever way that he gained their confidence made Grace melt inside. When his visit was due to come to a close, he stood speaking with the Headmistress outside her office and every so often he would glance in Grace's direction as she stood, 'busying herself,' just along the corridor. Grace's attempts to make it look as though she was very busy and couldn't possibly leave the corridor weren't fooling him, and she probably knew it. Grace could hear every word of his conversation with the Headmistress and was aware of anything said that might imply that he was going to be leaving the school. She was getting concerned that he was simply going to walk out and drive away until she got an unexpected stroke of luck.

'Miss Chambers, would you see our lovely Police Officer out please?'

Grace mumbled something incoherent as she hurried herself along the corridor towards the Headmistress's Office, dropping a textbook in her over exuberant attempt to hide her excitement and was all too aware that her eagerness to help made her appear rather transparent. The chat that she had been hoping for lasted a lot longer than a simple 'Goodbye'. In fact, it got to the point where she was getting worried that the Headmistress would start to wonder where she had got to. When Grace finally returned to her class, filled with excited children that were still enthused by the Policeman's visit, she tucked the piece of paper that she had been holding tightly in her hand into her jacket pocket. She would text *Marc* later on, but not before texting her dearest friend first.

'I hope she's not waiting for us,' she said as they turned into Bazeley Street.

'Hope who's not waiting?'

'Carrie.'

'Why would Carrie be waiting for us?'

'Because she's meeting us there, daft.'

'Is she? She never said anything to me about it earlier.'

'Well, she didn't *know* earlier, did she? I rang her on my way home.'

'You never said.'

'Well, I'm saying now ain't I? C'mon, slowcoach.'

Nothing surprised Sutton where Grace was concerned. She could have invited the Dalai Lama and she wouldn't have thought to mention it to him. Still, Carrie was alright. He had no problem with her being there. It wasn't as though it was a special occasion or anything and Carrie had become part of the furniture over the years anyway. In a way it would mean that the two of them would probably chat away merrily, saving him the job. He enjoyed Carrie's company, in all honesty, so it was fine.

'Hi,' shouted Grace as she spotted DS Carrie Linton standing outside the restaurant.

'Hi.'

Grace opened the door and, hand in hand, pulled Sutton inside with her. As he half-turned to hold the door for Carrie she spoke, 'Didn't know you were coming, Marc.' Sutton made his way in behind Grace to a free table, half expecting the Dalai Lama to be sitting there grinning up at them. He wasn't. Grace plonked herself down next to Carrie and the chatter began. Sutton decided that it would be nice for Grace to have Carrie here. His own interest followed the noise from a gathering upstairs which he could just see if he leaned back on his chair. Probably a birthday celebration or something similar. While he was gazing around Grace and Carrie had already chosen what they were going to order. Carbonara for Grace and something called Fettuccine Alfredo for Carrie.

'What are you having then?' asked Grace, as a stray balloon from the party on the upper floor came floating down and bobbed around on their table, only to be batted away by Grace.

Sutton turned his attention to the menu and predictably said that he'd have what he usually has, 'Spaghetti Bolognese.'

'You always have that.'

'Well, I like it.'

'C'mon Marc, be adventurous,' said Carrie.

'Oh, let him have it. He'll be happier that way,' said Grace.

'How could I not be happy spending an evening with you,' Sutton replied.

'What about me, then?' Carrie joked.

'I saw you at work,' he said, in a deadpan sort of way.

'Oh, cheers. I love you too,' Carrie said, enjoying the moment with Grace.

Carrie and Grace were quite the double act. It was never a bad idea to have Carrie along, it helped Grace relax more. He'd asked how the teacher training day had gone but Grace didn't say a lot about it. He guessed there probably wasn't a lot to say. Once the waiter had taken their orders and stepped away from the table Carrie made her excuses to Grace about talking about work things and asked Sutton about the missing girl.

'Any more on, you know, earlier on?'

'What?'

'About the commotion we had at the front desk this morning.'

'Ah, no, nothing more at the moment. The usual procedures have kicked off and we'll have to hope it turns out well. Before anything bad shows up.'

Sutton never felt comfortable talking about this sort of thing when they were out of work and especially in such a public place. Changing the subject, he asked Grace about her day again but the two of them were so busy talking and giggling that he didn't think they had even noticed. Better that way. When Sutton and Carrie had to be at work the next morning, they never stayed out too late. Grace too, would be off to school and back into the throng of a normal day. The alcohol consumption was under control tonight and after a nice satisfying meal and a few rounds of drinks they were heading back out into the evening air and ready to go their separate ways. Carrie had booked a taxi and after a short wait she saw it coming. The car stopped outside the restaurant, and they said their goodbyes. She gave Grace a hug and a kiss and turned to Sutton with a silly look and formerly held her hand out, 'Goodnight, Sir,' she said, much to Grace's amusement. Carrie always did this, just to make Grace laugh.

'Sod off, Linton,' was his default reply.

When they got home, Grace went straight into the kitchen and made coffee, 'Having one?' she called.

Sutton sat on the sofa and heeled his shoes off, 'Yeah, please,' he said with a sigh.

Grace could always tune in to when something was bothering him and sometimes, she knew it was best to let it pass, but this time she could feel that he wasn't quite right. She appreciated that whenever her and Carrie got together, he was going to be a bit out of it, but she knew he didn't mind. He loved having Carrie around as much as she did. As soon as she had returned from the kitchen with two mugs of coffee, she put them onto the table and reached over to the CD player. One touch of the correct button and the room was being filled with a soft and gentle tune. Grace had left one of her favourite cd's in the player. *America* soothingly played *I need you* which came from a live recording somewhere in California. She snuggled close to him and swung her legs onto his. She gave him a long kiss on the cheek and said, 'C'mon then, what is it?'

'What's what?'

'I know you, Marc Sutton. Ever since Carrie mentioned the 'commotion' at work, you've been stewing.'

Grace remembered, only too well, how severely affected he was 3 years ago when Haley Breen was found.

'It's that girl ain't it? The one you told me about when you got home, the one who's gone missing. It'll be alright. She's just gone around to her mate's, got plastered and doesn't want to face the music when she gets home.'

Sutton knew she was probably right, but he didn't like it. Looking at the photos of Haley Breen again today, had stirred up the demons that festered deep at the bottom of the pond. It was never so much what he knew, it was always what he didn't know that bothered him the most. Earlier in the day he'd sat looking at the photos of Haley Breen and gone over the questions that he wanted answers to, again and again. Each time he juggled the balls they always came down with a clatter. The image of her hands and feet, bound with tape. The once white bedsheet stained with her bodily fluids. The wounds. The post-mortem had shown that the only fatal wound was the puncture to her neck. She had no significant head injury; nothing more than evidence of a small contusion on the back of her head, perhaps from a struggle. Someone had stabbed something straight into her neck, and it seemed that someone had cut her hair. The so called 'tattoo' on her shoulder had been done before death. Was she conscious for that? And what did that mean? Did it matter that she was alive when that was done? Why was she wrapped up and not just dumped? Sutton was daydreaming by the time Grace had shaken his arm for the second time.

'Hey, I'm here you know. Talk to me, Marc. I love you,' she said as she gently cupped her hand around his bicep.

'Yeah, sorry,' he paused to gather his thoughts, 'When we've had this, let's go to bed, I'm knackered.'

'Promise me one thing, Marc Sutton,'

'What's that?'

'That you'll talk to me sometimes about this stuff. I know it's not my business to know all the details but...we're a team ain't we? I don't want you to be poorly over this stuff again. I know work didn't fully appreciate what it was like for you, but I did. Angelica whatsit will turn up soon.'

That's what worried him the most. *The turning up.*

SIX

Minneapolis, Minnesota.
Four years ago

The Minnesota winter could be extremely harsh. Frigid and snowy, according to the National Oceanic and Atmospheric Administration Climate Prediction Centre. Temperatures regularly dipped down to somewhere in the region of -40 degrees. The NOAA is a scientific agency within the U.S Department of Commerce which supplies environmental information pertaining to the state of the oceans and the atmosphere as well as the ecosystems and commerce. Its information is shared by a variety of sources, including The National Weather Service (NWS). The NWS is tasked with providing weather forecasts for the purposes of public protection and safety.

Gregory Bonner sat huddled close to his desk with his feet tucked well underneath and his arms across his chest in an effort to warm himself. The electric fire that he had brought into the office from home was positioned under his desk and was doing a splendid job of beginning to warm his feet and legs. His midday trudge to the Minneapolis Police Department on South 5th Street, east of central Minneapolis, was made extra difficult by the previous night's heavy snowfall. Of course, he knew it was coming. He would have been disappointed if it hadn't, in a strange kind of way. Bonner was a weather freak. He absorbed himself in the seasonal challenge that Minnesota offered him and got a weird buzz as winter approached. He sat studying the information on his laptop screen and fidgeted with a pencil, twirling it around his fingers and tapping it gently on the side of the screen. His attention was being taken up by the Twin Cities Snow and Cold Index (SCI). It was a bit like a comparison site for geeks like Bonner. It attempted to weigh up the relative severity of the current winter with winters of the past. The SCI assigns single points for daily counts of maximum and minimum temperatures within a specific range. For 8 points to be attributed to a given day, the minimum temperature would have to drop to -20 degrees or colder. Even snowfall totals of one inch receive a point. Bonner was hoping that last night's blizzard had managed to contribute enough of the white stuff to warrant the award of 8 or even 16 points. The points for snow were added to the points for cold to make a grand total. Bonner had formulated a league table on his laptop and regularly checked the status of this current year's total to see if it was heading for the top spot. The points total sat at just over 100 points, not enough for Bonner. He wanted more, much more. It was his hope that he would see a new record created in his lifetime. If he was to witness this, he would die happy. But the statistics would have to be boosted by a hell of an extreme blast of winter. Something that nobody else he knew ever wanted to witness happening in Minnesota, this winter or any other. Parts of the Mississippi River were already frozen or beginning to be. He would walk there quite often, observing the daily alterations in the frozen landscape, sometimes wandering back and forth on West River Parkway until his toes were numb, even when the advice from the NWS suggested it would be foolish to go out and become exposed to the severity of the weather. Not a particularly good advert from a Police Officer. The parks and woodland areas were like a winter wonderland with crystallised trees and bushes. Snow drifts had provided playgrounds for those who wished to slither and slide down them and chaos to those trying to dig out vehicles, providing that they could actually get out of their houses in the first place.

Bonner was thawing nicely now. His toes were tingling, and his fingers felt as though they belonged to him once again. As he viewed the latest NWS information on his screen something caught his attention. Another storm was being predicted for tonight. His heart skipped and he felt a glow inside him. He swiftly got his self-made league table up on the screen and looked again at the top of the table. Winter 1916-1917…305 points…*Wow*. He transferred to the Twin Cities International Airport site and checked on the current state of play. All measurements are taken from the Minneapolis-St Paul International Airport, hence Twin Cities. Nothing new was apparent but Bonner was hopeful. He knew that seeing the record broken was unlikely, but it didn't stop him dreaming.

'Get off that damned thing, Bonner.'

Big Toni was right there by his side. He'd spotted what Bonner was doing and had crept up behind him. Big Toni was Antonio Rodrigues, a very large Latin-American man. It was a miracle that Bonner didn't hear him coming but he guessed that he was too preoccupied in his fascination of the weather. Captain Rodrigues supervised the daily goings on in the station and generally made sure that everything that needed to be done, got done.

'What have you got under there? A fire? What do you think this is, a hostel?'

Big Toni wandered across the office towards his own desk but wasn't best pleased, probably because he hadn't got one under his desk. Bonner quickly shut down his laptop and waited for the next storm to come his way, this time it would be from Big Toni and not from the fierce and relentless Minnesota weather. Bonner's efforts to suddenly look incredibly busy were in vain. Big Toni was already on his way back with a wad of papers in his giant hand.

'You a trooper, Bonner?'

'A what?'

'Don't *what* me, I asked you if you was a trooper,'

'Yeah, I guess,'

'And don't *guess*, Bonner, for crying out loud.'

Big Toni was referring to one of the many descriptions of a Patrol Officer.

'Right, well, having established that you are indeed a trooper, I wonder if you can *guess* exactly what it is that I would *very much* like you to do next?'

Bonner knew precisely what was coming next, he'd heard Big Toni run this routine before.

'Troop?' replied Bonner with a certain amount of resignation in his voice.

'You damned right, Gregory. It's time for you to get your cosy little ass away from your cosy little fire and get on over to the far side of town.'

This really wasn't what Bonner wanted to hear. His afternoon plans of following the weather and the cloud formations in the vicinity of Minneapolis sounded much more like the sort of afternoon he really wanted. He glanced out of the window at the snowy-looking sky and began to feel rather apprehensive as he tried to second guess what his task was going to be. He thought that he would be best to try to get it over with quickly whatever it was. He wanted to be back as soon as possible and curled up with his laptop, checking the weather and praying for the record-breaking snowfall. If it came, he could stay at the station for the night and maintain a close watch on the activities of the storm on his laptop.

The address that Big Toni gave him was familiar. Why he was needed out there, he couldn't say. *Just get out there.* Reluctantly, Bonner gathered his jacket and his overcoat, his thick gloves and a beanie hat that covered his ears and prepared to make the journey. When he pushed open the door that led him into the car park, a waft of cold air made him grimace. He got outside to his car and found it to be at the phase where it was just starting to freeze. He de-iced the windshield that had only a light covering of snow and sat inside rubbing his legs. He started the patrol car. The screen began to show signs that the icy covering was turning to liquid, so he gave the wipers a go. They scraped against the glass making a loud rubbing noise which told him that he would have to wait just a little longer before he could attempt to move off. He felt this was preferable to stepping out of the car and spraying more de-icer. Inside, he adjusted the heater to deliver as much heat as it could. He knew he'd be ok once he'd got the car moving. The grey sky reflected as much light as possible for this time of the afternoon. The darkness wouldn't be descending for at least a couple of hours and by then he hoped to be well on his way back to his desk. He drove slowly out of the station, listening to the deep crunch of compacted snow beneath the wheels of his patrol car as he made his way through the local streets which would lead him to the outskirts of Minneapolis, on South Washington Avenue, heading towards his destination. His journey took him past a variety of restaurants that Bonner used to like to frequent when he got the opportunity. As Bonner drove, allowing his mind to wander, he wondered again about what might be so interesting at *that* particular house. He knew who lived there. Or at least he used to. As far as he could remember it had been just the old man who was there nowadays. Since the girls left. They were a little older than him, but he would always talk with them given the opportunity. Bonner's college days were memorable to him, not least for the friends he made whilst he was there. He was part of a large clique of students and had many good memories to fall back on. He turned to join Plymouth Avenue North and continued out towards the Golden Valley area. Just another 3 miles to go to where Betty and Elisha used to live.

'Bonner, you gettin' any closer by any chance?' Rumbled Big Toni's voice on the radio.

He fumbled for the button which would activate the handsfree device and took a breath to compose himself before replying.

'Here, Captain,' he said.

'Where's *here*, Bonner?'

'Er, North side of town, Captain. About 3 miles away now, I think.'

'Right, well, get a move on will ya? More calls are coming in and I want you there yesterday, got it? And, Bonner, I want you back here yesterday too, got it?'

Big Toni had made himself quite clear and so Bonner shifted down a gear and stepped on the gas as much as he dared, considering the conditions. The tyres spun on the crusted surface, and he slowed down to a safer pace. Big Toni would have to be patient. He hadn't made use of the sirens as he didn't consider this call to be classed as an emergency. The blue lights that flickered against the glare of the snow-covered streets and parked vehicles were enough for Bonner. They announced a Police presence and were illuminated as per Minneapolis Police Department Policy. To his right he noticed some children waving at the car. He raised a friendly hand to them as a snowball thudded against the side window making him jump. He cursed at them from inside his car and shook his head in disapproval of their act. He knew full well that it's exactly what he would have done as a child.

Few vehicles were brave enough or foolish enough to be out on the roads at this time of the afternoon. He hoped that everyone would be heading home especially as the forecast was for more snow. *Lots more snow.* Bonner was getting close to his destination now and began to regret that he would soon have to step out from the comfort and warmth of his patrol car. The snow was building up on his windshield and the wipers were battling valiantly against the onslaught that had been slowly increasing as he drove. As he approached the street, the patrol car's headlights shone against the bright snowy scene, he reflected again about the house and the people he'd known before the Police Department owned him, at least that was how it felt sometimes. He'd been inside on several occasions. He remembered the extravagant staircase; he probably remembered it to be much wider and awe-inspiring than it actually was. Fondly, he thought about the large kitchen, mostly for the cookies that would be left out by Mrs Nelson for him to take advantage of. He could picture the gardens and recalled how they always looked so tidy, thanks to old Mr Bones. The girls were nice too. Betty was the Vikings nutter, crazy about them. And Elisha, well, she was nice but was sort of mysterious in a cute way. He could never decide which of the girls was his favourite. Elizabeth had taught at a dance studio in St Paul after college and Elisha used to go along there sometimes. Bonner remembered seeing them there. He also recalled how he had once kissed Elisha even though she was a little older and several leagues out of his reach. It made him smile to himself. The kiss was nice but there was something else about it that he remembered most of all. The look she gave her sister afterwards. Weird, that. He couldn't recall what else they used to do. He could recollect Betty's dark hair and pigtails, she always had those. Elisha was lighter and a bit scruffier. Still, the pair of them had been gone for a while now. They used to shoot the bow too but that all stopped after the dog died, he could never work that out either. Maybe they just had other interests and it drifted away, the way things sometimes do. They never talked about shooting again. When he had heard that they were leaving he wasn't entirely surprised. He remembered how awful it was when their mother died and how he never really felt welcomed by their father. S*trange one, he was.* Bonner always thought that he was controlling the girls more and more as time went on. *Maybe he always had.* He had heard from some of the others that it caused quite a commotion when they told their father that they had made up their minds and that they were going to England to see places that they had only read about. A sort of gap year. But one or two of their closer friends didn't see it that way. Once they had actually gone, Bonner had no cause to visit the house again. It just stood there; only old Harry used to be around from time to time. Things were simply not the same without the girls there and definitely not the same without Mrs Nelson.

He turned into the drive and saw the big house and realised, again, just how impressive it was. It looked even more imposing with the snow on the roof and the icicles hanging from the first-floor balcony that circled around the house. When Bonner got out of the car, he donned his overcoat and beanie hat and slowly stepped towards the front door. As he got closer, he saw a familiar face. Old Harry Bones was cautiously walking towards his car, treading very carefully.

'Just checking on the place for any post that needed picking up. Got a key, you see. Been watching out for any water pipes that might have burst too,' he said.

'That's good of you, Mr Bones, but you shouldn't be out here in these temperatures. Might be a lot more snow tonight,' he hoped as the thought of a new SCI record flickered across his mind.

'That's what they say and they're usually right about it too,' said Harry.

Bonner wasn't really one for small talk and especially not right now. The wind was beginning to whip up the snow and was causing a white, very chilly dust cloud to batter Bonner and Mr Bones as they stood outside the front of the property. Heads down, they squinted at each other.

'Well, I was too late, however.'

'Too late?'

'Round the back,' said old Harry.

Bonner envisaged how much damage might have been done to the property and how much of it had become a frozen mess. If the water had been leaking for any length of time it would have created a frozen waterfall and if it had got inside the house, he dreaded to think of the damage that could be caused. He took Harry Bones' arm as they both slithered across the untrodden snow close to the house, supporting each other and leaning towards the building. It was a little less deep than the rest of the garden which was filling again as the fresh snow had just begun to compact the problem. Harry stopped before they got to the rear garden and looked at Bonner, 'Round there,' was all he said. Bonner prepared himself for the watery disaster that he expected would materialise before him and drew a torch from his coat pocket. As he turned into the rear garden a spray of snow blown by the wind hit him, causing him to turn his head away and wait for it to subside. The Red Pines were at the point where they couldn't hold much more snow before they had to let it fall from their laden branches that bowed under the strain. As the wind abated temporarily, he shined his torch towards the rear of the house. Nothing looked out of place immediately, so he glanced back at Harry Bones for confirmation. Old Harry wiped his nose and with a look of despair said, 'Up there.'

Bonner looked up towards the first floor. Something that his brain couldn't immediately process caught his eye. He took one more step to get a better view and stopped, slipping to his right as his boots grasped for some traction, and stood, motionless with his mouth open. The light from his torch beam illuminated the gently falling flakes of snow that were landing on his face, causing him to squint each time one hit his eyes.

'Called you guys straightaway,' said Harry, as he gingerly trod the same path as Bonner, appearing beside him and stood holding onto his left arm for some support.

Both men stared at the gruesome image just above them that barely moved, even in the wind that was whipping icy needles into their faces. Bonner released himself from Old Harry's grip and took a few more careful steps into the rear garden, checking his footing as he went. The snow crunched under his boots, and he began to sink a little deeper into the undisturbed layers that had carpeted the lawn underneath. Now he could see. Now he knew why Old Harry Bones had made the call which interrupted his leisurely afternoon in front of his laptop, studying the Snow and Cold Index.

'Is that…'

'Yep, that's him,' said Harry.

Wade Nelson, the girls' father, was hanging from the balcony rail. Frozen absolutely solid.

Big Toni arrived 30 minutes later. By this time Bonner had escorted Harry to the comparative warmth of his patrol car. He had run the engine and the men had thawed in the front seats. Bonner had called the local Fire Department too. Many of the trucks were already out helping people that had become stranded, but he was promised a response from a vehicle that would be with him soon. Just as Bonner had seen the flicker of lights from Big Toni's car, the Fire truck came into the street from the other end. Bonner stepped out from the comfort of his patrol car, leaving Old Harry safe inside, and met the Captain as he, in turn, opened his car door and began to brave the latest onslaught from the Minnesota winter. Bonner didn't relish dragging Big Toni out in these frightful conditions but felt he had little choice. Had he not, he would have been wrong either way.

'You better show me,' said Big Toni.

'Around the back, Captain.'

Big Toni stared into Bonner's patrol car and spotted the occupant in the passenger seat, 'Who's that?'

'That's the guy who found him, I'll take him home after we're done here…if that's ok?'

'You better do, Bonner. He looks as though he might not get there otherwise.'

As the two of them started towards the front drive of the house, they were joined by a couple of Firefighters from Fire Station 14. The snowfall was steady, and Bonner was keeping one eye on the sky, wondering if it would deliver anything *special* tonight. Bonner led the way, trying to keep to the previously trodden path, and shone his torch down ahead of them. As they approached the rear garden Bonner heard Big Toni curse. He turned and noticed that the Captain had dropped a glove as he was wrestling with them, trying to put them onto rapidly freezing fingers. Once Big Toni had picked up his glove, Bonner continued around the corner of the house, past the shed. It was then he heard Big Toni yell out, louder this time. As he looked back, he saw his Captain flat out in the snow, swearing away merrily and slithering as he tried in vain to get himself upright. Bonner and one of the Firefighters helped the big man to his feet as he dusted himself off, his coat now mostly white.

'What in hell was that?' Big Toni shouted.

Bonner noticed something half sticking up in the snow. Whatever it was, Captain Rodrigues had found it. Big Toni was back on two feet now. He stood holding the offending article in one hand and shone his torch on it with the other. The piece of wood had been painted white at some stage and as the Captain turned it around, he read the wording on it, "*Hastings*.' Who the God damn hell is Hastings?'

SEVEN

Now

Karter Swann aka Kevin Marshall carefully checked his appearance in the mirror. His head had been bowed over the sink for a while as he tried his best to apply the colouring. Slowly he looked up and focussed on the man in front of him. The sun-kissed mop of mostly blond hair now took on a much darker look. He hadn't had a clue how to do this but figured that it couldn't be that much of a challenge. Other men did it, so he could too. He had learned that there were two small bottles of solution to mix, that also needed to wait 5 minutes before they were applied. He had looked on YouTube for some pointers first and decided it would work…probably. He realised after that he would need to either stay clean shaven or dye his beard too. If he left it, he'd look like a two-tone weirdo. The advice that he had managed to glean from the search engine on his new phone had suggested that the hair colour would last approximately 4 to 6 weeks before the roots started to show through. Before he started, he rubbed a thin layer of Vaseline into his skin around the hairline to ease cleaning any unwanted residue that had run down from his scalp towards his face. He decided that he would keep a check on it and that the beard would be getting the same treatment next, as he had bought more than he needed. He was wearing an old t-shirt that could be thrown out if it got covered with dye and it also protected his upper body while he was experimenting. He wiped his skin with alcohol-free face wipes to clean some of the dye off. The information he had researched told him that his scalp would give the impression that his hair was darker than it was for a day or so until it was completely washed off. *Don't go too dark or it'll look black.*

Once he was happy with his efforts, he took off his old t-shirt, finding that it had got away with it and will survive another day. Before he stepped into the shower to rinse his hair, he looked in the mirror at the tattoo; the one on his shoulder that he couldn't really miss whenever he was bare-chested and in the presence of a mirror. The one that brought back a variety of memories. It hadn't ever been his idea to have it and although it wasn't exactly forced upon him, it sometimes felt as though it was, in a fashion. He had felt obligated and remembered the day he had it done, quite clearly. He could picture himself entering the shop and hearing the constant buzzing emanating out from the rear of the premises. Numerous designs of a variety of tribal markings and soulless demonic skulls stared back at him, as well as some very elaborate designs of Koi Carp and Japanese Bonsai trees. A couple of girls sat looking at magazines that displayed brightly coloured photographs of tattoo designs and a younger man sat opposite them in a gaze, looking across towards them but sort of mesmerised. When the heavily decorated young woman, sporting an array of studs and piercings, came up to the counter to greet him and asked if she could help, he barely had a chance to open his mouth before his companion spoke up. Betty Nelson was driving this. She had her own agenda to fulfil and although he'd agreed to have it done, he hadn't really felt that he had a lot of options. A flat refusal would bring about a torrent of questions about why he wouldn't do this. If he loved her like he said he did then there surely wasn't a problem, *was there?* Except, there was.

Karter Swann met Betty Nelson at the Cactus and Coyote, a pub in Brick Lane in East London, not far from Spitalfields Market and in close proximity to Shoreditch High Street. An area heavily populated by Bangladeshis and famous for its many Curry restaurants. The Cactus and Coyote was one of those buildings that had been converted from a disused warehouse. High up above the front doors was the old original pulley system that once hauled sacks of grain up to the floors above for milling. The extensive building work and décor downstairs was very impressive. Many of the walls were mirrored giving the impression of a full and bustling interior. Swann found this very useful as he could keep an eye on what everyone was doing from his position behind the bar. He could also see who was coming in. When he noticed Betty Nelson wander in, his interest grew. He managed to catch her eye as she approached the bar and confidently drew her in with a smile, seamlessly blending business with pleasure. He immediately liked her cute American accent and the way she dropped in those 'Americanisms' when she spoke. He thought she was very pretty, especially with her pigtails of brown hair that swished around as she turned her head. Establishing that she hadn't been in England for very long, he saw his chance to suggest that he might show her some of the tourist spots which would enable him to get to know her a little better. In another hour he would be finished for the night and free to grab some food, if she wanted to. Happily, for him, she did. They left the pub together, neither of them really planning on anything more than a chat and some company. They walked to an area where a number of eating houses and wine bars had sprung up, attracting a lot of interest from the local yuppies. The pavements shimmered from a light shower. As they walked, she told him all about where she was born, at a hospital she called 'The Mercy' in Coon Rapids, a Northern suburb of Minneapolis. She spoke about her time at college and how she used to work at a dance studio in St Paul, none of which meant very much to him. In fact, she just talked and talked.

'Do you watch American Football?' she asked.

'I've seen some,' he lied.

'Guess my team, bet you can't,' she said, teasing him.

He felt that he needed to make a genuine effort at this but really didn't know where to start. *Did Minneapolis have a team?* As they walked, he decided to see whether she would object if he took her hand as they crossed the road. As he did so, she looked at him for a short awkward moment. He wasn't sure whether he had done the right thing. When they got to the pavement on the other side, he kept hold of her hand, with a degree of uncertainty. After another couple of shopfronts had been passed, she released from his grip, ferreted about in her bag for something and placed her hands into the pockets of her coat. Before he had to admit that he didn't know any other teams than the Miami Dolphins or the New York Giants she rescued him, 'The Vikings, silly.'

It was only a rescue in part, as he still didn't know who they were, his face failing to deceive her.

'The Minnesota Vikings,' she explained, 'Purple and gold. I could see their stadium from my bedroom.'

'Oh. Right, those.'

Those? He hadn't gotten away with it. Not for a minute.

'You don't know who they are, do you? Oh, how can you not know the greatest NFL team ever?' she chuckled, almost disappointedly.

'Erm, well. I've heard of them, obviously.'

After a brief disagreement about which wine bar to try they settled for one near to Heneage Street, having passed several options and walked further than they really needed to. Inside, Betty suggested where they should sit, close to the window with a good view of the street. Once their drinks arrived, she sat close to him and finally asked about him, and his story. He told her about the fact that he was born in Germany and how he had come to live in England. His story didn't sound anywhere near as exciting as hers, but he didn't mind. She was so enthusiastic about her own stories that he just went with it. She told him all about the big house that she had lived in and how she had a sister who had come over with her and how he must meet her.

He reflected on that day, aware now, that he couldn't possibly know where it would lead him. He touched the outline of the tattoo with his fingertips, tracing the pattern of the bleeding heart. He ran his fingers over his shoulder, following the drips of blood to the ends. His gaze lifted to meet that of his reflection. His face looked drawn. His expression, heavy. Once again, he thought about having the tattoo lasered off or maybe, covered over with something that would completely hide it in an attempt to reverse the past. *Maybe, one day.*

How everything had happened so fast was always a puzzle to him. One moment he was in the throes of a new and exciting relationship with a young and attractive American girl, the next he was 'dead' and had become Kevin Marshall, the guy that ran and hid, forced into seclusion and the relative safety of anonymity. He removed the plastic gloves that he had worn whilst dyeing his once golden, sun-kissed hair a less conspicuous colour and decided to get it washed before repeating the process on his beard. He didn't want to leave it too long and find that it was darker than he desired. He nodded to himself as he considered that he would have to try to get the timing right in order that his beard was as near to the same shade as his hair, as possible. *It'll be worth it.* He told himself. He wasn't really sure whether any of it was worth it, but he had no choice but to keep going now. He stepped into the shower, his mind still whirring around. *If she hadn't walked into the pub, if he hadn't taken a fancy to her, if she hadn't had a sister.*

Karter Swann could no longer roam the streets freely. He was a marked man. Kevin Marshall would need to be on his guard.

EIGHT

DI Sutton had an important meeting at 11 o/clock. Mr and Mrs Rowntree would be expecting some answers about the whereabouts of their missing daughter, Angelica. Sutton knew it wasn't going to be easy. This was the fourth day of her disappearance and nothing substantial had come to light up to now. He and DCI Blackery had spoken with her parents before, but it was 'early days' and they just needed a couple more. Supposedly. Sutton felt the cloak of dread engulf him again as he remembered going through this, remarkably similar scenario, with the parents of Haley Breen three years ago, before the terrible discovery.

He had left the house at the same time as normal to ensure he got a seat on the busy bus, as he was still waiting anxiously for some news about his car. *Any day now.* He had kissed Grace and hugged her just a little longer than usual. 'It'll be ok, I'll be thinking of you,' she had said, supportively, as her kind eyes met his, wishing him luck. As he'd travelled along towards his stop, he had gone over how he thought he should play it. DCI Blackery had insisted that Sutton take the lead, leaving him to oversee the meeting, only interjecting when he thought he should. As Sutton had sat quietly, pondering how to explain that they had almost nothing more to offer than was already known, his bus jolted and stopped. He'd risen from his seat and made his way towards the front of the bus. The doors remained closed. He had looked out, further down the road and was able to see his stop close by. The bus driver had waved his arms in despair and muttered something relating to a small commotion that had unfolded just ahead. As Sutton peered through the misty windscreen, he saw a cyclist being aided to his feet by a couple of commuters. No broken bones or significant damage to him, apparently. Not the same could be said for his bike, though.

'Alright to get off here?' he'd asked.

'Yeah, chief,' the driver had replied, reaching to operate whatever it was that enabled the doors to open.

Sutton had disembarked, this time checking for puddles. He'd walked past the cyclist who was now upright and looking hard at the condition of his bike. He didn't have a lot further to walk and thought he would probably get to his stop well before the bus did.

The room that had been chosen for the meeting with Brian and Lesley Rowntree was on the ground floor of Old Clapton Street Police Station. On the door was a sign that read IR5. Interview Room 5 was situated conveniently close to the front entrance and yet far enough away from the front desk so as to avoid being interrupted by raised voices or the banging of doors. Sutton sat inside with the door closed and a folder in front of him. The magnolia walls did nothing much to inspire him as he pondered the information. DCI Blackery was upstairs. It was 10:47. Sutton was looking at the clock, hoping for someone to burst in and say that Angelica had been found safe. He knew this wasn't going to be easy. His clear recollection of the meeting that he had held with Raymond and Sylvia Breen was still fresh in his mind. Telling them that all he could offer by way of information was that nobody had seen her since she went missing and that they were 'doing all they could', was as inadequate and as useless as it sounded. He felt then that he was staring into a void and unfortunately, he didn't feel much better about this instance either. He opened up the folder and took out the photograph of Angelica Rowntree, placing it on the desk in front of him. Innocent brown eyes stared back. *For goodness sake, get a grip,* he told himself, posting the photograph immediately back into the folder. He studied the meagre amount of information that his team had been able to amass over the past few days and sighed. As many of Angelica's friends as could be found had been questioned repeatedly about her character and the likelihood that she may, even now, be with a friend somewhere. If any of them had mentioned any special or favourite or secretive places that Angelica liked to frequent, they were visited by Sutton's team. He had, himself, looked in Angelica's bedroom. All he saw were the usual pin-up pictures of pop stars and those of celebrities, neither of whom he recognised. Her wardrobe was full of outfits, her dressing table weighted down with a variety of different cosmetics. Her father had been one step ahead of him by having already spoken with some people at the local gymnasium, but to no avail. There was no report of a note being left or any other clue that might indicate her whereabouts. Particular attention had been paid to the garage where she worked and the people that worked there. Their lives had been probed into. *Was it one of the mechanics that had her held against her will somewhere close by? Was there a boyfriend after all, maybe one that one of her friends knew about, even if her parents didn't?* So far nothing significant had come to light. The local area had been searched as thoroughly as it could be. Her family members had been out, walking amongst the people at the local shops and had placed photographs of Angelica on lamp posts, billboards and just about anything that didn't move. Even the bus garage, especially the perimeters, had been comprehensively explored. Sutton himself had taken a look at the precise site where Haley Breen was found. Nothing up to now. It was 10:56 when DCI Blackery could be heard outside the door talking to someone. A shadow ghosted across the frosted window and as if in slow motion, the door opened. Mrs Rowntree walked in ahead of her husband and the DCI. Sutton thought that even 'good morning' sounded wrong but went with it anyhow. Very soon it was just the four of them, sitting silently, in the room that now felt incredibly cramped. Blackery and Sutton were on one side of the desk and two very sullen faces were on the other. Empty and frightened. It was very clear to see that the levels of stress being experienced by the Rowntrees was, naturally enough, at an all-time high. In reality, they had probably not lowered from the moment that it became clear that their daughter was unaccounted for. Sutton knew that they would have pinned all their hopes on the chance of hearing some positive and encouraging news from him this morning only to have them cruelly dashed. Brian Rowntree held his wife's hand throughout the whole meeting and offered all he could by way of an occasional crooked smile. Sutton could see just how brave they were both being in the face of what he hoped wasn't going to be a repeat of the Haley Breen outcome. He found it difficult not to go around in circles and tried, painstakingly to sound positive but inside he felt a deep and grave concern for Angelica's welfare. He told Lesley Rowntree that they were very hopeful of a lead that would aid the investigation and that they must all believe that it would come soon. After all everyone on his team was fully focussed on finding Angelica safe and well. Officers were out every day, talking to people and showing photographs of Angelica to all and sundry. Sutton felt sure that his eyes were not as convincing as his well-intended words of comfort. The Rowntree's said very little, just nodding in agreement every so often. The desperation was clear to see. Sutton got little help from Blackery during this meeting. He just sat beside him and made the odd gesture but that was about it. *How many ways can you say, 'we don't know'?* The only thing he could do for now was to repeat the only words he had. He knew that there were no guarantees, though. Not that he uttered *those* words. When the Rowntree's stood to leave Sutton noticed that the clock showed 12:15. How that much time had gone by in a flash surprised him. Blackery showed them out. Sutton sat down again and wondered what more could be done that wasn't already being done. The local CCTV had been studied too but without so much as a sniff of good fortune. Angelica Rowntree appeared to have disappeared from the radar completely. He saw Blackery's shadow pass the meeting room door and figured that he would be heading upstairs to his office, so he followed. When Sutton got upstairs Blackery was already behind closed doors. Sutton went into his own office and placed the Angelica Rowntree file back into the cabinet from where he had got it earlier. He stood silently for a moment before he felt someone's presence behind him and turned, half expecting to see the formidable shape of DCI Blackery. It was DS Carrie Linton.

'How was it?' she asked, her expression, full of empathy.

'Huh. You know, as tricky as ever.'

'How are her parents holding up?'

'About as good as anyone would expect, I guess. Terrified of every word I spoke, just in case.'

'Yeah. Well, the guys are out there, trying everything. Something will turn up soon, I'm sure. Look Marc, I know you have Grace but...well, you have me too, ya know.'

Sutton felt a glazing in his eyes and turned away from her. He picked up some papers from his in-tray and pretended to look at them, 'Cheers, Carrie. It'll be alright. She'll be ok.'

'Yeah. Hey, Grace has asked me round tonight, do you mind? I won't if you'd rather not.'

'Course not. You're always welcome,' he said with a genuine smile.

Carrie stepped towards Sutton but before she could squeeze his arm Blackery's door opened just across the hall. Carrie backed off, probably looking a lot more awkward and suspicious than the circumstances dictated. As Blackery stepped into Sutton's office, Carrie stepped out so as to avoid any sort of contact with the man that she really didn't like very much. Never had.

'You know who it is, don't you?' Blackery said.

'Do I know who who is?'

'The one responsible for all this.'

'No. Do you?'

'The same monster that killed Haley Breen. Swann. We should have had him locked away the first time.'

'Swann? How could that be? We had nothing on him. Anyway, I thought he was dead. You saw the mess that was left in his kitchen. I reckon he'd argued with the wrong sort.'

'Dead, my arse. I reckon it was him before. We just didn't have enough evidence, that's all. Look at the pattern here and look at the Breen girl,' blasted Blackery.

'Evidence? Just because he wore a tattoo? Apart from that there was absolutely nothing we could keep him on. We had nothing that tied him to the scene. It was all supposition. It was hopeless and we don't have a pattern anyway…without a body,' the words catching in Sutton's throat.

Blackery gave Sutton a stare and harrumphed. 'Well, you'd better find her then and when you do, you'll see I'm right.'

Blackery turned out of Sutton's office before another word could be spoken. Sutton stood looking at the doorway, a little shocked. A few seconds later Carrie poked her head around the door.

'Couldn't help overhearing.'

'Listening, you mean,' replied Sutton.

'Yeah, alright, listening,' said Carrie with a coy smile, 'So?'

'So what?'

'So, what did he mean about a pattern? There's no pattern with only one…Anyway, why did he mention Swann? I thought he was dead.'

'No idea. If Swann is dead then it won't be him, will it?' said Sutton, stating the obvious, 'And if he isn't then how do you explain the mess in his kitchen?'

'I am inclined to agree with you. It wasn't a pleasant sight. But what if Blackery knows something. Do you think he's still around?'

'Can't see it. I don't see how he can know any more than I do at the moment, either. Whoever we're looking for hasn't left anything by way of a trail to follow, that's for sure. But when we find her, we'll know, I guess.'

'Except we won't, will we Marc? Find her, I mean. Not in that way, at least. Cos she's gonna be ok, right?' said Carrie.

Sutton wanted to agree with her but just nodded instead. Carrie nodded back and left the office saying that she'd see him later, probably around eight. Sutton looked across at Blackery's closed door and pondered the conversation but decided to let it go. There were much more important things to be getting on with straight away than arguing with him about his guesswork. The morning had flown by, and he knew that every second counted as far as Angelica Rowntree was concerned. He had a team out this morning talking again to the neighbours that lived in the Rowntree's street, another officer checking for any text messages that Angelica may have sent to her friends and two officers out on the beat, poking their noses into anywhere and everywhere that might possibly throw up something that they could work with. *Doing all we can.* Fingers crossed.

NINE

At 16:30, later that day, Marc Sutton received two pieces of good news. The first came from DS Carrie Linton who had raced up the stairs to his office to let him know that one of the beat PC's had spoken to one of the mechanics at the garage where Angelica Rowntree worked. The garage on Trenton Street was easily accessed via a short underpass that linked the Lavender Road Estate to Trenton Street and was the quickest route for Angelica to take on her way to work. Apparently, the mechanic had been hurrying away from the garage to catch his bus at around the time when Angelica would usually have been expected home, at roughly 6pm, on the day she went missing. By all accounts, he had caught a glimpse of her talking to a man. The mechanic didn't think anything of it, of course, and had continued around the corner to board his bus that was already at the stop. His account explained that when the bus drove by the end of the turning, he looked into the street, but it was empty. Angelica and the man had gone.

'So why didn't he tell us this before, when the questions were asked the first time around?'

'I bet you can guess what he said'

'Yeah. He didn't think it was important.'

'You got it,' said Carrie.

'Damn,' shouted Sutton, 'What's the matter with these people?'

'That's just it, Marc. This guy suffers with a learning disability. From what the PC said, he was lucky to get anything from him at all. He almost clammed up as soon as this came to light. The PC had to gently coax it from him. Doesn't sound like much of a lead, does it?'

'No, Carrie, but it's something. Make sure somebody speaks with him again, maybe at his house,' offered Sutton.

'I don't think he has a house. Sounds to me as though he lives at some kind of Warden controlled arrangement; you know.'

'Ok. Well either way we need to follow this up, just in case. Maybe he can give us a description of some sort. Can you get someone on it as soon as possible and let me know if anything more useful comes from it?' he asked.

'Of course. I'll sort something for tonight and see if we can tease something more out of him, but it doesn't sound very promising. I think he'll be difficult to talk to going by what the PC said earlier.'

'Well, we gotta try, Carrie. We'll just have to be gentle.'

Even before Carrie Linton had left Sutton's office, she had already decided that she'd get a couple of WPC's to go to see the mechanic. She considered that perhaps they might pose a softer approach. She wasn't sure but she thought it would be worth a try. Maybe he would feel more comfortable, less in the spotlight.

'See you tonight, then. And try not to be late, Grace's cooking something special.'

'Is she? She never said anything to me,' said Sutton.

'Yeah. She texted me.'

Course she did, he thought.

Sutton's other piece of good news was waiting for him when he arrived, just in the nick of time, to collect his car at the local Subaru garage, moments before they were about to give up on him and close up for the night. His pride and joy had been washed and hoovered out. It sat gleaming on the garage forecourt, waiting for its master to arrive. Sutton felt a real sense of relief when he sat in the driver's seat and turned the key. Although not such a relief when he had paid the bill. The Subaru Impreza WRX STI sounded sweet. He had wanted one ever since he made DI. Grace had wanted one ever since she had met him, even though she wasn't entirely sure of the difference between one and another. The 2.5 engine sounded as though it had a lot more under the bonnet than that. 295 bhp, 0-60 in 5 seconds. If ever there was a car to impress Grace, then this was it. Her own Peugeot 108 was fine for what she needed it for, but she was always on the lookout for a chance to take the Subaru instead. That particular battle was always one that he won. Grace didn't mind, she loved it as a passenger just as much.

He turned out from the garage forecourt and began to head in the direction of home before something made him turn left instead of right at the junction. His intuition or maybe the demons in his head seemed to be forcing him to drive towards the street where Angelica had been spotted with *'the man'*. Once he thought of looking, his inquisitiveness had grabbed him, and he knew he couldn't just go home without at least one look. Stealthily, he drove the Subaru in the direction of the garage on Trenton Street where Angelica worked. As he turned into the street, he wondered why he was here, looking for a needle in a haystack, instead of going home to Grace and her 'something special'. Surely, nothing would come of it. He parked the car at the end of Trenton Street and sat for a moment trying to envisage what the mechanic must have seen. He imagined him leaving the garage and turning to see Angelica talking to someone. *Where would they have gone from here? Which way? Where did you take her, you bastard?* Sutton selected first gear and rolled the Subaru slowly along the street. Looking uncharacteristically suspicious, he peered into every crevice, every side entrance, every alleyway and every front garden, wondering, even though he knew full well that his team had been comprehensively combing the street. As he drove further along, he began to consider whether the man had a vehicle nearby, just waiting to take her away somewhere. The road veered to the left a little further down and the garage, in his rear-view mirror, went out of sight. Ahead of him, he could see the start of the underpass that led to the Lavender Road Estate. The underpass itself had been checked out by officers on foot as well as a team with cadaver dogs and those that specialised in indicating the presence of blood. Then on the left side of the road he saw a rough piece of ground with old chain-link fence that separated it from a disused car park. Tall grasses had grown between the cracks in the tarmac and claimed their place. Dandelions and a variety of other weeds occupied a lot of the bare ground. He could see that there was ample space for a car or a van to park there. He pictured that this could easily be where a vehicle had been lying in wait for him to return to with Angelica.

Sutton got out of the Subaru and stood beside the fence, peering across the open space as if searching for something, anything, to give him a clue. He turned and looked back towards the bend in the road. Nobody from Trenton Street could see anything. He looked around and realised that this particular spot was completely secluded from any houses or buildings nearby. It was entirely private. *Maybe this is where he abducted her.* Sutton started to look hard at the ground, walking slowly as he did. The area was dry and stony. He didn't notice anything which would indicate the presence of a vehicle. No fresh oil stains, no useful fresh tyre marks. He knew that his team had already been over this area, but he just had to look, anyway. *Got to check again.* He paced along the road, following the line of the chain-link fence, looking in bewilderment at the landscape. He stood with his hands in his pockets and stared across the car park. *Where are you, Angelica?* Bereft of a good reason to stand around helpless for another minute, Sutton decided to return to the Subaru and make his way home to Grace.

As he walked, head down, towards the car he noticed a small object on the ground next to his foot, almost buried in the long grass and in close proximity to something that he definitely didn't want to touch. *Dogwalkers. Why don't they pick up?* He bent down for a closer look and recognised the object to be an earring. It was tiny but something about it had caught his eye. Sutton quickly went to the car and looked for something that he could use to collect it with. Then it came to him. Grace always liked to keep a pen in the glovebox. His own were all on his desk at the station. *Never know when you might need one*, she'd say. *Grace, I love you*, he said to himself. He opened the glovebox and peered hopefully inside. A packet of tissues and a menu from the trattoria were all he could see immediately. He began to ferret around inside, shifting things forwards from the back. As he picked up a windscreen scraper, he spotted a pen underneath it and picked it out. 'Good girl,' he muttered. He knew that he would need something to put the earring into but was pretty sure that Grace didn't have an evidence bag in there too. He fetched out the packet of tissues, opened them and got a couple out. *They're gonna have to do.* He folded them into his pocket and with the pen in his hand, he made his way back to the rough ground. *Now, where is it?* Sutton bent over and stared again. *There.* He retrieved the tissues from his pocket and separated them, opening one fully. Holding one of the tissues, he lowered it close to the earring, making sure not to get anywhere near the item that was emitting the undesirable smell. Carefully, he guided the nib of the pen through a loop on the earring and lifted it slowly as he stood to have a better look. It was small by Grace's standards. She liked those with hoops and dangly bits, as he called them. He took a photo of it with his phone and with the earring safely wrapped he began to walk back to the car. Sitting in the driver's seat again, he hoped that this, seemingly, innocent piece of jewellery was going to be of use. Buoyed by his finding, he hoped that if this belonged to Angelica, that it may at least prove that she was here. Sutton put the tissue on the seat beside him and started the Subaru. *Just shows you,* he thought. Pleased that he had followed his intuition, he headed on to find a suitable place where he could turn around before making his way, not home, but back to the station. His finding had meant that he would have to do something about it before he could even think about getting back to Grace.

Back at Old Clapton Street he made his way inside, through the old Victorian entrance, to register the earring into the exhibit log. Scenes of crimes (S.O.C.O) would be able to take it from there in an effort to establish whether there was any useful DNA on the object which might link it directly to Angelica Rowntree. Her DNA had been gathered from a toothbrush that Angelica used. It would be studied in the lab and he would receive the outcome soon. His immediate thoughts were that it would be hopeful at best considering the rainfall that had been around lately. As he sat at his desk, he considered that he should give Grace a call.

'Thought you were getting the car back?' she said.

'I did but something else has delayed me. I've had to submit something into the evidence log and get the process started for it to be looked at in the lab.'

'Oh. Something about the girl?'

'Possibly. Don't know yet. An earring.'

'Ok, well, when do you think you'll be back, just so that I can get the dinner timings right?'

'I won't be much longer, just wanted to let you know, that's all,' he explained.

'If it's not hers, I'll have it,' she joked, 'Is it the sort that I like?'

'No, not at all. Too small for your tastes but I bet you'd still carry it off,' he said.

'I'd look silly wearing only one,' she laughed, 'Oh, and you're not keeping Carrie back, are you? We've got a girly night tonight.'

'No, she'll be there, never fear. Anyway, I'll see how this goes and hopefully I'll be home in an hour or so,' he said.

'Thought you said you wouldn't be much longer.'

'I did but I've just thought of something. I'll do my best and text you as soon as I'm leaving.'

With that out of the way and Grace reasonably satisfied that he'd be home soon, or reasonably so, he got his head into gear and had a look at the photo he had taken of the earring. It was definitely not Grace's style, but he knew she would still look good in ones like that. The question was, did Angelica Rowntree look good in them? Over the past few days her parents had provided a number of pictures of Angelica that he had kept with the case notes in his office. Sutton drew the folder from his cabinet, pulled out all the photographs and began to look through the available photos of Angelica. He found two photographs of her wearing earrings, but none matched the one he had on his phone. *Ok, so that didn't work.* Sutton knew that he would have to ask her parents whether they recognised the earring or get someone else to but decided to wait for the lab report. If they found any traces of DNA that were a match for Angelica, then he would definitely need to have a conversation with them. One he would not relish in the slightest. He spent the next half an hour going through all the photos that he could find on Angelica's Facebook page, staring closely at every image to see whether she was wearing earrings that would match the one in the evidence bag. There were a lot to scour through and many were inconclusive as to whether there were earrings on her or not. Hair got in the way, hats got in the way, people obscured a clear view. The only ones that showed her in earrings certainly didn't match up either. Sutton decided that his search was going to have to be over for tonight. *Maybe it wasn't hers anyway.* He put away the folder and left his office in darkness, remembering to text Grace.

When he got home, he could just about hear the girls giggling excitedly from the kitchen above the din from the stereo. Something smelt very nice, and he was ready for it. As he reached the doorway to the kitchen, Grace came bounding out followed closely by Carrie, both holding large wine glasses and giggling like schoolgirls.

'Hey, mister. Have you seen a policeman? He went out this morning and I haven't seen him all day,' Grace teased, playfully.

'Not as good looking as this one though, eh Grace,' said Carrie.

Sutton told them to behave, or he'd have them locked up, as he ran upstairs to get changed.

'Want us to follow you?' shouted Grace, as her and Carrie burst into fits of exaggerated laughter and made their way from the kitchen into the lounge.

Sutton shook his head and ignored them both. What he had in mind was to satisfy his rumbling stomach. Grace's games could wait until Carrie had got her taxi home later. Probably much later, it seemed. *If she even manages to get in a taxi.* It certainly wouldn't be the first time that Carrie had crashed at their house and needed coaxing into a taxi in the morning. The pleasant smell of something that had had him salivating from the moment he walked into the house, wafted upstairs. Grace and Carrie often joined forces in the kitchen to create a lovely meal. Girl's night wasn't really solely the two of them as he was usually present. Either he'd be in charge of changing the music or fetching nibbles from the kitchen to replenish the stock. Sometimes he'd simply slide away into another room and let them let loose on their own. He really didn't mind. As long as the girls were happy, so was he. His concentration on what was being said over dinner waivered from time to time. *The earring.* It was a thought that he couldn't shake off. In one way he wished that he hadn't gone driving off towards Trenton Street, but then in another way, he was glad that he had. He had it in mind to mention this discovery, if that's what it was, to Carrie tonight but the way things were going that had become pretty pointless. *Anyway, why bring work home?* Sutton knew that it would have to wait until the morning. He was itching to learn of the DNA results too. He knew that he needed to be patient and let things unfold in their own time. Dinner first.

Once Carrie had managed to get safely into the taxi that Grace had ordered for her, and not without a little help, Sutton and Grace began the task of clearing up before bed. It wasn't something that either of them wanted to face in the morning. When the job was almost done, Grace wiped a handful of suds onto Sutton's face and the war of bubbles began in earnest. This was almost routine; it was just a matter of which of them was going to start it first. In hindsight, it was nearly always Grace. She was definitely the biggest kid of them both.

'That's more like it,' she said.

'Like what?' he replied as he gently, wiped the biggest handful of bubbles on Grace's face, smearing the warm soapy cloud of fun over her nose and around her mouth, causing her to blow bubbles at him.

'I've been watching you, Marc Sutton. Where have you been half the evening?'

'I don't know what you mean' he replied as he defended another assault of foam, which by now was covering his head and shoulders and floating down to the floor.

Grace stopped and looked at him. Sutton stared back, knowing full well what she was referring to. He sighed and wiped soap from his face so that he could see her properly and leaned back against the worktop. He felt the coming admission clambering to get out as Grace put her arms around him and hugged him tightly.

'You promised you'd talk to me if something was bothering you,' she said quietly.

Sutton took her by the hand, and walked her, suds and all, into the living room. The pair of them stood face to face and hugged even harder, still dripping with bubbles.

'It's the earring isn't it?' said Grace, 'I'm right aren't I? You better not let this get inside again or I'll leave you and run away with Carrie,' she joked, causing him to smile.

'Might not be so bad,' he said, teasing her.

'Right Mister get up those stairs and you'd better put that uniform back on. This time I'm the one who's gonna be taking it off.'

TEN

Karter Swann alias Kevin Marshall, quite liked being 'dead'.

At least one half of him was at peace, for now. He was never able to relax completely, but it had taken some of the pressure off him. It wasn't the first time that he had considered that being dead might be his easiest, if not his wisest, option. He had thought about carrying it out for real on more than one occasion. Whatever it was that stopped him, he was glad of it.

The money that he brought home, as Kevin Marshall, from his part-time job, working during the evenings at a nightclub, was enough to top up the rent he had to pay for the modest room in a house in Tilbury, East London, down towards the docks. Mr and Mrs Turner, who lived in the main part of the house at 12 Countess Street, were pleasant enough and left him alone most of the time. The room was compact and had an ensuite but apart from that it was basic at best. Not that he expected or desired anything more. From the upstairs window he could see the towers that stood high above the Dartford Crossing Bridge which spanned between Thurrock in Essex, to the north, and Dartford in Kent, to the south. The sun was still just visible to the west as he strained to look beyond the bend in the river at Greenhithe and past the skinny necks of the cranes. Every so often he would see some river traffic through the gaps between the nearby warehouses. This was a busy stretch, or so he was told, although he had never considered that any part of the main sections of the River Thames were anything but busy.

The glass of Chianti that he had just poured himself was the last one that he would drain from the, now redundant, bottle. He contemplated making the effort to go to the local Mini Market to buy another but decided against it. Instead, he ambled closer to the window. The sun's brightness glinted off the water as he reflected on how many hot and sultry sunsets he had basked in during his stay in Crete, each one so precious and considerably warmer than the one he had been witnessing today. He missed the solitude of those days but most of all he missed the protection of being someone else on an island a couple of thousand miles away. The distance shielded him from the chaos that had entered his simple life ever since she walked into his view at the Cactus and Coyote. Whenever he allowed these thoughts back in, he could hear the constant buzz and feel the stinging burn of the tattooist's needle on his shoulder, as if it had been freshly carved into him, just this afternoon. *It was a curse.* One that he had carried with him, like an inescapable restraint that tethered him to the memories that had dictated the pathway of his recent life. One of them was punishment enough, but two of them was like a prison sentence. His new existence as Kevin Marshall had served to sever him from them but the memories are crystal clear. So too, the memory of the act that had started it all around four years ago.

    Swann remembered the image of the Travelodge with great clarity. The single-story building sat adjacent to The Gamekeeper's Rest, a public house that was used frequently by lorry drivers as a convenient stopover for the night on their journey out of London and eastwards towards the busy port of Harwich in Essex to catch the early morning ferry across to the Hook of Holland, one of the busiest routes across the North Sea. Swann had been to The Gamekeeper's Rest with Betty on more than one occasion. Each enjoying the lively atmosphere and the warm, cosiness that came with the comfort of the open fire. It wasn't exactly their local, nor anybody's really. Its location was simply popular with a host of different sorts of people that made every visit interesting and varied. It was a sort of 'out of town' retreat. On the night in question Swann arrived alone. He had finished his shift at the Cactus and Coyote and had been making his way out into the street when his phone alerted him to a text message.
    It was Betty.
    Meet me outside the Gamekeeper's Rest.
    That was it, no more. Swann looked down at his phone and wondered what she had in mind but didn't bother to question it. He sent an acknowledgement that told her he was coming, slipped his phone back into his trouser pocket and made his way to his car. As far as he knew she was going to be seeing her sister, Elisha, but obviously something had changed. He thought that she must be at a loose end and decided to meet up for a drink instead. Or maybe they were both going to be there tonight. Swann was perfectly at ease with the idea of going for a drink, earlier than usual. After a shift at the pub, he was always ready to 'lose his inhibitions', as Betty used to call it. He made it a rule that he would never drink at work, unlike some of the others.
    Swann drove off in the direction of The Gamekeeper's Rest, allowing himself to drift along with the traffic at a leisurely pace. He wasn't sure whether Betty would beat him to it but either way he assumed that she wouldn't be far behind him if he did arrive first. It was a twenty-minute

drive and seeing as they were going to be early, he knew he would easily find a parking space. The car park could be really busy on certain nights. He could never understand why it had not been made a lot larger than it was. He would have made it bigger if it was his place. He turned the volume down a little on the radio and just allowed it to become a background noise. He had been listening to music all through his shift at the pub and welcomed the peace while he drove. As he turned into the drive that directed him in an arrow straight line for the pub he peered ahead to see if he could see Betty's car. It was there. She'd beaten him to it after all. He parked the car in a space that faced the front of the pub and sat for a moment, waiting to see whether Betty was going to show herself. On more than one occasion he thought that he had seen her outside the pub entrance but each time, he was mistaken. After a few minutes, his phone sounded its message alert tone again.

Change of plan. Come to room 8. Door's unlocked.

Swann recognised '*room 8*'. It referred to somewhere that he and Betty had been before. It wasn't a regular thing, but they had, on occasion, stopped over at the Travelodge if they had had too much to drink at the pub and thought better of driving back. Swann always felt that there was something erotic, even lustful, about spending the night at the Travelodge. As if they were enacting some salacious and forbidden act of passion. He got out of the car and walked slowly across the car park towards the Travelodge. There was a swagger in his stride. An anticipation of what was to greet him very soon. *She was waiting.* When he reached the door to number 8 it wasn't only unlocked, it was slightly ajar. He stepped inside. Betty wasn't immediately in sight but the sound of water running from the bathroom solved the puzzle. The door had a large towel draped over it which held it slightly open but not enough for him to be able to see inside. *Already in the shower, naked.* He recognised her shirt on the bed which laid on top of a pair of jeans and some underwear. Swann called out to her, just to make sure she knew it was him, but there was no reply. His phone buzzed again.

Get undressed.

He smiled, impressed by her ingenuity and imagination. He was being enticed in and he liked it. He felt his pulse step up its pace as he began to remove his shirt, and almost simultaneously unbuckle his belt one-handed. He dropped his clothes to the floor. The steam from the bathroom was seductively wafting into the room, and as he stepped towards the door, the bathroom light went out. In no time, Swann was fully undressed and ready to claim his reward. The water must have been running for a while because the bathroom was filled with steam. He pushed the door gently and could just see Betty's outline in the shower as he stepped across towards the shower door, treading clumsily on a crumpled bathmat as he fumbled his way through the mist. He noticed her phone was on the toilet seat. Swann felt the excitement working its magic on him. He could almost feel her softness against his skin as he slid the door across and stepped into the cubicle. Before he could take her in his arms, she all but leapt at him, pushing him back against the wall. Her mouth was upon his in an instant, her tongue driving into his mouth with an exaggerated eagerness. He could feel her breasts pressed against him and her hand feeling around his groin, taking him in her hot, wet hand. He wrapped his arms around her body and gripped her bottom, pulling her even harder towards him. The kissing was erotic and forceful. Swann felt that something seemed odd, but he couldn't grasp what. That was the moment that their eyes met for the first time. Swann looked hard into her piercing blue eyes and froze, momentarily. *Elisha*. His heart jumped as she continued to kiss his mouth passionately, her momentum, uninterrupted. He stood, shocked, as she slithered down his body, licking at his stomach. Swann was as out of control as he had ever been. She was irresistible. She was making his body yearn for more and in a brief moment, he knew he was powerless. Swann reached under her arms and pulled her up from him. Looking into her eyes, he turned her against the wall wrapping her legs around him. He wanted her now. Any rhyme or reason of what was happening betrayed him. He was nothing more than her captured prey. They embraced in an unrehearsed, spontaneous act of frantic lovemaking until both of them slid slowly to the floor, panting in each other's arms.

Neither spoke as they composed themselves, their legs entwined. Swann stared at her waiting for some sort of explanation, but none came his way. He didn't know what to say. Elisha just smiled and got up off the floor, picked up the phone and walked into the bedroom, no towel, just wet and naked. Swann stayed on the floor for a few minutes, still dazed by the surprise that he certainly wasn't expecting. He tried to understand what had happened, but it was hopeless. The water was still running in the cubicle. He stood and reached in and turned it off. He grabbed the large towel that he first saw draped over the bathroom door and began to dry himself off with it. All he could think of was getting out of there but first he had to try to talk to Elisha again. He shouted to her but got no answer. Then he tried again. Still nothing. Swann wrapped the towel around his waist, covering his lower half and walked into the bedroom. There were no clothes on the bed, as before, and no sign of Elisha in the room. His clothes were still on the floor where he had left them, but he was very much alone. Betty's phone was in the centre of the bed, abandoned.

Swann drove back to Betty's. He was due to stay there tonight and couldn't think clearly enough to process a reason why he should change the arrangement. That would only lead to suspicion. *Keep everything normal.* He was in a constant sweat. Questions peppered his brain, but he had no answers to offer. His shock accentuated when he parked up and noticed Betty's car in its usual spot. Elisha had got back. He wondered whether she would be inside or whether she had made her way home. *What a mess.* Automatically, he made his way inside, not knowing what to expect next or having any clue of how to deal with it. His mouth was dry, and his brow was clammy. His heart was now thrashing for the second time in the last hour, not that it had calmed down very much on the journey back to Betty's. He stepped into the living room and saw Betty sitting on the sofa, engrossed in some television programme. He froze and instinctively scanned the room for any sign of Elisha. She didn't appear to be there. Then he noticed the shirt that he'd seen at the Travelodge, Betty's shirt. It was on the arm of the sofa at the opposite end to where Betty was sitting.

'Hi, good day?' she said without taking her eyes from the screen. Swann tried to answer but his mouth failed him. 'You ok? You look hot and bothered. Anything up?'

'No,' was all he could muster.

'Elisha's been round,' she said, calmly.

'Oh?'

'Yeah, her car has let her down again. Something about it making a funny noise, or something like that. I didn't really know what she meant. I said you'd look at it for her, tomorrow. She borrowed mine for a couple of hours. Went off with my lumberjack shirt too for some reason. Have you seen my phone? Can't find it anywhere.'

Swann stood motionless; his shirt was clammy on his back; still sweating. His mind was racing. He put his hand into his pocket to reach for his handkerchief, to wipe his forehead and found something solid instead. He brought out Betty's phone. He had instinctively picked it up off the bed. Staring hard at it as though it was some alien object, he swiftly came up with something believable.

'Here, down the side of the cabinet,' he said in a shaken state.

'Oh, I looked there as well. I spent ages hunting everywhere actually. I've been all over the house,' she said as he handed it to her. She began to look for any recent messages that she may have missed.

'Oh, that's odd. All my messages to you have been deleted,' she said, with a quizzical look.

ELEVEN

Now
Minneapolis, Minnesota.

Many of the Patrol Officers were being deployed at a huge public gathering. The Minnesota State Fair is the second largest state fair in the United States. Outdoor concerts, music festivals, movies in the park, pet shows, antique shows and art shows are some of the varied and popular events that are available that provide a great deal of fun and excitement for hundreds of families and thousands of people throughout the year in the greater Twin Cities area of Minneapolis and St. Paul. However, in the uncustomary quiet station, the afternoon was dragging for Gregory Bonner as he sat at his desk in the Minneapolis Police Department on South 5th Street. His mind was occupied with something that he considered important even if the Police Department didn't. The previous winter had not been up to his expectations and the Snow Cold Index (SCI) hadn't excited him one bit. The regular amount of snowfall had only served to tease him into thinking that something remarkable might happen at any time, but it didn't. He had plotted and planned his spreadsheets and graphs on his laptop, created a brand-new league table showing the previous ten years of SCI information and spent several evenings at home in his den preparing for another torrent of frozen blizzards to come his way. He knew that he would have to accept that not every winter would produce new records but, as ever, he lived in hope. *If only we could have another 1996 winter*, he thought. This afternoon Bonner was bored to the point where he had even created a database using Microsoft Excel to record his most disappointing SCI scores of the last fifty years. When Gregory Bonner gets bored, he tends to resort to his default interest and therefore doesn't stay bored for too long. The problem for him was that this was nothing to do with the task that had been set for him by Big Toni, Captain Antonio Rodrigues. Bonner also knew that the Captain would be intrigued to know just how he had got on this afternoon with the task at hand. Bonner decided that Big Toni must've been just as bored as he was, coming up with such a tedious and longwinded challenge. With a glance at the clock, he decided that it was probably time that he put his spreadsheets and databases to one side for a while and actually got on with some policework. If Big Toni happened to sneak up behind him and find him messing with Snow Indexes again, he just might be in a whole lot of trouble.

Bonner switched screens and gazed, half-heartedly at the BCA. The information on the Bureau of Criminal Apprehension Homepage displayed a number of administrative services ranging from Firearms to the Minnesota Duty Officer program, and from the Minnesota Crime Alert Network to the Minnesota Missing and Unidentified Persons Clearinghouse. This was his port of call. Big Toni had specifically requested that Bonner and the rest of the available officers should study the seemingly, endless list of missing and unidentified persons in an effort to get Deputy Police Chief Bolton off his back. Big Toni was never at his most cheerful when someone above his rank was pestering him for results. Minnesota had thousands of missing people on this particular database and Big Toni was getting the grief for some of it. His officers had been instructed to look at the last fifteen years and to concentrate on any missing persons from within the Minneapolis City boundaries. Bonner knew before he even started that this was a task and a half. He followed the links through to the dedicated page and gasped at the amount of information held within the MUPC. Casually, he began to scroll through the list and mentally ignore any that had been missing since before the specified timeframe. There were still hundreds there. *What a sad list it is. So many people*, thought Bonner, as he scratched his chin and wondered just how long this was going to take. The ages ranged from three to ninety- three. He looked into the eyes of each photograph wondering how so many people can just disappear. As each face started back at him, his far too active imagination conjured up a scenario to fit each missing person. *That one must have been murdered. That one was taken and held hostage for years in a barn in Wyoming.* Bonner's mind was far too inventive for his own good. *She killed her whole family and ran away to the other side of the States. Wow, she's pretty. What happened to her?* Before he knew it, he had gone completely off track and was drifting in his own dreamworld, imaging all sorts of crazy scenarios that he attached to each face that fitted his weird and idyllic realm.

Scrolling down the sea of faces, he eventually began to run out of scenarios and realised that he wasn't actually concentrating as he should be. Not knowing where to start he chose to scroll back to the top of the list and work through them in alphabetical order, noting the dates on his pad as he went. Although he enjoyed his little game, he was aware that he had just wasted more time and if Big Toni showed up, he would have a lot of explaining to do. A glance at the time displayed on his laptop screen made him shudder. Big Toni could quite possibly be back at any time. He wondered whether any of them would be someone that he knew or maybe, just recognised. As he stared at the top of the screen and allowed the empty faces to scroll past again, he became quite disturbed by just how many young people had been missing for so many years. The information showed their name, the location from which they were missing, the date they went missing and what their current age was now. Many of the faces had been unaccounted for, for a lot longer than the timeframe that Big Toni wanted him to concentrate on. A little boy that looked about 4 years old in the photograph was now 32. Even a guy who went missing in 1967 was given the current age of 111. Bonner was taken in by the thought that he could possibly be alive. *Where did you all go?* A lot of the locations that were recorded on the MUPC were places that he had never heard of. Then there were the more familiar ones. Places that he knew well. As he studied the list, he was able to disregard the ones that had been on the list for over fifteen years and stop at each of those that needed to be considered. As he reached each of the ones that fell into the right time frame, he wrote the details on a pad beside him. Bonner had no plan for how he might begin to trace such people that had been missing for so long, but he knew he would have to come up with something plausible when Big Toni turned up. There were a few that actually fell outside of Minnesota but were still on the list. A couple from North Dakota, one from Wisconsin and another from Iowa. Although he didn't recognise the townships that were given as their last reported location, he thought that these must have gone missing from locations very close to the border with those neighbouring states and were therefore included on this list. The dates interested him too. *How many went missing on Christmas day?* he thought. *That would be strange. Maybe they couldn't face washing all those dishes.* He allowed himself and little smile but soon realised how inappropriate smiling was in this instance. After twenty minutes of staring at the faces, their names, last known locations and prospective current ages, he sat back in his chair and looked at the details written on his pad that he had taken from the MUPC site and wondered where to start. *Minefield*, he thought. He decided to break the list down some more and write out the most recent entries in the hope that there might be a better chance of latching onto a slightly fresher trail of those people. The older people that had been gone for up to fifteen years were quite possibly dead anyway, depending upon their ages at the time of their disappearance. Bonner scrolled back to the top of the list and began to check the ones he had written on his pad against the faces on the list in case he missed one. He reread the details of each face, although this time without the fairy-tale scenarios, and ticked them off on his pad as he went. He was at least glad that this was helping to shrink the list considerably. Not as much as he would like, but it was getting smaller. *What if they don't want to be found? Shouldn't they be left alone to get on with their lives?* As he got halfway down the sea of faces for the third time, he heard a noise outside. *Big Toni?* Bonner's desk was close enough to the window that looked out onto South 4th Avenue. All he needed to do was to slide his chair across a few feet and stop it clanging into the radiator for a better look down into the car park. *Better not get spotted looking out,* he thought, as he peered slowly over the edge of the window frame. Big Toni's car was there. Big Toni, however, was not. Bonner pushed away from the window and back to his desk. With his eyes affixed firmly on the screen, he began to study the sea of faces again, this time with a renewed determination. Busily, he checked the names of those that fitted into the time frame with those already on his list. He went through the K's, L's and onto the M's, trying hard to concentrate on the details, whilst concentrating even harder on whether he could hear Big Toni entering the office. Then he heard Big Toni's voice. He was back. Bonner looked as studious as he could, assiduously working through the information on the MUPC and cross-examining it with the details he had written on his pad. When Big Toni noticed Bonner, seemingly, hard at work, he remembered the task he had left him to follow up in his absence. Big Toni made his way slowly across the office towards Bonner, intrigued to find him glued to the laptop. He took a slightly curved approach to Bonner's desk so that he could get a better view of precisely what Bonner was looking at. The first thing on Big Toni's mind was that he'd caught Bonner looking at the SCI and he mentally prepared to unleash his anger upon the unsuspecting Patrol Officer. In one way, Big Toni was a little disappointed to find that the scribblings on the pad beside Bonner were not about snowfall. He was quite looking forward to bellowing at him for disregarding the order he had been left to carry out. Big Toni stood behind him, certain that Bonner knew he was in close proximity. This would usually be enough to get some kind of reaction from Bonner, but not so far. Big Toni leaned his huge frame around to one side of Bonner's desk and into full view.

'Good afternoon, Bonner,' he said in a deep and soft whisper.

Bonner didn't react. Big Toni wondered what kind of game Bonner was playing and tried again, 'I said 'Good afternoon, Bonner,'' he repeated.

Bonner wrote some details onto his pad and looked back at the screen, apparently ignoring Big Toni. There was an icy silence as Big Toni frowned and looked hard at Bonner's face that was seemingly, absorbed with what was on his screen.

'I said...' began the increasingly impatient Captain.

'I knew her,' muttered Bonner, quietly, tapping his pen on his pad, 'She went missing.'

'No shit, Sherlock,' exclaimed Big Toni, with eyes now bigger and wider, in anticipation as to what gem Bonner would come out with next. Bonner was unphased by Big Toni's outburst and continued to stare at the screen. Big Toni looked at the screen and down at Bonner's pad and read the information.

'Caterina Marks...so?'

Bonner sat back staring at the screen, 'I'd forgotten about her,' he said, 'She went missing not all that long before the girls left the Nelson house. You remember? The guy that hanged himself from the balcony?'

'I remember,' responded Big Toni, his mind turning to the scar on his shin that he gained from falling over the piece of wood that had been sticking up out of snow in the back yard, 'So what? Who was she?'

'Someone that I knew once. I knew her from college.'

Big Toni shot his eyes back to the screen and read the details.

Caterina Marks. Missing person.
Missing from: Minneapolis, Mn.
Missing since: 04/26/2010
Current age: 27

'You remember where she lived?' Big Toni asked.

'I think so,' replied Bonner, who was deep in thought, trying to piece together some more details about her in his mind.

'Your friend, you say?'

'Not really mine. She was Betty's best friend.'

'And who is Betty?' asked Big Toni.

'Betty was a friend of mine. Her and her sister lived at the house where we found that guy, Wade Nelson. He was their father. The girls both left for England shortly after the dog died,' said Bonner.

'What dog? Now what are you on about, Bonner?' said Big Toni, losing his patience a little with Bonner's explanation of who was who.

'Hastings. You fell over his grave in the garden, under all that lovely snow,' said Bonner with a well-disguised smirk.

Big Toni had heard enough and turned to make his way back to his office. Before he reached his office door, he stopped and looked back at Bonner, 'You wanna follow this up?'

Bonner was surprised that this was a question and not an order. Taken aback slightly, he looked at Big Toni, then back at the screen which was displaying Caterina's photograph, 'Yeah, sure.'

'Well, make a good job of it. The Deputy Chief is all over my ass.'

Bonner nodded and watched Big Toni go into his office and close the door behind him. He turned his attention, once more, to the face that now seemed to be asking for help. It was almost as if the young girl in the photograph was pleading with him to find her. Her eyes were all of a sudden connecting with him. A chill ran through him as he dropped his pencil down onto the A4 pad. *Well, well,* he thought. *After all these years I get to chase after you again,* he said to himself and shook his head at how strange it all felt. Bonner clicked busily on the screen and waited for the printer on his desk to begin to whirr, signifying that the photograph of Caterina Marks was on its way. He collected it from the tray that dispensed the photo and looked at his old friend. *Where did you go, Caterina Marks?*

TWELVE

DI Marc Sutton felt eager to establish whether the earring that he found at the bottom of Trenton Street had shown any signs of DNA that might have belonged to Angelica Rowntree and had asked DS Carrie Linton to check on whether any information had come back from the laboratory yet. He was expecting a call from the lab to filter through to him anytime now. While he waited to hear the latest, he sat at his desk and considered what he might say to Angelica's parents if there was a positive identification that suggested that she may have been present at that particular site. In one way it would be *news*, but it wouldn't necessarily be received as *good*. The only news that Brian and Lesley Rowntree wanted to hear was that their daughter had been found safe and well. Despite sending his team out for another look at the area, they hadn't come up with anything substantial. The ground had received enough rain to wash away certain potentially useful information and the area had been driven over by numerous vehicles. Dog walkers and other passers-by had trodden everything flat too. Nothing had shown up on the fencing that divided the disused car park from the road, nor in the undergrowth immediately beside it. Just the earring. Earlier, Carrie had explained to Sutton that an officer had been talking, again, with Robin Greaves, the mechanic who caught sight of Angelica in the company of a man, as he hurriedly left the garage. By all accounts, Greaves was vaguer about what he had seen at the time than he had been initially. His description of the person he said he saw with Angelica wasn't helpful. Carrie explained how he had been asked if he was sure it was a man, to which he replied, 'I think so.' The only difference in his story this time was a comment he made regarding the fact that he thought the man was possibly showing something to the girl, but he didn't know what it was. 'Couldn't see,' he had said. Sutton sat upright and stretched his back. His shoulders both cracked. *Sitting was the new smoking*, he often thought. He opened a file and began to look through the summary reports on the interviews that had been conducted during the first few days of the investigation, such as it was. A list of Angelica's friends had been made at the top of the page he was now studying. Each of their accounts was similar and had failed to shine any glimmer of light on anything particularly useful. There was nothing unusual about her. She appeared to be just a regular young girl. Just like Haley Breen had been. He read through each of their interviews, more like informal chats, and found nothing more than a number of stories that reflected Angelica's kindness and popularity with her friends. The neighbours that knew her best had nothing out of the ordinary to contribute either. Sutton found himself sitting, gazing at the words, but not reading any of them anymore.

Then something, probably just desperation, started the cogs whirring in Sutton's head. Once again, and for reasons that he could not explain he was drawn to check some of the details in Haley Breen's file. This time he felt no desire to look again at the pictures of the unfortunate girl's body. It was the summary reports that he wanted to study. He considered that although the two girls had not been personally known to each other, maybe they had shared some of the same friends. Swiftly, he found the appropriate pages that included the statements that were given by some of Haley Breen's friends. Pointing with his index finger, he checked the names at the beginning of each interview and corresponded them to those on Angelica's file. The list was reasonably long for both of the girls. Had they been listed alphabetically; it would have made the task a whole lot simpler. Slowly, he ran his finger down the list of names on Haley Breen's file and checked across to Angelica's at each one he came to. He found just one name that corresponded on both lists. Emily Roache. He had no recollection of talking with her himself and checked the bottom of the statement to see which officer had signed their name as the interviewer. The names were printed as well as signed. Haley Breen's file showed the officer to be Dominic Strand. Sutton knew that he had left the force within months of the date shown at the foot of the page and certainly would not have been active in Angelica's case. He looked at the bottom of Emily's statement concerning the missing persons file of Angelica Rowntree. To his surprise the space for the signature had been left blank.

Sutton was about to head out of his office to find out where Carrie had got to when she appeared at the door with DCI Blackery.

'DS Linton has been pestering me about the DNA report regarding that earring you picked up, so I thought I'd tell you myself.'

'You've had word, then?' said Sutton, his eyes meeting Carrie's in an evenly matched expression of impatience.

'Yes, the lab phoned it all through to the Forensic Science Office and they in turn called me about half an hour ago.'

'Half an hour?' exclaimed Sutton, again exchanging glances with Carrie.

'Well, there was no point me charging in here, I had other business to attend to, you know,' Blackery said, dismissively.

'So, is it hers? The earring?' asked Sutton.

'No. It isn't. Wild goose chase, so you'd better try harder,' said Blackery.

Sutton felt an immediate wave of despondency wash over him. He looked at Carrie and quietly mouthed 'Damn it.'

'Now, I've got a meeting with the Lord Mayor of the borough soon, something about a parade, so I'll leave you to it.' Blackery turned abruptly and left Sutton's office without another word.

'Fat lot of help he is, lately,' said Carrie.

Sutton agreed but didn't comment. He turned his attention instead to a report that had come in last night about a series of damaged vehicles following a car chase. The stolen vehicle had been abandoned but not before it had careered into a number of parked vehicles. The owners of the said vehicles were, obviously, less than pleased and wanted answers as to why the Police were chasing it in the first place. *Should have prevented it from getting into the estate in the first place etc, etc.*

Sutton needed a plan, and he needed a fresh starting point. He didn't feel that Greaves, the mechanic, was going to have a lot more to offer although he still wanted to talk to him again, just in case. He sat in his chair, disappointed that his discovery had led them nowhere. Whoever the earring belonged to; it obviously didn't appear to be Angelica. *Dead end.* But Emily Roache may be worth revisiting.

THIRTEEN

Four years ago

Everything had changed from the moment that he stepped into the shower cubicle at the Travelodge and got the surprise of his life. One of them, anyway. The evening that followed, that he had spent at Betty's house, was surreal. The guilt from what had happened that afternoon swept over him, time and time again. *Should he tell her?* The more he thought about it, the more he knew that he had no idea where to begin. How could he say the words? *I screwed your sister in the shower.* Somehow, he had managed to get through the evening before leaving around midnight and going back to his own place. What he couldn't seem to shake off was Betty's insistence that he should check on Elisha's car the next day. It was the last thing he wanted to do and yet he knew he would have to comply for two reasons. One, is that he needed to behave as normally as he could until his distorted thought processes could reassemble, and two, he needed to know what on earth the whole shower fiasco was all about.

The following day he had arrived at Elisha's house, at Betty's request, to take a look at her car. But that was far from his mind. He parked his car next to Elisha's apparently stricken vehicle and looked at the front of the terraced house, sorely tempted to drive away again. He had no real plan of how to approach the subject or what to say when he came face to face with her, but he knew that he had to get it over and done with. Then, hopefully, he could get things back to normal. Even though he knew that things would never be normal again.

Swann walked from his car with his eyes rigidly fixed on the front door as if it were hiding some unavoidable fate behind its innocent facade. He stopped momentarily, and again, wondered whether to turn away and drive off, but he knew he would only be delaying the inevitable. *This is crazy.* He stepped up to the door and rang the bell. *This was not going to be very comfortable,* he thought. When the door opened, Elisha stood there, wearing a floral dressing gown, and smiling at him. Swann had no smile to offer. She half-turned and stood to one side, waiting for him to step into the hallway, and when he didn't move, she wandered back into the house, leaving him at the open door. He looked down into the empty hallway and considered that maybe he should follow her in but was not sure of anything. He could hear her moving about in the house and after a full two minutes it was quite clear that she was not coming out again and that he would have to either go in or leave. But he couldn't leave without at least trying to make some sense of this. He stepped into the hallway and closed the door behind him. He wandered casually into the back room and noticed her standing at a window, with her back to him. The atmosphere was tense, at least it was as far as Swann was concerned. He cracked first.

'Look, Elisha, I don't know what you were playing at but…'

'Playing?' she said, as she turned to face him, her expression, serious and intense, 'You think I was playing? Did it feel like I was playing, Karter?' she said, as her stern look allowed a sultry, almost sexy smile curl at the edges of her mouth.

'I don't know what you were doing, but whatever it was, it shouldn't have happened,' he said.

Elisha turned back and looked out of the window into the garden. More silence. Swann stayed routed to the spot. He could appreciate that she was breathing harder as if she were angered by his comments. He looked around the room at nothing in particular, seeing things but not registering anything. He had been here once before with Betty but had not really taken a lot of notice of the layout of the place. The rooms were fairly small, and the furniture seemed to be crowded into the meagre space. He certainly felt as though the walls were closing in on him today. The atmosphere in the whole house was unwelcoming. He remembered that he hadn't liked it the first time he was here, and he liked it a lot less now. As he stood, wishing that he could be somewhere else, his mobile phone buzzed in his pocket. He knew that it would be Betty, just checking that he was there and that everything was fine. His guilt overflowed again as it had been doing ever since he arrived at Betty's last night. He chose not to look at his phone. As he looked across the room, Elisha looked over her shoulder at him, pulled a chair out from under the dining room table, and sat down. Her blue eyes looked inquisitively up at him. Swann needed to break the silence and try to find a way of repairing the damage. Before he could think of something to say, Elisha spoke.

'What are you going to do? Will you tell her about us, or shall I?'

'What are you talking about? There is no *us*. Don't start saying that. You tricked me. You even took Betty's car. You took her phone. You set me up, Elisha.'

'Betty *gave* me her car to use, I didn't *take* it,' she said, calmly.

'I can't believe you did that. And sending me text messages so that I would think it was Betty. You stole her phone just to…'

'I didn't *steal* anything,' she said, interrupting him, 'May have borrowed it, that's all.'

'What the hell, Elisha?' he said, his voice gradually becoming louder.

She crossed her legs slowly, allowing her gown to fall away, exposing her underwear. Swann felt his eyes focus on her, just as she had intended. She knew he was looking at her and smiled. Swann looked briefly at her face, registering her pleasure, and looked away again, sharply. Her distraction tactics were having an effect and Swann knew that unless he could get control of whatever she was trying to do, he could be in trouble again.

'Tell me what's the matter with your car and I'll go take a look,' he said in desperation, as he took a step backwards towards the hallway. Swann's foot clumsily struck the edge of the door causing it to close behind him.

'Tell me that you didn't enjoy it, then,' she said.

Swann knew that he couldn't deny that, but it certainly wasn't something he was going get drawn into. 'I'm not doing this. I'm not going to do this to Betty.'

'Bit late for that, Karter,' she said, seductively, as she stood slowly from her chair and took a couple of paces towards him, Her long legs now fully on show. She tugged slowly at the tie around her waist, allowing the gown to loosen and open at the front, to clearly show that underneath the gown, she was topless. Swann reached for the door, but Elisha was already right beside him. He could smell her fragrant perfume as she put a hand on his. Elisha's gown was fully open and barely in contact with her shoulders. It was virtually falling off her. Swann could feel her touching him and tried to turn to get a grip on the door handle, but she already had one hand on it, holding it tightly. Swann didn't want to use force, but he was fast running out of ideas. Elisha pushed hard and his back hit the wall behind him, trapping him in the room. He could feel her mouth caress his neck and move towards his, kissing his cheek, softly. Swann turned his head away and pushed at her body with an arm, trying to get enough space between them that would allow him to open the door, but Elisha was all over him. Her gown had landed on the floor by their feet and her all-but naked body was pressing hard against him.

'Elisha, stop,' he shouted, as she continued to kiss his face and groan with pleasure, probing her tongue at his lips, 'For Christ's sake, stop it.'

She took no notice of his cries and grabbed at his groin letting go of the door handle. Swann took his chance to push her backwards. As much as he wanted to be careful, he needed to use considerable force to get her off him. Elisha fell backwards, but only momentarily, which didn't give Swann enough time to reach for the door handle. Her hair was across her face, but he could still see her wild eyes as she came back, panting, for another go at him. Elisha reached with both arms for his neck to pull him towards her just as Swann reached out to put his hand on her shoulder. As Elisha leapt forwards, Swann's hand struck the right side of her face, causing her to cry out. The impact was significant enough to cause Swann to react with an instant apology. For a long second, they looked at each other. Swann, backed up against the wall and, Elisha, almost naked before him. Her cheek was red on one side of her face. It was then that she smiled as she touched her cheek. Swann went cold. In the pause he turned towards the door and opened it. Nothing was said, but when he glanced back at Elisha, she was still smiling at him.

When Swann returned to home, his head was again, filled with indecision about whether he should tell Betty what had happened. The more he thought about it, the more of a tangled web it appeared to be. The story of the Travelodge was bad enough, but now his attempts at explaining himself to her would be doubly difficult. Swann sat outside his house in his car mulling over the idea of how Elisha had set him up at the Travelodge and then gone after him again this morning, but it raised far too many questions. Questions that he did not have satisfactory answers to. In his mind, he could hear Betty quizzing him, but the harder he tried to think of reasonable responses, the more confused he became. *Just tell her everything. Tell her nothing and hope it goes away.* Having got no closer to working out what he should do, Swann made his way inside. He angrily threw his car keys onto the sofa and went into the bedroom to lay on the bed in a feeble attempt to sooth his throbbing head. *Now what?*

When Betty Nelson left her house, her head was in turmoil. She screeched the tyres on the tarmac and weaved her car down the road, fishtailing as she went. At the end of the road, she turned out with hardly a glance for other traffic. It wasn't until she had travelled a little further that the tears of worry for Elisha began to trickle down her face. As she drove, her head replayed the phone call, like a discordant cacophony, tormenting her every thought, disabling her ability to think or process anything. *'I've hurt my face, there's blood on my pyjamas.'*

Drive, drive, drive.

As she steered her car onto the opposite side of the road, past a line of traffic, and turned hard right into Elisha's road, she could see the Paramedic's Rapid Response Vehicle outside Elisha's house, causing Betty to expel an involuntary muffled cry. She slammed the brakes on and stopped her car in the middle of the road, leaving it there, abandoned, with the driver's door still swinging, and ran straight past the open front door and into the house. When Betty reached the doorway to the room where she could clearly recognise the reflective jacket of the Paramedic, her run was reduced to a cautious walk. All the way there, her mind had been conjuring up images of what she might find upon her arrival and now she was about to find out for real. When the Paramedic attending to Elisha turned to see who had just entered the room, it enabled Betty to get her first view of her sister. She was sitting on the sofa holding, what looked like an ice pack, against the side of her face. Betty moved closer and gasped.

'Oh my God, are you alright?' she said.

'I'll live. I shouldn't have called you; I knew you'd panic,' Elisha mumbled.

'No, you must always call me.'

Elisha had something that Betty didn't recognise on her finger. Some sort of probe. The Paramedic told Betty that he had advised Elisha to get checked out at the hospital once the Ambulance arrives. He explained that she should have an x-ray on her cheek to check whether it had been fractured by the blow although his initial assessment suggested that there wasn't any obvious fracture and that she would be sporting no more than a bruise. *Best to be sure, though.*

'Yes, you must let them look at it,' agreed Betty.

'I'm not going. I don't need to.'

Betty stood holding Elisha's hand and began to take in the extent of her sister's injuries. She could not really avoid seeing the blood-stained pad that sat in the bowl next to the sofa or the red blotches that stained Elisha's pyjama top. When Elisha spoke, Betty could tell that her lip was a little swollen and was already turning a purplish blue. It appeared that the bloodstains were from her gums that had been bleeding but had now stopped. The split on her lip looked like it should heal in the next week or so.

'Tell me what happened,' Betty asked, as she knelt closer to her sister.

'Look it was nothing much. Karter was here, as you know, to help sort out my car problems. He had a look and found out that it was something to do with a belt or something, I didn't really get it, but anyhow he's going to get it sorted for me. He wasn't here all that long.'

'Was he here when this happened?' Betty asked.

'God, I wish he had been. He could've helped me. No, he'd already gone. I feel daft now, it's nothing, really.'

'Elisha, I'm worried about you. Tell me what happened,' Betty said as she put her arm around her sister and tried to encourage her to speak.

Elisha looked at Betty and then at the Paramedic. 'Look, It's nothing. I've already told the Paramedic anyway.'

'For Christ's sake, Elisha,' exclaimed Betty as she, herself, began to tremble.

'Oh, very well,' said Elisha with a tedious sigh, 'As I said, Karter had just left, and I came back into the living room. There was a stupid bag on the floor, and I kicked it as I walked in, and it sent me flying. Only had my bloody flip-flops on too. I hit my face on the door frame and fell onto the edge of the sofa, softened my fall, actually. Still bruised my bum, though.'

'You could have knocked yourself out. You didn't, did you?'

'No, I was fine. Sort of. I panicked and called 999 when I saw my face in the mirror and noticed the spots of blood on my top. I shouldn't have bothered anyone, really. I'm sorry.'

'Don't be daft. You did the right thing to call me,' said Betty.

'Yeah, and how fast did you drive here? I knew I shouldn't have called as soon as I put the phone down.'

After a few final checks from the Paramedic and some more of Elisha's protestations, he decided to go. Elisha's flat refusal to go to the hospital had left him with little other option. She repeatedly said that her face wasn't hurting as much and that she was sure it hadn't got a fracture. Betty argued with her, and the Paramedic tried to encourage her to have an x-ray to be safe, but Elisha was adamant that she wasn't going anywhere. She was given the usual advice about having it checked out if she was in pain or simply changed her mind but that was that. Betty stayed with Elisha for the rest of the day, playing nurse, and that evening Betty ended up sleeping at Elisha's house. They talked into the evening with the remains of a large bottle of cider and two bottles of Pinot Grigio for accompaniment. They had reminisced about when they were younger, back in Minneapolis. Betty spoke about when her best friend, Caterina Marks, had gone missing and how the Police had searched around the house. She curled into a ball and talked about how they had questioned her about Caterina and how she had not been much help. They talked and cried about how much they missed their mother and about how much they didn't miss their father. Neither had made the return journey for his funeral. It just became something that they had both chosen to ignore. At first, they were both shocked, but it was temporary to say the least. Later into the evening, once the wine bottles had become empty, Elisha and Betty sat in silence. Both were tired. Betty's decision, much earlier, to stay with Elisha had been the right choice as far as she was concerned. She had enjoyed the chat about the old days and the laughs about their old college friends. But now she had become suddenly aware that the mood had changed. Elisha's mood.

'What's up? Is your face hurting?'

Elisha had her hand up to her forehead and when she lowered it Betty could see the tears.

'Oh, darling, can I get you something? Do you need something cold on it?'

'No, it's not that,' Elisha replied.

Elisha's pained expression was followed by more than just a few tears. Now she was crying with her head held in her hands.

'Elisha. What is it? Oh, my love, tell me.'

Elisha's pitiful eyes looked up at Betty. Betty felt a coldness run through her as if there was something terrible about to happen. She was right.

'I couldn't say anything before when the Paramedic was here. I don't want to tell you now either, but…'

'It's ok,' said Betty, 'Just tell me,'

Elisha took a moment to compose herself and breathed deeply, 'It's about earlier. I lied to you, I'm so sorry, but I couldn't say it with that Paramedic here.'

Betty was confused and held her sister close, not really certain what was coming next or whether she really wanted to hear it. They sat quiet for another minute, Elisha dabbing her tears, before she turned slightly to look Betty square in the eyes.

'Earlier when Karter was here…he…hit me,' she whimpered.

'What? What are you saying?' blurted Betty.

'Look I swear I didn't do anything; it was just…'

'What? Tell me, Elisha.'

'He came over, as you know, and I started to tell him about the car, I was trying to explain what noise it was making, I wasn't really paying attention to him. Then I realised that he kept looking at me all funny. When I went to go upstairs to put something else on, he put his arm around me. So, I pushed him off. I thought that was it, I didn't know what was going on. Then he...' Elisha's voice cracked, and she tailed off.

Betty gasped and held her hand to her mouth, 'Oh, my god,' she said, 'What?'

'He tried to kiss me. He had a hold of my neck. He kept on grabbing at me, and I turned away and he banged my face against the door frame. Then when he held my top and pulled it, I swung around, and I felt his hand hit my mouth. I don't even think he meant it, but it hurt, I know that. I was scared and thought he was going to hit me again or try to tear my top off. It felt like a bit like an accident, but I don't know. I was shaking but I managed to tell him to get out. Then he just left. I laid on the floor and cried for ages...then I called the Paramedic 'cos I saw the blood and I didn't know what else to do.'

'For Christ's sake, Elisha,' exclaimed Betty as she, herself, began to tremble.

Betty sat holding Elisha's arm, her mind couldn't get anything in order. *This can't be happening.* But she knew it was. *The bastard. I'll kill him.*

'Betty, I didn't know this was in his mind. I didn't do anything to cause this to happen, I swear.'

'I know you didn't, my darling. It's ok, it's not your fault.'

'I thought he was trying to rape me. He pulled at my top and tried to open it up...I thought he was trying to put his hand inside...' she said, as she crumbled into Betty's arms and wept uncontrollably, 'I often thought that he looked at me funny, like he fancied me, but I couldn't bring myself to tell you. I'm so sorry.'

'Well, I know now, don't I?' said Betty, 'I'll ring the Police.'

'No, no. Don't. I'll get dragged through hell; they'll say I made it all up. He's bound to deny it all. I don't want all that. No. Please. We can deal with this ourselves.'

Betty looked at Elisha, everything was churning around in her head, 'You're fucking right we will,' she said, 'He'll pay for this.'

FOURTEEN

Minneapolis, Minnesota.
Now

Golden Valley, Minnesota, is a city in the suburbs of Hennepin County on the western fringes of Minneapolis. Home, once upon a time, to the Native American Sioux tribes that had encampments on nearby Medicine Lake and was founded in 1886. It's approximate population of 22,000 people was far too many for Gregory Bonner to have to sift through in his search for information pertaining to the sudden disappearance of Caterina Marks back in 2010. Having been surprised and quite pleased to be given the opportunity to delve into his old friend's disappearance, he now felt as though he would be looking for a needle in a haystack. A big haystack too. He had thought about her a lot since being given his task, but his memories were restricted to that of a young teenager and not a 27-year-old woman, as she would be today. He could recall quite clearly how she used to look. Light auburn hair that went to about halfway down her back. No curls. Nice teeth, he always thought she had nice teeth. And she was what he called, slender, not skinny. A fairly pale sort of complexion too, but pretty. *Definitely pretty.*

 Bonner had brought along a number of A5 sized photographs of the picture from the MUPC missing persons site but knew it was always going to be an uphill struggle. The Missing Person's Report Form had also enabled him to construct a fuller picture of how Caterina Marks might look today. The information that detailed her last known whereabouts had provided him with an age-progressed photograph of her which gave a computer-generated impression of how she may have looked at the age of 24 albeit she would be a little older now. Bonner could see the similarity to the girl he once knew. Additionally, the form supplied her date of birth, sex, race, height, weight, hair colour and eye colour. He was also aware as to just how much people can change over a short period of time, let alone a whole 10 years. The comments section at the foot of the page explained that she had disappeared on April 26th, 2010, having been last seen by both her parents to be leaving the family home after breakfast. There were no other witnesses to her disappearance, and she has not been seen or heard from since. She had not said where she was heading. The information on the form did not state whether foul play was suspected.

The ride out in his Patrol car had been a pleasant one. The traffic was light, and the sun shone brightly in an azure blue sky. His route along Golden Valley Road had allowed him a view of the north aspect of Theodore Wirth Regional Park; one of a number of recreational areas in and around the city. He had walked along the paths on many occasions and enjoyed the scenic open spaces. Mostly, of course, he had enjoyed the trudges through the park when it was knee-deep in beautiful fresh snow. He sat in his Patrol car and picked up an envelope that contained all the paperwork and photographs that he had assembled earlier this morning in readiness for his inaugural visit to Golden Valley and to what was once the home of Catarina Marks. He ran his thumb under the seal on the envelope and peeked inside. With his forefinger and thumb, he carefully prised out one of the A5 photos of the age-progressed Caterina. To Bonner, it was almost as if she was in the car with him. He had found himself talking to her photo when he sat in his den at home, as if he were trying to reach out to her, almost to ask her to help him find her. A few members of the local community, a couple and two young boys, slowed as they walked past his car and peered in at him. No doubt they were simply being inquisitive. He was aware of them, but his gaze never strayed from the face of his old friend for more than it took for his eyes to flicker to one side. After a couple of minutes, he put the photo back into the envelope and pressed the seal down once more. Bonner looked across at the house that he intended to visit. It all felt a bit surreal. He wondered what sort of reception he would get. He had driven to the neighbourhood that he was once familiar with. It didn't look vastly different to how he remembered it. He was hoping to be able to speak with Alexandria Org, the mother of Caterina Marks. Bonner's research had discovered that her mother had re-married in 2014 but had remained in the same property. Connor Org, her current husband worked locally at KARE, an NBC-affiliated television station serving the Twin Cities television market. KARE is situated just a few miles west of the Golden Valley Country Club. He didn't suppose that Mrs Org would be overjoyed to see him and have the painful memories dredged up from the bottom of the depths of such a murky pond. However, he felt pretty relaxed and was ready for his latest challenge.

Bonner thought that the house looked familiar to him but questioned his judgement immediately, thinking that maybe he didn't really remember it after all. He actually couldn't remember whether he had been inside before or not. He had recognised the Nelson residence though. That unforgettable double balcony. He had become absorbed with the prospect of finding Caterina Marks alive and being able to return her to her mother, but he knew that was a long shot, after an absence of 10 years and with no sign or glimmer of hope whatsoever. Bonner was glad that the report had not mentioned that she was seen getting into a stranger's car like so many of the others he had read about on the MUPC. He had spent a considerable number of hours in his den reading the aged statements from Caterina's family and friends in order to get a fuller picture of how the investigation had gone originally. It seemed that a thorough job had been done. Fruitless, though it was. Bonner found it difficult at times not to feel personally involved, not just with Caterina's story but with all of them. During his evenings alone in his den he had read through a lot of the different reports and exchanged glances with so many different faces. Each of them had a different story and set of circumstances that led up to their disappearance. It was a sad website, for sure. He knew that to remain fully focussed was the only way to approach this. He couldn't afford to allow his fondness for Caterina to fog the purpose of his investigation. So, with that in mind, he gathered some of the information that he brought with him and got out of the Patrol car. The warmth from the sunshine was immediately evident and filled him with a strange sense of renewed hope. His mouth felt a little dry as he stood and looked at the house where so much sadness and distress had occurred back in 2010. It probably still did. Bonner knew that he had to make a start and that once he got going that he would be fine. As he walked up the path, past the white-painted wicket fence that followed the contours of the manicured lawn, the front door opened. Connor Org, he presumed, gave a curious look. He was very smartly dressed. Bonner's first thought was that the man was ready to go to play golf or maybe he was off to the tennis club or maybe he always dressed smartly.

'Anything wrong?' he said, instinctively.

'No, Sir. Nothing is wrong. I was hoping to speak to Mrs Org. Is she at home?'

'Yes, yes, I'm her husband. What's this about?'

'Would it be possible to speak to her directly, Sir?' *Being her husband doesn't mean I want to speak to you,* Bonner thought.

'Yes, she's in the garden, I'll call her. Wait here.'

The front door closed again, and Bonner waited. He turned his attention to how he looked in comparison to Mr Org. He brushed his hand down his trousers and straightened his tie. He had left his cap in the car. It was never going to be the easiest of conversations and especially after so long since the original investigation went cold, but he knew that there was nowhere else to start. He had already given some thought to the fact that a lot of time had passed and that maybe that would change the dynamic in his favour, or so he hoped. Bonner glanced around behind him as a passing bicycle sounded its bell as a dog scampered across the road ahead of it with its tail tucked away, defensively.

'Hello, I'm Mrs Org. Can I help you?'

Bonner turned back towards the front door to set eyes on Alexandria Org. She was 50 years old, according to the information he had gathered over the past few days, but he thought that she looked a little older. *Perhaps that's understandable,* he thought. She was wearing a pair of dark blue dungarees over a white sweatshirt and held a pair of bright yellow gardening gloves in one hand. Her greying hair was a little ruffled and yet Bonner's first impression was one of a woman who had class. Just something about her. Her eyes sparkled and made Bonner feel more at ease than when he first arrived.

'Good morning, Mrs Org. My name is Gregory Bonner, I'm a Patrol Officer with the Minneapolis Police Department.'

'Yes?' she said, thinking that maybe he was familiar.

'I've been tasked with…err…trying to trace some of Minnesota's missing persons and your daughter, Caterina, appeared on my list. I'm sorry to bring this up but…' Bonner ran out of words. He stood silently and looked at Caterina's mother and hoped that she would say something to ease the awkwardness of the situation. She spoke but it didn't necessarily make anything much less awkward.

'We've been through all this many times, you must understand. It's so very long ago now and I don't have any faith left in her being found. Not alive, anyhow. I can't even cry anymore. We've used Private Detectives and all sorts of people, but nothing has ever turned up. I don't know if I can go through it all again. I'm sorry but I don't think I'll be of any help to you.'

'I went to college with her. She was a friend,' Bonner said, spontaneously, in the absence of anything else.

Alexandria Org changed her forlorn expression for a softer, welcoming one. She tilted her head slightly to one side as if she were considering what he had said and clasped her hands together in front of her, looking at Bonner with kind eyes. Bonner's unrehearsed comment seemed to have removed any of the clumsiness that he had initially portrayed and replaced it with a seemingly good-natured amiability. He hoped that he hadn't said the wrong thing as the silence between them grew. Alexandria Org let out a quiet sigh and smiled at him.

'Well, in that case, perhaps you could come in for a cup of tea or something. Please excuse the mess, I've not tidied up this morning. I've been busying myself in the garden. Come on in, I'll tell Connor we've got a visitor.'

Bonner thanked his host and stepped across the porch and into the hallway of Mrs Org's home. Caterina's home. As soon as he got inside, he felt just that little bit closer to Caterina. The atmosphere in the house made Bonner feel as though he had a right to be there and not at all like someone that was intruding. In reality, he knew he was intruding though. He was asked to take a seat in the conservatory which offered a delightful view of the garden which seemed to extend for some distance. Huge Rhododendron bushes filled the borders to his right and Roses of all sorts and sizes provided a sea of colour to his left. The grass had been left to grow and purposely mowed paths dissected the wonderland that Mrs Org had provided for the local insects. Bonner, who was no expert in this kind of thing, found it quite a spectacular sight. A kind of cultured wilderness.

'I don't suppose you have much time for gardening, do you Officer?'

'No, none really. Can't say it's my thing, besides I don't have any space for one, but I have to say that yours looks beautiful, Mrs Org.'

'Well, thank you. Now I'll get Connor to put the kettle on and then we can have a little chat, but like I said, I don't think I can help much, unfortunately. I wish I could.'

Bonner was left alone, in the conservatory, to sit and stare outside whilst Mrs Org hurried her husband along with the tea. He placed his envelope onto the table in front of him but didn't open it. *Not just yet*, he thought. After a few moments, he saw Connor Org wander out among the Rose Garden, armed with a pair of secateurs. He began to snip and prune. Bonner didn't understand the finer aspects of gardening and turned his thoughts to the contents inside the envelope again. He gave a little shake of his head as he pictured the photos of Caterina, as she might look today. He felt a tingle of panic wash over him as he realised that they might be very upsetting to look at. Certainly, for her mother. *Maybe he shouldn't get them out at all.*

'She used to sit in here and do her homework, you know. Sometimes she would be out here until dark, and I'd have to prise her away from it some nights and get her to go to bed. She did some beautiful work. Her writing was so neat and…' she paused and gave a tight-lipped smile, 'She loved the garden too. She loved the strawberry bushes, especially. Who wouldn't?'

'I can see why she loved it, it is beautiful,' said Bonner, looking out at the array of colour and noticing that her husband was barely visible among the Roses.

Alexandria Org placed a tray of tea down for them both, poured out two cups, and sat opposite Bonner in a wicker chair. 'Well, how can I help you?' she said.

'Firstly, Mrs Org, I want to thank you for agreeing to talk to me. I know it's been a while since the initial investigation and, well, the last thing I want to do is go dredging up the past for you.'

'You can't dredge it up. It never left. And if you wish, you can call me Alex, I won't mind.'

Bonner nodded politely, while he tried his best to pick up from where he left off. As he did so, his eyes fell upon the envelope that he had placed in front of him, prompting a question.

'What have you got there?' she said, gesturing with her cup in her hand, 'Don't tell me it's new information.'

'Err…No, not exactly. More like old information, really. There're some of the original forms that were submitted when your daughter was first reported missing.'

'Please call her, Caterina. You were friends after all,' she said with another smile, as she tried again to place his name.

'Yes, we were. Thanks. So, as I was saying it's just the early stuff and…' Bonner thought again about the age-progressed photos and wondered whether they would be appropriate to show. Again, his conscience decided that they might be left for others to see, further into his search, '…and…err…a few other bits and pieces. Mrs Org…Alex, the information on the original report said that Caterina simply left the house and disappeared. Is that how it happened?'

'Essentially, yes. We had finished breakfast, just about, I think, and she was off. It wasn't completely unusual for her to skip off on a Saturday morning. It was the day that she tended to visit some of her friends, even though she had seen them all week, but I guess it's different not being at college.'

'I'm sorry to go over old ground, but I take it from the report that she didn't say where she was going?' Bonner asked.

'No, she didn't but my guess would be that she was off to Betty's. Did you know her?'

'Yes, I knew Betty. Probably better than I knew Caterina, really. Did she go there regularly?'

'Oh, I had a job to stop her sometimes. I always felt that she might be overstaying her welcome. Just me being a parent, I guess. But, yes, they were very close at the time. They did a lot of things together. But they had their own interests too. Caterina was mad on roller skating, she'd go to the nature park and skate along the paths for hours, and Betty used to fire that crossbow thing. I didn't like to think about it. I don't like weapons, but her father was really quite insistent about it. Both of his girls used to go with him,' she said with a slightly disapproving shake of her head.

'Yeah, I remember. He was rather obsessive about it.'

'He was obsessive about a lot of things. I didn't like him much. Still, he's gone now. His wife was really lovely though, but he didn't treat her too well as far as I know. The talk among the neighbourhood never used to show him in a good light.'

Bonner recalled the sight that welcomed him, when he and Harry Bones walked around to the rear of the property, of Wade Nelson hanging from his balcony. Frozen solid. He allowed the additional rumours about his character to sink in as he gazed out towards the Rose Garden.

'How long have you known Mr Org?' he asked.

'Connor? Oh, a while now.'

'Did you know him before Caterina went missing?'

'Yes, I did, but we were just neighbours then. He lived in the house behind, at the end of the garden.'

Bonner looked in that direction, but the floral displays and tall bushes blocked any view of the property.

'Did he know Caterina at the time?' he enquired.

'Yes, he used to come into the garden from the end. There used to be a gate. It's a fence now.'

'Did Catarina ever go into his garden?'

'I don't think so, but I guess she might have from time to time, during the summer, perhaps.'

'So how was it that you two got together?'

Alexandria Org shifted in her chair, turning towards the window that faced into the garden, observing Connor Org at work.

'Well, after my husband died, I always said it was from a broken heart, Connor was a brick for me. He was so helpful, and he was so good with Caterina years ago. Things just sort of developed.'

'In what way was he good with her?' Bonner asked.

'Ah, you know,' Bonner didn't. 'He used to be a mathematics lecturer at one of the colleges in the St. Paul area, and so whenever Caterina got stuck, he would offer to help her out. He used to come over now and again. Sometimes he would be here for hours going over the maths problems with her.'

'And on the evening before Caterina went missing, was he here then?'

'Well, now that you mention it, he was. He stayed for dinner that evening and then he and Caterina sat out here going through her college books.'

Bonner looked up towards the Rose Garden and could see Connor Org wandering around with a trug full of cuttings on his arm. He took a last look at his handywork and headed back towards the house. Bonner met his stare as he walked closer.

'Did Caterina take a mobile phone with her when she left the house?' he asked.

'I think so. At least we never found it. I tried ringing it, I can't imagine how many times, but I never got an answer. I left messages but…nothing.'

'How long was Caterina out of the house before you became concerned?' he asked.

'She left around 9 o'clock and I wasn't concerned at all for hours. Why would I be? Oh, I suppose it wasn't until after lunch, maybe after 2 before I first tried to call her on her phone. When I got no answer, I kept trying. But then I just thought that her and Betty were together and that she'd probably call me when she saw the missed calls. Anyhow, the time dragged on into the late afternoon and I began to get a horrible feeling that something was wrong. I even went round to Betty's house. Neither Betty or Elisha were in, according to their father and he said that Caterina had not been near or by. So, I came back and then at around 6 o'clock, I was getting really worried, so I telephoned the search and rescue people out at Elk River. I probably shouldn't have called them, but they were very good, and they said they would record my call and then inform the local police for me, and well, so it began.'

'So, it was you that started the ball rolling, so to speak?'

'Yes, it was.'

'Did Mr Nelson say where the girls had gone?' Bonner asked.

'No, he just said that they weren't in. I never did have any sort of proper conversation with him all the years we lived here.'

'And I assume that the Police checked at Betty's too?'

'They called at all the houses, and they checked with most of the girls that Caterina used to mix with. The Police were very good, they tried everything to find her. They searched the neighbourhood day and night. They even went all over the golf course at the Country Club.'

'Is that somewhere that either you or Mr Org go to regularly? Do either of you play golf?'

'Oh, not me, but Connor does. He's been a member there for years.'

'If you don't mind, I'd like to ask one more thing and then I promise I'll leave you to your garden.'

'Of course, what is it?' she asked.

'Why did you say that Caterina was probably on her way to Betty's?'

'It just seemed like the most logical place for her to be going.'

'But I thought that the girls both went shooting with their father on Saturday mornings.'

'Yes, they did but Caterina said that they weren't going that day. Something to do with Betty being upset about something or other. I didn't get the full story, although she did say something about their dog.'

'Ok. Thank you for your time.'

Bonner held his envelope with its age-progressed photos of Caterina under his arm and wandered out to the front porch with Alexandria Org. The two of them looked out across the road and commented on the fine weather before they said their goodbyes. As Bonner took a few steps down the path he turned back to see Connor Org standing behind his wife on the porch.

'Ok, then. Goodbye,' she said, and closed the door.

Bonner got himself settled into his Patrol car and put the envelope on the seat beside him. Captain Rodrigues, Big Toni, had told him earlier that he would be needed today at a fairground that had been set up within the grounds of Minnesota University, on East River Parkway. Something to do with a number of fundraising events that were being run by the University. Bonner didn't mind that. It was a lovely day for it, and it was better than patrolling around the city in his car. He started up the vehicle and dropped the shift into drive. Gently he guided the car away from the sidewalk and smoothly began to merge into the centre of the road. As he did so, Connor Org appeared once more at the front of the house. Bonner continued on his way and checked his rear-view mirror. Connor Org watched Bonner's car until it went out of sight.

FIFTEEN

Grace Sutton turned her key in the front door, put her shoulder to it, and dropped her duffle bag down onto the carpet in the hall, with a thud, before turning and closing the door. She made her way into the kitchen, flung her car keys into an old fruit bowl, and filled the kettle with just enough water to fill two cups. One for her and one for Carrie, who would be along shortly, following her shift at Old Clapton Street that had begun before most people were fully awake. Grace usually got home between four and four-thirty on Friday afternoons providing that she could get out quickly and didn't get delayed by any parents wishing to chat to her at the end of school. The rear entrance to the school playground was often used as a pick-up point as the chances of finding a free parking space were better than that at the front of the building. Grace always preferred to monitor the rear door at the end of the day for two reasons. Firstly, her classroom was at the back of the building, and provided that all the children had got out on time, she could have her bag ready to grab to ensure a quick getaway, and secondly, her Peugeot 108 was parked just across the road.

Grace tugged opened the door to the freezer, reached inside, and searched around for something to have for tonight's dinner. The easiest thing that came to hand was some breaded fish that she could simply cook in the oven. She flicked the switch to the kettle and looked up at the clock. It was four thirty-five. She wasn't prepared to wait for Carrie. She needed that cup of tea. *Carrie could make the next one,* she thought. Once the kettle had boiled, she poured her tea, sat on a stool at the end of the worksurface and switched a miniature television on, putting her cup down in front of her. Grace rubbed her eyes. Her feet ached so she kicked her shoes off; it'd been a busy day. The television was silent, as if it had been muted. *Oh, great! Bloody golf,* she thought to herself, looking at the screen. Grace immediately lost the impetus to watch any television and switched it off again. She picked up her cup and walked into the lounge and plonked herself down on the sofa. *Maybe a bit of quiet was called for,* she thought. Her eyes were not closed for more than a minute when she heard a tap on the front door. Grace's legs didn't really want to move but she couldn't leave Carrie standing outside, so with a grumble, she forced herself off the sofa and went to open the door. She could see the top of Carrie's head through the small panes of glass at the top of the door.

'Nobody's in,' Grace called.

Carrie rose up onto her toes so that she could see Grace approaching in the hall, 'Come on Missus, I'm gasping,' she said with desperation in her voice.

Grace opened the door for Carrie and the two friends exchanged a hug. Carrie bundled her way in hooking her foot in a strap from Grace's bag and cursed it.

'Sorry, I always leave it there. I'll shift it,' said Grace, grabbing at one of the strings and casually flinging the bag onto the foot of the stairs.

'Didn't shift it very far,' remarked Carrie with a smile.

'Oh, bugger it. I'll sort it out later. Anyway, you'll have to do your own tea, I've started without you. Sorry, couldn't wait,' said Grace, as she headed for the sofa to resume her position.

'Oh, charming,' said Carrie, making her way into the kitchen.

'How's your day been then?' asked Grace.

'Long. Thought it was never gonna end, to be honest. Just one thing after another. It just didn't want to leave me alone today. Took me forever to get my reports done. Every time I sat down, someone wanted something. How about you?' replied Carrie, sparing Grace any of the gruesome details of the attempted suicide that she had attended. Even though there was a distinct degree of uncertainty about whether the attempt may yet prove to be successful.

'Mostly, it was good. That was until two of the boys clashed heads in the playground at morning break. Both ended up with 'eggs' on their heads. Then I had to explain what had gone on to each of their parents. Boys are always so boisterous. But otherwise, it was alright, I guess. Got a new relief working with me too. Gotta show her the ropes for when I take any leave…or just decide not to turn up.'

Grace put her empty cup down on the carpet beside the sofa and stretched her legs out with a sigh. Her feet were tingling and throbbing. Before she knew it, Carrie was lifting her legs up and settling down beside her, carefully balancing her tea with one hand and placing Grace's legs back down on her lap.

'Make yourself at home, won't yer,' said Grace.

'I'm here nearly as much as you,' Carrie said, 'Anyway what's for dinner?'

'Cheeky mare. Who invited you?'

'Your husband, actually,' said Carrie, sipping at her tea.

'Marc?'

'If he's still your husband, yeah,' Carrie said.

'He won't be if he carries on inviting every Tom, Dick and Harry round for dinner without telling me.'

'I'm not Tom, Dick or Harry. I'm Carrie,' she said, poetically, which started them both laughing.

'You're still a cheeky mare though,' said Grace playfully.

'I probably get it from you,' retorted Carrie.

Grace grabbed a cushion and swung it towards Carrie causing her to lift her cup up out of the way of the incoming projectile. Carrie did her best to stop any of the contents of the cup escaping and landing on her, but the corner of the sofa didn't fare so well.

'Mind the furniture,' shouted Grace.

'It's your bloody fault, you wally. Fancy chucking a cushion when I've got a cup of tea.'

By the time Marc Sutton got home, two hours later, the girls were pretty much in full swing. The cd was playing *Amy Winehouse* and the tea had changed colour to something more resembling alcohol. As Sutton turned off the hallway into the lounge, he could smell the dinner and, to an extent, the alcohol. Grace and Carrie were sitting next to each other on the sofa with a plate of fish and chips on their laps. A bottle of Merlot was on the coffee table. Cushions raised the plates up to a workable height and wine glasses sat on the floor beside their feet.

'There's none for you. Carrie's had it,' said Grace.

'Don't be rotten,' said Carrie, 'It's in the oven, Marc. Should be alright but the plate will be like it's been in a volcano, so mind yer fingers.'

Sutton took his jacket off and laid it over the back of an armchair. As he walked into the kitchen, he loosened his tie, removing it and leaving it on the top of the stereo. He put on a pair of oven gloves before tackling the plate in the oven and opened the oven door. The smell of the fish and chips was just what he needed. He could see that the dinner wasn't burned and looked just about right, although Carrie's warning about the plate was very welcome. He could feel the heat from the plate penetrating his gloves straightaway and put it down on a chopping board for a moment to readjust his grip.

'Good job I had *three* pieces wasn't it, darling?' Grace called with more than a hint of condescension.

Sutton knew what she meant, but he also knew Grace well enough to know that she was just playing. Carrie turning up for dinner seemed par for the course these days and something that Grace would expect at any moment anyway. He made his way back into the lounge and sat down with his dinner.

'Chuck a cushion over, would you?' he said to Grace.

'Mind what you ask for,' said Carrie with a snigger.

Sutton looked on, oblivious to the joke and prepared to tuck into his dinner. After a few mouthfuls he asked Grace how her day had been. She told him about the clash of heads which appeared to be the highlight of the day. Sutton nodded as he concentrated on his meal. When *Amy Winehouse* sang the last song on the playlist, Grace jumped up to find another cd. As she fumbled around with the stack and tried to decide upon something that she wanted to listen to, Carrie spoke.

'So, how was your day, Marc. Better than mine, I hope.'

'You know how it is. Blackery was out more than he was in so that was a blessing.'

'Any more on the Rowntree girl?' asked Carrie.

'Sadly not. We're well outside of the timeframe for clutching onto any early clues. It's going colder with every day. I don't like the sound of it.'

Carrie knew he was right. Her experiences of finding missing people relied upon things happening a lot faster. She knew that there hadn't been a great deal to go on right from the start. Just one fairly unreliable sighting of Angelica seen with a man in Trenton Street. If it was a man. Robin Greaves, the mechanic that worked at the garage where Angelica also worked hadn't been what they might consider a first-class witness. Once Angelica had been officially reported missing, the details of the incident had been made available to other UK police forces within 48 hours. All useful information had also been passed on to The Missing Persons Unit which provided a point of contact for anyone with information that might be considered important. The Missing Persons website also provided a Family Factsheet detailing agencies that can provide help and support to the aggrieved family.

'Here you go,' said Grace, 'let's have a bit of *Randy Crawford*.'

'Oh, I love her stuff,' said Carrie, 'such a nice voice.'

Grace put the cd on and poured herself another glass of the Merlot. Sutton finished his fish and chips and took the empty plate into the kitchen.

'Leave it on the side,' called Grace, 'Carrie's washing up.'

Sutton took no notice, placed the plate into a bowl of soapy water and gave it a quick scrub until he was satisfied that it was clean. He returned to the lounge and announced that he'd already washed it.

Carrie said he was 'a diamond' and Grace said he was 'too soft.' Sutton sat down and put his mobile on the coffee table rather than have it stick in his leg. Grace made short work of her glass of wine and asked if anyone wanted some coffee making, before wandering into the kitchen.

'Oh, yeah, go on. I can't have any more of this anyway,' said Carrie, 'I'll have a thick head in the morning otherwise.'

Sutton sat on the sofa next to Carrie.

'I was going to say, I was studying the lists of their friends; Haley and Angelica, and there was only one name that appeared on both lists. Thought it might be worth chatting to her again.'

'Yeah, could be. Never know,' said Carrie.

'Funny thing was that the girl's statement for Angelica wasn't signed by the interviewing officer. So, I don't know who it was that spoke to her.'

'Who signed Haley Breen's?' asked Carrie.

'Dominic Strand. Remember him, or was he before your time?'

'No, I remember him, lanky bloke. Played tennis or squash or one of those.'

'Yep, that sounds about right. Anyhow, I'll see if I can track her down. I want to check on Robin Greaves too. I know we've tried with him, but he might just come up with something else. After all he's the only one who saw Angelica that afternoon,' said Sutton.

'Who you are tracking down now, detective?' said Grace as she walked in with 3 coffee cups on a tray.

'Just someone called Emily Roache.'

'Really? What do want with her?' said Grace.

'Well, if I can find her…'

'Oh, you'll find her alright,' said Grace, 'she's the temp at school I told Carrie about.'

SIXTEEN

Karter Swann, aka Kevin Marshall, walked towards the river at its easternmost end of Tilbury Docks, close to Tilbury Fort, once a strategic line of defence against the French Navy and erected during the reign of Henry VIII. From this point the river would widen significantly and finally reach out into the English Channel after Shoeburyness. He had finished his evening shift at the nightclub and instead of making his way directly back to his rented room, he wandered in the opposite direction. The road took him south, away from the Riverside Centre where the nightclub had been built five years ago. The protests against it being built in the centre of Tilbury were extensive and ultimately, successful. He didn't enjoy it as much as the Cactus and Coyote, where he had worked some years ago, before all the chaos ensued, but it served a purpose and kept him out of trouble. A bit of bar work and a bit of minding the door.

The water looked dark and mysterious, and he could smell it, even before he could see it. To his left he could see a tall mast bobbing along, heading westwards and in towards the city with just another 25 miles to go before it would get to London Bridge. He wondered whether the bascules of the infamous Tower Bridge would have to be brought into action to accommodate its lofty mast and sails, presuming it was intending to travel that far. As the principal port for London, Tilbury has extensive facilities for containers, grain and bulk cargos. As he got closer to the river, he could see numerous floodlights, each glinting in the murky water and seemingly dancing on the tide. Tilbury Terminal that represented a ferry terminal on the north side was ahead of him. Gravesend Pier sat almost directly opposite across the river. On warm summer afternoons he would often make his way down here just to think and clear his head and to remain in a kind of self-inflicted isolation. A secure remoteness. It was a better alternative than sitting in his room and drowning his sorrows in whatever came to hand. He also liked the diversity of nature that had made this stretch of the docks its home in recent years. Maybe sometimes he could do without quite so many bugs, but it was a small price for him to pay. The birdlife interested him, even though he didn't know all the names. He definitely appreciated them, nonetheless.

And so, he was done with being Kevin Marshall for another day. But before he resumed as Karter Swann, albeit covertly, he perched himself on a wall, swung his legs over it, and looked out across to the south side of 'Old Father Thames.' The light was fading, and he probably had around half an hour of it left before he would have to embark on another dark walk back, reliant only on the streetlights for company and guidance. He didn't really know where his life was heading these days. As Kevin Marshall, things had calmed down considerably but he always had to think about who was watching him and constantly worried that he might be recognised. The hair colouring was all very well but it wasn't fool proof. When he had returned from Crete, he had ambitions to settle scores and straighten records, but it had fallen a bit flat lately. He had got himself into a day-to-day routine of how best to survive. Sometimes he felt that he was too tired for the fight. All he was doing was drifting from one day to the next but something inside him wasn't content with that. He accepted that he had made some big mistakes but to let it go was stupid. Betty had driven him crazy after she fell for the tales that Elisha had cooked up. Nothing he could say or do would dissuade her from believing every word that Elisha said. The accusations of attempting to rape her, the fights and the days spent wondering where it would all end culminated in something far more horrific than he ever could have imagined. He had tried to explain that it was Elisha who was crazy. He told her exactly what had happened at Elisha's house on the morning that he went round to supposedly fix a car in perfectly good working order. Nothing made any difference. But the one big thing that Elisha had on him were the events of the previous day at the Travelodge. It was never mentioned by Elisha, and it was never mentioned by him. She didn't need to. He didn't know how to. If Elisha said nothing, then, neither would he. It was her secret weapon. It wasn't exactly something that would do her a lot of good, especially in Betty's eyes, but it might do him even more damage if she was to turn the story around and become the victim. *Elisha took your car and your phone, and she entrapped me at the Travelodge pretending to be you. And we...* He knew it was like nursing an unexploded bomb but while it hadn't gone bang, he had chosen to sit tight. Maybe one day he might get his chance, not that it would really make much of a difference now. He could only think that Elisha was jealous and that she wanted to take something that Betty treasured. He had considered on many occasions whether things could really have become much worse if he had told Betty about the dreaded escapade at the Travelodge but since things had already taken another turn, he decided to leave it undisclosed. It would do no good. Things had moved on. Considerably.

He watched the tall mast getting closer as he peered out across the river that was beginning to glisten even brighter. He chuckled to himself at the thought of the Memorial Service at Cobbe's Chapel. *Karter Swann was finally dead*, he thought to himself. Swann knew that he was dead in one life and as good as dead in another. He sat and shook his head at the irony of it all and the decision to take such extreme measures that had become the only outlet that he could see working. *Disappear, just go.* Obviously, it brought with it a number of other problems and he knew that once he had embarked upon that track, that he would be looking down a one-way street, and he didn't know for sure where it would take him. Fighting and arguing with Betty over Elisha's tales had become a regular event. He had moved his belongings out of Betty's house, and, over a relatively short period of time, his visits had become more and more infrequent. He experienced a side to Betty that he had never known and could never have believed she had in her. The spontaneous flurries of aggression had meant that he could not see any path to a reconciliation. She had drawn blood on a number of occasions, her temper fuelled with a toxicity he had not expected. Swann also sported several scars that served as caustic reminders of her outpourings of vitriol. He had steered clear of Elisha too. There were a number of occasions where she tracked him down or followed him to work but he avoided contact. She had done irreparable damage to his relationship with Betty, and he was not going to allow her devious plan to result in his final capture. He could tell how this angered her, but he had not bargained for the depths to which she would go to poison his life as a consequence of his refusal to concede to her and become a trophy in her sinister, malevolent war of sibling jealousy. That particular phase of his life, which was to lead to a permanent change from everything he once knew, came just a few months after the tempestuous relationship with Betty finally collapsed.

Three years ago, Swann had returned home after having spent the previous evening at The Cactus and Coyote. The pub had been terribly busy that evening and he was exhausted. He showered quickly and made a cup of his favourite Columbian blend of coffee, the type that Betty liked. He wore a red hooded top with a *Nike* motif and a pair of comfortable jogging bottoms that advertised a New York boxing gymnasium, no socks. He sat upright on his bed against a couple of pillows and flicked through a magazine article about a tv series based on the life of a member of the French Resistance and his gallant efforts during a number of operations in the liberation of occupied France. He thought it might be worth trying to find it on one of the Catch-up TV channels. *Could be interesting.* The coffee was really hitting the spot, helping the tensions of the day dissipate away, when the knock on the front door came. Swann jumped slightly. More of a thump than a knock. A voice called out, but he couldn't determine the words. He lifted himself off the bed with a groan, slipped his feet into a pair of sandals, and slowly made his way out of the bedroom and along to the top of the stairs. Before he had put his foot onto the top step there was another knock, even firmer this time. As he got within a few feet of the door he could see at least three dark shapes waiting on the other side of it. Swann glanced at the sturdy walking stick that sat in a large vase in the hall. He had found it in the house when he first moved in. Something that had been left behind by a previous occupant. He always kept it there. It was something to grab if the visitors were ever the type that could be considered unwelcome. As a precaution he picked it out of the vase and held it halfway down the shaft in one hand, just to one side of his body and mostly out of sight, at least until he knew who or what he was dealing with. As he reached to turn the door handle with his free hand, he was aware of someone behind him. He turned to face them.

'Put it down, Swann. Get onto your knees…NOW,' said the figure in black. *Police?*

Before he could speak or make good sense of what was happening, he heard another shout, coming from someone a little further towards the rear of the house where they must have made their entry. He said 'Down. Drop your weapon.' This time he definitely recognised that they were Police, but in his confusion all he did was stand, frozen with the stick in his hand.

'What's going on,' said Swann, raising the stick as he spoke and holding it in front of him now as an object of defence.

The next thing he knew there was a loud crashing noise, and the front door was swinging on one hinge towards him. Glass fragmented and fell on the floor around him. A small picture frame clattered onto the floor near to his feet, glass splintered onto the carpet. He flinched and raised the stick to protect himself. As he did so someone or something hit him from behind, sending him forwards towards the incoming door. He hit it with his shoulder, the stick falling from his hand. The commotion around him swallowed him up in an instant. Instructions were bombarding him to the point where he didn't know what he was supposed to do first. He lay prone on the floor and could feel someone grabbing at his arms, pulling them behind his back. Swann turned his body to see three officers behind him.

'What the hell's going on?' he shouted above the chaos.

'Calm down and lie still,' he was told.

'What for?' he said.

'Do as you're told, Swann.'

With an officer holding his head to the carpet, his hands cuffed behind him, and a dead weight on his legs, he had no choice but to follow their orders. Voices were shouting at him, but he still couldn't properly decipher what they were saying. With his face pressed hard to the floor he could just about see out into the street. Several more feet were stomping their way into his house, entering through the front. Through the melee of legs, he could see the reflective stripes on one of the police cars, but not much more than that. Then he felt himself being lifted up onto his feet. As he tried to swivel his body around to talk to whoever was holding him, he was shoved hard up against the wall. The passage was now crowded with bodies that all seemed to be talking at once.

'You're in enough shit, Swann, so don't make it any worse. Threatening a Police Officer with a weapon and resisting arrest, they're just the start.'

'I...' was all Swann could get out.

'Save it. You're under arrest.'

It was the first instance that he had been able to see precisely who was doing the bulk of the shouting. The broad man with the accent was still giving out his orders as he held Swann still against the wall and quoted Judges' Rules at him, making sure that Swann knew, and fully understood, that he was being arrested. *Arrested! But for what?* The next moments were virtually a blur. He was quickly marched out of the house and pushed into the rear of a van. The doors slammed shut and he found himself in what resembled a stark white metal box. Just enough room to sit on a hard surface with his head almost touching the roof and his arms uncomfortably jammed behind him.

What followed when he arrived at Old Clapton Street Police Station was even more bizarre to him. After being 'booked in' upon his arrival he was ushered into a type of holding cell. Any pleas from Swann, asking for an explanation were ignored. A little later the cell door opened, and two officers took him to a room nearby. The handcuffs were still on. Swann noticed that it had said 'Interview Room' on the door. The broad man with the accent and one other, that appeared to be a lesser rank, sat opposite him at a table that was big enough to seat six people comfortably. It sat in the middle of a stuffy, windowless room. Both men were in their shirtsleeves. One of the officers that had delivered Swann to the room stood behind him as if to guard the only way in or out. First there was silence as the two men looked down at whatever was in front of them, only glancing up at Swann periodically, almost as if they were checking that he was still there. Swann didn't bother to continue to ask what was going on, he knew he would find out soon enough. He looked at the papers that were in front of the two men, but they just looked like standard forms to him. Lots of scribble. The broad man with the accent introduced the two of them but Swann wasn't listening to their names. Then he opened a blue folder. There was a photograph of someone but because Swann was slouching in his chair, he couldn't see the photograph clearly. He assumed that this might be something to do with Elisha. He had worked that out quickly, whilst sitting in the cell. Maybe some other fabrication that she had conjured up just to get at him and make things even more unpleasant. Swann thought back to when Betty had described Elisha's wounds, albeit he knew that they were self-inflicted, just for maximum effect. He was shocked that she had gone to these lengths just because she hadn't got what she wanted. But she was typical of a woman scorned. He'd had plenty of time to consider that she probably didn't really want him, it was more a case of wanting what she couldn't have. Something that was Betty's. Swann was never sure about what was churning over in her mind, behind the seductive eyes and the practised lure of her sexual advances. Perhaps, in her desperation to cause him grief she had done it again, only this time she had reported it to the Police. He began to think about his alibi. *When was the last time he actually saw Elisha? Could he verify exactly what he had been doing lately and where he had been?*

When the broad man spoke, his accent sounded ten times stronger than it had at the house. Maybe it was the acoustics in the room, or lack of them. He leaned forward with his elbows resting on the table and took a good long look at Swann. He seemed to be studying him as if he were searching for something specific. Swann sat it out and waited but what he heard threw him completely, to the point whereby he actually felt even more uneasy than he had up to now.

'I'd like to look inside your brain,' said the broad man, the higher rank of the two.

This generated a brief but definite glance across from the other officer, who then continued to look at the notes he had in his possession. Swann registered that he had also looked up, expressionless, at the officer standing by the door. Swann said nothing. Not that he could think of anything to say. The broad man sighed and reverted back to looking down at the blue folder on the table. He held it up in front of him and then placed it down again on the table, turning it so that Swann could clearly see the photograph.

'Tell me about her,' he said.

Swann looked at the broad man and then at the photograph. To his surprise it was not Elisha that he was looking at. It was a younger girl. Someone that he said he did not know, remonstrating that he hadn't even been told why he had been arrested.

'Oh, don't you worry, Laddie. I'm coming to that,' said the broad man with a degree of menace in his voice which was now a lot softer but no less sinister, 'Now, the girl. Where do you know her from?'

'I don't,' answered Swann.

The broad man left the photograph of the girl in full view, tapping his finger on the top of the blue folder and slowly leaned back in his chair again.

'How long have you had that tattoo of yours?' he asked.

Swann expressed more than a little confusion and wondered how the broad man could even know about it. *Did he see it at the house?* Swann didn't think so. He sat quiet and waited for the next question to arrive, while his head tried to work out what this was all about.

'Rather unusual, wouldn't you say?' the broad man said.

'Not really. Lots of people have hearts as tattoos,' said Swann, knowing that the broad man obviously knew what it must look like, or he wouldn't have referred to it in the first place.

'How many people do you know to have one just like it?'

'No-one, personally,' said Swann.

'You're lying to me about that, aren't you, Laddie? Because I know someone that has one just like yours…and I think that both of us know exactly how they got it too.'

He tapped his finger on the top of the blue folder again and stared hard at Swann. Swann wasn't any the wiser. He looked at the girl and shrugged his shoulders at the broad man who sneered back. It was then that the other officer spoke for the first time.

'Can you tell us what you were doing at the bus depot on 26th August?' he said.

The possibility of being able to accurately quote the approximate date given to Haley Breen's physiologic death according to the forensic pathologist's calculations is extremely difficult and may be considered grossly vague in the circumstances. However, it was the day that Swann was reported to have been seen at the depot and matched to the time that Haley Breen was missing.

'I wasn't at the bus depot. I never use a bus.'

'We've a witness that says they saw you running out of the bus depot on the date I mentioned. What were you doing there so late?'

'What witness? I wasn't at the…' began Swann as the broad man interrupted, 'You were seen, so we know you were there. You left your mark on her, didn't you?'

The room fell silent once more as the broad man pulled the blue folder back across the table towards him and flicked through some more photographs. Swann felt a numbness as the true gravity of what was happening registered with him.

'You marked her with your tattoo, didn't you? You scratched it onto her shoulder like some sort of a brand. Is that what you do? Brand them?' he said.

'I've no idea what you're on about,' shouted Swann.

The broad man shoved the blue folder back across at Swann, 'There,' he said, his voiced raised and angry.

Swann looked at the photograph that had been pushed close to him. His eyes focussed upon something that he recognised instantly. His tattoo, or at least a very rough attempt at it, stood out on the girl's shoulder. It looked brownish, almost black, not red as his was, but Swann quickly comprehended that this was because the blood that must have dripped from the wound was now dry. The heart was misshapen and distorted, unlike his professionally created example, but it was clearly a reasonable attempt at a replica. The right shoulder, the drips of blood that had run down onto the top part of her arm, mimicked his design closely. Swann stared at the photograph.

'Familiar now, is it?' said the broad man.

Swann said nothing, shocked by the image in front of him. The broad man reached and snatched the blue folder back again. He turned over to another set of photographs and looked up at Swann again who was still mesmerised by the image.

'We also made some interesting discoveries in your house earlier. You really should be more careful with what you leave around.'

The broad man showed Swann a photograph of a screwdriver. It wasn't one that Swann immediately recognised but then he had many of them. Swann returned the stare and shook his head as if to say *"So?"*

'This was found in your kitchen drawer. Recognise it? Of course, you won't. Look at the end of it, Swann. Sharpened to a point. Is that the one you used to carve your sordid mark on her?'

For the next 30 minutes, Swann continued to deny any involvement in the abduction and murder of the unfortunate girl. The questions and accusations grew wilder as far as he was concerned but they were no less traumatic. After going around in circles with the broad man and his partner, Swann was placed back in the holding cell. He used this time to try to understand what was happening. He sat alone and knew that he would have to be incredibly careful in regard to what he said. *A witness?* That part made no sense at all. He knew he hadn't been anywhere near the bus depot, but someone had other ideas. He wasn't even aware that a girl had been discovered there. He had no idea how he had missed that. Someone had made good use of this and was determined to involve him in a big way. Swann found it hard to imagine that even Elisha would try to implicate him in something like this. *I need to prove that I wasn't there.* He concentrated hard and tried to fathom precisely what day of the week the 26th was. *It was a Saturday.* Swann knew because he had been at work for that whole evening but could not be so certain of being able to verify where he had been during the day. Then it struck him. He remembered what the other officer had said when he was questioning him about his whereabouts. *"late," he said "late." I was at work.* Swann felt a sense of relief but did not want to rely on it too much, until he had got his alibi confirmed. His manager at the pub would definitely be able to vouch for him being at the pub all evening until after midnight. When Swann was collected by the original police officer and asked to return to the Interview Room, he had had time to think. He was able to offer an alibi and was prepared to fend off anymore wild accusations from the broad man, knowing full well that he had nothing on him. Swann wasn't bothered about the screwdriver. As far as he was concerned, it was nonsense. He didn't expect that there would be any trace of DNA on it, his or the girl's, as he'd never seen it before. It might have been at the back of that drawer for some time. Ultimately, Swann was held for the full 12 hours. Much of this time was spent sitting either, in the Interview Room or in the holding cell. He knew that the so-called witness scenario was a set- up, even if he didn't fully understand why. *Unless it was Elisha.* Once it had been accepted that his alibi was solid, he was released without charge.

The tall mast was led into view by the impressive vessel's bowsprit and stays as Swann started to prepare for the journey home in the dark. He swung his legs over the wall, away from the river, and began to walk.

SEVENTEEN

Minneapolis, Minnesota.

Harry Bones sat in his favourite chair, an old red leather recliner that he had treated himself to after retiring, reading *Joseph Heller's Catch-22*. He had lived alone at the marital home following the death of his wife, Mary-Ann, 30 years previous. The house was starting to show the cracks of old age and Harry did the best he could under the circumstances to keep it going. He managed to keep the garden under control, mostly. It was a challenge, but he had, over the years, been able to landscape it in such a way that the amount of work required to maintain it had been greatly reduced. Raised beds eliminated the need for him to bend quite so much and gravel paths had limited the amount of lawn to be mowed. The planting had been done with care so as to ensure that the bulk of the flora were perennial shrubs and bushes that only required trimming and keeping in shape every so often. Several large Heathers provided him with a grand display in the earlier part of the year and an area towards the rear of the garden had been left to grow wild on purpose. That way, Harry could do his bit for nature too. The, once productive, vegetable plot had become redundant since his wife passed away. Harry kept it going for a while but simply didn't need so much produce anymore and over the years, giving it away had become a chore.

 He had given up on any thoughts of forming a new relationship many years before, even though the thought still found its way into his head on certain occasions, more as a yearning for companionship than anything else. Harry never felt that it would be worth all the hassle of courting and settled instead for a peaceful existence on his own. People only brought problems. His world was his. Retirement had come some years ago and his days as a mailman were just vague memories. He didn't bother to keep in touch with the guys at the Sorting Office either, despite their invitations to annual reunions, even though he had worked there for a number of years roaming the streets and delivering the mail. Harry's life was simplicity itself. The most important part of it had been his collection of novels that he enjoyed reading, and his 'little job' as he liked to call it, tending to the garden at Poppy's. There was no doubt in Harry's mind that if the circumstances had been different, he would have displayed an interest in Poppy, one that she would have seen as unmistakeable. Instead, he held it all back inside, as painful as it was. There were many occasions whereby Harry tormented himself with thoughts of how it could have all been so perfect and how it had all turned out to be so torturous.

When Penelope Nelson died of pneumonia, Harry felt a sense of grief that he had never felt before in his entire life. Sometimes it made him feel guilty that he had not felt anything even close to it when his own wife passed away, but it was what it was. Harry had been broken into more fragments than he cared to remember. There was always something precious about her, something magical. Penelope Nelson, Poppy, was a special friend, someone that occupied a special corner of Harry's old heart. There were many moments when Harry would begin reading and, before he knew it, would end up in a trance, thinking about Poppy. His fondest memories were those of the days when they worked in the garden together. He would turn up at the house on most mornings, weather permitting, and hover outside in the garden with one eye on the house, waiting for Poppy to spot him out there and tap on the window. She would always bring him a hot drink on cold days and something refreshing during the warmer seasons. When he mowed the lawns, he would often have one eye on Poppy, watching how she lovingly tended to her flowers. How he wished that he could hear that innocent tap on the window again. Simple really, but there was something about the innocence of them both working side by side. Laughing. *Creating new life,* she used to call it. Every springtime, when the bulbs would poke their heads above the soil, Harry would feel a warmth inside him. Even when she had gone, he still looked out for the bulbs each spring and stood, glassy-eyed, in admiration of the new lives that he and Poppy had planted. He could almost see her there. *Bulbs were more reliable than people,* she'd say, *they never let you down.*

He also remembered the things he had seen, things that twisted in his head and tormented him to breaking point. He was never meant to witness such things but one day he was in the right place at the wrong time. From that moment on, Harry was vigilant. He saw things. He had registered the truth on restrained faces. He had unpicked a lock, one that would drive him to distraction, and one that he hadn't acted upon soon enough. By the time Harry had decided that he would do something about it, she had gone. Forever.

About two weeks before the girls had left for England, Harry had looked out of the front room window following a sound that he thought resembled that of a bell. Not his front door but something outside. A higher pitch than his doorbell. As he parted the curtains and peered outside, he could clearly see the culprit. A bicycle laid on his front lawn. It looked to him like Betty's bike. Before he could work out where the owner might be, his doorbell rang. No mistaking it this time. Soft and tuneful. Harry answered the door and was met by the rosy face of Elisha Nelson, Poppy's other daughter. Her face was flushed slightly from having been riding her bike. Betty's bike. Harry registered a concern on her face and invited her in. Elisha and Betty were both completely comfortable at Harry's house. They had both visited many times before. Usually with their mother and sometimes after school, before their father got back from the bank in Central Minneapolis. They liked it at Harry's. They used to tell their mother that Harry's house smelt of 'welcome', if 'welcome' could have its own smell. He had the best lemonade around, as far as they were concerned. Their mother told them that they could get it at the local store but to them it never tasted the same unless it came out of Harry's fridge. He asked Elisha whether she would like a glass of the 365 Pasteurised Lemonade, her favourite, but to Harry's surprise she declined. *Maybe she had finally grown out of it,* he thought.

'I don't have long, Harry,' she said, walking into the lounge and glancing at the old clock that sat on the top of an antique sideboard, 'I need to talk to you…about Mum.'

Harry's mind whirred and the cogs inside grinded as he sat down beside her on the couch, 'Your mother? Well, I'll help if I can,' he said, shakily.

'I want to know what you know, Harry,' she said with a purposeful look in her eye.

Elisha said it in a way that left Harry wondering whether the time had come where he was either going to have to tell Elisha the truth or cover it up for the rest of his life.

'I don't know what you mean, Elisha.'

Harry knew, alright, but was hoping that maybe he could allow this to slip through the net just once more, just for long enough until the girls had boarded their plane at St. Paul International Airport and were bound for Heathrow.

'I've seen the things that you've seen, Harry. I know.'

Harry went cold inside. He looked at her face that was almost pleading with him to open up at last, 'Elisha...'

'I know about the shed, Harry,' she said, as she dropped her cycle helmet down beside her feet, 'I know about a lot of things.'

'I don't know what you can mean, Elisha.'

'I know you do, Harry. We both know you do.'

Harry exhaled heavily and put his head in his hands. It felt like he was going to weep at the thought of having to relive the moment that he, himself had learned of what had really been going on at the Nelson house. He drew a deep breath and turned away from her on the couch, sitting side on. He wanted to tell her to go but didn't see how he could hide this any longer. He owed it to himself. No, he owed it to Poppy. He owed it to the woman that he had loved so dearly for so long, to tell the truth. Harry struggled to know where to start and so he turned it around to see what Elisha really knew.

'What, Elisha? Exactly what do you know?' he said quietly.

'I said, I know about the shed. I know about the affairs, and I know about the abuse.'

Elisha's face told Harry that he wasn't going to be able to bluff or coax her into dropping the subject. He looked down to the carpet and gently shook his head.

'How?' said Harry, his eyes now wet with despair.

'Same way you do, Harry. I saw things. I saw things when he didn't know I was there. When he thought I was asleep. But I wasn't. I hid, Harry. I curled up into a ball behind the sofa in the lounge and I listened to her scream when he hit her. I saw her face, swollen and red. I didn't question her when she said that she had a terrible toothache and that it had caused her cheek to redden. I heard her cry in the night when he was doing God knows what to her. I was there when he groped at the housemaid and struck her too. I was sneaking around when he had that woman from the bank, whoever she was, on the floor in the lounge. I saw it, Harry, and I can't unsee it.'

Harry stared at the ceiling and carried his gaze around the room, anywhere but towards Elisha.

'Does Betty know too?' he asked.

'She never saw any of it. She was mostly out with her friends or my friends that she had stolen. Even if I had told her, she wouldn't have done anything. She was always under his spell. She was the one he cared about. She was the one that got all the praise for her college results. I didn't see any point in telling her, she would never face up to him and I daren't even try. After all, she was the one that couldn't do anything wrong, so why would she jeopardise that. Anyhow, I'm here to talk about Mum, not Betty.'

Harry felt the pain at Poppy's passing again, as he had done so many times before. Tears ran freely down his old, wizened cheeks. He looked at Elisha, desperate for it to come to an end. But he knew that couldn't happen until she had been satisfied. He could tell that she wasn't going to leave before she had heard what she came to hear. His voice was just a feeble creak as he asked Elisha about the worst of it all.

'And the shed? How do you know about the shed?'

Elisha screwed up her eyes as if to be imagining the scene again. She was blank, almost as if she had removed herself from the reality of it. She sat almost statuesque. A few silent seconds passed before she began her tale.

'I didn't say anything because it didn't seem real. It didn't seem possible. I knew that something was going on but... After all, I'd seen all the other stuff. I would wake up most nights and peep out onto the landing, just to check it was all quiet. Betty slept like a log so there was little chance of her stirring. His bedroom door was often open slightly. I would check to see if they were both in bed, but on a few occasions, it was only him in the bed. Then I'd creep downstairs to see if Mum was there. I was afraid that I would find her beaten up, but sometimes I didn't find her at all. So, I would creep back to bed. In the morning I could see the marks on her, on her arms, not her face, not always. I didn't know where she had gotten to. But one night when I'd been looking for her, she appeared at the kitchen door. She didn't see me. I crouched down in case he was out of bed now too. She was filthy, Harry. Her nightdress was dirty with what looked like earth. As she turned away from me, I saw that the back of it was really mucky. I just watched as she made her way upstairs, tired and bedraggled. I didn't go back to bed, I kept looking around, wondering where she had been to get so dirty. Nothing made any sense. I went into the living room and could see through the window into the garden. I noticed that the shed door was open. I went outside and quietly tip-toed towards the shed. I don't know what I was expecting to find but I looked inside, and I saw a pillow. I just stared at it. It was so out of place. Then I saw that the floorboards were missing...not missing...all messed up like someone had lifted them. It was then that I realised that she had been sleeping in the shed. Not even on the boards but...under them in some kind of sunken shallow pit with the worms and who knows what else. That was when the horror of it all hit me, and I realised that this was just another act of his cruelty.'

'Oh, Elisha. My love, I'm so sorry.'

'I know you know, Harry. Now tell me the rest. Tell me how you found out about the shed...and all the other stuff. I want to know, Harry. I want to know what he did.'

Harry wiped his face with his handkerchief and moved himself around again to face Elisha. This conversation had played out in his mind more times than he cared to remember but nothing had prepared him for today. Harry stood up slowly, moved over to the window and looked out at the bicycle that Elisha had left strewn on the front lawn. The rain fell lightly.

'Harry,' she prompted.

'I know, I know. Let me think a moment, Elisha.'

He took his time, not because he couldn't remember the details but because it hurt him to speak about it.

'I have to get back soon. Before he gets home, but I'm not budging. If I have to be late, then I will. Tell me', she insisted with a sternness in her voice.

Harry continued to stare out towards the front of the property, holding a screwed-up handkerchief tightly in his fist. Elisha looked at the clock again and was about to get agitated and raise her voice when Harry dabbed his eyes again and turned to face her. Finally, he spoke.

'It was a Sunday morning, and I was in the garden as usual. Your mother was inside fetching us both a drink of water. It was a hot summer. We had been working in the garden all morning and edging the lawn. Digging the pieces of lawn out and lifting them into the wheelbarrow was hard going that day. Anyhow, I happened to look towards the house when I thought I had heard a cry of some sort. Didn't know what it was really. Thought, maybe, old Hastings had yelped. But it wasn't him. I saw some movement in the kitchen, through the window and…then I saw something that shook me to the bone. I didn't see the whole thing, but I saw your mother falling to the floor. Before I could even start to make my way towards the house, I saw your father come into view. I stopped moving because I thought that…well, if he was there then maybe I didn't need to worry. He would be picking her up and making sure that she was ok. But I was wrong. The next thing I saw was when he bent forwards and shouted something. I couldn't make out what. Then he stood up straight, still looking down at where she lay in front of him. Although I couldn't actually see her from where I stood. It was then that I saw him flail something at her. Again, I didn't recognise what it was…until he did it again. Then I saw the strap in his hand. I was so shocked that I thought I was going to be sick. My whole body went numb. I didn't know what to do first, but in the end, I didn't do anything. Elisha, I just stood there, paralysed. Then I saw your father walk away, out of sight, and your mother got herself up. I didn't know whether I should go into the house or stay outside and wait for her to come out. In the end, I waited. After a few more minutes, she came back out. I expected her to say something, but she never said a word. She just handed me a glass of water and carried on where she had left off. That was the first time that I knew something was going on.'

Harry seemed to have run out of tears. His recollections of a sad time had left him weary. He went on to tell Elisha that he too had seen more evidence of the abuse once he had known what to look out for. Again, he was sorry that he hadn't said anything about it. But it was too late now. Elisha, still with one eye on the clock, continued to glean more and more from Harry about what he had seen. As she sat exchanging the stories with him, she became angrier inside. Harry tried to calm her down but to no avail. She grilled him for more and more as if she was quenching herself with horror. One story led to another as the two of them matched their individual experiences. Stories of the bullying and physical abuse to her mother fuelled Elisha with a detestation for her father that even excelled the abhorrent dislike that she had amassed in the build up to her visit to Harry's house. Even Harry began to feel a torrent of loathing run through him as they compared their tales, and together, conjured up a fuller picture of how dreadful life must have been for someone that they had both loved so dearly.

'How did you find out about the shed, Harry? Tell me,' she demanded.

As Harry breathed in deeply, he arched his back and felt his bones crack and creak. Sitting down for too long was never great for a man that had been used to walking the streets with a mailbag filled with letters and parcels. He sat upright allowing his spine to unfurl. Elisha heard the clock in the hallway chime. She knew that her father would be on his way home soon and ideally wanted to be back before him to avoid a potentially uncomfortable situation. She did not want an inquisition to follow about where she had been and why. Not that Elisha was in any mood to give a straight answer. That is if he even bothered to talk to her. He was more likely to ask Betty instead, as if she would know.

'I found out by accident really. One night after I had gone to bed, I found that I kept thinking about your mother and couldn't get to sleep. Understandably, I was concerned for her. I decided to get up and dressed and go out for a short stroll. Just to see whether I would feel tired and be more likely to be able to sleep when I got back. Anyhow, I wandered towards your place, probably because I subconsciously wanted to check on things at your house. I got to the front path and stopped briefly to listen. The neighbourhood was completely silent, save for the odd dog barking or a car going passed the end of the street. But it was still quiet enough for me hear if there was a cry. But it was as I continued on passed the house that something caught my eye. I saw a figure come out of the side door, the one that was eventually boarded up. It was your mother and I watched her, wondering what she was doing at this time of night. She was in her night clothes, and I was surprised to see her outside in the dark. I was about to call out, but something stopped me. I decided to keep on watching to see where she was going. Didn't seem right, you know?'

'What happened, Harry?' said Elisha with an urgency in her tone.

'Well, I watched her go around the side of the house. In those days, that big pine was a lot smaller than it is now and you could see straight through to the back.' Elisha nodded so as not to interrupt.

'She seemed to be heading for the shed, which, of course, made no sense at all. Then she opened the door and went inside, closing it behind her. Well, I stood there perplexed. I waited for a few minutes, but she didn't come out, so I started to wander on back. It puzzled me but I got back, fell asleep and didn't give it another thought until I woke in the morning. It was the first thing I thought about. I didn't associate it with anything else that had been going on. So, the next morning I made my way to your place as usual ready to start trimming those Laurel bushes where old Hastings used to lay in the summer months, out of the sun. I was early so I didn't wait for your mum to spot me outside; I just went straight to the shed to get the strimmer out. That's when I saw the pillow, just as you had. The floorboards were crooked, like you said, but they didn't really concern me. But something else did…' Harry looked at Elisha with sorrowful eyes… 'It was the blood on the pillow, just a few spots, but it was unmistakeable. A little later on after I had started work your mother came up to me to say hello and I noticed that her lip was cut. It wasn't all that obvious, but I saw it, alright. My mind was working overtime and I didn't know whether I was imagining things or not, but then it all started to drop into place. So, I took the liberty of asking her about it. It was the only time that I had done something remotely positive. She denied that anything was wrong, of course, but I wasn't satisfied so the next morning I got up extra early, even before the dawn chorus began its morning song, and I sneaked around at the end of the garden, where I would be able to see the shed and then my worst fears came true. In the half-light, your mother came out of the shed, almost in a trance, grubby with dirt, nothing on her feet and clutching that damned pillow. I'm so sorry.'

Harry dropped his novel by his chair and reflected on the next thing that Elisha had said that day. Her words were so bitter and venomous that he still, to this day, shudders at the very thought of them. Only Harry really knew what happened on that fateful day in April.

EIGHTEEN

Having been let in through the padlocked entrance, DS Carrie Linton waved from the gate of the school playground, which was busy with excited children on their morning break, as she walked across the tarmac towards the back door to Grace's classroom. The sound of excited laughter and high-pitched shouts swirled all around her as if she was in the eye of a storm. The children barely took any notice as they ran and jostled with each other in their individual friendship groups, darting around Carrie as she tried valiantly not to get trodden on. Grace had been standing by the window, expecting a visit anytime, and waved back, smiling.

'I thought Marc was supposed to be coming,' Grace shouted above the din, with a hint of disappointment in her voice.

'He was but something came up, so I grabbed the chance to get out for a bit,' Carrie replied.

Carrie and Graced hugged briefly as Grace invited her into the classroom and away from the shrills of chaos that were unfolding outside. When Grace closed the door, the melee could barely be heard.

'Are they always that lively?' Carrie asked as she looked out at the children, swarming around in clusters of various happy, fantasy worlds.

'They are when it's windy like today. Never fails. It seems to have this effect on them every time. Then when they come back in it takes me a while to get them to calm down again. Like a whirling dervish, some of them,' said Grace.

'Rather you than me,' chuckled Carrie, as she took off her shoulder bag and set it onto Grace's desk, 'You did square it with the Headmistress, didn't you? You told her someone was coming?'

'Yeah, I sorted it as soon as I got in this morning, no problem. Actually, I should go and let her know that you're here. Give me a minute and I'll be right back.'

Grace hurried out of the classroom in search of the Headmistress, leaving Carrie gazing out at the playground activities. Carrie found her attention focussing on a particular group of 4 girls. They weren't charging about like many of the others, they were seemingly preoccupied with a bird, a young one, she guessed. It looked to Carrie like a Starling or perhaps a Thrush. She watched in the solitude of the classroom as they stood around the bird and formed a protective circle.

One of the girls was shouting something at a group of boys that were chasing a ball and coming far too close for her liking. The others appeared to remain on guard duty. Carrie smiled at their efforts to preserve a life. For all the turmoil going on around it, the bird didn't fly off or appear to be distressed. *Maybe it daren't move for fear of being squashed by rampaging feet.* Carrie wondered exactly what the girls were planning or whether they had a plan at all. Then another little girl with long blond hair that was being picked up and wrapped around her face by the wind, walked towards them pointing to the bird. She appeared to be showing an interest too. The group of 4 seemed to be quite happy for another opinion and the bird appeared to have a fan club. Then the newest member to the group bent down and gently scooped the bird into her hands. The original 4 stood perplexed. Carrie expected the bird to panic and fly but it didn't. She carried it to the school gate and managed to post it through a gap between the fence and the gatepost. All 5 of them stood watching the bird that had now hopped a little further along the pavement. Then all at once it took flight and soared between two houses, out of sight. Safe again. Carrie nodded her approval at the team of little rescuers and turned back towards the classroom door on hearing it open, as Grace returned.

'Right, we're all sorted then,' said Grace as she wandered back in.

'Good,' said Carrie.

'Do you want a quick coffee, I don't have long 'cos they'll be coming back in in a mo,' asked Grace.

'No, don't worry. I'll get something when I get back with a bit of luck. Shouldn't be too long.'

Grace asked Carrie whether they had all been behaving themselves and she told Grace about the saga of the bird. She expressed just how impressed she had been by the actions of the girl with the long blond hair.

'Oh, that's Chloe. She's a smasher,' said Grace.

'Shouldn't somebody be out there with them, you know, keeping an eye?' said Carrie as she scanned the playground again.

'Yeah, there is. I hope there is, anyway,' replied Grace, 'Yeah, over by the kitchen, next to the side door.'

Carrie looked across the playground in the direction that Grace had been pointing and could see someone standing motionless looking at their mobile phone. The young girl was probably about 20 years old, fair hair, quite thin, and more interested in her phone than watching the children as far as Carrie could tell. She had on a denim jacket with several patches sewn onto it, and a long multi-coloured scarf that hung either side of her willowy frame, almost to her feet.

'That's Emily,' said Grace. Carrie looked a little harder. 'As soon as break is over, I'll introduce you. You can go into the Deputy Head's office, she's not in today.'

'Cheers,' said Carrie, taking a long look at the girl she was here to speak with.

The Deputy Headmistress's office was situated towards the front of the school, near to the main entrance and on the opposite side of the corridor to that of the Headmistress's office. Grace had left Carrie in the room and gone back to tend to the 'whirling dervish's' following their windy playtime adventures. Carrie looked around the room and was quite impressed by the layout. Knowing that it was unlikely that anyone would suddenly come in apart from Emily Roache, she began to have a nosy around. Grace had told her that Emily would be along as soon as all the children were back in the classroom and that she would not be disturbed. Carrie didn't expect the Headmistress to appear unannounced either. So, she thought that she had at least 10 minutes to chill out and check out the décor. The ceiling was high and rather ornate. There was lots of wood, rustic looking cabinets and bookshelves on both sides of the room. There was an old fireplace that looked as though it was in perfect working order too. A pile of logs cut to a specific size were laying in a pyramid shape to one side. On the other side of the grate was an old-fashioned coal bucket, highly polished. Carrie peered inside it noting how clean it was. *No doubt it was only for show,* she thought. The room smelt fragrant. She spotted a vase of flowers that were likely to be responsible for the pleasant perfume. She could imagine just how cosy it must be in the winter months, fire lit, door locked, no interruptions. She wished that she had somewhere at Old Clapton Street that would afford her the same level of luxury. And the peace and quiet. Turning away from the fireplace, she looked across the room to a large window that provided a view of a garden. She tried to get her bearings, in order to work out which aspect of the school she was now looking out from. The garden was modest, not fancy, and overlooked by nearby houses. Some trellis had been fixed to a brick wall and was mostly smothered in Honeysuckle. Again, she reflected that it was a considerably nicer outlook than at Old Clapton Street. She walked over to a large Knowle settee, grey in colour and finished in what looked like velour. It looked as though it had never been sat in. Carrie pondered for a moment but resisted the urge to try it out just in case Emily came straight in. There was a solid looking desk with portholes for laptop leads to go through, and a number of books on it. Carrie noticed that there were two chairs beside it on one side. She was just moving one of the chairs to the other side of the desk when she heard a faint knock on the door. She was already on her feet, so she walked over to the door and opened it. The young girl that she had spotted in the playground stood before her. She had on black trousers and a crimson blouse. Her hair was now tied back in a ponytail.

'Hi. Emily, isn't it?' The spindly girl nodded without speaking, 'Come in, I'm DS Linton from Old Clapton Street,' she said. Carrie thought about introducing herself by her first name but chose not to. Not just yet. Emily walked in tentatively, looking down as if she was checking that there were no bear traps. Carrie closed the door and offered Emily a seat opposite her at the Deputy Head's desk. She looked rather uncertain and sat with her arms folded, a little reluctant to make eye contact with Carrie.

'Thank you for letting me have a chat with you. I'm sorry to drag you away from your classroom, I'll try not to keep you too long,' said Carrie.

Emily gave a shy nod and continued to sit defensively, with a thin smile on her lips. No words.

'You don't have to look so terrified,' Carrie said with a smile, 'I only eat little babies when I'm really hungry.'

This time Emily raised her eyes to meet Carrie's and her smile had curves at the edges. 'Sorry,' she said, timidly.

'It's ok, don't worry,' Carrie continued, 'How are you getting on working with Grace? Enjoying it?' *The icebreaker.*

'Yes, it's really fun, she's very nice.'

'Yeah, she is. I've known her for a long time. How many days are you at school during the week?'

'Three, at the moment, I'm still studying to become a teacher. So...'

'You'll be fine. Grace says you're as bright as a button, and I know that she's enjoying having you work with her because she told me so,' she said in an effort to ease Emily's nervous start, even though she had embellished the story a little.

Another encouraging smile beamed back.

'Right, so, let's get this bit over with, and you can get back to Grace. She'll shoot me if I keep you too long,'

More smiles. Carrie placed some paperwork in front of her on the desk and retrieved an A5 pad from her bag.

'Sorry, I should have been ready. I was too busy admiring the room.'

'I know, it's lovely. The Headmistress' office isn't as nice as this one. They swapped at the end of last term. Don't know why though,' remarked Emily who had settled a little more.

'Oh, you do surprise me. Bet the Deputy Head was happy about that.'

'Yes, I would have been,' said Emily.

'Right then. What I want to chat to you about relates to two separate things really. Of course, you will remember that you were interviewed twice in the past few of years regarding the two girls that went missing. Haley Breen and Angelica Rowntree.'

Carrie noted that the smiles had gone again, replaced by a concerned, serious look.

'The reason that I'd like us to have a quick chat is that you were the only one of their friends to give two statements. One for each event. We thought that it might be worth just going over a couple of things to make sure that we had not missed anything.'

'Do you know where Angelica is?' Emily asked, arms unfolded, hands clasped together.

'No, I'm sorry, not yet. But we will find her,' said Carrie without any real certainty, offering as much assurance as she could.

'I hope so. It was horrible before,' she said, her eyes a little glassy and tearful.

'I know,' said Carrie softly, pausing to let Emily gather herself again, 'Ok, so, I've got copies of your statements here and they are pretty much identical. I know that you have been friends with both of them and that you helped us as much as you possibly could, so I don't intend to go over all of that again.'

'I have been thinking more this time. In case I forgot anything, but I don't think that I have.'

'Well, you know what, Emily, sometimes we don't always ask the right questions in the right way. Now, I appreciate that you have been over the details about their characters and where they used to hang out and all of that, so I don't want to drag all of that up again because I think you answered everything in the best way that you could. I want to ask you something else.'

'Ok,' said Emily, feeling more at ease now.

'Seeing as you are the only person that we interviewed that was friends with both Haley and Angelica, I would like you to have a think and tell me if you knew anyone, or still know anyone, that both girls used to see or talk to? Apart from the regular crowd of friends, I mean.'

Emily had unclasped her hands and was sitting with her arms folded again but Carrie thought that she had relaxed considerably. Carrie sat back and gave Emily the time she needed to think. It was obvious to see that she was churning over thoughts in her mind, trying to picture whether she had seen them with anyone. Emily twisted her hair with one hand and looked up at Carrie.

'There's no rush, Emily. Just have a think for a few minutes. Would you like me to get you a drink of water?' asked Carrie.

'Yes please. Thank you.'

Carrie told Emily to have a think and not to let it bother her. She went out of the room and walked back down the corridor, adorned with paintings that various class members had created, towards a water cooler that she had spotted on her way to the Deputy's office with Grace. Carrie poured two cups of ambient water and made her way back to Emily.

'Here you are, Emily,' she said, handing her one of the cups.

Emily took the cup and thanked Carrie. Both of them sat quietly and sipped the water. Carrie studied Emily who was still trying her best to come up with something useful.

'It's really hard to think. I used to go about with both of them but not always at the same time. We were not really old enough to go to the pubs, but we still did. We always looked older than we were, so we used to have a drink 'cos we got to know the barmen.'

Emily realised that she had said too much with regard to going into pubs and looked at Carrie for approval or perhaps forgiveness but didn't get either. Changing the subject quickly, she carried on chatting about some of the people they had met when they were out in the evenings and those that lived nearby but didn't trigger any significant memories relating to someone that the girls both knew other than their circle of friends. Emily wore the expression of a guilty party for admitting to going into pubs and drinking underage, but she didn't think that Carrie was going to say any more about it, so she just carried on as if it hadn't happened. After Emily had gone around in circles a couple of times Carrie tried to focus her mind on specifics.

'Tell me a bit more about those evenings in the pubs? Which ones did you go to?' asked Carrie.

Emily blushed ever so slightly and must have given Carrie a look as if to say, *am I in trouble?* But she decided that if she was being as helpful as possible that it might be overlooked. Carrie wasn't interested in the slightest. Her aim was to make a connection between the Haley Breen murder and what she hoped wasn't going to be a repeat for Angelica Rowntree.

'We went to the local one at the end of Ridley Street a couple of times, but we didn't like it, so we used to go to either the one on Market Street or '*The Cactus*', that was the better one', said Emily.

'What sort of people would you find in the Cactus and Coyote?' asked Carrie.

'More young ones of our own age. Well, you know…nearly.'

'Yeah, well, forget about the age issue for the moment and think about who was in the pub. Did you see anyone that paid an interest in you and the others?'

Emily knew that considering the way they used to dress, there was quite a lot of interest but didn't really know the best way to explain that. She said that they used to talk to a lot of people and often met up with some of the older boys from the estate. Carrie wasn't entirely convinced that a young man was the one that they were looking for but considered them anyway. Emily gave Carrie some names of some of the boys from the Lavender Road Estate where Angelica lives and a couple from Church Close where Haley Breen had lived. Carrie was fairly certain without checking that they had probably been spoken to previously and thought that most of them would probably have moved away now and could be difficult to trace but far from impossible. Carrie asked Emily to tell her as much as she could recall about the pub evenings and continued to concentrate on the people that were in the pubs on a regular basis. As Emily explained, many of the regulars were older men whereas the younger ones used to flit from one pub to another depending on what took their fancy.

'Any weirdos?' said Carrie unexpectedly, with a smile so as to show Emily that she was still on her side and wasn't going to bother to labour the point about underage drinking.

Emily was taken aback slightly but smiled at how Carrie had suddenly come out with it. She flicked her hair back and took another sip of water before thinking about this new line of question that Carrie had come up with.

'What sort do you mean?'

'Any oddballs that used to be around the pub, say the Cactus and Coyote for example,' answered Carrie.

Emily smiled broadly for the first time as she thought of one such person who was a bit odd. 'There was one that I called 'the cameraman'. Only saw him once, but he seemed a bit…you know?'

'Why did you call him that?'

'Well, he took a picture one night. Don't know what of but we saw a flash, just once. It was a bit like he didn't mean to do it. He turned away from us and left. I watched him go but the others didn't say anything about it. I didn't even get to see his face.'

'So, he didn't come back another night then?' asked Carrie.

'He might have done but it was always really busy, so I suppose he could've been in there, I don't know. I never saw him.'

'Can you tell me what he looked like, generally?'

'Oh, I don't know. Average height not smartly dressed though. He didn't seem to talk to anyone or be with anyone. He was sort of on his own, I think. Nobody took any notice really. I just remember there was this flash and he scurried off, that's all. Like he didn't mean to do it. Never saw him at any other time.'

'Did the others ever say that they saw him again?'

'Haley saw him. Only once, I think. She was the only one that did as far as I can remember.'

'Where did she see him?' asked Carrie.

'I think she said that she saw him walking along the street when she was on her way back one night…you know, from the pub.'

'Was he following her?' said Carrie as she added more notes to her pad.

'No, well…maybe, but she just said she walked faster until she could get down by the streetlights at the end of her Close. I remember now that she said he crossed the road when she did, and it spooked her a bit. I'm sorry, I don't know anything else.'

'Did he speak to her?'

'I don't think so, but I didn't really ask her anymore about it. Angelica never said that she ever saw him again. He could've been in the pub anytime; we probably wouldn't have known anyway. He could've been watching us or maybe he just went in there for a quiet drink. Don't know.'

'Funny that he took a camera for his quiet drink, don't you think?' said Carrie.

'Yeah, a bit. But I only ever saw it flash that one time,' said Emily.

'Precisely,' remarked Carrie.

Carrie thanked her and told Emily that if she remembered anymore about him or saw him again, that she should call her. She handed Emily a card with her number on and apologised for keeping her for this long. She escorted Emily back to Grace's classroom and mouthed an apology to her for how long it took. Grace mouthed back that it was fine and that she would text her later. Carrie slipped through Grace's classroom and out of the same door that she had come in earlier. As she did so she noticed the little girl that had rescued the stranded bird in the playground. She was busy writing something in a textbook and looked up at Carrie. The little girl smiled at Carrie and said goodbye. Carrie said goodbye and went out into the playground. *Grace would love one like you Chloe,* she thought as she snapped the padlock, got back into her car, and set off back to Old Clapton Street.

NINETEEN

Minneapolis, Minnesota.

Alexandria Org looked out across the street where a familiar Patrol Car was parked. Although she conceded to herself that there were definitely more than one of them, she did wonder if it was that of Caterina's old college friend, Officer Bonner. As it turned out, she was right, but he wasn't in it. He was not far away, but as she looked left and right out of her front room window, he wasn't in sight. Bonner had been nosing around for at least 20 minutes, wandering from the front of the property, along the street to the left and back towards the house, pondering and trying to recreate Caterina's exit from the house on the morning that she went missing, ten years ago.

Bonner had been thinking hard for a number of days. His mind had been churning over the different scenarios that might have played out on the morning in question. One; had she been kidnapped? *By whom? From Where?* Two; had she gone somewhere and fallen into water and been taken away? *Surely, she would have been found by now.* Three; did she know the person that took her? *Maybe. That was fairly common.*

In most of the cases that Bonner found himself involved in, there was usually some degree of a thread that he could latch onto. At least to an extent. A rung of the ladder to cling to. But in the case of Caterina Marks, all he had was a memory of a girl he once knew and a period of time whereby any clue to her whereabouts had simply vanished along with her. Bonner had sat at his desk in the station and read and reread the reports from ten years ago until he just about knew them off by heart. Even Big Toni had remarked on how impressed he was at Bonner's dedication to the task that he had agreed to take on. Another shake of the head. Bonner had decided that morning that the only hope he had of getting anywhere close to finding out what had happened to Caterina Marks was to do the only thing that he felt was left for him to do. Start at the beginning. Play it out.

Bonner stood thirty metres from the front of Alexandria Org's property, just out of sight from the façade of the house and began to walk slowly towards it. The weather was fine and was predicted to stay that way. The blue sky canvassed over a crisp, slightly frosted ground. *Good,* thought Bonner, *winter's not far away.* His beloved Snow and Cold

Index would soon be warming him up with information about the current weather fronts and predictions of snowfall. He was looking forward to inputting his own spin on the possibilities of a harsh and relentless winter. The anticipation of building new league tables for this year and the ever-present expectation of record-breaking temperatures that would shatter those of previous years and give him the thrills that others only saw as mass inconvenience, were already causing an atypical glow.

C'mon Bonner, play it out.

As he got within sight of the front aspect of the Org's house, he concentrated hard. In his mind he saw the front door open and out stepped Caterina Marks. She was in a hurry. Bonner's memory of the detailed reports allowed him to see her white, flowing dress, just above knee height. Her cardigan was pale blue, and her hair was the same colour as the russet Maples of today that had shed a plentiful supply of deep red and orange leaves that were beginning to carpet the street. Her black minimalist shoes skipped beneath her towards the street as Bonner followed her. *Nobody saw her go.* The street was empty as she made her way down the path and turned right along the footpath. Bonner was still close behind. *Where are you going, Caterina?* Bonner's focus led him past the first turning on the right and across toward a small green that had benches and a small copse of young Sycamore trees. Bonner erased them from his scenario, they were too young to have blocked anyone's view of Caterina ten years ago. *She didn't stop here. Unless she was meeting someone.* She walked on and Bonner's overactive imagination followed. Hampshire Avenue North took him further on towards the Nelson property. The houses were becoming even more grand as he followed her beyond Bassett Creek. *Here? Did it happen here?* The water wasn't deep today but it might have been during the springtime, when Caterina went missing. The amount of meltwater that may well have fed into Bassett Creek following the winter would probably have caused the level to rise considerably. He stood for a moment and watched the flow. It was steady and moved quietly downstream. He knew, from local knowledge, that it ran between Northwood Park and Bassett Creek Disc Golf Course. There was also no record of any of her clothing being found anywhere along this stretch. *Maybe not here.* Bonner sensed that if Caterina had been followed, she may not have had any idea at all. The woodland thickened and seemed to grow with the houses as Bonner continued to imagine Caterina walking onwards towards Betty's house. It was quite a few blocks, but Caterina would have been in better shape than he was today. He stopped to take stock of his surroundings. *Did you come this far? Was there a car that stopped to ask for directions? Had a stranger approached you and used all their powers of persuasion to entice you away?* Bonner shuddered at the thought.

The reports had followed what Alexandria Org had said at the time, that she was most probably heading for Betty's. The top end of the golf course was only fifty metres away to his left. There was plenty of cover for someone to walk that way with her to a car waiting down one of the cul-de-sacs. A short ride in a car would take her away onto Douglas Drive North which had an arrow-straight route out of the city to the north of Minneapolis to who knows where. Bonner checked the immediate area around him and decided to continue to follow Caterina in the direction of Betty's house. *Where are you?*

Just another few minutes and he would be there. On checking his watch, he found that his walk with Caterina had taken about twenty-five minutes. Given that he had stopped and started on the way, she would probably have completed the journey in a shorter time. The relevant pages of the report pictured in Bonner's mind had confirmed to him that Betty's house had checked out as far as the search for Caterina had gone. Wade Nelson had not seen her, the girls were both out, he said. *Maybe Caterina never arrived.* Bonner stood looking at the front of the house that by this time was in an entirely different ownership. Flower beds had replaced much of the lawned areas, the main structure of the old rickety shed still stood there but had new roof felt and displayed a coat of preservative that was doing the old wooden frame some good. Bonner had come to the end of his walk with Caterina Marks for today and although he knew it was always going to be fruitless, he had given himself a few things to think about. Next time she might take him on a different route, *if she chose to.* Right now, Bonner dearly wished that his Patrol Car was parked just across the street instead of outside the Org's house. He gave one final look at what was the Nelson property, envisaging the bleak and frozen scene that he had faced at the rear of the property on the day he met old Harry Bones, and turned to make his way back to his car. But Bonner wasn't disheartened. If anything, it had made him more determined to find where she had gone.

Back at his car he sat inside and relished the comfort of his seat. He took off the radio that he had been wearing over his shoulder and placed it on the seat beside him. As he did so, Big Toni could be heard on the main scheme radio.

'You done yet, Bonner? You gonna take all day?'

He replied, telling Big Toni that he was on his way. He started the engine and looked across at the Org house. Inside, he could see Conner Org moving around.

I am gonna find you, Caterina Marks, he promised himself.

TWENTY

London

The familiar judder and whine of the tube train, as it applied its brakes, alerted its passengers that it was about to enter the station. The boredom of the dimly lit carriage changed to light as the colours on the billboard style advertisements flickered by the windows, too rapidly to be read. Those holding onto the pivoted grab handles swayed with the application of the braking system as those seated leaned and rocked with the motion. As soon as the doors opened, with a hiss, hundreds of passengers made their urgent escape, each reminiscent of a greyhound having been released from its trap. Not a second to lose. The platform that, moments ago, had been occupied by patient commuters, some gazing hopefully at the information being displayed above their heads, was now filled with a torrent of people, all moving in the same direction. The claustrophobic tunnels and walkways hummed with the drone of footsteps as the wind, generated by incoming and outgoing trains from adjacent platforms, gusted around. A busker could be heard playing a saxophone as the melodious echo was drawn along through the hive of activity; its tuneful acoustics bouncing off of the tiled walls of the hectic subterranean world.

    Karter Swann elbowed his way through the crowd as he ascended the escalator and crossed the ticket hall, surrendering his ticket to one of a phalanx of hungry ticket machines. Head down, and still feeling the need to avoid eye contact with anyone that might recognise a dead man, he walked out of the underground at Temple Station and looked across the River Thames towards the rooftop of The National Theatre on the South Bank. He welcomed the cooler air of the street as the instant sounds of a very busy Victoria Embankment invaded his head. The sirens from a fire engine were immediately evident, and to his left he saw the first signs of its blue flashing strobe lights flickering in his peripheral vision. He watched it thunder by and could briefly see the firefighters inside as the machine changed its piercing warning to a different tone. Staring further down the road he could see the tell-tale signs of acrid black, carbonaceous smoke billowing into the London skyline. His nose had also picked up the unmistakeable stench of it now, too. With a subconscious glance left and right he pulled his hood up and over his slightly faded blond locks. The dye needed redoing soon. He had allowed his beard to grow, and the roots were giving away his true hair colour. *Sloppy.* He turned right and began to walk slowly in the direction of Waterloo Bridge with one eye on the flickering rear lights of the fire engine as it pushed on to its destination, dissecting the traffic and becoming the master of the road as it advanced. He slowed his pace further to look at the impressive statue of Isambard Kingdom Brunel that sat, looking out along Victoria Embankment and across the old river, at the road junction with Temple Place. It crossed his mind that he might stop to read the inscriptions on his return later, if he remembered.

It would be several hours before Kevin Marshall would need to play *his* part in his life, later on, so he had decided on a trip into the city. Although Swann's journey was not without purpose. At a pre-determined rendezvous point, he intended to meet up with an old pal from years ago. One that he still owed a favour to, a big favour, although it would not be returned today. He had arranged to meet up at half past ten and was looking forward to an early lunch. This morning's breakfast had been limited to a hasty bowl of cereal and a cup of tea. The sausages that he had promised himself never left the freezer the night before and he couldn't be bothered with trying to defrost them in the microwave. By the time he had realised his error, he had lost the inspiration for them.

As he got close to the north side of Waterloo Bridge, he could see the reason for all the smoke that was now billowing around in the wind, encircling him and making numerous people veer away from the inconvenient, wafting cloak of soot. His intended path from Victoria Embankment and up onto Waterloo Bridge, which would lead him towards Aldwych Tube Station and onto The Strand was blocked, closed off by a diagonally parked Police car and the rear end of large fire engine; its engine roaring as its pump generated the water pressure. Cones and other warning signs were already occupying the footpath. The flames from the van fire were reflecting against the windows of the nearby buildings and an officer was steering people away from the road and waving them on, making it necessary for Swann to find another route. He walked on under the bridge and followed the crowd past the chaos and away from the smoke, that was fortunately blowing in the opposite direction to his newly acquired path. Most of the people headed right, onto Savoy Street, but Swann decided to follow a smaller group into the next turning and hope he could find a quieter cut through. His lucky dip seemed to be heading in the right direction. Savoy Place took him alongside the river a little further, past the rear of the grand Savoy Hotel, into Carting Lane and north again towards The Strand. By this time Swann had worked out that he could probably have shortened his walk by disembarking from a station closer to The Strand, but it didn't make a lot of difference in the end. When he emerged from Carting Lane and onto The Strand, he caught sight of the signs for the Vaudeville Theatre to his left, but his destination was straight ahead. With just the busy thoroughfare to conquer, he timed his move between the stream of London buses and across to the far pavement. The Irish public house was in Southampton Street, just across the road and so, he hoped was Odhran O'Connell. Pronounced Orin, Odhran O'Connell originally hailed from Victoria Street in Belfast, once considered to be an area of violent crimes, and was, to say the least, a handful. Previously a member of the 253 (North Irish) Medical Regiment, an Army Reserve medical unit located in Northern Ireland, he had become a skilled Combat Medical Technician. He had worked alongside many respected medics in a number of countries. Once he left the Army his choice of associates left a lot to be desired. His relocation to London was only one step ahead of his reputation that followed him wherever he went. Best known as someone you didn't want to upset, he had, at a cost, become a good friend of Swann's. It had been a mistake of Swann's to point out that Odhran meant *little pale green one* and although Swann himself was no push over, he soon found out why O'Connell, essentially meaning descendant of Con, and composed of the elements con, meaning *wolf* and gal, meaning *valour*, best described Odhran as someone *as brave as a wolf*.

Swann first encountered O'Connell after he had arrived from Germany, several years ago. The chance meeting at a summer fayre, where O'Connell was working at a shooting gallery, was the start of a tenuous and somewhat fractious relationship. It always felt to Swann, that unless you were in debt to Odhran O'Connell in some form or another, he was never entirely satisfied. What you didn't want was for the debts to mount up, because O'Connell had a knack of calling them all in at once, and if the tally had become a lengthy one, he had other ways of being repaid. None of which would be pleasant. Swann learned very quickly to decipher the main difference between O'Connell's generous nature, and his crafty way of drawing people into his sinister web of personal proprietorship. Swann had made good use of O'Connell a few years ago when, in a great deal of desperation, he chose to take Connell's advice in order to unchain himself from a situation that had escalated to an uncomfortable level. At a time when Swann was firmly against the ropes and had nowhere to turn, he had asked his old friend for his help, telling him that he needed to be invisible for a while.

'That's not a problem but are you absolutely sure?' said O'Connell.

'Yeah, I'm sure,' answered Swann.

'In that case I'll need a bit of time to make some arrangements. When I've got things in hand, you'll know. In the meantime, practice being invisible.'

From that moment, Swann had constantly questioned his choice, but at the same time, he knew that he had to make use of someone that, although unpredictable in many ways, would not let him down when it came to the details. It was the details that Odhran O'Connell was good at, and Swann trusted that part of him above all else. He knew that his plan had to be as watertight as it could reasonably be, and he had acknowledged, somewhat regretfully, that certain lines would have to be crossed in order for it to work out the way that he wanted. Once Swann had opened the door to O'Connell, he knew that there would be no going back. With Odhran O'Connell in the driving seat, it was time to buckle up and be brave.

At the time when Swann was coming under fire from a multitude of accusations, he had asked around about O'Connell, just casually in the pub. He knew that that was all he had to do. He didn't need an answer straight away. The grapevine would do the rest and one day O'Connell would slide out from under whichever rock he was currently living and appear. Elisha was still hunting him down and stalking him to or from his place of work at The Cactus and Coyote. Sometimes she was there on both his journeys, but although she was never close enough to be approached, he saw her, as she had intended. She would also send text messages to his phone. They would sometimes give the impression that the two of them were the closest of friends but there was always a hidden agenda to them. Swann became an expert at reading between the lines. The worst of them were full of pent-up anger. He considered changing his number but decided that he would rather have it this way than infuriate her further, not knowing to what lengths she might go if he tipped her over the edge. Her threats to tell Betty about their meeting at the Travelodge increased in frequency and each time she twisted the story just a little more. She would describe how they had planned it and how they had been together a number of other times. She threatened to embellish the event at her house even further, when she had accused him of hitting her, by saying that it had happened before and that it would only have been a matter of time before Betty had become his next victim of abuse. Regularly, she threatened to tell Betty. Swann was on the verge of telling her to do it; to call her bluff. But he wasn't confident about whether she would do it, purely out of spite, or whether it was all talk. Afterall, he didn't want Betty to be hurt any more than she had already been, and he didn't want to take the chance. Things were bad enough as they were. And then there were the notes that he would find. Sometimes tucked under his car wiper blade or in an envelope posted to the Cactus and Coyote, addressed to him. The owner of the pub would pass them on. *Thank God, he didn't open them.* These were always about how he had killed Haley Breen and how he would do it again soon. There were even photographs of her body included in the sordid mail. They didn't resemble the ones that he had seen in the blue folder when he was in the interview room at Old Clapton Street; these were decidedly more graphic. As if this wasn't all bad enough, he regularly had felt that he was under some kind of spotlight. The way people looked at him at the pub made him wonder what stories were being spread and by whom. *Elisha? Betty?* He couldn't even be sure that it was coming from them. Both were driving him crazy though. Their anger had physically frightened him in the past. The Police were never too far away either. He would see a car roll by his house often. *Was it just coincidental?* He didn't know and couldn't stop himself thinking that they had not finished with him just yet. *Another fabricated witness would bring havoc.* He was aware that if the owner of the pub opened just one of those highly damning letters and showed it to the Police, he would have nowhere to hide. The whole Haley Breen nightmare would re-emerge like a returning plague and if the owner of the pub was persuaded to alter his story about his alibi, he could be in deep. He had put up with the uncertainty of how far Elisha would go and the fear of those damned letters at the pub for long enough. The unstable timebomb that had ticked in his head daily had to be defused and finally he had reached the end of the line. Swann made his decision and O'Connell hatched his plan. And it was to change his life.

The instructions he had received from O'Connell, just under three years ago, had been crystal clear. When Swann was told to prepare, he was to ensure that his house looked lived in, just as normal. He was to turn on any lights that he would normally have on and ensure that all the curtains and blinds in the house were closed. He was to prepare dinner for himself and leave it on the worktop in the kitchen and to make sure that he had eaten and drank before he returned home. He was to leave the television on with the sound low but audible. The house keys were to stay wherever they usually could be found. All that was required was that the door to the rear of the kitchen was unlocked and the key left in the lock. He wasn't to pack anything; no clothes, nothing. He wouldn't have to worry about money or clothes, he was told. Swann figured that this would be all part of his debt to O'Connell. That and a big favour that he was sure that the Irishman would call in one day in the future. He was to leave his car parked in its usual spot and make sure that it had a full tank of fuel, even though it wouldn't be going anywhere. O'Connell was insistent that Swann should act completely as normal, especially in the days leading up to the day that he had chosen for his plan to be put into action. Finally, Swann was told that he should leave O'Connell to worry about the rest. And that, as much as anything, was Swann's biggest worry. The rest.

Swann had told O'Connell everything. He knew how Odhran O'Connell worked by now, and if he had left anything out, then he might just regret it somewhere down the line. Swann knew that once he had deployed the services of O'Connell that he was going to be at this man's mercy. He had little doubt that O'Connell would do a good job, he just didn't know precisely what it would involve. So, on the day in question Swann had returned home from the Cactus and Coyote following his evening shift behind the bar. He had parked his car and mentally checked the fuel level. Almost full. *That will be ok.* He entered his house and locked the front door behind him. He walked through the passage and into the kitchen and turned the key in the rear door, unlocking it and remembering to leave the key in the door as instructed. He guessed that O'Connell would slip in via the alleyway that ran at the back of the houses. The passage that led from the cul-de-sac, thirty yards from his front door, was overgrown and secluded from any view of the neighbourhood. Then he hung the rest of the house keys up on a hook in the hall. He walked into the living room, switched on a table lamp, turned on the television and set the sound to a low volume. Now dinner. He microwaved a meal and removed it from the appliance, sitting the hot plate on the kitchen worktop and placed a knife and fork beside it. The kitchen light was off, and the blind was fully down. Swann wasn't sure exactly what time to expect O'Connell to show, but he was certain that he would do. Swann sat in the living room, nervously checking the clock like he had a compulsive disorder. He was sensitive to every sound outside. He didn't like the feeling of being completely out of control of the situation and as he sat, he became more and more edgy. His shift had finished at midnight, and he had arrived home at 00:30. It was now 2a.m.

A noise. The clock showed 02:55 and Swann realised that he had dozed off in the chair. Beside him, Odhran O'Connell stealthily, appeared in the doorway. All in black and wearing a beanie and gloves, he stood in silence. As Swann opened his mouth to speak, O'Connell flicked his head towards the kitchen, encouraging him to follow. Swann heaved himself out of the chair, his body wanting nothing more than to ascend the stairs and lay down on the bed, and obediently followed. O'Connell stood next to the rear door in the kitchen, which was dimly lit by the shared light from the table lamp in the living room and scanned the preparations that Swann had made. A black duffel bag was on the worktop. O'Connell asked Swann to confirm with him that he had followed his instructions and that he had done precisely as he was told. Swann acknowledged that everything was ready.

'Right then,' said O'Connell, his Northern Irish accent, gritty and sinister, 'You've done your bit, now I'll do mine.'

Before Swann could ask about any of the details and before he knew what was happening, he was grabbed from behind and felt the rib-crushing bear hug squeeze the air from his lungs. His arms were trapped beside his body and whoever was applying the hold was incredibly strong. Swann's brain filled with a thousand different scenarios as he stared at Odhran O'Connell like the proverbial rabbit in the headlights. O'Connell reached into the duffel bag and brought out a coiled tube and a small bag along with some other smaller items that Swann didn't recognise in the half-light. After setting the things out on the worktop, he turned to Swann.

'Now, do as you're fucking told, and I'll have you out of here in a jiffy,' said O'Connell as he fiddled with the tubing, 'Give me your arm,' he ordered.

'Why?' asked Swann.

'Shut up and give me your fucking arm.'

The bear hug increased in its intensity as the strong guy squeezed tightly. O'Connell grabbed at Swann's arm, pulling it towards him.

'You ever given blood?' O'Connell said quietly.

'What?' Swann gasped.

'You fucking heard me. Have you?'

'Yeah, a long time…'

'Right then, you'll know what it's like won't you?' said O'Connell.

'What do want with my blood?' said Swann, with a tremor in his voice.

'Listen to me. You fucking shut up and get this done or I'll sedate you and do it anyway. Got it?'

Swann said nothing, wishing that he had never began this deal with O'Connell.

The constant bear hug was stifling his breathing and whoever it was that was applying it was a powerhouse. Swann knew that he could not overcome both of them. Even one of them was out of the question. O'Connell prepared his equipment as Swann watched on, helpless, trying to work out what this was all about. O'Connell applied a tourniquet to Swann's outstretched arm and began to prepare the needle.

'How much you going to take?' asked Swann.

'Still now,' said O'Connell, as he carefully put the sharp needle into Swann's arm, 'There. Clench and unclench your fist until I tell you to stop.'

Swann was quietly grateful that O'Connell appeared to be acutely adept at the procedure. In the grip of the man behind him, Swann relaxed as much as possible and went with the flow. Seeing as his heart was racing a little, it didn't take long for O'Connell to collect the amount he wanted and within 8-10 minutes, O'Connell had removed the needle and stuck a plaster onto the wound site on Swann's arm. He sat the bag of blood on the worktop, dropped the needle into a yellow plastic box and the other used items into a plastic bag. Everything went back into the duffel bag.

'Thanks,' said Swann, instinctively.

O'Connell didn't respond, he just looked hard into Swann's eyes and said, 'Now the fun part.' Swann realised now why he had been instructed to eat and drink before he got home. The bear hug continued even after the procedure had ended, making sure that Swann didn't move or maybe that he couldn't collapse. O'Connell took the blood bag and bent down, carefully spilling some of the collected blood onto the kitchen floor, creating a pool of the sticky substance in the centre of the room.

'Lay down on it, on your back,' he said.

Swann looked at O'Connell and acted out his instruction. *At least the bear hug had been released.* Laying down he could now see the face of the other man. It looked to Swann as though the man had a lump of chiselled granite on his shoulders. Unshaven, with the features of a comic book villain. Even the scar on his cheek that ran from his eye all the way down to his chin looked like it had been freshly carved especially for tonight. He filled the room.

'Don't move,' said O'Connell.

O'Connell then gave a deft nod to the musclebound giant who slowly bent down and lifted Swann's legs up, holding his feet in the crook of one elbow, similar to a headlock. From where Swann lay, it appeared that the man kept bending and bending, he was so huge.

'Now, just relax and allow yourself to be slid out. Let your arms flop beside you, like you're dead. Understand?' said O'Connell, opening the rear door to the kitchen and stepping to one side, allowing enough space, 'When you get out, don't make any noise. He'll take you to the van. You make a fucking sound and I'll know. Got it?' he said in an assertive whispered tone.

Swann nodded silently. The next second Swann felt the big man begin to slowly drag him across the floor creating a smear of blood across the kitchen and out of the doorway. Swann lay as limp as possible, allowing his arms to trail above his head. As dramatic as it was, he was now beginning to get the gist of what was happening. The journey on his back continued right until they reached the alleyway. Once he was at the end of the small back yard he was hauled to his feet and escorted through the overgrown brambles and saplings that had invaded the unkempt alley. Drips of blood fell from his clothing and were wiped onto the brambles as he stooped low along the alleyway, his head pushed down by the giant.

Swiftly, Odhran O'Connell got to work. Standing well clear of the slimy smear of blood he carefully tipped some of the freshly drawn blood into a small garden sprayer. By adjusting the nozzle, he could aim the blood to replicate an arterial spurt or blood spatter onto the cupboards, the cooker and the then tip as much as he desired from the bag onto the floor near the head end of the smear, allowing it to run and settle into the spaces between the grouted floor tiles. Just enough. By the time he had finished, the scene looked authentic. It hadn't been the first time that Odhran O'Connell had created such a gruesome sight and not always with the aid of the garden sprayer.

TWENTY-ONE

Within a very short space of time, Karter Swann had been driven through the dark of night to a house in a tree-lined street, just outside of Finchley, in the north of London. From the back of the windowless van, he had been able to peer through a gap between the rear and the front compartment telling him that, although his perspective of which way he was heading was nothing more than a wild guess, there were very few vehicles on the road. Lying against what appeared to be a large roll of carpet he had, briefly, fallen asleep. The trauma of the 'voluntary' blood donation had tired him more than he had realised. On arrival, the giant man had swiftly escorted Swann inside. In an upstairs room of the house Swann had sat on the end of the bed and began to check the contents of a large holdall. His shirt was clinging to his back with dry blood, and he had yet to clean himself up. The big man had spoken very few words, but those he had uttered were ingrained with a deep Northern Irish accent. There was an A4 envelope in the bag that he took out and opened. Inside he found that the new passport that he was now holding and studying closely was informing him that his name was Kevin Marshall. Everything about it looked professionally done. It was Odhran O'Connell after all, and if anyone had the sort of contacts needed for such a thing, then he did. The large holdall also contained various items of clothing. Just about everything that he would initially need to survive was there, anything beyond that he would have to buy himself. A new wallet housed a Travel Money Card, that had been loaded with enough money to get him settled and on his way in his new life, and a small amount of cash in Euros. *Euros?* There was also enough Sterling to get him by for now. As he looked around the unfamiliar room, he heard a phone ringing from inside the holdall. His attendant, the giant man, said nothing and turned away and out of the room, almost as if it was his signal to leave. A familiar voice spoke into his ear.

'Get showered and changed and leave your old clothes in the refuse bag that you'll find in the holdall. My man will clean the room and tidy up everything later. By now I expect you've had a chance to check your new identity too. Pick something suitable to wear from the bag that won't make you stand out in a crowd. You'll check it in as light luggage and keep it with you. Are you paying attention to me?'

'Yeah, I…'

'There's enough money on the Travel Card in the wallet to get you up and running. If you should run into difficulties, then I don't exist. You got that?'

'Yeah, I…'

'That is something that you need to remember, my friend. From now on you need to be careful. Once you're out of the country then it's up to you. In the holdall you'll find the travel documentation that you'll require. The taxi will be with you in one hour. Don't fuck up. Any questions?'

'Yeah, I got some questions…'

'Good. Enjoy the sunshine, Kevin.'

With that Odhran O'Connell hung up.

Swann had felt as though the evening's events had been a bad dream and if it wasn't for the irritation that the plaster on his arm was causing, he might have been able to believe that it had been. After having followed his latest batch of instructions, Swann was ready. He was clean, he was shaven, and he was presentable. Now all he had to do was wait about 15 minutes for the taxi to take him to the airport. He hadn't even considered which one he would be going to fly from but from the information on his travel documents he could work out that LSA was referring to London Stanstead Airport and that he would be heading around the M25 and up the M11 to his point of departure. The documents also filled in another gap in the proceedings by telling him that his destination was HER. The flight time and O'Connell's parting comment of *"enjoy the sunshine, Kevin,"* had been enough for Swann to work out that the HER probably referred to Heraklion in Crete.

O'Connell's promise of getting him out of the way for as long as it took had, so far, gone without a hitch as he sat in the rear of the taxi. A fresh member of the O'Connell clan, a smaller man with a flat cap, drove. A minimum of dialogue was exchanged on the journey and Swann had felt the tiredness rapidly catch up with him again.

'There's a big floppy hat in your bag. Put it on and keep it on. Avoid the cameras as best you can.'

The experience of checking in at the airport had definitely raised his blood pressure but he had gotten through it unscathed. Sitting in the departure lounge, he had stared up at his flight number and waited apprehensively for the departure gate to be announced. His arm itched again as Swann found himself feeling reluctant to look at anyone. Being recognised now could prove fatal once O'Connell found out. *Fatal for a dead man.* It had all felt so surreal. Fortunately, the waiting time had gone quickly and before he had known it, he had climbed the mobile stairway and found himself at the doorway to the aircraft that would take him far from his current troubles. His boarding pass informed him that he should sit in seat F3. When the cabin doors were closed and checked by the cabin crew, he just wanted it to go.

The flight Captain had promised a quick departure, thanks to a slightly earlier slot that had become available at the last minute. Only a few minutes later, Swann was feeling the immense force of the aeroplane charging down the runway. Still, he dare not look at anyone for too long. His mind had been working overtime as he had mentally scrutinised every face that he had set eyes on since arriving at the airport in the hope that he simply didn't know them and, more importantly, that they didn't know him. As the aircraft thundered at speed and lifted from the tarmac, the bright early morning sunlight flickered across his face at the emergence of a new day. A bead of sweat trickled on his temple as he quickly wiped it away. He had wondered just how long it would take him to get used to being dead. He was airborne and for the first time in a long while he had felt a sense of freedom. Freedom from the strain of looking over his shoulder for Elisha. Freedom from worrying about the letters arriving at the pub, and freedom from the death of Haley Breen. He had wished that he could get to Crete instantly in order that he may work his way through the airport and out the other side. Just 9 minutes later, Karter Swann was asleep only to awaken as a new man.

Karter Swann was dead, and Kevin Marshall had been born.

TWENTY-TWO

Ahuja Industries, East London.
Now

As the evening began to cast its shadows across the silent ironwork of the largest building on the desolate old site, another swirl of grey cement dust whipped up in the wind. The whole area was no more than a deserted expanse of disused buildings, abandoned machinery and discarded metalwork, that had not seen any sort of industry for around 15 years since the owners had abandoned their business and gone, leaving 200 workers unemployed and desperately angry. The most regular visitors nowadays were fluffles of wild rabbits and several hundred birds that would return each evening for the night. Fluffles are also referred to as colonies but with a word like fluffle, why would you want to use anything else. Foxes were also on the site, scurrying around for a meal. Their young and vulnerable cubs would occasionally play in the thickest of the overgrown areas that mostly bordered the site. An occasional piercing cry might be heard as they fought with each other or perhaps befell an unfortunate end in the mouth of a large weasel. The days of the seemingly constant flow of lorries that entered and left the dust-clad site had long gone. The gates had been chained and bolted together and a number of heavy plant vehicles had been left to rust. Giant hoppers sat in silence with their gaping mouths hopefully open, like ravenous Humpback whales, to whatever fell from the sky. Conveyor belts that once fed the hungry rock crushers were now motionless. Fixed in place by rust. All that could be seen from the road of the old, once industrious landscape, was the roof of the tallest of the giant buildings. The trees and bushes that surrounded the area had, over the years, provided a thick and almost impenetrable screen that relegated the once impressive hive of activity to a barren and forgotten wasteland. Various smooth-barked saplings now occupied the cracks along the once busy roadway that led in and out of the plant. Weeds had done what weeds did best and had self-seeded across the disused site. Whether it had become a wasteland or a wilderness, the stark dustbowl of cement had conceded to nature, which had a way of taking back what was rightfully hers.

Inside the main building, the gloom of darkness slowly began to cloak everything. The wind blew around the ill-fitting gates that once provided the security and wafted suffocating clouds of cement into the vast ghost-like factory. Everything that remained inside was coated with a fine powder. The sound of jagged metal scraping against concrete, that had become an all too familiar daily reminder of her plight, echoed and creaked around the largest of the cold, heartless buildings. Rainwater dripped from the roof way above her head and created small puddles on the dust-laden floor. The damp stench was a constant reminder of this hell that she found herself in. It was always there, like a ubiquitous poison that infiltrated every breath she took, causing a spontaneous cough to develop. The air was cold. It was the only reliable indication she had of the time of day. Colder usually meant that the sun was in the process of setting, and she knew that she would have company soon. The pattern had not changed for days. The grating of metal either meant that she was going to be alone all day in the unfriendly and desolate building or that she was going to be fed before being left for the night. A morning visit might mean another blanket for her with any luck, but they were brief affairs. It was almost like it was no more than a check to make sure that she was still alive. At her lowest moments she often wished that she wasn't, but she knew that was one fight she must never give in to.

The welcome slivers of moonlight that punctuated the metalwork high up above the floor of the building offered the merest hint of illumination and allowed her to get some perspective as to how enormous the space around her was. *No wonder it's so bloody cold.* Her perception of the size of the building changed as she tried to grasp where she was. Echoes from pigeons, cooing in the half-light, fooled her into thinking that they were closer than they were. She had been sure that she had seen a rat two days ago and had felt its presence at every tiny noise since. She also knew that it was highly likely that there was more than just the one. She sat on a pile of dank and musty blankets and listened, quietly, to the footsteps, pulling one of the blankets over her legs to help against the chill. Her hair was dirty and lay in strands across her face. It felt like it was becoming matted. As she touched it, she felt the bump on the back of her head. It had stopped bleeding but there was definitely still a little lump that reminded her of the day that everything changed. The memory of the moment that everything had gone black brought a tear to her eye. She could smell her own body and it repulsed her. The chain that had been tied around her waist and her ankles was firmly fixed to a bracket on the wall and dictated the distance she could move from the corner where the blankets had been placed, allowing her just enough travel to reach the bucket that had been positioned at the furthest reach of one wall. The footsteps were still in a different part of the building to her, or so it sounded, but they were becoming louder, as they approached. She knew that from the sound of the gate opening to her first sight of somebody, was usually about 3 minutes. Her time alone was, once again, about to come to an end. The food that she was offered usually consisted of either cold pizza or, if she was lucky, a bag of warm chips. A plastic bottle of water was all she had been offered to drink. During the first day and parts of the first night she spent some of her time shouting out in the hope that her cries would be heard. From then on, she had attempted this only periodically as her hopes waned. She often walked to the end of her chain in every possible direction and looked around in the gloom, hoping to see something that would tell her where she was, but each and every aspect of the building that she could see looked identical. Each wall seemed to reach high up to the roof. She could just about make out some railings above her on all sides. *Perches for pigeons.* She could see that they were the edgings to walkways that seemed to stretch the length of the building. Every so often there was a ladder surrounded by a safety cage that provided access to the individual levels. There were two or three large funnels in sight, further down the factory, that reached up high towards the roof. Everything was grey; the roof, the walls, the floor, everything, not least her clothes. The area where she sat for most of the day and night was secluded from the view of the funnels. Her corner was under a sort of half roof, lower than the main roof. It wasn't intact enough to prevent the rain occasionally landing on her, depending on how the water fell after it had dripped and bounced off of the railings above. There were wooden pallets and a pile of sand which didn't look like the right colour to be sand, but whatever it was, she didn't want to touch it. Not that she could reach it. There was what looked like a hard hat on the ground. She had tried to reach it before, but it was slightly more than half a metre outside of her range. An hour ago, she had managed to stretch herself to the furthest point that she could possibly reach and get two fingertips to touch a bar of some sort. *Steel or iron,* she thought. It only moved the slightest amount. Twice, she wanted to give up trying to move it towards her, but she persevered. Her fingers scraped on the rough factory floor, breaking a nail and causing one of them to bleed and become instantly sore when the dust entered her skin. Then with three fingertips she started to move it very slowly towards her, almost hooking one finger around it. Her hand ached and was becoming weaker with every strain. She even thought that her shoulder was going to pop out, at one point. She panted and groaned with the effort it was taking to be at full stretch, resting periodically and allowing a tear to roll down her cheek. The hard floor hurt her arms, her knees, everything. The bar moved painfully slowly, but it did move. Then finally, she could wrap her whole hand around it and drag it closer, scraping her elbow on the gritty surface. With a gasp, she pulled it into her arms and sat inspecting it. It was about three feet long and pointed at one end. Her best guess told her it was made of iron. Not too heavy but solid enough. First, she thought of using it as a line of defence, or attack if she got the chance, although they never came that close to her. She scurried back to her corner, dust wafting as she dragged herself on her bottom. In the silence she tried to work out what to do with her prize. If she did manage to strike the masked person, then what? She knew that she would have to kill them or face the consequences, and that didn't bear thinking about. If she did kill them, then what? *Nobody knows where I am,* she thought. She didn't even know where she was. *I could starve or be eaten by the rats or both,* she thought. She decided to hide it among her grubby blankets and see what happened. *Maybe I can break my chain with it...tomorrow. Or tonight. Then I could get to a road, if I can find one. If I can get out at all.*

Sometimes, when the dark had fully descended on her ghastly nightmare, she thought she could hear someone else in the factory. A sort of distant cry of despair. Maybe somebody else was here too. Nobody ever responded when she shouted out, but she was sure that she heard something or someone. Sometimes she thought that she had been dreaming in desperation of company. At various times during the day or night, she dreamed about her family. She dreamed about waking up in her own bed instead of in this living nightmare. She had seen an inquisitive fox staring at her when she woke, this morning. She had clapped her hands and sent it running. *Maybe it was that. Maybe that was the noise.*

Her clothing: a sweatshirt, jeans and trainers, were almost completely grey with a coating of something that reminded her of cement. Her face felt dry, and her lips had started to become sore and cracked. Every time she licked her lips, she could taste it. Her hair had become matted with it thanks to the drips of rainwater and the dust in the air, and the wind blew it around constantly. Some of the water that she was given to drink, she had used to wash her face. It made her feel marginally better. The tears of utter despair had dried and recently had failed to flow anymore. She knew that it would do no good. Each time that her food had arrived, she had shouted abuse, but she rapidly learned that screaming and shouting meant less pizza. The water that had been brought for her had been half poured out onto the dry floor in front of her. Whoever it was beneath the ghoulish mask never spoke, not even one word. *Are you a man or a woman or what are you?* They just walked in, put the food and water bottle on the floor within the reach of her chain, and stared at her, almost inquisitively. They never stayed within range of her for long. The bucket was inspected, and the contents strewn across the floor before being thrown down into the same position again. Each time, she tried to engage in conversation, but nothing ever came back in return. She was desperate to know why she had been taken away from her home, her parents, her friends. The most she ever got from the person was a sort of curious sideways glance. They would tilt their head like an inquisitive Praying Mantis or like they were from another planet. Like an animal that was trying to work out what to do with its prey. Then they would turn away and be gone again. She screamed for mercy until they were out of sight and until she heard what sounded like a large door or gate being dragged open and closed. Then she was in silence until the next time.

Now she could see her visitor. Colourless dusty jeans, dusty boots, dusty jumper and to her surprise, a different mask, but nonetheless fiendish and creepy. Like the other one it covered their head completely, hair and all. *What are you?* She felt the iron bar beneath her blankets and watched as her 'evening meal' was pulled out from under the jumper. Immediately, she could smell it before she saw it. *It's hot,* she thought. She knew the smell and her heart skipped in anticipation of something sustainable at last. The meal was in a plastic container. *Chinese.* It was placed down on the ground in the usual place, right at the end of the length of her chain. There was a plastic fork on the top of the little box. A bottle of water beside it. They stepped back, once again, and watched her. She didn't move. She was conscious now of her metal bar and didn't want to disturb it and make a noise that would clearly raise suspicion.

'Thank you,' she said.

Her mind was saying, *now go, now go.* But they just stood there waiting for her to move towards her meal. Eventually she slowly slipped the top layer of blanket off her legs with one hand holding the bar still underneath and began to move across the floor on her side, finally standing. This wasn't going down very well with her visitor as she had always hurried to pick up the food before, and they seemed uncertain as to why she was behaving differently.

'My leg's gone to sleep,' she said and began to rub it.

She dragged her leg a little for effect and bent down to pick up the meal. Worried that they might go to her corner, she made her way back a bit quicker and sat with her meal, feeling the bar under her blanket and sitting carefully so as not to cause it roll on the gritty floor and make a sound. *Still there.* She didn't care what it was, but her tastebuds told her that the food was chicken. There was rice and there were noodles. *Chow Mein?* she thought. Her hungry stomach was in such demand for food that she hurriedly ate it, almost without taking a breath, and certainly before the situation changed and she lost it. The water bottle was still across the floor. She looked at it but didn't move. *The bar,* she thought, *I'll get the bottle when I'm alone.* Then she jumped as she heard foot stomping and looked up to see that her attention was being brought to the fact that the water was still there.

'I'll get it in a minute', she said, not wanting to appear ungrateful.

Too late! The bottle was kicked so hard that it split as it sailed across the factory floor and out of her sight. She could hear it bouncing along and striking a wall and in an instance her company for mealtime was walking towards her. Her heart leapt into her mouth as she froze, one hand instinctively on the metal bar, still out of sight. *I'm chained, I can't do anything.* She cowered into a fetal position on her blankets, trying to protect herself as much as possible. Then she felt a hand on her shoulder. Just as she was about to cry out, she felt a hand gently stroking her head. Then the plastic container was slapped out of her hand. There was very little left of the meal but what was left, scattered over her. On her face and in her lank hair. To her massive relief, the beating never happened, although mealtime had all of a sudden become rather unpleasant and rather creepy. By the time she opened her eyes and unfurled her body, she found herself alone in her corner under the half roof, near the pallets and next to the pile of sand that wasn't sand. But the footsteps were not footsteps now. They sounded like someone running, *and crying?* She raised herself up and stood, listening. Then she moved away from her corner and looked down the factory, but nobody was in sight. Then she heard the scraping of metal on concrete. Evening mealtime had finished. Another lonely night was descending upon her. She sighed heavily in relief that she had got away without any real trouble and turned towards her corner, her blankets and her new friend, 'Iron bar'. Then again, she heard it. A whimper, it was unmistakeable this time.

Somebody is here, she thought. She shouted 'Hello,' but there was no reply. *Am I going mad?* Sitting huddled in her corner, one hand still caressing the metal bar, she wondered what the point was of her being here. The thoughts of what might happen to her made her feel sick. *Don't be sick, don't be sick.* She knew that she had to keep the Chinese down so that she had some energy. The water would probably come back next time. With one hand on her metal bar, she withdrew it from its secure place and looked at her chain. The bar was too big to fit in the rings of the chain and be twisted. She began to try different methods of breaking the chain, but it was strong. The fitting on the wall was a metal plate with a large D-ring. She knew that she didn't have the strength or the energy to break that. After striking the chain with the bar a few times the vibration that she felt in her arms started to become too much. The shock of the impact hurt her hands. She collapsed exhausted and the tears returned. But the single, most important thing that she clung feebly to, was the fact that Angelica Rowntree was alive.

TWENTY-THREE

The canteen at Old Clapton Street Police Station seemed to get more and more crowded with people these days. The main desk was one thing with its seemingly constant flow of enquiries, but since the new training rooms had opened on the first floor, it had become a matter of ensuring that an early chase to the canteen was the only way of securing a table. Thirty extra people rushing to get fed at lunchtime posed a challenge for everyone, not least the kitchen staff. The canteen had always permitted people that brought their own lunch to sit at the tables, but that meant that some of those on the courses had to wait until there was space before they could get a seat. It seemed that the introduction of more bottoms for the same number of seats had somehow slipped by the Head of Internal Courses, who had been complaining that his students needed feeding like everyone else but had failed to raise the issue of how this was going to be accommodated until it was too late. If you were delayed, then you would probably have to queue into the corridor. The potential for the day staff to be called away on business also added to the furore and tension. DI Marc Sutton pushed his way past the queue and peered hopefully into the canteen, looking for DS Carrie Linton, in the hope that she had got there first and had managed to grab a table for them both. As Sutton's head came into view around the doorframe at the entrance to the busy room, with his eyes scanning frantically for Carrie, she spotted him. A few seconds of exaggerated waving finally got his attention.

'Thank goodness you got here before me, it's nuts today,' he said as he sat opposite her.

'Yeah. Nuts every day, lately. Daft trying to squeeze everyone in at once. They should have introduced staggered lunchtimes or got the course to come in earlier or something. Mind you, forward planning has never been a strong point around here.'

'Sometimes you wonder where good old-fashioned common sense went.'

'Now you sound like my old Mum,' said Carrie.

'Well, she wasn't wrong,' replied Sutton as he took a bite from a sandwich.

A stream of white shirts lined its way from the serving counter back to the door and into the corridor. The course instructor could be heard harrumphing in general complaint, but the situation wasn't going to improve today, or probably for the duration of the course.

Carrie and Sutton tucked into their respective packed lunches. Marc's lovingly packed by Grace the previous night, and Carrie's rushed together by Carrie that morning, which threatened to cause her to be late for the start of her shift.

'You're bloody spoilt, you are, Marc,' she said under her breath.

'I've just got a good system, that's all,' he said.

'You've got more than a good system, you've got Grace. You don't know how lucky you are to have her. She's a diamond, that girl.'

'Well, yeah, I know,' he said with a mouthful of sandwich.

'Sometimes, I wonder. She's devoted to you, you know. You ever upset her, and you'll have me to deal with.'

'Alright, steady on. Anyone would think we're married,' he said.

'I'd rather marry Grace,' she said.

'Sometimes I think you two *are* married,' Sutton remarked with a smirk.

Stares from the line of white shirts at the joviality occurring in the room were loaded with hints that they wanted to use the table where Carrie and Sutton sat, but the icy look from Carrie made it clear that they were out of luck this time. After all, she was a fixture, and they were only visitors.

Once Carrie and Sutton had finished their lunch, they returned upstairs to Sutton's office and shut the door. This is something that they often did if they had the time. It provided a few moments of solitude from the mayhem of the station and allowed them to relax before the afternoon agenda took hold.

'I'm worried that we're hitting a dead end with the Angelica Rowntree case,' said Carrie, as she wrapped her hands around a mug of hot chocolate and stretched herself out between two chairs.

Sutton looked up from his newspaper and sighed as he folded it, knowing that now Carrie had raised the subject, that he would have to engage with her over it. His leisurely perusal of the crossword had just been shot down in flames. The concentration he would need to work out the anagram in 12 down that had bugged him all morning was no longer achievable. He looked across at Carrie who was as relaxed as a person could get.

'Make yourself comfortable, won't you?' he said sarcastically.

'You know it,' she replied, with all the cheek of someone that knows they can get away with it.

'I bloody *do* know it,' he responded, but with no malice. It was Carrie, and there were few boundaries she wouldn't push, so he left it. Not that he actually minded anyway. She spent enough time at his house with a completely free rein, playing whatever music she wanted to hear and playfully ordering him around.

'I actually woke up in the night because I...'

'What? Needed a wee?' he interrupted.

'No, you pudding. I thought about her,' she said, looking over to him.

Sutton looked back at her but didn't speak. Carrie took a sip of her comforting drink before she spoke again.

'What do we know, Marc?' she said, giving him a sideways glance.

'Well, we know that there has been no movement on her bank account and no activity from her on Facebook or any of her other social media haunts. We also don't know the whereabouts of her mobile phone but there doesn't appear to have been any activity from it. None of her friends have heard a word either which is all rather alarming. We've checked with all the local hospitals, and she hasn't been admitted to any of them.'

Sutton stood and walked over to a large whiteboard. Work had recommenced. It had replaced an old-fashioned corkboard that he favoured but had eventually got rid of at the insistence of DCI Blackery. On it he had stuck a photograph of Angelica Rowntree, the A4 one from the folder that he had referred to previously. Beside the photograph were a number of lines that, in a spider web fashion, branched out to meet headings such as Trenton Street. Under the heading was a list of facts that pertained to all they knew about the sighting of her by Robin Greaves, the mechanic from the garage where she worked. There was no record of Greaves on the Police database. Also, there were comments relating to the discovery of the earring that Sutton had stumbled upon when he was checking out the narrow lane at the end of Trenton Street. Next to the photograph was a list of Angelica's friends and associates. Emily Roache seemed to have been the most useful but even her story fell well short of anything like a breakthrough. The event that Emily had described in the pub regarding the 'unknown photographer' and the fact that she had mentioned that Haley Breen had been followed made Sutton suspicious of whether there was a link between the two instances. There was the reported sighting of Karter Swann that had been tenuously linked to the Haley Breen murder and although Sutton knew that he had provided an alibi, he still wondered about it. DCI Blackery didn't seem to believe that Swann was dead, despite all the blood at the house where he vanished from, and Sutton couldn't help considering that there might be something in that too. He knew that Swann had worked at the Cactus and Coyote and was pretty sure that he would have generated a degree of interest with the female clientele.

'Did we fail with Haley Breen?' he asked Carrie, out of the blue.

'No, Marc. We didn't stand a chance of doing anything to prevent that, but we do have a chance now, with Angelica.'

'I know, you're right,' he confessed.

Carrie lazily swung her rested legs back down from the chair and sat looking straight at Sutton. She knew as well as anyone, and probably better than most, that Sutton hadn't managed to shift the Haley Breen murder from his head in the way that many officers usually do.

'We have to find her for the sake of her parents. Dead or alive. As awful as it is, we can't leave them in limbo, they need closure to be able to move on,' she said.

'I know,' he said, returning to his desk and spinning his chair to face the whiteboard.

'Maybe the Haley Breen incident has nothing to do with this,' offered Carrie.

'Yeah, maybe. The time gap between the cases doesn't always indicate that they're separate though. Perhaps whoever has taken her was just letting the dust settle before they struck again. Anyhow, we found Haley Breen fairly quickly because she was left where somebody could find her. Although I'm not saying that the two cases are definitely connected, but if they are and the same person has taken Angelica, why hasn't she turned up in the same sort of time frame?'

'I have wondered that too…if they are connected. Either way, whether they are connected or not, she's not coming to us, so we've got to go to her.' said Carrie.

Sutton was already flipping through a file with Angelica Rowntree's name on the top of it.

'We've already checked the railway tracks and the sidings and the sheds and found nothing. The bus depot, obviously, got checked out thoroughly. Even the dogs didn't indicate anything,' he said.

'Maybe she's been dumped out of sight for a reason. Unlike Haley Breen, they might not want her to be found so easily,' said Carrie.

'We've had divers in the canal, and we've had our people wading across the lake. I've had 40 officers on overtime, which upset Blackery's budget, sniffing down alleyways, under bridges, and in disused car parks and who knows where else. They've opened bins and looked around the rear of the supermarkets too.'

'I know…and the helicopter has been up with its heat-seeking device.'

'Thermal Imaging Camera,' he said.

'That's what I said. Anyhow, what would make her go off with a perfect stranger, though?' said Carrie.

'Greaves said that she was talking to a man…'

'…which he wasn't sure wasn't a woman,' interrupted Carrie.

'Yeah, well, that wasn't helpful. But maybe she did know this person.'

'And what sort of person? What makes them tick?' said Carrie.

Sutton mumbled under his breath and although Carrie didn't catch what he said, she left it. Sutton pulled his mobile phone from his trouser pocket and began to study it closely. Carrie thought he had either been distracted by an incoming text or was planning to make a call. If so, she might have to leave him in peace to get on with it.

'There you are,' he said, to himself, sounding quite pleased, 'Carrie, I'm going to do some investigating into just that very subject and see whether that helps us to understand. I know someone who can shed some light on it.'

'Well, that's good. Ok, then. I'll go and have another word with Robin Greaves, just to see whether he's remembered any more about whatever he says he saw. I'll run another check on her friends, just in case they have seen or heard anything new.'

'Maybe he goes to the same pubs as our underage drinkers. Maybe he knows someone who carries a camera with them,' said Sutton.

'I'll ask but don't get your hopes up. It wasn't easy getting a straight answer the first time.'

'Well, if you can't persuade him to be a little more accurate about who he saw then nobody can. I've every faith in you,' he said, smiling in her direction.

'Ah, that's nice. So, what's behind the sudden spurt of compliments?'

'Nothing.'

'Except?'

'Except, Grace told me that you're cooking round our house tonight and I don't want to get indigestion,' he said, jokingly.

'Bloody cheek. I'm a good cook. Anyway, if you were my husband, I'd put poison in your tea,'

'If you were my wife, I'd drink it,' he swiftly replied.

TWENTY-FOUR

When DI Sutton arrived at the gates of Freedland House, which was situated just outside of Amberley Chase, a quaint market town on the edge of the Essex countryside, he realised that he had forgotten just how imposing they were. Made of solid walnut and hung on thick posts, they presented as a portal to another world. The house secluded behind them had been erected in 1824 and was once occupied by the family of a very wealthy landowner. No longer under the ownership of Robert Freedland, it was nowadays shared as office space by a number of different companies ranging from chartered accountants to insurance companies and law firms. At the rear there was an enormous conservatory that hosted business meetings, conferences and forums. There had even been wedding receptions that had spilled out onto the lush lawns at the rear that led down to the trout lake with its unmissable fountain. The perimeter of the grounds at the front of the building was landscaped with Norway Spruce that had been underplanted with a variety of spring bulbs. A Western Red Cedar commanded its place centrally in the gravel driveway, reaching as high as 30 metres to date.

Sutton chose to park the Subaru outside on the long driveway that had spurred from the main road. He had phoned ahead and forewarned against an unexpected appearance rather than just show up unannounced. It felt to him that things would be more relaxed and a whole lot less awkward than if he simply popped up out of the blue. He had visited Freedland House on a number of occasions in the past but not for some time and knew that this was likely to be at the forefront of the conversation. Sutton strolled slowly towards the house, gravel crunching underfoot, and looked up to the second-floor window noticing somebody walk from view. He had been spotted from the oriel window with its pretentious corbels jutting out underneath the structure. He was a stickler for being punctual, especially when he came with cap in hand in search of a favour. He also knew that the person he was here to see would be expecting nothing less as their punctuality had always bordered on obsessive.

The heavy entrance door that led into the foyer opened silently as he stepped inside. Sutton felt that he knew where to go but checked the location of the office layout with the lady at the reception desk in case there had been any switching of offices since his last visit. Nothing had altered, which confirmed to him that the person spying out of the window was indeed his intended acquaintance. He had only caught a glimpse, but it told him all he needed to know.

'You'll find the office on the second floor, sir. All the doors are clearly marked,' she said, her voice echoing in the impressive, marbled entrance hall.

The polished stone staircase spiralled up towards the first floor and provided him with a splendid view of the gardens beyond. He could see a large and wide patio with a gate in the centre that encouraged its guests to walk along the decorative stone path towards four symmetrically arranged Box hedges that encircled a full and flourishing flowerbed. Lawns that spread left and right blended into the countryside. The ceiling above him, or lack of it, allowed an uninterrupted view of the roof structure. Huge wooden beams, stained black, with exposed bolts, stood out against the rest of the off-white ceiling. It was quite a sight to behold. He wrestled with his memory, trying to recall if this was a new thing or whether he had simply forgotten about it. As he slowly climbed the stairs, he passed numerous certificates that decorated the walls pertaining to the personal achievements of various lawyers and accountants. He nodded politely to a passing secretary, her arms overloaded with files, as she skipped lightly from one office to another, appearing not to even notice him. Her suit was smarter than his and probably cost significantly more too. When he reached the second-floor level, he was faced with four doors but only one room faced out towards the front of the building, and only one bore the name that he instantly recognised.

Dr Patricia Toussaint, PsyD (Hons), MA. Forensic Psychologist.

As he tapped on the sturdy door, he tried to recall exactly how many years it had been since he had spoken with his sister other than at Christmas and the like. As he lowered his hand, and before he could reach for the door handle, the door opened. She was taller than him, and although she was 12 years older, she had never lost that radiance that seemed to come hand in hand with her professional demeanour. He wasn't at all surprised to see her wearing a very stylish black trouser suit, the jacket open at the front, over a white shirt. Her necklace reminded him of a mayoral chain, far too extravagant for his liking. But then none of this was designed to be for *his* liking. She had always been one for first impressions and making a memorable one. Everything about her spelt success. Her heavily tinted and dyed blonde hair was perfect, and so too, was the fake smile that greeted him.

'Marcus, such a pleasure to see you.'

'Hello, Patricia.'

'Do come into my little office.'

Little, it wasn't but it wasn't unlike her to play it down in the hope that someone else might express just how large and beautiful it was. So, he didn't.

'Thank you. It's cosy in here,' he said, as sincerely as he could.

Her face failed to hide her attempts to shrug off the comment. The slight, but noticeable break in her cat-walk-like stride told him that his response had landed perfectly. She invited him to sit at her desk but remained standing by the window which filled most of the wall space at that aspect.

'How's Gracie?' she said, without turning her attention from the world outside her window.

Sutton knew only too well how much Grace detested being referred to as 'Gracie'. It sounded so pretentious and that was something that Grace certainly wasn't. A more down to earth and honest girl, you could not find.

'Grace is fine, thank you.'

'Oh good. Still teaching?'

'Yes, she's very happy there.'

'Good.'

Sutton knew that making small talk was something that disinterested Patricia immensely, unless of course, she was the subject matter.

'And how is…Rebecca?' he said floundering for the name of the woman that Patricia had moved in with the last time he had spoken with her.

'Rachel,' she said, correcting him with a huff.

'Ah, yes, Rachel.'

'I left her if you must know,' not that Sutton really wanted to know, 'and I'm back with Gordon, and don't ask because I shall not tell you. Far too messy,' she said, flicking her hair from her forehead as she glided back to her desk and began to tap a fountain pen on her desktop. Subject closed.

He allowed the silence to drag on for a moment and waited expectantly for the inevitable subject to arise. Rather than attempt to engage in the conversation he had come here for, he thought he'd get it over with sooner rather than later. He didn't have to wait long.

'How long is it, now?' she said, maintaining a solid stare in his direction.

He knew precisely what she was referring to and as he tried to remember with a degree of accuracy, he noticed just how green her eyes were. *Had they always been so bright?*

'I think I saw you last about three years ago,' he said from memory.

'More like seven, I think you'll find. Although at least you have remembered to send a Christmas card each year.'

'That's down to Grace, she's the one who's on the ball with that sort of thing.'

'Well, she has her uses then. Quite the little woman.'

Sutton knew also that Grace absolutely abhorred being referred to as 'the little women,' especially by Patricia. He decided to sidestep the comment and change the subject away from Grace and on to the reason for his visit. The sooner it was over, the better.

'Patricia, I know just how busy you are,' he said, already preparing the ground for an easy escape, 'so allow me to come to the point of my visit,' he said.

'I didn't expect for one moment that it was going to be a social call. Do carry on,' she said, as she relaxed back into her leather-bound recliner fit for a princess.

'Right. I'm here to pick your brains, if I'm honest. I have a case currently and would like to know a little more about the type of person that I am looking for.'

'Are they missing?'

'*They* aren't but a young girl is, and I believe that she has been taken. Now, obviously, I'm hoping that we're still going to be able to find her safe and sound, but so far, we've drawn a blank.'

'So, what is your suspect like? Describe them to me,' she said.

'I don't have one,' he said, sounding somewhat defeatist.

'Oh. Then who exactly am I helping you with?'

'Well, I was hoping that you could help me to understand what characteristics this person might have and what causes them to take a girl in the first place. Also, about how they behave, generally.'

Sutton realised just how sketchy his words sounded. He almost regretted coming into Patricia's lair, but he also knew that she was good at what she did and that her knowledge might just give the case the kick-start it desperately needed. Sutton respected that she had not wasted her years at the University of Birmingham working towards her Forensic Clinical Psychology Doctorate. Not for the first time, he felt that he was starting from scratch. Patricia picked up her spectacles and put them on. Something about that slight alteration in her appearance made Sutton feel as though she had suddenly transformed into work mode.

'How long have you had those?' he enquired.

'What? Oh, these. Ever since I realised that my squinting was becoming more frequent. Rachel pointed it out first, but naturally enough, I shrugged it off. At least I did until one day when I misread the cooking time for a Sussex Pond Pudding. I was never the Delia Smith of the family, as you know, but I was trying desperately to make an effort. Rachel was out at her tennis club, and I decided to make something nice for dessert. I had everything I needed and all my instructions. Sadly, I did not read them quite right and accidently extended the cooking time which allowed the saucepan to steam dry. The first I knew of it was when the smoke alarm went off. I was in the bath and came rushing down wrapped in my gown to a wispy, smoke-filled kitchen, a blackened pan and an unmitigated disaster. That was the turning point.'

Sutton tried in vain to hide his smirk and refrained from dwelling on Patricia's disaster for any longer than necessary. Enjoy it, though he did.

'Oh,' was all he offered.

'Anyway, that was then. As you know, Gordon is an excellent and award-winning chef, and so I am now relieved of my kitchen duties. Why would one need to get their hands dirty when one has a highly respected Michelin star chef at their beck and call, 'eh?'

Patricia had met Gordon Toussaint in Paris whilst on a weekend break, ten years ago. She had only frequented L'avant Comtoir de la Mer on one previous occasion but having struck up a friendship with the head chef, she planned her strategy.

'Yep, I suppose so. So anyway…'

'Forgive me, Marcus. To business. Where do you want me to begin?' she said.

Sutton told Patricia what he knew with regard to the Angelica Rowntree disappearance, and it wasn't long before he could see that she was beginning to look at him a little blankly. He decided to bring up the Haley Breen case and although he insisted that there was no evidence to suggest that the two cases were connected, this definitely got her attention. He pushed on with the details of Haley's case and it seemed to be just the sort of thing Patricia needed to be able to formulate some kind of opinion.

'And you don't have a suspect or a conviction for that one?'

'No, unfortunately, not yet' he said, with a sigh.

'Then, I can help you with that one, although it's obviously a little late in the day to bring forth a positive result for the poor girl. But if we consider that they may indeed be connected then at least I can paint a picture for you of the type of person that you may be seeking.'

'That might just really help,' he said hopefully.

Sutton knew enough to realise that the best thing he could do now was to let Patricia speak uninterrupted. After all, her favourite pastime was telling people how much she knew about her subject and therefore just how damned clever she was.

'Good. Well...That's a starting point. Ok, so I'll try to put this into layman's terms as much as possible. I hope that doesn't sound too condescending.'

'No, not at all,' he lied. *As if.*

'Right. More often than not, you're going to be looking for a man. They tend to commit around 80% of violent crimes and significantly for you, about 76% of women killed knew their killer. Which doesn't help if it's a random attack. The statistics are all very well and can be useful, but they don't help you to construct a picture of the person that you are looking for. Which is where I come in,' she said, peering over her glasses at him, 'I think it will help you greatly to understand that they tend to think differently to us. The reasons for this can be manyfold but as a rule the factors that affect their early life very often dictate the psychological path of the potential murderer.'

'Such as what?' Sutton said, immediately realising that he had pledged to himself to keep quiet. He also knew full well that Patricia was not going to leave a stone unturned once she got going.

'Such as...Abuse, neglect, trauma, jealousy, rivalry, anger etc. All these things can make a big difference and present as triggers for the sort of person that you're looking for. Look, their brains work a little differently. What we recognise as something that is clearly wrong is masked for them. Their brains calculate things in a different way.'

Looking at Sutton's expression, Patricia tried a different tack.

'Ok, look at it like this. In order for them to carry out a crime like the one you described about the young girl, Haley, their brains will, if you like, provide a smoke screen whereby their choices are being driven by an internal force that takes control of their ability to decipher right from wrong. Although sometimes they know the difference and still cannot control it. Also, they invariably display a distinct lack of emotional awareness. It's called Alexithymia. It's symptomatic of some of the things that I've already mentioned.'

Patricia paused at this point to give Sutton a chance to respond but he only smiled and nodded so she continued onwards.

'Maybe worth noting that people that have sustained head injuries are four times more likely to be violent and as young people that have witnessed violence, they are four times more likely to commit it.'

'So, what is going on in their heads then? I mean in their brains,' Sutton asked, now becoming intrigued to learn more.

'More long words coming, Marcus,' she warned. 'A lot of it has to do with this loss of emotions that I mentioned just now. Bear with me. The Amygdala is near the base of our brains and is highly responsible for our emotional attachment to events and memories. It plays an important role in fear and anger. So, with your suspect, if you had one, they may not be feeling fear and therefore they do not have that association with what they are doing. A scan might show a shrunken Amygdala,' she said, now standing and beginning to pace around the room, 'Think of it like this also. A sustained lack of fear reduces the concern for getting caught and makes the incident easier to commit because they are unafraid of the consequences of their actions,' she explained.

'Got it. Wow, that's interesting. So, would that apply to why Haley was left at a site where she would be found fairly soon after being placed there?' he asked.

'Indeed, it could do. Sometimes the reason for the chosen location of the unfortunate victims also relates to the sense of achievement they might have.'

'Sorry?' Sutton said.

'To your killer, it was just somewhere to leave her. She was his trophy and perhaps he wanted her to be displayed. Her being found was inconsequential to him, or her. In their mind, they had not necessarily done anything wrong and certainly were not over concerned with being caught for it. They sometimes will seek rewards too and there is no greater reward than revenge. But where they find it might be from someone who is innocent and unrelated to the origins of why they are looking for it.'

'So, are they trying to account for some event from their past?' Sutton asked as Patricia returned to her seat.

'This is relative to those childhood events that I mentioned. They often like to dominate too. Sometimes that can be a reaction to having been bullied in their younger life. I am afraid that it is a toxic combination of risk factors, Marcus.'

'That's certainly given me food for thought.'

'Well, I hope I've been able to help a little but, Marcus, I'm going to have to unceremoniously shove you out very soon as I've got an appointment in about ten minutes, so I'm really sorry that we cannot talk for longer.'

'Patricia, you've been very helpful.'

'Well, of course I have.'

'Right then. Thank you for your time and I'll see you.'

'I don't suppose you will, but if you wish to email any further questions, I'll be pleased to answer them.'

'I'll do that. Thank you again. Goodbye.'

Back in the Subaru, Sutton sat for a moment and digested the details that he had rattling around in his head. Fortunately, he understood virtually everything that she had said. It was almost dark now and time he made his way home to Grace. As he joined the main carriageway, he remembered that Carrie was cooking tonight. He hoped it was something substantial because he was as hungry as a bear.

TWENTY-FIVE

Minneapolis Minnesota.

Gregory Bonner was back on the trail of Caterina Marks. Big Toni was dubious as to whether his efforts were going to reap any sort of reward but decided to let him run with it anyway. At least he could tell his superior that he was following orders and attempting to trace the untraceable. Captain Rodrigues and Bonner had discussed that she may have left the county or even the state after all this time, but Bonner couldn't help feeling that she was somewhere close. Perhaps it was nothing more than wishful thinking. At the time of her disappearance there was nothing to imply that she was going to actually run away. Her homelife was pleasant enough and she was a straight A student. She had a normal circle of friends and enjoyed the usual social activities that any young girl did. She was popular, not an outcast. Bonner could find nothing in her make-up that caused him to doubt that Caterina was anything other than just a normal young lady. More than that she had been his friend and he knew deep inside that that was what this was all about. Gregory Bonner had had a soft spot for Caterina Marks all those years ago and had never plucked up the courage to tell her. How he regretted that. Now, after so many years, the pangs of young love were starting to hit him again. This time it was no more than a memory but if he could find Caterina then he would feel as though he had done a good job. He needed to help her.

The current temperatures aided Bonner's decision to do his patrol from his vehicle so he purposely avoided walking behind Caterina in the cold air. *I could only just keep up with her the last time,* he thought, ironically. With Bonner snugly sat in his Patrol Vehicle and Caterina skipping happily down the path, he cruised along the street. He was following the same route as before and considering all the possible turns and changes of direction that she may have made.

If not Betty's, then where else?

Bonner parked his vehicle for a moment and looked across the street at where he imagined Caterina standing, frozen in time between a world of innocence and a world of mystery. Her auburn hair glowed against the backdrop that the dark privet hedges were providing. Two boys on cycles raced by her and as Bonner watched them go, she began to move again. Hampshire Avenue North. *Surely, she was heading for Betty' house.* Nothing else made any sense to Bonner. Her mother had commented that she thought Caterina was on her way to Betty's, "Something about the dog" she had remarked. Bonner remembered Old Hastings. He was a lovely old fella. A real loveable old hound. He appreciated just how painful the loss of him would have been to Betty as he was always more Betty's dog than Elisha's. As Bonner reflected, he couldn't resist a smirk at the sight of Big Toni sprawled out face down in the snow having fallen over Hastings' grave.

He shook his head and concentrated on his job of trying to establish what had happened to Caterina. The fact that so much time had elapsed since her initial disappearance ruled out Bonner spending a lot of time searching the areas within the district that the police had already paid attention to. He knew there would be nothing left to find. The dogs hadn't had any success so why should he? The wooded areas of the golf course where Connor Org played had been meticulously searched by man and dog. Every inch. He was beginning to feel as though it didn't matter what he did, he was never going to find her. *10 years.* The envelope with the photographs of the age-progressed Caterina were beside him. Maybe he should give them a try. Maybe there was a slim chance that somebody had seen her. Maybe he was trying to hit a Fighter Jet with a peashooter. He would drop in at the Org household and courteously let Alexandria Org know that he had issued a few posters. She would either understand or hate him for it. He wondered which. Either way he questioned his actions. He looked towards the start of Hampshire Avenue North, at its junction with Golden Valley Road, and in his mind's eye, could still see Caterina standing on the corner, almost as if she was saying, *which way now? C'mon, it's cold.* The image of her in her white dress and pale blue cardigan saddened him.

'I don't know, I don't know which way. I'm sorry,' he said quietly to himself.

Bonner grabbed at the envelope and left his vehicle by the side of the street. He felt the levels of desperation rise in him and decided that even though it was destined to fail that he would ask some of the local shop owners to put some of the posters in their windows. He walked to the local leisure centre and did the same. The looks that he received when he made his request were a mix of surprise and delayed empathy. They were all happy to give it a try, but each had commented upon it being a long shot. They were sentiments that Gregory Bonner already knew.

The poster was basically a photo of the 24-year-old, age-progressed, Caterina with the wording above her photo that read: **MISSING PERSON.**

Beneath her photo was the following information:

> **This is an age-progressed photograph of Caterina Marks who went missing on April 26th 2010. She was 17 years old. Last seen in the Golden Valley area wearing a white dress with a pale blue cardigan. Brown eyes / Auburn hair / 5' 4" / 130 pounds.**
> **IF YOU HAVE ANY INFORMATION, PLEASE CONTACT YOUR LOCAL POLICE DEPARTMENT.**

Bonner knew that similar posters had been put up in the area when she initially disappeared, but he just thought he'd try the age-progressed version in case anyone had seen her in her adulthood. *Just maybe.* It was a despairing attempt, but he knew it was still a possibility and anyhow, he had nothing else. When someone vanishes in the way that Caterina had, there is very little to work with and little hope to cling to. If he hadn't been scanning the MUPC when Big Toni walked up to him, then he would very likely not be feeling sad today. But there she was, looking back at him, her eyes pleading for help.

Bonner had one hand on the car radio with the intention of telling Big Toni that he was on his way when he decided to roll past Betty's house for another look before he made his way back to the Minneapolis Police Department at South 5th Street to declare to Big Toni that he could not see how he was ever going to find any information that could lead to the answer to the Caterina Marks mystery. He slowly drove past his imaginary vision of Caterina standing on the corner of Hampshire Avenue North and almost apologised again. *To whom? To nobody.*

He continued onwards and battled against the emptiness inside him. When he had first taken on the task of searching for her, all he could imagine was the joy of finding her alive and returning her to her mother. But no longer. As the enormity of the task became a reality, he began to cave in. *Maybe I didn't think this through.* The Nelson property, as it was once known, was just a couple more blocks away. As he approached it, Bonner could see the colour of the house through the trees before he got right up to it. It still looked fairly good. He parked his vehicle opposite the property and sat staring at it, taking in all the little differences that he noticed, before he got out, pointed the key fob at the vehicle, and listened for the tell-tale clunk of the locking mechanism. He ambled across the street and took another good look at the house and the new arrangements in the garden. The old shed stood defiantly but the sign that marked Hastings' resting place was gone. Of course. He was glad that nobody came out of the house to ask if he wanted something. *Maybe everyone was at work,* he thought. He felt a real attachment to the property or maybe it was to the time when the girls used to be here, and Mrs Nelson would invite him into the kitchen to sample the cookies. Bonner sighed and crossed the street back to his transport and as he shifted into D and crept gently from the kerbside, he thought that he could almost hear the girls outside in the garden, laughing as Caterina squirted them with water from the garden hose. Bonner glanced across and noticed the front door begin to open. He felt that, maybe, he would have to explain why he had been hovering around outside after all. When he saw who it was, he stopped the vehicle, and selected P for park, switching off the engine.

'Mr Bones, Harry,' Bonner shouted, with one hand raised through his open window.

To Bonner's surprise Old Harry Bones was heading slowly down towards the street. His movements were cautious as he was being careful not to slip on any autumn leaves. He was aware that a fall at his age could be serious. Harry looked up when he heard the shout, and once he had recognised Bonner, he began to smile and walk across the street to the Patrol Car. Harry didn't look a great deal older than the last time that Bonner had seen him, albeit the circumstances were less fraught.

'Good to see you Mr Bones. Do you know the new owners, then?'

'I do now,' said Harry with a glint in his eye, 'I've just got my old job back. I'm going to be helping Penelope, I mean helping out with the garden. No heavy work though, just some planting and general tidying up. I realised the other day just how much I've missed the old garden.'

Bonner knew who Penelope was but couldn't see why Harry had referred to her like that though. *Slip of the tongue,* he thought.

'Great, Mr Bones. It'll be just like old times.'

'No. It won't be like old times. Those lovely old days when we planted the bulbs together are gone now. But the new owners have purchased a lot of nice equipment for me to use. All the old spades and other tools got thrown out after…well, you know.'

Harry stood beside Bonner's window and sighed a little. He seemed to be a little trance-like and lost for a moment. Bonner tried to change the subject slightly.

'Well, I'm sure it'll work out for you. Would you like a ride home? I can take you if you like, it's no trouble. Save you walking.'

Harry gave this a little thought but readily accepted. The air was chilled, and he didn't want to get too cold on the walk back. It took him a lot longer to re-warm than it used to. Old Harry walked around to the other side of the vehicle and opened the door. He settled into the front seat, enjoying the benefit of the warmth from the heater, and all of a sudden felt quite important. He studied the radio and the display screen that had a variety of information that he didn't understand. The seating position was higher than most of the vehicles Harry had been in before. He liked the elevated view of the street and the comfort of the seat that wrapped itself around him. The engine started and Harry wanted nothing more than to go around the block a few times first, before getting home.

'So, did they advertise for someone to help out with the garden?' asked Bonner, as he drove away.

'No, I just went up to the front door and took my chances. I hadn't been back here for a long while and yet I'd walked by it enough times. I like to see the bulbs coming up in the spring and summer. They are…special to me.'

'I expect you must have planted most of them, Harry.'

'I did. I did.'

'I guess the old place holds a lot of memories for you,' said Bonner.

'More than you can imagine, young man. Too many sometimes,' said Harry, sombrely.

'I thought you enjoyed doing the garden in those days,' said Bonner, a little confused.

'Oh yes. We worked, that's Penelope and I, and put lots of effort into creating a lovely display. Yes…'

'I bet you miss her, Harry,' said Bonner, wishing that he could suck the words back in. It was obvious that he did.

'Terribly,' he said quietly, 'Even now, I don't know if I've done the right thing by knocking on the door. I'm afraid that working there again might stir up old thoughts. And yet…Oh, I don't know.'

Bonner pulled the vehicle into the kerbside and looked across at Harry who was wiping his eyes with his handkerchief. Bonner was unsure what was going on, but he'd known Old Harry Bones for a long time, and it looked to him that his old friend needed his help. He turned the radio volume down so that he could still hear it in case he was called, but quiet enough that it allowed the relative silence to create a calm atmosphere before he asked Harry if he could explain if there's a problem that he could help with. To Bonner's surprise, Harry looked to be struggling to find the right words. Finally, after the two old friends had sat quietly for a few moments, Harry spoke.

'Nobody knows this, and if I didn't think that I could trust you then I wouldn't be telling you either, but we've known each other for a good while and if I can't trust a police officer then who can I trust?' Harry paused and then said, 'I was very much in love with Penelope. It was not that we had a relationship or anything like that, but we just had a very close friendship, like dear friends do. Except, it was a lot more than that for me.'

Bonner was looking straight out to the front of the vehicle and wondering just how much it must have hurt Harry when she died. Harry continued.

'I knew some other things about her life that I am not proud of. I mean, I'm not proud that I kept it all to myself. In fact, only one other person knows about these things and I'm not going to say who that is. It turned out that we both knew and did nothing to help matters. I was the one that should have done something though. That's why it's ground me down for all these years.'

'Harry, if you want to share anything then I give you my word that it'll remain in the strictest confidence. It's not my job to go spreading tales.'

'I know it isn't. I have wondered whether it could actually do any harm to say something, but it wouldn't do any good either, not now. It's too late. Although it might unburden me somewhat.'

Harry sat pensively, considering his options and wondering whether it would matter if he did say something. He pondered, not for the first time, whether it would make him feel any better about the whole thing. He knew that he couldn't alter the past, as much as he would like to, and he had often sat at home wondering whether he was silly to store it all up in his head. It wasn't as though he would be breaking a confidence, not really. *Penelope wouldn't mind.*

'Bonner, you there?' Big Toni's voice blurted out of the low-volume radio.

'Yes, Captain.'

'When you gonna be back, Bonner? You staying out all night?'

'No Captain, I'm just with a motorist. Bit of a disagreement between a couple of guys. No big deal. I'll be on my way very soon.'

'Ok, then. Sure you don't need any assistance?'

'I'm fine, Captain.'

'Thought you were gone for good, Bonner.'

'Thank you for caring, Captain.'

Bonner replaced the handset with a slight chuckle and looked at Harry, 'What he doesn't know, won't hurt him.'

'Thank you,' replied Harry.

'So, Harry. I won't push you but if you think that I can help, then I'm all ears.'

Harry Bones sat quietly in the comfortable car seat and tapped his fingers gently on his leg.

'You know, I think I want to tell you about the shed,' he said as he turned to face Bonner.

'The shed?'

TWENTY-SIX

Tilbury, East London.

It was noticeable that the afternoons were beginning to merge into evening a little sooner than they had just a few weeks ago. The rush hour was dragging out at both ends. It started a little earlier but did not seem to end any sooner. The traffic thickened daily, like a coagulating lava flow, as the night-time temperatures lowered, and the street lighting illuminated like beacons in the gloom. The huge numbers of heavy goods vehicles that spewed from the large distribution centres on the west side of the A1089, journeyed to and from the A13, rumbling on relentlessly, pouring in and out of London. Shoppers packed the stores in neighbouring Grays, just a couple of miles from where Karter Swann, aka Kevin Marshall, was living. He had recently returned from a shopping trip of his own and, as he put his items into the cupboards, he muttered to himself.

Swann thought that he was becoming paranoid. He also felt like an idiot. From his bedroom at the Turner's residence, he sat crouched by the window and peered outside at the people and cars passing by. Only 20 minutes earlier, in the guise of Kevin Marshall, he had had a shock. He did not know for sure whether his mind was playing tricks on him or whether he had caught sight of Elisha, staring at him, from the far end of the superstore. As he paid for his groceries at the checkout, the moment made him go cold.

Although his view wasn't perfect, and he couldn't be absolutely certain that it was her, as soon as their eyes locked, he froze. He had paid for his items and turned away from the checkout desk when he began to stare into the shop to see if he could get another look. Whoever she was, she had gone out of sight. Swann figured that if it was her, that she would surely follow him out of the store. Nobody did.

The image in his mind of the woman with the knee-length brown coat and red neck scarf, which covered most of her face, was fixed in place. He had been able to see that she had light-coloured hair, similar to how he remembered Elisha's to be, and she was about the same height. He was just too far away from her to get a really good look at her face. But it was enough to put him on red alert. He felt surprised at the ease of which an innocent glance across the superstore could have rattled his cage to such a degree. Goosebumps, and the feeling of a weird numbness, had come over him in an instant. The more he tried to pass it off as a ridiculous episode of unfounded anxiety, the more he convinced himself that she had found him and was going to begin to plague his life again.

 He changed from the light green hooded sweater that he had worn, less than half an hour ago for a dark, indistinguishable raincoat. He donned a beanie hat, and recklessly decided to drive back to the superstore for another look. He could not validate that his choice was a sensible one, but something inside him simply needed to know if it was her, although he had no idea what he was going to do if he got the confirmation that he dreaded.

 Swann studied the cars that were leaving, as he turned into the vast parking area, concentrating on the faces of the departing drivers. He drove slowly around the superstore car park in case he caught sight of the woman that had made his heart skip a beat. His beanie hat was pulled as low onto his forehead as it could be without hampering his ability to see where he was going. He had recently re-dyed and trimmed his beard. His dark hair was becoming almost long enough to sport a ponytail. He liked the new look. Once he had circled the car park and was sure that she was not immediately in sight, he parked the car in the next available space. He got out as discretely as he could with his head slightly bowed and started to carefully check out the shoppers that were at their cars, unloading their trollies and placing their bags into their vehicles. He knew the make of her car but fully expected that it may have been changed by now. His radar was searching for a woman with a brown coat and red neck-scarf but nobody in the immediate vicinity was fitting the description. Swann slowly made his way towards the entrance to the store, keeping one eye on the car park and the other on the people that were exiting the building. He much preferred it if he could spot her out in the open, but as time went on, it became increasingly evident that he was going to have to commit to going inside. When he reached the entrance, he half-turned as he knew that once he was in the store, he would miss her if she was still outside. There were a lot of cars to keep an eye on, all in one go. Swann was reasonably certain that she had not been in the car park and so he turned his full attention to the occupants of the interior. First, he scanned the checkouts to see whether she had, perhaps, finished her shopping. Seeing as he had been home and returned again, he reasoned that there would have been enough time for that to have happened. There were 12 checkouts at this end of the superstore, and he could see all the way to the end. Although the final few were a little more difficult to see clearly, he was certain that the woman he was looking for was not at any of them. Swann knew that he was taking a chance and that if he bumped head on into her, that he would be leaving himself wide open, but the nagging feeling inside him told him to establish whether it was her or not. It was a risk, but he thought that it had to be taken. If he found the woman to be someone else then he would sleep at night, if not, then he felt as though he might not ever sleep again.

Swann decided to go to the nearest point at the end of each aisle and take a look down them in order. All he could do was try. He knew that there was a chance that as he looked down one aisle that she could move to the next and he might miss her. But, short of causing an evacuation of the store, he didn't have a lot of options. He moved into position at the first aisle carefully and peered down it. There were plenty of people but none of them were the woman in the brown coat with the red neck-scarf. He moved on to the next, checking everyone around him as he went. His eyes were darting around in a sort of frantic panic. He was aware that he probably looked quite suspicious, like a customer with unlawful intentions in mind who was checking out where the staff and the security guards were, before he grabbed his intended items and made his bolt for freedom. What he didn't need were distractions. He couldn't afford to worry about the impression he was making, he just had to make sure that he didn't mess this up. He refocussed his thoughts and began to scrutinise each customer as they innocently went about their business. The crowded aisles were the most difficult to judge. His radar was set to identify the colour of her coat. The next five aisles didn't raise any alarm bells and he was beginning to think that she had more than likely already gone. He continued on, with the same cautious peeping down each aisle but he did not see her. Finally, he decided that he should give up and go home. At the furthest end of the store, he sidled, obliquely through a self-scan till and began to make his way back towards the exit. The first thing that he was aware of was that three members of the store staff were watching him closely. He knew that he had not done anything wrong but conceded that his actions may have appeared a bit strange. If asked, he would tell them that he was looking for someone, which of course, he was. The fact that he wasn't trying to conceal anything probably limited their interest in him to nothing more than curious suspicion. Nobody spoke as he walked past them and approached the exit to the car park. This was fine by him as it would give him a final opportunity to check the exterior one last time. As he exited, he became immediately aware that the daylight had now, been completely lost. It was also raining lightly. The floodlights that surrounded the perimeter of the parking area, reflected in the raindrops that sat on each of the vehicles and shimmered in the wind. Rainbows of oil in the puddles decorated the tarmac. Swann found his car, opened up, and got inside. Even if she were out there now, the rain on the car windows would blur her view and offer only a distorted perspective of the man with the beanie hat and dark beard.

The amount of traffic had increased substantially since he had frequented the superstore, for an unplanned second time during the afternoon, and made for a slow drag to the roundabout. Although the ASDA Superstore was a lot closer to where he lived, he had chosen to shop in Morrison's as he was desperately low on fuel and didn't want to risk getting snarled in traffic before he had a chance to get to the more local store. Had Swann not been out in his car, and had he paid attention to the fuel level, he may have filled up elsewhere and not ever found himself in this predicament. He followed the traffic at a snail's pace as it gently merged into increasingly busy roads. What frustrated him the most, was not the repetition of words from *Buggles,* telling him that *Video killed the radio star,* from his stereo, but not being able to be certain that it was Elisha who caught his eye. *It could have been anyone,* he thought, *Maybe I'm losing the plot.*

Swann arrived home and managed to park the car in the same space that he had driven out from 40 minutes ago. He sat in the car for a moment and shook his head at the absurdity of the whole scenario. He had not set eyes on Elisha for some time and anticipated that she must have moved on by now. *Probably tormenting some other mug,* he thought. A quick, unexpected flashback of Betty's face jolted him. He walked towards the front door and entered the Turner's residence, realising that, maybe, his brain had not quite secured those feelings under lock and key after all. Betty had meant a lot to him, and he had to acknowledge that he may not ever find anyone as lovely as her again. *Lovely in a crazy way.* As he began to ascend the stairs, he realised that he still had his coat on and turned back to hang it on a set of hooks by the front door. Swann slipped out of the coat and noticed an envelope, facedown, on the door mat. He bent down and picked it up, taking it upstairs with him to the portion of the house that he rented. He didn't consider that it may not be for him, and probably wasn't. His mind was somewhere else. Sometimes he forgot that the Turner's were even there, they were so quiet. He put it on a table, switched on the kettle, and got a mug from the cupboard, into which he dropped a teabag. Once the kettle had boiled, he poured the water into the mug and sat on a stool beside the table. Inquisitive about the envelope, he turned it over to see who it was addressed to. As Kevin Marshall, he did not tend to receive mundane items in the mail, or anything else. It was blank. Just an envelope. He felt it to work out whether there was anything inside but ultimately decided to slide a finger under the flap that was tucked in and not glued.

Swann's blood ran cold as he prised out the photograph. Reluctantly, he found himself studying it. At first glance he couldn't make sense of it. The clarity of the photograph left a lot to be desired. It was dark and he even questioned whether he was holding it the right way up. Swann turned it sideways but that didn't look right either. *So, what am I supposed to be looking at? Something like a roll of white material,* he thought. He took the photograph over to his bed and switched on the lamp. Holding it now, in better light. He held it closer and tried to make out exactly what it was that he was studying. The white roll of material looked as though it was somewhere without much light as the picture seemed to have been taken using a flash. The white reflected sharply back at him. Swann couldn't be certain whether the undecipherable object was large or small as there was nothing else in the photograph that would provide any scale. Dropping it onto the bed, he took a mouthful of tea from his mug and wondered again about the potential Elisha sighting. He knew that he wasn't going to be able to shake it from his memory any time soon. His mug of tea seemed to suddenly lose its appeal. His unwanted return adventure to the superstore and the discovery of the mystery envelope were definitely beginning to spoil his day. He set the mug down on the bedside table and picked up the photograph, concentrating on the less than reliable detail again. As he stared at it, he noticed that something else was becoming visible to him and held it a little closer once again in order to study it further. Something red was marked on it too. Near to one end of the roll was a fairly innocuous sort of blemish or maybe a stain on the material. The mark looked like a kind of smudge but the more he scrutinised it, the clearer it became. Swann suddenly got a sickening feeling that he knew what this might be. He didn't want to think it, but his brain was running riot with dystopian thoughts and images. Images that he had seen before. The red mark was beginning to make sense. It was a distinct pattern that he now recognised. Swann swore out loud as he identified what he was looking at, throwing the photograph down onto the bed. *Another photograph.* It was similar to the ones that had arrived at the Cactus and Coyote. *How?* The afternoon was going from bad to worse. Swann sat heavily onto his bed, his face now drained of colour, and tried to accept what this meant. *Somebody has found me.*

TWENTY-SEVEN

The dulcet tones of the satnav sounded pleased with its final announcement as DS Carrie Linton parked her car outside the premises at 38, Rodina Close, where Robin Greaves lived. She checked her appearance in the rear-view mirror. Carrie was always very well presented on the occasions that she left the confines of Old Clapton Street, especially when she was meeting someone in particular, such as she was hoping to, today. It was a different story when she was chilling round Grace's. *Anything goes,* was their motto. Both of them were completely comfortable to wander around the house in whatever felt right at the time. Sutton often walked in on a pair of scantily clad women. Mostly, he just didn't look or take any notice anymore. It was Grace and Carrie, and he knew the motto. Sometimes he wondered whether it was his house or Carrie's. Over the years she had left various articles of clothing at Grace's and knew that if she needed to change into something different that there would be something of hers in Grace's bedroom, or even something of Grace's. Sutton called the bedroom 'Carrie's wardrobe'.

Her hair was neatly tied in a short ponytail and clipped into place. She looked back at herself approvingly and checked that the remnants of her lunch with Marc Sutton were not still evident on her teeth, even though they had been brushed before she left the station. It was simply one of Carrie's pet hates. She looked across towards number 38 and wondered whether he would be in or even that he would answer the door. Before she got out of the car, she opened her bag and got out an A4 pad that had a copy of the report that had been previously taken when Greaves was last spoken to. The details of which were scant. *It might have been a man or a woman.* Carrie was convinced that it was definitely one of those two. She replaced the pad in her bag, opened the car door and stepped out turning to view the properties in the Close. The first thing that she appreciated was the stony silence. Even the traffic noise from the nearby main road seemed to be absorbed by the solitude of the Close. There were a number of identical looking abodes, all with very neat front gardens and clean-looking facades. Most were bungalows like 38, with the exception of a smattering of two-story houses. She calculated that one of the houses was probably where the Warden for the residents lived.

Not bad, she thought, as she took a look around her at the secluded rows of properties, each with a carefully clipped privet hedge to the front aspect. The window cleaner, whose van she had parked behind, looked at her via the reflection in front of him, and nodded to her, calling 'Afternoon' in a slightly too friendly tone. Carrie wasn't in uniform. She had on a smart dark blue suit, trousers and a jacket, black shoes. Her raincoat was in the car, just in case. Carrie nodded back. Not one to miss the details, she turned to see the name displayed on the side of the van. She logged *Willow Window Services* into her memory. The name at the bottom of the signage read *P. Goodacre*. Whether P. Goodacre was up the ladder she didn't know, but she decided that she didn't really care enough to find out.

As Carrie was halfway along the path that led to the front door of number 38, somebody came out. A woman. She was probably around 50 or 55. She wore a kind of apron with a silly motif of a dog seemingly pushing a vacuum cleaner. *Ridiculous*, thought Carrie. She had with her, a carrier bag that swung against the doorframe as she exited and hurried out towards Carrie, who was approaching down the path. Carrie considered that the woman must have seen that she was on her way towards the front door but still closed it behind her. Carrie's expression generated a comment.

'I'm sorry but we always encourage the residents to keep their doors closed. We never let anyone in without the resident seeing who it is first. You never know who's about these days,' she said with a smile.

'Oh, that's ok. Very wise,' replied Carrie.

'Just done my good turn, well, one of them, anyway. Bit of cleaning and tidying up and making beds, never stops. The residents are supposed to do their own, but I like to help out if I've got a spare minute or two.'

'Are you a neighbour, then?' asked Carrie.

'Oh, no. I should have said. My name is Dorothy Walton, I'm Graham's wife.' Carrie's rather blank look said that she had no idea who Graham was and prompted a further explanation.

'He's the Warden. We live over the road in one of the houses,' she explained, pointing in the general direction of one of the two-story properties.

'Oh, right,' said Carrie.

'Not seen you before. Are you a relative of Mr Greaves or just a friend? Excuse me being nosey but we like to know when we see a stranger on the Close. And you are?'

'And you are?' Nosey wasn't the word, more like pushy, thought Carrie.

'I'm Detective Sergeant Linton, from Old Clapton Street Police Station,' she said, with a confident smile, and her warrant card visible in her hand.

The woman, Dorothy, was taken aback a little and all of a sudden, the run of questions came to an abrupt halt. She smiled back with a look full of curiosity and could only muster a stifled 'Oh'. Dorothy stood affixed on the path between Carrie and the front door to number 38, her eyes still following Carrie's warrant card as it disappeared back into the inside pocket of her jacket.

'Is Mr. Greaves in?' asked Carrie.

'What? Oh, yes. You know he's a bit slow, don't you?'

'I am aware that he has a degree of learning difficulties, yes.'

'Don't be surprised if you meet his mother either,' she replied.

'His mother?' said Carrie, but Dorothy was on her way across the road and oblivious to the enquiry.

Carrie turned back to face the front door, not entirely sure what she had meant, unless, of course, he had a visitor. She rang the doorbell which chimed its tone loud enough that she could tell that it was operating functionally and waited. Carrie startled slightly at the clatter of the window cleaner's ladders being repositioned against the wall of the upper story of the house next door which took her attention from the front door. P. Goodacre, or whoever he was, held his stare on her until Carrie looked away, unimpressed. *No chance, mate.* A shadow was now visible from the other side of the door and in another moment the door began to open very slowly. The door chain restricted the amount of movement and only allowed enough space for Robin Greaves to cautiously, peep around the door, his face only partially coming into view. He looked quite pale, and his receding hair was dishevelled. Carrie noticed that he was also unshaven, and his eyes were a little blurry as if he had just woken up. He wore dark blue jeans and a light blue vest. *Old man's slippers*, thought Carrie. The mustiness of the bungalow wafted out into the air causing Carrie to wonder whether she really wanted to go inside at all. He didn't speak, he just stood motionless to one side of the doorway.

'Mr. Greaves, I'm Detective Sergeant...'

'I know who you are. I could hear you outside,' he said.

'Then you'll know which Police Station I am from too. May I speak with you?'

'Depends. What's it about?'

'It's about the sighting of Angelica Rowntree that you spoke to us about previously. I would like to ask…'

'I told you what I saw,' interrupted Greaves, dismissively.

'Yes, you did but it wasn't really very helpful was it, Mr. Greaves?' said Carrie forcing the upper hand.

Carrie saw a flicker in his face which was all she needed to know that she had regained control.

'Well?' he said.

'May I come inside for a moment?' Carrie asked reluctantly, given the atmosphere in there.

'It's not convenient,' said Greaves, looking back inside.

Thinking back to what Dorothy had said, Carrie asked what the reason was.

'I've got my mother here and she's asleep,' he said.

Carrie saw something in his expression, something in his eyes, that made her doubt his words but then Dorothy had implied that she might *'meet his mother'*, so maybe it added up after all. She looked at Greaves and tried again.

'It would be much easier so that we could go over what you saw again and…'

'She's asleep.'

Not willing to take no for an answer, Carrie delved a bit further.

'Then we could speak quietly in the living room so as we don't disturb her. I'm sure that…'

'She's on the sofa in the living room. She's old.'

Carrie realised her slip having inadvertently created a scenario that Greaves appeared to have picked up on and turned to his advantage. Unless, of course, she really was asleep on the sofa in the living room.

'Ok,' said Carrie, with a kind smile, 'Then we'll do it here instead. Tell me once again exactly what you saw in Trenton Street on the day that Angelica went missing. You remember, it was when you left the garage. Tell me again what you saw.'

Carrie waited patiently as Greaves looked past her across the road. His expression had barely changed since he had opened the door to her. *Don't be surprised if you meet his mother.* Carrie was about to repeat herself when Robin Greaves spoke up.

'I saw Angelica.'

'Yes, and…' said Carrie, in her imperturbably polite way.

'What?'

'You saw Angelica. Was she with anyone?' asked Carrie, knowing full well that his previous story implied that she was.

'She was talking to someone and then I got on the bus.'

'Yes, but before you walked away to go to the bus stop, what else did you see?'

'What do you mean?'

Carrie had had about enough of the go-slow that Greaves was playing but she knew that playing it too aggressively with him was not going to work either. Uncertain of precisely what his learning difficulties were, Carrie was fairly sure that learning how to be evasive wasn't one of them.

'What was Angelica wearing?' she asked, 'Surely you can remember that, can't you?'

Carrie knew what Angelica was wearing when she went missing. The report from her parents confirmed exactly how she was dressed. A dark red sweatshirt, blue jeans and white trainers.

'Yes. She had a pair of jeans on.'

'What else Mr. Greaves? What was she wearing on her top half?'

'Like a...like a...a thick jumper, like a sweatshirt.'

'And what was the person she was speaking to wearing?'

'I couldn't see. It was getting dark.'

'Except it wasn't really all that dark, was it?'

'*Getting* dark.'

'But it was light enough for you to clearly see what Angelica was wearing wasn't it? Perhaps you could think again about the other person that you saw. It's very important.'

Greaves facial expression seemed to go a little vacant and Carrie wondered whether she was starting to exceed his already diminished attention span. However, having made the effort to drive over and having also got him talking, she was reluctant to give up now.

'Was she talking to a man or a woman? You must know that don't you?' she asked.

Greaves looked at Carrie and nodded, 'It was a man,' he said.

Carrie wondered whether to ask him if he was sure in case he changed his mind again but decided to try to confirm it with him anyway.

'Definitely a man, Mr. Greaves?'

Greaves nodded.

'What was he wearing?'

After another pause, he said, 'I don't remember anything else because it was getting dark,' he repeated.

'How often did you used to go to the Cactus and Coyote?' said Carrie, deciding to change tack.

'I don't drink,' responded Greaves.

'I didn't ask you whether you drank, I asked you how often you went there.'

Greaves barely appeared to be bothered by the question but appeared to be giving his answer some thought.

'Only a couple of times,' he said.

'Which nights did you go there?'

'I don't know,' he said.

'I think you do. After all it's not something that you would forget is it, Mr Greaves?'

'No, well, it wasn't always the same night.'

'Who did you used to see there? What were their names?' asked Carrie.

'No-one. I went on my own,' he said, glancing indoors again.

'And when you got there, who did you see?' asked Carrie.

'I don't know really,'

'Was Angelica there on the times you used to go?' she asked.

'She might have been, I don't remember,' he said.

'How about her friends? Did you see them there?'

'A lot of people were there. It was very busy,' said Greaves.

'Angelica and who else, what were their names?'

'I don't know their names.'

'But you do remember seeing them there?' asked Carrie.

'They…Sometimes…I don't know,' said Greaves, a little more rattled now from Carrie's rapid questioning.

'Ok, Mr Greaves. I won't keep you away from your mother any longer. If you remember anything else that could be useful, please get in touch. Here, this is the number to use. Please remember that if we need to talk to you again, it might be easier to do it at the station.'

'I haven't done anything wrong,' he said, defensively.

'I'm not suggesting that you have, it just might be easier, that's all. And warmer,' she said turning to look at the dark clouds that were fast approaching, 'Oh, and Mr Greaves, do you own a camera?' she asked.

As Carrie turned back towards Greaves, and before she could say anything else, he began to close the door. She didn't see any point in stopping it from closing, as tempted as she was. She felt that the answer would likely be either 'I don't remember' or 'I don't know.' She knew that she had got as much as she was likely to get from Robin Greaves for now. For what it was worth, he had confirmed that Angelica was talking to a man. She knew that nothing he said could be considered completely reliable and that maybe, he might enter the picture again at some point in the future.

Carrie sat back in her car and placed her bag on the front passenger seat next to her. As she started the engine, she began to doubt how much good it had done talking to Robin Greaves. She checked her mirrors and began to drive her car out of Rodina Close. She wasn't all that happy with her afternoon and hoped that Sutton had had more luck than her. As she approached the main road at the end of the Close, her phone rang. It was DI Marc Sutton. Carrie steered the car to the kerbside and picked up her phone.

'Hi Marc, how has it gone?'

'Carrie, meet me at the Cut, at the end near the weir.'

'What's happening?' said Carrie with her heart in her mouth.

'Someone saw a roll of white material bob up beside one of the old, abandoned houseboats. The guys are down here now and I'm arranging for it to be retrieved from the water.'

'Oh, shit, not Angelica?'

'I don't know. Get here as soon as you can.'

Carrie was only three miles away. With her heart in her mouth, she floored her car's accelerator.

TWENTY-EIGHT

The crowd that had quickly gathered on the bridge was already four or five people deep. The talk of something in the canal, and the wild assumptions of what it was, were rife. As soon as the police vehicles showed up and the urgency of their actions became apparent, the curious on-lookers had begun to amass in their droves. Those that had ventured nearer to the site where the hub of the commotion was taking place, had been moved back to a more respectable distance from where they continued to stretch their necks for a better view. The news of the initial discovery by an elderly couple that were doing no more than enjoying the exercise as they walked along the towpath, had spread onto social media with exceptional rapidity. This proved, again, to be out of anyone's control and whilst it could sometimes be an adventitious occurrence, it could also be considered to be a hindrance. The movement of traffic on the Limehouse Cut, a tributary of the River Lea, had been stopped at the previous bridge, only 35 metres upstream, and likewise had been blocked in the opposite direction.

Sutton's actions had been swift, and the scene had been secured quickly. Many of the available officers in the immediate area had been mobilised to the scene, including the Forensic Team, the Forensic photographer and the police pathologist. Once Sutton arrived, his suspicions of having another unfortunate murder on his hands were heightened when he saw the roll of white material resting, silently beside the canal boat and moving gently with the moderate flow of the water. It appeared to have snagged against the side of the boat and become entangled in a length of rope as well as several strands of weed of some sort. His mind reverted to the discovery of Haley Breen at the bus depot and his innermost thoughts that Angelica Rowntree was wrapped inside it were immediately disconcerting.

'DS Linton', she said, presenting her warrant card to the police officer that was standing beside the crime scene tape and preventing anyone entering the scene. The words, POLICE DO NOT CROSS, could be clearly seen on the blue and white tape as it wavered in the breeze. Without speaking, the officer reached forward and held the tape up to shoulder height for Carrie to duck under and make her way along the towpath towards a group of officers. She thanked him and tried to decide which route to take in order to avoid the worst of the slippery mud. She wasn't exactly dressed for traipsing along a wet and muddy towpath. It had been her intention to return to Old Clapton Street where she would be able to change into something that resembled her usual workwear. As she carefully picked her way along the path, and concentrated on avoiding treading into anything unpleasant, she had her mind firmly fixed on the hope that this wasn't going to be the discovery of Angelica Rowntree. Obviously, she would rather it wasn't anybody.

Among the group she could see the figure of DI Marc Sutton. He was simultaneously speaking into a police radio and giving out instructions to those around him with exaggerated hand gestures. Carrie could also see 3 police divers in full rig walking along the towpath from the opposite direction. Stepping around the deepest of the puddles, Carrie approached the line of houseboats that had been bobbing about, unattended, at this site for quite some time. Once loved, they were now mostly abandoned. The pots positioned on the rooftops of the old disused properties that once displayed an array of colours were now full of weeds, and the garish paint on many of them was peeling badly. The wooden windowsills showed obvious signs of rot and they had all definitely seen better days.

A white crime scene tent, about three metres square, had been erected at the top of the bank, no more than 20 metres away from the edge of the canal, and a number of officers dressed in white coveralls were standing beside it, looking down towards the water. The single word, POLICE, was clearly printed on the side. Sutton saw Carrie approaching and broke away from the group of officers that surrounded him, handing his police radio to one of them, and taking a few steps towards her. His face was full of concern.

'Glad you're here,' Sutton said, his voice raised slightly to combat the sound of the rushing water that was pouring down from the top side of the weir.

'I didn't hang about,' she explained, 'Any idea yet?'

'Not yet, but we'll know soon enough,' Sutton said as he walked back towards the scene.

Carrie followed enabling her to get a better look at the white object in the water.

'All too familiar,' she said.

'Yeah. So far. We won't know if this is the same MO until we get her out and into the tent. Then it should all become a lot clearer.'

Carrie tuned in to Sutton's referral to the person in the water being female, but then acknowledged that he was probably right in his assumption. The white roll of material taped at one end and the length of the object, pointed to a replica of what they found at the rear of the bus depot 3 years ago. Sutton and Carrie stood looking down at the bleak and cold canal as the police divers talked over their precise plan to retrieve the object. There was no need for instant action as life for anyone inside the object would certainly be unsalvageable.

'Who else is here?' she asked, looking around her and back towards the rubber-neckers at the bridge.

'Just us and the usual turnout. The pathologist and his assistant are setting up inside the tent. Blackery is on his way.'

'Nice,' said Carrie, sarcastically.

'Yeah, well, he won't be here in time to see it lifted out. We'll have that pleasure to ourselves.'

'How come?' Carrie asked.

'He's been in Nottingham since this morning. Expecting him to roll in before we can tidy all this up though. Obviously, he's been informed so I expect he'll come bowling in before long. He left there a couple of hours ago, I think. Maybe longer. Anyway, how did you get on with Robin Greaves?'

'Ah, not great really. He confirmed that he saw a man with her, but even that took some prising from him. He didn't help at all with a description of him though. Said it was too dark.'

'Wasn't, was it?'

'Not in my book, no. I pointed out to him that he managed to see exactly what Angelica was wearing but he still didn't think that he could see well enough to describe the man. Apparently, he had his mother there with him and obviously wasn't keen on me going in, so I spoke to him on the doorstep.'

'Ok, well, we may need to speak to him again, but it doesn't sound as though it'll get us far.'

'No,' said Carrie, wondering whether the search was about to come to an end.

The Police divers were in position, sitting on the edge of the towpath and ready to enter the water. They had their masks on their faces, and were already under air, waiting to get the word that they could begin the retrieval of the white object. The demand valve that led from their facemasks to the air cylinders was in position and their breathing just audible over the background noise from the weir. The black diving suits were baggy with a number of folds and creases. Each had a yellow torch hanging from a waist belt and a gauge that looped around in front of them. A length of yellow line was coiled around the arm of one of the divers and each had a number of carabiners clipped to the waist belt. Both divers wore a large knife that was strapped to one of their legs. Their fins were just about touching the surface of the water as they sat on the side of the towpath. Sutton and Carrie were anxious for them to get in and retrieve the object and yet apprehensive as to what they were about to learn.

'I thought we had this area searched properly,' she said, looking across the canal and back up towards the road, half expecting DCI Blackery to come charging down the path, despite Sutton's confidence in him not turning up just yet.

'We did. The divers went right across the weir from one side to the other and spent a good couple of hours searching underwater. I saw them myself. If anything was evident then, I reckon they would have found it. The Cut has a fairly strong undercurrent so maybe it floated down to this point from another location,' he said.

'Or maybe it was dropped in later, after the search,' offered Carrie.

'That's also possible. Or maybe it was just in a place that they couldn't see. I don't know,' he said.

'Well, they have something now, for sure. We should get dressed if we're going to go into the tent soon,' she said.

'Yeah, let's get up the bank and get suited. We'll still be able to see from there.'

Sutton and Carrie clambered up the bank of sodden turf to the crime scene tent. It wasn't a steep slope, but it was wet. The cursory examination by the forensic pathologists prior to the deceased being moved for autopsy, would give Sutton and Carrie enough information initially so that they could possibly tie this crime to that of Haley Breen. The tent only had a floor covering inside. It was purely a convenient place for the pathologists to inspect the contents of the object before it was removed. When Sutton and Carrie were appropriately suited, they both stood outside the tent and watched as the divers, now in the water, untangled the white object and began to move it in the direction of the towpath. Slowly it got closer. Screens had been placed to either side of the immediate area where the object would be lifted from the water using a simple A frame and initially, placed on the ground before being moved to the tent where Sutton, Carrie and the two pathologists waited. The far side of the Limehouse Cut flowed right up to a factory wall so there were no onlookers from that side. At least that was one problem that took care of itself. Several people had gathered at the point where Sutton and his team had been allowed access to the towpath but once the object had been lifted from the water, it would be out of sight and most likely they would begin to disperse. The scene was as secure as it could be.

As more of the white object became visible, Sutton and Carrie grew more apprehensive as to whether this was going to be the unfortunate discovery of Angelica Rowntree. The natural sequence of events upon her discovery would obviously include telling her parents, and that was not something that any officer relished. Sutton had chosen not to alarm them at this very early stage but to wait until he knew the outcome. He didn't want to put them through hell, only to find out that it had been unnecessary. Had the Detective Chief Inspector been here, he may not have had the luxury of taking that decision.

The divers were now in a position whereby the object, that was looking more and more like a human shape, might be lifted out of the water and lowered onto the towpath at any moment. The line securing it was securely affixed to the A frame via a number of carabiners. Sutton and Carrie tried to look around the bodies that were now getting into their line of sight. Murky canal water began to drain from the shape as it was lifted above the level of the surface and turned in mid-air by one of the divers into a position that those on the towpath could reach. The strands of weed that had wound their way around it, were plucked from it and dropped back into the foul and turbid water. Once the roll of material was out of its watery grave, the degree of discolouration became a little more evident. It had certainly appeared to be white against the black of the canal water but was now, looking a lot greyer and filthier. It was laid on the towpath in a puddle of water that gradually found its way back into the dark and dingy abyss. The divers positioned themselves in order that they could be assisted from the canal and, once again, step onto relatively dry land. The process for transporting the object into the tent was already fully organised. A large black body bag was standing by for it to be placed into. Once zipped securely inside the bag, it would be protected from any further potential damage. It would then be carefully carried up towards the crime scene tent and placed inside. After an inaugural inspection by the pathologists, it would be transported to the laboratory for a thorough autopsy to be carried out at the appropriate time. Sutton and Carrie looked on in anticipation, saying little and yet eager to establish some answers, however grim. After some careful manoeuvring, Sutton and Carrie, along with the two pathologists were joined in the tent by the black body bag. Those that had brought the object gently up to the privacy of the tent left as soon as they had arrived. Their job was done. The front of the tent was zipped shut and in a strange moment there were now five people in the crime scene tent. One of whom may well hold a number of secrets. Whilst they both hoped it wasn't Angelica Rowntree, they fully expected that it was.

The two pathologists introduced themselves as Dr Martin Overton and Dr Rebecca Franklin, insisting that first names were used. Sutton and Carrie returned the niceties. Before the bag was unzipped Rebecca went over some of the preliminaries with regard to what they might find. She acknowledged that Sutton and Carrie had probably seen it all before but as a precaution she needed to explain that the contents of the bag might not exactly be pleasant. Both Sutton and Carrie had witnessed a lot of unpleasantries during their careers but neither had dealt with a body that had been immersed in putrid canal water before, although they had both seen photographs of such things and were fully aware of what being submerged for a length of time can do to the deceased's appearance. Rebecca continued by explaining the stages of putrefaction, the process by which the deceased will decompose following death.

'The extent of damage to the deceased will depend largely upon the length of time that he or she has been exposed to their surroundings, and in turn, what their surroundings were. In this case, water. Canal water, that is obviously filthy, will do a couple of things. There will have been exposure to plenty of bacteria and waterborne critters that may or may not have found their way inside the sheet. Yet on the other hand the lowered temperature of the water will have slowed putrefaction somewhat too. The cold isn't a perfect breeding ground for bacteria. As I mentioned, the length of time the deceased has spent in the water will also make a difference. That is something we will establish once the bag is unzipped, and we see the extent of the damage.'

'Also,' Martin added, 'we may be able to establish whether the deceased drowned or was, perhaps, already dead when they entered the water. Usually, when the deceased has drowned, their lungs fill with water. The air sacs in the lungs act like a sponge. In such an instance, the body is more likely to sink because it becomes heavier. Seeing as this example was found nearer to the surface it may become apparent that they were deceased prior to submersion. The other reason for that, of course, is that gases will escape from the deceased and that may be why they have floated to the surface.'

'So, having said all that, are you ready for us to unzip the bag and see what we find?' Rebecca asked, tentatively.

Sutton and Carrie glanced at each other with some uncertainty but confirmed that they were ready. They had to know.

'Rebecca, would you grab a couple of clips for Marc and Carrie please? And some latex gloves.'

'Of course. Here put these on your noses. You never know. Sometimes it can be quite overwhelming,' she said with a smile.

Sutton and Carrie gratefully donned the nose clips and put on the gloves. They stood watching Martin and Rebecca prepare to go to work. Following the words that Rebecca and Martin had spoken, the atmosphere in the tent had quickly turned from one of anticipation to one of trepidation, at least as far as Sutton and Carrie were concerned.

Martin knelt down beside the bag and took hold of the fastener, drawing it slowly along the zip. Rebecca stood beside Sutton and Carrie and watched. As the zip unfastened, more of the sheet could be seen. Once he had the bag fully unzipped, it was fairly clear for all to see that the figure inside the sheet resembled that of a human form. The sheet clung to the deceased, outlining its shape. Rebecca passed a sharp knife to Martin who checked with Sutton and Carrie that they were ready for him to expose the deceased before cutting the tape away from the head end. With the tape off, the sheet was free to gently pull away from the deceased. Dark hair, long and matted, came into view followed by pale, insipid looking skin. The deceased was lying on its back with one arm mostly underneath. The person's hair was wrapped around the face, eliminating any immediate view of their features. The top half of the body was partly clothed by a t-shirt that appeared to have been ripped or cut open at some point. The lower half wore jeans, but no footwear was present.

'We have a female,' said Martin, 'and at first glance I would say that she hasn't been submerged for very long. Certainly no more than, probably 3 to 4 days, even less but remember, as Rebecca said, the process may have been slowed down by the cold temperature in the water and the diminished exposure to air.'

'Can we see her face?' asked Sutton.

Delicately, he picked up the soaked strands of hair that were lying across her face and lifted them to one side of her head, allowing a proper look at her features for the first time. Sutton and Carrie could tell that she was a similar age to Angelica. Naturally, she was very pale, and her eyes were also closed. The skin had the resemblance of a slightly marbled pattern and discolouration, in accordance with the decomposition process. Sutton and Carrie leaned forward in an unrehearsed synchronised movement and peered at her face. Fortunately, there was no horrific damage to her that may have been caused by her decomposition. Martin looked up from his kneeling position and waited for one of them to comment. Sutton spoke first.

'That's not her,' he said.

'Are you sure,' said Rebecca, 'they don't always look quite the way they used to after being submerged for a while.'

'Oh hell,' said Carrie, 'that's not her.'

'Well, I'm glad it's not her but I'm guessing that probably means that you've got yourself another problem,' said Martin.

The atmosphere in the tent altered as Sutton and Carrie allowed the latest twist in the tale to register. The relief that this was not the body of Angelica Rowntree seemed to be short-lived and unexpectedly stressful in the weirdest of ways.

'We'll take her back with us to the lab and have more information for you soon,' said Rebecca.

'We can establish cause of death and provide some sort of timeline with regard to the actual time of death too,' added Martin.

'Wait,' said Carrie, 'I want to look for something else before you go.'

'Ok, what do you want to see?' said Martin.

'Can you check the side of her neck? Both sides.'

'Sure,' said Martin as he began to carefully draw the abundance of wet hair away from her neck and up around her ears.

'That,' said Sutton, pointing now at her neck.

Martin shone a torch for some extra light as the darkness was just beginning to fall outside. He shone his torch on a distinctive mark on the right side of her neck.

'What is it?' asked Sutton.

Martin stared closely at the dark blemish that Sutton had spotted. Blood had coagulated at the site.

'That,' he said very slowly, 'looks very much like the point of entry of something that could, quite possibly, have killed her before she became submerged.'

'Is that significant,' asked Rebecca.

'Yes, it could be,' said Carrie.

'Well, that could well account for her death, it's quite deep too,' said Martin, inspecting the wound closely, 'We'll be able to inspect both sides of her properly, so I'll have all the details for you when we have completed the full autopsy. We'll get the DNA results that you're going to require if you're going to find out who she is.'

'Anything else for now?' asked Rebecca.

'Yes, there are a couple more things that we really would like to check before you go,' said Sutton.

Martin and Rebecca said that they would help in any way that they could.

'Would it be possible to roll her over slightly so that we can see her upper arm? On her right side, if possible,' he said.

'And can you check whether her hair has been cut at the back?' asked Carrie.

'Sure, but we don't want to move her unnecessarily, you understand,' said Martin.

'We understand but this is really important,' remarked Sutton.

'Please be really careful where you tread,' said Rebecca, handing another torch to Carrie.

Rebecca stepped closer and knelt down beside Martin. Both were now on the same side of the girl, her left. They explained that they would roll her gently towards them in order that Sutton and Carrie could see a clear view of her arm that was mostly hidden from view. Together they reached across the girl to hold her right side. They both used the sheet that she had been wrapped in to move her in order that they didn't inadvertently cause any damage to her.

With both of them in position and Sutton and Carrie standing where they could get a good look, Martin and Rebecca slowly drew the girl up towards them in a controlled manner until she was just far enough over to her left for them to see clearly. They only raised her a few degrees, but it was enough. Sutton and Carrie looked at her arm and saw the mark that they were suspicious of.

'What's that supposed to be?' asked Martin.

'It's supposed to resemble a tattoo, not that it's exactly a professional job,' said Sutton.

'Gross,' said Rebecca.

'Why would anyone do that?' asked Martin.

'We might ask the same question,' said Carrie.

'I'll check her hair for you,' said Rebecca, once they had both gently lowered the girl down again.

Rebecca felt around the back of her neck and held her hair in order to establish whether it was cut in different lengths.

'Yes, it is. It's definitely shorter at the back, just about in the centre, I'd say. Yes, definitely,' she said.

'That fits then,' said Carrie.

Sutton nodded in agreement.

Martin and Rebecca confirmed with Sutton that they could zip the bag and prepare to move her to their van that was parked on a track that ran beside the canal, just 20 metres from the tent. Sutton offered the assistance of the waiting police officers outside the tent and thanked them both for their help. Carrie and Sutton stepped out of the tent and arranged for the officers to assist the pathologists with their next task. The police divers had packed up and gone.

'Well, now what?' said Carrie, as they slowly walked down the slope to the towpath.

'Indeed,' replied Sutton.

Sutton and Carrie wandered down the towpath and back towards their cars, away from the scene. The crowds that had assembled earlier had lost interest long ago and dispersed. The police crime scene tape was still in place as the scene would need to be protected for a while longer yet. The Scene of Crime Officers (S.O.C.O.) and the Forensic Team would still be hard at work. The fact that the girl had probably been put into the water a number of days ago, according to the pathologist's first assumption, combined with the rain that had fallen, made the likelihood of any reliable traces of DNA a little more doubtful. Sutton and Carrie were aware that they had gleaned nothing from the site where Haley Breen was found and didn't hold out a lot of hope this time, but everything would be thoroughly checked. Additionally, they couldn't be certain whether she was placed into the canal at this point or further upstream. The sheet that was wrapped around her would probably offer very little help seeing as it has been underwater.

Sutton and Carrie reached the road just as a recognisable car pulled up on the bridge. DCI Blackery had arrived. Sutton and Carrie waited until he had got out of his car in order to fill him in on details of the discovery so far. Blackery walked towards them, zipping his coat against the chill of the evening.

'Evening Sir,' said Sutton.

'Sir,' said Carrie.

'I assume I've missed all the fun,' he commented.

'Not exactly fun, Sir,' said Sutton.

'No, but you know what I mean. So, what did you find? Is it her?' he said, looking around behind him to check that nobody was close enough to hear.

'No. It's not her,' said Sutton.

'What? Not another one.'

'I'm afraid it does appear that way, Sir. Another young girl. Same MO. We both managed to inspect the deceased at close quarters and the signs are that this is very much a copy of the Haley Breen murder.'

'Are you telling me that she had that ghastly tattoo scratched on her as well?'

'Yes, Sir,' said Sutton, 'same place, upper right arm.'

Blackery reddened slightly and cursed. He leaned against the wall of the bridge and looked down towards the illuminated scene where the tent that the pathologists had used was just being dismantled. The black body bag had been locked securely in the rear of the pathologist's vehicle. The light from the searchlights that sat upon tripods, shimmered and reflected in the canal. Blackery thumped his fist down on the top of the wall. Sutton knew precisely what was coming next.

'We have to find Swann,' he said, through gritted teeth, as Sutton and Carrie exchanged doubtful glances. 'I'm telling you, it's him,' he said as he turned back towards his car.

'We'll get on it, Sir,' replied Sutton.

Blackery made his way back to his car without another word and drove away leaving Sutton and Carrie considering the prospect of finding a dead man.

'Do you think it's him?' asked Carrie.

'I didn't. Now, with the discovery of this girl, I'm beginning to wonder,' said Sutton, turning to face the water and stare across towards the where the police photographer was at work.

'But…' said Carrie.

'Yeah, I know. He's dead.'

'We need to find out who the girl is too. Hopefully, the pathologist will find something in the way of ID,' said Carrie.

'Get somebody to check the CCTV around here for the last week. We'll know once we learn how long she has been in the water if we need to extend it. Also check the ANPR and see whether we can establish the number plates of any vehicles that might have parked on the track alongside the Cut. With any luck she'll show up once her fingerprints and DNA are put into the system, if not, well, we'll cross that bridge when we come to it,' said Sutton.

'Ok. I'll speak to Martin or Rebecca tomorrow morning and see whether they have found any personal effects, jewellery or tattoos. Real ones that is. If nothing useful comes from them then I'll organise a door to door around here and see if anyone knows who she is.'

'Good. As for Swann, I really don't know. That tattoo is too much of a coincidence and I'm beginning to like it less and less,' said Sutton.

'I know it is,' responded Carrie, 'But the blood in his kitchen was definitely his according to the DNA database,' said Carrie.

'Hmm…doesn't mean he's dead though. And if he is responsible for this, then what better cover would you need than being dead?'

Carrie and Sutton began to walk back towards their respective cars, deep in thought, the pictures of the dead girl replaying in their minds. When they reached their vehicles, they turned to look at each other in silence, although their eyes were shouting precisely the same thoughts.

'Doesn't help us with Angelica, does it?' said Sutton.

'I was just thinking the same thing,' responded Carrie.

TWENTY-NINE

Ahuja Industries, East London.
6 Days Ago

Angelica Rowntree lay wrapped up in amongst a pile of fresh-smelling blankets. Three underneath her to protect from all the grit and the cold floor and three on top of her to keep her as warm as possible. She didn't know whether they were new, but she didn't care either. They were clean and that alone, made her feel slightly more human. She had slept better last night than any night since she found herself here. She had gathered up a pile of the grey dust to make a sort of pillow under her head and laid one of the blankets over it. The blankets had been brought to her yesterday evening when she received her customary evening visit from the person in the mask. It was the only welcoming thing about the event, that was otherwise very routine. Once she had heard the gate scrape against the floor as it opened and echoed in the factory, she had sat on her pile of blankets and waited for someone to appear into view, hopefully with her dinner. The footsteps had told her that someone was close. This time, however, the person had a black bin liner with them too. The bag had been placed on the ground and untied. The blankets were pulled out one by one and thrown *at* her rather than *to* her. Three of them. Angelica had thought that she would be expected to throw the existing ones back but hoped that she could keep them too. No indication had been made that she should do that so she sat tight, hoping that she would be warmer tonight.

This afternoon she had been walking as far as her chain would reach and back to where she otherwise sat, slept and ate. *Lived.* She looked at her arms that were showing the dark, tell-tale signs of the bruising that she had got from wrapping her arms around the chain and pulling at it or simply from laying on it in her sleep. It wrapped loosely around her neck too, and she could feel the pain from it pressing against her skin when it became too tight as she moved uncomfortably during the night. Sleep was a luxury that Angelica didn't benefit from as much as she would like. Often, she would wake during the night, each time the reality of where she was would hit her hard. She was tired from asking herself why she was here and wondering whether she would remain so for much longer. *What is this all about?* She had, of course, asked many times but she had never got so much as an answer. Sometimes, not even a look.

Her legs had felt cramped from sitting for long periods and the lower region of her back was becoming painful. She knew that she needed to move or suffer even more if she did not. She was the sort of person that would rather walk than ask for lifts or take the bus unless it was absolutely necessary. Sitting for long periods and having little other choice in the matter, hurt her physically and mentally. As she walked, stopping to stretch her back and legs as much as possible in order to relieve the aching, she came to an abrupt halt when she spotted a fox staring back at her. She had seen them earlier when one of the smaller ones had inquisitively studied her as she sat trying to keep warm. Angelica stooped down slowly to see whether she could entice the fox over to her. Its fur looked so soft even in this murky environment. It had a sheen that she yearned to stroke, although she didn't expect the animal to come close enough. Then another one appeared, noticeably smaller than the first. Then three others had wandered into view, each staring with bright, wide eyes. Angelica smiled at their apparent innocence. She could tell that some of them were not incredibly old. Probably a couple of weeks. *Or months.* Down on one knee, she spoke softly to them as they stood, seemingly, in bewilderment. She guessed that they probably had not expected to encounter a human here. Now she found herself to be the main attraction. The largest of them edged a little closer to her whilst the others held their distance. She quietly, whispered to it and held her hand out. *I'll call you Dad and the other large one will be Mum,* she thought. Realising that she had nothing to offer it, she decided that she would keep a little of her dinner aside from tonight in the hope that they returned to her corner of the factory again. 'I might give all of you names', she said, quietly.

Then something startled her little visitors. All at once they turned to look further down the factory, back towards where the sound of the gate usually came from. Angelica did not expect anyone to be here at this time of the afternoon. It was still a little too early. She stood slowly so as not so frighten them, but they were fully focussed on something else and did not appear to be interested in her anymore. Angelica could not see what they were looking at, but she assumed it was probably another fox. Perhaps a rival had come looking for them. One by one the young cubs began to wander tentatively away, each of the small ones behind the larger foxes. Angelica turned towards her pile of blankets but froze when she heard a sound that reminded her of a pitiful cry. Just like she had heard once before. Or thought she had. This was not the cry of a fox. *The pitch was different*, she thought. She stood still and listened hard. She could just about hear somebody talking as if they were talking under their breath. She could not make any sense of it. Could not pick out a single word. Angelica was frightened and did not know whether she should shout out to try to communicate with this person or not. If it was a person. *Maybe I don't want to know*, she thought. A cluster of thoughts were running through her head. *What if it's someone like me that is trapped here? What if something bad is happening? I don't want to draw attention to myself.*

Angelica wanted to know what was going on, but she was not prepared to make any noise. She walked quietly, to the farthest reaches of her chain, checking her footing as she went so as not to tread on anything that might make a sound. She knew that if anyone came that she could not exactly run away but as a last resort she still had Iron bar that she kept out of sight under her blankets. Then something caught her eye. She had not noticed it before but just in front of her was a piece of broken glass. A triangle of glass that she could see the roof in. *A piece of mirror*, she thought. Angelica slowly bent down to see whether she could reach it. *Maybe I can look in the reflection and see what is going on.*

Another faint cry made her stop. She calculated that if they were busy then they may not be concentrating on what she was doing. The more she heard the noise, albeit very indistinct, the more she thought that it was another girl. A shiver ran through her. *What if I'm next.* Angelica reached as far as she could but the small piece of mirror, was a good eighteen inches too far away. *Iron bar, you are going to come in handy after all,* she thought. Hurriedly, but as quietly as possible, she made her way back to her pile of blankets. The chain dragged and made some noise, but she decided that she didn't care now. After all, they knew she was there, she just didn't want them to see that she was spying or at least trying to. Finally, there was something else to concentrate on rather than just sitting, trying to keep warm, and crapping in a disgusting bucket.

Angelica stopped and listened for a brief moment before she retrieved Iron bar and stepped back to where the piece of mirror lay. It was almost silent but for the sound of someone moving about further down the factory. *How am I going to do this?* She knew that if she was to stand a chance of managing to see what was going on, that she needed to reach the mirror before it was all over. She lay Iron bar flat on the floor and decided to try to sweep it across the floor in the hope that it might move the mirror into a position whereby she could reach it. With an outstretched arm, she began to run Iron bar along the dusty floor. At the end of each individual movement, she stopped moving and fell silent in order to listen in case she could hear footsteps. *Still just the noise of something going on further away.*

Angelica carefully swept the bar along the floor and managed to make the piece of mirrored glass move sideways. *Sweep it in an arc.* The mirror moved steadily across in the dust as Angelica concentrated. It was definitely getting closer to the point where she could pick it up. *Not far. Bit more.* Then, Angelica jumped as a sudden, stomach-churning shrill echoed in the factory. It lasted only a second, and then absolute silence, but it went right through her. She felt herself go rigid and she held her breath so as not to make a sound. Her arm was still in view as she quickly scraped Iron bar along the floor and frantically grabbed at the piece of mirror, placing Iron bar beside her. *If I'm caught now, I'm going to cave their head in,* she thought in panic. Holding her prize, she felt the sweat run on her cheek and saw a droplet drip from her nose onto the dry floor. She was sweating through nervous energy rather than because of the temperature inside the factory. Her hair, now filthy and unpleasantly matted, fell on her face. With a dirty hand she wiped it away. Her heart was racing, and she had tears of fear in her eyes. Angelica looked at the piece of mirror with thoughts of wiping it on her clothes when she noticed the blood. Her hand was cut. Angelica was one of those people that tended to bleed well at the slightest injury, although fortunately she controlled it quickly when she applied direct pressure. *No time for all that now,* she thought. A quick wipe on her jeans and Angelica was trying to find the right angle to see what was going on.

All she could see was more of the factory. Steel railings and the slots and gaps higher up where the sunlight and moonlight seeped through. 'Tilt it down, silly girl', she whispered quietly to herself. The blood from her hand was now on the glass and it was becoming difficult to see. Angelica wiped it quickly against one leg of her jeans and tried again. *It's just a nick, I'll deal with it in a minute.* She had no idea how much time she had for this. The factory had fallen into silence apart from the sound of someone present but still out of sight. Hardly any sound now. Angelica tilted the piece of mirror and caught sight of something other than steelwork, railings and the big funnel-shaped things. Something moved in her mirror. *A person.* This time there was no obvious mask, but it was impossible for Angelica to make out any features. Her arm ached at the awkward angle that she had to hold it and the blood dripped annoyingly from her fingers. She lowered the mirror to check on the cut. It was not deep. It had not even hurt her, and she had no recollection of doing it.

Angelica took the mirror in her hand and raised it slowly and precisely. This time she wanted to get the view that she needed. She knew that she may not have the luxury of lots of time in case the person came her way, and so she tried to get it positioned exactly right. *Steel railings. Lower*, she thought. *Nearly there. Got it.* She held the mirror as still as she could using her other hand to steady it as she leaned against the wall with her hands just in the open. Her arms were exposed, should anyone look this way but there was no other way of doing this. Her cut hand was now beginning to sting, but she drove the pain out of her mind. She could tell that the person was standing with their back to her. Their clothes were dark but then the light was fading in the factory and the vision was only going to get worse. Some kind of hat was being worn. From where she stood and with the reduced view that she had, that was the best that she could glean from whoever it was.

Then they moved, almost out of sight. She could just about tell that they appeared to be bending forward. *What are you doing?* They were only just visible. But they were definitely bending down and fiddling with something. She lowered one hand just for a brief moment, to give it a rest and allow the numbness to reduce in her fingers. Angelica could see that something was happening now. The person was moving about a lot more. They were standing again but she still had no view of the front of them. No look at their face. Something was pulled along the ground into view. *Something white. And long.* Angelica puzzled as to what this was. The object lay on the floor. The person stood and got something out of a pocket. She couldn't see what it was. Her arms were aching again, but she couldn't put them down now or she would never know what was happening. If she missed it after all this, she would be cross with herself. Then a glare flashed in her mirror and startled her. She gasped slightly. She withdrew her arms and rested them by her side, out of sight. *What the hell was that? A photograph?* She remained absolutely still and silent in case her gasp had been heard. Angelica was beginning to tremble a little, partly because she was getting cold as the sun set, but mostly through the adrenaline that was pumping through her arteries and around her body. *No footsteps.*

She raised the piece of mirror to the same position and angle as before. Her muscle memory was now in charge. *Got it. Just about there.* This time it was a whole different ballgame. The white object had been dragged out into the middle of the factory floor. Whoever was doing all this was bending over it and grabbing at it. In her mirror, Angelica saw the person lift one half so that it sat in an L shape on the floor in front of them. Then swiftly, they lifted it onto their shoulder. She could see that the white object was draped over this person. Half in front, half behind. It looked as though the lift had been executed with consummate ease. *Can't be heavy*, she thought. Holding as still as she could and trying her best to ignore the pain in her arms, Angelica stared into the glass.

Something else. Something really easy to spot. Red. Angelica realised that this was probably the first time that she has seen any colour since her own clothes became grey and horrible. Perhaps the foxes with their russet tones were the only other colour she had seen. Even the rats were grey. This place was as bland and uninteresting as anywhere she had ever had the misfortune to frequent. She could not tell what it was, but it stood out even in this gloom. The person began to move with this thing over their shoulder. She noticed that it wasn't exactly a struggle, but she was still feeling puzzled as to precisely what it was.

Until it happened.

A moment frozen into her mind that changed everything. Angelica's eyes widened as she witnessed something that for her was absolutely terrifying. On the far side of the white object something came into view. As much as Angelica didn't want it to be so, her brain wouldn't let her deny what she was certain that she saw. *An arm.*

Angelica dropped the piece of mirror and with one hand tightly covering her mouth, she scurried back to her blankets and collapsed onto them. She pulled them over her and began shaking. *A bloody dead body*, she thought as her eyes filled with tears. She lay down with her head sticking out of the blankets and listened for a long time. It was quiet. She hadn't heard the gate scrape its way across the factory floor but then she was in no condition to detect any normal sounds. Her head was swimming and she felt absolutely sick.

As Angelica waited for her dinner to arrive that evening, she tried to gather herself together. The image of the trailing arm, and the red mark that she now thought must be blood, played on her mind continuously. She had got this far and knew that she could not show that anything was different. She had to compose herself and just behave exactly as she always did. Only this time, she knew that her evening meal was going to be served to her by a murderer.

THIRTY

Minneapolis, Minnesota.
Now

The rain had just started to fall gently onto the roof of the conservatory. Almost secretly, it announced its arrival. It was hardly visible outside. The tip tap on the roof always made it sound as though the rain was falling heavier than it actually was. Even the backdrop of the Yew trees with their dark green leaves did not show that it was actually raining, but Harry Bones could hear it even if he couldn't actually see it. This section of the conservatory, that had always been referred to as *the den*, had been separated from the main area ever since Harry's wife had insisted upon a dividing wall being built. She always felt that it would be nice to have two rooms in the conservatory instead of just one large expanse. Her idea was that the smaller area could be used as a sort of craft room, somewhere where she could paint and spend quiet afternoons. The larger part could be used for sitting in comfort and reading or just staring out into the garden and providing a form of escapism. Eventually, Harry had given in to her demands and began the work. He knew that he could not possibly take on a project such as that these days as much as he would like to think it. Often his mind would write cheques that his body couldn't cash. Harry had enough common sense to know his limits and lived a much more leisurely life nowadays, except of course for his little part time job at the old Nelson residence.

Harry sat at a small table in the den and thought about many things. His late wife's paintings adorned one wall. He always made sure that they were free of dust and often admired her work. He would lose himself in the detail of the paintings which were generally scenes of mountains and rivers. She used to love watercolour and Harry had to admit that she had become quite proficient in what he considered to be a fairly short time. Harry remembered how she used to fuss if he moved anything out of place. Her paints used to sit in a row of colours that were graded from light to dark. Her brushes were always cleaned after use and set out on the table in a line. Every part of her hobby had become regimented over the years. Things were not quite so formal with Harry, although he did spend a fair amount of his free time busying himself with a variety of modest enterprises. The table had a multicoloured plasticised cover on it that allowed him to make as much mess as he wanted and not have to worry about marking the surface underneath. It had become spattered with drips of paint and blobs of glue over the years that all added to the stories that it could tell, if only that were possible. Harry's mind would freely go wandering and he would often end up mulling over a variety of daydreams. Somehow, though, his memories of Penelope Nelson were never far from the forefront of his mind. Harry had got over the feelings of guilt for thinking about Penelope instead of thinking about his dear departed wife. They were different people, and he knew that he had never really let either of them down. At least not in a bad way, although he still thought that he just might have been able to intervene in the episode regarding Penelope and the shed had he been braver and a lot more decisive. That still bothered him, and he was fairly sure that it always would, even though he had finally shared the tale with Officer Bonner. That day, sitting in Gregory Bonner's patrol car, had lifted a huge weight from Harry's mind but unfortunately, he knew that nothing he did would be able to change the past. Wade Nelson, Penelope's husband, had also departed and could not be questioned about the cruelty that burned deep inside Harry. Too late now.

As the rain became more audible, he sat quietly and carved a piece of old log. He would collect pieces of a suitable size and shape as he walked and dry them in his house on top of the boiler. Sometimes he would go out purposely searching for just the right piece and other times he would simply spot a piece and pick it up. He was not always certain of what the outcome of his creation would be, but he didn't always feel that he had to know either. Harry just carved. Therapeutic, he called it. Sometimes the wood would begin to resemble the shape of an animal or another indistinguishable object. Harry just went with the flow. The table would end up covered in strips of wood and shavings, some of which made it to the floor. Harry always kept his knife really sharp and was proud of the tools that he had acquired over the years. Everything in Harry's tool shed had a place and was rarely out of it. Perhaps he wasn't so different from his late wife in that respect. Harry called it being 'old school'.

He put the knife down next to two chisels and an array of rasps of differing sizes that lay on the tablecloth in front of him. He had been cutting away at the piece of log for twenty minutes and had no idea of what he was supposed to be trying to create, other than a mess on the table and around his feet. He had got up from the chair and walked around the house, from the den to the front room window and back again, but the inspiration that he searched for still deserted him. When he reached the window, he looked out onto the street. It was quiet but for a couple of small groups of youths that were trying to grab the lowest of the spindly branches from a sapling. Harry watched as they took turns to jump up but fortunately for the little tree, its delicate young branches were just out of reach. He watched them move on, full of chatter. One of the boys in the group wore a Minnesota Vikings hat, reminding Harry of Betty and her fascination for the team. He smiled slightly at the memory of her obsession over them and her collection of so much memorabilia. She had shown him all her favourite photos of the players and her entanglement of scarves a number of times in the past. He nodded his head to himself and just before turning away from the window and preparing to make his way back to the den, he looked down at the lawn immediately outside the window where Betty's bike had laid on its side on the day when Elisha had turned up unannounced. The conversation was as fresh in his mind as if it had happened yesterday. If the only thing that had bothered him all these years was the part about the shed, it would have been bad enough, but Harry recalled more than just that part. That was just the beginning.

Back in the den, he sat again and looked out into the rear garden and watched a Black-capped Chickadee sitting on the rim of a dish of water that he had placed outside that morning. The bird, a passerine member of the Tit family, cautiously looked around before quickly dipping its head towards the water. Harry remained still and watched the bird, admiring how beautiful it looked to him. They were common in his garden, and he counted himself lucky to get to see a variety of other feathered visitors throughout the year too. The bird rarely stayed for very long and in a trice had flitted away. Harry refocussed on his part-carved piece of log. As he picked up his knife and sat contemplating what to try next, the real reason for his disrupted thoughts were once again, realised in his mind. Opening up to Gregory Bonner felt good but did not free him of all of the worries that had haunted him for a number of years. None of this would have been possible if were not for that day when Elisha turned up on Betty's bicycle and came in to speak to him about her mother. Harry had held onto the secret about what went on at the Nelson property for so long that it was burning away inside him like some caustic poison. Although he had finally spoken, willingly, to Bonner about the truth behind some of the scenes at Elisha's house, he had not told the whole story. There was more that he did not say. Much more.

The episode regarding the shed and how his beloved Penelope had been so cruelly treated was bad enough, but Harry knew that what he had not said was far more damning. It had become a kind of challenge to him, not to think about it. He tried hard to simply get on with life and did his best to forget the whole conversation with Elisha, but it wouldn't go away. Although he could go for weeks and not think about it, somehow it triggered in his mind at the strangest of moments. He could be reading or carving or even walking to the shops and bang! There it was again, like a lance through his body. Harry knew that this issue was not going to leave him alone, as much as he wanted it to. He was reminded too often. Far too often. After speaking to Bonner, Harry had given a lot of thought to whether he should tell him the rest but it felt like a bridge too far for him and so he regularly had to reconsider. He tried to second guess how Bonner would react and sometimes sat for hours during the evening pondering what he would say and how Bonner would reply. He knew that it probably wouldn't pan out the way he had dreamt it might. Harry knew that Bonner would have no option but to act and that frightened him. There was no way that he could be expected to just sit on it as Harry had done. Although he had somehow managed to shrug off the thoughts time after time, he realised that the way he felt was leading him closer and closer to the most awkward of conversations with his friend Gregory Bonner. He would play the scenario out in his mind and invent ways to tell the story differently so as not to make it sound as bad as it was but each time his efforts failed. It was what it was. A mess. It did not feel like Elisha's mess anymore. It felt as though he owned it now. It had passed over from Elisha to Harry on the afternoon that Elisha rang the doorbell and Harry was starting to lose the fight for keeping it all quiet. That afternoon was just the beginning.

THIRTY-ONE

Old Clapton Street Police Station.

The station was buzzing with talk about the girl that had been discovered not far from the weir. S.O.C.O. (scene of crimes officers) had been amassing as much information as they could muster at the scene and the Forensic Photographer had taken photos of the area in great detail including any tyre tread markings on the track that ran beside the waterway. These were added to the photographs of the girl that were taken immediately after Sutton and Carrie left the crime scene tent, and before Martin and Rebecca had transported her away from the scene. The locals had already spread the news via social media. When Sutton had returned from the Limehouse Cut to the station, he had immediately telephoned the Rowntree's to confirm with them that the girl did not identify as Angelica. He found that the 'jungle drums' had beaten him to it by at least 30 minutes but at least he had the task of being the bringer of good news as far as they were concerned. It was a form of good news, anyway. Angelica was of course, still missing.

Marc Sutton was at his desk when his mobile phone rang. It was Carrie.

'Hi,' he said.

'Hi, Marc. I'm just about to leave the Pathology Unit.'

'Ok, did you find out anything interesting?' he asked.

'Yeah, a number of things but I'll fill you in on everything properly when I get back. But for now, it seems that our girl may have been weighed down in the water. Rebecca showed me where there were signs that her skin had been rubbed around both of her ankles, as if they had been tightly tied together. When they removed the sheet, they found a piece of string that they think had come off her feet. Maybe the string had broken, and the weight had come off at some point. If so, whoever did it hadn't made a very good job of it.'

'Right. I assume that considering that wound on her neck that she was already dead when she went into the water? This hadn't come off because she struggled, had it?' asked Sutton.

'No, they don't believe so. If they are right, then it looks as though she wasn't supposed to be found floating around in plain sight. At least not as soon as she was. There was also a wound on the back of her head which may have been received when she was first abducted.'

'Like Haley Breen,' said Sutton.

'Seems so. Also, her jeans. One of the labels wasn't in English.'

'You mean not bought in this country?'

'That's what I'm thinking but we can work on that. Listen, I'm on my way. I'll talk to you soon,' said Carrie.

'Ok. See you soon.'

Sutton replaced his phone in his pocket and walked across the corridor and into DCI Blackery's office. He explained the initial findings that Carrie had just reported to him and said he would update him as soon as he had heard more from Carrie. Blackery was in an uncharacteristically good mood, or so it appeared to Sutton. He said that he was looking forward to reading DS Linton's full report on her morning with the pathologists. He then explained that he would be out of the office for the rest of the day. Something about a meeting with the Chair of the City Council but by now Sutton had pretty much switched off. Blackery's meeting wasn't anywhere near the top of his priority list. He knew the news that Blackery wouldn't be around to aggravate Carrie was going to be well received by her on her return. He also knew that she wouldn't be more than another twenty minutes and decided to get himself a coffee in the meantime. As he wandered out of his office and towards the coffee machine, he began to run the next process in the identification of the unknown girl through his mind. Sutton was hoping that there would be a record on the database of her DNA or perhaps fingerprints but knew that if she was a new arrival to the country that this might not be available. Dental records may also be scarce although at least the visual identification possibilities had not been removed due to decomposition. She might even show up on the missing persons database, but this would all be established in time.

After a quick refreshing coffee, Sutton returned to his office, closed the door, and waited for Carrie to get back. He stood beside the whiteboard and moved the photograph of Angelica Rowntree to one side of the board with the idea of making space for the unknown girl and began to make notes on the board in reference to her discovery. He drew a line from the short list of similarities regarding the discovery of Haley Breen and stopped short of the space where the unknown girl's picture would go. Filled with uncertainty, Sutton was becoming more and more eager to speak with Carrie.

Stepping back to his desk, he sat and decided to text Grace.

Hey, how are you doing? Any news from this morning? xx

Sutton didn't often text Grace during the day, didn't usually find a spare minute, but he knew that she had had a meeting arranged with the Headmistress for as soon as she got into school and was keen to find out what it was all about. Grace had just been told as she left school the previous afternoon to go to see her first thing but didn't know why. It wasn't exactly unusual as there could have been any number of reasons, so Grace didn't worry about it, unnecessarily. He sat looking at his phone and the message that he had just sent, waiting for a response. *Maybe she was too busy.* Sutton knew that she would reply when she could and returned his screen to the homepage. He cleared his desk of some of the paperwork that had built up from yesterday and waited for Carrie. He didn't have to wait for long.

'Hi,' she said as she came bounding into his office without knocking.

'Do come in,' said Sutton, condescendingly.

'Oh yeah,' she said, 'Sorry.'

'Doesn't matter. What have you got to tell me?'

Carrie noticed the adjustments that Sutton had made to the whiteboard, as she dropped her coat down onto the floor beside his desk and put her bag down onto a chair. She opened it up, retrieving a notepad, and placed it on the desk in front of her.

'Ok, so,' she said, 'It was interesting.'

'How lovely for you. Anything you'd like to share?' he said, jokingly.

Carrie sat opposite and squinted her eyes at him as if to say *you're not funny.*

'So far, we don't have a positive ID, but her fingerprints and DNA have gone into the system, and we'll get the DNA results in about a week. There was nothing on her person in the way of jewellery or personal effects but when they checked her jeans back pocket, they found a receipt. It wasn't in what you might call good condition considering where she was found but it was just about readable. It looked like it was for a purchase of a mobile phone although there was no actual phone to be found. It was really hard to see the name of the shop but there was a date on it. It was only two weeks ago, so it's something that we can look into.'

Sutton continued to nod and make notes as Carrie spoke.

'She had a scar on her left knee that may have come from an accident of some sort, but according to Martin, it was a few years old. They found a tattoo of a fish, like one of those Japanese koi, on the small of her back and this was also an old one. They said her blood group was O positive so nothing out of the ordinary. But it was the label on her jeans that was unusual. It was in another language which I'm pretty sure was Italian.'

'So, couldn't they have been bought here? Don't we have Italian brands?' said Sutton.

'We do, but it wasn't the brand label that drew our attention, it was the washing instructions. They were all in Italian. At least I'm thinking that it was Italian. They were of good quality, and I reckon they'd have cost over £100, maybe 200,' explained Carrie.

'Hmm…Well, that might prove to be significant then,' said Sutton, still writing.

'They reckon that she was about twenty years old. They had already taken all the photos that they wanted by the time I arrived. And the dental photos. Also, there was no evidence of any sexual interference either and, as I said, there was the bump on the back of her head and of course there was the stab wound to her neck as well as the so-called tattoo. Martin said that the bump on her head could have occurred at any point after she was taken but seeing as Haley Breen had corresponding wounds, I think that we should consider that the similarity might just be too coincidental, plus there's the sheet and the tape.'

'Sounds just like an exact repeat of Haley Breen,' said Sutton.

'Yep, increasingly so.'

'Except Haley Breen was in full view and this girl was destined to stay undetected. Or so it seems,' he said, 'I wonder where her footwear went to?'

'No idea. Also, she didn't have anything like contact lenses, but these could have been lost given the circumstances. No rings either, unless they were removed, of course, although her fingers weren't indented. And Rebecca said that there was evidence to say that she wore a watch, but it wasn't there.'

'Ok. For now, we can work on this receipt. We may not know the shop she used but we can start local and spread from there. Hopefully she shopped around which would give us more of a chance of at least one of the shop assistants remembering her,' he said.

'Is Blackery still harping on about tracking down Swann?' asked Carrie.

'He's preoccupied at the moment but I'm sure that he'll get back to it. Personally, I think we need to concentrate on getting some of our guys out to the mobile phone shops. Without a name, we can only use a description of her for now. Maybe she had an Italian accent, that could trigger a memory,' said Sutton.

'True. I'll check the missing persons again and take a punt at the nearest universities and colleges in case they have a student that has mysteriously disappeared. Then I'll get out to the shops.'

'Fine. You get onto that, and I'll get the team together for a briefing. See if we can make some headway. Oh, and Blackery wants to read a report of your morning with the Pathologists, sorry.'

'Yeah, well, ok. I'll knock something together later,' she said.

As Carrie left Sutton's office, he felt his mobile buzz in his pocket. He drew it out to read the message. It was from Grace.

Hey, I'm ok. My meeting was good xxx

Glad to hear it. What was it about? xx

Let's just say that I've got some news for you when you get home xxx

Sounds intriguing! Why don't you give me a clue? xx

That would spoil the surprise! You'll have to wait until later xxx

Now you're teasing! xx

Nah, you'll know if I'm teasing xxx

Oooh! That sounds even better xx

Stop it! Behave yourself, you've got work to do. I'll see you later. Love you, Detective xxx

Love you too, Miss xx

THIRTY-TWO

Tilbury, East London.

Karter Swann stood rigidly at the top of the stairs and gazed down at the front door where two plain envelopes were visibly poking through the letterbox like evil intruders attempting to sneak in unnoticed. *Not again,* he thought. His shock at receiving the weird photograph of the mysterious white object was still buzzing around his system. The thought that someone had found out where he was living was bad enough but now, for the first time since he returned from Crete as Kevin Marshall, he felt truly exposed and vulnerable. *Who knows where I live?* The puzzle didn't get any easier to solve, and the more he thought about it, the more panic-stricken he became. He considered that it was Elisha that had tracked him down after spying on him at the Superstore but didn't want to accept it. *Was she really responsible for the photographs that turned up at the pub too?* Since the photo of the white object had arrived, he had been trying to fathom out when he might have let his guard down. He was sure that he had been careful, extra careful, but obviously, at some point he had slipped up. He had put the latest photograph back in its envelope and placed it in a locked drawer with the others that he had managed to intercept at the Cactus and Coyote before anyone had seen the contents. He had thought about destroying them way before he turned his life upside down by making the secretive arrangements with Odhran O'Connell but for some reason, had held onto them. There was just something about them, apart from the gruesome images, that made him keep them. He conceded that they had become a sort of bizarre fascination. If he ever found out precisely who had sent them, then maybe they would be useful at some point as evidence in some way, should he need it. Sometimes, he didn't know whether they might clear his name or serve to convict him of some heinous act. Either way he had kept them, and now he hoped that he was not staring at two more. Clearly, there was only going to be one way of establishing what the contents of these two envelopes were.

Swann slowly walked down the stairs; his focus did not stray from the two envelopes that were three quarters of the way through the letterbox. He was already hoping that they would be displaying the names and address of the Turners. If so, he could simply leave them on the hall table and forget about them. As he got a little closer, he could see that they were different sizes. One appeared to be a little squarer than the other. Both were white. It was at times like this that he wished he could still feel the warmth of the Cretan sun on his skin and be lost in the escapism of the relative isolation of the Mediterranean isle, whilst acting out the pretence of being Kevin Marshall, beach bum and waiter.

Swann plucked them both from the letterbox in one hand allowing the flap to slap shut and instinctively flipped them over to show two blank envelopes. No address. No names. Just two curious communications, their concealed secrets as yet unrevealed. He felt there was no value in opening the front door. Whoever had been responsible for the delivery was hardly likely to be standing on the doorstep for him to identify and if the arrival of the other envelope was anything to go by the mysterious postman or woman was not going to be standing outside with a warm smile. He turned back towards the stairs and studied the envelopes as he walked. The longer thinner one felt like it could contain a letter of some sort. The other, slightly squarer, had something rectangular inside. *Like a photograph*, he thought. He also realised that he had no idea how long they had been there. *Were they even posted by the same person?* That thought sent a shiver down his spine. *More than one person knows where I live!*

Swann sighed and made his way back to his upstairs retreat. He shut the door and dropped down onto the bed, envelopes in hand. He decided to open the smaller one first. Dreading what it might contain, Swann slowly teased the envelope open and clamped the contents between a thumb and forefinger. As the item became exposed to the outside world, he could see that this was indeed another photograph. Swann's heart sunk as he prepared himself for whatever gory sight was about to intrude into his mind. He checked the back for any words but there was nothing. Tentatively, and with a degree of trepidation, he turned the photograph over to reveal the captured image. This time it was relatively easy to understand what he was looking at. No strange white object, and on closer inspection, no red mark. But this was no less of an ordeal. Swann could feel the blood draining out of his face as the image conjured questions in his head. None of which, he had any answers for. There was no appreciation of looking at a possible dead body as before with the photograph he saw at the Police Station or of those sent to the Cactus and Coyote. No gauged tattoo. This time he was looking at what appeared to be a youngish female. Her long hair hung across her face and completely obscured a good view of her features. He studied her and thought, without much certainty, that she could be familiar, but he immediately dismissed it. He could tell that her clothes were dirty, and she looked bedraggled, but she looked as though she was alive. At least she was alive in this image. As he studied the image further, he picked out that she was wearing jeans and a dark sweatshirt, possibly red in colour, and it looked like she had trainers on. She resembled a tramp, or even somebody that had been living rough. *Maybe she had*, he thought. But he knew it wasn't as simple as that. The sight of this latest torment brought back the images of the girl that was discovered at the bus depot. He couldn't remember her name, but he certainly remembered setting eyes on the photos, both at the Cactus and Coyote and at Old Clapton Street Police Station. *Why me?* Unsurprisingly, this wasn't the first time that Swann had asked himself this. Each time he pondered the question, he wondered whether this was all Elisha. As crazy as it seemed, he never came to any other conclusion. *Who else? Why?* There had been so many occasions when he had thought about going to the police and trying to explain that these photographs were being sent to him but each time, he relived the interview with the big man who had the accent and decided that it just might be more trouble than it was worth. He had made it quite clear that he intended to pin the girl's murder onto him, and Swann didn't fancy putting himself in the firing line again. *A witness saw him running from the bus depot.* Swann knew that this was impossible and after all, how could he even begin to explain his faked death at the hands of the menacing Odhran O'Connell, not that he could afford to mention *his* name. That really wouldn't end well. A false passport and a new identity would be too much to explain. *A guilty man on the run?* He knew that they were never going to let that go. It was also his thought that his innocent story about being the recipient of these photographs would be twisted into something far worse. *I would probably end up on a murder charge. Or even three. Maybe that was the idea. But who was doing this? And who on earth was this girl?*

Swann dropped the photograph onto the bed and lay his head onto the pillow. His mind had become clouded with more confusion than normal, and he knew that he was only halfway through opening his unwanted mail. Swann tapped his fingers on his chest and tried his best to think hard about a believable conclusion to this bewildering episode in his warped life but however hard he tried to make some sense of it all, he always ended up at a dead end. He had questioned himself a number of times as to whether the whole Odhran O'Connell chapter had been the right move, although it had definitely felt like it at the time. He had reflected on the depth of his dilemma and often wondered whether he should have brazened it out rather than look for an escape route, one that was to take him out of the country and into a completely new persona. Not that he had been entirely in control of his destiny. He knew that he had landed himself on the wrong side of debt as far as O'Connell was concerned. Returning to the UK may also have been a decision that he had taken too soon. Whatever the reasons for his return, Swann knew that as a dead man, he would have to live with the consequences. *Maybe I should move on again.* If he wasn't careful, he could find himself running into an even darker and more sinister alleyway than he already trod. *Why didn't I just stay in Crete?*

THIRTY-THREE

Three weeks ago.

Betty Nelson rubbed her eyes and poured another glass of white wine, holding it, almost protectively, in both hands. She sat in silence not really thinking about anything in particular, apart from getting drunk. The room to the rear of her house was illuminated by a single reading lamp of low wattage, that sat in one corner, offering just enough light. A Helen Reddy cd had just finished playing although Betty hadn't really noticed that the silence had taken over. She tilted her head back and looked up at the drab ceiling, which looked more like an overcast sky, and pictured the 'stars', as they were known, that lit her beautiful bedroom ceiling back in the family house in Minneapolis. She could almost see the deep blue sky that was punctuated by the tiny spotlights. It all seemed a world away now. Her eyes were heavy, and her head was becoming more and more woozy, but she had no intention of stopping tonight. The bottle of Chardonnay; purchased from her local off license, was more of a comfort blanket than a treat and had more recently become a habitual custom. The first bottle lay empty on its side beside the coffee table and would soon have a companion. Betty's eyes blinked a slow and lengthy flicker. Her head dropped forward and immediately righted itself when she was disturbed by the acute, piercing sound of a knife landing uncontrollably on a dinner plate. Elisha was in the kitchen preparing some cheese and crackers. She knew it was probably the only thing her sister would agree to eat at this late hour, and she knew that she had not eaten very much today.

'Do you want any help?' asked Betty, more out of politeness than sincerity.

'No, I'm fine.' *As if you could*, thought Elisha.

'You sure? You only have to ask, you know. Anyway, you don't have to bother for me.'

I think I do, thought Elisha in silence.

Elisha didn't bother with a response; besides she was about to take the snack into the living room and begin the task of persuading her sister that she was hungry. She wandered in and noticed Betty's head beginning to nod again. Elisha purposely allowed the plate to land a little heavier than usual in order to startle her sister back to full consciousness.

'Here. You're going to help me demolish this lot,' she said.

'I don't...' began Betty.

'And don't think for one minute that you have an option because you don't, apart from being force-fed that is.'

Betty saw the determination in her sister's expression and gave a grumble. Reluctantly she reached out for a cracker. Elisha met her eyes with a purposeful glare and Betty knew that she would have to take some cheese with it. Elisha had buttered eight crackers and had put a selection of cheeses on the plate, including Boursin, Stilton and Wensleydale. She knew Betty liked all of these so there would be no excuse and both girls knew that however much Betty complained, there was only going to be one winner. The ephemeral resistance was over quickly. Elisha picked up the bottle of Chardonnay and drained the last of the wine, looking squarely at Betty as she did so, as if to say *really?* Betty gave a slight, uncaring shrug. What Betty didn't know is that whilst preparing them both a late-night snack, Elisha had removed the remaining two bottles from the fridge and placed them into a carrier bag, ready to take them home with her when she left, and out of Betty's reach. This certainly wasn't the first time that Elisha has resorted to such measures, and she knew that it probably wouldn't be the last. There had been times when Elisha realised that if anybody looked in her fridge at home, they might easily draw the conclusion that it was her that had the drink problem. Of course, Betty's fridge would be restocked the next time that she visited but there was only so much that she could do.

'Do you still think about him, Elisha?'

'Who?' said Elisha, knowing perfectly well who her sister was referring to.

Betty and Elisha did not mention Karter Swann very often but if his name did pop up, it was usually Betty that mentioned it. Whether it was fired by desire or distain, the corrosive potion had not completely drained from her system. Despite Elisha's act of being the innocent victim, it was Betty that had been hurt the most. She was very aware that Elisha had 'suffered' at the hands of the person she referred to as 'that monster' and only introduced his name into conversation when she felt that Elisha would cope with it or in this instance because she was well on the way to being drunk. Betty had stood by her sister through all the dark days that had followed the attack that she had endured when Swann had tried to take advantage of her, leaving her bruised and shaken. Betty admired just how brave

Elisha had been and how she had made such a concerted effort to overcome the mental trauma that had followed her terrifying assault. *Or so it seemed.* There had been several occasions that Betty had stayed at Elisha's house and comforted her during the times when she felt vulnerable and alone. Naturally enough, Elisha had played it very well.

It had been Elisha's intention from the start that Swann would be hers, but things had not quite gone to plan. To Elisha's mind the steamy episode at the Travelodge had been perfect. Taking her sister's mobile and using it to lure him into her sordid web worked beautifully, along with the pretence with regard to her stricken car that had provided her with Betty's. It was the ideal cover to convince Swann that Betty was waiting for him. Naked in the shower. Desperate for him. The passionate encounter had made Elisha feel that she had finally got her man. The next morning, when Swann arrived at Elisha's to 'fix her car', was supposed to be the icing on the cake. But when he shunned her advances, Elisha turned from the amorous lover into a rejected and scornful woman, incensed with fury. As far as she was concerned, he was hers, and above all, she needed to ensure he wasn't Betty's anymore. Not everything could be Betty's. The disturbing memories of childhood at the hands of her vindictive father were perpetually rumbling just beneath the surface. Almost uncontrollably.

As small children, the girls had always managed to stay close but when their mother died it all changed. At least it did in Elisha's mind. She knew that it was Betty that got her father's approval for everything, no matter what. Whether it be college grades or shooting the bow, it had all become about how successful Betty was and never about her. She found it hard to resist the feelings of jealousy and betrayal even though she knew deep down that she loved Betty, and that the problems were not being directly engineered by her, there was still an underlying resentment festering away that misguided her to an irrational hatred of her sibling. Parental favouritism is a toxic source of sibling rivalry, and even in adulthood, is often found to re-emerge when least expected. Elisha had suffered in silence for years and yet inside she was constantly competing for attention. It was always Betty's bedroom, even though they both slept there. And although Betty had welcomed her sister into her room and had no issue with Elisha using it as her own, in her father's eyes it was Betty's, and she was just there. *The other one.* They were Betty's things that adorned the room, not hers. Betty's bike was better, her hair was more beautiful, her clothes were of a better quality and

Elisha was the one that was given all the difficult and unpleasant tasks; like digging that hole for Hastings on the evening before he was so callously shot by their father with his beloved bow. But for all the reasoning and effort that Elisha put into trying to understand why she was the one that could never gain the love of her father, she only came to one conclusion. She was worthless. She didn't want to have to compete with her sister, but she was backed into a corner, desperately trying to define who she was as an individual. Whenever she felt as though she was making headway, her father would demoralise her confidence by showing her up in front of people; neighbours, other family members, whoever happened to be around at the time.

'You know; that monster.'

'He's gone, Betty. You need to drop it,' answered Elisha, taking a sip of wine.

'Why, because he wants you more than he wants me?'

Wants? Elisha was slightly taken aback at this unexpected conversation. She looked at Betty and shook her head, disapprovingly. *Drunk again.* Betty slumped back in her chair and sighed; her eyes, reddening by the second, still fixed on Elisha's.

'Maybe I should make some coffee,' said Elisha, quietly.

She stood and turned towards the kitchen but stopped when Betty spoke again.

'And what about that girl in the bus depot? Marcie said he was taken in for questioning.'

'So? That was years ago.' said Elisha.

'So, he must have had something to do with it or what was he doing there? She said he was seen running away from the depot, or that's what she was told.'

'As far as I know, he wasn't charged with anything. Anyhow, Marcie has a big mouth. How would she know?'

'I bet he did it,' said Betty, with a scowling expression.

'Betty, for crying out loud. If he had done it, they wouldn't have let him go, would they? Anyway, he's dead and gone.'

'Hmm, is he?'

'What's that supposed to mean?' asked Elisha, becoming less patient, 'We both went to his funeral, didn't we? I suppose you've forgotten that?'

Betty leaned forward and sneered as she inspected the, now empty, bottle of Chardonnay, dropping it on the floor with a thump, beside the other one.

'Get another one out of the fridge when you make the coffee, and I'll tell you something else too,' she said, 'and it wasn't a funeral, it was a memorial service. There was no body, remember? He was still missing.'

Elisha sat back down and studied her sister, saddened by what she was becoming. She considered that it may well be all her fault. Probably was. She was the one that ruined her relationship with Karter by trying to take him for herself. She knew he wouldn't say anything about what went on at the Travelodge either, anyhow, she would say that it was all part of the game; pretending Elisha was Betty. All his idea. All part of his kinky game. She had only gone along with it because she wanted to try to talk him out of it, but he forced her into the shower and stripped her. She was frozen with fear. Terrified of what he might do if she didn't comply. The Travelodge, Elisha's car the next morning, the sexual attack that Elisha had tried to stop. But she was sure that it would never come to that. She was confident that she held all the cards. She could make Betty believe it.

'You are kidding me, aren't you? You heard about the state of his place when he went missing. Didn't sound like he'd just gone out for a walk, did it? He must've been in with the wrong sort. Maybe he owed them money, I don't know. Either way, he's dead. And if he isn't, where would he have been all this time?' said Elisha.

'I don't know where he was, but I know where he is now,' said Betty, her eyes were glazed by the wine, but her face was ice cold and stern. She stared straight ahead, mesmerised.

Elisha was now paying full attention to her sister. Her mind began to whirr. Immediately, she was thinking that if this was true, she could have another real chance at capturing her man. Betty's man. It had always meant more to her that he was Betty's. A prize possession that she could claim for herself.

'What?'

'You heard me.'

'How?'

'I saw him, at least I thought I did, so I had a better look. It was him, alright. He'd dyed his hair, but it was him. He didn't see me. I followed him in the car and saw him go into a house down by Tilbury Docks. Same height, same stature. It was him.'

Elisha sat with eyes wide open. She was trying to process all the possibilities at once. She wanted to believe it but wasn't really sure whether Betty had dreamt the whole thing up. *Could it really be true that he was still around after all this time?*

'Why didn't you say something? Why wouldn't you tell me?' asked Elisha.

'I thought about it, but I didn't want you to worry that he was still here. I didn't want you to think that he might try to hurt you again. Sorry, but I thought it was the last thing that you would want to hear after…before.'

'He doesn't scare me anymore. Anyway, if he did try anything I'd go straight to the police. I'm sure they would be interested to talk to him about his little disappearing act.'

'I thought about that too, but I decided not to. Dead or not, he's dead to me. Besides, now I know where he is, should I ever need to,' said Betty.

'Need to what? You going to share it? Surely, it's better that we both know, isn't it?' said Elisha, still contemplating what to do next.

'Maybe,' said Betty, giving Elisha a look that made her think that she shouldn't sound too eager.

'Look, I'm only saying because it feels like it makes sense that we both know. I don't want to get the shock of my life one day. At least I'll know so I can steer clear of that area,' said Elisha, who was already thinking that she was saying it all wrong. *Still too keen to know.*

'You fetch me another bottle and I might tell you.'

Bingo. Elisha thought just for a moment and decided that it was a fair trade. One more bottle and she would know where to find Karter Swann. *Yeah, that's a good deal.* Besides, she knew that Betty wouldn't drink much of it. She had already had enough for one night. Elisha stepped out of the room and went to make herself a coffee and fetch her bargaining tool. *Perfect. Now don't screw it up.* As Elisha waited for the kettle to boil, she hoped that Betty wouldn't have succumbed to the alcohol in her system before she could get the answer she wanted.

THIRTY-FOUR

Elisha sipped her coffee and tried not to smile. She had the address and was already plotting what to do next. As intrigued as she was about the whole discovery, she decided to drop the subject. After all, she didn't want Betty to become curious as to the level of her interest in Karter Swann. Betty always bought Columbian blends of coffee and Elisha loved them. She often wondered why she didn't buy them herself, but she never seemed to remember to add them to her shopping list. Betty unscrewed the top of the third bottle of Chardonnay and filled her glass. Elisha's glass had already been washed up and was outside on the kitchen drainer. The room was quiet with the latest Karter Swann revelation hanging, mysteriously in the air. Elisha nibbled a cracker and took a couple of pieces of cheese. All of a sudden, she had an appetite, and it wasn't only for food.

'And here's another thing, just to make your night. Do you remember my friend, Caterina?'

Christ what now? 'Well, yes, of course, but why do you ask?'

'They never found her, did they?'

'No.'

'Would you like to know something?' asked Betty.

'What?'

'Well, I've never mentioned it before, sort of forgot really, but before we left for England I bumped into Gregory Bonner. You remember him? The Patrol Officer.'

'Yes, he was at college with us, so?'

'He told me that on the day Caterina went missing the police came to our house, although we didn't realise it, obviously searching for her and asking questions like they would do, and father said that she hadn't been here and that we were both out. But we weren't both out, were we?'

'I can't remember,' said Elisha and began to walk out of the room to go to the bathroom, happy that there was nothing that Betty could possibly say that would top her having Karter Swann's address etched deep in her mind.

'Hold on, you must remember. We were upstairs in the bedroom nearly all day. You came upstairs all filthy with mud and blood and dog hair all over you and I helped you get cleaned up. And you had that wretched tail in your hand, holding it like it was a prize for a good deed or something. Another of father's sick jokes, I assume.'

'Yeah, ok, so what?' said Elisha, dismissively.

'So, we weren't both out.'

'Well, it hardly matters now does it?'

'But why did he say that we were both out, when we were both upstairs?' asked Betty.

'Maybe he was protecting us from all the questioning, I don't know.'

'But we still had to answer questions later, although now we had to lie,' said Betty.

'Look, I don't know why he decided to say that we were out, but he did, so leave it, ok?'

Elisha only got as far as the doorway out of the living room before Betty continued.

'She was coming to see me because I was so upset about Hastings. Father knew she was coming because I remember saying so, but he told the police that she hadn't.'

'Look, I know it wasn't' nice but something happened that we don't know anything about. She went missing. I'm sorry. I liked her too.'

'But she sent me a message,' said Betty.

'What? What message?' said Elisha with an alarm in her voice.

'When she got there. Before she reached the house, she sent me a message just to say that she was here. I've never told anyone. Nobody. Not father or the police or anyone, even you. When he said that we were out I just clammed up. I deleted the message but surely, he must have seen her. She was almost on the front lawn by then. You must have seen her...'

'Nobody saw her, Betty. She didn't show up. I don't know what happened, but she vanished. The police searched everywhere and found nothing. They didn't find her or her phone or anything. Look, I'm sorry, and I know that she was your best friend, but it happened. You have to leave it. I'll make some more coffee and eat another one of those while I do.'

As Elisha walked out to the kitchen, she tried to absorb what Betty had just said. She knew that the text message placed Caterina at their house or very nearby. She knew her father had lied to everyone. She also knew that only her and Harry Bones held the answer to the puzzle and that it needed to stay that way.

THIRTY-FIVE

Now

DS Carrie Linton negotiated her way through the busy revolving doors that swished as she pushed against them and made her way into the newly refurbished shopping precinct on Camber Gate. Three storeys of shop units branched out from a central point and above it all were another four levels used for parking. The noise of raucous shoppers filled the air, resonating from every hard surface that surrounded her. As she walked through the entrance, she looked up at the roof of the atrium that pointed skywards like a cathedral spire; every pane of glass capturing the brightness of the morning sunshine. As if any further illumination was needed, bright lighting shone from every shop in the unimaginatively named Market Centre. It was Carrie's first time in here and although it had been open for at least a couple of months, she had never bothered to make the effort to traipse around it. After her shifts at Old Clapton Street the last thing she had on her mind was trudging around the shops and engaging in combat with hundreds of people. She always favoured the local shops in the High Street where there was less glass, fewer of the ice-rink-like shiny floors and less pretence. The service always felt more personal, more genuine. At first glance she could appreciate why such a fuss had been made about it in the local media, but it still wasn't her cup of tea, and she knew that Grace wasn't all that keen either. Carrie would have preferred it if the money had been spent on upgrading the shops in the High Street, but she also conceded that that would not have attracted many new money-laden customers and somewhere like this would make a bomb at Christmas.

Carrie had studied the plans that showed exactly where the shopping units were situated and having researched where to find the mobile phone shops, wasn't particularly interested in investigating any other type of retail establishment today. In the absence of a photograph of the girl found in the canal, other than those taken by Martin and Rebecca at the Pathology Unit, none of which were suitable for display to the public, she would have to do with a general description of the unknown girl and a tenuous enquiry as to whether she might have had an Italian accent. Carrie knew the girl's height and eye colour as well as what her hair colour was but didn't have much else to work with currently. She was aware that her information was rather insubstantial, but it was all that she had.

Checking the faces of people as she went, Carrie was on the lookout for a colleague that would be joining her. When DC Steve Kingham wandered into view at the far end of the concourse Carrie decided to meet him halfway along where there was more space and somewhere to sit. She began to stroll towards him. Kingham was 6 foot 5 with shock-white hair, worn with a short flat top and bristled at the sides. Pretty much unmissable. He had been in the job for 18 years and was popular with most people, even with Carrie, who was choosy to say the least. Kingham saw himself as a bit of a modern-day George Peppard from the old TV series, The A-Team. Carrie saw him as a likeable dickhead and she knew that she could have him flat on his back in a heartbeat, regardless of how big he was. She could take him or leave him, but she still liked him more than not. His work was good and that would do for Carrie. She got to the seating area ahead of him and grabbed a table on the perimeter of the circle where he would be able to see her as he approached. A number of popular eateries encircled the rest area that was at least three quarters full of people with shopping bags and push chairs. None of the mobile phone shops were in view at this point but Carrie had them mapped in her mind. The background hum generated by constant chatter competed admirably with the sound of ABBA emanating from huge speakers high on the walls of the domed circular chamber. Carrie gazed up and noticed the impressive expanse of steel walkways crisscrossing above her that guided people from one side of the Centre to the other. *Ok, it's smart,* she conceded, as she watched Kingham until he caught her gaze and nodded his acknowledgement. She looked around at the occupants of the tables that were nearby and wondered how many of the younger people might know the identity of the unknown girl but for now her hopes rested with the mobile phone receipt that was found by Martin and Rebecca, and the possibility of some details about her being stored online.

'Morning,' said Kingham as he sat opposite Carrie, almost blocking her view of the rest of the Centre.

'Morning,' she responded with a smile.

The pairing, that were thrown together by DI Sutton had worked together before and were familiar to each other. Kingham wore a black jacket, dark blue shirt, black trousers, black shoes and a smile that beamed confidence. He wasn't Carrie's first choice of partner for searching for a needle in a haystack but there were plenty of others that could be worse. He had never upset her, and she had often wondered whether she needed to be a little less judgemental, sometimes.

'How many phone shops are we checking out?' he asked.

'All of them, which is four. Three of them are quite close to each other and the other one is at the south end of level 2. Shouldn't take us long though,' she said.

'Hopefully we'll strike lucky.'

'That would be nice,' said Carrie, raising her eyebrows across the table at him.

'Is there much detail left on the receipt? I've not seen it,' he said, keeping his voice down.

Carrie delved into her bag and retrieved a photograph of the receipt that had been enhanced to show as much of the remaining detail as possible. It had been expanded to A5 allowing the fine print to become as readable as could be expected seeing as it had been lying flat in the back pocket of her jeans and submerged into a dirty canal.

'Here. The name of the shop from which she purchased her phone is almost impossible to read but the length of the name tells me that it probably wasn't one of those with just a couple of letters, like EE or O2. Can't really give a good guess as to exactly which one it is but I think we should check them all in case she shopped around. Maybe someone might remember her. It's dated from about two weeks ago so with any luck it might trigger a memory with one of the shop assistants. You can see that there are some numbers just about visible at the bottom of it, so maybe the correct shop will recognise it as their own. Who knows, but it's something.'

Kingham took it all in and nodded in agreement as Carrie went along.

'If we could find the phone it might help too. I can't imagine that it would have still been in her possession when she was disposed of. Surely the perp wouldn't have taken any chances and had got rid of it before,' he said.

'You would think so, but if it is in the canal, it'll take some finding. There must be so much sludge at the bottom. Like you say, I can't see it being down there. C'mon, let's make a start. We'll stay together,' she said.

Carrie replaced the photograph into her bag, looped the strap over her head, and stood at the same time as Kingham, although it didn't take her as long to get upright. Carrie wasn't small but she felt as though she was walking beside a giant. They began to walk towards the north end of Market Centre on the ground floor where three of the targeted shops were situated, when Carrie's phone rang in her inside coat pocket.

'Marc, hi,' she said, as she walked along.

'Sorry to disturb your shopping spree, but I was wondering how you got on with the Universities and Colleges. Any joy?'

'Ah, sorry, I meant to call you. No, nothing from them. I spoke with the nearest two unis and colleges before I came out but neither reported that any of their students had gone missing and none were aware of any Italian girls of that age on campus. I asked them to keep their ears to the ground and to call me if they found out anything.'

'Ok. Is Steve there with you?'

'Yes, he's here.'

'Fine. Just checking. I've briefed the team with the information that you brought back from the Pathologists and I'm preparing something for the media. Good luck with it. If you have anything to pass on, don't forget to give me a bell,' said Sutton.

'I didn't forget, Marc, I just didn't remember,' said Carrie, cheekily, knowing full well that Sutton would forgive her instantly. Besides she hadn't failed to pass on anything crucial. That might be a very different story.

Carrie returned the phone into her coat pocket and kept on walking purposefully towards their starting point. Kingham didn't bother to ask about the call, he'd got the gist from what he heard. The North Aisle was about 150 metres long and as they approached the end of it, they could both see the first of the mobile phone shops that they wanted to visit. Fortunately, the shop was quiet, and they didn't have to wait to be seen. As soon as they entered the shop, they were approached by a young Asian girl named Anipe, according to her name badge. Carrie introduced herself and Steve Kingham, both showing their warrant cards to affirm their identities. Anipe's beautiful eyes widened a little more. Carrie had no idea exactly where her name originated from, but she couldn't fail to notice the girl's long and multicoloured fingernails that tapped against the top of the counter as she nervously listened to Carrie's questions. When another shopworker appeared at the rear of the premises, Kingham moved towards him and continued with the investigation into whether either of them had any recollection of seeing a girl, about so high, with dark hair and possibly, an Italian accent that might have purchased a phone from either of them around two weeks ago.

Carrie showed the A5 photograph of the receipt in the hope that it might help but neither of the assistants recognised it as coming from their shop. The conversations weren't proving to be fruitful so Carrie left them both with a contact number for her so that, if anything changed, they could get in touch with her. They moved on to shop number two.

Carrie and Kingham knew that the chances of getting a good result were fairly slim, but the phone had come from somewhere and the new shopping precinct was as likely as anywhere. The next shop had a few more customers in, but it also had more staff, so Carrie and Kingham managed to get to work quickly. The same routine played out without them getting a bite. One of the young boys that worked there did say that the description, as far as it went, reminded him of someone but his recollection was extremely vague. Again, contact numbers were left before they moved on to shop number three. The third shop on Carrie's list was jam packed with customers but her and Kingham didn't want to walk to the opposite end of the Centre and check out the final one, and then have to come all the way back again, so they made their way in and waited until one of the shop staff became free.

The signage above the entrance to the busy shop simply said *The Phone Shop*. The facia was best described as teal blue with white lettering. The obligatory bright lighting shone down from sunken spotlights onto a main console displaying all of the latest gadgetry. There were numerous *Pay As You Go* phones decorating the walls, many of which were being pawed by several inquisitive shoppers. Staff members were constantly watching every move and continually replacing the phones into their correct place on the display. Visible towards the rear of the shop were a number of laptops, perched on small white desks, each with metal-framed chairs, should any of the customers require the attention of the staff for advice with regard to the accessories on show or information about the products and services available to them. Much to the apparent disappointment of Lisa G, whose name badge proudly announced that she was the Manager, Carrie and Kingham were not here to become potential customers of *The Phone Shop*. Once Lisa G had discovered the true purpose of Carrie and Kingham's visit, she invited them to talk in a small room at the rear and away from the flurry of activity in the main part of the shop. Again, Carrie took the lead and Kingham watched on. The low ceiling in the small room, that was used as a storeroom, just about accommodated DC Kingham, who was trying not to flatten his haircut any further. Carrie showed Lisa G the A5 of the shop receipt.

'That might be one of ours, although they are all very similar. Not in particularly good condition, is it? Where did you get it from? I can barely read it,' added Lisa G.

Carrie was not about to explain its origins. Instead, she asked whether the numbers on the bottom of the receipt were of any use in its identification.

'I think it could be one of ours. Let me confirm it with my colleague.'

Before Lisa G could leave the room with the A5 photograph in her clutches, Kingham stopped her and insisted that it stayed in the room. If she wanted to show her colleague, they would have to come to her. Lisa G obliged without any fuss and called her colleague over. Carrie read the next name badge that told her that Geoff, a man, approximately in his fifties with flashes of grey in his thinning hair, had entered the room. He was the polar opposite in stature to Kingham and was dwarfed by the imposing build of the detective. Now Kingham was feeling claustrophobic. Carrie allowed Lisa G to explain the basics of their visit and show Geoff the A5. He took it from her and lifted his glasses into position on his nose.

'Yes, those numbers are ours, at least I think they are, they all look alike,' he said.

'Thought so,' said Lisa G, unconvincingly.

Carrie gave Geoff the best description she could of the unknown girl and watched intently as the information sunk in. Geoff screwed up his face and thought hard. His efforts seemed exaggerated and caused Carrie and Kingham to exchange covert glances. He was making the most of his few minutes in the spotlight. Finally, he spoke.

'Rings a bell, but this receipt looks like the sort from a Pay As You Go purchase. I doubt there's any record of the customer who bought it. I'll check the computer and see if I can find anything, but I don't think I'll be able to. Won't be a minute,' he said, handing the A5 to Kingham.

Having made a mental note of the sparse detail on the receipt, Geoff scurried out of the room and over to the nearest laptop. He inserted his log on details and began tapping away. Carrie and Kingham swapped another glance that implied they didn't fancy their chances of learning anything new or useful, other than that the girl had, perhaps, bought a phone here. Carrie replaced the A5 back into her bag and stepped out of the small room back into the main part of the shop. Kingham followed. Both of them stood patiently, watching the hubbub take place in the brightly lit shop until they noticed Geoff approaching them again. When he returned with the news that there was no news, and no personal details of any sort that would further the investigation, Carrie and Kingham felt the chill of the line of enquiry going cold.

'And you're sure that you don't recall seeing her, either of you?' said Carrie, accepting that it was difficult without a photograph of the girl to show.

Both shook their heads and apologised for not being able to help more. Carrie and Kingham thanked Lisa G and Geoff for their time and made their way out of the shop. Once outside they rejoined the throng of people on the North Aisle concourse and headed for the stairs to take them to Level Two.

'She could have still got it from there,' said Kingham.

'Yeah, she could. Wasn't exactly a positive ID of the receipt though.'

'No.'

As they ascended, the atmosphere altered and the noise level abated, creating a calmer ambience. There were definitely fewer people on this level. They walked along the elevated section of the north aisle until they reached the central point from which they were able to view the seating area below. It had filled to capacity now and the noise of chatter could be clearly heard, albeit quieter than if they were sitting amongst it. Being higher up and nearer to the large speakers dulled the humdrum from below too. Their path curved with the architectural shape of the eye-catching domed centrepiece and led them onto the south aisle of Level Two. Some of the shop units in this section of Market Centre were still unoccupied and some were still undergoing refurbishment. One or two looked completely finished but had still not been officially opened for business. After another couple of minutes, Carrie and Kingham spotted their final destination and made for the doorway of MCR, which the small print beneath explained, stood for Mobile Computer Retail. This shop contrasted dramatically with the previous three. It was relatively tiny. The frontage consisted of one pane of glass that filled most of the width of the shop and a single glass door. Inside, it was like an old curiosity shop but with slightly less clutter. However, the contents virtually covered every wall. There appeared to be hundreds of different mobile phones in plastic packaging hanging up in all directions as well as numerous leads, headphones, printers and USBs on the shelving. The shop appeared to taper the further Carrie and Kingham ventured in towards the rear, where a glass counter housed an array of mobile phones. Two young people, a girl and a boy that both looked about eighteen years old, sat on stools behind the counter and chatted quietly, glancing up just briefly in acknowledgment that somebody had entered the shop. They were surrounded by more phones and other gadgets that hung on the back wall and down from the ceiling above them. The young girl had red highlights in her blond hair that she flicked from her face as she welcomed them both and asked if she could help them with anything. Carrie decided not to concentrate on the identity of the receipt in the A5 photograph as it appeared that any useful details would be untraceable, and that the unknown girl had quite likely purchased her phone from the previous shop. Instead, she was more interested to establish whether she had frequented this shop during her search for a phone.

'Actually, you might be able to,' said Carrie, reaching once more for her identification, 'I'm DS Linton and this is DC Kingham. We're both from Old Clapton Street Police Station and we're wondering whether either of you might be able to help us with the identification of a young girl, about twenty years old that may have visited your shop about two weeks ago.'

'We'll try, obviously, but that sounds like most of our customers,' said the girl, with a giggle.

'I'm sure it does. This girl was about your height with dark hair, brown eyes and we think she may have spoken with an accent, maybe Italian.'

'Is she in trouble,' asked the boy.

'No, but it would help us a lot if you had seen her or knew her name,' said Carrie.

'If she did come in here then I can't remember her. We get so many young people in here,' said the girl, smiling broadly.

'I might,' the boy said, rising from his stool.

'Oh, why? Has she been in here?' asked Carrie.

'No, I don't think so, but I do know a girl that sounds like her. Not me, personally but…'

'Ok. What can you tell us?' Carrie asked.

'Well, I don't *know* her, like that, but I know where she works, if that's any help. Although my brother hasn't seen her for a while so she may have quit.'

'Well, that could still be useful. Do you know her name?'

'Yeah, but I can't think of it. My brother will know.'

'So, what's your brother's name and how does he know her?' asked Kingham.

'Robert. Robert Holbrook. She works with him, or she has been, anyway. I'm Nick, well, Nicholas really.'

'Where does he work, Nick?' asked Carrie.

'At the builder's merchants on York Street. Brady's. He'll be there now. He said she's nice. Kept talking about her when he came home,' he laughed.

'Ok, thank you Nick and…'

'Serena,' said the girl.

'Nick and Serena. Thank you both,' said Kingham.

Carrie and Kingham made their way back towards the front of the compact shop, being careful not to knock anything off any of the crowded shelves as they went. They stepped back onto the concourse and headed for the stairs, once more, but this time they felt as though they could be getting somewhere at last. Before they reached the top of the stairs a voice called after them.

'Excuse me.'

Carrie and Kingham turned to see Nick running from the front door of the shop towards them.

'I remembered her name. It's Claudia but I can't remember the rest. D something is all I can remember,' he said.

'That's great, Nick. Thank you very much,' said Carrie.

'Hope she's alright,' he called, as he headed back into the compact little shop.

Carrie and Kingham proceeded down the stairs to the ground floor level and headed for the exit onto Camber Gate. The noise of the traffic was amplified by the rain that had fallen whilst they were inside Market Centre. Cars and buses could be heard splashing through puddles but in some ways, it was a change from the echo within the precinct that was beginning to give Carrie a headache. She welcomed the fresh air.

'Right, well, I'm glad to get out of there. Is York Street that one up by the old brewery?' she asked.

'Yeah, Brady's is next to the wood yard, just before the bridge. It's got a big yellow sign outside.'

'Ah, yes. I knew that,' she said with a smirk.

'Never doubted you for a moment,' replied Kingham, with a grin.

'Let's hope young Nick may have steered us back on track.'

'Yeah, let's hope so. Bit of luck if he has,' said Kingham.

'It might work out. He said that she fitted the description, and it was the accent that nudged him to speak. Plus, his brother had said that she had been absent recently so…maybe.'

'We'll know soon enough. Then we'll have something to work with.'

The pair walked away to their right and along Camber Gate, passing Vitruvius Way and to the junction with Lancaster Gate. From there they crossed the road and turned into Fox Lane; York Street was just another few minutes away.

THIRTY-SIX

Tilbury, East London.

He laid on the bed and pondered his options, few that they were, but it was the uncertainty as to how secure his identity had become that bothered Karter Swann most of all. He definitely hadn't planned on becoming exposed quite so soon or at all if he could help it. Shaken by the image on yet another unwanted photograph, he looked at the second envelope, that laid beside him, with apprehension, as if it possessed something demonic. He was reluctant to open it. He thought that when he returned as Kevin Marshall, he had made himself invisible. Rather Odhran O'Connell had. He had been sure that he had taken all the necessary steps to remain concealed. He had relocated in an area that he had previously not lived or frequented, he had changed his appearance, he had taken great care to continue his existence as Kevin Marshall, and yet here he was, looking at the second batch of mail that had been pushed through the letterbox in a matter of a few days, all of which had a sinister feel to it. He recalled how he had felt when the photographs of the girl that had been found at the rear of the bus depot arrived at the Cactus and Coyote. *Horrible images*. If they were somebody's idea of fun, then Swann wasn't impressed. But once he had been dragged in for questioning, they took on another perspective. Whether his reasons were right or wrong he saw them as damning and decided to keep it quiet. He recalled how shocked he was at finding the recent photograph of the white roll of material that he had put out of sight with the others. Now this. A girl, that appeared to be alive, was looking straight at him. Her face was pale and pitiful. Perhaps she had been captured by some weird creature and was being held somewhere against her will. Or maybe she was already dead. Swann hoped that he wasn't going to receive any images to confirm his worst thoughts. And now something that looked as though it might be a letter. *But from whom?*

Swann picked up the second envelope and knew that he was going to have to open it or forever worry about what it might contain. *Another plain white envelope*. He could not be sure whether the two envelopes were connected in some way or not although he didn't think that he was going to see another photograph. *Maybe it was just an innocent circular that had been poked through the letterbox. Maybe all the houses along here had one.* The more he delayed opening it, the more he doubted that he was going to be that fortunate. Swann was beginning to feel as though he had gone full circle. From being plagued by Elisha and the thoughts of being rearrested, to whatever this new dubiety was. Either way, the Cretan sunshine seemed a distant memory and was something that he yearned for again.

He got off the bed and, holding the envelope, he walked over to a chair that he had positioned by the window from which he could see the River Thames, and sat down. He took a long look out at the old waterway and noticed a fishing boat, heading out towards Shoeburyness and the open sea beyond. He stared at it and noted the motion of the craft, allowing the peacefulness of its rhythmic movement to distract him from the object he held in his hand. He wished he could swap places with the fisherman that was sailing out to sea, seemingly without a care in the world. After a minute or two he looked away. *This is silly*, he thought. Swann began to open the envelope. He slid a forefinger along the top edge and revealed what looked to be a letter and, thankfully, not another sordid photograph. He could feel his heart racing with anticipation. Again, his mind told him that nobody knew he was here, and yet the arrival of the envelopes confirmed otherwise whether he wanted to accept it or not. Finally, Swann acquiesced to the inevitable and took the paper from the envelope, opening it up and sitting with the answer to this latest enigma in front of him. There was less than a full page of print. The words upon it were typed in a font that he was unfamiliar with but was intelligible enough for him to read. He began to read it quietly under his breath to himself.

> You must be wondering who I am and why I sent you the photographs. I hope you liked them.
> Sometimes, Karter, you can't run away from the things you have done. They have a way of popping up when you least expect them. Just like that tattoo of yours.
> How interested the police would be to see them.
> I'll be in touch, now that I know where to find you.

Swann dropped the letter at his feet and realised just how much he had begun to sweat. He felt as though his universe was beginning to curl at the edges. Names began to run through his mind; Elisha, Betty...O'Connell? Was this O'Connell's way of showing Swann that he thought he should have stayed in Crete instead of disrespecting the job he had done and the help he had arranged? He didn't know and he was in no state to try to understand. He got up off the chair with slightly shaky legs and walked into the bathroom. He leaned against the sink and looked up into the mirror. The man in front of him looked a ghastly shade. Sickly and weak. His eyes were glazed with tears of panic, and he hardly recognised himself at all. He turned away from the mirror and reached for the door handle to steady his shaky legs and slowly made his way back to where the letter lay on the floor. Confusion reigned again as he thought of burning it or tearing it into pieces but all he did was stare at it. His emotions switched dramatically from anger to a strange, helpless calm. Swann stood beside the window and noticed that the lights were beginning to come on down by the river. Old Father Thames was getting ready for bed, even though it never really slept. He had become exhausted by the emotional drain but couldn't stay still. His mouth was dry and so he poured himself a glass of water, noticing how much his hand was trembling, and contemplated what to do now. He hadn't eaten and although his appetite was shot, he knew he needed to have something.

He decided that if this person knew where he lived then hiding away was pretty pointless. But seeing as he didn't know who they were he still needed to maintain his Kevin Marshall pretence. He put a pair of boots on and donned a coat. The evening air was cool enough for him to wear a beanie hat whether he was in hiding or not. Oceans fish and chip shop on Stanley Street, was only 200 yards away and he thought that he would be able to stomach something like that with ease. Comfort food. Swann stepped out of the Turner residence and paused to look up and down the road although he knew that nobody would be there now. Even though he knew it, his suspicions grew more and more each time a pedestrian strolled, innocently, passed him. He walked with his head down, more out of habit than anything else. *'I'll be in touch.'*

As he turned the corner, he could see that the queue of people that often lined the pavement outside the fish bar was not there. For once Oceans wasn't too busy, and he managed to walk straight in. He studied the options that were written in white chalk on a black board behind the counter as if he was going to ask for anything other than his regular choice. He ordered a large cod, small chips and a pot of curry sauce. The smell of the frying fish excited his dampened appetite and so he added a couple of pickled onions and a pot of mushy peas to his order. All the drama had made him hungrier than he first thought. As he had done before, he found himself sitting on a cheap and nasty couch that had been provided for the customers while they waited for their order, engrossed in a large poster that had been taped onto one of the tiled walls. The heading at the top of the poster read British Shore Angling Fish Identification. Swann was no fisherman, but he found the different varieties displayed on the poster fascinating. There were 33. He had counted them before. Repetitively, he subconsciously marked off the ones that he had eaten, the ones that he fancied trying, and the ones that looked too frightful to even consider putting in his mouth. The one that held his attention the most was the Scorpionfish. A tough-looking character that, as its name suggests, had a type of sting in the form of sharp spines coated with venom. Swann was still absorbed in reading the information he had found on Google when he heard his name being called for him to collect his order.

'Here you are, Mr Marshall,' said the woman who was holding a red and white Oceans bag on top of the counter.

Swann paid for his meal and turned his back to the counter, as he waited for his change. He looked out onto the street. It was fairly quiet apart from a few cars that trundled slowly past every few seconds, as they joined the queue to escape to the A13 and probably join another, longer queue.

'Thanks,' he said, as his change was dropped into his hand.

As Swann took the bag from her, he noticed somebody in the mirror behind the fryers. A man in a duffel coat was looking in from the street. As Swann turned, the man locked onto his gaze for a few seconds. Swann made his way towards the door as the man in the street walked away. Swann stepped outside and watched him walking further up Stanley Street, away from the main road. The man didn't look back and Swann decided that he was being paranoid, in just the way the supposed sighting of Elisha in the Superstore had affected him. Not that he had been able to confirm that it was ever her. He'd had enough of over-thinking all of this and really needed to get himself off the streets and locked indoors. He tucked the warm bag inside his coat and nursed it as he walked back to his retreat for the night.

THIRTY-SEVEN

DS Carrie Linton and DC Steve Kingham turned into York Street just as a noisy flatbed truck laden with six huge bags of what looked like sand reached the junction with Fox Lane. The brakes hissed as Carrie and Kingham crossed the road in front of it, both raising a hand in gratitude towards the driver. The single occupant, an oldish man with a full ginger beard, sat at the wheel. He wore a bright yellow reflective jacket and a black knitted hat and peered at them both as he crunched the gearbox into submission and engaged first gear, ready to continue his journey. The vehicle had a yellow cab with BRADY'S displayed in bold black lettering just above the front grill. The truck complained and groaned loudly as it juddered onwards, causing the cab to vibrate violently. One of the pair of rear wheels climbed carelessly onto the kerb as it turned left, causing the bodywork to roll from side to side testing the reliability of the rachet straps, and splashed down into a puddle that had gathered over a drain that was no longer capable of doing its job. The contents on the flatbed held firm as Carrie and Kingham heard another gear crunch into place as it began to go out of sight.

'It's a wonder there are any gears left in that,' said Kingham, as he watched the back end of the truck move slowly out of York Street.

'Did you notice he was colour coded?'

'Yeah,' laughed Kingham.

Brady's builders merchants had occupied the first two floors of the site for the last thirty years following a large fire in the premises which caused severe damage to a big portion of the structure, mostly to the rear. It was once a factory that manufactured milling machines, used for machining custom parts to precise tolerances, and exported them to Germany and Switzerland. Nowadays, the top two floors of the old building remained empty, despite rumours of them becoming occupied by a textiles firm, currently based in the west of London. Even a nightclub owner had enquired about the available space, but he never showed again. The yard gates, also painted yellow, sat to the left of the frontage. The brickwork on either side of the old entrance was scarred and scraped from previous encounters over the years, of reckless delivery trucks going either in or out. Much of the brickwork had lost its original right angles and now looked much more rounded and smoother. As Carrie and Kingham stepped past the open gateway that afforded them a brief glance into the back yard, they noticed another of the yellow lorries approaching at speed from the other end of York Street. It didn't appear to be slowing down a lot, until, at the last minute, it braked hard and swung across the narrow, cobbled pavement and into the yard entrance.

'No wonder there's brick dust on the pavement,' observed Carrie.

Kingham acknowledged with a 'Yep' and pushed the shop door open, holding it for Carrie.

'Cheers,' she said, entering the shop and feeling a welcoming blast of warm air from a heater above her head.

The whole of the ground floor was a well-lit open expanse with a counter at the far end that stretched across the entire width of the shop. It looked well organised, with the usual items that would be expected to be found in a builders merchants, assembled upon the shelves. A stack of buckets stood at the end of a row of pots of paint and thinners. The buckets, seemingly only available in red or black, stood taller than Carrie and had been painstakingly arranged in alternate colours. She wondered whether this may have been the work of Robert Holbrook. She was 10 yards into the shop when she turned to talk to Kingham but he was standing with his back to her looking at an arrangement of power tools that sat on display in the front window.

'Hey,' called Carrie, 'Anything interesting?'

'Yeah, actually. I need a new drill. Mine's seized up. Think it over-heated. Well, I know it over- heated. The smoke gave it away,' he said.

'Ah, well, I guess it would do,' she replied.

'Hmm, not a bad price either.'

Carrie wandered back to where he stood, tugged at his arm, and playfully told him that he could come back another day if he was a good boy. They walked further towards the counter, beyond the stack of buckets, and passed a long shelf of general hand tools and saws. Looking towards the counter at the end of the shop, they could see through a door that led to an office where a woman wearing a bright blue jumper and black trousers sat touch-typing and staring at a laptop screen. As they reached the counter a man popped into view from behind it. He was short with hair that had flecks of white either side of his head, just above his ears. His cheeks were flushed, and his bushy eyebrows looked too full to stay in position. He looked briefly at Carrie and Kingham, acknowledged them with a nod of his head, and walked briskly towards the office door with a handful of paperwork.

'Be with you in one moment,' he said, with a smile, and vanished out of sight into the office.

Carrie could hear him relaying something to the woman in the blue jumper about a delivery that hadn't been registered on the system and her, in turn, remonstrating that she had entered it yesterday when it came in. As quickly as it had begun, the conversation fell silent, and the man returned into view from behind the partially closed door.

'Sorry about that. How can I help you?'

'I'm DS Linton and this is DC Kingham from Old Clapton Street. Are you the manager?'

'Yes, I'm Victor, Victor Terry.'

'And do you have a Robert Holbrook that works here, Mr Terry? We would like to speak with him too, if possible,' said Carrie.

'Robert? Err, yes, he's loading in the yard. Is there any trouble?' said the concerned man.

'No, he's fine. We would like to ask you both a few questions about a girl that works here.'

Maybe 'worked', thought Carrie but continued to aim a pleasant smile at the shop manager.

'Don't have a girl here. Just Leana in the back but not a girl really. We have had in the past though. Is something wrong?' he said with a frown.

'Let's hope not. Would you mind fetching Robert for me?' she asked politely.

'Yes, yes, of course' he said as he returned to the back room and could be heard asking Leana to put a call on the tannoy for Robert to come into the shop.

Carrie and Kingham waited only a few seconds before they could hear the request on the tannoy echoing from the yard. The manager re-entered the shop and announced the blatantly obvious, that a tannoy had been put out for Robert.

'We heard, thanks,' said Kingham.

'Ah, yes. Right,' said Mr Terry, 'Shouldn't be long.'

Carrie preferred to wait patiently in silence until Robert arrived rather than go into a conversation with the manager that would only have to be repeated for the benefit of Robert Holbrook. Purposely, her and DC Kingham turned their backs on the counter and looked around the shop until they could hear somebody approaching through the office at the rear. A door that led out into the yard opened and closed, allowing the sound of a forklift truck echoing its warning to permeate the shop as it reversed over the rough ground. A moment later a young man of about 23 came into view still wearing thick gloves that he had obviously been wearing whilst loading the lorry in the yard. He pulled at them vigorously and tugged until they came free, jamming them into two large pockets in his trouser legs. His hair was light coloured and rather dishevelled. He wore a black t-shirt with an Iron Maiden print emblazoned on the front showing something that resembled a black horse being ridden by some kind of warrior carrying the Union flag in one hand and a sword dripping with blood in the other.

'This is Robert,' said Mr Terry, as if nobody could ever have guessed otherwise.

'I gathered. Morning Robert, I'm…' said Carrie.

'My brother text me. He said you were coming,' interrupted Robert.

'I expect you know why we're here too then,' said DC Kingham.

'Yeah, it's about that girl, ain't it?'

The shop manager gave a look towards Robert and flitted his eyes back and forth between Carrie and Kingham with a growing look of concern on his face. 'What girl?'

'It's alright, I ain't done nothing,' said a defensive Robert Holbrook.

'We aren't saying that you have, Robert. We just need to find out some more about her. Could you describe her for me, the one your brother mentioned?' asked Carrie.

Robert scratched his head and looked at Mr Terry, as if for approval.

'Go on then. Tell the lady officer what she looked like,' he said.

Lady Officer, give me strength, thought Carrie, noticing a crafty smirk on DC Kingham's face.

'She had dark hair, quite a lot of it and it was sort of brown really. She was about as tall as you, I reckon,' he said, looking at Carrie, 'She was about my age, 22. Don't know what else really.'

A lot of dark hair rang true with Carrie from her memory of the first time she saw the unfortunate girl in the Crime Scene Tent, who may yet turn out to be Claudia.

'What was her name?' asked Kingham.

'My brother said he told you her name.'

'He did, at least part of it, Robert, but I'm asking you,' said Kingham, whose stature was winning the day.

'She's called Claudia,'

'Oh, I remember her. Don't reckon she'll be showing up again,' said Mr Terry.

'What makes you say that?' asked Kingham.

'Well, she finished here a couple of weeks ago and hasn't been back since. Probably packed it in, I reckon.'

'Finished?' said Carrie.

'I mean finished for the day. I didn't sack her or anything. She just hasn't shown up since.'

'What was her other name, Robert?' asked Kingham.

'De Luca. D E not D A, I remember her telling me that,' explained Robert.

'Thanks,' said Kingham as he noted this in his pocketbook.

'Unusual surname. Do you know where she was from, Robert?' asked Carrie, hoping that he might say 'Italy'.

'I asked her once. I asked her out once, too,' he said with a wide grin.

'Did she say 'yes'' asked Carrie, playfully.

'No, unfortunately not.'

'So where was she from originally?' said Kingham

'She said she used to live in Rome when she was growing up.'

'Anything else?' prompted Carrie, pleased with the Italy reference.

'Yeah, she wasn't born in Rome. She went to school there. She said she was born in somewhere called Tivoli. I don't know where that is though.'

'Rome is in Italy,' offered Mr Terry, coming to life.

'Yeah, I know *that*,' responded Robert.

'Do you know how long she has been in this country?' asked Kingham.

'Not very long. If she wanted to go out with me, I was gonna show her up town. West End, you know.'

'So, do you know how long?' asked Carrie.

'Not really but I think it was just a couple of months. No more as far as I can remember. She worked here for about a month or just over. She didn't seem to know her way around all that well.'

'Mr Terry, do you have further details on record about Claudia, such as where she lived for example?' asked Carrie.

'I'll have a look for you now. I'll have to go into the back and ask Leana to bring up the details on the computer. It's all on computer nowadays, isn't it? Anyway, I won't be a minute,' he said, as he squeezed behind Robert and curled himself around the doorframe into the office, never taking his eyes off of Carrie and Kingham.

With Victor Terry out of the way, Carrie and Kingham were left alone with Robert Holbrook.

'So, what else can you tell us about Claudia, Robert? Did she have a circle of friends she used to go about with?' asked Carrie.

'I never really saw her with anyone else. I only saw her when she came in here to work.'

'What did she do here?' said Kingham.

'Mostly office work. Sometimes Mr Terry would get her to put some of the delivery out in the shop, that sort of thing. I'm out in the yard a lot so I only saw her when I came in to collect something that was part of an order.'

'How many days did she work?' asked Carrie.

'She did Monday, Tuesday, and Wednesday.'

'You sound sure of that,' remarked Kingham.

'Yeah, well. They were my favourite days,' said Robert with a twinkle in his eye and a slight flush to his face.

'Ah, I see,' said Carrie, with a knowing smile, 'Did any of the other lads here pay her any attention?'

'No, the others are all older with girlfriends,' said Robert, implying that he was the only eligible person that might be in with a chance.

'Here we are. I've printed off all we have about her. There's not much though. Well, Leana printed it off, but still,' said a returning Mr Terry with only a single page of printer paper.

'Thanks,' said Carrie, taking the information from him.

The information about Claudia De Luca was scant to say the least but it did show an address that both Carrie and Kingham recognised as being in the vicinity of the Lavender Road Estate where Angelica Rowntree had been living, and not a million miles from where Haley Breen had lived either. It was also fairly local to Old Clapton Street Police Station. They both knew that the address on the paperwork, which read as 24b, White Horse Street, related to a low-level block of council run properties, no more than two storeys high, that were situated on a raised embankment with a war monument to the front of the building. It was generally occupied by single parent families and a host of young children. Her date of birth did indeed place her at 22 years old, the same as Robert Holbrook had suggested. There was no known phone number and nothing that related to any bank account.

'How did you pay her, Mr Terry,' asked Carrie.

'Cash,' he said.

'Why cash?' asked Kingham.

'Well, she didn't have a bank account, you see,' said Mr Terry.

'And you have all the appropriate documentation to show that the right amount of income tax and National Insurance contributions were deducted in line with the employment laws, I assume,' said Kingham.

Carrie could see this line of questioning coming a mile off as soon as cash payments were mentioned. She knew that DC Steve Kingham had spent a number of years working in the Fraud Squad as part of the City of London Police Economic Crime Department. He had gained a wealth of experience tracking down banking frauds, insurance frauds and investment frauds. Not that she thought for one minute that Mr Terry was actually in any danger. Carrie assumed that once it was under his skin then any mention of something such as cash in hand was always likely to make Steve Kingham's ears prick up.

'Yes, of course. I've got it all on the computer, Officer. Leana could find it for you if you like,' said a slightly shaky Victor Terry, his eyes wider than they had been up to now.

Kingham didn't bother to follow up on Mr Terry's offer but instead continued to jot down notes in his notebook. Carrie guessed that the mere mention of potential tax evasion had done the job and she knew that Kingham wasn't here for that today. She continued reading the piece of paper in front of her but unfortunately there wasn't a huge amount to go on. On the flip side, Robert Holbrook had given a good description of her which corresponded with the timeline and the girl found in the Limehouse Cut, as well as the confirmation of an Italian connection, and now they had an address to work with. Carrie was as certain as she could be that her mystery girl was probably going to turn out to be Claudia De Luca from Tivoli, Italy. Time would tell.

'Ok,' said Carrie, 'One more thing for now. Did either of you see anyone come into the shop and, maybe, speak with her or seem to be watching her closely at all?'

Both Robert Holbrook and Victor Terry looked at each other and ummed and ahed for a moment. Carrie and Kingham were pretty sure that the answer was going to be 'no'. As expected, both of them had no more to offer. Carrie and Kingham thanked them both for their time and left a contact card with her number on should anything else worth mentioning crop up. As they began to make their way out of the shop Carrie reached for her phone and pressed the quick dial button on her mobile that would put her through to DI Marc Sutton. She relayed the conversations at Brady's and the information that had been gleaned during their visit and informed him that they were on their way to check out 24b White Horse Street next. Sutton told her that he would get on to Interpol and see whether they could supply any information from their extensive DNA database on a Claudia De Luca, aged about 22, from Tivoli, Italy.

A DNA profile provided by the Forensic Pathologist would have been submitted as an alphanumerical code and would hopefully be able to match with the information on the database. As in this case, Sutton decided that searching for a method of positively identifying the girl found in the canal would require further assistance and that international police co-operation would be needed. If the database held information from the mystery girl, then it would be able to return a positive hit. Usually this was fairly quick, depending upon the extent of any backlogs.

Fairly satisfied with the morning's work up to now, Carrie began to feel as though she was actually getting somewhere at last but before her and DC Steve Kingham could get as far as the front of the shop, she heard somebody call after her from behind. Carrie looked around towards the counter where her and Kingham had been speaking with Mr Terry and Robert Holbrook but neither of them were in sight. In fact, nobody was in sight initially, until the top of a lady's head could just be seen moving towards the front of the shop on the other side of a dividing row of tubes of bathroom sealants, mastics and glues. Due to his height advantage Kingham was able to see that this was the lady from the back office before Carrie was able to identify Leana.

'Hello, I'm Leana, Leana Turnbull. I could hear what you were all saying from the back, so I thought you should know that I have seen someone in the shop when Claudia was here.'

'Ok, so what can you tell us?' said Carrie, hoping for a bit more information.

'Well, if the office door is open, I can see straight into the shop and I noticed somebody standing around behind where Claudia was putting some of the 1 litre paint onto the shelf. I didn't think anything of it, well, you wouldn't, would you? Anyway, I saw him again another day, might have been the following day but I don't really remember that well.'

'Can you describe him for us?' asked Kingham.

'I didn't really get much of a good look. He had his back to me, but he did seem to be watching what Claudia was doing. What bothered me is that as she moved further up towards where we're standing, he moved up with her. I don't know how she didn't notice, but I suppose she was just getting on with stacking the shelves.'

'You say that he came in again soon after that day?' said Kingham.

'Yes. Now thinking about it, that must've been a Wednesday because that was the last day that Claudia came to work, before she, you know, disappeared,' said Leana, assuming the worst.

'Did you get a better look at him on that day?' asked Carrie.

'Not really,' she said.

'Do you have cctv?' asked Kingham.

'No, we only have a movement sensor thing that goes on at night. I'm not even sure that it works properly,' she said.

'So how sure are you that it was a Wednesday?' asked Carrie.

'Oh, I'm sure it was. Her last day, you know,' said Leana.

'How long did he hang around in the shop?' asked Kingham.

'The first time that I saw him, he was in for about fifteen minutes, I think. When I looked up again, he'd gone so it couldn't have been much more than that.'

'And the second time?' asked Carrie.

'Not as long that time. Now thinking about it, the first time he left a few minutes after Claudia finished putting the paint on the shelf. Mr Terry said she could go as soon as she had got them out. It was a late delivery that day. The second time he walked out pretty much as she did. She was a bit over her time so he said she could go when she was done. Then we didn't see her again after that.'

Carrie and Kingham thanked Leana Turnbull and left with the knowledge that a man was in the shop and that he left when Claudia did. It was not very much use to them without cctv or a definitive description of him, but it did raise their suspicions that this may well be relevant to the fact that she had gone missing and turned up the worse for wear. They left Brady's and began the three mile walk to White Horse Street. Had the weather not improved significantly whilst they had been speaking with Victor Terry, Robert Holbrook and Leana Turnbull, they would have considered walking to the nearby taxi rank outside Market Centre. Once they had finished, their return to Old Clapton Street would not take too long as it was not far from their next port of call; 24b White Horse Street.

THIRTY-EIGHT

Minneapolis, Minnesota.

The Minnesota Search and Rescue Dog Association (MinnSARDA) which is situated on 223rd Avenue NW, Minnesota, took Gregory Bonner no more than the suggested 43 minutes to reach. The weather was bright, the roads had been gritted, and his patrol car covered the 38-mile journey with ease. The route which had taken him onto I-35W and US-10 W before leading him onto I-94W and Northern Boulevard NW, ran freely today and without so much as a single broken-down vehicle to interrupt his journey. A covering of fresh snow provided a bright canvas of white on the fields as his patrol car glided from Interstate to Interstate. He had been cruising at not a single mph over the allotted speed limit as it smoothly ate up the tarmac. Inside, Bonner had been singing along to the radio and feeling completely relaxed. The solitude of his patrol car was just what he needed considering that the start to his day had been somewhat tense and stressful. Big Toni had reluctantly authorised his request to pay a visit to MinnSARDA after Bonner had won an argument that he looked like losing from the outset. He had proclaimed that the journey was necessary and pertinent in relation to his search for the truth behind the disappearance of Caterina Marks. The conversation had at one stage become rather heated as Bonner tested his Captain's patience further than he had ever done before. At several stages of the quarrel Bonner thought he had blown any hope of hearing Captain Antonio Rodrigues agree to letting him go and felt it was much more likely that he would find himself getting admonished for his insolent behaviour. Bonner still didn't know what possessed him to stick his neck out further than he ever had but having steadied his racing heart as he drove, he was pleased that he had persevered.

    Since he began his search for answers, he had gone through an array of different emotions from optimism to utter despair. Mostly it was the latter. On a number of occasions, he had begun to wish that he had never volunteered himself for the desperate task and yet he just could not leave it alone, however ridiculous his chances were of discovering something substantial that may lead to Caterina's mysterious story becoming clear. Bonner felt a commitment to helping his friend and that alone drove him on. The image that he first recognised on the MUPC website, was firmly etched in his brain, her young innocent face that looked back at him, almost pleading for him to help her. When he shut his eyes, he could imagine her leaving her house, just as he had when he decided to 'follow her' on the day that he traced her presumed route towards the property where Betty Nelson had once lived. In order to control the pre-occupation, he had spent many evenings in his den, scanning reports of predicted snowfall for the region and creating new and more intricate Excel charts. None of which solved his recurring issue. Bonner wanted to know the answer more than almost anything else and it was starting to bother him to the extreme.

'Why, Bonner, that's all I'm saying. Tell me why I should send you off on another wild goose chase?' Big Toni had insisted.

Bonner had been remonstrating with Big Toni for 20 minutes. The rest of the department that were within earshot of this morning's entertainment were just as curious to know, and just as baffled as to why Bonner was bothering at all. Nobody gave him a hoot of finding the answer to her disappearance.

'I've said, Captain, because something's just not right about this. There's got to be more to it. She didn't just vanish into thin air. She was on her way to Betty's and...'

'...and I've said that somebody took her, Bonner. Nobody knows, but she's gone.'

Bonner grimaced at Big Toni and could feel his temper rising to the surface. Even though he had not previously thought about her in ten years, he now could not accept that she had simply 'gone'. He knew that losing it with Big Toni would probably close the incident for good and so he had to count to ten before he continued. The rest of the office on that floor had fallen silent. Bonner and Big Toni realised simultaneously that they were the focus of everyone's attention.

'What you lot staring at? Get the hell back to work,' Big Toni yelled.

Captain Rodrigues stormed into his office and closed the door. This was the inexplicable moment that changed the game. As Bonner had driven onwards towards his destination, he had tried to understand why he had spontaneously followed the Captain and shoved the door open, causing it to strike a cabinet and rebound towards him, without hesitating to knock first. Nothing came to mind. Maybe stupidity. Desperation. Whatever it was, the event, remarkably, had not made things any worse. Bonner acknowledged that had he not risked everything at that very moment that he probably would not be driving on the Interstate and feeling quite so smug about the outcome of his traumatic morning. A lot of raw luck and a huge chunk of fortunate timing turned things in Bonner's favour when he and Big Toni least expected it. Bonner's unscheduled appearance in his Captain's office stunned Bonner just as much as it had Big Toni, whose eyes glared with surprise as he began to rise slowly from his chair like a King Cobra preparing to strike. Once the Captain's office door had stopped bouncing between the cabinet and Bonner's arm, there had been a moment of anomalous stillness that neither man knew how to react to. Big Toni's stare was filled with a rage that was ready to unleash a venomous barrage. Immediately, Bonner's blood pressure began to drop through the floor in realisation of the fact that a forbidden line had just been unexpectedly and recklessly crossed.

'What the fuck, Bonner,' Big Toni had said, somewhat shocked by the interruption.

But before Bonner could contemplate something to say in response, the intercom on Big Toni's desk clicked and the soothing tones of Sharon Kwasniewski, an admin clerk who regularly intercepted the Captain's calls, cut the tension in the room.

'Captain Rodrigues, I have Deputy Chief Bolton on the line for you.'

Big Toni stared at the intercom and cursed, knowing that he would not be able to shrug this call off. Bonner stared at the intercom and mentally thanked the Lord. What Bonner did not know at this stage was that the Lord was about to answer his prayers in a way that he had not expected.

'Hellfire Bonner, don't you move. Not one inch,' said the irate Captain, '*Now*, Sharon?'

'Yes, Sir. He's already called once this morning, but I didn't get a reply from your office,' she responded softly as if the Deputy Chief himself was listening.

Big Toni knew that he could not defer speaking with the Deputy Chief and that his dealings with Gregory Bonner would have to wait.

As Bonner stood perplexed in Big Toni's office, he recalled hearing a distant voice coming from behind him during the heated exchange with Big Toni and gathered that it may well have been Sharon alerting his Captain to the initial call from the Deputy Chief. As Bonner remained motionless and tried hard to come up with a reasonable argument as to why he should continue to pursue the Caterina Marks mystery, he remembered that he had done something else that was also completely spontaneous and completely out of character. He had sent an email to Deputy Chief Bolton entirely off his own bat. The morning's mayhem had caused this to slip from his mind. It was done during a moment of madness when he had convinced himself that he was finally going to solve the Caterina Marks case. Even as he had composed the email, twelve days ago, he could not really warrant why he thought this was a good idea or precisely what it was that had made him believe that he had any chance of successfully resolving the unresolvable. He had come up with an idea after reading through the paperwork from the initial investigation that had taken place ten years ago.

Dogs, he had thought, *why didn't the dogs find something at Betty's house if she was really there?* Bonner considered that this inexplicable and random inspiration which had prompted him to dare to send an email directly to the Deputy Chief, in the absence of Captain Rodrigues, who was on a spell of short leave, had, talking of dogs, finally returned to bite him. He knew that he had not needed to send anything to Deputy Chief Bolton when he was fully aware that Lieutenant Svoboda, was his commanding officer when Big Toni was not immediately available, but something had triggered a memory in his mind of where this difficult trail had begun. Maybe it was all because the Deputy Chief had been pushing Big Toni for some results regarding the list of missing people that came under his area. *Maybe that was it.* Either way, having read and re-read the initial findings, or lack of them, from the report that was submitted by the team of dog handlers, he had swallowed hard and sent it.

'Good morning, Sir,' said Big Toni, his eyes still piercing Gregory Bonner's skull as he stood with the telephone pressed firmly to one ear.

Bonner had wished that he could have heard the conversation in full although listening to Big Toni's half had ended up being sufficient. The first mention of Search and Rescue dogs had made Bonner's ears prick up and also made Big Toni thump down into his chair, knocking an empty mug onto the floor of his office. The Captain could not hide his disappointment at the timing of the call just when he was looking forward to giving Bonner a roasting. As the exchange between the Captain and his superior unfolded, Bonner had felt himself getting the edge and the inevitability of being scolded by a disconsolate Captain Rodrigues had gradually begun to filter away.

'But…but no Sir. Yes, Sir. No, Sir,' was all that the Captain could offer as the Deputy Chief had made his recommendation.

But right now, Bonner no longer cared. He drove along the Interstate with a contented smile and the consolation that an officer of a higher rank than Big Toni had come out in full support of his spontaneous proposal that he should extend his research into why the Search and Rescue Team had discovered not a trace of the presence of Caterina Marks at Betty's house when Bonner himself, was so adamant that she was heading there as previously arranged. Somehow, Bonner had managed to convince the Deputy Chief that the most likely scenario had been that Caterina had arrived at Betty's and that the dogs had completely missed this. The response to Bonner's email that had been delegated via the telephone of a disgruntled Captain Rodrigues had indeed been music to Bonner's ears, even if it had been completely out of the blue. Big Toni had reluctantly passed on the wishes of the Deputy Chief and Bonner had wasted no time in scurrying out of the building and heading off to MinnSARDA in Elk River, Sherburne County, Minnesota.

The road into MinnSARDA wound around in a big curve which took him over the road he had approached on and swung round into a spacious parking area. He parked his Patrol Car in one of the allotted visitor's spaces at the front of the building. There must have been about one hundred slots, sixty or so of which were occupied. From where he sat, he could see that the main doors that led to the reception were virtually straight in front of him across a wide pavement. The view of the section of the building that Bonner could see from his vehicle, was mainly of a glazed frontage with a large, wide sloping roof. *Wow, that could hold tons of snow,* he thought. He could also see a few people exercising dogs around the perimeter of the building and a few more in the distance. Some of the people wore reflective jackets with K-9 SEARCH TEAM printed on the back in bold black lettering. Others were purely dressed in heavy overcoats that provided protection against the air temperature that was forecast to drop below -12c tonight. Even the dogs wore padded coats, and some were even wearing boots. Bonner recognised the German Shepherds and the Retrievers but was not entirely sure what the other breeds were. He stepped out of his vehicle, hearing the door locks clunk as he pressed the key fob with one hand in his pocket, and wandered slowly across the pavement towards the main doors. The sign above the main entrance read:
   WELCOME TO MINNSARDA. SERVING THE MINNESOTA AREA AND BEYOND SINCE 1981.

Bonner pushed the large swing door that led him into a light and airy reception area. It was busy. Several people were standing at the reception desk so rather than queue behind them, Bonner decided to sit at the nearby seating area and wait until the queue had diminished a little. Nobody had noticed him enter so he chose to sit and look around, giving himself a few moments to reflect on how it was that he had even managed to be here at all this morning. Bonner also considered that having received his welcome surprise from the Deputy Chief, who had actually championed his request to continue to follow up on what had happened to Caterina Marks, that he had better come up with something and not return to Big Toni's office with no more than that he had had a nice day out. Several glossy magazines and leaflets were spread out on a low-level table beside him. A discarded and stained coffee mug sat unattended on a table a few feet away. He reached for one of the leaflets that he thought looked informative. He was not disappointed. The information within explained to him that MinnSARDA was the oldest canine search and rescue unit in Minnesota and that it specialised in providing trained canines to assist public safety agencies, such as the Police, in the search for lost persons as well as in homicide investigations. Bonner read that MinnSARDA does not offer private dog training classes but does have a specialised cadaver dog facility. He raised his eyebrows briefly at this and mumbled to himself that it had not worked in the case of Caterina Marks. Then he realised that for possibly the first time since all this began, he had considered that his friend, Caterina, may be dead. Bonner dropped the leaflet down onto the table and wondered whether he was, indeed, wasting his time as Big Toni had tried to tell him earlier, although he felt a strong reluctance to finally admit this to himself. Bonner shook the thought from his head and took a moment to watch the activity in the reception area as people, some uniformed, others not, accessed and egressed the building.

'Good morning, Officer. My name is Derek Grant. Can I help you?' said a smartly dressed man as he approached Bonner.

'Yes, good morning,' he said, standing to shake hands, 'Forgive me for not calling ahead this morning but I wasn't sure that I would make it. My name is Gregory Bonner, I'm a Patrol Officer from downtown Minneapolis. I'm currently working on the case of a missing person.'

'Well, you've come to the right place.'

'I hope so,' said Bonner, assuming that he very likely had.

'We do specialise in that sort of thing as I'm sure you know. Why don't you come through to my office and I'll see what we can do for you,' he said, cheerfully.

Bonner had no precise plan other than to follow Derek Grant through a set of double doors that led them into a long unlit corridor with numerous rooms off to either side. As the two of them advanced further along the corridor, the in-built PIR sensors illuminated in turn as they reached the point from where they could be detected, causing the lighting to operate in sections as they walked. Bonner looked behind him to see the lighting nearest to the double doors had already gone out.

'Do you like it?' asked Grant as he stopped and put his hand flat onto the door numbered 24.

'Neat,' said Bonner.

'They say it saves money but considering the number of times people walk up and down these corridors, the lights are on and off like a disco. Come on in, take a seat,' said Grant.

'Thanks,' he said.

Derek Grant's office was about the same size as Bonner's den where he sat and plotted the information that he gleaned from the SCI. It was considerably lighter and a great deal tidier too. The generously sized window offered a view of the kennels where all the resident trainees were housed. Bonner could hear them barking.

'Do you like dogs?' asked Grant, noticing that Bonner seemed drawn to the activities outside.

'Yes, I do.'

'Well, you would like it here then. We have several that are in training and many others that are fully available for work. It's a busy compound.'

'What makes a good search dog?' asked Bonner.

'Several things. For a start they have to be able to withstand the extremes of weather that we get in Minnesota. Then they have to be tough enough to work in all sorts of challenging terrains, from floodwater to the urban jungle in the cities too,' answered Grant.

'How long does it take to train them?'

'Well, what happens is that we get them from when they are puppies and it usually takes a couple of years to get them up to scratch,' explained Grant.

'And then they are ready?' said Bonner.

'Nope. Then they are ready for certification. If they do not pass, they do not get to be part of the team. Not all make it, either.'

'What happens if they get too old?'

'They don't get too old. They get retired. Usually, they work up until they are about 8-10 years old but that's only half of it. The handlers need training too. No good having a trained dog if the handler isn't up to speed also, so they have to go through a stringent process too.'

'What sort of training do the handlers have to go through?' asked Bonner.

'We start with a thorough background check, then there's the theory stuff, like scent theory, navigation and maps, first aid, radio comms and crime scene preservation. It is a tough course. It has to be. We have to make sure that the handler is as good as the dog they are relying on. As with the dogs, they have to be able to withstand the weather extremes too.'

'What's the pay like?' asked Bonner.

'Pay?' Grant laughed, 'There ain't no pay, this is all voluntary work. Most of these people have fulltime employment but when they are required to despatch, we expect them to be out there instantly. If they cannot be released from work, then they are not much good to us. Let's face it, we never know what time of day or night someone might be reported missing and in what type of terrain we might find ourselves. It's a full commitment, Officer,' said Grant.

'What about all the kit they need?' asked Bonner.

'They have to buy that too. And we expect that they will be out training at the weekends. You see, if we are to be expected to find somebody's loved one that has gone missing, or perhaps locate an elderly person that may have become confused and lost their way, we have to be on the ball. And then there's the re-certification that happens annually to the field teams and, of course, we have to keep our dogs in tip-top condition too. Anyhow, let me get you a coffee and then we can see how I can help you.'

Grant made his way back out of the office and back into the corridor and left Bonner to stand by the window and watch the dogs being escorted in and out of their kennels. Some were indeed quite small and others, he imagined, might be at the other end of their rigorous training programme. He returned to his chair and sat for a moment to allow all this new information to be absorbed. He had only been here for a short time but, already, he felt as though he had learned quite a lot. Grant's office was decorated with various certificates and Bonner could see the name of Derek Grant printed on them. He assumed that he must have gained a wealth of experience and that with any luck he was going to be particularly useful. Bonner stood and began to wander slowly around the office, checking out the certificates and admiring the achievements of Derek Grant. He read the certificates as he walked slowly along the wall. There must have been at least fifteen and he presumed that these were not all of them. Some were specific, such as Mountain Rescue and then he spotted one that caught his eye. A qualification that licensed Derek Grant to work with cadaver dogs.

'Here we go. I brought you a couple of sachets of sugar and a little pot of milk. I should have asked but, never mind,' said Grant.

'Thanks,' replied Bonner.

'It's pretty busy out there today,' said Grant, looking out towards the kennels, 'We're having an Open Day at the weekend and so everyone is actively cleaning and preparing everything for when the public come storming in,' he said.

'Right,' said Bonner.

'That's one of our Malinois, right there,' pointed Grant.

'One of your what?'

'Belgian Malinois. Like a German Shepherd, but I find them even better. Just my preference, you understand. You see, they're intrinsically motivated. In other words, they train and work because they love it. I had one for a number of years. Her name was Cilka. We went to plenty of jobs together. She was the best I have ever had. Brilliant in the woods. Her nose was simply perfect. A real professional. You see that black face? Don't they look beautiful?'

'They sure do,' said Bonner, admiring the appeal of the Malinois on just the other side of the glass.

'Yeah. They are my favourite breed. I guess you can tell. Anyhow, you haven't told me how I can help you.'

Bonner picked up his coffee, took a sip, and looked to his left towards the certificate that he hoped would mean that Derek Grant may be of use to him today. He briefly saw Caterina's face in his mind and for the first time for ages, he felt as though he was getting back on track.

'My missing person,' he said, almost to himself.

'Ah, yes. Right then, let's see if I can help you with that. I've dealt with the police department a number of times so it shouldn't be a problem. Best hurry up with the details 'eh?'

'Hurry up?'

'Yes. It's always best to move as quickly as we can with these things before the trail goes cold. Not that it would stop the dogs picking up a scent. They can detect a human presence years after they were missing, even under water. So, when did the person first go missing?' asked Grant.

'Actually, ten years ago, to be precise,' replied Bonner.
'Oh. Well, perhaps there isn't a rush after all.'
'Yeah. Not a recent one, exactly,' said Bonner.
'I don't understand. Why are you looking now?'

The words *she was my friend and I used to really like her* shot into Bonner's head, but he held firm and composed something less gooey.

'The department are having a drive in an attempt to solve as many of the mysterious disappearances as they can, and I got this one. It's come down from the Deputy Chief.'

'Jack Bolton? Right?' said Grant, putting his pen down beside his notepad and leaning back in his recliner chair, as all the urgency in his demeanour dissolved in an instant.

'That's him. Anyway, I think I know where she was going and I think the dog team may have possibly missed something,' said Bonner, instantly regretting the insinuation.

Grant looked at Bonner with an expression of doubt that his team could possibly have missed anything. For a brief few seconds, the pair exchanged uncertain glances. Grant asked Bonner for the details of the event, such as the date and the address of the property where Bonner was so convinced his missing person had last been known to be.

Bonner looked to his left again and made reference to the certificates that he had been reading whilst Derek Grant was out of the room fetching the coffee. Grant was always happy to talk about his personal achievements and the awkwardness of the moment passed without any further incident. Grant gave Bonner a run-down of the dates when he became certificated in all the different disciplines and told him a story that seemed to accompany each and every one of them. Bonner nodded politely as he watched Derek Grant in full flow, but he was only really interested in one incident. It was a matter of waiting until Derek Grant finally got around to his certificate that licenced him to work with the cadaver dog.

'Cilka was my cadaver dog. Although she had been trained in various other techniques because she was such a highly capable animal. Seven years we spent working with cadavers. Searching for them, anyway. Not many escaped her sensitive nose, I can tell you. So, tell me what you meant about my team 'missing something'.'

Bonner shuffled in his chair and wondered how best to wriggle out of his recent Freudian slip. Grant was obviously extremely proud of his team and Bonner had basically suggested that they had missed Caterina Marks completely.

'I'm not trying to suggest that your team had failed to locate somebody, just that I am as sure as I can be that she turned up at the property where the search was carried out and that it was the last place she would have been seen,' said Bonner.

'Doesn't mean she was there though, does it?'

'I think she was, at least some evidence of her DNA should have been,' insisted Bonner.

'DNA, huh. If her DNA was there at the property when you say it was, then our team would have found it. What did the report say about your missing person? Surely it showed that a thorough search was conducted, and I assume there was no DNA present,' said Grant, with an air of superiority about him.

'It detailed that a search had taken place, but I still don't think it went far enough.'

'My team went *'far enough'*,' said an agitated Grant.

'But surely there have been occasions where someone has been missed before,' said Bonner, sticking to his guns but feeling that he was heading for a disappointing end to his day.

Bonner was used to being up against unbeatable odds, especially where Big Toni was concerned, but he reminded himself that he had won a significant battle today already and that he shouldn't back down now.

'You're an expert in working with a cadaver dog,' said Bonner in an effort to butter up Derek Grant, 'so tell me how the search is usually conducted,' he said.

'Ok,' said Grant, a little reluctantly, 'When we get to the area that requires searching, we will set the dog free with a command. Usually the handler will simply say 'search'. The search takes the same form as the training. The dog will scan the area and once it finds the scent it will indicate, usually by sitting or lying down at the site where it has found the scent. Sometimes they will be trained to bark. The dog, similar to a child, is taught that good behaviour gets rewarded. That gives them an incentive. It's just like any old training day as far as they are concerned. When we train them, we use human remains or blood as a source of scent. They have an inbuilt ability to find this stuff. Bones are detected too. The animal's sense of smell is far superior to ours and they rarely miss anything, so I don't think your missing person was ever there in the first place. You gotta understand that these canines are capable of locating the scent of death even after many hundreds of years. I'm telling you, there was no mistake.'

Bonner was still convinced that something had gone wrong. He didn't bother to express this to Derek Grant again though. He could tell that no amount of time with Grant was going to change his mind. As Bonner looked beyond Grant and out of the window at the movements outside, he came up with another idea.

'Do you know who may have been on the team back then?' he asked.

'Well, let me think. I was here but I didn't attend to your missing person. I remember all the locations that Cilka and I have been to. If she had been there, then there would be no mistake.'

'So, are you saying that a different dog, one not as good as Cilka, might have missed something?' said Bonner, seizing the opportunity to step into the doorway that he felt Grant had just inadvertently opened for him. He reasoned that if he implied upon a possible mistake whilst crediting Cilka for her professionalism, that he might be more inclined to get an answer.

Grant raised his eyebrows and sat back in his chair. He wasn't happy with the implication that anyone from his team might have erred, but he found himself caught between defending his team and taking the opportunity to express how much better than the others Cilka was. He explained again to Bonner why Cilka was the best and that had she been there, that all doubt would have been removed. Grant didn't like it, but he felt that it couldn't possibly do any harm to disclose to Bonner, the name of the handler that would have attended to a call for that area in those days. After all, he didn't feel that it was going to do Bonner any good in his quest for the impossible. Impossible, because there had been no mistake, as far as Derek Grant was concerned. None at all.

Thirty minutes later, Bonner rang the doorbell at 3452, Cardamon Avenue, on the outskirts of Eden Prairie, a city twelve miles south-west of downtown Minneapolis. The home of Ken Toft.

THIRTY-NINE

Ahuja Industries, East London.

A male fox yelped its high-pitched cry somewhere in the factory as Angelica Rowntree stirred from yet another patchy sleep. She had become accustomed to the foxes and accepted them as her only friends in this dystopian world. She had made up names for them and always spoke to them softly whenever they ventured close enough to her little corner of the factory. There was Mum and Dad, but she had been a little more inventive with the young ones. The one with the white on its paws, she had named Socks. Another with a spotty chest, she had named Speckles and the third of the young ones she had named Stripe due to a distinctive black line on its back.

Every bone in her young body ached, as it did most mornings. Sleep was never a pleasure on this hard stone floor. Thankfully, the blankets managed to keep her reasonably warm, but she had not had any quality sleep for days. *How many days?* She had no idea anymore. She tried to turn over, but her arms would not move properly. Maybe she had laid awkwardly and stopped the blood flowing properly into them. Her mind was asking her far too many questions at once. She struggled in a misty cloud of confusion before she reached a level of consciousness that permitted her to begin to make sense of her surroundings, swiftly realising where she was. *Still here.* She licked her lips and registered the taste of dry cement again. It was light. *Early*, she thought. Angelica accepted that it was still her fate to remain here, maybe until she too was disposed of, just like that girl. *Why am I still alive?* She knew that this was not a question that she wanted to keep revisiting, and that she was just thankful that she still was.

She tried again to open her eyes fully, but they felt as though they were stuck together, as if she had slept so deeply that she could not perform the most basic of tasks. Her head swam around, as she laid still, hoping to fully recover soon. One eye and then the other flickered up and down and then both together, allowing as much of the daylight that there ever was in this dusty, filthy place, to pierce her mind. Sunlight shone through one of the windows high above her which instinctively made her grateful that she wasn't going to get dripped on from above today. She tried to raise one arm to wipe her eyes, but her arms still felt as though they were detached from her in some weird way. Angelica began to roll to her right in an attempt to stretch her aching body into life, but she could not move without twisting and turning excessively. She instinctively lifted her head a little to look down towards her feet, to see why she felt so confined, so cramped. Her first thought was that she felt as though she had extra blankets laying on her. Then the horror of the situation hit her hard, like a sudden unexpected explosion in her head. She saw that she was wearing white. *No, not wearing it. Wrapped in it.* Having spied on the goings on regarding the other girl when she had painstakingly held the piece of mirror in her hand, she knew what this probably meant. Angelica opened her mouth to cry out, but her sounds were stifled by her dry throat. She was so terrified that she could not catch her breath. Her chest was pounding, and her heart thudded within it pulsating blood around her body, fuelled by a massive surge of adrenalin as her lungs were crying out for oxygen, but she had lost control. She could not even breath in properly in order to scream out. She began to feel light-headed and started to shudder as the horror rushed through her body and began to make her feel numb and nauseous. Sweat ran down her face. A cold deathly sweat. *No, not me. Please, no.*

She laid herself flat onto the ground and tried to kick her legs but all she experienced was pain. Her ankles were tied tightly, and as she struggled; she could feel something cutting into her skin, just above her ankles. Her arms felt as though they were being held close to her body just above the elbows. *Really tight.* With her eyes now fully open and taking in everything around her she tried to scream again. *Someone will hear me. Nobody will hear me.* Her efforts echoed around the cold metal structure. Tears ran down her face and as she shook in sheer panic, unable to release herself from the torture into which she had awakened. Then she heard it. The unmistakeable sound of the metal gate scraping across the gritty floor, penetrated into the factory. Angelica froze. Her mind swiftly thought about Iron bar that she had concealed successfully under her blankets, but it would do her no good now. *Probably gone anyway. Was probably found.*

Oh, God. He's coming for me, she thought. Angelica had decided that when she saw the ease with which the person had lifted the other girl up, that it was probably a man. She looked about her immediate surroundings for any hope of a way to free herself, but there was none. She knew that all she could do was lie there like a wounded, defenceless prey and await her fate. Silently, she listened to the approach as she had done so many times before. The echoes were familiar to her now. The opening and closing of the gate with the rush of cold air, and the steps that grew ever louder as her captor approached. This time it all felt very different. Sinister. When he came into view, Angelica startled. The grubby clothing and the mask no longer bothered her and even though she knew precisely when he would be walking into her sordid little world, she still jumped. Her eyes watched every tiny move intently. *That sheet on the girl had blood on it. He's going to kill me.* Then she experienced a delayed mental image as she fought with the reality of her probable fate. *Haley Breen was found in a sheet too.* She had heard the rumours at the time.

He stood at her feet and stared. Angelica stared back, as defiantly as possible, hoping to win some kind of pointless battle of wits that might save her. She looked hard into the eyes that peered out from behind the mask. *Can I recognise who this is? What is the point?* He had a small red and black rucksack over one shoulder that he placed down on the ground beside her. Close this time. No need to worry about her causing any problems. *Iron bar would be completely useless now.* Angelica grimaced as he touched her right shoulder and shuffled himself into position towards her head. Sweat continued to glisten on her forehead. She had long-since stopped worrying about her hair. It was a mess now as far as she was concerned and would probably need to be cut off. If she survived. Her breathing accelerated and every muscle in her frightened body tightened. *No, no,* she thought, but no words came out. The grip on her shoulder wasn't firm, it was gentle. Angelica didn't know whether this was good or bad. She knew that he didn't need to restrain her any further than she already had been, that was certain. *Maybe he put something in my food.* She laid flat and looked up at the mask. She had gotten used to seeing it since she had been incarcerated by...whoever it was.

'I'll do anything you want. Please, you can do anything you want to me. You can touch me, I won't tell anyone,' she said, in an act of complete and utter desperation, although Angelica knew it would not alter anything. She was sure that she was going to die today.

He reached into the rucksack as her eyes followed every tiny move his hands made. He still had his left hand on her shoulder in a weird, uncomfortably caressing manner. He put something down on the ground and shuffled closer again. Angelica clenched and squealed as he grabbed forcefully at the top half of her body with both hands and raised her up and back against the wall, into the corner where she *lived.* The chain was still on her, and she heard it clink against something underneath her. *Iron bar,* she thought. With her arms secured, she knew that she would not be able to even hold it, let alone wield it. *Pointless, I'm chained here,* she thought. Whoever was doing this reached slightly behind them and took the object that had been placed onto the ground in their hand. Angelica didn't want to look at what it was. Her body shook again as he moved really close now. So close, that for the first time, she could smell alcohol on his breath. *Him? Must be.*

'My Dad has money, please don't do this. Just let me go, I won't tell, I promise,' she begged, her voice trembling now.

He held her chin; his thumbnail dug into her cheek. She could feel the sharpness of it on her face. Angelica considered trying to bite his hand but all she did was begin to squeal pathetically, quietly this time like an animal begging for mercy before the impending kill. It felt as though this was all she had left to give. She felt her head being turned away from her captor, exposing the right side of her neck. The grip was firmer now, there was no mistaking the difference. She felt the pain and thought that something was about to happen. There was no mistaking the strength in his fingers and the intent with which he clawed at her. The odour of alcohol was making her feel sick as it washed over her at such close quarters. *Whiskey.* Angelica continued to beg and promise that she would never tell a soul about any of this if she could be set free. Nothing she said changed anything. The silence that had been there from the very beginning still existed. He was not going to leave her alone and he certainly was not going to do what she was asking. Out of the corner of her eye she could see that he had something in his hand. She couldn't tell what it was, but she was already thinking that this was what he used to kill the other girl. Still, he held her head away from him, pushing it against the rough surface of the wall, the thumbnail still digging into her cheek. Angelica began to try to wrestle herself away from him by wriggling on her bottom, but it was pointless. She was as far into the corner as it was possible to be. Her captor was in full control. He knelt across her thighs and put some of his weight onto them. She was going nowhere. She felt her chin be released and the flat of one hand be laid against the side of her face, so that she was still facing away from him. *Why doesn't he want me to look at him? Stupid question.* The fierce grip and pressure released a little more as something touched her head. On the top. Her head was tugged backwards, and Angelica waited for the pain to follow and the sense of blood oozing down her neck and onto her shoulder. The pulling sensation on her head carried on as she tried to prepare herself for the worst. *One last attempt at wriggling free might save me,* she thought, but she didn't really believe it.

Then it stopped with a jolt as her head recoiled forwards. The hand on her face began to stroke her cheek. Angelica froze. *He's playing with me.* Again, something touched the top of her head and caused her head to be tugged backwards. Her skin felt prickly and tingled all over her body. She could hear it too. Her hair was repeatedly being pulled. *I know what he's doing.* She could not believe it. Her hair was being brushed. *Am I being prepared for death? Did he do this to Haley too?*

She tried to turn her face towards him, so as to try to speak again. Anything to save herself. But the hand pushed her face away again. The tugging at her hair continued as she sat leaning against the wall in her corner, the corner that had become home. She wanted to wee. *Maybe I should ask to be untied so that I could walk to the bucket.* Angelica's mind raced as she tried to compose herself and find the words that just might enable her to be released from the deathly white sheet, but before she could speak, she heard a faint sound in her ear. It reminded her of the strange pitiful whimpering sound that she heard when she spied on the other girl. Something dripped onto her cheek. *Sweat,* she thought. But something felt wrong about it. Angelica appreciated that this moisture had not run from her forehead and down her face; it had dripped. *He's crying,* she thought. Then the volcanic eruption in her head returned and another shockwave hit her as Angelica tried to interpret the muffled sound. *Marry me? Did he just say, 'Marry Me'?*

FORTY

Old Clapton Street Police Station.

DI Marc Sutton knew precisely what time it was. He didn't need to check his watch, check his mobile phone or lift his eyes up to confirm the time on the clock on his office wall, he just knew. He looked up from his desk, towards his open office door for what felt like the umpteenth time this morning as his concentration was once again disturbed by the tiny ping from the small carriage clock that DCI Blackery had brought to work with him earlier today. He had sat it to one side of his desk and spent many moments admiring the precision of the works within that were visible through the glass case. Sutton couldn't see it from where he sat but he certainly knew it was there. Blackery had wedged his own door open which was unusual for him, as he generally left it closed. Not this morning. Sutton had been cursing it each time the segment of fifteen minutes passed. He even found himself glancing up, subconsciously, at the wall clock in his own office, almost to prepare himself for the next high-pitched, silence-shattering ping. It was a small carriage clock with a voice like Blackery's; persistent and annoying. Sutton thought that if the sound it made penetrated into his office in this way, then it must have been deafening in Blackery's, and even if it was, the big man would never concede to admitting so. Sutton had said how he liked it when it had been shown to him earlier, but now he couldn't care less if it fell from Blackery's desk and smashed into a thousand fragments.

Sutton's morning had been going very slowly and had felt a lot slower since the torturous carriage clock arrived. He had been thoroughly consumed with an investigation into a new spate of attacks and sexual assaults that had steadily increased in frequency since the arrival of a fairground that had set up on the local park. Whenever these forms of public entertainment appeared, it always meant that the resources of the local police would be stretched a little further. They rarely went smoothly. There were often injuries suffered from the misuse of the rides and theft of personal belongings reported. A police presence, even a small one, was required during certain periods of the day and more commonly at night when the pickpocketing tended to take place. The organised handbag snatch followed by the escape of the perpetrator was as frustrating for the Police as it was traumatic for the victim. Sutton found these types of public attractions to be a headache from start to finish. If it was up to him, he would never grant them permission to enter the park in the first place.

The majority of the offences that had been reported had taken place on the site, or within the boundaries of the park, which stretched from the large ornamental gates at the main road, all the way to the edge of the High School playing fields, where a rigid barrier of chain-linked fencing provided a boundary between them. Most of the problems seemed to have taken place behind the largest of the rides that stood furthest from the road, close to a row of trailers and camper vans. Yesterday he had sent a team of officers to talk to the owners but, as usual, nobody knew anything about these accusations. *The girls were lying.* Unfortunately, one such girl was currently in hospital, having fallen from a four-lane slide. Her story suggested that she was being assaulted when she fell, having been enticed to the top of the apparatus by one of the men that worked in the fairground. This man, however, was not on the site and according to the owner and his family, was unknown to them and had never worked for him. Her description of him wasn't exactly filled with clarity either. Her account of what took place, when she was admittedly drunk, didn't make it easy for Sutton's team to establish precisely who they were looking for. She admitted that she couldn't remember half of what happened but was nevertheless insistent that the amorous affections of that evening were being forced upon her after she was coaxed onto the slide. The man's hands were reportedly touching her despite her complaints, but she went along with it because she was frightened not to. The tears in her clothing were blamed upon the fall which was significant. One broken ankle and a broken wrist attested to that. In the past three days there had been three such reports, none of which had been substantiated by Sutton's team. The other girls concerned had provided scant details but all of them had been insistent that the attacks were real. The first of them allegedly took place a couple of days ago during the late evening, just as the fairground closed. Tonya McKell had explained that a man had pulled her by the arm and forced her to follow him behind one of the trailers, out of sight from the rest of the park. It was there that she reported how he began tugging at her clothing and attempting to force his hand down her top. Tonya had described how she had let out a loud scream and managed to free herself from his grip. Melanie Fletcher had a similar story to tell. Her account described how the man had offered her cans of lager during the evening which she, by her own admission, had foolishly accepted. As darkness fell, he became, in her words, over-friendly, and soon she had found herself wrestling with him behind one of the trailers. Had the girl that was currently in hospital not fallen then who knows what might have happened to her. Maybe Jilly Reed was lucky to have got away with a couple of fractures after all.

When Sutton heard DS Carrie Linton and DC Steve Kingham talking in the corridor outside his office door his attention turned to even more pressing matters. *About time*, he thought. Sutton had been eagerly awaiting some more news from Carrie on Claudia De Luca and had become ever more certain that she was the girl that had been discovered in the canal. Everything Carrie had told him during her brief phone calls that morning, had led him to become sure that a positive identification was imminent. He raised from his chair and met Carrie and Kingham at his office door.

'Hi. Come on in,' he said, as he ushered Carrie and Kingham into his office and closed the door, wondering why he hadn't closed it earlier to shut out the sound from Blackery's new toy.

'I'm as certain as I can be that it's going to be her,' said Carrie.

'Sit down, both of you. How did you get on at White Horse Street?' asked Sutton.

'The people we spoke to were very helpful. It turns out that she did indeed reside at 24b. She hadn't been there very long though which fits with what Robert Holbrook, the young lad at Brady's, was saying. It's a first-floor maisonette-sort of place and they confirmed that she had been seen around until fairly recently too,' said Carrie.

'Did they offer any connection with regard to her having come from Italy?' he asked.

'Yep, that too. One of the neighbours was more friendly with her than the other one and she specifically remembered having had a good chat to her about her time in Rome and how much she missed it,' she said.

'Did they say whether she had any visitors? A man, maybe?'

'I asked but neither of the women had seen anyone come to her door,' said Carrie, 'It appears that she went out at around 8a.m on Monday, Tuesday and Wednesday, and returned between 4 and 5p.m. That ties in with the information we got at Brady's too. As for the rest of the week they didn't see much of her until the weekend, then she would sometimes knock and go in for coffee, but it wasn't exactly a regular routine.'

'Did she ever speak about meeting anyone, maybe after work?' asked Sutton.

'No. They didn't have any more to say about her movements. Just that she was a quiet girl.'

'Do you think the account from the lady at Brady's about this man she said she saw watching Claudia is our man? What was her name? Leana Turnbull?' asked Sutton.

'Yes, Leana Turnbull. Well, she said she saw him twice and both times he seemed to be taking an interest in her. Could be the man we're looking for,' said Carrie.

'Right. Well, it does sound as though it's going to be her. Just need the DNA results to give us a positive match, if we're lucky, then we can be certain of her identity,' said Sutton.

'Martin and Rebecca from the pathology lab have started the ball rolling on that so we'll see,' said Carrie.

'Let's hope so. In the meantime, we still have to find Swann, if he's still alive, of course,' said Sutton.

'Do you think he killed them both then? Haley and Claudia?' asked Carrie.

'Blackery does. When we interviewed him the first time around after the Haley Breen discovery, Blackery was adamant it was him, even after he came up with a fully supported alibi. At the time I thought I saw something in Swann's face, something devious. It was more than just the discomfort of being arrested and interviewed. There was something on his mind about this whole scenario. He didn't comment but I know something was bothering him. He almost seemed distracted when we were interviewing him. As if he was trying to work something out.'

'And what do you think now?' asked Carrie.

Sutton paused in thought and looked in turn at Carrie and Steve Kingham, trying to read their thoughts as to which preference they had. Neither was displaying any sign as to what they were thinking. Probably, neither knew. Sutton scratched his chin and shuffled some paperwork on his desk before looking at them both and speaking.

'I don't know,' he said, with a sigh, 'But if it is him, he's gone to a lot of trouble to avoid being caught.'

'That's not unusual though, Marc,' said Carrie, 'Going to a lot of trouble is often what they do.'

'No, it isn't, but did he really set up the scene at his house? All that blood that was identified as being his, the fine spray on the units and the trail of his body being dragged out into the garden, he'd have needed some help to set that up. And the disappearance. If he did fit it all up, then he did a good job. It feels more likely that he got mixed up with the wrong sorts and they decided to pay him a visit. Maybe he owed them money, or it was drug related. I don't know. What we do know is that the MO for these two murders is identical and if we don't get cracking and find out who's behind this there might just be a third, maybe there already is and we just haven't found her yet. Or whoever's doing this hasn't wanted us to find her yet.'

'I can understand how Haley Breen might fit with that because she was pretty much left somewhere where she was going to be found fairly soon after she was dumped but Claudia, if it's her, could have still been under water if it wasn't for whatever was tied to her feet coming loose,' said Carrie.

'Unless...' said Kingham.

'Unless?' repeated Sutton, looking at DC Steve Kingham with interest.

'Well Sir, this could be wrong but...unless it was only meant to look as though her feet had been tied to some heavy object. Or, although her ankles were marked, maybe those wounds were received during the time when she was being held captive. Perhaps there never was something to hold her down. In that case maybe it was the killer's intention that she should be found, just like Haley Breen, after all it appears that she hadn't been in the water for very long,' explained Kingham.

'Two girls of a similar age and build, two identical MO's, both almost put on display. Then what about the third girl? Why haven't we found her in the same timeframe?' said Sutton looking at his DS and his DC.

'Angelica Rowntree,' said Carrie.

'Quite. Angelica Rowntree,' said Sutton.

FORTY-ONE

Betty and Elisha Nelson strolled out of Georgette's, on Harriet Road, and into the bright afternoon sunshine. Each were holding a large orange carrier bag that sported a bold capital G in red. It had taken Elisha a long time to finally persuade her sister that she should 'let her hair down', come out shopping with her, and have a 'spend up'. Georgette's was a favourite High Street shop of theirs, where they rarely failed to find something to catch their eye as the styles were suited perfectly to their individual likings. They had walked in together and split up, not meeting again until they were ready to pay at the till, save for an occasional glance across the dress rails in search of an opinion. A simple nod, a flicker of the eyebrows, or a screwed-up expression sufficed to pass on the relevant message. Betty had never been very dressy despite Elisha's insistence that she ought to 'glam up', as she called it. Betty's clothes were sometimes ridiculed by Elisha as being 'comfort clothes'; dull and safe. But Betty wasn't the glamorous one, at least as far as she was concerned, she wasn't. Elisha had always admired that Betty could look good in almost anything, even a black dustbin bag, she had joked. Probably because when they were younger, it was Betty that had the opportunity to wear a variety of different things, even if she wasn't over-bothered about it. Elisha had always been the one to go without after their mother died. She was also the one who didn't cry any real tears when she learned that her father had died at the end of a rope, hanging from the rear balcony, frozen in time, during a snowy Minnesota winter a few instantly forgettable years ago.

Betty's style was born out of years of throwing on her favoured Minnesota Vikings sweatshirt and baggy pants and then snuggling under a throw, designed for the furniture. Elisha would often wear some of Betty's things. Betty never minded; she was happy to see Elisha looking smarter than she usually did. Betty also knew that it wasn't a matter of Elisha not having the will or yearning to look good, it was more that she didn't like to rock the boat. Challenging her father about why Elisha didn't get new clothes of her own was not something Betty wished to do. She felt that the privileges that she could possibly lose were not worth risking. Betty didn't tend to show much of an interest in boys either, not until she came to England and met Karter Swann at the Cactus and Coyote. All of a sudden, she began to take a little more time over her appearance. Her chestnut hair shone a little brighter and her eyes sparkled a lot more than they used to. Elisha noticed the difference immediately and once she noticed that Karter Swann was the reason for her sister's change of heart, the trouble began.

'Did you see him?' asked Betty.

'Who,' replied Elisha.

'That man.'

'What man?' said Elisha, looking around behind her.

'No, in Georgette's, the weird one, looking through all those dresses? He was right next to you, you must have seen him,' said Betty, with a giggle.

Elisha linked her arm with Betty's as both of them waited at the edge of the pavement before crossing the street at the traffic lights. The two of them ambled across once the lights had changed in their favour and swung their orange bags beside them as they walked. As it had been Elisha's idea to come shopping, she was going to be the one picking a coffee shop too. It was going to be an easy choice. She had told her sister that another time Betty could organise a day when they could go out together and she could find somewhere for coffee or lunch. A surprise location, she had requested.

The sun was low in the cloudless sky. Its brightness flickered across their faces as it appeared and disappeared between the buildings making it difficult to see. They walked close to the buildings and underneath the canopies that jutted out from the front of the shops so as to avoid the worst of the glare until they reached *Beans,* Elisha's favourite coffee shop, which was situated just off the main road, in a secluded lane called The Brambles. Once inside Elisha told Betty to grab a table and mind the bags whilst she fetched the coffees from the counter. Two flat white coffees were ordered and prepared within just a few minutes and soon Elisha was sitting opposite Betty.

'Thanks,' said Betty, 'Did you then?'

'Did I what?'

'See that bloke looking at all the dresses?'

'Erm…I guess so,' said Elisha.

'I thought he looked dodgy,' said Betty.

'In what way…apart from the fact that he was looking through the dresses?'

'Well, how many men do you know who go out dress shopping for their wives?'

Elisha had to admit that she couldn't think of any.

'Did you see what he was wearing?' asked Betty.

'No wonder you haven't bought as many things as me, you spent all your time watching him.'

'No, it wasn't like that,' said Betty.

'Well, it sounds like it was to me. So, what was so interesting about what he was wearing then?' asked Elisha, as she stirred her coffee.

'Let's just say he was hardly dressed to come shopping.'

'What's that supposed to mean?' asked Elisha.

'He looked like he had just walked off a building site.'

'He didn't. Anyway, so what! Perhaps he had,' said Elisha.

'It's a wonder you didn't get covered in dust.'

'Dust?'

'Yeah. His boots were leaving footprints all up and down the shop.'

'Well, I didn't notice. Not as much as you, obviously,' said Elisha, beginning to disbelieve the whole thing.

'What would a man be doing buying women's clothes, anyway?'

'I'm sure his wife was in the shop somewhere. Maybe he was going to treat her and didn't want her to see what he was looking at,' said Elisha, taking a sip from her coffee cup.

'Well, I can't believe you didn't notice. He was right next to you when you were trying to decide between that dress with the flowers and the plain one. He was watching you when you were trying on that leather jacket too. Gave you a right stare, he did. You must have had your eyes shut not to notice him and his boots,' said Betty.

'Why are you so interested in him and his boots?'

'Well, they were filthy. Fancy coming into a shop like that and treading cement dust all over the place.'

Elisha shook her head at her sister in exasperation and sighed out loud. Betty looked at Elisha briefly but decided to take the hint and drop the subject of the man who was looking at the ladies garments and leaving grey powdery residue everywhere he trod. She had to concede that it probably wasn't worth worrying about. However, something else that had been on Betty's mind recently, was. Karter Swann. *Monster or not,* she kept wondering. Betty tried to let it go but something kept rushing this dilemma to the forefront of her thoughts. For days, ever since she had established where he was living, she couldn't shake off the thoughts. Betty couldn't help thinking that something was wrong with the way it all ended with him, and yet, her mind plagued her with reminders that she was doing the right thing. *He tried to rape her sister...Didn't he?* She was over him...until she saw him again. And like the dregs having been stirred up from the bottom of a muddy pond, thoughts of how there must be some mistake kept on surfacing. On the night that she had opened up to Elisha about having spotted him, or at least believing that she had before getting the confirmation she desired by following him to his house, she had been trying very hard to conceal her innermost thoughts. On the one hand she considered him to be a monster and yet on the other she knew that a distant candle was still flickering away in her heart. That and a lingering, niggling doubt. She went from hating herself for it to almost acknowledging that her only hope is to yield to her emotional torment. So many times, since accepting that he was not dead, she had re-run the events of that day at Elisha's house when she had received the call and driven at a ridiculous speed through the traffic to her sister's side, finding her bloody and stressed.

'Penny for 'em,' said Elisha.

'What?'

'Your thoughts. Penny for 'em. You haven't heard a word I've said, have you?' she said.

Betty realised that Elisha's coffee cup was empty and began to play catch up. She downed the lukewarm mixture as Elisha began to pursue the reason for Betty's blank look.

'Still thinking about that bloke that you seem infatuated with?' asked Elisha.

Betty's eyes widened as her mind questioned how Elisha could know what she had been thinking about. *Could she possibly know that I had been parked outside his house in wait, hoping to see him?*

'No, no, nothing like that,' she said defensively.

'What then? Must be something interesting,' asked Elisha.

Betty had not been the only one of them that had been thinking about Karter Swann. Ever since Elisha had learned of his address from Betty, she had been plotting and scheming about what to do with this especially useful information. As far as Elisha knew, Betty was not concerned with him anymore, which left the door wide open to her. She had driven by the house on more than one occasion, intrigued as to whether it was really him, but had not seen him yet. *Maybe it was time for that to change. Maybe it was time to force him out.* If Elisha was going to finally get her man, then she would have to make her move soon, just in case he should happen to move on and disappear from her sinister radar.

'Well?' said Elisha.

'Oh, nothing really…just…'

'Just what?'

Betty pushed her coffee cup towards the centre of the table and placed the two saucers on top of one another. Then she put the two cups on top, one inside the other. She looked up at Elisha and made an exaggerated sigh. *It can't do any harm to find out what she's thinking.*

'Have you thought anymore about Karter? About him being around?' asked Betty, tentatively.

Elisha sat back in her chair and started straight at her sister. *Surely, she doesn't know that I've been driving by his house.*

'No, have you?' replied Elisha.

'No.'

'You must have, otherwise you wouldn't ask,' said Elisha.

'Ok, so I have. But I was only thinking of you. I just don't want you to…'

'Thinking of me?' interrupted Elisha, 'Sounds to me like you've been thinking about *him*.'

A stony silence ensued for at least half a minute. Betty was sure that Elisha would still be horrified at the thought of him ever getting close to her again, after what happened but the feelings that Betty had inside were becoming intense and whilst she did not want to upset her sister, she was finding it hard to just ignore them completely. Betty had been wondering that if she spoke to Elisha on neutral ground then she might be able to make her understand that her longing for him had not gone away, even after everything. It was a big risk.

'I *have* been thinking about him,' said Betty.

Elisha's mind began to evoke all sorts of scenarios but ultimately, she knew that she could not let this happen. She knew that if Betty got to Karter before she did, that she just might be able to win him over. *Would she believe his story about what happened at the Travelodge? Would he be able to convince her about what really happened to Betty's phone and why her car had become a crucial part in Elisha's plan?* Elisha was convinced that Betty hated him and that she would never accept his account of what went on, especially as Elisha had played her part so well the following day. But, if she loved him, there could be a chance that she might believe him still. After all, what went on the day before the events at her house just might make a lot of sense to Betty, and if she accepted his story about the Travelodge then she would be likely to see through Elisha's act at her house. She could not take that risk. One way or another Elisha was determined that it was going to be her that wins his heart. She needed a plan to ensure that Betty would not be a stumbling block for her.

Whatever it takes.

'Well, you can just stop then. He tried to rape me. He beat me. You saw what he did,' she said.

Betty felt the eyes of the people sitting nearby upon them. She glanced sideways and gave an awkward, almost apologetic smile. Elisha had been too loud for Betty's liking, and she had seen her sister in this mood before. Once Elisha got riled, she took some calming down. It was like throwing a switch. Betty remembered only too well how Elisha had behaved on one occasion when she got into a fight at the college. Except it wasn't with a girl, it was with a boy. He had been tormenting one of Elisha's classmates for a few days, a girl that Betty didn't consider to be a true friend of Elisha's, but she still came to her rescue and faced the boy head on outside after the classes had finished for the day. The last thing Betty can remember the boy doing was smiling at Elisha and mocking her for being a girl. He was putting on a show for his mates who were all giggling at his act of bravado and his efforts at continuing to try to make Elisha look feeble. Betty's next clear recollection was how she startled when Elisha hit the boy full in the face, sending blood and fragments of teeth across the sidewalk. But that wasn't the worst of it. Betty never forgot the degree of rage and savagery she witnessed on Elisha's face as she mercilessly punched and kicked the boy until he was all but unconscious. Despite Betty's cries for Elisha to stop, the ruthless onslaught continued. Those watching began to gradually fall silent and step away, creating a sinister feel to the whole episode. Every punch could be heard as it landed on the unfortunate boy's face and body. Thankfully, a passer-by intervened and pulled Elisha off the stricken boy. She had his blood all over her hands and on her shirtsleeves. There was even blood spatter on her face.

'Anyhow, if you hate him for what he did then why would you even think about him? I thought you hated him as much as I do. I thought we were together on this one. I remember that you said that we were going to make him pay,' said Elisha; hands now flat on the table, body leaning in towards Betty, eyes as cold as diamonds.

'We are together,' said Betty, doubting her own words.

'Then we need to finish this,' said Elisha, in a much more controlled, muted tone.

'What do you mean?' asked Betty, in a whisper, almost fearful of the response.

'We need to finish him; for good.'

It was time to go. Time to bring an end to the conversation. Betty rose from her chair, without another word, grabbing a handful of bags as she did so, and began to make her way for the front door of *Beans*. Elisha followed with her bags. Outside the two of them walked away from *Beans* as if nothing had happened, but Betty had received the message loud and clear. The question on Betty's mind was what to do about it.

Whatever it takes, was the answer.

FORTY-TWO

Eden Prairie, Minnesota.

When Ken Toft opened the door, he was surprised to see the uniform of a Minneapolis Patrol Officer standing on his porch. He didn't recognise the man in front of him. Over the years, he had gotten used to seeing a number of Officers at the scenes of several missing persons locations, but they didn't usually turn up at his door. He tended to meet the same old faces and had, in the past, become quite familiar with many of them, but not this one. This one was a new face to him.

Toft was dressed in a green and black check shirt and faded blue jeans. He didn't have anything on his feet. He stood at about 5 foot 3 inches, considerably smaller than his visitor. Toft looked Gregory Bonner up and down and as if he was inspecting his dress and was about to speak when Bonner piped up ahead of him.

'Good afternoon, Sir. My name is Gregory Bonner. Am I speaking to Ken Toft?'

It was established that he was and soon after Bonner informed Toft that he had come straight from MinnSARDA, the search and rescue dog association, he was invited inside Toft's home. The property gave the impression of being a warm and cosy type of house. The furnishings were mostly of dark oak and were complimented by a large dark leather three-seated chesterfield. The upholstered armrests gave it a sturdy appearance and Bonner immediately began to imagine just how good it would look in his den, providing that he could actually fit it in there. Two matching tables stood at either end of the couch, like book ends, and each had an elegant reading lamp sat on them. A low-level coffee table sat in the centre of the room with a generously stocked wooden fruit bowl on it. Bonner noticed his reflection in a large mirror with a wooden surround that was situated on the wall above the chesterfield. As Toft offered him a seat, he asked Bonner whether he would like some coffee that he had heating up in the kitchen. Bonner had smelt the inviting aroma as soon as he stepped inside the house and gratefully accepted.

While Ken Toft was out of the room, Bonner checked his phone for any messages from the station, specifically from Captain Antonio

Rodrigues. There were none. Bonner allowed himself a little smirk in regard to his moral victory earlier today and nodded to himself with a certain amount of satisfaction. *All quiet from Big Toni*, he thought, although he did wonder what sort of mood the disgruntled Captain might be in when he returned.

Looking around the room, Bonner noticed a large plant in a white ceramic pot that seemed to be happily climbing up the doorframe to his right. Bonner's knowledge of plants was limited to whether it was big or small or green or had flowers; the names of which were a mystery to him. This one was big and green and that was all he knew. To left and right of him were large single-seat chairs in the same leather as the chesterfield. There were no magazines on the coffee table or underneath it, in fact nothing looked out of place at all. Opposite where Bonner sat was a dresser or bureau made from dark-stained oak. It had multiple parallel horizontal drawers stacked one above the other. On top of the impressive piece of furniture was a photo frame. It was a picture of two dogs that Bonner reasoned were owned or once owned by Ken Toft. He rose from the irresistible comfort of the chesterfield to take a closer look. Bonner picked up the frame and began to study the photo within. He assumed that the photo had been taken outside in the garden of Toft's house. He could see a neatly kept lawn with a backdrop of a large shrub of some kind. Not that Bonner recognised it, of course.

'Ah, you've found Hansel and Gretel', said Ken toft as he re-entered the room with two steaming mugs of delightfully smelling coffee.

'Er... yes, I guess so,' said Bonner.

'Well, just like the fairy tale, they were found in a forest, except my house isn't made out of gingerbread. I think the pair of them would have eaten it all long ago. Anyway, I was out on a training mission with a fellow dog handler and there they were. I couldn't believe what I was seeing. Two beautiful puppies abandoned in the wilderness. It was only by chance that I found them. Actually, I didn't, it was my dog, Susie, that found them. She's gone now, sadly, but she was on the ball that day. I had sent her into a bit of a thicket to have a sniff around and when she didn't come out, I knew something was up right away. For Susie not to come when I called her was unheard of. Anyhow, I decided to take a look to see what was keeping her when I saw her indicating. You know what I mean by that?'

'Yes, like she wanted to tell you that she had found something,' said Bonner.

'That's it. I can tell that your time at MinnSARDA wasn't wasted. Well, Susie was one of those dogs that held her position, almost as if she had been frozen in time. Some bark but not Susie, she just froze in close proximity with her nose aiming straight at the object, inches away. So, I looked and there were two little heads peeking out of a suitcase. I reckon somebody had left it very slightly open so that the dogs could breathe or something like that. I was horrified.'

'I bet you were. What happened?' asked Bonner.

'I carried the case, with the dogs still in it, to my car and put them in the rear. I couldn't leave them there now, could I?'

'No, not really. Did anybody ever claim the dogs?'

'Never. The local police never heard a word from anyone. They put the word out, but they got no responses whatsoever. I have to admit that I was rather pleased about that. I'd taken a liking to the little guys. Rather than them be sent to a dog pound, they let me keep them here. I'm sure that they weren't supposed to, but I knew a couple of the officers and, well, because of my knowledge of how to care for dogs, they fixed it for me,' explained Toft.

'Lucky for you and the dogs. Are they still around?' asked Bonner.

'Yes, they're outside. Both are in retirement from the search and rescue game nowadays. I don't allow them into the house, you understand. I don't think the leather would last long, do you?' joked Toft.

'No, I don't think it would. Do you have a dog that you still use, Mr Toft?'

'A dog? Yes, absolutely. I couldn't be without one. I don't go out as much as I used to, but I still have one. He's outside, of course, round the back of the kennels. There wasn't room for three in one kennel, so I had to build a new one.'

'What's his name?' asked Bonner.

'I called him Leo. When he was younger, his eyes reminded me of that of a lion. I never changed it because it seemed to fit after a while.'

Toft and Bonner sat, and Bonner began to enjoy the coffee. It was much more pleasant than the coffee he had been offered by Derek Grant. Toft continued to tell Bonner about how Hansel and Gretel had become search and rescue dogs and how successful they had turned out to be. After another round of stories about Hansel and Gretel and their exploits, Bonner decided to try to turn the conversation back to the reason that he was here.

'So, Mr Toft, as I said I have been to MinnSARDA this morning and when I was there, I had a chat with a man called Derek Grant and...'

'Ah, yes, I know Derek.'

'Well, it was him that suggested that I might like to speak with you about an incident that I am re-investigating. It's a bit of an old case but he told me that you were there at the time and so...here I am,' said Bonner.

'An old case? Crickey! Don't know if I can help you. The old memory isn't what it used to be,' laughed Ken Toft.

'I'm sure you'll be fine, Mr Toft.'

'Call me Ken, young man. Much more friendly,' he said.

'I will. Thank you. So, if you don't mind, I'd like to ask you about a case that occurred back in 2010.'

'2010, you say,' said Toft with an element of surprise in his voice.

'Yes Sir...er, Ken. To be precise this particular girl went missing on the morning of April 26th. She was on her way to her friend's house, I believe, and she didn't arrive. She was 17 years old at the time of her disappearance. I've spoken with her mother and told her that the case is being re-opened.'

'Why?' said Toft.

'Well, Sir...Ken, it's actually just by chance that this case cropped up when I was asked to check on some of the information that was held about several missing persons on the MUPC. That's...'

'I know what it is. I've looked on that site myself over the years. I have to admit, I found it quite intriguing,' interrupted Toft.

'Yeah, that's one word for it. However, as I said it just came up by chance and I was assigned to it by my Captain. I didn't know whether there was likely to be any good to come from it but I, kind of had to do it.'

'Had to do it? What do you mean?' asked Toft.

'I knew her, when I was at college. She was, well, a girl that I liked a lot before I was doing this for a living.'

'Gosh. Ok, well, I will try to help you where I can, but I don't know how you're going to find her, to be honest. That's a long time for her to be missing and then the outcome isn't usually too favourable in such cases. Didn't the team search for her back in the day?' said Toft.

'They did, Ken, and that's why I want to talk to you specifically. Yes, there was a search team from MinnSARDA that were deployed to find her, but they drew a blank. It's just that...' said Bonner, hesitating.

'Yes?' said Toft.

'Well, Ken, I think there was a mistake. I think they missed something.'

Toft sat upright and took a good look at Bonner. He put his coffee mug down onto the coffee table and scratched his head. Bonner did not speak. He decided to wait to see what Toft had to say. What he expected was for Toft to defend the search and rescue team in a similar way that Derek Grant had. He knew how proud these people were of the standard of the work that they did, and he had a fair understanding of the detail that went into their searches, as well as the training for both the dogs and the handlers. He had witnessed the impressive set up at Elk River, Sherburne County too. MinnSARDA set a high standard and Bonner knew that Toft, just like all the other volunteers, would be ready to uphold the reputation of the teams that had been produced over the years. He wasn't wrong.

'Mistake? Are you kidding me?' replied Toft.

'No, Ken. With the greatest of respect, I think that something may have been missed on this occasion. I know it seems unlikely, but I cannot help thinking that there's something wrong here. I am sorry, I don't mean to be disrespectful. I know how good you guys are at this stuff, but I can't…,' said Bonner.

'What? You can't stand the thought of this girl being taken…because she was your friend? Let me tell you, young man, when you've seen the things that I've seen on these sorts of jobs, it leaves little to the imagination as to what can happen in these cases. I'm not saying that any harm came to her but if the team were there at the time, then I'm sure something would have turned up. She must have been taken away in a car or some other vehicle, far from that area. Or maybe she ran away from home, a lot do that, you know.' said Toft.

Bonner had got the response he expected. The case for the defence. He sat and considered what Toft had said but as hard as he had tried, he could not force himself to accept that she had just vanished into thin air, without a trace. Nothing. Nothing at all.

'She had a good and stable family life, so I have no reason to think that she just ran away. Anyhow, her mother was positive that she was on her way to her friend's house and that's what I believe too. I take it you were there, just as Derek Grant said?' asked Bonner.

'I think so. At least the date matches with the time that I was working for MinnSARDA, and if Derek says that I was there then I will not argue,' said Toft.

'Do you remember which dog you would have been working with at the time?' asked Bonner.

'Yes, easily. That would have been Gretel. Hansel was active too, but I tended to use Gretel a little more. She was still a youngster then, but she was one of the best I have ever worked with. Maybe even on a par with Susie.'

'Do you remember being at the Nelson house?' asked Bonner, who was now digging a bit deeper.

'I think so,' replied Toft with a kind of uncertainty.

'So, you do remember the incident then? After all, I only gave you the date,' said Bonner.

'Look, would you like anymore coffee? I've got plenty in the pot. I can fetch some more if you want.'

Before Bonner could answer, Toft had leapt up and made his way into the kitchen. Bonner heard Toft switch on the coffee pot and sat pondering at the way in which Toft appeared to stall a little when he asked him about the Nelson house. Bonner closed his eyes and imagined Caterina turning up at Betty's house, but he could not picture her going inside because nobody had seen her or heard a word from her. Sometimes he was not exactly sure why the images of her appeared to him with such clarity. He would sit in his den at home and imagine her sitting beside him, trying to tell him where she was. His imagination would conjure up ghostly images of her as he drove through Golden Valley and then on other occasions, he would even consider telling Big Toni that it was hopeless. Bonner snapped out of his trance when Toft returned with more coffee and placed the mugs on the coffee table in the centre of the room.

'There you go,' he said.

'Thanks,' said Bonner.

The conversation that followed generally consisted of Bonner talking about the search that took place at the Nelson house and Toft talking about his dogs. Bonner felt that he didn't need to push too hard straightaway because he had a trick up his sleeve that only came to him as he had been drinking his second mugful. It would all be in the timing. Once the coffee had been consumed by them both, Bonner began to set up his plan.

'How did Gretel used to indicate to you, Ken?' asked Bonner.

'Gretel? She was another quiet dog. Like Susie. The team can train their dogs to indicate in ways that suit them. When they are trained from such a young age you can get them to behave exactly how you want. Gretel would lie down as if she were guarding the find. She would stay motionless, and then I would know that she had found something. Obviously, I would keep her in view the whole time.'

'And did she? When you were at the Nelson residence, I mean?'

Toft looked a little uncomfortable, just like before and so Bonner prompted him.

'Ken?'

'Erm…I'm just trying to remember what happened on that day. Long time ago now.'

'Well, you've remembered just about everything about the dogs. Where they were found, the training they had, the way they indicated to you. And you knew that I was speaking about the Nelson residence. So, what about this one? What about the way that Gretel indicated at the Nelson residence?'

'Well, she was very good and if there was anything to find, she would find it,' he said.

'What did she find, Ken?' asked Bonner.

Toft looked around the room, and everywhere except straight at Gregory Bonner who was reaching into his jacket pocket. Toft watched him as he brought out a piece of paper, unfolded it and turned it to face Toft. It was a scale drawing of the Nelson residence and the gardens. The impressive house sat in the centre of the grounds and the boundaries were clearly marked out. It was obviously the Nelson place, and Toft could see it. He looked at the drawing and then finally looked at Bonner.

'So?' he said.

'So, Ken. Where did she indicate? How about you point a finger at the spot for me,' said Bonner.

Toft began to hold out a finger but hesitated. He was uncertain about something on the drawing. The same something that Bonner had purposely left out.

'The shed's not there,' he said.

'Is that where she indicated, Ken?'

'Well…the indication was compromised,' he said.

'What does that mean, Ken?' asked Bonner.

'It means that there was another influence in the vicinity that interfered with the indication,' explained Toft.

'And what would that have been, Ken?' Bonner continued to use his name at the end of each sentence to keep the pressure on his host.

'The shed was the problem,' he said.

'And how did that make a difference, Ken?' asked Bonner.

'Gretel…'

'Yes, go on, Ken.'

'Well, she was put off by the shed. You see, the previous evening Mr Nelson's dog had died, and he had put him in the shed before he buried him. I think that Gretel was indicating at the old dog,' said Toft, looking up at Bonner for approval.

'And where was the old dog on that day, Ken?'

'He was buried…next to the shed. I think she became confused and so I had to declare the indication void.'

'Oh dear, Ken. How embarrassing for you and Gretel,' said Bonner, with a certain amount of condescension.

'And there was the odour. Wade, Mr Nelson, had used some acid on the grave to help to dissolve the old dog and accelerate the decomposition of the body so that the foxes stayed away.'

'Acid, Ken?'

'Yes, he used it to clean metal in his shed. Sort of a hobby for him. Don't ask me why, but that's what he did. It was sulphuric acid. He always kept a 25-litre drum of the stuff in his shed. It was known as oil of vitriol, dreadful stuff. He told me that he had poured some over old Hastings and then watered the grave with the hose to cause an exothermic reaction, you know, to cause heat and make the process take place faster,' said Toft.

'Were you good friends with Mr Nelson, Ken?'

'I knew him.'

'First name terms?'

'Yes, I guess so.'

'So, what happened about the indication at the shed, Ken? Did you follow it up? Surely you would have had to double check, you know, just in case. After all you would never leave anything to chance, would you Ken?'

'No, that's true. I wouldn't,' he said.

'So?' said Bonner.

'Well, the next thing to do was to put Gretel back in my van. As far as I was concerned, she had done her job and I was sure that there was nothing to find here. Then I asked Wade if I could take a look in his shed.'

'Go on, Ken. I'm listening.'

'When I looked, I noticed that there were new floorboards and so I asked him when they were put down and why he had changed them. He told me that he had spilt some of the acid and that it had burned into the floor, so he had replaced the damaged boards. He said that every time he stepped into the shed, he could smell the stuff. That sounded plausible to me, so I didn't doubt him.'

'So, you didn't lift the boards?' asked Bonner.

Toft looked straight ahead and simply shook his head, 'No. No need. I could trust Wade.'

'Really?' said Bonner, 'What made you so sure that he hadn't put the girl under the boards of his shed?'

Toft turned sharply to Bonner and said, 'Because Gretel would have found her, that's why. Are you suggesting that Wade killed the girl and stuck her under the floorboards?'

'Did you check Hastings' grave, Ken?' asked Bonner.

'What? No. She didn't indicate at the grave. I would have known if she had found anything.'

'So you have said. But you said that she did indicate, and that the indication was compromised,' said Bonner.

'Gretel was confused from the odour of the sulphuric acid and the fact that old Hastings had been placed in the shed and was now in the grave. These factors compromised the indication. Look, I've already explained this to you,' said Toft.

Bonner wasn't happy. And yet in a bizarre and curious way, he was. *A mistake*, he thought. He laid the drawing of the Nelson residence flat on the coffee table and asked Toft to point to the precise spot where Gretel was laying down when she, apparently, indicated.

'Ok, Ken. One more thing. Show me on this drawing where the exact spot was that Gretel was laying down. Imagine the shed is on the drawing, in fact, I'll draw it on for you. There, that's close enough. Now put a cross on the spot, Ken, and be careful, I want to know the *exact* spot.'

Bonner was adamant that he knew precisely where the shed should have been on the drawing. He knew its exact position in relation to the corner of the property that led into the rear garden. After all, he had been to the house numerous times over the years. Toft looked at Bonner and paused for a moment before taking the pen from Bonner. He held his hand above the drawing and looked at it. Toft sighed, still pondering where to put the cross.

'Ken? The exact spot in relation to the shed, please,' said Bonner.

Then he drew it. Bonner took the pen from him and put it back into his jacket pocket. He folded the drawing and placed it in his jacket without making any reference to it. Out on the front porch, Bonner thanked Ken Toft for his time and assistance in the matter. The men exchanged the usual pleasantries and Bonner turned towards the street, before stopping and turning to Ken Toft.

'Oh, just one more thing, Ken.'

'I don't think I can help you anymore, I don't remember anything else,' Toft said.

'The girl,' said Bonner.

'What about her?'

'Her name is Caterina Marks. You never asked me. Maybe you remembered after all.'

Bonner left Ken Toft motionless at his front door and walked slowly away towards his Patrol Car. Inside the car, he took the folded drawing from inside his jacket and opened it up. Bonner studied the point where Toft had placed the cross. There was the shed and there was the cross. Not as close together as Bonner might have expected if Gretel was indicating at the shed. He felt that she would have been right up to it, closer than the drawing showed. He remembered how Toft had described the way in which Susie had indicated at the suitcase where Hansel and Gretel had been so cruelly left. *Nose pointing right at it, inches away.* Bonner could clearly recall the location of Hastings' grave, especially as he had such a precise recollection of seeing Big Toni flat out in the snow on the evening that they found Wade Nelson, frozen, beneath the rear balcony. He had no reason to assume that Ken Toft would train his dogs any differently. He couldn't be absolutely sure, but if Susie was trained to indicate in a particular way, then surely, Hansel and Gretel would be no different. A trait of Ken Toft's dogs. Bonner carefully positioned his forefinger on the spot where Hastings' grave was found in relation to the shed. He allowed himself a satisfying nod. He could not swear to being unquestionably accurate, but he was as certain as he could be that all these years later, he had just taken a huge step closer to finding his friend, Caterina Marks. Now all he had to do was prove it.

FORTY-THREE

Old Clapton Street Police Station

Had Claudia De Luca not volunteered to have a sample of her DNA taken during an investigation into a fatal assault by a group of girls at the gymnasium that she regularly frequented a mile from her home in Tivoli in order to eliminate her from suspicion, she may never have become a match on the database. When the details of the match arrived at Old Clapton Street, DI Marc Sutton was not in his office. He was attending a monthly meeting of the Resident's Association that had been formed by a number of the local people to discuss and address a variety of local issues and concerns. One such concern was the recent troubles that had been taking place at the fairground where the girls had reported their assaults. This morning, Sutton found himself under fire from several irate members of the local community that wanted the fairground shut down and moved away from their park. It had been DCI Blackery that had agreed to support the request from the Chairman of the local Council that the fairground should establish itself on the park as it had for a number of previous years, without incident. The previous applications had never met with any resentment, and it appeared to be a simple matter of authorising the current one, as Blackery had done. This time, however, events had turned rather sour.

Sutton's task of placating the vociferous audience was not as simple as he would have liked. He knew that the removal of the fairground would not be as straightforward as it appeared to be from the residents point of view. Sutton was well aware of Blackery's personal association with the Chairman of the Council which meant that its removal would become challenged at every turn, culminating in it staying until the current licence ran its course in just another ten days. Ten days that could not come fast enough for DI Marc Sutton. He too had had enough of the attacks on the girls. The fact that the fairground would vacate its present location in the foreseeable future was the straw that Sutton was prepared to clutch to in order for him to buy just a little more time in the hope that no more unsavoury incidences took place in the dark hours at the park. His promise of providing extra Policing after 6pm each evening seemed to just about do enough to calm the mood in the Assembly Room, adjacent to the Town Hall. The building had been the home to many bouts of wrestling that were extremely popular in the 1960's and 70's. Twice weekly, the crowds would gather and vent their anger towards their favourite grappling mat performers. The added incentive of the contests being televised on Saturday afternoons, would regularly ensure that the large room was filled with excitable and sometimes mercurial audiences, depending upon whether their preferred gladiatorial hero appeared to be winning or losing. Echoes of the atmospheric old days of grunts and groans seemed to be aimed mercilessly at DI Marc Sutton, much to his dislike.

When Sutton left the meeting, he felt as though his pyrrhic victory was as much as he could expect, given the tension in the room. The inevitable reputational damage to the Police, as a consequence of him making the promise of extra Policing; a promise he was not entirely confident of fulfilling, felt tantamount to defeat. Sutton was pleased to be out of there. Now he could reach for his phone and try to establish why he had received four text messages: one from Grace and three others plus a voicemail, each from DS Carrie Linton. He pressed the quick dial button with one hand and the key fob to unlock the Subaru with the other, without reading the messages first. Carrie picked up on the first ring.

'Marc,' she said.

'Hi, what's up?' he responded.

'Good news, for a change. The DNA results are back, and they confirm that the girl found in the Cut is Claudia De Luca,' she said.

'Wow,' said Sutton, a little taken aback, 'Well done. You were right about the Italian connection.'

'It seems so,' she said.

'Ok, look, I'm on my way back to the station. Where are you right now?'

'I'm with Grace,' she said, as if it was the most normal thing ever.

'With Grace?'

'Yes. Remember? She told you I was coming round this morning. It's her day off and I'm not supposed to be in until two, so we are having a bit of girly time together. Honestly, you never listen,' she said.

Sutton could hear Grace laughing in the background.

'Right. So how did you know about the results?' he asked.

'Steve Kingham called me.'

'Why didn't he call me?'

'You have to ask? I had to leave three messages and a voicemail, that I assume you haven't listened to, as it is,' said Carrie.

'Ok, fair point. Carrie. I need you back at the station. I'll make it up to you.'

'You never say that to me, Detective,' shouted Grace, leaning her head against Carrie's, as she burst into more laughter.

Sutton knew better than to try to match his wit against Grace and Carrie when they were in this mood. They were a formidable team once they got going. He started up the Subaru, never tiring of the throaty rumble of its engine, and pulled out into the traffic to begin his relatively short journey back to Old Clapton Street.

'I'm sorry, darling,' said Carrie, 'but I'm going to have to go. We'll catch up soon, yeah?'

'Don't worry, I'm used to it after all the years. Better than it used to be though. There was a time when I never knew when I was going to see him or for how long,' said Grace.

Back at the station, DI Marc Sutton pulled into the station yard at precisely the same time as DS Carrie Linton. Each of them acknowledging the other with a nod through the car window as they arrived. Once parked they made their way into the station; Carrie following Sutton up the stairs and into his office. As Sutton closed the door, DC Steve Kingham opened it and entered the room carrying a folder that contained the details of the DNA database profile match that confirmed that the unfortunate girl was indeed Claudia De Luca.

'Right, all here,' said Sutton, as he sat behind his desk.

'These are the results from the database,' said Kingham, placing an open folder in front of DI Sutton who studied the findings whilst Carrie and Kingham sat patiently.

'Ok,' said Sutton, as he closed the folder in front of him, 'Now we know who she is.'

'Yeah, but we're not any closer to knowing why it was her that we found,' said Carrie.

'Unless she was just selected at random. Maybe there isn't a 'why',' said Kingham.

'It does appear to be the case. Currently we don't have anything to indicate otherwise,' said Carrie.

'What we do know is that both Haley Breen and Claudia De Luca were subjected to an injury on the back of their heads and a stab wound in their necks. Both had a piece of their hair removed at the back and both were wrapped in a white sheet, similar to a bedsheet. Both were found fairly easily and had not been at their locations for very long. Neither were sexually abused or physically beaten beyond the wound in their necks,' said Sutton.

'Both right side,' said Carrie.

'So, are we looking for a right-handed man, assuming he grabbed them from behind when he hit them on the back of the head?' said Kingham.

'That narrows it down to several million,' said Carrie, '90% are right-handed.'

'Who says he stabbed them when he caught them? He could easily have hit them to gain control and then transported them somewhere. The stab could have occurred later. Perhaps they were only wrapped up in the sheet after they were dead and before he was ready to dispose of them,' said Sutton.

'Has the analysis of the girls' clothing or the sheets shown anything?' asked Kingham.

'No, nothing that you wouldn't expect to find and no direct connection between them either, other than the obvious similarity,' replied Sutton.

'Whoever has done this has been very careful not to leave even the slightest trace at the scene and nothing turned up on the local cctv near the canal. There was nothing from the tyre tracks by the canal either. He probably dumped her upriver and she ended up next to the houseboats. Both crime scenes were contaminated by their surroundings. Anything that might have been useful was either washed out or destroyed by rats. What worries me is where Angelica Rowntree is. If she's still alive,' said Carrie.

'If she is still alive, we have to do everything we can to find her, so we're going to have to go over the search areas again in case we missed something. We'll pour what resources we have into this and hope that we can dig something up. Maybe a second look in the same places will turn up something that will give us a start. Steve, I want you to try to trace Karter Swann again. If he is alive after all, as Blackery believes, then someone will have crossed paths with him at some point. Use the photo we have of him and put the feelers out. Talk to your contacts out on the street, will you?' said Sutton.

'Of course, Guv.'

'Carrie, go over the people you spoke to before and reinterview if you have to. See whether Leana Turnbull recalls anything else about the man at Brady's and talk to Robin Greaves again. I'll organise some teams to revisit the places we looked before. Let's see what happens. I know it's a bit of a shot in the dark, but we have to keep trying.'

Kingham and Carrie stood and left the office, leaving Sutton at his desk feeling more empty than enthused.

FORTY-FOUR

Ahuja Industries, East London.

The weirdest thing for Angelica to work out was why she was still alive. She didn't mind the fact at all, of course, but she was becoming increasingly puzzled by it. Each day she woke, her first thought was that she was still here, still clutching grubby blankets, still cold and still wondering just how long this would go on for. She had been given fresh blankets on more than one occasion, had been fed regularly and had even had the luxury of toilet roll. Even the white sheet had been pulled off her and discarded to one side of where she sat, in her corner. Her arms and feet had been freed too since the plastic ties had been snipped off. *It's almost like he changed his mind,* she thought. The chain, however, remained. Her captor had still not spoken to her after all this time, aside from what she thought was a very spooky proposal of marriage. *Marry me.* They were the only words she has heard throughout this nightmare, and she couldn't even be certain of that. She was beginning to feel that she was going to be spared and yet she dare not believe it. *That girl. The sheet. The blood. Who was she?* These were the thoughts that repeatedly played on her mind, but she had no answers to them. Only a vivid memory of the reflection of the sheet that she saw in the broken mirror.

Not everything about her encounter had been unpredictable. The foxes were back. She could almost set her watch by them, if she had a watch, or her phone, if she had a phone, or if she even knew what day it was. Angelica actually thought that she recognised a difference in them, as if they had grown in the time that she had been here. *Maybe they had,* she thought. Dad was looking more dominant than she remembered from when she first set eyes on them and even Socks, Stripe and Speckles did not seem so small anymore. Their coats were lighter too; more golden. She liked the foxes, especially the little ones but even Mum had a lovely way about her; the way she nudged the little ones around as if to say *C'mon, time for bed.* They were Angelica's only companions after all. Sometimes she had managed to keep some food back and waited until they came by. She would throw a few scraps onto the dusty factory floor and watch them with interest as they became more and more confident of her being present on their territory. Angelica often worried that if the foxes didn't eat everything up, her captor might think that she didn't want the food and stop feeding her. Fortunately, the foxes were always hungry, especially Stripe. That one never left anything spare.

Since her worst fears of being prepared for death had passed, she started to become a little cockier when her food arrived at breakfast and dinnertime. Over the past two days Angelica had spoken to him; previously, she would have been too terrified to utter anything. She had ceased screaming and crying for mercy a while back once she realised that it was getting her nowhere. It was nothing much, but just enough to try to get him to speak. *Maybe I'll recognise the voice,* she thought. *Maybe he's not that stupid.*

Angelica reasoned that she did not have a lot to lose in trying to tempt him to speak. It was obvious that 'Good morning' and 'Good evening' had got her nowhere, save for a stern look from beneath the mask. She knew that she had to be careful so as not to upset him and make things worse for herself than they already were. She had recapped the situation she was in over and over in her mind. *I'm not injured, the bump on my head had gone. I'm not starving. I haven't been assaulted…yet. That girl has gone, I'm still here.* Angelica stopped short of thinking any further thoughts about the whereabouts of the girl in the sheet. That part of all this was too much to bear. *She's dead, I know it.*

When Angelica awoke earlier this morning, she had realised that she had come to terms with something, which caused a chill to run through her. Why she had not cried immediately when this thought entered her mind, also caused her some concern. She tried hard to accept why she had felt so comfortable with a thought that should have horrified her, but somehow didn't. She had to acknowledge that even her most precious memories were beginning to blur into obscurity, dampened by the overbearing reality of her desperate situation. Somehow, unbelievably, unforgivably, Angelica had not thought about her parents for days. She had not even dreamt about life outside of the cold and bare factory. She was beginning to forget what it was like to feel the warmth of the sun on her skin, to hear the birds sing, to feel the loving touch of people, and to see her friends. This dystopian world had become her home. She had even stopped hating the vile bucket that had been left for her to use as a toilet. She had, without realising the transition was happening, accepted her fate and no longer felt the urge to fight back, at least not physically. Her prison was beginning to feel normal. Too normal. *I'm never getting out of here,* she thought.

When her breakfast arrived, Angelica had not even heard the scraping of the metal gate that signified that he was coming. She was wrapped in her blankets like a desert dwelling Bedouin, with her head down as if to protect her face from the inexorable sting of needle-like sand blowing across the desert. When she heard a bag drop down onto the cold factory floor, she opened her eyes and peered up at her visitor with distaste. The bag had been placed right at the edge of her reach. Over the days, Angelica had made a semicircle in the dust which marked her territory. She had not done this on purpose, it was just that this was as far as she could go thanks to the chain that ensured she stayed captive. She would pace up and down the perimeter of her available space just to stop herself from becoming set in one place for too long. Her bones ached enough as it was. It created a boundary between her enforced surroundings and the rest of the factory, the rest of the world. Angelica did not move towards her meal as she had done on just about every other occasion since she had been here, picking the bag up or hooking it with her foot. She made no effort to retrieve the bag. It was a risk in case he took it back and left her with nothing, but she found herself in a state of insentience, numbed by the utterly depressing acknowledgement of her recent thoughts. She just stared. *C'mon you bastard, speak,* she thought.

He stood, perplexed that she had not moved immediately to claim her breakfast as she always had. He pointed at the bag. Angelica saw this as a positive gain in her new game. *I made him do something that he didn't want to do,* she thought. She looked at him again, at risk of losing her meal. Slowly, she drew one arm out from the confines of the blanket and, with one hand and a raise of her eyebrows, beckoned him to bring it to her. To step inside the arc, into her world. A ten second stalemate followed, culminating in him pointing at the bag again. Angelica beckoned him forward again and waited for his reaction. After only a couple of seconds, he drew his foot back as if in preparation to kick the bag towards her.

'No,' she said, 'I'll get it.'

What Angelica had in mind frightened her, but she felt that unless she tried to break the sequence of events that had become the new normal for her, she may never get the opportunity to find out who he is. Even then, she knew that she may not actually know him, but she was just hoping that the stories of the victims knowing their attackers might just be true. Angelica had learned that 80-90% of victims knew their attacker. That was high enough for her. Her sketchy plan was to try to establish who he is without him knowing it. If he became aware that she knew who he was then she felt that her life would definitely be in jeopardy. It would change the state of play completely. It was her plan to gain an advantage without him knowing, as difficult as that may be. Angelica unwrapped herself from the blanket and dropped it in her corner. Her clothes were so ingrained with cement dust that she was hardly able to distinguish the colours that she was wearing, and her hair was becoming knotted with filth. The last thing Angelica wanted to see was her reflection in a mirror, it would be too upsetting. Her appearance had become something that she had given up on many days ago. The once attractive Angelica Rowntree was closer to resembling a tramp.

She walked slowly towards the edge of her arc, dragging her chain along behind her with her eyes fixed on him. When she got within touching distance of the bag she stopped and looked down at it. Instead of picking it up as he fully expected her to do, she stood upright and looked at him hard again.

'Would you pass it to me, please?' she said, politely.

His head jolted up a little. Angelica had his attention.

'Please. My back hurts from sitting on this cold floor and I can't bend down very well. Could you lift it up for me?' she asked, 'Please.'

His eyes darted up and down from Angelica to the bag, as if he was considering what to do next. He bent a little but stopped, seemingly uncertain as to whether this was some kind of trap. Angelica knew that this was a pivotal moment. If she played it wrong now, he would be gone. So too would her breakfast and she would not have heard him speak. She needed something extra. She needed inspiration.

'Please,' she said, again, but it wasn't working.

He took a step back. Angelica was not sure whether he was going to kick the bag after all or simply begin to walk away. What came next was the flash of inspiration that she had been hoping for. She noticed the red and black rucksack on his back. She thought back to the time that she found herself wrapped in the white sheet. Her preparation for death. The words almost did not come out but then from somewhere she found a burst of adrenaline, and almost stuttered her request.

'Would you brush my hair for me? Please,' she said, quietly.

His head twisted around, his eyes almost burning into hers. Still, he did not speak. But a line had been crossed, Angelica could feel it. And for some reason she did not feel under threat. He nodded at the bag on the floor between them. Angelica remembered to feign her sore back and carefully picked up the bag containing her breakfast. She even let out a slight cry of pain as she did so. She walked slowly back towards her corner and to her surprise, he followed. He was inside her arc. He stood until she was down on the ground, taking no chances, before he knelt down slowly beside her. Angelica adopted the same position that she had before when he had sat her up against the wall. She had to trust her luck now. She turned her head away to her left so that he could see the back of her head. *Please don't hit me,* she thought. She heard him drop the rucksack down onto the ground and open the drawstring. *He's getting it.*

Angelica moved her left leg into a more comfortable position and could feel Iron bar beneath her blankets. *Nice to know you're there, but you're not much use to me right now.*

Angelica tried to control her fears and yet still flinched slightly when he touched her shoulder, just like he had before. His hand touched her head and then it began. *The brush. He's doing it,* she thought. Angelica immediately recognised a difference in the way he was brushing her hair this time. *He's being extra gentle,* she thought. Now she needed to be clever. She wanted to hear his voice. Angelica allowed the brushing to go on for a few minutes in order to create a calm atmosphere. *Am I really dictating this?* The brushed snagged every so often in her unkempt hair but she simply bit her lip each time so as not to stop him. Angelica slowly tilted her head as if to show that she was at ease with what he was doing. Each stroke of the brush actually made her feel more relaxed. It had been something that she had wanted to feel for so long, although she would rather it was not him that was doing it.

'You're very good at it,' she said, 'I wish you would do it for me every day.'

He stopped. Angelica froze slightly. Then he started again but it wasn't so gentle. There was something wrong. The brushing was becoming faster and catching in her hair more often than not. Angelica winced as the brush pulled at her hair. She was worried now. She could feel the blood pulsating through her veins in a panic. This was not a comfortable situation anymore. His actions had become frenzied.

'Stop, you're hurting me,' she cried, as the brush seemed to completely snag in her hair, 'Ouch! Stop it.'

Angelica blindly flung an arm around towards him, striking it against the side of his face. She gasped at what she had done and turned her gaze towards him. All she could see were a pair of eyes looking straight into hers. But there was something else. *Watery eyes? Was he crying?* Before Angelica could think of anything to say, he was up off his knees. She lifted her arm up to protect her face, fully expecting to find herself on the wrong end of his retaliation, but he was on his way. He trod clumsily over her legs as he got to his feet and scampered away from her into the factory, kicking up a cloud of dust as he went. Angelica could hear his footsteps becoming gradually softer and then as she heard the unmistakable scraping of the metal gate, she heard something else. He shouted. It was muffled and unclear, but she thought that she could decipher it. Angelica sat back against the wall and listened intently, in the hope that the factory would fall silent signifying that she was, once again, alone and relatively safe. All she could feel was her heart thudding in her chest. She tried to control her breathing and in two minutes she was calm again. Something touched her shoulder, making her jump, and as she turned her head, she could see it was the hairbrush, still dangling in her hair. She teased it out carefully and sat looking at it. Strands of her hair were trapped amongst the bristles, survivors of a traumatic experience.

Angelica listened again. It was quiet. He had gone. She looked down at the bag that contained her breakfast and began to untie the knot in the top of the bag. Angelica's survival instinct kicked in and she decided that she should eat in case he returned and took it away. She put a couple of pieces of bread under her blanket for the foxes and started on her meal. As usual, there was ham and tomatoes, cheese and a bottle of water. *Hope this isn't my last meal,* she thought.

As Angelica ate, she began to think about what it was that he had shouted as he arrived at the metal gate. It didn't take her long to recall the sound and to make sense of it. She had heard it before. *Marry me. No, it sounded more like 'Marry them'* she thought. Angelica pondered over this as she devoured her meal. She was hungry enough to have eaten the foxes share but she didn't. Even the scare of what had gone on this morning had not done anything to discourage her appetite. She knew that it was so important to keep her strength up, for what it was worth. Angelica felt the soreness on her shin where he had stumbled over her in his haste to get out. She pulled up the leg on her dirty jeans and could see a scrape on her shin. The skin was rucked a little and there was a spot of blood. *Not too bad, I've had worse.* Just another thing to remind her that she was still alive. She would keep it clean, as she had done with the cut on her hand, by using the bottled water.

That was the moment. *He spoke. He did. I didn't imagine it.* Angelica sat up and replayed the few seconds when he trod on her, just before the dust flew up. 'He said 'Sorry'. I'm certain of it,' she said out loud to herself. Angelica's head was suddenly filled with questions. Questions that she did not have the answers to. *They really were tears in his eyes,* she thought, *this is getting weirder.* She sat eating the rest of her breakfast and tapping the hairbrush lightly against the wall, trying to put a face to the voice that she had heard. Nothing was springing to mind. Then a glossy nose and a pair of bright eyes peered around the corner at her. The foxes were back. First, she recognised Mum and Socks, then Speckle. She knew that Dad and Stripe would not be far behind. 'Is it breakfast time?' she said.

FORTY-FIVE

Tilbury, East London.

'See you tomorrow night, Kevin. Same time?' said Ray Keller.

'Yeah, I'll be working again, so why not?' responded Karter Swann.

Keller closed the front door to the pub and locked it, giving it a firm push to ensure it was secure. He stood in the half-light and watched his new drinking companion wander towards the road before turning and heading in the same direction. The after-hours drink at the *Snare and Cymbals* had become a regular occurrence for the pair of them over the past couple of weeks. They had struck up a friendship of sorts; the first that Swann had allowed himself in a long time. Swann had crossed paths with Ray Keller on a couple of occasions, on his way back from the Riverside Centre, where he worked. Keller had explained that he worked late at a nearby factory that made screws and bolts. The men had got on well and it was Keller that first suggested they pop into the pub. Swann enjoyed Keller's company and felt that there was little to no chance of him establishing who Kevin Marshall really was. Keller, who was around the same age as Swann, had said that he used to work at the pub and had always claimed that he was related to the owner who allowed him to come in after closing time. Swann did not really fully understand what the arrangement was but decided that he could not be bothered to find out, provided that it remained discreet, and nobody poked their nose into it. He felt that he had seen Ray Keller around occasionally but could not place exactly whereabouts. He wondered whether he had some sort of connection with Odhran O'Connell and was keeping an eye on him but was not completely sure. Swann knew that ever since he had 'employed the services' of O'Connell, he would never be truly out of debt. One day O'Connell would reappear from some dark and sinister place to request a favour or two. He also knew that the return of a favour could turn out to be more expensive than actually paying him in cash.

Swann walked away from the pub, trying to avoid a tumble with the pub furniture that had been placed outside in the street, and into the night air. The wind was wafting a strange odour his way from somewhere down by the docks. The streetlights had been recently upgraded to the new LED version and had already switched off automatically as part of the new energy saving programme in the area. As he wandered past the rear of the nearby factories and towards the end of Brickhouse Street, he could see the lights from the floodlit warehousing, polluting the sky. When Swann reached the end of the street, he turned to look behind him, fully expecting to see Keller wandering along, but he was out of sight. Swann frowned, wondering how Keller had managed to apparently vanish in a street with no other obvious exits. He stood for a moment and studied the layout of Brickhouse Street. A single yellow line was visible at the edge of the cobbles. Swann peered into the darkness, still expecting Keller to emerge, but nothing moved apart from a cat that scampered swiftly across the cobbles of the old East London thoroughfare. Swann gave up on Keller, assuming that he must have gone back into the pub for some reason and carried on walking towards the removable black and yellow bollards that separated the old street from the main road, restricting access to anything wider than a bicycle.

Swann had never been much of a drinker, even during his time in Malia when the temptation was to let himself go. He had ample opportunity to get into drinking with the customers at the café or in any of the ubiquitous bars and other nightclubs along Beach Road, but he had always refrained. He would enjoy a moderate drink from time to time but tonight he had had more than his usual limit. He wasn't drunk, exactly, but he was looking forward to getting back to his room at the Turner's residence and curling up in bed. Half a mile later he turned the corner into Countess Street and made his way along to number 12. The Turners would be asleep, and Swann was always courteous. As he always did, when returning to the house late at night, he held the gate firmly to ensure that it didn't rattle, and quietly closed it before venturing towards the front door. He inserted his key into the lock at the second attempt and turned it slowly. Fortunately, the front door was not prone to creaking or making any noises that would penetrate the silence in the house. Nothing louder than Mr Turner's rumbling snore. Swann stepped into the property, opening the front door just enough to enable him to enter the hallway, and being careful not to knock into anything that the Turner's may have left unattended. He carefully closed the door and turned his key in the lock. At Mrs Turner's insistence, a spare key hung on a nail next to the door in case of an emergency at night.

When Swann looked down at the item that was laying on the doormat, he felt a familiar sensation as his heart skipped a beat. He looked at it for several seconds as if in denial of the knowledge that he knew precisely what he was likely to find inside the white envelope. This envelope was a little larger than the others had been. More like an A5 size. Swann shook his head and bent down to pick it up. He instinctively flipped it over in the improbable hope that the other side would show that it was addressed to Mr and Mrs Turner. It wasn't.

Swann sighed and quietly made his way up the stairs to his room, again wondering who had been responsible for posting these damned letters. Once inside, he flung the envelope onto his bed and put his coat over the back of a chair. The room was in darkness, but he could see a flickering light from the other side of the river from his window. To his right he could see the much brighter lighting from the Dartford Crossing; the Queen Elizabeth II Bridge, that stretched across the expanse of the River Thames. Swann sat down by the window and, all of a sudden, wished that he were still in the pub with Ray Keller. But he knew that nothing was going to change the situation. He turned to look at the envelope and decided that it could not wait until the morning. Swann knew that he wouldn't sleep until he knew what was lurking inside it. He picked it up, pulled the chair closer to the window, and sat. The moon was full, and its reflected light was just enough to assist him in reading. The combination of the tiredness and the alcohol made him feel wearier than usual and the apprehension associated with opening another envelope made him feel sick at what he might find inside. Swann tore one corner of the envelope and ran his finger along the seal, tearing it apart. Two items fell from it and dropped at his feet as he angrily screwed the envelope into a ball and discarded it onto his bed. Two photographs.

As Swann picked them up his eyes widened. He felt his heart jump. He stared at the images and saw that he was the prominent figure in both of the photos. Him and a girl in each one. It did not take him a second to recognise the décor of the Cactus and Coyote either. Puzzled by the reference, he double-checked the surroundings on the images. *Definitely the pub. What the hell?* He could clearly see himself, that part was unmistakeable, but didn't immediately recognise either of the girls at the bar. There were so many young girls that frequented the pub in those days that he couldn't usually distinguish one from another. Swann could see that he was wearing something familiar. It was the white capped-sleeve shirt that he often wore when he was working there. His tattoo was visible in both photos as he leaned forward and appeared to be in conversation with his customers. His hair was lighter than it was today, and he wasn't sporting any sign of the Cretan suntan. All that was still to come. Swann reflected that these were the days before he contacted Odhran O'Connell and committed himself to a rather bloodthirsty end to his life before being reborn into his new one. It felt as though he was looking at a man that he didn't even know. He had become so used to being Kevin Marshall that weirdly, his spurious identity sometimes confused even him. Having realised who the man in the images was, he turned his attention to the girls. Swann was grateful that there wasn't any evidence in the photographs of girls that were murdered or captured. That was one blessing. He glanced onto the bed and looked at the screwed-up envelope, double-checking that there was definitely no sordid typewritten note amongst the remains of it. There wasn't this time. He placed the photographs on the corner of the bed and studied the first of them.

The girl had dark hair with coloured beads that dangled against the side of her face. She was wearing a yellow cotton shirt, mostly unbuttoned. She had light blue denim shorts, probably some that she had cut herself from a pair of jeans going by the frayed edges. There was nothing visible on the photograph below her shorts. Swann gave up on that one for the moment and picked the second photograph from the corner of the bed. He could see a little more of this girl's face but not all of it. She also had dark hair and wore what Swann would call a summer frock, quite colourful and free flowing. He wondered whether that was the correct description of her clothing but decided that it didn't really matter. *Frock, dress. All the same to me,* he thought. He picked up the first photograph and held the pair of them side by side, switching his attention from one to the other, hoping to be able to make some reference as to who they were. Because he so often wore his white shirt, he couldn't really be sure whether the photographs were from the same night. Neither of the girls were visible in the other photograph. Swann looked at his tattoo in the images and wondered whether that was the reference he was looking for. In each photo, it was clearly visible, and he appeared to be in the centre of the image. *Tattoo,* he thought.

Swann dropped the two photographs onto the floor and looked towards the locked drawer, where he had previously placed the other images; the original ones from the Cactus and Coyote and the ones that had turned up at 12 Countess Street more recently. He stepped across the room to the drawer and forgetfully tried to open it. *Locked. The key,* he thought. He opened the kitchen cupboard, ferreted about behind a selection of jars and felt for the key that he had placed there. He put the key into the lock and opened the drawer. There was the collection of envelopes. Reluctantly, he picked them up and returned to his chair in the moonlight. It was only then that he appreciated that his hands were beginning to shake a little and that the adrenaline rush was stemming the tide of his tiredness. He leaned back against the backrest of the chair and took a long, deep breath and exhaled slowly. Concentrating on the photographs, he took them all from the envelopes and placed them on the corner of the bed, nearest him. He turned each of them face up and placed them in the order that he had received them. The Cactus and Coyote images were by far the most distressing of them all. In turn they reminded him of the ones that the Detective had shown him at the Police Station when he was accused of her murdering the stricken girl.

He gave another quick look at the two most recent and studied the two girls. Then he picked up the one of the white object, and knowing it would be of no use, placed it back on the bed. Next, he looked at the one of the girl sitting on her own in the dingy surroundings. The girl in the sweatshirt. He held her picture and compared it with tonight's Cactus and Coyote ones. There was a resemblance to one of the girls although it wasn't absolutely clear cut but there was something about her. He picked up the one of the other girl at the bar and compared it to the girl in the sweatshirt. *Definitely not her,* he thought. He turned his attention to the grim images that were sent to the Cactus and Coyote and looked hard at them both. 'Could be,' he mumbled to himself. After switching the photographs around and staring at them for the next few minutes he was able to conclude that the girl in the sweatshirt did look very much like one of the girls at the pub; the one in the dress, and that the other girl at the pub just might be the girl found murdered at the bus depot. *Both pictured with me.*

Swann's brain started to do the sums and the results were not good. Photographs of him with the two girls, his tattoo in full view. One dead with a nasty version of his tattoo scratched into her arm, another, who knows where, and then there was the object rolled in the white sheet with the blotch of blood on it. *Another girl. Another jagged tattoo? That had to be what the red mark was. Was that the girl that was found in the canal the other week?*

Swann gathered the photographs together and locked them away in the drawer. He replaced the key behind the jars in the cupboard and sat back down on the chair. His head was spinning. Somebody had not only found out where he was living but had come up with a plan to try to set him up for the murder or murders. Swann didn't want to take this to the police, he felt that this is just what this person wanted. Besides, he would have to explain his fake death too. Having already been arrested and questioned about the girl at the bus depot, he didn't feel that a repeat performance was going to go down well. They would say that the photographs were his souvenirs and if the girl that, at far as he knew, was unaccounted for, was to show up dead with a tattoo on her arm, it would become even worse for him. *There are probably two already,* he thought. The big Detective had already suggested that he had used a weapon to scratch his tattoo into her arm. If it wasn't for a solid alibi, Swann knew that he would have had a real job convincing them of his innocence. *You killed before then you faked your death, but you couldn't leave it, could you Swann? You had to come back and do it again. What have you done with the missing girl, Swann?* He cursed his tattoo again, the one that Betty had insisted upon.

Karter Swann laid down on the bed and stared up at the ceiling. So much was whizzing around his head but the biggest question of all was *Who?* He allowed his tormented mind to go through a short list of people. *Elisha? Betty? Surely not O'Connell. Ray Keller? Somebody else?* It didn't help and before many minutes had passed, Swann, still fully clothed, was asleep.

FORTY-SIX

The continuous flow of the local traffic rumbled past her, causing reflections to flicker across the windscreen of her car. Fortunately, the noise of the passing vehicles was muffled by the nearby trees and bushes, affording her a degree of peace. DS Carrie Linton was sitting in her car with a notepad on her knee and a few scribbled words written on it. She stared ahead, concentrating on nothing in particular and tapped her pen against the steering wheel in time with the song that was playing in her wireless earbuds. Twenty minutes earlier she had left home and driven to a quiet spot on the edge of Epping Forest. Hollow Pond was situated close to Whipp's Cross Hospital which was once utilised to treat wounded troops during both WW1 and WW2. Nowadays it boasts to be one of the busiest A&E departments in the country.

The ponds are sandwiched between Walthamstow and Leytonstone in London's east end and are popular as areas for picnicking and boating during the summer months. Carrie came here often as a child; so many memories were attached to it for her. Latterly it had become her favourite place to think and allow her mind to relax in order to make sense of the latest conundrum. Today should have been her day off but the way things were going she knew it was not very likely to pan out that way. The mystery that surrounded the whereabouts of Angelica Rowntree was at the forefront of her thoughts yet again. Whilst DI Sutton had his teams of officers revisiting previously searched areas in the vicinity of Angelica's address, Carrie's task was to decide who of the people she had already interviewed or spoken with, to talk to again.

Carrie checked her phone for text messages and saw that she had received one from Grace whilst she had been driving. She opened the message and read it. As expected, Grace was enquiring whether Carrie would be popping by later once she had got home from school. Unfortunately, Carrie didn't really know how the day was going to go and decided to send a rather non-committal response. At least that way, if she made it, Grace would be pleased and if she didn't, she would not be too disappointed.

She looked down at her notepad where she had listed the names of the people that she wanted to revisit in relation to the disappearance of Angelica Rowntree. Frustratingly, the list was not extensive. The trail behind Angelica had been so faint that it was almost invisible. Carrie's scribbled names included those that she had already spoken with and a tick if she felt they were worth talking to again. There were not many ticks. She contemplated what she was likely to get out of each of them; Emily Roache, the young girl that was temping at Grace's school, and had reported a man in the pub with a camera and a story that Haley Breen was followed towards her home one night was fairly unlikely to contribute much more. Robin Greaves, the mechanic, had left the garage on Trenton Street and reportedly seen a man talking to Angelica before catching his bus and noticing that they were gone as he rode past the turning. He wasn't the easiest to speak with. Even Leana Turnbull, the lady from the back room at Brady's, was on the list. Although her connection within the investigation related solely to Claudia De Luca, Carrie was highly suspicious of a connection between the discoveries of the girls. Leana had only half a story about a man that appeared to be paying close attention to Claudia De Luca. What Carrie felt certain about was that the *modus operandi* regarding the discoveries of both Haley Breen and Claudia De Luca were a match and indicative of the crimes having been carried out by the same person. A copycat was always possible, but Carrie felt this unlikely. She was as certain as she could be that if they found the perpetrator for one of the murders, they would have found the person responsible for both of them. The reason for the killings would come out in time. *Where are you, Angelica?* she thought.

She raised her head from the notepad and watched a dog-walker wrestle with four dogs on one of those split leads. *Rather you than me*, she thought, as she witnessed the dogs getting the better of their handler by wrapping themselves around the lady's legs, almost bringing her to the ground. As partial as she was to a spot of schadenfreude, Carrie couldn't afford to waste time on other people's misfortunes. With a sigh she held her pen above the notepad and closed her eyes. She decided to hunt for this particular needle in a haystack by randomly picking a place to start. When the pen jabbed onto the notepad, she made the decision to get moving. Within a couple of minutes, Carrie had put the notepad away, reversed her car out of the dusty parking area with a spin of the wheels, and turned out onto Whipp's Cross Road into the busy traffic and was heading for 38, Rodina Close, the residence of the Trenton Street mechanic, Robin Greaves. She decided to try his home address as she would have to drive past it to get to Trenton Street. 'Day off, my arse,' she said to herself.

For some reason, the front desk at Old Clapton Street was busier than usual. On each occasion that Desk Sergeant Rick Green watched the ground floor lobby doors close, they seem to be being pushed open again within seconds. If it wasn't missing pets, it was attempted break-ins or differing degrees of vandalism. He really wasn't in the mood. Having heard the news that his expected replacement later in the day had phoned in sick, he knew it was going to be another long one.

Upstairs in the comparative sanctuary of his office, was DI Marc Sutton. He returned to his desk, having just closed his office door to block out the ear-piercing sound of DCI Blackery's blessed carriage clock and sat down. Earlier today Sutton had composed and sent an email to his sister, the Forensic Psychologist, Patricia Toussaint. He had been thinking about asking her for her expert opinion since the previous evening. He had decided that rather than wrestle with the thought of how she would become even more self-righteous at receiving his communication, she would, most likely, be especially useful and able to help him to understand the type of person that he was so desperately, if not successfully, attempting to hunt down. He had conceded that he needed her help. The next three times that an email alert sounded on his laptop; Sutton had checked to see if it was her reply, but it wasn't.

The fairground at the local park only had another day to run before it's licence finally expired and the unsavoury owners, along with the problems of the girls that were assaulted by the man that nobody on the site knew, would be able to go away. Efforts would continue to be made to track down the assailant, but it was never easy in these circumstances. Without a man to interview and possibly charge, he knew he was fishing in the dark. Only one of the girls had provided any sort of reliable description and the CCTV in the area had not shown them anything. It was also proving to be futile to ask questions of the unhelpful fairground owners. He had arranged for the same level of additional security by way of a Police presence to be in attendance after dark but unless the man returned and was recognised by somebody, which was hardly likely, his identity would remain a mystery. Sutton was adamant that the licence would not be awarded to them next year, whatever DCI Blackery and the Chairman of the local Council had to say about it.

It was at this moment, as Sutton pondered on what to do next, that the email from his pretentious sister arrived. His request had been centred around her opinion of the murderer in relation to what she thought that he was thinking in leaving Haley and Claudia at those specific crime scenes. *Why there? Why so easy to find?* Patricia's response was as thorough as ever. Three whole pages of her explanation regarding how she comprehended the situation that Sutton had described. As soon as he saw the length of her email, he knew that he should probably have spoken to her earlier. It was her field of expertise, after all. Sutton read the email exhaustively, studying every word. He reviewed the sections where Patricia had referenced other cases of a similar genre and concentrated on everything that she was implying or, more often, telling him outright. As for why the girls had been found in the locations they were, she described the girls as his trophies. *He was showing off to you,* she wrote, *look what I have done.* She described the level of violence as his anger, but not towards these girls, specifically. Patricia felt that all this, from the abduction to the murder, was, in his mind, being directed at someone else. Her thoughts about the pattern of his crime led her to believe that this was related to some event in his past life. *It is not uncommon,* she asserted. Sutton was engrossed in her descriptions and the more he read, the more he accepted what she was saying. *Angelica is different,* she wrote. *If he has her, he feels no anger and it's my honest opinion that she is most likely still alive because the purpose for her abduction is markedly different from his reasons for taking the others. You have not found her because he does not want you to, unlike the others; Angelica is his.*

That line sent a shockwave through the body of DI Marc Sutton. *His,* he thought. He desperately wanted to understand the difference between Angelica and the other two girls in order to know where to start from. All three girls seemed to be very alike, and Sutton could not distinguish any particular dissimilarities between them. Each of them had dark hair and each were in their early twenties. Haley and Angelica were friends and lived close to one another, but Claudia was from an entirely different background; in fact, from a different country all together. *If he was intent on simply discarding the girls, then he might have placed them in similar locations. Haley Breen was apparently dumped, whereas he seems to have gone to extra lengths with Claudia De Luca. I believe that this could be noteworthy,* she wrote.

The locations of the discoveries of the bodies were, indeed, quite different. Sutton pondered on Patricia's comments regarding the extra lengths that he had taken to dispose of Claudia. He hadn't previously thought that it might be significant but had to acknowledge Patricia's point. He was equally interested in her suggestion that Angelica may be being treated completely differently to the others and that Patricia intimated that Angelica may still be alive. It was her feeling that, somehow, she was *his.* Sutton hoped that this might be the case and that there was still a chance of finding her, if only he knew where to look.

FORTY-SEVEN

DS Carrie Linton drove into Rodina Close and parked precisely where she had on her previous visit; directly outside number 38. The Close was quiet. A couple of ladies could be seen chatting outside one of the properties further into the cul-de-sac. Neither seemed to have noticed Carrie turn up. She unclipped her seatbelt, shuffled sideways in her seat, and reached for her notepad. Carrie flipped the pages until she arrived at the page containing the notes that she had made about her previous chats with Robin Greaves. She reread her notes about Greaves' sighting of the man with Angelica and was immediately reminded of how sketchy his account of it all was. *It was getting dark.* She remembered that part.

Carrie looked across to the front door of number 38 and, hoping that her journey had not been wasted, wondered whether he was going to be in. Then, as she turned her gaze back towards the Close, she noticed somebody familiar. She turned a page in her notepad and found the name that would not immediately come to her. Dorothy Walton: Carrie recalled that she had addressed herself as *Graham's wife*. Dorothy was now looking at Carrie's car and was most likely sizing up who had arrived in the Close, unannounced. *As if permission was required.* Par for the course, Dorothy was armed with her mop and bucket and had a roomy bag hanging over one shoulder; everything she required for her cleaning duties, and what's more, she was now heading in Carrie's direction. Carrie got out of the car and began to walk towards the path that led to where Greaves lived. She was in two minds as whether to approach the door and ring the bell or whether to wait a few moments longer and encounter her welcoming committee, otherwise known as Dorothy Walton. In the end the decision was made for her.

'Hello there. Back again?'
'Apparently,' said Carrie.
'Sally, isn't it?'
'Carrie.'
'Oh, sorry. I'm usually good with names. Are you here to see Mr Greaves again?' said Dorothy, stating what did appear to be the obvious.
'Do you know if he's in?' asked Carrie.

'I don't think so. You're a bit early for him. He's not usually home for a few hours yet.'

Carrie checked her watch; it was midday. Obviously, this was not one of the days that Greaves spent away from the garage. Carrie knew that he did not work every day and had taken a chance on catching him at home, knowing that she could always head off to Trenton Street if need be.

'I'm going in there next, as it happens. I like to get all the cleaning done without any interruptions. I can get on better that way,' explained Dorothy, 'pity you missed him.'

Knowing that Dorothy was going to be opening up at any minute, Carrie was all of a sudden extremely interested in getting herself through Greaves' front door and was hoping that Dorothy was going to help with that. Carrie knew that she did not have a warrant to search inside but it might be different if she was invited in by a kind cleaning lady. Carrie was also very aware that her efforts to gain access to the front door of number 38 were not part of a criminal investigation and that she currently had nothing that she could provide as supportive evidence for her interest in getting inside but what she did have was Dorothy Walton, and she intended to make the best use of her. Carrie kept herself close to Dorothy as she fumbled with the keys to number 38. She seized her chance and insisted upon holding Dorothy's mop and bucket for her. Unaware of Carrie's frail plan, Dorothy gratefully accepted the help. As she turned the key and opened the front door, Carrie was already edging her way inside with Dorothy's cleaning equipment.

'Where shall I put it for you, Mrs Walton? I'll put it down in the kitchen,' said Carrie, striding through the living room.

'Oh, ok. Thank you,' said Dorothy, a little overwhelmed by all the sudden acts of kindness.

Carrie was scanning the property like an echolocating bat in search of an unsuspecting mosquito. Her eyes were checking everything and everywhere. The furniture, the flooring, the items on show hanging on the walls and sitting on shelves awaiting Dorothy's duster.

'Alright then?' said Dorothy in a feeble attempt to shift Carrie from the residence, but she wasn't shifting; not yet.

Carrie's curiosity was in full flow. Before Dorothy could string together another sentence, Carrie had walked her way in and out of the living room and back into the kitchen. She studied the unwashed cups and plates with a slight sneer of disapproval but apart from that nothing really stood out to her. She really wanted to get to the bedroom.

'Thank you, Mrs Walton,' she said, almost without any relevance to what was happening.

Dorothy Walton didn't have a response because it all seemed to have happened very quickly. One moment she was gently pushing the door and the next her helper was whizzing around the place like a whirlwind. Carrie barely acknowledged Dorothy as she began to say something. Whatever it was, Carrie was not particularly interested in it. She was already heading for the bedroom. Instinctively, Carrie pushed the bedroom door closed behind her and began to scan again. It looked like a typical male domain as far as she was concerned, not exactly the way Carrie would allow things to get. *Very untidy,* she thought. There were clothes that had been thrown over chairs and a pair of shoes that looked as if they had been thrown from one side of the room to the other. Carrie wasn't too bothered what Dorothy was doing outside as long as she kept on doing it for just a little while longer. Carrie noticed a garment that seemed rather out of place but assumed it was probably something that belonged to his mother and had been left here from when she last visited. Carrie had just put one hand on the wardrobe door when Dorothy opened the door to the bedroom and interrupted.

'I'm sorry to disturb you but you're not really supposed to be in here,' she said sheepishly.

'No, well, you're probably right. I'll leave you to your cleaning,' said Carrie, reluctantly, as she backed out of the room, still scanning as she went.

'You understand, don't you? I can tell him you came by if you like?'

'No, better not. We wouldn't want him to think that you had been letting somebody into his room, would we? That would be against the rules of privacy for the residents, wouldn't it?' said Carrie, guessing that there was such a thing in Dorothy Walton's world.

'No, I suppose not. He would think it very unprofessional of me. You won't tell Graham, will you?'

'Yes, he would. And no, I won't. We'll keep it just between us,' said Carrie, smiling without the least bit of sincerity.

With Dorothy Walton fully placated and assured that her little misdemeanour was not going to be spoken of again, Carrie made her way to the front door.

'Just one thing, Mrs Walton. The dress on the bed. His mother's, I take it?' asked Carrie.

'Yes, I think it is. He has a few of her things here; dresses, jewellery, all sorts,' answered Dorothy.

'Right, well, it was nice to see you again. I'll show myself out,' said Carrie as she closed the front door and wandered back to her car.

Before leaving Rodina Close, Carrie sat in her car and replayed her quick but fairly thorough scan of Greaves' rooms in her mind. Mostly, it was a normal set up. Only the ladies dress was out of place but, as Dorothy said, it belonged to his mother. *If she is as untidy as him, she probably doesn't even miss it,* she thought.

Carrie checked her phone for messages, started her car, and did a U-turn in the junction just ahead of her, swinging the car around and heading off towards Trenton Street Garage.

FORTY-EIGHT

The unpleasant end to the coffee morning at *Beans* had been at the forefront of Betty's thoughts over the past few days. It had disrupted her sleep and left her feeling drained. It was one of those events that, as hard as she tried, she just could not shift to the back of her mind. There had been little contact from Elisha other than the occasional text which Betty read as purely by virtue of sending a message for the sake of sending a message. Arguments with Elisha were not entirely uncommon, but Betty had always brushed them off as nothing more than silly sibling squabbles, flashes of teenage emotions. But they weren't teenagers anymore. They never had lasted long and sometimes seemed to cement their relationship, but not this time. This time it all felt quite different, alien almost. Betty regretted ever saying anything about Karter Swann, knowing that she should have kept her feelings under wraps. How she could have expected Elisha to assent to her admission of having thought about Swann, she could not fully understand. It felt, now, like a rush of blood to the head.

When Elisha had said 'We need to finish this,' Betty had noticed a glint of something in her eye that sent a shiver down her spine. She had seen it before, albeit not very often, and she knew exactly when. It was when she witnessed Elisha batter the boy outside the collage. She looked almost demonic and was so full of hate that for a moment Betty did not recognise her. She remembers being frightened of her for the rest of the day and keeping herself to herself during the evening when the girls reached home. The blood on Elisha's shirt was put down to a nosebleed. True really.

The confusion that Betty felt about what to do regarding Karter Swann had become a puzzle that she didn't want to have to solve alone, but she knew that she was very much on her own with this one. There was no way that Elisha was going to support her secretive desire to rekindle her relationship with Swann. Betty had lost count of the number of times over the past few nights that she had woken up from a disrupted and restless sleep, wondering how this whole episode might end. She had felt a crippling sense of guilt about how her intentions would affect Elisha, especially after all that had gone on between Swann and her sister, and how they would influence her future relationship with her. The only certainty in Betty's mind was that she was no longer in control of her innermost thoughts and desires and that the overwhelming and impulsive impact of her recent decision was likely to be a disruptive and distressing one.

Betty made her way into the kitchen to retrieve another bottle of Chardonnay from the refrigerator. As she walked across the living room, she accidently kicked an empty bottle against the table leg of the coffee table, causing the bottle to spin and roll as if it was in search of a hiding place, eventually halting its pirouette under the table. She hardly noticed.

Giving the refrigerator door a shove and holding the cold bottle by the neck, she ambled back into the living room and placed it onto the coffee table as she let out a tired sigh and flopped onto the settee, wiping her cold, wet palm on the furniture. She sat staring into space, too weary to concentrate on anything in particular. After a few minutes her conscious level resumed to somewhere resembling a state of awareness. The brief period of absentmindedness had passed, and she refocussed on the issue that had been virtually the only thing on her mind for days. The bottle top cracked as she twisted it free from the foil around the neck and began to look for the glass that she had been using the previous night. Betty mumbled and cursed to herself as she tried in vain to locate the glass. *Not on the table. Not on the floor.* Another lengthy sigh. Another wipe of her wet hand. She grasped the bottle and raised it to her lips, gulping the cold liquid and taking a decent mouthful before swallowing and leaning back among the cushions, resting the base of the bottle onto her thigh as she did so. The shock of the cold caused her to lift the bottle back onto the table, leaving a circular mark that was created by the punt of the bottle on her now equally cold thigh. This time she didn't bother to wipe her hand, at least not onto the arm of the furniture. Instead, she rubbed her hand over her face, making use of the cold condensation in an attempt to rally her senses. It seemed to have the desired effect. Betty continued to swig generously, knowing full well that she could easily cope with her liquid breakfast. It was nothing that she had not done before. The fruity tang coated her mouth and its freshness appeared to help to revive her from her fatigued state. It may not be everyone's idea of breakfast, but it was working for Betty Nelson this morning.

Out of the corner of her eye she noticed a flicker of light in the hallway. She watched it change and dance against the wallpaper as she downed another mouthful of 'breakfast'. It took her a few more seconds to realise that it was coming from the muted television that she must have left switched on when she hauled herself out of the chair and upstairs to bed the previous evening. As soon as it had entered her mind to go and switch it off, the thought had gone. Only two things were now important to her; her liquid breakfast, and what to do about her feelings for Karter Swann. Whatever her decision, it was going to have to happen sooner rather than later. She stared across the room at the bookshelf opposite her and allowed her mind to meander through the titles, hoping that she would find the inspiration she needed to come up with some kind of plan. Most were crime thrillers with dark and sinister titles that seemed to invade her cloudy mind and stimulate a variety of thoughts. Her eyes followed along the spines of the books from left to right, probing for something, anything. One of the books had fallen onto its side and laid with the title upside down. Betty kinked her head to one side and then the other, trying to focus on the word that stretched its way along the length of the spine. When she worked out what it said, she looked away and stared at the wall above the bookshelf in an attempt to make the word fit into her troubled life. *Separation.* Another hearty swig of 'breakfast'. And another, and another until the cold bottle was almost empty.

Questions began to course through Betty's mind as she sat, feeling refreshed by the cold liquid and roused by the stimulation of her quest to establish a plan. *Separation.* She disregarded the thought that she should give up on Karter Swann. Betty knew what she wanted and the longer that she considered what had happened between him and her sister, the more she felt ready to forgive. Crazy, but that's just how it kept on coming back to her. *Maybe Elisha exaggerated. Maybe.* Betty recalled the cut on Elisha's lip and the stressed state that she had found her sister in but somehow it no longer mattered to her. A once unthinkable situation seemed to be approaching fast. She wanted Karter Swann again. She knew where he lived, but so did Elisha.

'*'We Need to finish this.'* Surely, she wouldn't go near him', she said quietly to herself.

Betty downed the remains of the Chardonnay and let the bottle slip from her hand onto the floor beside her feet, guiding it under the table with her toes. *Separation. It's her that I have to separate from.* Betty was certain that if she didn't take this huge step then Elisha would always be in the way. And if Elisha got to Swann first, then she didn't know what might happen. Betty's alcohol-fuelled mind battled with the concept that Elisha was going to try to take Karter from her, one way or another. That was what troubled Betty most of all; not knowing exactly what Elisha had in mind.

FORTY-NINE

Minneapolis, Minnesota.

Gregory Bonner had not slept well. In fact, he had had an awful night until he had finally faded into a deep sleep at a time when the earliest of the City's workers were rising. When he stirred again, he found himself staring straight at his work shoes. His vision blurred and cleared as his brain tried to make sense of precisely what was going on. His head hurt from a lack of sleep, and he could feel the inflexible resistance of the floor beneath him. The bedclothes that should have been keeping him warm and snug were trailing from the mattress to the floor like a frozen waterfall. Bonner was cold and sweaty. As hard as he had tried to shake the thoughts and dreams from his troubled mind, the more intense and twisted they had seemed to become. His trip to MinnSARDA, his afternoon at the house of Ken Toft, the shed in the garden of Wade Nelson's property, and Caterina Marks, always Caterina Marks. Not for the first time, he had dreamed about finding her and woken feeling exhausted, as if he had been chasing her along the street in an effort to catch her up and put his arms around her. Sometimes he even dreamed about having a conversation with her mother, Alexandria Org, only this time, he was crying and apologising that he had failed to provide her the answers that she so badly needed, even if she didn't really expect any good news.

Bonner rolled over onto his back and felt every bone and joint in his aching body creak. As tempted as he was to clamber back into bed, Bonner knew that the glint of daylight that was invading his room through the gap in his poorly fitted curtains spelt that it was high time that he was upright. After another attempt to stretch his body into action, he sat up, reached across to the edge of the mattress and heaved himself up. Bonner couldn't believe quite how old and rickety he felt this morning. He had heard Captain Antonio Rodrigues moan and grumble about his recurring aches and pains on many occasions; now Bonner was beginning to feel a little sympathy. The coffee enabled his body to react as Bonner had hoped and after a quick shower, he was ready to haul himself to his patrol car and begin to join the traffic that would escort him towards the police department once more.

As Bonner's patrol car approached South 5th Street, he could see The Stars and Stripes fluttering in the gentle breeze. America's pride and joy hung proudly outside of each and every police department across the entire United States. Big Toni was considerably more fanatical about it than Bonner ever was, or ever would be. His office windows were immediately above the flagpole that projected from the brickwork and Big Toni would often stand at the window, looking down towards the street with the flag that he termed as Old Glory, in full view. Bonner remembered the first time that he met Big Toni when he had been posted to the department as a probationer and the lessons about the flag that Big Toni had relayed to him in his office. Bonner had not realised that there was so much to it or that anyone could be quite so passionate about such a thing. He recalled how he was quite taken aback to learn that the Stars and Stripes should be illuminated during the hours of darkness. Bonner could not see what difference it made. But he would never forget the reaction he received from Big Toni when he had dared to question why. Big Toni had drilled a list of flag etiquette into Bonner for the next 30 minutes and Bonner had sat in virtual silence while he had done so. Of all the intricate details regarding the flag and how it should be presented, and there were many, there were a few that Bonner still found rather odd. In particular, the fact that the flag is worn facing backwards on Police and Army uniforms when it is worn on the right shoulder. When Big Toni was in full flow about this, Bonner had kept his lips tightly zipped and decided that he should simply keep his thoughts concealed. He had learned that in these situations, the flag would give the impression of being flown in the breeze when the wearer is moving forward. Bonner remembered only too well how he had fought with his facial muscles and averted potential disaster by stopping his eyebrows from raising in a show of surprise or even mild disapproval which would have been received by Big Toni as a display of disrespect.

The office was busy and bustling with people this morning and Bonner, as he often did, aimed straight and true towards his desk in the hope that nobody would notice him arrive. He wasn't late, he just wanted to get through the throng unscathed. Smartly dressed, official-looking people, carrying clipboards and manuals roamed around the office with intent. Bonner had no idea precisely what was going on, but he expected that he would soon find out. The less fuss the better, as far as he was concerned. Bonner sat at his desk and switched on his computer screen. He nudged his bag under the desk with his foot as the green light from the screen announced that his computer was active. He looked into the reflection on the screen and could see Big Toni glance up from his desk and look in his direction. *It won't be long now,* he thought.

Before he could turn his attention to the screen, Bonner was aware of somebody standing over him. Except it wasn't Big Toni.

'Right, you're next,' said the man in the crisp white shirt and perfectly creased black trousers as he immediately began tapping on Bonner's keyboard.

'What am I *next* for?' asked Bonner.

'You're being upgraded to the new system,' said the smart-looking man, as he continued to tap furiously, enabling all manner of pages of complex numbers and patterns to appear and disappear on the screen with frightening regularity and in a way that Bonner knew he could never acquire the skills for.

'Oh,' was all Bonner could offer by way of a rather suppressed response, all the time hoping that the records he stored on there from the Snow and Cold Index would be safe. Plus, of course, there were the charts and graphs that he had lovingly created about the extent of the snowfall across several winters.

'Right, this should be done fairly soon providing it all runs smoothly. Now don't touch anything until I get back.'

'You won't lose my work, will you?' asked Bonner in desperation.

'I won't lose anything,' replied the man, sternly.

Bonner gazed at the screen that was dancing through a variety of self-perpetuating instructions, seemingly without any external intervention. He knew better than to *'touch anything'*. In the absence of anything to do, he turned his attention to the hullabaloo that was circulating the office like a haze of dull, indeterminate mumbling. As the sounds resonated through Bonner's brain, he wished that he could be back in bed, catching up on the sleep that had deserted him. He had rallied during the drive to work but now that he was simply sitting and staring, Bonner began to yawn and feel extremely jaded.

Officers were at their desks being attended to by the people that had infiltrated the workplace, men and women were fussing over keyboards, and Big Toni was sitting at his desk with a lady in a long white dress who appeared to be reading something from a manual. Bonner expected that Big Toni would probably be required to have a certain level of understanding with regard to whatever the new system was. *Rather him than me,* thought Bonner. As he watched the strange activity, he noticed somebody approaching. Not the man from before but the lady from Big Toni's office. Her dress seemed to swish as she walked towards him, performing a neat sidestep around the tables every so often.

'Hi, my name's Riley. This is your manual. You'll need to refer to it if you should have any problems in the coming days but we're hoping that it should all transition smoothly and with any luck you won't need it. Sometimes takes a day or two for everyone to become accustomed to the system but I'm sure you'll be fine. Ok? And if you need any assistance you can talk to Captain Rodrigues or alternatively call the number on the back of the manual.' she said.

'Is that it? Can I use it now?' asked Bonner.

'No, I didn't say that you could use it. You should have been told not to touch it while it's downloading,' said Riley with some concern.

'I was,' replied Bonner.

'Well then...' said Riley, as she flicked her hair from her forehead and scurried off into the assemblage of chaotic downloading, her dress swishing even more than before.

Bonner sat, feeling perplexed. *I won't then,* he thought to himself. He considered that he actually didn't mind the delay to the start of his working day. He wasn't exactly on his best form after such a torrid night of disturbed sleep. He picked up the manual that had been thrust into his hand and sighed. *I'm not in the mood for this,* he thought. Bonner dropped the manual onto his desk, stood, and with one glance at the busily downloading computer, he decided to get some much-needed coffee from the machine in the hallway in the hope that it might provide the spark he would need to get through the day or at least the morning. As was Bonner's luck, he only made it halfway across the office when, out of the corner of his eye, he saw Big Toni standing in his doorway.

'Hey, Bonner. Here a minute.'

A minute. It's never a minute, thought Bonner.

He ruffled his hair and turned away from his intended destination. The coffee would have to wait, however badly he wanted it. He weaved his way towards Big Toni's office, passing a number of computers that appeared to be at various stages of the morning's download. None of the flickering information on any of the screens meant a single thing to him. *Just a load of jargon.*

'Come in, Bonner,' said the Captain, as he held the door open for his patrol officer and to Bonner's slight dismay, closed it behind him.

'Take a seat.'

Bonner sat opposite Big Toni. The sunlight was shining in from the window behind his boss as it ventured over the Matrix 12 Building that was on the other side of the street. From Big Toni's window, Bonner could see the top of the Grain Belt Beer sign that had been lovingly restored and stood proudly next to the Hennepin Avenue Bridge on Collett Island in the middle of a narrow section of the Mississippi River. That too was illuminated at night although not for the same purposes as 'Old Glory' that flapped in the wind outside the police department.

'Quite a morning,' said Big Toni, who seemed to be remarkably chilled considering the start to the day.

'Yeah,' said Bonner, apprehensively.

'How are you, Bonner?' asked Big Toni.

'Tired,' replied Bonner, wondering why Big Toni was asking.

'Didn't you sleep well last night?'

'No. I had a lot on my mind.'

'Anything that I can help with?' said the Captain, with an expression of genuine concern that Bonner was really not used to, and just a little suspicious of.

This little unaccustomed exchange batted back and forth for a few more minutes leaving Bonner slightly unsettled before Big Toni eventually got to the point.

'The Deputy Chief has been asking about you, Bonner. He wants to know how you got on at that dog centre you went off to the other day,' Big Toni said with a sour face.

Bonner could sense that the tone had changed and recalled how he appeared to have gone over Big Toni's head in order to get what he wanted. It was never his intention but the very fact that his Captain had not been available at the time did rather play into his hands. The extremely well-timed call from Deputy Police Chief Bolton had come out of the blue but it had released Bonner to go to MinnSARDA and start on a fresh trail for the whereabouts of his friend, Caterina Marks.

'Oh,' said Bonner.

'Yes, oh,' said Big Toni, 'I take it you had a nice day out.'

Bonner didn't really want to rub this in Big Toni's face, but he knew that he had indeed had a very nice day out. *Best not to mention it.*

'I learned a lot about how the whole rescue dog procedure works. It was very interesting. It's an impressive centre,' said Bonner, keeping his response clipped and not really knowing how much to elaborate on his day without sounding smug at his personal victory.

'And has it got you any further to finding out what happened to that girl?'

That girl.

'Caterina?' said Bonner, insistently.

'Yes, obviously.'

'Well, I don't believe that she was simply taken off the streets, if that's what you mean. I think there's more to it. I believe that she did turn up at the Nelson residence, but I haven't got the full picture yet.'

'Do you think you might have the full picture anytime soon, Bonner?' asked Big Toni, his mood switching back to the Captain that Bonner recognises daily, by the minute.

'I do, Captain. Soon.'

'You do?' said Big Toni, with an element of surprise.

'Yes, Captain. I'm going to work it out. I learned a lot at MinnSARDA and I've spoken to one of the Rescue Team that was directly involved with her disappearance at the time. I feel like I'm getting somewhere. There are a few bits of the puzzle that I'm not happy about and although this is a stone-cold trail, I'm determined, Captain.'

'Well, well, Bonner. You do surprise me. I never thought you had it in you.'

'I'll find out, Captain. I just need a little more time and I'll find out. I owe it to Caterina. She was…I mean, I…it doesn't matter. I just need…' he said with a slight but noticeable quiver in his voice.

'Bonner! I never saw it coming. This girl, Caterina, she means more to you than just a missing person from the MUPC doesn't she? She's not just an old friend from your college days, is she, Bonner? You really felt something for her, didn't you, Bonner?'

Bonner looked down from Big Toni's gaze. He sat quietly and felt an impromptu shudder bubble up from far below inside him. One that was infused with the truth about his love for the girl that he used to dream about during his college days and continues to dream about even now, albeit with an unbridled sadness. The girl he never got close enough to, despite so many attempts to pluck up the courage he needed to even speak to her. Ok, he spoke to her, but he didn't manage to say the important things that he wanted so desperately to say. When she went missing all those years ago, Bonner had cried every night for a week. He couldn't sleep, eat properly or put his mind to anything else. Caterina Marks filled his head every day. They say that time is a healer and over such a long period it did its job. But when the face of Caterina Marks appeared on the MUPC website, Bonner was thoroughly shaken. He tried not to show it at the time, but it hit him like a train. When Big Toni asked him to look into her disappearance and try to establish whether he could tie up a very cold loose end, he was numbed and shocked, but it was going to be the easiest decision of his entire life. *Yes, Captain.*

'Bonner? Are you ok?' asked Big Toni.

Bonner raised his head and instinctively wiped a tear from his cheek. Captain Antonio Rodrigues only stared. It was all falling into place in Big Toni's head. This wasn't just another routine missing person, at least not to Gregory Bonner, this was personal. Big Toni shifted in his chair and let out a sigh. He knew that it was time to play good Toni and leave bad Toni out of it.

'Bonner?' he whispered.

'I'm ok, I just had a sleepless night. Just a bit tired today, Captain. I could do with a coffee to get me going again. Is that all for now?' he said.

'Well, let me tell you what's going to happen next. No, it is not all for now. I want you to do something for me. I want you to go get *two* coffees and bring them both back in here. I'm going to help you, Bonner. Together we are going to find out precisely what happened to Caterina Marks, and we are going to solve this thing once and for all. How does that sound?'

Bonner's eyes could not hold back the emotion anymore. He was beyond that now. Big Toni was on board and Bonner felt that there was real hope for the first time in ages. He knew deep inside that they were not going to miraculously find Caterina Marks alive and well and living in some kind of rural location, unnoticed by everyone around her, and although that would be wonderful, he knew it wasn't to be. But something almost more important was going to happen. Gregory Bonner was going to find Caterina Marks and fulfil the promise that he had made to her so many times in his dreams since this whole episode began; since he began talking to her in his den and since he began seeing her everywhere he went and since he started following her image along the street towards Betty's house.

'I'm going to find her,' he said, looking up at his Captain through glistening eyes.

'No, Bonner. *We* are going to find her…and you will sit right there whilst *I* get the coffees. And that's an order,' said Big Toni.

Big Toni left the office, and just as Bonner was turning and trying to say thank you, he heard the door lock behind him.

FIFTY

Ahuja Industries, East London.

Angelica's meagre collection of items that she kept under her blankets in the dusty corner rested on her lap, as she sat, huddled with her blankets pulled up to her neck, trying to dodge the spots of rain that fell like guided missiles from the openings in the factory roof. There was nowhere within her scope that would provide a completely dry area, so she made the best of it. The most useful item she had with her was the hairbrush. At least that made her feel a little more human. She had tried to use some of the bottled water to brush through her hair in a feeble attempt to cleanse it, but it was just a token effort in the end. Whilst it didn't make her hair much cleaner, it did assist her in straightening some of the curls that had naturally formed over time. Iron bar, that she had concealed days ago was still there too. Angelica had tried a number of times to jam it into the chain somehow and twist it in the hope that it might just break one of the links, but they were still proving too sturdy. She had caught her knuckle against part of the chain the last time that she had attempted to damage it. All she achieved was to damage herself. *I'm still alive. Why, why?*

One thing that Angelica knew was different was that something had altered with regard to the relationship between herself and whoever was behind the mask. At long last, a form of contact had been made. However weird it was, she somehow felt safer. Her thoughts of becoming just like the girl in the white roll of material had waned over the past few days. Angelica reasoned that if he was going to so much trouble to feed her and keep her reasonably warm, she must have a chance of survival. *Why otherwise?* Very little else made sense to her.

Another drip of cold rain hit her head. They landed with quite a bang when they had fallen all the way from the roof. Thankfully most of the rain had fallen just beyond her semi-circle of dust, at the perimeter of her world. She had slept for longer than usual today, until the first drip had splatted on her face. The foxes had come and gone, as usual, and she had performed her daily routine of stretches and star jumps; anything to stop from seizing up on the unforgiving cement-coated floor. She had become an expert at recognising the various sounds of the factory too. The creaks and groans that it made in the wind, the echoes of the foxes' cries, and the noise of the pigeons flapping high up in the ironwork out of sight. Of course, only one noise was important; the scraping of the metal gate which signified that her next meal was on its way.

But this morning it was later than usual and although none of her meals completely fulfilled her appetite, she was eager to receive them. Angelica could, literally, only dream of tucking into a Sunday roast with all the trimmings. Her memory of the table at home being formally set and the smell of the Sunday roast wafting into the living room from the kitchen triggered recollections of happier days, but they were short-lived as she soon became saddened by the harsh reality that jolted her back to the present. Everything about it made her yearn for home even more than ever. Her defence was to do something, anything to take her mind off it. She made up songs and sang softly to herself or walked around in her corner until she was bored, which didn't usually take all that long. Other times she would replay the words in her mind that she had heard him utter or shout, as if from a tape recording in her head. She so wanted to put a name to the voice, but it just wouldn't come to her. Sometimes she thought she had it, but her mind was just playing cruel tricks. She thought of everyone she knew, even people that she didn't think could possibly be the answer. She drew up a short list of suspects in her mind but none of them really fitted that well. Too tall, too short, too unlikely. It was pretty hopeless really.

Then she heard it. The metal gate. Breakfast had arrived. *Thank goodness, bloody starving.* Angelica reorganised the items under her blanket, keeping Iron bar well out of sight. She wasn't so bothered about the hairbrush, and although she didn't want him to take it away, she thought that if she left it on show, there might be a chance of him brushing her hair. Not so that she could get her hair brushed, she could do that herself, but so that she might get him talking again.

The sound of his boots scuffing their way along the factory floor was followed by a faint cloud of dust as he came into view. Same clothes, same mask. Angelica couldn't decide whether to speak or not. She didn't want to appear too forward and upset him. After all, the most important thing of all was to get her meal. She had enough sense to know that going without because she had been too pushy would be stupid. She pushed herself back with her hands and feet, sliding her bottom further into the corner and as she did so she felt the tip of Iron bar sticking out from its hiding place. He looked her way as she shuffled. Angelica placed the palm of her hand over the exposed metal end and sat still, waiting for him to look away so that she could post Iron bar back under the blankets. But she had a bigger problem.

From his back he slung a bag down onto the ground in front of her. It wasn't her breakfast, that was in a carrier bag just inside her perimeter. It was a bag of fresh blankets. Iron bar wasn't where she usually kept it, not concealed enough. *Today of all days,* she thought, *oh shit.*

Usually, Angelica would manage to take one blanket at a time from the bag and when he wasn't watching, switch the one that concealed Iron bar. But he was watching far too intently for her liking and if she moved her hand, he would see it. As hard as she tried not to, she knew that her face was giving something away. He began to act as if he was suspicious about something, even though she was sure that he had no idea what to be suspicious about.

'I'm sorry, they got wet with the rain,' she said in a desperate attempt to divert his attention from getting the blanket switch done right this minute, 'Can you pass me the bag and I'll swap them over?' she said.

Angelica began to feel sweaty. She knew Iron bar was useless to her unless she was free from the chains, but she could not afford for him to find out that she had been concealing it under her blankets. No more than she could afford for him to find any evidence of her keeping food aside for the foxes, not that it usually remained on the floor for more than a few seconds. After a brief moment, he stepped towards the bag of blankets and picked it up by the handles. He was inside her world now, just like he had been when he terrifyingly started to brush her hair. Just as he motioned to drop the bag beside her, he stopped. Angelica realised that he was no longer looking at her. He had spotted the hairbrush. Now she was wondering whether it might have been better to hide it properly after all. Somehow, when she was concentrating on hiding Iron bar, she must have moved the hairbrush into full view again. It was a very odd moment. He remained motionless; his eyes fixed on the hairbrush; the bag of blankets held off the ground. Angelica realised her opportunity to tuck Iron bar out of sight and deftly slid it back under cover; coughing loudly as she did so in order to muffle any scraping sound of iron on concrete. He put the bag down next to her and pointed at it. This was all the instruction Angelica needed to know what to do next. She pulled out a couple of clean, fresh-smelling blankets and laid them on her lap. As she did so, she dragged the wet, dirty ones out from her corner. Iron bar remained out of sight the whole time. She gathered the replacements and laid them out in her corner whilst keeping one eye on him, in case anything changed. When she had finished organising the new blankets, she looked at the carrier bag that contained her breakfast. He nodded and she reached for the bag, bringing it close and untying the top of it. Then it all got weird again. He stepped closer. Angelica watched him closely, and as she ate her breakfast, he knelt down close to her. Angelica froze. She didn't know whether to speak or just stay quiet. Nothing bad happened immediately so she continued to eat in silence, hoping that he wasn't going to take her breakfast away. *Does he just want to watch me eat?*

Right then, as she sat, wedged into her corner, Stripe and Socks peered around the wall. Her heart jumped. Their keen sense of smell must have latched on to the fact that breakfast was here. She didn't mind the foxes being there, but she was more concerned about what he would do. When he noticed them, he did nothing, immediately. He just watched them. Stripe and Socks didn't seem bothered that there was an extra guest for breakfast and began to slowly creep towards Angelica. *No, no, not now boys.* She knew that they could smell the food, but she also knew that she couldn't give them any right now. That would not go down well with him. *Soon, soon. I'll feed you all soon.* It had taken her days to entice them closer and although she had not yet managed to get them to feed from her hand, she knew that she had been making progress towards it. She could imagine just how soft their sleek coats would feel and longed to stroke them, if they would let her. *Please come back later.*

Angelica jumped, her heart pounded in her chest, and the foxes scattered as he waved his arms erratically and shouted at them. No words; more like a roar. He kicked his leg out at Socks but missed. Dust flew up and she could hear their claws scratching on the factory floor as they tried to gain the traction that they needed to make their escape. In a moment the startled foxes were gone. She was horrified and wanted so much to hit him with Iron bar. But as usual she knew it would be no good. For a moment she imagined herself battering him with it and not stopping until the cement dust was flooded with blood, and he was dead. She hated him now. Not that she had ever liked him at all.

Then everything took another turn. Without her asking, he grabbed the hairbrush and started to brush the tangles in her hair. They pulled and snagged and caused her to wince. This wasn't pleasant. For a brief moment she put up with it, but Angelica didn't feel like making out to be friends with the man that had just terrified her real friends, her only friends in this gruesome world, the foxes.

'Get off,' she said, abruptly, pulling her head away from him.

He stopped. She could feel his eyes burning into her. No words. Angelica could barely look his way. She had stopped him from doing something that he wanted to do, and she didn't know how he would react or what was going to happen next. New territory. Then she felt the pain in her shoulder as the hairbrush struck her hard. *He hit me. This is it. He's finally going to kill me like that other girl. Like Haley.* Angelica was determined not to cry. She did not want to let him see that she was weak even though she could not control the shaking in her legs. Her stomach knotted as she turned to face him and look him square in the eyes. She raised her hands to protect her face as another blow came her way. This time she felt pain in her elbow as the hairbrush glanced off her arm and fell uncontrollably to the factory floor, spinning to a halt in the dust.

Angelica cradled her breakfast bag and sat awaiting her fate, squinting her eyes in anticipation. She was sure that he was going to strike her again and again. She imagined herself wrapped up like the other girl. Dumped like Haley Breen, or worse. But it didn't come. Instead, there was an eerie silence. She heard his foot scrape on the gritty surface as he rose from his kneeling position and began to walk away without looking at her. Angelica tentatively opened her tightly shut eyes and saw the back of him moving away, almost rounding the wall and going out of sight. *Go, just go.* In another two minutes she heard the metal gate play its signature tune on the ground and the factory fell silent. Angelica felt confused and sat shaking but she definitely had the feeling that he was not about to hurt her. She knew that there had been plenty of opportunity for him to do so if he had really wanted to. Why he hadn't was still a daily puzzle. In five more minutes, her furry friends were back peering at her with rumbling tummies and eyes filled with expectation.

FIFTY-ONE

DS Carrie Linton flicked the wipers again as she approached the right-hand turn that would lead her into Trenton Street. She parked her car out of the direct line of sight of the garage entrance. If Greaves was there, she didn't want him to be pre-warned of her unscheduled visit by spotting her car across the street, just in case he might have a sudden desire to become invisible. She walked up to the large blue doors that were mostly closed and peeped inside. She saw what she expected to see. Cars on ramps with mechanics stood beneath them, rows of various sized tyres on metal shelving, and a couple of customers standing around watching what was happening to their pride and joy, but there was no immediate sight of Robin Greaves. Carrie checked out the mechanics again and confirmed to herself that he wasn't any of them. None of the mechanics had noticed that Carrie had entered so she stood near the door and waited in case Greaves appeared from the rear of the premises. He didn't. After a few more minutes she decided to make it known that she was there. She wandered a little further in, past the waiting customers and stood at the door to the office hoping to gain the attention of the man sitting inside at a computer. It worked.

'I won't be a minute, sir,' he said without looking away from the screen.

When he turned to see Carrie, he was full of apologies and genuinely a little embarrassed. Carrie wasn't too bothered by his little error even though she was tempted to ask whether it was only men that brought their cars to his garage or whether there was a special ladies day that she should know about. But she didn't. *Why be bitchy?* she thought.

'I'm sorry but you'll probably be waiting for ten minutes before I can get your car inside. Probably after we get the red one down off the ramp and out,' he said.

'My car won't be coming inside today,' she said, 'I don't need your skills for this visit, fortunately. I was wondering whether Robin Greaves was here.'

Carrie had considered whether to make her visit official but decided to just see how it went.

'Robin?' he repeated.

'Yes. If he's around I would like to speak with him for a moment.'

The man gave Carrie a closer look. Carrie raised her eyebrows.

'You've come on the wrong day, I'm afraid. Robin isn't here right now,' he said, 'If you had come this morning, you would have bumped into him, but he left earlier,' continued the man.

'Do you have any idea where I might find him?' she asked.

'Well, he doesn't say much about what he's doing or where he's going but I can tell him you called the next time I see him if you like.'

Carrie gave herself a moment to consider whether this would be of any advantage to her but decided that it wouldn't. Neither could she see any point in hanging around. He wasn't here and he wasn't expected to come back by the sounds of it. She thanked the man for his time and walked back to her car without giving her name. Once inside the car, she sat for a couple of minutes to gather her thoughts and decided to go back to Rodina Close and wait for him. Dorothy Walton had implied that he would be back fairly soon and having wasted part of her day driving to and from Trenton Street she thought that she may as well try to get something out of what was left of it even though there were times that made her wonder whether she was barking up the wrong tree by bothering to speak with Greaves but there were certain things that kept niggling away at her. She wasn't happy about his sketchy story of seeing Angelica with a man in Trenton Street on the day that she went missing and she was also bothered about finding his mother's clothes and other bits and pieces at his house. That might make sense if Dorothy was right about her visiting there but there was something in Dorothy's expression when she was telling Carrie that she might see his mother that didn't feel quite right. As Carrie turned the ignition key to begin her journey back to 38 Rodina Close, her mobile rang. It was DI Marc Sutton.

'Hi Marc.'

'Hi Carrie. Where are you?'

'I'm sitting in the car in Trenton Street. Greaves wasn't at home, so I've popped down to the garage to see if he was here, but I drew a blank here too.'

'Typical. Look I've had a report from one of the beat guys that a woman was seen walking along the canal a couple of days before Claudia was discovered. Apparently, she walked up and down the stretch where Claudia was found and seemed to be paying particular interest to the water.'

'You sure she wasn't just feeding the ducks?' asked Carrie.

'Ha, ha,' replied Sutton with all the contempt that Carrie's feeble attempt at humour deserved.

'But seriously, she could have been doing anything,' said Carrie.

'I agree that it might be nothing but I'm going to have another look at the CCTV and check out the days in question. You never know,' said Sutton.

'Ok. But a woman?'

'Yeah, I know, but it appears that she spent a while studying the water as if she was looking for something. I'll check to see whether she was there on any other days around that time too. I know it seems a bit hopeful, but I want to see for myself, just in case.'

'Ok.'

'Also, Patricia has been calling me. Most unusual, but she was helpful before, so I think I'll give her a call back. See what she wants. It's not like her to want to spend her time chatting idly with her brother.'

'Ok. I'm going to go back to Rodina Close in case I can catch him at home.'

'Alright. Take care. Oh, and Steve Kingham thinks he's getting closer to locating Karter Swann.'

'Blimey. Well, if he does it'll prove Blackery's theory right. How has he managed that?'

'He has his own contacts and he's been digging deep. According to him, there was a memorial service for Swann at Cobbe's Chapel, out in the sticks, a while ago, and whilst that tied in neatly with his apparent murder, he's discovered that a few of Swann's associates at the time always had their doubts about the legitimacy of the whole thing. No proof of course, but by all accounts, one of his friends swears that they saw Swann working abroad when he and his family were on holiday. They never managed to get close enough to be absolutely sure and never crossed paths with him again while they were out there. Crete, apparently. Another reportedly saw him driving a car, somewhere near the docks at Tilbury but they only got a brief look in passing.'

'Hmm, well that might be an interesting meeting if it comes to fruition. Ok, well, I'll be careful. See you soon.' Said Carrie.

FIFTY-TWO

Tilbury, East London.

Karter Swann turned off the water, stepped out of the shower, and reached for a towel to wrap around himself, checking his hair in the mirror to make sure that his recent attempts at dyeing it had been successful. With practice he had got used to the exact amount of dye that he needed to use to acquire the desired shade. He had dyed his beard too which he always felt was a bit of a tedious job, but he decided that he would rather have it than shave it off. He wondered just how long he could expect to stay anonymous to most of the world. *Somebody knows where I am,* he thought. Again, names flashed across his mind. He didn't think that Ray Keller was aware of exactly where he lived because, as far as Swann was concerned, Keller had never followed him all the way home from the pub and Swann had never divulged the location of his residence either. He'd never even told him his real name. Anyhow, the envelopes had arrived before he met Keller.

He dried himself and began to get dressed. Black trousers and a long-sleeved shirt that would cover his tattoo, laid on the bed. Ever since the discovery of Haley Breen at the bus depot, he had made sure that it had stayed out of sight since his return from Crete. Tonight, he was at work at the Riverside Centre and would meet Ray Keller at the Snare and Cymbals later. He sprayed the deodorant under his arms and across his chest and picked up the red and navy checked shirt, putting one arm into it before passing it around his back. Swann checked his appearance in the mirror as he continued dressing for his shift. He was going in a little earlier tonight because he wanted to get the bar organised the way he liked it. Those that worked there during the day did things differently and they certainly didn't leave the place as tidy as Swann liked. Today's delivery of bottled beer would have been placed in the chillers but not to his liking. When Swann worked, he always ensured that the bottles stood neatly in rows and had their labels facing out towards the customer. Presentation was key, as far as he was concerned. The Riverside Centre, down by the docks in East London didn't compare to The Honeycomb in Malia Old Town or even to the Cactus and Coyote but he couldn't do much about that now. Needs must. Karter Swann was dead, and Kevin Marshall needed to go to work.

DC Steve Kingham sat in his car opposite the entrance to Brickhouse Street as the rain beat loudly on the roof, and watched the front of the Snare and Cymbals, flicking the windscreen wipers occasionally. His route to this point had been filled with dead ends and false hope but he was starting to believe that the man inside the pub was someone that he would benefit from speaking with. Kingham's monotonous enquiries had led him to Tilbury and although he didn't have an address for Karter Swann, his intuition was telling him that he must be around here somewhere. He could feel it in his bones that Swann was nearby. Kingham's connections to the sleazier members of society had been developed over a long period of time and had been very useful to him on a number of occasions. They had got him into a few difficult situations too, but he had always managed to squirm out of them. The challenge to locate Karter Swann, who appeared to have disappeared from the face of the Earth, or as some would prefer to believe, been murdered in his kitchen and had his body disposed of, had provided him with several headaches, but tonight he hoped that the net was closing in. Kingham knew from experience that if he put enough pressure on the right people, that they would usually crack. Not all of the criminal fraternity were as hardened as they would like people to believe, and Kingham was an expert in deciphering the difference.

When the rain began to subside, he lowered the window slightly, just enough to be able to peer over the glass. All was quiet in Brickhouse Street. Occasionally, one of the locals had ambled past him and scurried into the Snare and Cymbals and out of the rain, but none of those folk interested Kingham. He expected that his target would already be snug inside and blissfully unaware that Kingham intended to pay a visit. Basing his hunch upon no more than a supposed sighting of Swann in the area, Kingham had called in a favour from a contact that lived in the vicinity. He was only ever known by the underworld as Spider, but Kingham also knew him as George Sullivan, an ex-submariner who moved to London from Portsmouth in the 1980s and soon became familiar with the wrong side of the street. Kingham had arrested Sullivan on a number of occasions during his days in the Fraud Squad but most of the time he had used his knowledge of who was really behind the criminality to find the perpetrators. George Sullivan was no snitch, but he wasn't stupid either. His connection to Kingham had kept him on the street and away from Her Majesty's less than desirable establishments on more than one occasion. Kingham knew that Sullivan was of greater value to him on the outside than he was locked up in prison.

A week ago, Kingham had appeared suddenly from a well-trodden woodland path and stood in front of George Sullivan who was walking his brown Labrador. The awkward silence was broken only by a defensive throaty grumble from Tide.

'Good morning, George,' said Kingham as he stepped out from behind a laurel bush.

'Mr. Kingham,' replied a surprised George Sullivan, 'fancy seeing you here.'

'Yeah, you never know who you might bump into in these secluded spots do you, George?'

'So, what is it you want this time?'

'Really, George. So suspicious.'

'Well, if you're going to tell me that you are out for a morning stroll, you can save it.'

'I'm looking for someone, George, and I was hoping that you might be able to help me,' said Kingham.

'Depends. People that don't want to be found aren't easy to find but I can give it a shot.'

'Karter Swann,' said Kingham.

George Sullivan stopped in his tracks and looked inquisitively at Kingham, as Tide pulled impatiently at his leash.

'The one that was accused of killing that girl at the bus depot? He's dead, right?' said Sullivan.

'Maybe, maybe not. It depends on who you talk to. Nobody has seen him for a while but there have been a couple of rumours that he's not as dead as he'd like to make us think he is.'

The two men walked on quietly. Another dog walker passed them with a courteous nod. Her Jack Russell taking a wide berth from Tide.

'Why do you want to speak with him?' asked Sullivan, 'He's not involved with that other girl, is he?'

'There are a lot of similarities, let's say that, George.'

'What about the Rowntree girl? Is she still missing?'

Kingham looked at Sullivan and nodded. 'Uh huh.'

'Nasty business, Mr Kingham.'

'It always is, George. So, are you going to help?' asked The Detective Constable.

George Sullivan sighed as he ambled on, head down, seemingly in thought.

'It doesn't give me a lot to go on, does it?' he said.

'I was hoping you could do what you're good at George. Ask around for me, see what pops up.'

'Is that all? Find a dead man, that hasn't been seen for ages?' said Sullivan.

'It'll do for now. Find out if he's still around, George. If he is, then I'll be interested. You know how to get me.'

Kingham sat in his car at the end of Brickhouse Street and checked the mobile phone that he used as a method of contact with people like George Sullivan and scrolled down to read the message that he had received yesterday.

Snare and Cymbals. Brickhouse Street. Ray Keller. One of O'Connell's. Best I can do.

Steve Kingham was more than familiar with the name of Odhran O'Connell. He hadn't had many direct dealings with him, but he had heard all about his reputation. Some people called him *The Magician* because of his penchant to make people disappear. Kingham had no good reason to suspect that O'Connell might be involved in Karter Swann's disappearance, but he knew that if Swann had set it up, then he would have needed some help. He couldn't have dragged himself out of his kitchen, leaving a slimy trail of blood. To Kingham it looked like a case of Swann having upset the wrong people. Maybe somebody else was keeping him quiet about the murder of Haley Breen or maybe he had pushed the boundaries just a bit too far and got in over his head. But if he wasn't dead then somebody had gone to long lengths to hoodwink the police and just about everyone else. Kingham had been as convinced as anyone that Swann was dead and with him the truth about what had happened to Haley Breen and why. But since the discovery of Claudia De Luca and the similarities of the injuries to the bodies, the whole thing had turned on its head. Kingham knew that Sutton and Carrie couldn't be any more certain than he was that Swann was behind this, but at the same time he knew they had their doubts. One thing that was certain was that if this latest dark alley did lead to the whereabouts of the elusive Karter Swann, then it would become a whole new ball game.

The heavy clouds and the rain had darkened the early evening ahead of time. The streetlights had been activated by the gloom at least two hours ago and Karter Swann was not looking forward to walking to the Riverside Centre and risking a soaking. The thought of arriving damp for the beginning of a shift was enough to make him want to stay at home but he knew he had to brave it and get moving. He had made his decision to go in and prepare the bar to his liking, so it was best to just get out there and start walking.

Swann donned his favourite winter coat and took the beanie hat out from the side pocket before reconsidering and putting it back in favour of the large hood. The hood had helped him feel anonymous whenever he was outside and with the potential accusation of murder still hanging over him, he knew it made sense to wear it. He left 12 Countess Street and turned left towards the river. The walk usually took him at least twenty to thirty minutes depending upon which way he went and whether he was in any sort of a hurry. He strode past Brickhouse Street and kept his head down as he passed a car that was sitting at the end opposite the bollards. As he walked by, he could see the light from the screen of a mobile phone that offered a modest glimmer of light in the interior of the vehicle. He walked on. The rain seemed to have stopped for now.

DC Steve Kingham lifted his attention from his message and switched from the text message screen, placing the phone back into his pocket as a man in a sturdy coat walked by the car. He decided that he had sat for long enough and that it was time to try to locate Ray Keller. Kingham didn't know Keller but by process of elimination, he thought he would be able to work out which one he was in the pub. Not many people had entered in the time he had been sitting and waiting. He got out of the car, thumbed the remote locking key fob and walked into Brickhouse Street to meet a man he had never met about a man that might be dead.

FIFTY-THREE

Old Clapton Street Police Station.

DI Marc Sutton could clearly see a woman in a long coat and wearing a headscarf, walking along the canal towpath. The CCTV provided a good quality picture. The time and date at the top of the screen showed this to be two days before Claudia De Luca had been discovered by the couple that first spotted her, or at least, spotted the white roll of material. It was 16:23 in the afternoon. Sutton looked closely at the woman and watched her walk and stop, walk and stop. Her coat was dark blue or black and she wore dark trousers and what looked like appropriate footwear for a mucky towpath. The headscarf was mottled with a variety of colours and what could be seen of her hair appeared to be of a light shade. She occasionally bowed her head over to apparently get a better look at the water, just for a moment. What Sutton could not determine was whether she had been looking on the other side of the bridge too. If Claudia had been carried by the undercurrent, then she may have moved from her original position and if this person knew where that might have been then they may have been looking in more than one place, but unfortunately, the available CCTV didn't stretch to the other side of the bridge. As hard as he tried to stare at the screen there was never an opportunity to see her face. The woman strolled slowly and only stopped briefly. Satisfied that he wasn't going to learn any more from this recording he forwarded the CCTV to the next day; one day before Claudia's discovery. He allowed the recording to scroll slowly through the day but disappointingly he didn't see the woman or anyone that resembled her. *I must have missed her.* Sutton played the recording back to the start of the day until the time showed 05:09. *There. That's her. Same coat. What is she doing out by the canal at this time?*

Sutton didn't have the answer to his own question, but he knew that there weren't going to be too many options to choose from. Sutton watched as the woman walked slowly and purposefully along the towpath, her face pointing towards the water. This time she didn't stop. She continued slowly along the edge of the canal and sat on a bench that was obscured from view by a large Oak. Sutton knew it was there even though he couldn't see it clearly on the screen because he remembered it from when he and Carrie had endured the gruesome discovery. She stayed on the bench for another 14 minutes before moving and Sutton gazed at her feet, which was all he could see of her. He didn't want to miss the chance of getting a better look at her were she to suddenly shift her position. Then, eventually, the woman stood and, as she did so, she held a newspaper up against her face as she began to walk back towards the bridge, which concealed her features from the CCTV. *My God, does she know the camera is there?* Sutton studied her as closely as he possibly could until she went out of shot but he never once saw her face. *Maybe she was shielding her face from the wind.* Sutton checked the previous day again but, in a way, there was nothing to be suspicious about. She walked along the canal path and looked into the water. *So what?*

He slumped back into his chair, folded his arms and stared at the screen, wondering whether any of it really meant anything at all. It was difficult to say. As he sat, he took his phone from his pocket and checked it in case Grace had sent him a message. She had, and there was another from Patricia. *Damn, I should have called you,* he thought. He prioritised Grace and quickly responded to her usual, general enquiry as to whether he was ok and sent it, promising that he would text her again later. Then as he searched his recent calls for Patricia's number, he tried to think of a good excuse for not responding to her sooner. He found her and noticed that the entry said *Patricia (3)*. Sutton hadn't realised that she had tried to get him three times.

The phone rang at least six times before he heard her voice.

'Hello Marcus.'

'Hi Patricia, I'm sorry that I took so long to get back to you, but you know how it is,' he said.

'I know precisely how it is, but I did find the time to call you.'

Here we go, he thought.

'Yes, I know, I'm sorry. How are you?'

'I'm well, thank you, and how are you?'

'I'm fine and Grace is fine too,' he said, knowing that Patricia wasn't going to ask, 'What can I do for you?'

'Nothing, I shouldn't wonder. I was actually just wondering how you were getting along with your search for a needle in a haystack,' she said.

'We're working on it,' said Sutton, not wishing to have to go into a lengthy explanation about how he and his team were coming up against more dead ends than a mazed convolution of hedges and paths.

'I should hope you are.'

Sutton knew that Patricia had a good reason for calling him three times but getting to the point was always an onerous task where she was concerned. He also knew that Patricia's time was invaluable and that if she really was going to be helpful, he would need to prompt her a little. *All part of the game,* he thought.

'So, Patricia, I don't want to take up too much of your precious time. Is there something you wanted?'

'There's nothing that I want, Marcus, but I think that it sounds as though you may need my assistance.'

Pretentious, precious, Patricia, he thought.

'I'm sure it will be valuable,' he responded.

'Of course, it will, Marcus. Now, are you any closer to pinning this down to one person?'

Finally.

'Not exactly but I'm sure that he will slip up,' he said.

'Why should he slip up. He is playing this exactly as he wants to. He's shown you his hand on more than one occasion and he is no worse off.'

'What do you mean by shown his hand?' asked Sutton.

'The two girls that were left for you to find, of course.'

'Left for us?'

'Yes. Left for you. All part of his control. The first one, Haley Breen, she wasn't found ten years hence in the middle of a forest, was she? She was left in a location where she was always going to be found. That's what he wanted and that's what happened.'

'Yeah, ok. But Claudia, the second one was submerged and may have stayed out of sight for much longer,' he said.

'Nonsense. That was another deliberate scenario.'

'But what about the marks around her ankles. The Pathologists thought that she had probably had some kind of weight tied to her to keep her down and prevent her from floating to the surface.'

'Thought? Probably? No. Did your divers find anything to substantiate this theory? No. My conclusion is that he knew it would only be a matter of time before she was discovered. If he had wanted those girls to remain hidden, then he would have made certain and would have chosen entirely different locations to place them. You may never have found them,' she said.

'So why hasn't Angelica Rowntree been found?' asked Sutton.

'She's a different kettle of fish, that's why. He's playing this one slightly differently. The others weren't important to him. They were nothing more than symbolic. If he was just your routine serial killer then you would have found her by now, because he would have wanted you to. But Angelica is being kept out of sight for a reason.'

'Do you think that she is still alive then?'

'It's not out of the question, Marcus. For now, the discoveries and reports of missing girls have stopped, which doesn't mean he's finished, but there is still a reason that she has not been found,' she said.

'Why would he alter the pattern?'

'The two that you have found are insignificant to him. They played their part in his fantastical mind, but they had no further meaning to him. Once he had finished with them, they were discarded and left for you.'

'So, are you saying that Angelica is special to him in some way?'

'I believe so. If I'm right, then you may be looking for someone with a family history of violence towards them or maybe a form of mental torture. These heinous acts may be retribution for past events, revenge for personal trauma, perhaps.'

'But not Angelica?' he said.

'I don't believe so. Remember, she is only a substitution for the real thing, just like the others.'

'So, if he doesn't feel hatred towards her in the same way as he does with the others, why take her?'

'If his mind has been twisted by past events then there could be a number of reasons, but I suspect she represents somebody that he cares for or did once.'

'Well, we'll find him,' said Sutton.

'You may, Marcus. You may not. And who's to say that you haven't already met him or perhaps one of your officers has. Killers look like everyone else, Marcus. They have normal lives, jobs, families. They can be silent and uncommunicative or gregarious. But the façade has cracks and it's up to people like you and I to recognise them. Would you even know if you had seen him or even spoken to him? Would any of your team know? I believe in the science, but I believe in gut feelings too, Marcus. Don't ignore them.'

Sutton paused on the phone and considered what Patricia had said. *Could we have already been that close? Gut feelings.*

'Remember, Marcus. These people have little conscience. They don't process guilt in the way we do. Guilt is no more than a social constraint to them, an inconvenience. They are brazened. They are not afraid of being caught because what they did was acceptable to them. I think I've told you all this before. Like revisiting the scene of the crime,' she said.

'What?' said Sutton, abruptly.

'What?' repeated Patricia.

'You said 'revisiting the scene of the crime'. Why would he do that?'

'Power, narcissism, maybe to prove to himself that he is smarter than you. These girls are trophies. They are representative of some kind of achievement. The trophy cabinet is the location that they were left at. He would be admiring his work.'

Sutton's mind flashed back to the CCTV of the woman on the towpath of the Limehouse Cut that was looking into the water.

'Patricia, could our man be a woman?' he said.

'It's possible, but I doubt it.'

'How are you able to be sure?'

'I'm not. Gut feeling, Marcus. It's possibly my most reliable source,' she said.

'So, if they are trophies in a cabinet, then we have to find the cabinet that he keeps Angelica in,' he said.

'Well done, Marcus. You're beginning to think like a Psychological Profiler, heaven forbid you should ever reach the dizzying heights of a Forensic Psychologist.'

'Quite. One of those in our family is quite enough,' he said.

FIFTY-FOUR

DS Carrie Linton was already bored of waiting outside 38 Rodina Close. She had rung the bell, knocked on the window, and peered inside, but nobody came to the door. Dorothy Walton was not in sight and as much as Carrie wanted to get inside Robin Greaves' abode, she couldn't just yet. She was fully aware that she didn't have the right to enter the property or the right to force entry without a greater reason than merely having a dislike for his attitude, which wasn't sufficient, sadly. Carrie didn't have the grounds to suspect that an offence had been committed and no magistrate in the land would grant her a search warrant just because she wanted one. She knew that she needed something more. *40 minutes, I've been here,* she thought.

Her dampened enthusiasm flickered into life momentarily when a car drove into Rodina Close but unfortunately, it wasn't him. She phoned Grace.

'Hey, beautiful.'

'Hi Carrie. What you up to?'

'Presently, I'm perched outside somebody's house, waiting for them to come home so that I can ask a few questions.'

'Sounds exciting,' said Grace.

'You wouldn't believe it. I'm bored stiff. I've been to and from this place already today and I've drawn a blank both times.'

'Sounds about as productive as my day. You remember Emily Roache?'

'Yeah, the girl I spoke to at school.'

'She walked out today. Decided that she didn't want to be a teacher after all. Left me completely in the lurch,' said Grace.

'Charming. Sounds like we need a girl's night pretty soon to drown our sorrows.'

'I'm always up for one of those,' laughed Grace.

'Let's fix it up then. What about Friday night?'

'Definitely. Although Marc is home that night, does it matter?'

'No, he's used to us by now,' said Carrie.

'That's true. Friday it is then.'

'Ok. Listen, I better go. I'm supposed to be at work, if that's what this is.'

'Alright. Talk soon, darling,' said Grace.

'Bye, you gorgeous girl,' said Carrie.

Carrie ended the call and put her phone back inside her coat pocket. The time was dragging, and she was ready to give up for the day and go back to the station. She had been thinking about the CCTV footage that Marc Sutton had been looking at and she wanted to have a look for herself. *Right, that's it.* Carrie turned the ignition key and started the car. As she held the gear lever, she looked in her rear-view mirror and spotted Dorothy Walton going into a house, further into the Close. Carrie didn't know whether it was the house that Dorothy lived in or whether it was one of the resident's but either way she felt the urge to have a little chat. She wondered whether Dorothy might be useful seeing as the rest of her day had been very uneventful. *Why not?* Carrie locked the car and left it outside number 38. It was unmarked so even if Greaves came home, it would look like any other car. She decided to take the chance this time and walked along the Close and up to the door where she had seen Dorothy. She rang the bell. A surprised Dorothy Walton answered.

'Oh, it's you. I did wonder if that was your car,' she said.

'Well, you were right,' said Carrie.

'I'd invite you in, but Graham's got a cold, and I wouldn't want you to catch it.'

'Oh, ok. Best I stay out here then,' said Carrie.

'Is there something you wanted? Sally, isn't it?'

'No, it's Carrie and yes, there is something. I don't suppose you've noticed if Mr Greaves has been back since I was here earlier, have you?'

'I haven't seen him much at all today, no. Not since he went out earlier this morning. I've been changing the bedding today and getting it all prepared for the laundry van that comes tomorrow. Such a lot to get through.'

'I bet there is. Any idea where he went?' asked Carrie.

'I expect he went to work, unless he was popping to see his mother.'

'How often does he do that?'

'Oh, a couple of times a week, not much more than that, I don't think'.

'Well, she comes to see him too, doesn't she?' Said Carrie.

'Oh, no,' said Dorothy.

'Pardon?'

'No. She doesn't come here.'

'Oh, I thought she did. Wasn't she here when I came before, and you said that I might meet her?' said Carrie.

'Oh, no,' laughed Dorothy, 'That wasn't what I meant at all.'

'Then what did you mean, Mrs Walton?'

'I don't know if I should say, really. It's just that…'

'What?' asked Carrie.

'Well, sometimes he likes to dress up in women's clothes. I meant that he looks like he could be his own mother. She doesn't come here. She's in a Care Home,' explained Dorothy.

'Have you actually seen him?' asked Carrie.

'Through the window, yes.'

'So, when I saw the things in his place, they weren't actually hers at all.'

'They probably were, just that he puts them on sometimes,' said Dorothy with an awkward grin, 'but it's not my place to intrude so I don't say anything.'

'Right,' said Carrie, a little surprised at the news, 'Where is the Home?'

'Oh, now you're asking me. Hang on, I'll ask Graham, he's better with directions and things than I am.'

Dorothy Walton took a step back into the passageway and called out to her husband as Carrie tried to process the latest news about Robin Greaves. She reached in her bag for her notepad in case Graham came up with an address for Greaves' mother and opened it up to a new page. Carrie could hear Dorothy and Graham talking, and within a minute, Dorothy was back.

'Right, here we are. It's The Pavilion in King Edward Road. Do you know it?' asked Dorothy.

'I think so, but I can certainly find it.'

'Tell her about that bloody bedding,' shouted Graham, with a cough and splutter.

'She doesn't have time for all that,' shouted Dorothy.

'Time for what?' said Carrie, inquisitively.

'Oh, he's got his knickers in a twist about the bedding. He's not the one that has to deal with it either.'

'What about it?'

'Well, you see I don't usually allow the residents to remove any of the fixtures from their rooms and I include things like the bedding in that, but then I noticed that I was short of a few items from number 38, but they always came back after a few days or so. So, I turned a blind eye. Well, you do, don't you sometimes?'

'What did he want them for?'

'Well, as you know, he works at the garage, that one in Trenton Street, you know. Anyway, I think he must lay them on the floor in the garage when he's working under the cars. I can imagine how cold that floor would be. So, consequently, they get grubby and then I find them all mucked up with dirt. Graham doesn't think I should let him use them, but I can't have him feeling the cold when he's at work, so I don't say anything,' she explained.

'I see. They must get very dirty.'

'They do. Graham says it's not like dust from a garage, but I say it is. You know, when they bang the side of the car, and all the rusty bits drop down. I've seen it when Graham used to do his own maintenance on our old cars.'

'It's not rust, Dorothy, I've told you before. One day Catchpole's are going to refuse to take them.' shouted Graham.

'There he goes again,' said Dorothy, with eyebrows raised to the sky.

'What does he think it is?' asked Carrie.

'Rust is darker,' shouted Graham, over-hearing the doorstep conversation, 'Like brake dust. This is lighter and more like the texture of flour. It's fine and dusty.'

'You haven't worked on cars for years,' shouted Dorothy, dismissively, 'I expect he's forgotten what it was like,' she said turning to Carrie.

'Perhaps. Ok, well, thank you for the address,' said Carrie as she turned away from the door and said her goodbyes.

Carrie walked back to her car and sat inside. She checked her phone for directions to The Pavilion and jotted the address on her pad along with the story about the bedding from Graham and Dorothy Walton. As she left Rodina Close, she touched the phone symbol on the media screen in her car and called Marc Sutton. He answered after two rings.

'Carrie, how's it going?'

'It's not, really. Greaves never showed but I did have a chat with the Warden at Rodina Close. It seems that Greaves' mother doesn't visit him after all even though he implied that she did. I've got an address for the Care Home that she lives in and I'm going down there now. I reckon I stand a chance of getting more out of her than I do out of Greaves. Also, there's a chance that I might run into him,' she said.

'Ok. Sounds like another long shot but I'll go along with it,' said Sutton.

'I know what you mean but I just know he's hiding something, and I might be able to get something from her.'

'Alright. Stay in touch. I'll still be here when you get back so you can have a look at the CCTV footage if you like.'

'Oh, yes, definitely. I'll see you soon, hopefully,' she said.

'Oh, and another thing. I hear it's girl's night on Friday.'

'Oh, yeah. You up for it?'

'Sort of. I'll be upstairs,' he said.

'Thought you were serving the drinks,' said Carrie, with a chuckle.

'You watch it, Detective Sergeant, or I'll change your shift,' he joked.

'And I'll tell Grace, I'm being bullied.'

'Ok, you win. Take care, see you later.'

'Will do, bye.'

FIFTY-FIVE

Minneapolis, Minnesota.

Captain Antonio Rodrigues unlocked his office door and carefully nudged it open with his knee as he balanced two cups of coffee on a small tray. The boisterous noise from the office intruded into the room. Some of the computers had finished uploading or downloading, he was never certain which it was. Neither for that matter was Gregory Bonner. As the door clicked shut and the hubbub remained outside, where it belonged, several eyes looked up as they saw Big Toni disappearing out of sight and wondered why Gregory Bonner might be on the wrong end of a lecture from the Captain.

'Here we go,' he said.

Gregory Bonner sat in silence as his Captain lowered the tray to the desk. Big Toni walked around the desk to his chair and took one cup for himself before nodding at Bonner, inviting him to take the other. Big Toni took a careful sip and replaced it on his desk.

'Ok, then, Bonner. Where do we start?' he said.

Gregory Bonner was certainly not accustomed to taking the lead or even being offered the opportunity to contribute so freely on any sort of investigation when Big Toni was in the room, so he just looked at him, waiting for a prompt. All he saw was Big Toni's vacant expression.

'So, what have you got, Bonner?' he said.

'What do you want to know about first?' said Bonner, slightly nervously.

'Give me the trail you've been following. What happened at that search and rescue centre? What was so important about you going there in the first place?'

'Oh, ok. Well, I knew from the original reports into her disappearance that the Search Dogs had been deployed but I couldn't understand why they hadn't found anything. There didn't seem to be anything. Nothing to say that she had been there on that morning. The two Nelson girls, Elisha and Elizabeth, had said that they were out and didn't see her, but I don't understand why Betty would be out if she had asked Caterina to come to see her. They were close friends.'

His story stalled before it had really got going. Bonner envisaged his walk behind Caterina on the day that he imagined her walking to Betty's house. The day when he 'followed her' from her door towards the Nelson residence. He could picture her pale blue cardigan and her white dress flapping as she walked along briskly to Betty's. She was so determined to get there. Betty had asked her to come so she wouldn't let her down. *I followed her.*

'Maybe she wasn't there. Maybe she didn't get that far. Didn't Wade Nelson say that he hadn't seen her?' said Big Toni.

'Yeah, I know what he is supposed to have said. Anyhow,' said Bonner, returning to the original subject, 'when I arrived at MinnSARDA, the search and rescue training centre, I met with a guy named Derek Grant. He took me to his office and gave me quite an insight into how things work there. The training that the dogs go through is extensive, but it's not just them, the handlers have to be trained too. It takes a couple of years before the dogs are ready and then they have to be certificated. They don't just go out and start working. He explained to me that there are annual re-certifications too. They have a variety of skill sets, like cadaver dogs. It's a big operation.

'So, if it's such a big deal, then why didn't they find something at the Nelson place?' asked Big Toni.

'Well, that's the thing. I think they made a mistake,'

'A mistake?' said Big Toni, cocking his head to one side.

'Yeah, there's something not right,' said Bonner.

'You didn't suggest this to Grant, did you?'

'I did actually.'

'Wow. I bet that went down well.'

'As expected, I suppose,' said Bonner.

'Tell me, Bonner, what is it about this whole situation that has you second-guessing the outcome? You have to give me something more than just your suspicion,' said Big Toni.

Bonner knew that he simply couldn't tell Big Toni that it was Caterina telling him that she was there; coming to him in his dreams and at times when his mind wandered into a trance. He sat with her staring into his eyes, begging him to find her, but he just couldn't put it that way to his Captain. 'After I had been educated in the world of search and rescue, I asked Derek Grant who was on duty with the dogs that morning, and he told me that it was a guy named Ken Toft. These people all have their own dogs so as to be able to create a real tight connection with them. Grant had one called Cilka. You would think that the sun shone out of her, the way he went on about how amazing she was. He was incredibly protective of her reputation. But it wasn't her that was there that day. It was a dog owned by Ken Toft, called Gretel, like in the nursery rhyme. He found two dogs in a suitcase in the forest when he was on a training mission or something. Anyhow, he took them home and after nobody had claimed them from the police, he named them Hansel and Gretel. It was Ken Toft and Gretel that went to the Nelson house.'

'Ok, so what happened next?' asked Big Toni.

'I asked Grant where I could find him, and he gave me Toft's address, out at Eden Prairie. So, I went to pay a visit.'

'Full marks for determination, Bonner,' said Big Toni, sipping some more of his coffee.

'He seemed a nice enough guy. He didn't kick me out, anyway.'

'Good job, he didn't. So, what happened then?'

'He invited me in, and we got talking. Like Grant he was very proud of his dogs and, as expected, he didn't really like the idea that a mistake might have taken place. He was about as impressed with the idea as Derek Grant had been. Anyhow, we continued talking and I pressed him about the accuracy of his dog that day. You see, Gretel indicated to Toft that she had found something.'

'Indicated?' said Big Toni.

'Yes, it's something that all the dogs do if they should discover something. Their sense of smell is remarkable, and they indicate in a number of different ways. Some will bark, some will stand, and some will lay down facing the spot where the find is. Ken Toft's dogs would lay down quietly and he would recognise that they had found something.'

'So, did this Gretel do that?' asked Big Toni.

'She did. And for me, that was the start of the problem.'

'How do you mean, Bonner?'

'Well, when I questioned what had gone on at the Nelson house, Toft seemed to be looking for excuses. He told me that the indication had been compromised and therefore could not be trusted. He said that Wade Nelson had used sulfuric acid on the grave of Hastings, the old dog that he had buried, to ensure rapid decomposition and to keep the foxes from digging around at the site. He also said that Wade Nelson had put the old dog in the shed before he buried him.'

'So, what does that have to do with anything?'

'So, Toft said that the indication was compromised because Gretel became confused by the strong odour and the fact that the old dog had been in the shed. He said that Gretel was indicating at the old dog and not at anything else,' explained Bonner.

'And you don't believe it.'

'No. But there's one more thing. Before I left, I showed Toft a scale drawing of the Nelson residence and I asked him to pinpoint precisely where Gretel had laid down to indicate her find. It took a bit of doing, which also concerned me, but eventually Toft made a mark on the map.

Now the grave for the old dog and the location of the shed were marked out as best I could manage, but when Toft made his mark, it was at neither point. So, what I'm wondering is that if Gretel is such a good dog, and as far Toft is concerned, faultless, why didn't she indicate at one particular spot.'

'Like he said, she was confused.'

'No. I don't buy it. These dogs are amazing at what they do. Something's wrong,' said Bonner.

'What can be wrong, Bonner? The dog indicated but because of the smell that was lingering, and you said they have a fantastic sense of smell, it was put off. The Nelson dog was in the grave and this Gretel was picking up the scent. I don't see what's wrong,' said Big Toni.

'It's like you just said Captain, they have a fantastic sense of smell. They go through extensive training and attend extra training days; it's not making sense. I think Gretel indicated because she had found something, but it was Toft that failed, not the dog. I believe that the canine was superior to the human. I think Gretel was definitely onto something. It's the accuracy of the mark that Toft made that I don't trust. That's what's wrong.'

Big Toni had to concede that Bonner made a good point. Although the search and rescue world was new to him, Big Toni was beginning to understand. He had to accept that if the dogs had acquired such high-quality skills and had been trained at such an elite school, there might be more to the whole thing. Slowly, Big Toni was beginning to feel that Bonner just might be onto something, but proving it was going to be messy.

'Just give me a minute. Drink your coffee,' said Big Toni, as he stood and turned to face the window, looking out across towards the Mississippi and the Hennepin Avenue Bridge.

This pause allowed Bonner to reflect on what he had said. It hadn't been his intention when he left home this morning to try to convince his Captain that there might be more to the Caterina Marks case than the reports were showing, but it had turned out that way. He was grateful that Big Toni had listened to him and for the first time he believed that his investigation might have a chance of divulging the truth behind the Caterina Marks mystery. As he sat and waited for Big Toni, Bonner realised that he had lost interest in his coffee. Too much was at stake to think about coffee as much as his tired body was crying out for a lift.

'Bonner, have you got that map of the Nelson residence to hand?' said Big Toni without turning around from the window.

'Yeah, it's at my desk.'

'Get it. I wanna look for myself.'

FIFTY-SIX

Ahuja Industries, East London.

Angelica pulled the sleeve of her sweatshirt down over her wrist and wrapped it around her painful right hand. Trying to find a clean part was impossible. Tears trickled gently down her cheeks. *That really, really hurt.* On inspection, the evidence that she had been wrenching the chain in an effort to pull it away from the wall was apparent. The chain that she had held tightly and wrapped around her hand had slipped as she tugged violently at it. Her hand had bruised quickly, and a couple of her knuckles were bleeding. She had pulled at it so hard that it had raked across the back of her hand causing it to begin to swell. She had felt her wrist strain too and was sure that she heard it click. She sat down in her corner and tucked her hand tightly under her armpit to keep it warm. The throbbing pain caused her to screw her face up and grit her teeth. *I had it then,* she thought, as she looked over her left shoulder at the point where the chain connected to the wall. There was a dusting of brick dust on the floor beside her and a little that clung to the uneven surface of the wall immediately beneath where she had been pulling. She would probably have to clean it up before it was seen by *him.* Angelica was certain that she had plenty of time to have another go before she was likely to get another visit. She didn't want to waste time resting her hand, even though it hurt her. *It'll calm down in a minute.*

She looked at her hand and noticed that the bleeding had slowed down considerably. The pressure on it had helped. She would have to clean it properly when she next got some water. Iron bar lay on the floor beside her, and she decided that she would try to make use of it again. Previously, she had failed to break the chain with it, but it was worth trying to use it to damage the brickwork around where the chain met the wall. Her problem was that she didn't want him to see that she had been causing damage. He would know that she had been using something and would start searching amongst her blankets. He had remained mostly calm up to now, save for a couple of weird episodes with the hairbrush, but she was still alive, and she wanted to keep it that way.

What have I got to lose? If I get free, I'm off. Angelica felt a renewed strength deep within her. She couldn't judge time anymore and had no recollection of exactly how long she had been here in this cold and depressing echo chamber of a hell hole. The thought of being free made her start to cry. She was certain that her parents and her friends had all given up hope by now. *I bet no-one is looking for me anymore.* She tried to refocus her thoughts and push away the idea that she was never going to get out; never going to hold her Mum and Dad ever again. The tears ran. Angelica looked down at Iron bar and sighed. *C'mon old friend. Let's do this.*

When she held Iron bar in her hand she could feel the pain shoot through it, sharply. She winced as she realised that this was going to have to be a left-handed attempt at freedom. Not something that she had a lot of confidence in. Angelica held Iron bar in her left hand and looked at the point where the chain met the wall. She raised the bar and aimed it. With a clumsy, ungainly movement, she swung Iron bar at the wall. The noise of it striking the bracket that fixed the chain to the wall reverberated around her, it's sound bouncing off of the steel walls of the factory. *Missed.* She wiped the tears from her cheeks and prepared for another attempt. When she swung again, she hit the same spot. Iron bar fell from her hand and bounced against her shin, just above her ankle. 'Shit, shit,' she shouted. She put her hand onto the part that hurt and held it for a moment until the worst of the pain had subsided. Angelica picked up Iron bar and looked at the task again. She had to hit the brickwork immediately beside the bracket and keep hitting that point to wear it away and hopefully loosen the bolts that held it in place. Once it was loose, she could use Iron bar to try to displace it. But she was a long way from that moment right now. She swung at it again and caught it perfectly. She looked at the bracket, hoping to see some indication that she had made a difference. It didn't look any different. In fact, hardly any brick dust had fallen at all. Her mood swung from the anticipation of escape to the resignation of dying here before anybody found her. *Nobody is looking.*

She was getting cold again as the late afternoon cooled the factory even more than usual. Iron bar had made her hand hurt and feel cold too. Every blow that she attempted caused a shudder to vibrate along her arm and make it ache. As much as Angelica wanted to beat the wall over and over until the bracket finally yielded to her, she knew that she couldn't keep it up indefinitely. She couldn't keep it up for very long at all. *Maybe, I'll try again later or tomorrow. Maybe when I've eaten, I'll feel stronger.* She looked at her injured hand and cursed it. The burst of physical activity had tired her so much that she closed her eyes, just for a moment, just long enough to re-coop some of her enthusiasm and strength.

The next thing she knew was when she startled as she heard the metal gate bang loudly. She realised that she had fallen asleep. It was darker now. *He's coming. The wall. Shit.* She hurriedly grabbed at a blanket and started to rub the brick dust from the wall and sweep the dust from the floor in her corner. The dust that she had created was darker than the coating of cement that encrusted just about every part of the factory. *He mustn't see this.* Angelica worked fast to hide the evidence. As much as her hand hurt her, she had to get this done. Her breathing rate increased at the thought of what he might do if she got caught. She felt that if she didn't cause him any trouble then she might survive for longer, but what she didn't know was how long this could go on for. *Why is he keeping me?* She could hear him now. His footsteps across the floor were getting louder. He was close. Angelica began to panic. Then he appeared. There was no carrier bag with her food, no water bottle. *Something's wrong.* Angelica froze. She sat in her corner, motionless, and stared at him. The routine that had played out since she found herself here, in this dirty place, had not changed up until now. Breakfast and dinner had always arrived at about the same time each morning and evening. She couldn't work out why there was no bag for her to untie and find her food in. Then she noticed that he wore his rucksack over his shoulder. *It must be in there.*

For a brief moment, Angelica felt reassured as he took the rucksack off and placed it on the floor beside him. He didn't usually get quite so close to her unless he had anymore weird ideas about brushing her hair again. He loosened the string at the top of the rucksack and reached inside. Angelica breathed a quiet sigh of relief in anticipation of a much-needed hot meal. Then he looked straight at her, and with a single rapid movement pulled out something white. Before Angelica could react, he was forcing it over her head and pulling it tight around her neck. She could feel the weight of him on top of her, squeezing the air from her lungs and making it impossible for her to move. *This is bad. He's come to kill me.* Angelica's mouth dried. She could feel the blood draining from her face. She tried to kick out, but now he was kneeling on her legs, stopping any movement. She was aware of him grabbing at her hands and could feel something tightening on her wrists. He clambered all over her and seemed to be kneeling across her chest now. Then he stopped moving. *This is it; I'm going to die.* She began to whimper and braced herself for pain, but the sound she heard next made her think of only one thing. A loud crack and the sound of the chain dropping to the floor. Part of it landed on top of her, glancing off her head. Angelica's brain was working overtime as she tried to comprehend what was happening. *Is he letting me go? He's taking me somewhere. He's going to kill me.*

She could feel him pulling at her roughly and dragging her to her feet, but she couldn't see a thing. *The chain is off.* Sharply, he tugged her forwards. Angelica stumbled onto one knee, but he didn't stop moving. She was being dragged along whether she liked it or not. After being dragged for a few more paces, she managed to get herself onto two feet again and keep up with him by stepping blindly along. *I'm outside my circle of dust,* she thought. Angelica didn't know whether this was good or bad. *I don't like this hood.* She kept up, occasionally stumbling over unrecognisable objects on the factory floor. The further they went, the more Angelica thought about trying to escape, somehow. *Got to get this hood off first. Then I can run.*

Then her foot kicked something solid that made her fall abruptly forwards, landing flat on her face. The fall knocked the wind out of her, but immediately, he grabbed at her arms and dragged her up again. Feeling his hands on her made her shudder. *Can't run with this hood.* The next thing she knew, she was being pulled up a flight of stairs.

'Where are you taking me?' she said, choking back the tears, trying to gauge her footsteps.

But there was no response, other than more pulling at her tied hands. To Angelica, it felt as though they were going up for ages. She had no perception of how far they had come or where she was in the factory in relation to her corner. But she knew she was still in there somewhere. The hood was thin enough for her to appreciate light that every now and then would appear and disappear. *Windows,* she thought. Angelica had seen some windows that were high up above her corner. Some were broken where the pigeons got in. So did the rain. Then she could feel the surface beneath her feet change. It felt like metal grating to her. *I'm on one of those landings, high up. What the hell am I doing up here?*

As Angelica continued forwards, trying not to fall again, he jolted her to a stop. She felt him push down on her shoulders, forcing her to sit. *If he takes this hood off, I'm going to fight and run,* she thought. But Angelica didn't get the opportunity. She felt him tying something around her waist and arms and then she felt it pull tightly towards one side of her, holding her in place. Lastly, he tied her feet. Next, she felt his hands around her neck. He was untying the hood. Angelica knew that her idea of flailing out at him and making herself just enough space to get to her feet and run was already a failed plan. When the hood came off, Angelica's hair was all across her face. She shook her head and for the first time since being removed from her corner, she could see where she was.

Angelica gasped.

FIFTY-SEVEN

Minneapolis, Minnesota.

A steaming cup of tea sat next to the sofa, on a small, rickety round table. A book about the ruins of Pompeii sat beside it. The explosion of Vesuvius in 79CE and the consequential disaster had become a fascination of late, for the reader. The book also touched upon the history of the Roman Empire and its relationship with life today which had provided many hours of stimulating reading. The evenings were long, and the days weren't much better but at his age, time was precious, and so filling some of it with reading made sense to him. It kept the brain active.

Outside, the debris from a hard afternoon's work in the garden sat visible from the patio doors which faced out onto the garden. The overgrown Honeysuckle that clung relentlessly to the fence had finally yielded. The tea was a sort of incentive to get the job done. Having showered and changed into some comfortable clothes, Harry Bones rested with his feet up. The gardening enabled him to think of nothing in particular for a couple of hours, but the longer time went on, he found that his old memory would keep replaying his torrid conversation with Elisha Nelson on the day that she turned up unexpectedly on Betty's bike. Harry felt a sense of guilt. He knew something that he knew he should tell his old friend Gregory Bonner, the patrol officer, but each time he thought about this, he arrived at the same conclusion; it would do no good. In fact, it could only, possibly, do harm and he didn't want that. There were a lot of questions to answer about the morning that poor old Hastings had been put to death. Harry also knew that it didn't stop there.

Harry sipped at his refreshing tea and stood from his sofa. He wandered slowly into the front room with one hand rubbing his back. 'I'll be alright tomorrow,' he told himself. He often found himself wandering around the house without really knowing why. Perhaps it was a combination of boredom and the need to simply move occasionally rather than sit and get set in one position. *You're a long time dead, Harry,* he thought. As he stood at the front window and looked out at the street, the old clock in the hall chimed three times. The school kids would be coming by soon. Harry watched sometimes and fondly remembered the days when Betty and Elisha would call by for lemonade. Not anymore. Those days were long gone. A lot of things that Harry enjoyed were long gone. He waited to see the first of the school kids start to amble past, some dragging their school bags, some walking their bikes, before he turned away from the window.

In front of him, on the opposite side of the room, was the bureau where he often sat and wrote lists of jobs he wanted to do around the house. He had owned the bureau for forty years. He and his late wife had chosen it together. As with many things that Harry owned, it was in perfect condition.

Nowadays, though, it served as another reminder of something that troubled him. He walked over to it and rested his hand on the top. It had been lovingly polished so many times that his hand glided over it with ease. It had been made from Danish walnut and the handles to the five storage drawers were made out of brass. There was plentiful storage for stationary. Harry had organised the drawers into various items; paperclips, pens, a stapler, and rubber bands like the ones he used when he delivered the mail. Inside the pull-down top section were a number of small box-like drawers that over the years had become filled with all manner of bits and pieces.

He loved the old thing. The top drawer contained a box of articles that he had so often thought about burning when he had a fire going in the garden, but he never had. They meant too much to him, and yet their purpose had not been entirely innocent. If they fell into the hands of someone that understood their original intention, they might cause him more trouble than they were worth. Harry used to get these out every so often and look through them, even though they were only copies, just to bide the time. Many of the originals were usually destroyed by the recipient after being read but sometimes Harry found them in the bins or screwed up in a drawer. He removed the ones that he found. In a way it had a greater effect. They gave him a feeling that retribution had been served, however right or wrong that may be. Retribution on behalf of his beloved Penelope Nelson; Penny. He knew that if he burned the lemon-coloured envelopes, that he couldn't be tempted to look at them or read them ever again, but he never mustered the will. It would be like breaking his final connection to the woman that he still loved dearly. Harry had given it a lot of consideration before he began to write the letters that hid, secretly inside the lemon envelopes. He couldn't have carried it out if he hadn't freely had access to the Nelson residence.

Penny used to keep her envelopes in the study and Harry knew where to look. He could never be entirely certain that they had the effect that Elisha had wanted him to achieve, but he knew in his heart that they definitely played their part. When Harry reflected on what he had done, he always found himself wrestling with mixed feelings. Guilt and satisfaction. Whether he would ever tell Gregory Bonner about them was another matter. Maybe not.

What made Harry's mind up about his secretive venture was that he and Penny had formed their letters identically. He would often leave her notes about their daily jobs in the garden and even Harry couldn't tell the difference sometimes. It was just as though she had written them. That, of course, was the point. It was a wild idea and not without risk, but the more Harry thought about it, the more he liked the sound of it, and the more he so wanted to inflict discomfort upon Wade Nelson.

Harry had sat at his old bureau and written several short notes on scrap paper before he was satisfied with the content. His memory of seeing Penny being beaten or the thought of her sleeping in the shed kept him focussed on the task. When Harry made his first attempt, he wasn't sure that it would work, but he was pleasantly surprised by the effect it had. So much so that he wanted to do this over and over and cause as much trauma to Wade Nelson as possible. Penelope was writing to him from the grave.

Whenever the opportunity arose, Harry would ensure that he could slip one of the lemon envelopes in with the morning's post. This was easy, most of the time. He was always around early to tend the garden. All he had to do was time it right.

On the first occasion he had arrived exactly on time. The mail had only just been deposited in the mailbox and he knew that it often sat in there for an hour or so. He slipped the envelope in with the morning's delivery and wandered in as normal. Harry collected whichever tools he wanted from the shed and watched from the side of the house.

Before very long he could see Wade Nelson sit in his usual chair with a handful of mail. Harry watched closely as Wade Nelson picked through the mail until he got to the first lemon envelope. His reaction was even more dramatic than Harry had hoped it would be.

Initially, he expressed a degree of confusion, but then he opened it. What Harry witnessed was terror in his face. He threw the note down and walked out of the room. Harry saw him make for the stairs and took a risk that he knew would be worth doing. He quickly entered the property. He could hear Wade Nelson upstairs. Harry rushed into the room as quickly as he could and retrieved the note and the envelope, hiding it in his overalls, before swiftly returning to the garden to take up his vantage point again, and wait.

Sure enough, Wade Nelson returned. He began to look for the note, but it had gone. He looked pale as he became more frantic, throwing cushions onto the floor as he searched the area where he had sat. But nothing. It worked. Harry didn't always manage to retrieve the evidence, but he was successful more often than not and Wade Nelson never had a clue. As far as he was concerned it was Penny that was somehow, mysteriously communicating with him. Harry continued with his plan right up to the day that he found Wade Nelson swinging from the balcony.

FIFTY-EIGHT

Tilbury, East London.

She hadn't spoken to her sister for nine days. Even the text messages had dwindled to a halt with a gradual lethargy. Ever since the whereabouts of Karter Swann had been shared between them, the atmosphere had noticeably altered. Neither was certain of what the other was thinking anymore, or more likely, what their intentions had become. But there was an overwhelming urgency to act before the other did.

    She parked her car close to the house and got out, looking around her to ensure that her sister wasn't anywhere in sight. She carefully studied the other cars in the vicinity in case she recognised one of them. Content that she was alone, she approached the house, stepping around the puddles, and knocked on the front door of number 12 Countess Street and waited, feeling immediately uncomfortable. She was certain that this was going to be the right house, going by her sightings of him in the past, but she had never committed to getting this close before. The pavements were wet and drops of rain fell from the guttering at the front of the house, landing on the shoulders of her coat. She looked up and could see the broken guttering; the culprit that was responsible for her being dripped on. The curtains to the upstairs rooms were closed. She wondered if he was up there. *Did he see me?*

    The occasional car could be heard behind her as it drove through the puddles in the road. She nervously looked around behind her as if to check that nobody was watching her. It was quiet. *I should go.* Then she heard a faint noise coming from inside the house. *What the hell am I going to say if it's him?* She questioned why she was even here and why she hadn't thought this through more clearly, but something was driving her to be first. First to make contact. Trying to prepare herself for the inevitable awkwardness of the situation, she mumbled rehearsed words quietly to herself, as another nervous shudder chilled her body. The time and effort that she had spent on her appearance felt like a waste of time now. Her face felt devoid of all colour; pale and clammy. She considered turning away, but it was too late now, as the door chain could be heard jangling on the other side of the door. *Oh God! What am I doing?*

A shortish gentleman opened the door and peered defensively around the frame. He looked as though he was trying to work out whether he recognised her or not. His brow was furrowed, and he looked almost cross and more than a little confused.

'Yes. Can I help you?' he said.

She tried to speak with a dry mouth, but the words stuck. Quickly she moistened her mouth and gave a little cough. *It's not too late to run,* she thought.

'Sorry. I wonder if you could tell me if Mr Swann lives here?' *Mr Swann? What am I saying? I've never called him that.*

'Erm.... No. Nobody lives here by that name,' he replied.

'Oh! Are you sure?' she said, immediately realising how ridiculous that sounded.

'I should know. It is my house. Perhaps you have the wrong address,' he said.

She was as certain as she could possibly be that this was the house that she had seen him enter on more than one of her spying missions. *This is the house.*

'No, this is the house,' she said, as her mind began to work overtime as she tried to make sense of what was happening.

'I'm afraid there is no Mr Swann here. Perhaps you have the wrong name,' he said.

Wrong name? Yes, why not. His hair is different and there's the new beard. Why not.

'Yes, that must be it. I must be getting him confused with somebody else. I haven't seen him for a long time, and I must have got his name mixed up.'

'Well, I'd like to see the look on Kevin's face when he gets his surprise. Two surprises!' he said.

'What?'

'It's none of my business but I assume that you're not his girlfriend too?'

'What?'

'She was here earlier. Nice girl. Just in from the States, she said. I guess that's America,' he said.

'What? What girl?'

'She said that she wanted to surprise him, but he wasn't here, so I told her where he worked. She said that he didn't know that she was here and that it was all a big surprise for him. If she has come all that way, she doesn't want a wasted journey. Funny thing. She called him

Karter. I took it to be her pet name for him. Perhaps she prefers it to Kevin. She's gone to meet him at work and give him a surprise.'

'Kevin?' she said.

'Yes. Kevin Marshall. That's who you're looking for isn't it?'

'What? Yes. Kevin.'

'You sound a bit like Elizabeth too. Pity. She only missed him by about five minutes or so.'

'Who?'

'Elizabeth. Kevin's girlfriend. You have that same twang in your voice.'

'Right. I need to know where he works too…so that I can join in with the surprise,' she said.

'Of course, you do. Goodness, he will be shocked to see you both. He never has visitors. Hardly even gets any mail. A bit secretive, is our Kevin. Anyhow, it's the Riverside Centre. Not far. If you turn left at the traffic lights, you can follow the signs from there. They should lead you straight to it. Easy enough. It's down on the left-hand side before you reach the river,' he explained.

'Thank you,' she said, turning towards the gate at the front of the house.

'Have you brought a present too?' he said.

'What?'

'A present. It looked as though Elizabeth had a present in her rucksack. Not really a rucksack, more of a holdall. It was over her shoulder. I'm only guessing really but I noticed it as she walked away. Funny shape too, with an E on the front. It looked like she had a small axe in there. Obviously, it wouldn't be that, but it was shaped a bit like it. Anyway, I hope you find him,' he said as he began to close the front door, 'Oh, what did you say your name was? In case you miss him, I can tell him later,' he asked.

'I didn't. You said an E. In a circle?'

'Yes, I think it was. Hope you haven't bought him exactly the same thing.'

'No, hardly. Thank you, again.'

She hurried back to her car. Her head filled with images of what was in the holdall. Except it wasn't a present and it wasn't actually a holdall or a rucksack. She was sure of what it was. The shape that Mr Turner had described to her could only be one thing as far as she was concerned. As soon as he had said it, her blood chilled. The shape of the case that she imagined was so recognisable to her. Years ago, she had become very familiar with these items. The ones that she used were larger and heavier, but it would be no less deadly in the hands of someone that knew how to operate it. She could be wrong but everything about this was shouting to her, warning her of the danger that she was sure she was about to face. She knew that her sister had always been smitten with the thought of owning a Cobra RX. She could remember the pictures that she had of them and the way she used to talk about the damage that she could inflict with one. 130lb draw weight, self cocking, self-loading, plenty of power for its size; she had heard it all before. If she was right, then Karter Swann was in real danger. Betty Nelson slammed the car into first gear, revved the engine hard and drove the car fiercely, wheel-spinning in the wet as she went. Things had just become serious.

FIFTY-NINE

When he left the pub, Brickhouse Street was deathly quiet. He briefly turned his head to see a single car parked opposite the bollards, only noticeable by a dim glow from the interior. He had sat by the window that looked out onto the street, waiting for him to walk past. He knew that he wouldn't enter the pub as he would be on his way to work. What he hadn't expected, was for him to be early. Without the luxury of a clear view of his face, Ray Keller relied on instinct. He had seen the hooded coat before, all part of a deterrent that would assist him from being recognised. Once he got into his stride, he could see the size of the man and was able to recognise the way in which he walked. Apart from being a little early, he was convinced that this was Kevin Marshall, or as he knew him, Karter Swann. The invisible man wasn't quite as invisible as he thought. Odhran O'Connell may have made people disappear, but he never took his eye off them.

The luminescence from the streetlights and the numerous factory floodlights shone across the road in the lengthy puddles as the thick and miserable clouds blanketed the sky above. It was dark and there were plenty of alleyways to hide in if necessary. Keller could only see him when the twists and turns in the road were favourable. He didn't want to be seen so he made sure that there was sufficient distance between them. He knew exactly where he was going and how long it was likely to take before he saw his man arrive at his place of work. Keller's dark clothing helped him blend into the grey and gloomy surroundings. He reasoned that even if Swann did turn around, that he wouldn't be able to discern the outline of the distant shape of the man following. Keller walked with his hands in his deep pockets. His right hand on the handle of a self-made cosh. Odhran O'Connell's instructions were clear. *Use your imagination, but don't kill him. Just deliver the message that nobody throws a favour back in the face of Odhran O'Connell. Remind him that I don't exist.*

Keller knew enough about precisely why he had been called on to carry out the task. The phone call from O'Connell had been short and sweet, but also entirely intelligible. When O'Connell had gone to great lengths to do a favour for Karter Swann, he didn't expect him to return and risk the chance of his 'disappearance' becoming known as a fake. The whole operation, including the acquisition of the bogus passport and the money, could prove very inconvenient if the police got hold of it. Then the trail could possibly lead back to O'Connell and that simply wasn't tolerable.

DC Steve Kingham entered through the front doors of the Snare and Cymbals. It wasn't exactly a welcoming atmosphere. Perhaps only as many as six people were inside. There was no music and no chatter. Just a few folk sitting in various snugs, minding their own business. His first look around didn't draw his attention to anyone that might have been Ray Keller. He took a further moment to study the clientele and was able to rule almost all of them out straight away. Kingham suddenly began to doubt the information from George Sullivan, although he had never let him down before. He checked his text again and waited at one end of the bar in case Keller was to appear, but nothing changed. The barman exchanged glances with Kingham but didn't immediately move towards him. Kingham wasn't drinking anyway. If he didn't think that Ray Keller was here, then he would be leaving. He didn't intend to spend more than a couple of minutes to establish whether Keller was present. His instinct would tell him if it wasn't obvious. The place was dead and Kingham thought that his chances of meeting Ray Keller were too, but he thought that there could be no harm in asking. His short conversation with the barman gave his adrenaline a shunt and he was out of there in a heartbeat. The majority of the people in the Snare and Cymbals hadn't even registered that Kingham had walked in.

Having established basically which way Keller was heading, DC Steve Kingham got moving in the same direction. Initially his intention was to catch up with Keller and try to speak with him but as he travelled further along the road, he decided to just follow for a while and see where he was going. Perhaps he might even learn where Ray Keller lived, which might be useful to know for the future. Kingham was tall and had a lengthy stride pattern, so it didn't take him long to catch sight of the man ahead of him. He reasoned that seeing as there were so few people around this area at this time of the evening, that the silhouetted shape ahead of him was very likely to be his intended target.

Kingham eased his pace a little in order to maintain a suitable distance from Keller whose own pace hadn't varied up to now. When the road straightened out, as it got closer to the river, Kingham could see another man ahead of Keller, approximately equidistant from him.

As he followed Keller, Kingham had no idea where he was aiming for. Before long they would begin to run out of road and so whichever Keller's destination was, he knew that it couldn't be too far away. Kingham could see that there were definitely no houses in this area which altered his first thought that he might be following Keller home. Nothing but large factories and wide factory gates.

Then he noticed the man up ahead turn left into a gateway and go out of sight. As he did so, Keller stepped up his pace and headed straight for the same gateway. He didn't stop to look around, he just seemed to follow the same route into the yard. Kingham increased his pace too and when he reached the entrance, he could clearly read a large sign. Riverside Centre. It didn't mean anything to him, but he was now feeling highly suspicious that the man ahead of Keller might be someone that Keller was interested in speaking with, or worse. The two men had vanished from sight and Kingham supposed that they were most likely to be inside the building, so he headed across the yard and towards the door at the front of the premises.

As Kingham walked through the gates, he spotted a single car parked up to his right. No occupant. He looked up and down the yard that stretched the full length of the building, but it was all quiet. As he stepped forward, he saw a light flicker to life from a window on the first floor. A shadow drifted across it. For the first time he wondered whether Keller had been following Swann. *Surely, I won't be that lucky.*

When he reached the door, he saw a smaller sign that sat above the doorway, again announcing that this was the Riverside Centre. Above the sign, a few wires hung down from the position where a small strip light should have been. After another quick look around him, Kingham decided to go in for a closer look and gave the door a gentle nudge, allowing it to creep open slowly. He was faced with a narrow passageway that extended about 30 feet ahead of him. A single door at the end was just visible. The walls and the ceiling of the passage were painted in a matt black paint making it as dark as possible. Above his head he could just make out the shape of a box that he assumed might be where the main fuses were. He ducked his head to avoid a part of the ceiling that hung down, supported only on one side, barely preventing it from falling to the floor. Kingham stood still and listened but didn't hear any sounds. Whoever was inside wasn't making any noise.

Seconds later, he was at the end of the passage. The single door was ajar. He peered cautiously around the frame and could see the beginnings of a stairway. A smidgen of light that was filtering through from the floor above enabled him to see that the staircase was made of concrete. Now at the foot of it, he could see that it terminated after approximately twelve steps. The small landing appeared to only have one exit; a set of double doors that he reckoned would lead him onto the first floor. Kingham fought off the scintilla of doubt regarding the intentions of Ray Keller and began to ascend the stairs.

SIXTY

20 minutes ago

It hadn't taken her long to persuade the man that opened the door to let her in. Her eyes did all the work. After all, she had explained that she was Kevin's girlfriend, and he hadn't wanted to be the one to stand in the way of a special surprise for him. He had told her that she could leave her car there too if she wanted, as there were no beer deliveries expected to arrive on the site tonight.

'Just pull the gate to when you go. The security is rubbish around here anyway,' he had said.

After she had finished using her most reliable flirtatious tactics, he would probably have shown her where the nightclub safe was and opened it for her too. He had considered hitting on Kevin's girlfriend but hadn't fancied facing the consequences if it all went wrong, which it invariably did, where he was concerned. He had told her to go up the stairs and through the first set of double doors on the left, which would lead her to the nightclub and the bar. She was welcome to wait for Kevin there. He even suggested to her that she might want to switch the lights off as part of her surprise. Besides, he would be on his way home very soon and didn't really care that much what went on after he had left work.

An unbridled desperate longing had led her to this point and there was no going back. She was completely convinced that her sister had eyes for Karter Swann, and intended to make him hers, and she just couldn't let that happen. Her hand had been forced and she had to act before Betty did. Only this time, losing him to her was not an option. The anguish that had built up ever since Betty had told her that she had been thinking about him had regularly plagued her mind. That day in the coffee shop had replayed over and over in her head. *Betty still thought about him, wanted him. Everything was Betty's. Everything always had been. But not this time.*

Elisha had felt his passion at the Travelodge, and she had wanted more but she had become deeply affected by the wretched hurt that she felt when he rejected her the following day. It twisted her mind and engineered an explosive desire for revenge, despite what she might have told Betty. If she couldn't have him, then nobody will have him.

She knew that she didn't have long before he would also be climbing the stairs, but there was just about enough time to decide whereabouts to wait. A quick look around enabled her to see that he would have to walk from the double doors and across the floor towards the bar. The empty space where people would gather and dance much later in the evening was far too exposed. She needed somewhere much more secluded for what she had in mind. She turned off the lights and relied on the torchlight on her mobile phone to help her to see, noticing a flicker of red brake lights as a car left through the gates to the outside yard. She needed to get him trapped so that he couldn't just turn and run. She followed the light around to the back of the bar and found a large storeroom. As she raised the light up it reflected against a mirror. Her own reflection startled her. There were spare chairs and tables stacked up to the ceiling and a large, refrigerated cabinet half filled with bottles. Behind the door to the room was an empty space, spacious enough to stand in and wait. But Elisha wanted somewhere even more private and secluded. She walked back into the bar area, glanced quickly out of the window to check if he could be seen approaching the building, and then noticed another window that looked out across a courtyard to the rear. It was dark but she could see a large sliding door with several windows in the top half of it. A number of beer barrels sat stacked up outside it. *A storeroom.* It looked perfect, and he would definitely be alone when he came to replenish the stocks. Elisha knew that he would have to go there to bring the beer across to the bar before anybody arrived. *If I can get in there.* Her brain began to concoct a plan.

SIXTY-ONE

Pavilion Care Home, King Edward Road.

Twenty minutes after leaving Rodina Close, DS Carrie Linton was standing at the reception desk and waiting for the lady on the telephone to finish her call. The building which sat well back from the road outside, had a large canopy which was supported by several angled struts that Carrie thought looked ugly, and stretched the full width of the façade. There were also attractive flower beds either side of the path that led to the front door. The reception area was bright with two vases of cut flowers that were situated at either end of the counter. An old-fashioned Grandfather clock delivered a subdued chime as she waited patiently. The atmosphere inside was peaceful, which was how Carrie had expected it to be, and only a handful of staff, including a member of the cleaning company who was wrestling with a temperamental vacuum cleaner, could be seen from where she stood. She heard the front door behind her give a positive click as a release lock allowed one of the staff to exit the building. She hadn't seen anyone press a switch to open the door and guessed that the staff might have a remote way of unlocking the door when they needed to leave. A form of remote key fob would certainly assist in preventing any of the residents from taking an unscheduled stroll outside. A line from the Eagles' song 'Hotel California' played in her mind. *You can check out any time you like, but you can never leave.*

As Carrie pondered the security measures at the Pavilion, the lady who had been preoccupied on the telephone spoke to her.

'Yes, can I help you?'

'Yes, I hope so,' said Carrie, turning to face the receptionist, 'I wonder if it's possible to speak with Mrs Greaves?' asked Carrie.

'Are you a relative?' she asked.

'No, I'm just a visitor,' said Carrie.

'Mrs Greaves,' repeated the lady, whose badge that Carrie could now read, said that she was Valerie.

Valerie reached under the counter and retrieved a large book with an orange cover. She opened it and began to flick the pages. Carrie assumed that perhaps Valerie was checking to see which room Mrs Greaves was in. She considered that with several residents it could be hard to keep track of all the room numbers. As Carrie waited for Valerie to come up with the answer, a slim young girl with shoulder length brunette hair walked up to the counter and placed a bunch of keys down on it.

'Here you go, Valerie. That's me done for today,' she said.

Valerie didn't respond immediately, engrossed as she was in her search in the large book. The young girl, whose badge said that she was Aimee, smiled at Carrie as they waited for Valerie to finish her search.

'Have you lost someone?' said Aimee.

'Yeah,' said Valerie in a long-extended sigh, as she referred to the computer screen, 'Mrs Greaves.'

Aimee lent across the counter and looked at the open page in the book that Valerie had spread open. While Valerie stared at the computer, Aimee ran her finger down the page and studied a list of names. When she got to the bottom of the page, she looked at Carrie.

'Are you sure of the name?' she asked, with a quizzical countenance.

'Yes, absolutely. Her son Robin comes here to visit her,' she said.

'Did you say, Robin?' asked Aimee.

'Yes,'

'I know who you mean,' she said, 'Robin's mother.'

Carrie gave a look that said *Well, obviously!*

'Ah, I know now,' said Valerie, as the proverbial penny dropped.

Carrie was a little bemused at the oddity as she tried to make a connection between Mrs Greaves and Robin's mother, whilst wondering why this wasn't the easiest of all conundrums to solve.

'I'll take you to her,' said Aimee.

'Ok, thank you,' said Carrie, none the wiser.

Aimee led Carrie down a corridor and apologised for the confusion. She explained that Robin's mother doesn't seem to acknowledge his name but always sees him. According to Aimee, she can be kind of reserved and distant at times. Sort of aloof, was Aimee's description.

'Are you family?' Aimee asked.

'No, no. I'm a police officer. I'm rather hoping that she can give me a few answers. Some information really.'

'Oh. Intriguing. Is anything the matter?'

'Not really,' said Carrie, 'More routine than anything.'

'Why Margaret? She can't have done anything wrong,' said Aimee.

'No, she hasn't.'

'Well, I'm not sure what you'll get from her. I'm not saying that she's not with it, just that she sometimes seems to be a bit confused to me. Especially when Robin is here to see her.'

'Does he come often?' asked Carrie.

'A few times each week. Maybe four times, depends.'

'Does she have any other visitors?'

'Not these days,' said Aimee.

'Does that mean that she used to have more,' asked Carrie.

'Not many, just the girls. They used to come when she first came to stay here but haven't been around for a while. Robin is her only regular visitor nowadays. She should be in here,' said Aimee, opening a door to a room that had numerous comfy chairs in; ones that were high-backed and looked out onto the rear gardens. Carrie followed.

Turning to Carrie, Aimee said, 'I think it might be best if you don't mention that you're a police officer. It's just that she will probably jump to the wrong conclusion and get herself all het up. Maybe we'll pretend that you're from the Befriending Service. Sometimes people come along to just sit and talk to the residents for a little while.'

'Fine. I can do that,' said Carrie. *Very inventive.*

Many of the chairs faced away from the door so Carrie couldn't immediately judge how many people were in the room. Aimee led her past a wide window that was flanked by extravagant looking curtains with a rich and colourful design, similar to that of a Peacock's train. As Carrie and Aimee ventured further into the room a few inquisitive heads turned to observe the unexpected visitor. Carrie smiled back at the blank faces and noticed that the light was just beginning to fade a little outside. She was aware that she wanted to get back to the station to see Marc Sutton and take a look at the CCTV, so she didn't want to spend any more time than was absolutely necessary talking to Mrs Greaves. Then as Aimee led the way, Carrie could see a lady sitting at the end of the room. The lady recognised Aimee and smiled up at her, offering her hand. Aimee held the lady's hand and spoke softly to her. Too softly for Carrie to hear. *Perhaps a whisper about the lady from the Befriending Service.*

'Somebody to see you, Margaret,' she said, 'I'll sit here if you don't mind, we don't let our guests alone with strangers, at least not until we know who they are,' she said, looking at Carrie.

'No, that's ok, although I thought you said that this was the end of your day. I don't want to keep you here,' said Carrie, hoping to speak with Mrs Greaves alone.

'I can stay for a little while longer. Just a few minutes. I'll catch up the time one way or another,' Aimee said with a wink.

Carrie set eyes on the face of Mrs Greaves for the first time. She looked quite frail, but her expression was one of curiosity. Her hair was extremely thin, and her face was quite pale. Her legs were well wrapped up under a blanket that displayed a Christmas scene. A little out of season but perfectly suitable for Mrs Greaves. Carrie introduced herself and, as Aimee had preferred, she didn't mention her profession or the reason for her visit. Carrie knew that at Aimee's request she was just going to have to bluff her way through it and see what happened.

'Did you say Carrie?' said Mrs Greaves.

'Yes, Carrie.' she replied with a kind smile.

'That's nice. I'm Margaret. Please call me Margaret, won't you?'

'Hello, Margaret. Nice to meet you,' said Carrie.

'Have you got any children?'

'No, I haven't,' replied Carrie.

'I have. I've got two daughters and a son. They don't come to see me though,' said Margaret.

Greaves has two sisters, thought Carrie.

Aimee exchanged glances with Carrie and smiled.

'Your son comes, doesn't he?' Aimee said to Margaret.

'Yes, their brother comes. But they don't come anymore,' she said.

Carrie looked at Aimee and mouthed *why?* Aimee shook her head slightly, indicating that she didn't know the reason. Carrie had logged that Aimee had mentioned that Robin's mother sometimes showed signs of confusion when her son was here to see her and wanted to know why.

'How often does your son come to see you, Margaret?' asked Carrie.

'I wish they would come again, but it's only him now,' she said.

Carrie looked at Aimee briefly, but persevered.

'Your son comes though doesn't he, Margaret?' she asked.

'They used to come. I miss them now,' said Margaret.

'Why did they stop coming?' said Carrie, following the thread that Mrs Greaves appeared to be happier to talk about.

'They didn't always get on in those days,' she said, drifting slightly, 'Pity, because he loved his sister.'

Sisters, pleural, thought Carrie.

'Why didn't they get along, Margaret?' she asked.

'Oh, usual things, I suppose. They were always taking sides. They used to tease each other and lock the bedroom door, and he used to get back at them. They could be rather unkind at times too. He could be so loving but not always. Life was hard with the children to look after and no husband to help out.'

'What happened to your husband?' asked Carrie.

'He passed away.'

'Oh, I'm sorry,' said Carrie.

'That left me with all of them to look after. I didn't manage very well, even though I had them there. The girls did their bit, but it wasn't easy. They stayed with me after he left the house but when he came back, they left. There was a lot of tension in the house at that time too. Filled with bad memories, it was.'

'Do they live nearby?' asked Carrie.

'Not far. Bournemouth, I think. Is that far?'

'That's a shame,' said Carrie, ignoring the geographical poser.

'Yes, it was a shame. Can't change the past though, can we? I would if I could,' said Margaret.

'What are the girls' names, Margaret?'

'They are Jennifer and Joanna,' she responded.

'Are they close in age?'

'About four minutes apart,' said Margaret, with a smile, 'Their brother is older.'

'Oh, twins then,' said Carrie, stating the obvious.

'Yes, I couldn't believe it. They used to all get on ok, but then something gradually changed. Before long I was having to sort out their differences and I was forever stepping in between the pair of them. They never seemed to stop winding each other up.'

'I guess it's normal to have a bit of sibling rivalry, isn't it?' asked Carrie.

'Not like this it isn't.'

'What made it different?' asked Carrie.

'They always seemed to always go too far. If somebody hadn't been around to rescue the situation, it could have turned out badly on more than one occasion.'

'Goodness me. Sounds a bit serious.'

'Well, can't change it now,' said Margaret.

'I'm sorry but I will have to go soon,' said Aimee.

'Oh, forgive me. Of course,' said Carrie.

'Ask for me another time and I'll make sure you get to see Margaret again if you wish to,' said Aimee.

'Oh, thank you. That would be helpful. I'll come again if I think I need to.'

'We'll make her welcome, won't we, Margaret?' said Aimee.

'Yes, we will. I'm sorry you that you can't stay longer. It was nice to talk to you,' said Margaret.

'Margaret, thank you for having a chat. I have to go now, but I might come to see you again,' Carrie said.

'Oh, please do. I'm not going anywhere. Thank you for coming.'

'I'll see you in the morning, Margaret,' said Aimee.

As Carrie and Aimee walked back towards the reception area, they both admitted that they felt as though Margaret was sometimes having a different conversation to the one that they were having and although Carrie didn't feel as though she had learned very much more about Robin Greaves, she was still inclined to think that Margaret had more to tell her about his past and that another visit to the Pavilion would be firmly on her agenda.

'I hope that was useful,' said Aimee.

'It was interesting for sure. There were certainly things that she said that I'll have to have a think about,' said Carrie, 'Pretty sure that I'll be back at some point. Here, take my card. It's got the station number and my mobile, just in case.'

'Ok, thanks. I'll keep it handy,' said Aimee.

SIXTY-TWO

Minneapolis, Minnesota.

When he finally managed to drag his tired body out of bed and downstairs into the Den, he was abruptly reminded why his head felt as though it was filled with shrapnel. The odour of stale beer alone was enough to make him want to throw up (again). He held onto the stair-rail and guided his fragile body from side to side down the stairs. Scarcely had the journey from one level to another felt so precarious. When he reached the main area of the den, one hand rested on the doorframe whilst the other tentatively explored the wall in search of the light switch. Even though the bulb was of a low wattage he shielded his eyes in readiness for the shock. He was sure that he wouldn't like what he was about to see. Reluctantly, he switched on the light and predictably, the sight that presented itself to him only highlighted one thing; that he really did go a little too far last night, as if his fragile head needed any confirmation.

He carefully trod his way through the detritus, meticulously checking for any sharp-cornered objects that may be lying in wait on the floor for his unsuspecting bare feet. He rubbed his face again and looked at the mess around him, wondering how he had even managed to get upstairs at all the previous night. Needing to get a window open as soon as possible to try to clear the air and at least begin to expel the worst of the stench, he gently made his way across the dimly lit space. He could smell the lingering odour of his late-night attempt at cooking himself a few sausages as it pervaded into the room, before he had finally given up, turned the grill off, and surrendered to his desperate desire for sleep.

The drapes in the Den were purposefully black, almost like blackout curtains. He had chosen to hang these in order to provide a completely secluded feeling. It was his space and, on the occasions when he wanted to shut the world out, they were perfect. Even on a bright day they didn't allow any light to permeate into his private territory. He wouldn't describe himself as a hermit, but there were just times when it made him feel secure and sheltered from all the troubles in the outside world and especially when he needed to think clearly, which was proving to be rather challenging at the moment.

Having slowly and successfully traversed across the obstacle-filled room, he finally arrived at the window. However, he hadn't prepared himself for the shock of what was coming next. He tugged at one of the drapes and was struck by the unforgiving glare of piercing sunlight. He yelped as he covered his eyes and remained motionless, holding on to the nearest stable object, for fear of falling back onto the floor. Slowly he began to lower his protective hand to allow the inevitable message that it was morning to enter his delicate head. The brightness seemed exceptional, even more than he expected it would be. The morning sky was as clear and blue as Gregory Bonner could ever remember seeing it. But there was another contributory factor this morning. It had snowed.

Bonner's squinted eyes stared at it. The more he focussed on the scene before him, the more he thought that it had been a moderately heavy fall. The sight jolted his body into an unexpected recovery phase, or at least the beginnings of one. Immediately, his attention turned to the details of what was outside of his window. *Do I need to record this?* Whether it was worthy of adding to the extensive documentation that his personal computer had stored away regarding the Snow and Cold Index would be something that he would think about as soon as he could stand unsupported. Bonner stared outside, tolerating the pain in his eyes.

'It's a post-holer', he said to himself. Only fanatics such as Bonner would comprehend what he was referring to. It was a reference to the depth of the snowfall. He couldn't be entirely sure without going outside to check, but from what he could see, it looked as though it might be a significant amount. In an instant, Bonner had forgotten about his morning struggle and was keen to explore the depth of the fall. He started to make his way towards the front door, but stopped abruptly, realising that he wasn't exactly dressed for going outside. His boxer shorts and bare feet were hardly suitable. Bonner dragged himself upstairs with a much-inspired athleticism and grabbed at his jeans and a pair of boots, putting them on swiftly, before returning downstairs much quicker than he had earlier. When he reached the bottom of the stairs his delicate stomach churned, reminding him again that perhaps he should take things a little slower. What Bonner wanted to see, was whether the snow that had fallen was deep enough to step into, leaving behind a hole that would be deep enough for a wooden post. *At least knee height,* he hoped.

As Bonner opened the front door, he was confronted by the formidable, silhouetted shape of Captain Antonio Rodrigues, who stood at his door with one hand raised in readiness to knock. The two men appeared to have startled each other. They stood without speaking for a few seconds before Bonner broke the awkward silence.

'Captain,' he said.

'Bonner, you look like shit,' he responded with a grimace.

Bonner's brain stumbled into gear, and he mumbled something about the snow in reference to Cat Tracks. His face was filled with disappointment at the realisation that the snowfall had actually been only enough to show animal tracks and not enough to warrant him getting excited after all. Big Toni looked down at his snow-covered boots and kicked them against each other.

'Can I come in now?' he asked.

'Err…I was just…Yes, ok,' said Bonner.

Bonner stepped back to allow Big Toni to squeeze past. As he closed the door, he took one more look outside but to his dismay the snowfall didn't look as impressive as it had at the rear window, and he feared that his expectations had got the better of him. Bonner ambled back inside and continued to mumble something about a snow drift, which was what he thought must have occurred at the rear window.

'Jesus, Bonner. Have you got a dead moose in here?' exclaimed Big Toni.

'Err…What? No, sorry. It was a bit of a night.'

'You're telling me,' said Big Toni, as he scanned the disordered den.

Bonner made his way towards the kitchen and offered to make some coffee for them both. Big Toni accepted and looked around in the den, desperately searching for somewhere to sit, but there was such a lot of clutter that he decided he would simply stand instead.

'How many people did you have here last night?' he asked.

'What? Oh, just me,' said Bonner. *Just me and Caterina.*

'You made all this mess on your own?' asked Big Toni.

'I guess,' called Bonner from the kitchen.

'Well, I'm glad my invitation didn't arrive.'

Bonner couldn't imagine that he would ever think to invite his Captain, but the thought made him smile. The smell of the coffee seemed to be acting as an instant fix and Bonner began to feel a little more alive. He carried two mugs of black coffee into the main part of the den and handed one to Big Toni. His preoccupation with the Snow and Cold Index, was now in the back of his mind.

'Don't you have any milk?' asked Big Toni.

'Oh, sorry.'

As Bonner turned back towards the kitchen, Big Toni stopped him and told him not to bother. He said that the strength of the coffee might help to dispel the odour that was infiltrating his nose. Bonner had to agree that his Captain had made a good point.

The unexpected arrival of Captain Rodrigues at his door began to stir up questions in Bonner's mind. It had been a long time since Big Toni had been to Bonner's house. So long that he could hardly remember when the last time had been. But at this precise moment, Bonner was more concerned with the work the black coffee was doing to aid his recovery. He knew that Big Toni would not be paying a visit purely out of kindness. There would be a good reason and he would find out soon enough. He didn't have to wait long.

'Look, Bonner. I haven't come here to experience the delights of your hospitality, or search for whatever it is that has died in here. I've had a phone call from Deputy Police Chief Bolton. He thinks that it might be time for me to move on, but he'll let me know.'

'Move on?' said Bonner.

'Yes. Move on. Change precincts, change departments, that sort of thing.'

'Why?' said Bonner.

'Because I've been here for quite a while and sometimes some room has to be made for younger men to replace the old wood. I've had a feeling that it might happen, but I was hoping to hang on for at least another few years before I was put out to graze,' explained Big Toni.

Bonner felt an immediate sadness waft over him. He had only ever had one Captain and although they had had their disagreements and their differences, Bonner was so used to Big Toni that he really didn't want to have anyone else in charge of him. In a rush of realisation, Bonner suddenly knew that all the arguments and badgering were just part of the make-up that enabled the team at the department to gel. He knew it wasn't personal. He instantaneously knew that it was all part of how Big Toni did things and how he got the best out of people, even if it had made Bonner feel a bit aggrieved from time to time.

'I'm sorry to hear it, Captain,' said Bonner, with an empty expression.

'Yeah, well, me too, Bonner. But we're not finished yet.'

'We?'

'Yes, we. I've been giving a lot of thought to the Caterina Marks case ever since you and I had that little chat in my office.'

'Really?' said Bonner.

'Yes, really. The more I thought about it, the more I could understand what you were saying about the whole search and rescue fiasco that took place at the Nelson property,' he said.

'Fiasco?' said Bonner.

'Yeah, fiasco. Do I have to repeat everything, Bonner?'

'No, sorry.'

'I think you are right about it. Something *was* wrong. I read over the initial report from the investigation all those years ago and I just kept coming back to what you had told me about the dogs and the expertise and all of that. I may have been a little stubborn about you heading up to Elk River and I may have doubted your intentions but that's by the by. Also, there was the whole Ken Toft thing. The way he was stalling with uncertainty about where to mark the cross on the map. If he was the professional that he portrayed himself to be, he would have had no trouble marking the exact spot even after all these years. I don't like it, Bonner.'

Bonner stood, slightly bemused, and slightly perplexed. But in no time, he could also feel an indescribable surge of hope. *He understands, he really does.*

'So, now what?' said Bonner, agog with anticipation.

'So now, you had better get yourself into shape. Like I said, I'm not here for the coffee or just to tell you about my current situation. Believe it or not, I'm here to tell you that I'm on your side about this Caterina Marks case and I think that we need to get our heads together and get it sorted. I've been thinking it over and I agree with you, something *is* wrong.'

'I don't know what to say, Captain.'

'I don't want you to say anything, Bonner. I want you to get ready for work.'

'But, Captain, I'm not really in any condition to…'

'Don't argue with me, Bonner. Leave that concern to me. Anyway, you're not going to be driving today. We'll take my car.'

'Where are we going?' said Bonner.

'Eden Prairie. We're going to have another little chat with Mr. Ken Toft.'

SIXTY-THREE

Ahuja Industries, East London.

From her elevated position, she could see the foxes. They looked tiny in comparison to her usual view of them. *Like little rusty dots.* She could also see that they were all out today, Mum, Dad, Socks, Stripe and Speckle. *I'm up here.* Angelica hardly dare twitch for fear of falling. She hated heights and had barely even glanced down to the factory floor from the moment she realised where she was; perilously suspended in the highest part of the factory. A weird falling sensation had overcome her each time she had peered down. She couldn't work out why she was up there. *So high. What's wrong with my corner?* She inspected the rope that tied her hands and feet and held her tight against one side of the raised platform. *I guess, I can't exactly fall. Could be pushed to swing like a pendulum though.*

She tried to expel the thoughts from her mind and just concentrate on not moving. Although she had never considered her corner to be exactly comfortable, by comparison with this position, it was palatial. She hadn't been grateful for many things since she had been here, but right now she was grateful for the blanket that he had left her wrapped in. It felt a bit colder up here and she couldn't exercise to keep warm either. *He won't keep me up here for long, I don't even have a bucket,* she thought. Then Angelica's mind went into overdrive. *That's it. He's getting ready to kill me. That's why there's no toilet. And I haven't had dinner or anything.*

She heard a soft whimper and her attention turned to the foxes. When she looked down in their direction, she could see Stripe looking straight up at her. She could recognise his distinct pattern anywhere. He had found her. It was a very odd moment. Angelica thought that she could feel his concern for her. *Help me, Stripe.* But he just looked away and followed Socks to search out some titbits that would usually be waiting for them in her corner. *Sorry boys. Can't help you, any more than you can help me,* she thought.

She shifted her bottom that was fast becoming numb on the hard gridded surface. Even that small movement made her tremble slightly at the thought of falling. *You can't fall, you silly girl.* The foxes were out of sight now. *So much for teamwork,* she thought. Angelica looked up as much as her restricted movement would permit and could see the sky through a gap in the roof. Access to the possible escape hatch was going to prove very difficult but if she could just get free then she would have all night to work her way up there. But each and every potentially courageous plan had its flaws, and this one would most likely turn out the same as every other thought of escape that she had had. She tried to remember whether she had seen the sky since she had been here but couldn't recall. She began to study the layout of the upper landings and could see that they were exactly the same on the far side too. She had never seen the factory from this angle and could, at last, get some perspective of the size of the place. There was less dust up here, but it was no less unwelcoming. Angelica had just about given up trying to work out why she was here or who it was that had taken her. She had all but forgotten about how she looked or how dirty she was, and in truth, she was beyond caring. Every now and then a whiff reminded her. She thought about the chain in her corner and wondered just how close she had been to breaking it from its fixing on the wall. She looked at the back of her hand where the chain had rubbed on it and could see a bruise forming. *Lucky that's all I have to worry about,* she thought. Her mind switched to the other girl that she had seen him carry away and the spot of blood on the white sheet. She closed her eyes and tried to dispel the image even though she didn't think that she would ever be able to forget it. The question of what happened to the girl ventured into her mind every so often, but Angelica had no answer. It was best not to think too much about it. She would find out soon enough if she was going to be next.

    Then the unmistakeable sound of metal scraping across the factory floor echoed high up in the factory. He was back. *Dinner?* Angelica looked around her, trying to get her bearings in order to keep an eye out for him approaching. It dawned on her that this was the first time that she would see him coming. Previously she had had to wait until he appeared around the corner of her little dust-laden world. She couldn't understand why this was so interesting, but it was something that had not happened in all this time. *However long that was.* Out of the corner of her eye, she noticed some movement. Way down to her left, on the ground floor, she saw him. Over his shoulder was the usual red and black rucksack. *Dinner?* He wore the same stupid mask that she so wanted to rip off and throw to the ground. *What if it was someone that I don't know? Then what? All my wild guessing would have been pointless.*

Angelica rechecked the rope and the knots that held her. They were tight. All she was worried about for the moment was that she got fed. That would signify to her that she was still going to be held captive and that he still had a reason for keeping her here. *Unlike that girl.* She realised that he would have to free her hands for her to be able to eat too. A number of random thoughts were rattling around her head. If he was close enough, she might be able to push him over the edge. She also knew that she wouldn't get more than one attempt at such a high-risk manoeuvre. She would have to be absolutely certain that it would work. Then she would worry about how to free herself afterwards. It might take hours or days, but it would be worth it. If it didn't work out right and he survived, then she knew that she would be in real bother. It didn't bear thinking about. Her latest little daydream was disturbed by the sound of him climbing the stairs. His boots tapped out every footfall. She could see him more clearly now. Step by step, he got closer. He was on the level just below her. He was mumbling something, which Angelica didn't like the sound of at all. He had never done that before. There were just the couple of occasions when he had briefly spoken. *Marry me?*

She watched intently as he came into full view. The red and black rucksack was off his shoulder now and was swinging freely in his hand. Angelica felt as though this scenario was different from the regular visits that he had made; the atmosphere was different. Maybe it was just that she wasn't in her familiar corner. Iron bar was not under her blankets and the morsels of food for the foxes were not hidden away. She didn't like it, but she had no choice but to get through it.

He stopped just out of her reach, as usual. Angelica didn't think that there would be any hair brushing today. She was feeling too anxious to broach the subject anyway. What she really wanted, apart for him to miraculously fall to his death, was her dinner. She looked at the rucksack that he had placed on the gridded floor beside him, hoping to find that it contained a hot meal of some description. Anything hot would do. Angelica was hungry. She raised her hands as far as they would go to show him that they were tied and that she would need to have them free to eat with. He didn't react to that. He just stood looking at her. It was just like some weird Mexican stand-off. Angelica was no fan of western movies, but she had heard her Dad say it enough times and she knew what it was in principle. And this felt like one of those.

She knew that she was powerless to make the first move and even if she could, she didn't know what to do for the best. So, Angelica sat, tied, and waited. Then he moved closer and pushed her body to one side a little, enough for him to get to the rope that was holding her fast to the railing. *Don't tell me we're going for another little walk,* she thought. He fiddled with the rope and then grabbed Angelica under the arms. *He wants me to stand. I am being moved somewhere. Back to my corner, I hope.* She stood, terrified of falling over the edge. Then he took a step away from her, back along the walkway. For a long moment neither of them moved. Angelica had nowhere to go anyway. She glanced down and immediately wished that she hadn't. Then as she spotted the foxes looking up at her she realised that all five were watching whatever it was that was unfolding above them. Her feet were tingling, and her body was becoming numb at the fear of falling. Then he stepped towards her. He had his arms held out in front of him as if he was going to grab her. Angelica heard a faint *'No'* whisper from her mouth, almost subconsciously. Before she had a chance to do anything he had her in his grasp, and she could feel herself being driven backwards towards the vacuous space behind her. One foot trod helplessly into fresh air and Angelica squealed out a high-pitched shriek. She braced instinctively for the fall, and her blood pressure seemed to drop like a stone. Her mouth was dry. All these things happened so fast, and he was grumbling something incoherent. Then she felt him start to shake her as she hung mercilessly over the drop below with her toes desperately trying to grip onto the edge of the walkway. She stared, petrified, at the mask that was close to her face, looking directly into his eyes. She thought that she could hear the inexplicable words again. *Marry me.* Seconds later everything went black.

When Angelica awoke, she thought that she was in her corner but after a few moments she realised that she was lying on the cold metal grid on the same level as before. Her hands were free, but her feet were still bound, although she was able to move her arms more than before. When she realised that she must have fainted, she shook her head slightly in an attempt to rally her senses. Angelica looked at what was preventing her from moving freely and saw that the rope had gone and that she was being restricted by a chain again. It wasn't as thick as the original one, but it looked very strong. Too strong for her to simply tug herself free from. The plastic carrier bag that contained her food was close by. She could just about appreciate the odour of food. *Something warm.* For a moment she remained still, too scared to move. It was deathly quiet in the factory. Angelica could only gauge the amount of time that had passed by the fact that the food was still warm. She managed to sit up and lift the carrier bag onto her lap. Eating had become the last thing on her mind, but she had learned that it was one of the most important things for her to do. She had to eat. If she was ever going to get out of here, she had to have some strength. She looked inside and found a container of what looked like, rice with a number of small pieces of meat in. 'Chinese again', she said to herself. But she really didn't care what it was. If she could taste it, then she must be alive.

Angelica ate the whole thing and dropped the container beside her. Instinctively, she looked into the bag again, and there was the bottle of water. Even after what had happened, he had still fed her and given her some water to drink. Angelica sat pale-faced and bemused. The fear from the terror that she felt had slowly seeped out of her. She was exhausted and didn't know whether she should laugh or cry. The food, combined with her fretful experience, had made her feel sleepy. Angelica rested herself back against the railing and began to feel her eyes close. Her head nodded a couple of times as her body began to surrender to her need for sleep. She thought about the foxes and how they would cope without their evening meal. *Sorry everyone.* Angelica assumed that there was plenty of food for the foxes outside the factory and that they only came to her corner because they could get an easy meal; one that wouldn't be running for its life. She took one more look up at the sky. It was darker now. As she shifted into a position that she thought would allow her to get off to sleep, she noticed something beside her. A blanket. Folded like new. She only had to shift herself a foot to her left to reach it. She took it and lifted it to her face. She could smell the freshness of it. It was clean and going by the way it was folded, probably unused. Angelica unfolded it and spread it across her legs and up her body. By the time she had finished wrestling with it, she felt even more tired, but it was covering most of her. As she sat in as comfortable a position as she could manage, she could see something on the blanket. *Some letters or a word.* Angelica fiddled with the blanket in order to turn the word around so that she could read it. *Catchpole's. Who do I know that works at Catchpole's?* She recognised the name. It was the big building at the far end of Farnborough Drive, not all that far from where she lived. *Or used to,* she thought.

Her thoughts turned, once again, to home. A sadness flooded over her, and tears welled up in her eyes. She didn't want to believe that her parents and her friends had actually given up on her, but as she sat staring helplessly around the dusty expanse, she couldn't stop those morose, depressing feelings swallowing her up. There had been a number of times when Angelica had wondered what was to become of her. Everything changed when she had seen him carry that girl away in the broken piece of mirror. But there were certain things that still gave her a sliver of hope, even if she didn't understand them. Every time her food arrived; she knew she was going to see another day at least. She was also given water to drink and blankets to keep her warm. She knew that she was being kept here for a reason, but she had no idea why. Her mind began asking questions again about how many other girls had been here before her. *Did they all end up like that other girl? Why haven't I?*

Angelica's thoughts returned to her family, and she found herself reciting a letter out loud to her Mum and Dad. It had been swirling around in her head for days, but she had resisted the upset of thinking too hard about it. Now she had to let the words out. She so wanted her rescuers to appear and whisk her away back to those that she loved. Angelica mumbled the words through her tears and felt an intense emotional pain grip her body. She put her hands over her face and began to weep uncontrollably. A few moments later she heard a yelp from below. It was Stripe again. She rubbed the tears from her face and looked down at him. It was almost as if he had known what she was thinking about. As if he understood. His eyes glistened as he stared up towards her. *Thanks Stripe.*

Angelica pulled the blanket over her again and hunkered down for what she hoped was some assemblance of sleep. She glanced up to the roof to check that any rain would not fall directly onto her, and then she saw the bucket, a little further along the walkway. It was within reach, and she knew that she wasn't going anywhere just now.

SIXTY-FOUR

Old Clapton Street Police Station.

DCI Blackery was in Marc Sutton's office discussing a house fire that had occurred in Folger Street that had all the characteristics of an arson attack. The item had appeared on the local news channel, the images showing the extent of the damage to the front facade of the blackened property. Fortunately, no injuries were sustained by the occupants who had escaped the danger via the rear garden of the house. At least not on this occasion. There had been a considerable amount of loathing for the family ever since the accusations that they had contributed to the injuries that were discovered on their two young children when police officers and paramedics had attended the property a week ago, following a neighbour's claim that she could hear cries coming from inside the house. Despite an initial investigation by the police and the social workers, nothing had been proved, but that didn't stop the local rumours spreading around the Golding estate. Sutton had thought that with the children in temporary care pending further investigations, there was always a chance that something might happen. Blackery was as sure as he could be that the locals had taken matters into their own hands. It was an opinion that Sutton couldn't disagree with.

When DS Carrie Linton stepped into the corridor outside Sutton's office, she could hear Blackery chuntering away. She didn't really want to stumble straight into his path, so she did an about turn and went to get a coffee before speaking with Sutton. The canteen was empty. Even the tables were bare of any free nibbles that the cook tended to leave out for any of the officers. Sadly, the evidence that the scavengers had devoured whatever may have been left was all too clear to see, in the form of the litter that they had inconsiderately left behind. Carrie walked in and tutted at the mess before making use of the free vend on the drinks machine. She took her coffee and sat down at one of the clean tables. She could hear some noises coming from the offices nearby but not clearly enough to warrant even trying to listen to the conversations. She had other matters on her mind. As she sipped the coffee, she thought about some of the things that Mrs Greaves had said during their brief chat. Most of it was pretty general but there were parts that Carrie didn't fully understand. Parts that raised queries in her mind. The more she thought about it, the more inquisitive she became and wanted to talk with Margaret again. She sat nursing the warm mug in her hands and allowed her mind to run through some of the conversation.

Firstly, she recalled the news that Robin Greaves had two sisters. Whether they would be of any use to her, even if she could find them, she had no idea. Carrie also thought about how Margaret seemed to be almost reluctant to speak directly about her son. She referred to him as 'their brother' when Aimee was speaking about when her son visited, and then steered the conversation back to her daughters, and then she had said 'sister' instead of 'sisters'. Carrie wondered whether this is what Aimee had insinuated when she mentioned how Margaret could be a bit confused when Robin was present.

Carrie screwed up her face and thought harder about the moment when Margaret had said that the house had been filled with bad memories. *Why did he leave and then only return when they had gone?* Carrie felt that there was still more to learn about Robin Greaves but seeing as he was so difficult to talk to, and Margaret tended to change the subject halfway through, she was groping around in a vacuum devoid of answers. As Carrie held onto the remnants of warmth from the mug, another thought dropped into her head. Margaret had said "It was a shame," as if she was referring to a specific occurrence, and that she wished that she could change the past. Carrie let out a sigh and thought about going back upstairs to speak with Marc and take the opportunity to watch the CCTV footage from the camera at the canal. If Blackery was still there, she decided that she would tolerate it. She took her mug around to the sink at the rear of the canteen and gave it a quick wash out, not wishing to discard it as others had. It was then that she noticed just how many mugs and plates had been left in the sink by those that couldn't be bothered to take a few moments to wash the things that they had used, instead of leaving it all for the cook.

Jennifer and Joanna were twins, she thought, as she dried her hands on a tea towel. *Somebody had to step in to 'rescue the situation.'* Too much of this didn't add up for Carrie's liking. With these conundrums rattling around in her head she made her way up the stairs and along the corridor to Marc Sutton's office. She couldn't hear any voices, especially that of DCI Blackery, and wandered into Sutton's office with a cursory tap on the door as she entered.

'Ah, Carrie. How was the care home? Have you booked yourself a spot by the fire for your old age?' he said,

'Ha, ha, very funny,' she said, sarcastically.

Sutton allowed himself a self-satisfying smirk and began to prepare the CCTV footage for Carrie to view. She flung her bag onto a chair and pulled another closer to his desk.

'So, how did you get on, then?' asked Sutton.

'Not so well at Rodina Close, although when I spoke to the Warden, Mrs Walton, she did mention that Greaves has been taking some of her blankets to work to lie on when he's underneath a car.'

'Don't they have hydraulic lifts for that sort of thing?'

'I guess so. Her husband didn't think that the dirt on the blankets was from the garage, something to do with the fact that the rust from cars is darker than the stains on the blankets,' she said.

'Maybe you should ask to see one of the blankets for yourself.'

'I will do the next time I'm over that way.'

'So, what about the care home?'

'I got to see her. A nice girl named Aimee took me through to the lounge.'

'And?' asked Sutton.

'…and, Greaves has sisters. Two of them. They don't visit their mother anymore and it feels as though there's some kind of history that is stopping them and causing them to avoid him. In fact, I think they are avoiding each other but I'm not sure what's behind it all yet,' she said.

'Anything else?

'Yeah, I got the feeling that Mrs Greaves was always on the verge of saying a bit more than she did. I could be wrong. It might be nothing, but my gut is telling me that there's something else,' she said.

Gut feeling, thought Sutton, *that's what Patricia trusted.*

'Well, maybe you should pay another visit to Mrs Greaves and continue your little chat,' he suggested.

'I think I will. Anyway, where's this footage?' said Carrie.

Sutton flicked his head to one side, inviting Carrie to sit closer to him. She moved her chair next to Sutton's and waited for him to locate the appropriate date and time on the screen. They both watched as the information across the top of the screen displayed the dates and times. Sutton moved the footage onwards towards the correct place and when the date finally appeared on the screen, he stopped.

'Ok. Here we are. Now let me move it on to the part where she appears. I want the afternoon, after four. This is the first day, when she was peering into the water,' he said.

Carrie and Sutton looked on intently at the image of the woman in the dark coat and colourful headscarf as she moved slowly along the towpath. Occasionally, she paused to look into the water.

'Have you zoomed in?' asked Carrie.

'Don't you worry, I've zoomed in and out of this until my eyes hurt. Unfortunately, there doesn't appear to be one moment when her face is visible,' he said.

'Convenient,' Carrie said.

'Possibly,' replied Sutton.

The pair of them watched closely until the woman finally went out of shot and was gone for the rest of the day.

'There doesn't appear to be much for us to learn from that so let's try the next day,' said Sutton.

Again, he forwarded the recording until the appropriate time of the morning showed on the screen. Carrie leaned in to get a closer look. Sutton's office was silent as the two of them studied the footage and watched the woman walk along beside the canal. Gradually, she went out of sight, obscured by one of the large trees.

'What's she doing now? Said Carrie.

'She's going to sit down on that bench behind the tree, just up from where the pathologist's tent was set up,' said Sutton, 'She sits there for a little while and doesn't appear to be doing anything in particular.'

'Ok,' said Carrie.

'Here we go again, she's coming back towards the camera, but look…,' said Sutton.

'What's that? A newspaper or magazine or something?'

'Yep. And she's holding it up beside her face,' said Sutton.

'So, maybe, she does know there is a camera.'

'Maybe,' he said.

'Hmm, crafty.'

'Crafty or coincidental, we don't know for sure,' said Sutton.

The woman went out of sight again and Carrie slumped back into her chair. Sutton could see the disappointment registering on Carrie's face, and gave a nod, agreeing that this did seem like another dead end. Sutton left the screen frozen on the scene from the second day and posed a question to Carrie.

'So, if this woman is involved in this in some way, we may never know how but I wonder if we're wasting time by watching her when all along, we've suspected that a man would be the most likely person to have carried out the crimes. What do you think?'

'I think it is a man that's behind all this. Isn't it something like 96% of murders worldwide are carried out by a man?' she asked.

'Something like that,' said Sutton.

'So why should this one be any different? Whoever she is, she did appear to be looking for something in particular. Why else would you pay such attention to this stretch of the canal? It's definitely odd, but I don't think it would be a good use of our time trying to track her down, do you?' she said.

'I'm inclined to agree. Listen, while you've been out and about lately, I've had a team revisit Angelica's friends to see whether there has been any sort of contact. There has not been anything from her since this whole thing began. Her mobile phone hasn't pinged on any of the phone masts, at least not since the day that she went missing. Her bank account has still seen no action either. Everyone has been told to stay vigilant and keep rechecking the places that have already been checked. Karen and Tony walked the whole of the railway line again yesterday, and the perimeters of the parks and playing fields have been checked again too. Still nothing new. I even sent a team of six to that old warehouse down by the new supermarket. They had a thorough look and didn't find anything to report. Understandably her family are becoming more and more despondent by the day.' he said.

'It must be horrible. Worse than horrible,' said Carrie.

'Yeah, it must. Oh, I nearly forgot. I had another phone call from Patricia when you were out at the home.'

'Heavens, you're honoured,' said Carrie.

'Aren't I just. She was just asking how things were going. Lately, she's being surprisingly helpful.'

'Maybe, that's because she loves her brother,' said Carrie.

Sutton gave Carrie a dubious look and closed the laptop.

'So, what did she want?' she asked.

'Actually, she did say something that made me think.'

'What?'

'When I spoke to her before, she talked about how our *man* had made it easy for us to find Haley Breen and Claudia De Luca. She sort of implied that he was, kind of, leaving the girls for us to find on purpose. It made sense because, as she said, if he had wanted them to stay hidden then we might not have found them, even now.'

'So, how does that fit with Angelica?' Carrie asked.

'That's what I questioned. She said that Angelica was different. At least different from his perspective.'

'How so?' she asked.

'Special in some way. Patricia said that she meant something to him for whatever reason.'

'And the others didn't?'

'No. They were just representations of someone else, something like that. She was inclined to think that they might not be simply random victims. To him they could be more than that. She also spoke about the specific locations that the girls were discovered in. Angelica, on the other hand, could be like a substitute for him. She also said that he may have come from a traumatic background. I know that's not exactly unheard of in our job, but maybe he has had a number of bad things happen to him in his younger years and Angelica represents somebody that he cared for or cared for him. I don't know, but that's the sort of thing she was saying.'

'Well, if he's keeping her somewhere, then let's just hope that she's unharmed,' she said.

'We need to increase what we're doing and keep getting our officers out there. If she is being held, then she's somewhere and we simply have to find her. There was something else that Patricia said when I spoke to her the first time about how some of these people revisit the scene or the place where they left them. She said that they are proving to themselves that they are cleverer than us. She spoke of Angelica being some kind of trophy for him.'

'If that's so then maybe she is still alive, and if so, he might have been feeding her otherwise she couldn't have survived this long,' said Carrie.

'She must have access to water, I guess. Let's hope that Patricia's impression of this is correct.'

'I hope so.'

'She also said something else today that was interesting too. When I relayed the steps that we had taken, and the latest searches that have been ongoing, she said that we might try to make him come to us. She said that we might consider not announcing that she has been found. Her thoughts were that if we had not got him in custody or if we didn't have enough evidence against him at that time, that if he got wind of the fact that Angelica was free, that he would be gone in a flash, and we would have to start over. She also explained that sometimes these people are so narcissistic that they crave the attention of being infamous to the point where they expose their hand and become neglectful of the very things that have kept them concealed,' he said.

'Do you think he will lower his guard like that?'

'I bloody hope so, Carrie, because at the moment we don't seem to be making enough progress and it's becoming very difficult to talk to Mr and Mrs Rowntree and keep telling them that we don't have anything new or encouraging to report.'

'I understand. Marc, can I have another look at the CCTV another time? I just want to check something. But first of all, in the absence of any other possible suspects, I think I need to talk to Mrs Greaves again.'

'Fine, but why don't you go home and get some rest. Mrs Greaves won't be available to you at this hour. You can start afresh tomorrow,' he said.

'Rest? Not much chance of that.'

'Why not? Are you out tonight?'

'I'm shooting straight round to see Grace. Didn't she tell you?' said Carrie, as she swiftly gathered her bag from the chair and headed for the corridor, 'See you at home.'

Sutton sat for a second and allowed this to sink in before shouting after Carrie.

'Home? Whose bloody home do you think it is?'

'Mine and Grace's,' shouted Carrie, already on the stairs.

'Sometimes, I bloody wonder,' muttered Sutton, with a broad smile.

He checked his phone, still giggling at Carrie's cheeky repost and saw that he had two messages from Grace. He opened the first.

Hi, darling. Hope you're having a good day. I'm just at the supermarket, but I'll be home before you. Love you loads xxx

Secondly…

Me again. Carrie's coming round tonight. Hope you don't mind xxx

Sutton couldn't help but grin. He loved Grace so much that she could do whatever she wanted, and, of course, Carrie was always welcome. It had become a bit of an in-joke between him and Carrie. He just shook his head and prepared to make his way home to whatever it was that Grace had planned. As long as it involved food, he didn't really care.

See you at home, indeed, he thought.

SIXTY-FIVE

The Riverside Centre, Tilbury, East London.

Betty Nelson blamed her unwanted detour towards the old Tilbury Fort on the fact that she was unfamiliar with the area. She had also had to drive in the rain on her way to and from Countess Street and she detested driving in the wet, day or night. But especially when it was dark and dingy. Betty really didn't want to be here, but she had found herself being propelled into an undesirable set of circumstances by her unyielding fascination for Karter Swann and the manic behaviour that she knew her sister was capable of displaying. Even Betty couldn't make any sense of it at this moment in time, but here she was. It wasn't until she saw the lights from the factories on the opposite side of the river that she realised she had gone wrong, and despite her frantic attempts to find her way out, she only succeeded in running into dead end after dead end. As she sat staring at another set of chained factory gates, she became angry with herself for missing the sign that would have got her into the Riverside Centre a lot sooner. To her left, the reflections from the factory floodlights shimmered in the water. She cursed out loud and reached for her phone to try to use the maps on it in order to find her intended location, rather than blindly head back where she had come from and probably get lost again. Betty hated getting lost at this time of night in a strange area that felt very sinister to her, and she soon became frightened. Betty knew that she wasn't exactly lost but the panic that she felt rapidly building inside her, was getting the better of her ability to remain calm and she was fast losing her sangfroid. Once again, she questioned her sanity at the very thought that she was here at all, chasing after Elisha, chasing after Karter Swann. *What am I doing?* What concerned her the most as she pondered her predicament, is what she might be getting into.

As Betty became increasingly agitated, she looked at the phone and tried to make sense of how to find her way back to the main road. *I must have driven straight past.* She gave a cautious look around her. All she saw was the light pollution from the factories that shone on the river and the wet road. The huge factories stood silently in the gloom. Nobody else was in sight, not that she wanted anyone to be anywhere nearby. If she had seen a strange figure walking towards her car she would have gone into a fit of terror. When she found the Riverside Centre on her phone map, she couldn't believe that she was so close, and cursed again that she had been so stupid as to drive straight past it. Betty took one cursory glance in her rear-view mirror and reversed hard. She spun her car around in the space at the end the road, causing the rear end to drift across towards the kerb, and raced back towards her intended destination.

She expected Elisha to be there, ahead of her. As Betty saw the large gates and the sign that she had inexplicably missed, her mind turned to the contents of Elisha's bag. She felt that she was sweating and dragged the back of her hand across her forehead, wiping the glaze of moisture on one leg of her jeans. The thoughts of what she might walk into when she arrived caused a chill to run through her. Once upon a time she could predict how Elisha was likely to react to certain situations. She knew her sister in those days. Although Elisha had an inbuilt defence system that prohibited her from crying and showing her innermost feelings, Betty could still tell when Elisha was hurting, especially when it was in response to something that their father had said or done. Betty had always been fully supportive and had often felt a sense of empathy for her sister's plight, but today, right now, she was scared of her, and completely uncertain of what was coming next. The very mention of the whereabouts of Karter Swann and the fact that Betty had been thinking about him had changed everything in a very short space of time.

Betty decided not to go through the gates and into the yard. She parked her car outside on the road and switched off the engine, sitting quietly for a moment and considering what to do next. A deafening silence surrounded her. The Riverside Centre was wider than it was tall, and she could see a number of bays at the front where she assumed the lorries would reverse up to. She had no idea what type of business the Riverside Centre was involved with and right now she didn't really care. The man at 12 Countess Street had told her that Karter was there, and she was as certain as she could be that unfortunately, Elisha was too. And then, as she scanned her eyes across the frontage, she spotted it. Elisha's car. It sat there like some kind of demonic depiction that represented the attendance of something menacing. Having come this far, Betty knew that she had committed herself to seeing it through. She took another look up at the windows on the upper floor and, in the hope that nobody was watching her, opened the driver's door and began to make her way quickly across the wet yard towards the building.

Betty saw a door ahead of her that appeared to be the way in and slowly opened it. She could see that the passageway in front of her was dark and narrow. She illuminated her mobile phone and pointed it down towards the other end of the passage. She had no idea whether this was the way in that Elisha had used, but she assumed that it had been, and walked quietly along the passage until she reached the end. When she reached the turn at the end, she listened hard in case she could hear Elisha or anything else. Betty heard nothing. The silence made her wonder whether she might have chosen the wrong entrance, but she was in now, and didn't want to waste time hunting around for another entrance.

She trod lightly up the stairs to the top and listened again. The fact that there were no lights on made her think that she was in the wrong part of the building. If the double doors in front of her had been locked, she would have probably turned away and gone back down to the ground floor, but they weren't, so Betty gently pushed the right- hand door and looked around it. She entered the room and held onto the door as it self-closed behind her, ensuring that it didn't slam shut. A certain amount of borrowed light from the nearby factories radiated in through the windows, and she could see a single light that was on at the rear of the bar area ahead of her which allowed her to establish the layout and to appreciate exactly how big the floorspace was. The bar area at the far end reminded her of when she first set eyes on Karter at the Cactus and Coyote, but there was no Karter Swann to be seen. *This is useless,* she thought.

Just then Betty heard a noise. Like a dull thud or something similar. Whatever it had been, she definitely heard it. She remained motionless, looked ahead of her, and tried to work out which direction it had come from. She glanced out of the windows that overlooked the forecourt of the Riverside Centre. She could see her car outside the gates and Elisha's in the yard, sitting amongst the glare from the puddles. Betty stepped forwards, checking behind her as she went. Again, she wondered whether Karter was in a completely different part of the building and that the sound she had heard was going to turn out to be something entirely innocent. Although she wasn't sure whether she was in the right area, she didn't want to give herself away. She didn't really have a plan for if she happened to meet Karter in the half-light but reckoned upon that scenario being the easier to manage than if she was to bump into Elisha and the contents of her bag.

For the umpteenth time she thought about leaving and just hoping that no harm would come to Karter. She hadn't been able to find him yet so maybe Elisha wouldn't either and she would just give up and go home. *Who am I trying to kid?* she thought, *Elisha doesn't just give up.*

In front of her, she was soon able to see an open door that appeared to lead out of the room. She couldn't decide whether she was being foolish or brave, but either way, she found herself walking towards it, intrigued as to what was on the other side of it and what the obscure noise had been. *Where are you?*

SIXTY-SIX

Fifteen minutes earlier

DC Steve Kingham reached the top of the stairs and softly leaned his shoulder against one of the double doors. As it silently opened, he stepped around it. The room that he now found himself in was empty with a bar area at one end. The light that he had seen flicker on was emitting from a fluorescent light behind the bar. Kingham listened for any indication of where Ray Keller or the other man might be. At first there was no sound and then he thought that he had heard a brief sound that reminded him of glass breaking. Kingham had not reported back to DI Sutton since he had left the Snare and Cymbals in his pursuit of Ray Keller, and thought about an update, but he didn't really have anything substantial to say at this time so he decided to wait until he could at least make contact with Ray Keller about where he might find Karter Swann. If he learned the answer to that then he would definitely have something worth sharing. George Sullivan's contacts were usually trustworthy, so he didn't worry about it. Kingham turned his attention back to the sound that he had just heard and walked slowly to the other end of the room. He checked behind the bar and noticed an open door. He figured that the light had, obviously, not switched itself on, and that Ray Keller or the other man had come this way too.

Kingham looked around the door and saw an iron staircase that led down into a small yard at the rear. One building with an open sliding door could be seen just across the yard. It looked as though there was a dim light coming from somewhere inside the building. *Maybe that's where he is,* he thought. Kingham stepped, as quietly as possible, onto the staircase and began to descend. When he reached the bottom, he had a better view through the windows but couldn't see anyone inside. At this point he reconsidered his decision about the phone call and decided to call DI Sutton to let him know the progress and inform him of his whereabouts. He took his phone from his inside pocket and looked to see if he had any messages before making the call. None were present. He looked around him at the low-level buildings and up at the main structure to see if there were any lights on anywhere else, but all the windows were in darkness. A steady stream of water fell from what looked like an overflow pipe further along and splashed onto the courtyard thirty feet ahead of him. The whole area was almost in darkness which made it difficult for him to establish very much about his surroundings, other than they were distinctly unpleasant and gloomy. As Kingham held the phone up to the light and turned slightly to find enough light to see which buttons he was pressing; he thought that he heard a footstep somewhere close to him. He wasn't able to distinguish who was nearby, but he was just about able to see a shadow appear and disappear about thirty yards away. He paused what he was doing and waited to see if anyone appeared. There were no footsteps to be heard and no indication of anyone casting a shadow. Kingham thought that he might have imagined it, but he wanted to be sure, so he walked slowly towards the spot where he thought he had seen it. He wondered if he was going to find Ray Keller or even the other man. *Karter Swann?*

The glimmer of light from the building with the sliding door petered out as he walked further from it. He was pretty much in complete darkness now. The rain had subsided but the flow of water from the blocked guttering up above him persisted to overflow. He held his mobile phone and used the torchlight to check out his surroundings. All he could see was a huge factory wall and a number of downpipes, most of which were no longer doing what they were intended to do, going by the number of splashes that fell from just about every joint along their lengths. There appeared to be more water running down the outside of the pipes than there should have been on the inside. A solid brick wall in front of him determined that there was nowhere else to go in that direction, so he gave one final look at his immediate vicinity and turned back towards the foot of the staircase that he had just descended.

As Kingham concentrated on the buttons on his phone and pressed the numbers that would allow him to speak with DI Sutton, he heard another faint noise coming from behind him but when he glanced around, again, he saw no movement of any kind. The phone rang twice in Kingham's ear as he waited to hear the voice of Marc Sutton.

There was only just enough time for him to notice a shadow in the puddles beside him before something struck his face and sent him crashing sideways into a factory wall and heavily down onto the wet floor. The phone that a moment ago had been in his hand, was sent sprawling across the yard, its casing skidding on the hard surface, causing it to flip and bounce on the cobbled ground. As Kingham rolled over to see who had attacked him, another fierce blow struck the back of his head. His head spun as the pain radiated into his neck. All he could manage was a muffled groan as he felt the warm trickle of blood run down the side of his face. Somebody kicked him hard and as he curled up, like a defenceless animal, and when a final thud landed remorselessly on the side of his head, Kingham fell unconscious.

SIXTY-SEVEN

*Eden Prairie, Minneapolis, Minnesota.
The home of Ken Toft.*

Ken Toft turned off the outside tap which had fed the hosepipe that he currently had coiled around his feet. He had just finished cleaning out the kennels at the rear of the property. It was a job that always seemed to take longer than he thought it should do, generally because he was finding the task a lot more of a physical strain than he used to. The kennels ran across the whole width of the rear garden. Toft preferred it when he could take the dogs out in his van each day in the summertime and let them 'do their thing' amongst the trees and in areas where he didn't need to take the responsibility for clearing up after them. The Belgian Malinois is a breed that has plenty of energy to burn off and ideally needs exercising two to three times a day, and Ken Toft knew that to neglect them could create an unhappy and possibly aggressive dog. He had always paid strict attention to their requirements and had never encountered a problem with any of them, but since Leo had joined the group, he knew that he hadn't kept up the routine as stringently as he should have done. As Toft became older, he accepted that he had not managed to exercise them all as much as he should have, which is why he was desperate for the first signs of spring whereby he could get back to the old routine. Hansel and Gretel were older now and Leo was a good, honest dog, so Toft felt that everything was going to work out just fine.

He coiled the hose up, hooked it over an old fence post, and took a look at his work. He liked to see that the kennel was clean, even if it didn't stay that way for very long. With three of them there wasn't much hope of that. As he started to wander back towards the rear door of the house, he heard a neighbour call to him from the other side of a thick row of conifer trees. Nick Hillier was around the same age as Toft and had been a good friend of his for at least twenty-five years, ever since he had moved into the neighbourhood from Bloomington, which is located 10 miles south of downtown Minneapolis and on the north bank of the Minnesota River, close to its confluence with the Mississippi. Hillier had worked for many years at the Mayor's Office in the centre of Bloomington and had seen the mayoral position change hands on a number of occasions. He also had a liking for dogs and owned three Dalmatians. Toft often referred to them as 'crazy dogs'. He regularly heard them barking and had seen Hillier being dragged down the street by them when he took them out. He often wondered how he ever coped with their lively characters in the house and was more than happy to acknowledge that he would never have to deal with such an energetic breed indoors. At least when he took Leo out with MinnSARDA, he didn't have to walk too far as Leo would be off doing his own thing as soon as he had been given the command. It had become necessary for Toft to establish an easier method when it came to exercising Leo seeing as he was the younger, sprightlier one. As the active dog of the group, he needed to maintain a training regime.

'Kenny. You've got visitors.'

'Visitors?' replied Toft.

'Yeah, there's a car out front. A couple of gentlemen were just about to begin walking up to your front door. I saw them from the front window,' explained Hillier.

'Gentlemen?'

'Yes, what have you been up to?'

'What do you mean?' asked Toft.

'Well, it's a police vehicle and they look like police officers to me. More search and rescue stuff, is it?'

Ken Toft scratched his head and paused for a moment as he tried to reason why any police officers would be calling today. He hadn't been out with MinnSARDA for a couple of months and hadn't been alerted to a new case recently. He wondered whether he was about to learn of a new missing person. He thanked Nick Hillier and made his way into the house, kicking his outdoor boots off as he went. When Toft reached the kitchen, he heard the doorbell ring. He didn't like it when people turned up unannounced and considered staying out of sight but then thought that his plan might capitulate if the men at his door knocked at Nick Hillier's house, so he decided that he'd better answer it.

When the door finally opened and the figure of Ken Toft appeared, Big Toni spoke first.

'Good morning, sir. Can you just confirm that I'm speaking with Ken Toft?' he said with an officious tone.

'Yes, that's me,' said Toft, looking past Big Toni at the officer he recognised from a previous meeting.

'You already know Officer Bonner. May we come in, sir? We would like to have another chat, if that's ok?' said Big Toni, edging closer to the doorway.

Toft nodded and stepped back into the hallway to allow his visitors to enter. He didn't really want to but couldn't see another option. He thought about asking why they were here, but he suspected it was going to be about something in relation to the previous visit. He showed Big Toni and Bonner into the lounge and gestured towards the Chesterfield for them to sit. Toft remained standing and asked whether they would like a drink.

'Two black coffees would be very welcome, sir,' said Big Toni, knowing full well that Bonner's need was even greater than his.

Toft nodded and stepped out of the room. Bonner pointed to the photograph of the two dogs, Hansel and Gretel, and briefly told his Captain the story that Toft had relayed to him about how they were discovered. The room was just as tidy as Bonner had remembered it to be, without a thing out of place. He told Big Toni that the dogs were kept out the back in kennels. Big Toni grumbled that he couldn't understand why anyone ever had dogs in the house. It was not something that he would tolerate under any circumstances.

When Ken Toft returned with two mugs of coffee, Big Toni asked if he was having one for himself. Toft explained that he had to go out soon and didn't want to drink just now.

'Uh, huh,' was all Big Toni said, knowing full well that Mr Ken Toft would not be going anywhere until he had finished with him.

The men sat in silence and sipped their drinks while Ken Toft watched on. Bonner was especially grateful for his. He had felt a little queasy on the journey from his house to Eden Prairie and was glad to get out of the car. The short spell outside Toft's house had allowed Bonner to stretch his aching body and take a few deep breaths of the cold but refreshing air. He was hoping that the coffee might reinvigorate him enough for him to survive the return journey in the car without the need for a potentially unpleasant and unscheduled stop.

Big Toni placed his mug down on the coffee table in front of him and reached into his jacket pocket. Ken Toft could tell that the officers were showing no signs of hurrying and knew that the questions would come soon enough so he sat down in an armchair and waited. Big Toni unfolded the map of the Nelson property that Bonner had shown him and laid it down onto the coffee table. Toft recognised it immediately, but as far as he was concerned, he had already been over that with the other officer and didn't see the relevance of it.

Bonner was still wrestling a little with his delicate condition and decided to stay quiet for a little longer in the hope that Big Toni would take the lead. He needn't have worried.

'Mr Toft,' said Big Toni, 'Do you recognise this?'

'Yes, your officer had it with him last time but…'

'Fine. We'll get to it in a moment,' said Big Toni, cutting Ken Toft off in mid conversation.

Ken Toft just shifted in his chair and looked around the room, almost in the hope that a wormhole would appear for him to jump into and escape.

'I'm fully aware that you have already spoken with Officer Bonner, but I would like to go over a couple of things myself. You don't mind, do you?' said Big Toni.

'I suppose not,' said Toft.

'You suppose not?' repeated Big Toni, without pushing any further as he already knew that he had the upper hand.

Big Toni nudged Bonner and asked for his notebook. It was the one that Bonner had had with him when he initially called on Ken Toft. Big Toni opened the notebook and flipped over a couple of the pages until he reached the part he wanted. Again, Toft looked on, without a murmur.

All that could be heard in the room were the deep breathing sounds that were coming from Big Toni as he took his time to read the pages and digest the notes that Bonner had made. Bonner was pretty sure that this was all for show and that Big Toni knew precisely what he wanted to ask Ken Toft. He sat, quietly enjoying the performance. Bonner hadn't had very many opportunities to work directly with his Captain and felt quite privileged to have him beside him today, especially as he had declared his belief in Bonner's suspicions regarding the search at the Nelson property. As the silence grew, Bonner's mind began to drift and before he knew it, he was thinking about Caterina Marks, the very reason for them being here.

At the lonely party in his den last night, she had 'been there' again. Bonner doubted that a party for one was even possible. He had sat beside her and talked to her, even danced with her…except, of course, he hadn't. When Big Toni spoke, Bonner snapped out of his daydream.

'Mr Toft, can you just confirm for me that you attended the Nelson property on April 26th, 2010?' he said.

'I think so. It's a long time ago.'

'I didn't ask you if it was long time ago, I asked you if you were there,' responded Big Toni.

Bonner was wide awake and switched on. He hadn't realised that Big Toni was going to push this hard. He was enjoying the trip a lot more now.

'Yes, I did,' said Toft.

'And were you there as a representative of MinnSARDA, the search and rescue dog association?'

'Yes, but…'

'How many dogs did you take with you, Mr Toft?' asked Big Toni.

'What?'

'How many dogs?'

'Just one. Gretel,' said Toft.

'Was one dog sufficient?'

'I thought so at the time.'

'How did you transport your dog?' asked Big Toni.

'In my van, like I always do.'

'Where did you park the van?'

'What? Outside the house, I think.'

'How long have you known Wade Nelson?' asked Big Toni.

'What?'

'How long?' said Big Toni.

'Oh, about fifteen years, I guess.'

'I don't want you to guess, Mr Toft. Is it fifteen years or longer?'

'Well, yes, fifteen,' said Toft.

'How did you first meet him?'

'I don't know…erm…I can't remember.'

'Try. You must have had something in common for a lengthy friendship to develop,' said Big Toni.

'It must have been the time when I went into the bank where he worked. We got talking and seemed to get on quite well. Then I bumped into him again when I was out doing some training with my dogs.'

'Where were you?'

'In the woods, not far from where he used to live in Golden Valley,' said Toft.

'What was he doing there?' asked Big Toni.

'He was shooting with his girls.'

'Shooting?' said Big Toni.

'Yes, Captain. The girls, Betty and Elisha, used to go with him and shoot the bow,' said Bonner.

'Shoot the bow?' said Big Toni.

'Yes. Captain. The crossbow. He was fanatical about it, and he taught the girls how to shoot. They used to go out on a Saturday morning. It was a regular thing. Betty told me all about it. She wasn't all that keen, but he made them go,' explained Bonner.

Big Toni absorbed Bonner's story before turning his attention back to Ken Toft.

'Mr Toft. Did you tell Mr Nelson that you were coming on the Saturday morning in question?'

It wasn't the morning when the search took place, thought Bonner, as he half glanced at his Captain.

'Erm… No, I don't think so. It wasn't really necessary,' said Toft.

The report said there was a call to the Nelson property to inform the house owner that the team would be coming, thought Bonner, *why did he go in the morning?*

'Why not?' asked Big Toni.

'Well, erm… I don't know.'

'Did you always used to attend to these things so promptly? After all, she had only gone missing that morning,' said Big Toni.

She wasn't actually officially missing until later, thought Bonner, as he enjoyed the Captain's line of questioning.

'When we receive a call, we react to it. The sooner these things are put into action, the better the chance of finding the missing person,' said Toft defensively.

'When you attend an incident like this do you have to fill in any paperwork afterwards?'

Yes, as soon as practicable, thought Bonner.

'Well, not always straight away. We have to record what we found. Or not, depending upon the outcome.'

'How do you usually receive the call, Mr Toft?'

'Usually, it comes from the police or the fire department or maybe mountain rescue, it depends on the…'

'And on this occasion?' asked Big Toni.

'Erm… It was directly from the police.'

'Is that what MinnSARDA told you?'

'Yes, they said the police had called them to report a missing girl.'

Alexandria Org made the call herself before the police got involved, thought Bonner.

Big Toni jotted something on Bonner's notebook before continuing.

'What was the weather like that day, Mr Toft?'

'What?'

'The weather, on the day you attended the Nelson property,' said Big Toni.

'I can't remember. It was raining, I think.'

It was cold and dry, thought Bonner.

'How long were you there?' asked Big Toni.

Bonner's eyes widened slightly in anticipation of the answer. Just by chance, on the way from his house, he had mentioned to Big Toni that Betty had peeked out of an upstairs window and told him that she saw a van outside the house and that it had gone after about fifteen minutes. He also told Big Toni that the girls may have been in their bedrooms and not out of the house like Wade Nelson had said. Big Toni wasn't unduly concerned by the lies. It was a long time ago and the man was dead. He didn't feel that it would help to locate Caterina. Maybe he was right, maybe not.

'I don't know…erm…I can't remember exactly. Must have been at least an hour or more. A search takes a long…'

'Were the girls, Betty and Elisha, there too?'

'Yes, they were inside the house,' said Toft.

That's not what the report said, thought Bonner, *Mr Nelson told the police that they were out.*

'How did you know?'

'I saw them through the window from the garden. Look, why are you asking all this?' said Toft.

That wasn't true, thought Bonner, *Betty said they were told they had to stay in their bedroom and keep out of sight. He couldn't have seen them. Anyway, as far as the report was concerned the girls were out.*

'And finally, Mr Toft, why does the report that I have contradict everything you just said?' said Big Toni.

Ken Toft reddened in the silence. Big Toni pulled out a set of pages from his inside jacket pocket and placed it on the table. As the silence continued, Bonner began to wonder why he hadn't asked these things when he initially visited Ken Toft after his trip to MinnSARDA but decided that he had had no reason to doubt any of the things he said at the time. He was more focussed on the exact spot where Gretel had indicated. It wasn't until after that he had begun to have a few doubts run through his mind.

'Well, I…' muttered Toft.

Big Toni picked up the papers again and started at page one.

'What time were you called by MinnSARDA?'

'Time?' said Toft.

'What time, Mr Toft?' said Big Toni, coldly.

'It must have been in the morning sometime, I don't know exactly,' he said.

'Do you find it strange that the report I'm holding says that the initial call came from a Mrs Alexandria Org, the mother of Caterina Marks, at 18:09. In the evening of April 26th, 2010? Because I do, Mr Toft.'

Ken Toft's throat dried up instantly.

'You mentioned that the team always respond quickly to these reports of missing people. Is that right, Mr Toft?'

'Yes, they do because…'

'So, could you tell me why you responded so quickly that you attended the Nelson property at least eight hours before the call was received at MinnSARDA, before it was passed to the police department? What were you doing there?' said Big Toni.

Ken Toft reddened even more, if that was possible.

'Did your Gretel like to work in the rain?' asked Big Toni.

'What? Not really.'

'Good job it wasn't raining that day then wasn't it, MrToft?'

'I thought…' was all Ken Toft could manage now.

Big Toni leaned forward and dropped the notebook on top of the map, allowing it to go down with a thud.

'You didn't even take your dog, did you? Why would you have taken your dog to a search that had not been authorised because it hadn't even been called in? That's why you couldn't pinpoint the location on the map, isn't it?' said Big Toni, in a tone that increased in volume as he went along.

Ken Toft didn't speak, he just sat there, perplexed.

'What were you doing at the Nelson property, Mr Toft, tell me that, because right now you're implicated in the case of Caterina Marks and if I don't start getting some answers, things are going to get a lot worse.'

Gregory Bonner's heart warmed, his fuzzy head cleared, and his desperate hope of discovering precisely what had happened to Caterina Marks reached a new height.

I will find you, Caterina. I promise you.

Nothing came back from Ken Toft. Just a blank startled look. The game was up.

SIXTY-EIGHT

Old Clapton Street Police Station.

DI Marc Sutton sat at his desk and viewed the evidence that had been provided by the Crime Scene Investigation Team from last night's fire in Folger Street. The blaze was a repeat of the recent arson attack at the same property and had first been reported to Fire Control via a 999 call by the owners at 03:22, earlier this morning. The photographs in front of him showed the extent of the damage to the house in explicit detail. The Fire Investigation Team and the Police officers at the scene were in full agreement as to the cause. Once again, it was very strongly suspected that the cause was arson. A squeezy bottle, similar to that which was originally intended to contain washing up liquid, was found to be discarded in the front garden. Following a simple investigation, which involved little more than a well-tuned nose, it was discovered to have contained petrol. It appears that the item had been used to squirt the flammable fluid over the front door and through the letterbox into the hallway.

On ignition, this in turn set fire to a pair of curtains that previously hung just inside the property and so began the fire that deeply charred the front door and rapidly engulfed the hallway, spewing toxic smoke up the stairwell and towards the unsuspecting, occupants that were deeply asleep in the bedroom on the first floor. The photographs that were taken of the melted smoke alarms that had had their batteries removed explained why the early warning system failed. This is something that he had seen all too often. Unfortunately, it was not uncommon.

Sutton turned each photograph over in turn and gradually appreciated how quickly this incident had escalated. From previous experience he knew that the spread of fire in a domestic property can accelerate within less than a minute into something unmanageable. Many things in its way can soon become a new ignition source and feed the voracious flames. But as with many incidents of this ilk, he also knew that it was the acrid smoke that could be responsible for the potential loss of life. When the occupants finally awoke, they discovered their upstairs rooms were already thick with life-threatening fumes. If their actions had not been so expeditious, they may well have fallen victims to the black cloak of death that was gathering around them. As it was, the male and female occupants both suffered from smoke inhalation and required oxygen at the scene, which was initially provided by the Fire Service before they were assisted into the rear of the first ambulance to attend.

Sutton gathered the photographs together and placed them to one side of his desk. He would be taking them into a meeting with him soon. At that point his DS, Carrie Linton, strolled into his office.

'What time did you two finally stop last night?' asked Sutton.

'You don't want to know,' said Carrie with a yawn, 'Didn't wake you, did we?'

'No. The first thing I knew was when Grace got into bed. Don't know how long I'd been asleep, but it felt like it was hours.'

'Good job she was going in a bit later today then, eh?' said Carrie.

'I guess it was.'

'Listen, Marc, before I head out, can I have another look at that CCTV? There's something that has been bugging me about it.'

'Sure. I'll set it up. Just click on the appropriate video on the screen.'

As far as Carrie was concerned, the previous night at Grace's had been a riot. The two of them had started off quite restrained and were very reserved throughout dinner but after a few glasses of their favourite tipple, they had become a little louder. Carrie and Grace were well aware that Marc wouldn't relish being kept awake by their frivolity but at the same time they knew he would be the most tolerant of people if they did exceed what they thought would be an acceptable level of clamour. Neither of them were drunk by any means, especially as Carrie knew that she would be at work in a matter of a few hours, it was just that they would set each other off laughing with all manner of silly stories. Unbeknown to him the time that Grace crawled into bed beside him was around 03:45. Carrie left quietly shortly after 05:30 having grabbed a few hours on Grace's sofa. She was hoping to get through the day without anything traumatic testing her to the limits.

'Here you go. Close it all down for me, will you,' he said.

'Are you going somewhere?'

'Yeah, I've got to go to a meeting with Blackery and the Incident Commander from the Fire Service about the arson attack last night in Folger Street.'

'Another one?' exclaimed Carrie.

'I'm afraid so. The occupants weren't so lucky this time either. Smoke inhalation, mostly though. Keep me posted. Catch you later,' he said.

'Of course, have fun,' she said, whimsically.

'Always,' he retorted, as he grabbed his jacket from the back of his office chair and left Carrie to peer at the video of the mysterious lady in the dark coat and multicoloured headscarf.

Carrie began to look at the information on the screen and clicked the curser on the video that she wanted to check again. It was something about the second day that bothered her. She skipped the footage from the first day and then slowed the video down as the woman in the shot began to walk out of sight behind the large tree. She watched as she sat on the bench and leaned in towards the screen to get a really good look. Carrie zoomed in on the only part of the woman that she could actually see at this time. Then she played the video back again and watched as she walked towards the bench. Carrie almost held her breath in anticipation.

'Now, sit yourself down,' she said to herself, as she held her finger, ready to pause the footage just where she wanted to.

'There,' she said, and stopped the video at just the right point.

Carrie sat still and looked at the screen for a few moments before she did anything else. The part of it that had bothered her was now clearly on the screen. It was such an innocent and possibly insignificant thing, but it had stuck in Carrie's mind right from when she first watched the footage with her DI. She had accepted that Sutton wouldn't have spotted it because she felt that it wasn't necessarily something that a man would notice. Carrie shook her head slightly at the likelihood that she had even found anything relative to the case, but something about it was niggling away at her. She questioned whether she was on completely the wrong track and the more she looked at it, the more uncertain she became. But if she was right, it could just make all the difference and if it played out the way she was thinking, it could help to bring a killer to justice.

She closed down the laptop and allowed the image to replay in her mind again. *I think I'm right; I just don't know I'm right,* she thought, as she left Sutton's office and made her way down the stairs, past the interview room where Sutton was talking with Blackery and the Fire Officer, and out to her car. If things developed as she hoped, she would inform DI Sutton, but if they didn't, she would keep it to herself. Carrie didn't want to raise anybody's hopes until she was as certain as she could possibly be that she was right, and her suspicions could be substantiated. And to establish that she first needed to have a worthwhile conversation and then secondly, she needed to pay another visit to Dorothy Walton at Rodina Drive.

When Carrie arrived at Pavilion House, she began to make her way past the colourful flower beds and towards the front door. Somebody was carefully watering the plants with a controlled, fine sprinkle of water from a bright yellow hosepipe. Carrie could see the rainbow of colour being reflected in the water as the light refracted in the droplets. Going by what Aimee had said, she should be on duty again today, and Carrie was hoping to see her. As Carrie got within reach of the entrance doors, one side opened towards her, and a member of staff wearing her white uniform with the word *Pavilion* printed in red on the breast pocket, exited the building. It wasn't Aimee. Whoever it was, was kind enough to hold the door open for Carrie. She thanked the staff member and went inside. The same lady that Carrie had spoken to before was standing behind the reception desk. She recalled the confusion about Mrs Greaves and how the lady had referred to her specifically as Robin's mother, which still didn't make any sense to Carrie. She decided to ask for Aimee at reception and walked towards the desk.

'Hello again,' said the woman, 'are you here to see Robin's mother again?'

'Is it possible to speak with Aimee before I do?' Carrie asked.

'Oh, I expect so, providing she's not busy. I'll check for you.'

'Thanks,' said Carrie.

'Aimee Richards to reception. Aimee Richards.'

'You've got a tannoy,' said Carrie, a little surprised.

'Yes. It's only on trial. The owners are trying it out. We've never had one before, but to be honest I like it. They said it's only to be used in emergencies, but I don't see what harm it'll do as long as I speak into it softly and don't alarm any of the residents. Nobody has complained so far and besides it saves me scurrying up and down the passages trying to find the person I want. And if there is any sort of emergency, it lets our people know in an instant. Good idea, if you ask me, not that anyone ever does,' she said with a chuckle.

'I'm surprised you have one but maybe they'll let you keep it,' said Carrie.

'Well, it's been fine so far, and it gets my vote. Not that anyone will be interested in what I think. Anyway, she shouldn't be too long.'

Carrie waited and watched as a couple of staff members helped to escort some of the residents from one area to another. Carrie wasn't sure where they were all off to but as she watched them, she didn't see Mrs Greaves among them, so that was fine by her. A few seconds later, Aimee appeared from behind her and walked up to the desk.

'Hi. You're back,' she said.

'Yes. A glutton for punishment, as they say,'

'If you want punishment, you should try working here, isn't that right, Valerie?' said Aimee.

'You can say that again,' she responded from the other side of the counter.

'Oh, it can't be that bad. At least you're in the warm,' said Carrie.

'Too warm for me,' said Valerie.

'How can I help you? Are you here for another chat?' asked Aimee.

'I am. Is it possible to see her?'

'Yes, I'll take you to her.'

'Just one thing. I need to ask a few questions. I'll try not to go on too much for her, but it is important,' said Carrie.

'I'm sure it'll be fine,' said Aimee.

Aimee began to lead Carrie down the corridor just as she had yesterday afternoon. When they reached the doors to the restroom, Aimee kept on going.

'Somewhere different today?' said Carrie.

'Yes. She's in her room. Ordinarily, we don't permit visitors to see the guests in their rooms unless they are unable to come out, or ill or something. We usually insist they see them in the communal room, like you did before, but seeing as you're, you know, 'in the police', I don't think it'll be an issue. I won't tell if you won't,' said Aimee.

'Thanks,' said Carrie.

They continued a little further along the corridor before Carrie spoke again.

'I hope she's not unwell.'

'Margaret? Oh no, she's fine. It's just that today is the day when some of the ladies, and it's mostly the ladies, sit in the restroom and play cards. Sometimes they play right up to lunchtime. They get quite vocal, and Margaret finds it all a bit too much. She said she doesn't like all the exaggerated laughter, as she calls it, so she prefers to stay in her room until it's over with. Right, here we are, 29. Would you mind waiting here for a moment while I make sure she's happy to see you?'

'Of course not,' said Carrie.

Aimee slowly opened the door and called out softly to Margaret as she went inside. Outside, Carrie waited and mentally prepared her questions. She wasn't sure what she might gain from her visit but there were just too many loose ends and things that didn't add up for her liking. She needed to clarify a few things and go over the things that Margaret had said. The situation with her daughters and their relationship with Robin was a bit mysterious and that was just the start.

A few moments later, Aimee reopened the door to room 29 and popped her head around the doorframe. Carrie was hopeful that Margaret would be content to see her again and waited for Aimee to give her the good news. When Aimee smiled and nodded at her, Carrie knew that she was going to get another chance with Mrs Greaves. Her and Aimee made their way into the room and Carrie could see Margaret sitting in a chair next to her bed. She wore a pair of soft and comfortable looking tracksuit bottoms and a similar hooded top. Carrie thought that she looked quite smart. She noticed that the television was on with the sound muted.

'Hello again,' said Margaret, cheerfully.

'Hello. I hope you don't mind me disturbing you again,' said Carrie.

'No, not at all. Switch that off for me, would you, Aimee. I'm not watching it anyway.'

Aimee switched off the television and both her and Carrie sat on the bed next to Mrs Greaves.

Carrie proceeded to make small talk with Margaret for a few minutes before approaching the subject regarding some of the things that were spoken about previously. Firstly, Carrie wanted to learn a bit more about the relationship between Robin and his sisters, Jennifer and Joanna.

'Am I still ok to call you Margaret?' she said.

'That's my name, so go ahead,' said Margaret with a laugh.

'Thanks. Ok, so, when we spoke before, you mentioned that the children didn't always get on together so well. Can you tell me why?' asked Carrie.

'Well, mostly it was your typical squabbling. They used to get up to all sorts of pranks.'

'Like what?' asked Carrie.

'Locking him in his room. I said that before, didn't I? And then there were the arguments over who liked who and all sorts of things.

I had to rescue him sometimes and get him out if his sister hadn't already let out him out,' she said.

'Did it ever come to blows, Margaret?'

'Oh, no, not exactly. They could be cruel sometimes though. Like the time Jennifer went out and she came back on her own. I went spare and it was lucky that he found his way home before it got dark. Even though he was a bit older than her, I still didn't like them becoming separated,' she said.

'Where did she take him?' asked Carrie.

'She said that *he* took *her*, and she didn't like being there, so she ran off.'

'Where did they go?'

'To the local tip of all places. Good job he managed to get back. I tore her off a strip when I got hold of her. Filthy, he was.'

'That can't have been very nice for him,' said Carrie.

'He didn't seem that bothered at the time, but then I could never tell with that one,' said Margaret.

Carrie referred to her notes for a minute or two whilst Aimee carried on chatting to Margaret and filling her in on what was on the lunch menu today.

'Margaret. You said that the girls stayed with you after he left the house, but they left when he came back. Why was that?' asked Carrie.

'Well, it wouldn't have worked with all of them there. It was bad enough before but then things just got even more tense between them. He always wanted to take charge of everything. And they used to continually blame each other and argue about it for hours. Drove me round the bend, it did. I ended up screaming for them to stop bickering,' she said.

'What did they blame each other for?'

'Her death, that's what. Her death,' blurted Margaret.

Carrie and Aimee looked at each other with widened eyes and the room fell eerily silent. As Margaret reached for a tissue to wipe her eyes, Aimee gave Carrie a look that seemed to suggest that, perhaps, the conversation should come to an end. But Carrie wasn't going to give up now.

'I'm sorry to upset you, Margaret, but who are you talking about?' she asked.

'Marion, of course.'

'Who is Marion?' asked Carrie, softly.

'She was his sister.'

'I thought the girls were Jennifer and Joanna,' said Carrie, becoming more confused.

'They are. I had three girls altogether.'

Carrie tried to process what was happening and fit all the pieces of the jigsaw together.

'So, you had three girls and one boy?'

'Yes,' answered Margaret, 'they were mine.'

'Do you mind telling me what happened to her?'

'I wish I knew. Whatever happened took place when I was out. I had only gone to the butcher's on the corner for some chops for tea because it was local and I didn't like to leave them for long, and when I got home…there she was, right in front of me…at the bottom of the stairs. I screamed the place down. It was a picture that will haunt me until the day I die. Her leg was all bent the wrong way and she just laid there, all twisted…completely lifeless. I knew she was dead. I could see it in her face. The other three were in their rooms, alone in the house, and the place was in silence. To this day, I don't know what happened. When I asked, all they did was blame him. The girls blamed him, he blamed them, but I still don't know. All I know is that they never forgave him and that the feeling was mutual. It was a horrible atmosphere. She was the one that used to care the most about them all. She rescued him more than once; I can tell you.'

'Margaret, I'm so sorry,' said Aimee.

'So am I, Margaret. That's awful for you. I assume there was a police investigation too?' said Carrie.

'Thank you both, but I have learned to deal with it. That's why I have the television on. Even without the sound, it gives me a distraction sometimes,' explained Margaret, 'And yes, there was a lot of questions from the police, but it didn't get me any closer to finding out what happened. I think the death certificate said misadventure or something like that. Like an accident, I suppose.'

'You said she rescued him. What happened?' asked Carrie.

'Oh, Joanna said it was Jennifer and he said it was Joanna, but either way, all I do know is that it was Marion who pulled him out of the bath.'

'The bath?' said Carrie.

'Yes. I don't know who did what to whom, but one of them held him under. Playing a bit too hard, I expect. Marion said she heard a commotion going on and could hear water splashing about, so she went to look and there he was, almost unconscious. The others were out of sight, and I never found out who the guilty party was. Anyhow, after Marion died things were becoming almost unbearable. Eventually he left and for the time being I had some peace. I'm can't blame him or them really because I don't know who did what. On the one hand Jennifer and Joanna said he pushed Marion down the stairs because she told him off for going into her room. Nobody knows really, or at least nobody is saying. Even after all the investigations, they couldn't tell for sure. She, that's Marion, had some marks on her but it appeared that they had possibly all been fighting and squabbling, so it was impossible to say that anyone in particular had pushed her. In the end it was put down as an accident. They were always sporting bruises and scrapes.'

'That's terrible, Margaret,' said Aimee.

'Yes, it was,' she said.

'What happened when he came back?' asked Carrie.

'You could cut the atmosphere with a knife. The arguing had stopped but the tension was awful. They didn't speak to him, and he didn't speak to them. To be honest, I didn't even know where to begin. He was strangely close to Marion and with all the goings on in those days, he would never hurt her. I never really worked out why he took to her like he did. It was funny but he was the only one that she would allow to brush her hair.'

'Really? I wouldn't let anyone brush mine,' said Aimee.

'Yes. I'm sure that he really loved her because I'm sure I could see it in his eyes when he came back. The hurt, that is. It hadn't gone away. He wasn't the same, as I said. There was something very different about his character.'

'Margaret, when your husband was alive, did he have a good relationship with the children?' asked Carrie, trying to dig a bit deeper.

Aimee looked at Carrie, as if to imply that she wasn't sure that she needed to drag up any more of the past and possibly cause any more stress for Margaret. But Carrie was too far down this particular road.

'He loved them all, of course…but…' began Margaret.

'Yes?' said Carrie.

'Well, there were just a few occasions when I thought he went a bit too far.'

'What do you mean, Margaret?' asked Carrie.

Aimee was becoming even more edgy.

'Well, I didn't think anything of it at the time but there were a couple of times when I think he was a bit too heavy-handed. It hadn't been the first time, either. Not with the girls, you understand. Never with them but sometimes I used to see him give his son a pasting.'

'Did he ever hurt him?'

'He did sometimes. I used to tell him not to hit him around the head. I didn't like it when he did that. That wasn't right,' she said.

Carrie's mind was twisting and turning with all the new information. *Robin had three sisters.* She could understand how much pain must have been caused by Marion's death, especially as it appeared that she was his favourite. She was also reflecting on the taunting and the possible bullying from Jennifer and Joanna. She wondered how far they took things and whether they took things too far. Maybe even further than Margaret appreciated. *The tip, the bath. What else?* Carrie knew that the division that had been created over the years between Robin and his sisters for the blame of Marion's death must have been corrosive. *But what did it do to him long-term?* Carrie found herself conjuring with a picture of somebody that had held a massive grudge for years. *But who pushed Marion?*

'I think…maybe…' said Aimee, looking at Carrie with a concerned expression.

'Yes, yes, ok,' she said.

Carrie had to agree with Aimee that this sort of upset had to stop. Margaret had given Carrie plenty to think about. The question now was what she was going to do with it. Then Carrie had another thought.

'Margaret, what colour hair did your girls have?' she asked.

'I think…that we should go,' said Aimee.

'Brown hair. All were very dark,' said Margaret.

Oh, God. Three girls, all with dark hair. The tip. The bath. And one he loved. Just like Patricia said, they represent someone to him, she thought.

'I couldn't believe it happened again,' said Margaret.

'What happened again?' said Carrie.

'Two sets.'

'Two sets?' said Carrie.

'Yes,' said Margaret, 'two sets of twins.'

Carrie and Aimee looked at each other.

'So, you had Jennifer and Joanna and then you had Robin and Marion?' said Carrie.

'What? Who is Robin?' said Margaret.

'Your son, Mrs Greaves,' said Carrie.

'Who is Mrs Greaves?' said Aimee.

'What? You know, Robin, Margaret?' said Carrie.

'Who is Mrs Greaves?' repeated Aimee.

'She…' began Carrie.

'I don't know a Robin,' said Margaret.

'This isn't Mrs Greaves,' said Aimee, who was now completely confused as to why the person who visited his mother that they all knew as Robin, apparently wasn't actually Robin.

'What? Then who is it?' asked Carrie.

'I don't know a Robin,' repeated Margaret, getting visibly upset now.

'I think you should go,' said Aimee, who was becoming extremely uncomfortable with the whole thing.

'No. Sorry, I mean, wait a moment,' said Carrie, turning to Margaret, 'What are the names of your children?'

Carrie waited for the answer as Aimee stood up, ready to escort Carrie out of the room. Margaret looked down at the floor for what seemed like an age before raising her head and looking straight at Carrie.

'Jennifer, Joanna, Marion and Michael,' she said, slowly, 'they are *my children*.'

'Michael?' said Carrie.

'Yes. His name is Michael Abbot. He comes to visit me,' she said.

'And this is Margaret Abbot, not Mrs Greaves. I thought you had that wrong when you asked at reception but when you said Robin, I recognised the name and he does come to visit her,' said Aimee.

'Who does?' asked Margaret.

'Robin,' said Aimee, making things worse.

'No Aimee,' said Carrie, 'he doesn't, but Michael Abbot does. He just calls himself Robin when you're around.'

'And he's always been an untidy little devil,' said Margaret.

'So, Robin is not Robin,' said Aimee, looking at Carrie and trying to catch up.

'And I don't know who on Earth Mrs Greaves is,' said Margaret.

'Pardon, Margaret. What did you call him?'

'An untidy little devil. Always was. Well, boys are, aren't they?'

'Please. Can we…' began Aimee.

'Why do you say that?' asked Carrie.

'I think I know,' said Aimee, suddenly.

'Why then?' said Carrie, looking straight through Aimee with eyes that were insisting upon an answer.

'Because every time he comes here, he leaves dusty footprints from his boots. I have to hoover up after him when he's gone. It goes right through the…' she said, as Carrie cut her short.

'Dust? What sort of dust?' asked Carrie.

'It's from where he works. The garage in Trenton Street. He's been working there for years, apparently. That's what he told me, anyway,' said Margaret.

Dorothy Walden's blankets have rust on them. Unless her husband was right, thought Carrie.

'Margaret, I'm sorry if I upset you. I have to leave now. Goodbye, and thank you both for your time,' said Carrie as she hurriedly made for the door, leaving Aimee and Margaret in the room.

'That blessed boy was nothing but trouble,' said Margaret.

Carrie quickly followed the corridor back to reception and ran straight through it and headed for the main door. When she got there, she pushed at the door but ended up crumpled against it. It was locked and she realised that it needed to be released by someone so that she could leave the building. She looked to the reception desk, but Valerie wasn't in sight. As she looked around for a staff member that might be able to help, Aimee came running into the reception area.

'Is something the matter?' she said.

'Can you let me out?'

Aimee fished inside the pockets of her uniform but didn't find her remote key fob.

'I've lost the stupid thing now. I bet it jumped out of my pocket when I ran after you. I'll have to go and...'

'No. I need to go now,' said Carrie.

'Don't worry, I know where the spare is. Valerie keeps one here somewhere,' said Aimee, and headed for the other side of the reception desk, 'So what's going on?'

'I can't tell you, Aimee. Sorry.'

Aimee walked towards Carrie with the spare remote fob and pointed it at the front door.

'There,' she said, as the door gave an audible click.

'Thanks,' said Carrie, 'and I'm sorry about all that. Just that one thing led to another. Thanks again, I've got to fly.'

Carrie left Pavilion House and ran towards her car. As she got to it, her phone rang. It was DI Sutton.

'Hi Carrie. Listen, I've had a missed call from Steve Kingham, can you give him a call and check on where he is, I'm going to be tied up with this fire investigation this afternoon,' he said.

'I'll check his tracker in a bit. I've got to go to Rodina Close, then I need to talk to you. I'll explain in bit. I just need to check one more thing. Then I need to talk to you about the CCTV. Look, I've got to hurry, I'll talk to you soon,' she said.

'I'll be in the meeting, and you don't have a warrant. Don't do anything stupid.'

'It'll be ok, I don't think I'll need one if it goes to plan. Just answer your phone. This is more important.'

'I don't doubt it. Listen, do you need back up? It all sounds a bit dodgy,' he said.

'I'll cross that bridge when I come to it, but it'll be fine. I'll call in if I do, but I'm sure I don't right now. If I'm right, then I think we might get a lead with regard to finding Angelica. I just need half an hour. I have to be sure. I'll call you as soon as I can.'

'Christ, Carrie. Ok, call me in 30 minutes without fail. I'll prioritise your call,' said Sutton.

'I will.'

Carrie started her car and aimed straight and true for Rodina Close.

SIXTY-NINE

DS Carrie Linton drove passed number 38, the residence of Robin Greaves aka Michael Abbot. As she went by slowly, she looked across at the premises to see if there were any signs of movement that could be seen through the front windows. It appeared to be quiet. Carrie's interest in what may or may not be behind the doors of number 38 would have to wait for, what she hoped was, a short time. Without a warrant she wasn't entitled to gain entry to the house unless she intended to affect an arrest or retrieve evidence that would support her suspicions. Nobody was in danger as far as she could tell so busting in had to stay off the menu for now. *More's the pity,* she thought. Carrie also knew that obtaining a warrant could take time, and currently she still felt that she didn't have a good enough reason for one that would convince a judge. Currently, all she knew was that he had used a different name, had removed some of Dorothy Waltons blankets, and caused Aimee Richards to get the hoover out after he had visited his mother.

When Carrie rang the doorbell at the house where she had previously spoken to Dorothy Walton, she turned away from the door in order that she could keep a constant vigil on whether there was any movement at number 38. It was still all quiet. Carrie heard somebody moving about on the other side of the door to the Walton house. When the door opened, Graham Walton asked whether he could help her.

'Hello, Mr Walton, is Dorothy in?' asked Carrie.

'No. You've only just missed her though. Cleaning day, you see. She's doing the rounds today. She came back to get the next batch of keys. She likes to do one half of the Close at a time. I keep telling her that she should have a spot of lunch before she starts again but she doesn't,' he said.

'Right. I didn't get to meet you properly before. I'm Detective Sergeant Linton from Old Clapton Street. I've spoken to Dorothy a couple of times before.'

'Oh, yes. The blankets. You were asking about the blankets,' he said.

'I was asking where to find Pavilion House, I think.'

'Ah, yes. That was it. It was Dorothy that was going on about the blankets. I wouldn't let him take them if it was up to me,' he said.

'No, I don't think I would either. You don't happen to have one of them here, do you?'

'I do actually. Hang on, I'll get one out of the laundry bag and you can see for yourself.'

Graham Walton went back into the house to find the example for Carrie to see. As she waited for Graham to return, she spotted Dorothy walking across the road towards number 38, although after a second glance it looked as though she was a bit further down. Carrie watched her go into one of the properties with her cleaning kit hanging from one shoulder.

'Here you are. I decided it would be better to bring the whole bag rather than get one out and shed dust all over the place. I wouldn't be very popular if I did that,' said Graham, as he opened the laundry bag for Carrie to peer inside.

'Oh, I see what you mean. That is dusty.'

'Yes. Dusty not rusty,' said Graham, with a knowing wink, 'You can take it if it's any good to you. I can put it into another bag for you, just don't tell Dorothy, eh.'

'I think I will, thanks.'

Carrie hadn't necessarily expected to be collecting potential evidence, but she wasn't going to turn it down. She hadn't needed to gain entry to number 38 or even ask for anything. She knew that if, by any chance, there was any connection between the blanket and Angelica Rowntree, that Graham's gift could prove very useful. She would definitely send it away to be tested for any trace of the DNA that belonged to Angelica as soon as she got back to Old Clapton Street.

'It's not for me to pry into why you might have an interest in the blanket but if you wanted to take a peek in number 38 then I wouldn't object. In fact, I could give you a spare key if you promise to bring it straight back. And if you promise not to tell Dorothy about that either, or I'll be in all sorts of trouble,' he said.

'Are you sure?' she said.

'Well, I trust you. It can't hurt, can it?'

'No, not at all, it's just that I don't have a warrant and I have to be careful,' said Carrie.

'Well, I'm giving you permission and I'm the Warden. So, it's up to me,' he said.

Carrie knew that she wouldn't be able to resist the opportunity to take another look in number 38. She wasn't forcing entry or doing anything without permission. In fact, she had been encouraged to take a look.

'I'll come with you, if you like,' said Graham.

'Ok, that would be helpful,' said Carrie.

Carrie saw Dorothy Walton walk back across the Close into another property as she waited for Graham to get his coat and change into his outdoor shoes. Dorothy looked towards the house but didn't seem to notice her. Carrie was certain that if Dorothy had spotted her, she would have been scurrying towards her in an instant. Once Graham was ready to go, Carrie placed the large carrier bag containing the blanket into the boot of her car, and they both headed off along the Close towards number 38.

Graham allowed Carrie access to Number 38, closed the door and stood in the living room. He invited her to 'do whatever she needed to do.' Carrie checked her mobile phone to check on the time. It had been 22 minutes since she had spoken to DI Sutton. *Another 8 minutes*, she thought.

'He won't be back, by the way,' said Graham.

'Who won't?' asked Carrie.

'Mr Greaves. He goes shopping after work and then he goes to visit his mother today.'

'Oh, right. Good,' she said, 'Do you speak with him, then?'

'Not a lot but he is a creature of habit, as they say. I can see most people coming and going from my house and he has a routine like everyone else.'

Carrie took a look around the living room with Graham watching on with interest. *Dorothy isn't the only nosy one, it seems,* she thought. She quickly drew her phone out to check the time, knowing full well that she was supposed to call Marc Sutton by now. His request for her to establish the whereabouts of DC Kingham had gone completely out of her mind. *I'll call him in a minute,* she thought.

The room wasn't too dissimilar to when Carrie had managed to gain access the last time, when she had helped Dorothy carry in her cleaning equipment. With a little more time, she thought that she should be able to have a more thorough look around. She began to slowly walk around the room and wondered how much Graham would be bothered if she was to delve into cupboards and the like. She decided to find out. She reached into her pocket and pulled out a pair of latex gloves which she pulled on. Carrie opened the door to a unit that had a tv sitting on top of it. The clutter inside looked like the normal sort of thing that one might discover; magazines, a tv remote, and a booklet that explained how the tv worked. She was sure that the empty beer bottles shouldn't have been there, but it wasn't her job to organise the house.

Carrie entered the kitchen and skirted around opening and closing the wall units as she went. There were the predictable objects like cups and plates but really nothing that Carrie thought was unusual. She checked the contents of the drawers, finding nothing out of the ordinary. Previously, Carrie's peek around the bedroom had been cut short by Dorothy. She thought about the irony that, at that time, Dorothy hadn't wanted her to tell Graham that she had gained access and now Graham was asking exactly the same with regard to Dorothy, albeit Graham had actually volunteered it.

Carrie entered the bedroom. She instinctively looked at the bed. The last time she had seen something that she had thought belonged to Robin's mother. Michael's mother. There was no female garment today. The floor was more or less empty, apart from a pair of socks that appeared to have been discarded under a bedside chair and a pair of slippers that were protruding from underneath a small chest of drawers. The carpet was beige and uninteresting. There were lots of bits on the carpet which resembled fluff and cotton balls that may have come off of the bed sheets. A single mattress stood, slotted neatly between the wardrobe and the bedroom wall. Carrie couldn't remember whether she had seen it before or not. She looked up above the wardrobe doors and noticed a pillow that had been wedged between the top of the wardrobe and the ceiling. She couldn't imagine Robin, aka Michael, having a guest to stay over. *Maybe that was there before too.* She glanced out of the bedroom door that had been left ajar and could see Graham in the living room. He didn't seem in the slightest bit interested in what she was doing. He was standing patiently with his hands clasped behind his back and appeared to be gazing out of the front room window towards the street. *Probably keeping a look out for Dorothy,* she thought.

When Carrie opened the wardrobe door, she found the missing item from her previous visit. A women's dress. Then another. The rest of the clothing looked as though it was the property of a man, although she only had Dorothy Walton's word that he sometimes dressed as his mother. Carrie pushed the garments to one side in order to check the back of the wardrobe. His jeans were filthy. They were the type that had padded knees which would fit with him working at the garage. Two dark overalls hung at one end of the rail, both quite grubby looking. With one finger she drew the material towards her, and with her other hand she rubbed the tips of her fingers along the sleeve of one of the overalls. Carrie studied the faint mark on her gloved fingers and rubbed her fingers and thumb together. Whatever it was felt like a soft texture, not gritty. It was also light in colour. *The same as the dust on the blanket?* she wondered.

Carrie recalled that Aimee had commented on the mess he left in his wake when he visited. She let the overall fall back into place among the other clothes and closed the wardrobe door. She hadn't been able to see anything else of interest hidden in there, but then she didn't really have any idea what she might be looking for. She stepped to one side and looked down the side of the wardrobe, where the single mattress stood. There didn't appear to be anything else tucked into the space. Carrie pulled it towards her in order to see down the side. As she did so the top of the mattress caught against the pillow on the top of the wardrobe and spun it 90 degrees, almost toppling it off. Carrie stood back a few steps for a better look. There was something else up there. A box, like a shoe box, that had been obscured by the pillow. She could just make out the picture of a trainer on the side of the box. Carrie stood close to the wardrobe on tip toes and reached up. Her fingers were able to touch the box, but she couldn't get a proper grip on it. All that happened when she tried to retrieve it was that it turned a little more but not enough for her to be able to pull it towards her. Carrie looked around her for something that she could use to reach it. Then she noticed a coat hanger hanging on the back of the bedroom door. She took it off the hook and bent the parts that are designed to support the shoulders of a garment together. Using the hook to draw the box towards her she began to reach up to the top of the wardrobe again, probing and jabbing at it, still on tip toes.

'Are you ok in there?' called Graham.

'Yes, I'm ok,' she said as she struggled blindly to reach it.

'It's just that Dorothy could be over any minute and, you know, I don't want…'

'Give me another moment. I'll be done in a sec,' she replied.

As Graham continued to mumble to himself about how Dorothy would be displeased to find Carrie in there, etc, etc, she stretched herself a little further and then she felt the box move. Only a small amount, but it definitely moved. It felt as though it only needed one more, hard poke with the coat hanger and it would be within reach. Carrie took a swing at it and hit the box hard on one side with the hook of the hanger, in an effort to slide it across the top of the wardrobe, and felt it snag. She wondered if she had punctured it and, keeping a hold on the hanger, dropped down onto the soles of her feet, giving her calves, which had become tight, a chance to stop hurting. As she did so, she stumbled against the foot of the bed, striking her heels and fell backwards bringing the coat hanger, which was still in her tight grip, with her, and in turn, the box, which landed heavily on her shin. Carrie cursed it, and as she reached down to rub her shin, she froze. She didn't even register that Graham had called out to ask if she was ok.

The box had spilled its contents out over her feet. She could now see what had struck her shin. A camera had bounced off her and rolled across the bedroom carpet, coming to rest at the foot of the bed beside her. Strewn around her feet were a number of photographs. Carrie put her hand down to take a look at them, but before she even got that far, she felt a chill run through her. She grabbed at the photos and held them in her hands, frantically sorting them. Her throbbing shin was no longer foremost in her thoughts. There were several of them, and all of them showed images of young girls. She turned them one at a time so that she could see who was featuring in the pictures. Immediately, she recognised Emily Roache, the girl that she had interviewed at Grace's school, but the others unfamiliar to her. Another showed a scene in a pub with some girls at the bar. As Carrie's mind began to place this new information into the puzzle, she noticed another couple of photographs that had not fallen out of the box. Carrie turned the box out onto the floor and gasped. There was no mystery about these ones. There was no mistaking what she was looking at. *White sheets.* Carrie knew instinctively that these were the images of the white material that had been used to wrap up the bodies of Haley Breen and Claudia De Luca.

She slumped down, fully sitting on the bedroom floor. 'Got you, you bastard,' she whispered to herself, at which point Graham opened the bedroom door. Carrie quickly looked around at him.

'Are you ok?' he asked.

'Yes. I've got to make a phone call. I want you to stop Dorothy from coming in here too,' she said.

'What? I can't do that, she's got to…'

'I mean it. Nobody is to come in here. You need to step outside and stop Dorothy from entering. I'm getting a couple of officers to secure the property. Somebody from the station will be here soon.'

'The station? What's going on?' he asked.

'Don't ask questions, Graham. Just do as I say.'

Graham Walton huffed and mumbled to himself for a couple of seconds before Carrie caught his eye with a look that left him in no doubt that she meant every word that she had just said. She pulled her phone out from her jacket pocket and pressed the quick dial which would connect her to the mobile of DI Marc Sutton. She listened to the phone ring and for whatever reason, swung the wardrobe door open again. She looked at the grubby, dusty overall and then saw something new; something that she had missed the first time. On the floor of the wardrobe was a large carrier bag. Carrie stooped down to inspect it, opened it wide with the coat hanger, and peered inside. She lifted something out of the bag with the hook of the coat hanger. On the end of the hook dangled a mask.

'Carrie, you're late calling. Are you ok? Did you get through to Steve Kingham?'

'Oh shit, I forgot him. Sorry. Marc there's something else more important. I'm in Greaves house…'

'What? Without a search or arrest warrant? What's going on? How did you get in?'

'Listen, Marc. I promise I'll explain all that it a bit. I've found something.'

'What exactly?' he asked.

'A couple of things. I've found a camera and a box of photographs of several girls. Emily Roache was amongst them too. There's also an overall that he has been wearing that is coated with the same dust that I've found on the blankets that he's been taking somewhere with him. And there's a mask. Look, I'm sorry, I know it all sounds a bit mixed up, but I will explain. There's something else that I've been meaning to tell you about too. Greaves likes to dress up in women's clothing. You remember that earring that you found at the end of Trenton Street, near to the underpass that leads through to the Lavender Road Estate? Well, I think this is where it has come from. Also, Marc, the CCTV.'

'Carrie, you're rambling. Slow down a bit,' he said, trying to assemble all that Carrie was saying.

'Sorry. I'm as sure as I can be that it wasn't a woman in the canal footage.'

'Why?'

'It was that part of the video where she sat down on the bench, almost out of sight from the camera. I knew something was wrong with it and when I looked again, I saw it. I saw what it was that was bothering me.'

'Any chance you're going to tell me?'

'Yes, sorry. It was when she sat down. Women don't sit like that, with their legs splayed out. Men do. I don't believe it was a woman at all. I believe it was Greaves…Oh, and, he isn't Greaves, He's Abbot…Michael Abbot.'

'For crying out loud, Carrie, anything else?' said Sutton.

'I think we should bring him in.'

'Because of the photographs, and the way he sat on a bench?'

'Because of two photographs. They showed rolls of white material. I think he had taken photographs of Haley and Claudia after he had killed them.'

'Christ, Carrie. Leave the best 'til last, won't you?'

'I've asked the Warden to stop anyone coming in until we get a team here. Can we get someone here to secure the place? It'll need a proper search too,' she said.

'I know that.'

'Yeah, sorry,' she said, her heart racing.

'I'll get a couple of our guys over there straight away and I'll sort the search warrant plus a warrant for Greaves' arrest…or Abbot's, or whoever he is. Do you know where he is now?'

'The Warden said he would be out shopping and then going to visit his mother at the Care Home,' she said.

'Ok. Give me the name of the Care Home. I'll send a team to intercept him there. Once we have him in here then we can try to establish a bit more.'

'This means that it wasn't Swann too. We need to tell Steve Kingham,' she added.

'Don't jump to conclusions just yet. Leave Steve to me. If he doesn't answer, I'll get someone to check on the location of his phone and get somebody to him as soon as possible. Leave it all as you found it and lock it up until I get somebody to you, I'll make sure they are quick. Then get yourself back here, I want a few things explaining. And Carrie, if Greaves turns up, be careful. Someone will be with you asap. If he really is our man, then we don't know what he is likely to do. I don't want you getting hurt, karate black belt or not,' said Sutton.

Carrie watched Graham Walton lock the house and stood next to him in the gateway.

'I heard some of that. What happens now,' he asked.

'You should go home and I'll wait for my colleagues,' she replied.

'And what if Mr Greaves comes back? What if he gets nasty?'

Carrie wrapped her fingers around a canister of pepper spray that she could feel in her pocket.

'Leave me to worry about that.' she said.

SEVENTY

The Riverside Centre, Tilbury, East London.

The old storeroom smelt dank and musty. The walls were stained from the rain that had run down them creating streaks of dirty lines. Years of grime and dirt had coagulated in every corner of the outbuilding. There was evidence that mice and rats had used the structure as somewhere to call their own on many occasions and the remnants of discarded birds nest were also visible in every nook and cranny of the aged guano-stained wooden rafters. Once upon a time the brick walls had been whitewashed but there was scant evidence of it left today. The majority of the original brickwork was now exposed once more, and the remains of the paintwork laid around the floor in its flaked and peeled format. Approximately twenty barrels of beer were stacked up against the walls like a phalanx of shiny soldiers. A large, dilapidated row of shelves stood at the far end of the room with a variety of bottles of wine and spirits standing precariously upon them. The floor was concrete, and the atmosphere was icy. The rear of the building had an extra extension that had been added many years ago as an extra storage space at a time when it housed several collapsible tables and chairs, and even a marquee that was used by a nearby company that organised weddings and other party events in a local community centre. Neither the company nor the furniture were in existence anymore. All that remained from those days was a stack of metal barriers that had been used to help guide people into the correct part of the old community centre on the days when such receptions were taking place. As cold and unwelcoming as it was, it served a purpose.

When Karter Swann had arrived at The Riverside Centre earlier, he had made his way up to the bar, flicked on the light and immediately checked to see whether the refrigerator in the rear storeroom had been left full of bottles, as was the arrangement. It was no surprise to him that it was half empty. Swann chuntered to himself that it really wasn't too much to ask for it to be replenished and therefore save him the job of going straight outside to the store and carrying several crates of beer bottles back up the stairs and then having to refill it before he checked how much beer was still in the barrels. If the empties had not been replaced at the end of the previous night, he would be having words. There was a primitive pulley system that had been bolted to the wall just outside the rear door that led to the rear courtyard. Swann would usually make good use of it, with one eye on the metal plate that was bolted to the wall as it strained under the weight. If he felt strong, he would often shoulder a barrel and ascend the stairs, grunting and groaning. During his time at The Cactus and Coyote he had often raised a barrel onto his shoulder and marched it through to the bar. The fact that there was a host of impressionable young ladies to show off to may have had something to do with it.

Tonight, there would be no showing off. Tonight, things had taken a very different turn from the usual routine. Karter Swann sat in the extension, with his back against the wall in the dim light, not moving. His eyes were fixed upon the crossbow that was clearly visible and was pointed directly at him. Swann had gone cold when he had heard a noise behind him as he reached to grab a crate of beer from one of the shelves and had turned to see a figure pointing something at him. When his brain rebooted a few seconds later, he couldn't believe who was standing in front of him, holding the weapon. He had stood, motionless, and stared at the worst person that he could ever have wished to see looking at him. Elisha Nelson's cold eyes burned through the gloom. Questions rattled through his head at speed, one after the other, none of them accompanied by answers. *Surely, she wouldn't,* he thought.

She was dressed in a black leather jacket with a dark hoodie underneath it, black jeans and black boots, and of course, gloves. The hood covered her hair and part of her face. The light wasn't favourable, but Swann could see enough to recognise the face that he had been avoiding ever since he left for Crete with the assistance of the menacing Odhran O'Connell. Elisha had dipped the crossbow towards the floor, by way of instructing Swann to sit. He had obliged. For a few short moments that felt like a decade of torture to Swann, Elisha didn't speak. The pair of them stared at each other, Swann trying to take stock of the position he now found himself in, and Elisha aiming her Cobra RX straight at him.

'Hello Karter. Or should I say, Kevin?' she finally said, with a noticeable sneer.

Swann didn't know what to say. He felt his years of living as Kevin Marshall crumbling around him like a weather-battered, spalling sandstone cliff. The self-imposed safety net that he had become so reliant upon now had a big, gaping hole in it. Swann sat in the dingy surroundings and looked towards the sliding door, beyond where Elisha stood.

'Don't think about getting out of here. You won't get past me, not without a bolt in your chest,' she said.

'What do you want?' he said, nervously.

Elisha stepped to one side, without taking her eyes off of Swann, and perched herself onto one of the beer barrels. The Cobra RX held its position and its aim.

'Not you anymore,' she said, softly.

'Then why are you here? How have you tracked me down?'

Elisha gave a quiet, sinister laugh and then remained silent. She stared at Swann. It was almost as if she was trying to work out the answer for herself. But Elisha knew precisely why she was there. Swann was no longer the central principle that occupied her thoughts. He no longer was the first thing she thought of each morning and the last thing at night as he had once been. Although the pain and anger that Elisha had experienced following his humiliating reaction to her advances at her house four years ago continued to burn and fester inside her, the reason for her appearance tonight wasn't about an attempt to revive the intimacy that she once yearned for; a relationship that she once desperately desired. It was no longer about unrequited love or a once unquenchable longing.

'I didn't track you down. That part was done for me. I can't take the credit for that one. Sure, I put the final touches together and managed to establish exactly where you were tonight but let's just say that I had some help,' she said.

Who else knows where I am? he thought. Swann thought about the letter that had landed on the doormat at 12 Countess Street and the sordid photographs of those girls. *Was Elisha behind those things? Was it her in the supermarket?*

Swann looked to his left and noticed a single brick. It was almost within reach. He wasn't even sure whether he could reach it let alone what he was going to do with it if he got the chance. He looked back at Elisha. Her position and her demonic stare were unchanged.

'So now what?' he said.

'How fast do think my bow can fire its bolt, Karter? Or is it Kevin these days?' she said.

Swann didn't respond. In truth he didn't know what to say and certainly didn't want to find out.

'I'll tell you,' she said.

'I don't really want to know, Elisha. Just get out of here.'

'This bolt can exceed speeds of 280 to 350 feet per second. That's about 150 miles per hour, *Kevin*. Just a little faster than you can reach out for that brick, wouldn't you say?' she said.

Swann knew that she hadn't missed his glance towards the brick and also that he would, very likely, not get the chance to make any use of it. He folded his arms in front of his chest, drew his knees up, and tried not to look at the crossbow.

'So, why don't we start by you telling me where you disappeared to,' she asked.

'Nothing to do with you,' he said.

'Are you sure? I would've thought it had a lot to do with me. I wouldn't have given up, you know. Not in those days. If you hadn't ran away, I would have got through to you. You would have yielded to my advances eventually. I knew you wanted me.'

'No chance,' he said.

'Huh. Like you didn't want me in the shower,' she said.

'You tricked me.'

'You loved it.'

'You're mad,' he said.

Elisha raised the bow and pointed it directly at Swann's head. He dropped his hands down and tensed his body. If she fired, he knew that he wouldn't stand a chance. As far as he was concerned, from this range the bolt would go in one side and out the other. He had to get her talking again to buy some more time. Anything to delay her releasing that bolt. Swann checked his watch. It would be another hour and a half before any of the punters were likely to start to arrive. By that time, he would have had the bar ready for them, but not tonight.

'So, if you don't want me anymore, what are you doing here?' he asked.

'Putting an end to something before it starts.'

'What are you talking about, Elisha? An end to what?'

'I'm not prepared to lose you again, you know,' she said.

'Lose me? You don't have me to lose.'

'Losing you once was bad enough, but I can't allow that again. I won't stand by and watch that happen,' she said.

'You knew that I was with Betty. What did you think you were playing at?'

'Did you forget that when we were at the Travelodge? Did you forget that when you made love to me?'

'Stop it. That was a mistake,' said Swann.

Elisha stood up and leaned forward, pointing the crossbow at Swann.

'That was no mistake, Karter. That was real. Why did you have to go and spoil everything?'

'There was nothing to spoil.'

'Don't you *dare* say that,' she said, with an explosive tone to her voice.

Even in this chilly storeroom, Karter Swann felt his shirt clinging to his back and a trickle of sweat run down his cheek. Every slight movement that she made with the crossbow caused him to panic that her finger was going to put just a little too much pressure on the trigger. He even began to hope that she had forgotten to release the safety mechanism, rendering it harmless. But this was Elisha. He knew that he was already clutching at straws.

'How did you find me?' he asked again.

'Like I said, I didn't. Betty did. She's still got a flame burning for you. Did you know that? That funny little landlord of yours was ever so helpful though. When I explained that I had come all the way from the States just to surprise you, he couldn't resist telling me where you worked. He didn't want to be responsible for spoiling your surprise. So very kind of him, don't you think?'

'If anything happens to me, he'll be able to identify you.'

Elisha smiled and lowered the crossbow slightly. Swann could judge that even at this angle, it could still do extensive damage. Probably kill him. She raised her left hand and pulled gently at the hood that had been covering her head the whole time, exposing her hair. Swann saw that her hair colour was dark, just like Betty's. The mousy colour wasn't there at all. She stepped forward just far enough that Swann could see her eyes more clearly in the light. They were brown, like Betty's. *Contacts,* he thought.

'Will he?' she said, 'I gave him my name too.'

'Your name?' questioned Swann.

'Yes. Elizabeth.'

'You won't get away with it,' he said.

'On the contrary, Kevin. He has no idea what Betty looks like. Although, in a funny way, I suppose he does now. She has never been to the house, until today, that is. Elizabeth knocked on the door and asked to find you so that she could complete her surprise visit. Then she drove here, entered the building and well, the rest is history, as they say. She killed you out of jealousy. She always knew that you loved me much more than you loved her, and she finally cracked.'

'What about the CCTV in the yard? I assume you arrived in your car,' he said.

'I did. But it had already been reported missing two days ago. Dear Betty must have stolen it. A few of her things are even inside it. I gathered a couple of bits and pieces the last time I popped in to see her, weeks ago. She never missed any of them. There's a half empty wine bottle too. She really does drink too much these days. And I've been very careful since I've been here waiting for you to arrive. As quiet as a mouse. Oh, and there was this young man who kindly showed me into the building as he was leaving. I made sure he got just enough of a look at me. I think he liked Betty's lipstick that 'Kevin's girlfriend' was wearing, something that I never wear. I don't even own any. I think he wanted to stay really. Kevin's girlfriend, with the dark hair, dark eyes, and the stolen car.'

'What about the weapon? You own that, I assume.'

'Ah, sadly not. I would love to have a Cobra RX all to myself, but you see this one belongs to my dear sister. I took an old credit card from her purse too. I knew she didn't use those things very often and that she had changed to a different one, but this one was still valid, so I thought that she ought to make good use of it. This beautiful killing machine is owned by Elizabeth Nelson. I have no idea that she has bought a crossbow, or what on earth she would want with such a thing…unless. Maybe she had something in mind.'

'You're nuts, Elisha,' he said.

'Elisha? Oh no, Kevin, she's not here.'

Just then Elisha heard a noise coming from behind her, out in the courtyard. Swann heard it too and considered shouting out but held his tongue. He was hoping that whatever, or whoever it was, would distract Elisha just enough for him to make a move. Swann knew that the risk of trying something right now was very high. If she pulled that trigger, he was dead.

'Hush, my darling,' she whispered, seductively.

Swann could tell that she was switching from being Elisha to being Betty. The whole thing sent shivers through him. He couldn't think of anyone that he would have expected to be outside at this time of the evening. He didn't know whether to warn them or just to use their presence as a distraction. In the end, the decision was made for him.

Swann didn't have a clear view of the doorway from his sitting position, but he knew that somebody was nearby. Elisha moved stealthily, back towards the door, keeping the crossbow aimed at Swann. Now was not the time to be a hero. Swann waited to see what would happen next. Elisha squatted down to one side of the doorway. Swann could still see enough of her to know that she had her eyes on him too. The footsteps were getting closer. Swann was sure that Elisha hadn't planned for this. He noticed a shadow cast itself onto the wall near the doorway. Somebody was coming in. Then the silence broke. Swann heard a man's voice say 'Kevin?'

'I'm in here. Look out she's got…'

There was a shuffle of feet and a loud *TOCK*. Then a brief moment of silence, before Swann heard the man thud to the floor. He leaned to one side in order to get a better view of the doorway and saw the shape of a man lying prone and a steady flow of blood which began to puddle beside his head. The man didn't move. The only movement came from the slow trickle of dark liquid that was running into the crevices in the concrete floor from the wound in his throat. A crossbow bolt was lodged into the wound. Swann could just see enough of the man's facial features to acknowledge precisely who he was and to know that, beyond reasonable doubt, Ray Keller was dead. He had no idea why he was there. He looked back at Elisha. She had a cold demonic expression that sent a chill through him. It was almost as if she had enjoyed the kill. Swann thought that he was going to be her next victim at any moment. Then he noticed another shadow. It appeared briefly and vanished. *Someone else's out there.*

Swann tried not to give anything away. He didn't want to witness another murder right now, or ever again, and he had no doubt that Elisha wouldn't hesitate to fire. Elisha turned her head towards the door and then back to Swann.

'Well, that was unfortunate,' she said, coldly.

Swann braced for the worst. He looked around him for anything that he could use to defend himself but there was nothing to hand, at least nothing within reach that he could deploy faster than a crossbow bolt.

'What now? Are you going to do that to me too?' he said.

'When I'm good and ready. Don't rush me, Kevin. Wouldn't you like to talk a little more before Betty kills you?' she said.

'You're not Betty.' *But she is,* he thought.

A head popped into his view close to where Ray Keller lay. It was Betty with her hand pressed over her mouth. Swann tried to convey a message with his eyes, but Elisha was watching him too closely for him to try anything too clever. He didn't want any harm to come to Betty and had to find a way of protecting her from Elisha. He was sure that Betty knew Elisha was there in the gloom so hopefully she wouldn't come any closer than she already was.

'Ok, then, Elisha. You want to talk, let's talk,' he said.

'Ok, Kevin. What shall we talk about?' she said, moving closer to him and sitting on another barrel.

'That day at your house, after the day when you took Betty's car. The day when you lied to her about your car having some mechanical problem. Why don't we talk about what really happened when I came round to take a look at the car?' he said.

Swann knew that if Betty was in earshot, then this could be his chance to get Elisha to admit that she was the one behind the alleged rape attempt at her house. His biggest concern, other than the crossbow that Elisha had pointed in his direction, was that he needed to avoid the subject of the Travelodge.

Outside the Storeroom, Betty perched herself out of sight, and continued to offer her support and hold a handkerchief tightly against the gaping wound that was on the head of a man she had never met.

SEVENTY-ONE

Ahuja Industries, East London.

Angelica Rowntree was beginning to think that she was finally going mad and that the long days of talking to herself were actually causing her brain to become demented. She had realised that she had begun to forget the names of some of her friends and was finding it increasingly more difficult to recall them. She also thought that she was becoming hallucinatory. *I'm cracking up*, she thought. She edged as far along the walkway as her restraints would allow her and peered over the side of the metal structure. *I can't fall, I'm tied to it,* she thought to herself. Her light-headedness made her feel dizzy, but she had to have another look. *I'm sure I heard someone. I can't be dreaming it this time.*

'Hello,' she shouted, hearing only her own echo by way of a response.

There was no reply. Then she heard another faint noise from below. She was certain that she heard it, but she couldn't pinpoint what it was or even precisely where it had come from. *I did hear someone.* Angelica called out again. Nothing. *I'm imagining it. Maybe the foxes made a noise,* she thought.

'Socks, Stripe, Speckle. Boys,' she called.

Angelica shuffled her way back along the landing towards her blanket and sat huddled on top of it. At least it served as a cushion against the hard surface. She sat and stared around her, bored with the same view day after day. But she knew that if she could see it, then she was still alive. She tried to remember the name of her friend who used to hear things that weren't really there. *It began with G. Gina, that was it,* she thought. Angelica recalled that Gina used to call it ACP. *Auditory something or other,* she thought. She knew that it was because of Gina's epilepsy. She had explained it all to her once when they sat on Gina's bed and were having a really good chat. She used to see people and odd things like cars or buses that weren't there at all. But she couldn't recall all the details now. *Maybe that's what's happening to me. But I don't have epilepsy,* she thought.

When Angelica had been in her corner, she used to flick tiny stones across the floor to see if one would hit the other, for something to do. A bit like her own version of marbles. She would sing softly to the foxes when they appeared after her meals in the hope of some scraps. She really missed them coming to see her, even though she knew that they were only there for the small pieces of food that she reserved, especially for them. Angelica sighed at the boredom again and rubbed at her scalp with her knuckles. Some days she felt lousier than others, and today was one of those days. *God knows what I look like,* she thought. In one way she was happy that she couldn't find another piece of broken mirror. The resultant reflection would probably cause her to wish that she hadn't bothered to look.

Just then she heard another noise and out of the corner of her eye, saw the foxes shoot across the floor below her, raising a cloud of dust as they went, as if something had spooked them. *It's alright, boys.* Angelica watched them. They were all together except for Mum and Dad. They were elsewhere. The three boys stopped as quickly as they had appeared and turned back simultaneously and looked in the direction they had come in from. They looked like gundogs that were fully focussed on their prey. A light dust cloud wafted silently in front of them and settled slowly to the floor. They were looking at something. *Or someone,* she thought. Whatever it was that had spooked them was still there. The foxes held their motionless position without a sound. Their tails were lowered between their legs. *Something really did scare you all,* she thought. Angelica moved slowly and as silently as she could to gain a better view. Socks was the first to break his stare. He had heard her chain clink quietly as she had moved. Angelica's eyes locked with Socks' for a moment. And for that moment she was part of their team. Or so it felt.

'What is it, Socks?' she said quietly to him.

All he did was resume his stare, along with his brothers. Then Angelica saw Stripe and Speckle move in the direction from where the sounds had come. They looked like they had regained their bravery and were walking slowly with their tails up again. Maybe they could see what it was, but whatever the reason, their confidence had returned. Socks followed a few paces behind, just in case, bringing up the rear guard. He wasn't always the bravest, even if he was usually the most inquisitive. Angelica watched the troop slowly go out of sight and listened for any sounds. *Maybe they saw a rabbit,* she thought. She knew that there were rabbits and stoats and rats that entered the factory from time to time. But the silence continued, and Angelica assumed that the foxes and whatever it was that had gained their attention, had gone. So, she repositioned herself on her blanket and sighed. *Now what? Only heaven knows how many hours before I get fed again,* she thought. Angelica wasn't feeling too hungry, but she knew that it would be foolish to turn it down. There had been so many occasions when she had wondered whether she was eating her last meal, but so far he had continued to return morning and night. How long for was the burning question at the forefront of Angelica's mind.

As she settled into some sort of relatively comfortable posture, she began to feel tired. She knew it was down to the utter boredom that went with her desperate predicament, and she tended to spend a lot of time dozing these days. If she had a preference, it would be to be back in her corner. It was moderately more comfortable, but more importantly, she could talk to the foxes and watch them nibble at the titbits that she secretly saved for them. As she allowed her eyes to close momentarily, she had an overwhelming feeling that she was being watched. Angelica thought that she was being ridiculous, but glanced down to the ground floor, expecting to see her favourite skulk of foxes looking up at her, with their innocent, sweet faces and glistening eyes, but they weren't there. Instead, as her gaze fixated on the dusty floor, she saw something move in the furthest reaches of her peripheral vision. Angelica went cold. But this time she was certain of what she had just witnessed.

'A man. That was a bloody man,' she said to herself.

The thought of being set free washed over her like deluge and filled her immediately with hope, so much so that a few uncontrolled, spontaneous tears fell onto her cheeks. She could feel her heart begin to thump rapidly in her chest. *Christ, I'm going to have a heart attack.* She hadn't been able to see him very clearly, but she knew that this time, she hadn't been hallucinating like Gina. Angelica instinctively hauled herself up, and without a thought for her restraints, tried to run along the walkway. The fierce tug on her waist hurt her, jarring her body, and reminded her that the chain was there, as she collapsed backwards onto the metal landing, striking her elbow and the side of her head against the grating as she fell heavily. She winced at the instant pain that she felt and was sure that she saw stars. Angelica permitted herself a brief moment to gather her senses before she called out desperately.

'Hey. Hello. I'm up here. Hello.' She panted, almost breathlessly, and laid on her side as her weakened body reacted to the sudden burst of adrenaline and the even more sudden, unexpected pain. Angelica waited for a friendly voice to respond to her but heard nothing.

Her head and her elbow both throbbed as she lay there, stretching her neck to get a better view of the ground floor level. She pushed herself up with her painful arm and grabbed at the metal landing rails to draw herself closer to the edge and peer over the side.

'Hello. Help me. Hello,' she shouted, as loudly as she could.

Nothing. Not a sound. Not a movement. Not even a fox. The factory was silent again.

SEVENTY-TWO

Minneapolis, Minnesota.

Ken Toft sat silently in his van. The engine was running, and the heater was gradually beginning to have an effect on his cold feet. But however warm he managed to make it; the remainder of his body still felt icy cold. Leo, his newest search and rescue dog, laid down quietly in the rear compartment. The warm harness and snow boots that Toft had him dressed in would keep away the worst of the weather, not that Leo would give a care to the temperature. Toft sat motionless and looked forward, out of the front windshield, at the rear of Big Toni's patrol car as the Officer stood, talking on his phone. He waited, as he had been instructed to do, for it to move off from the sidewalk outside his house in Eden Prairie. The outside temperature wasn't what he would consider tropical, not by a long way, but Toft was sweating, and it wasn't due to the heater in his van. His mind was empty of thought and his expression was completely blank. Only the final, seething words of Captain Antonio Rodrigues, as he had sat on the chesterfield and glared at Toft, were present in his head. *Get your dog. You're coming with me.*

Toft had held onto the charade for as long as he could, but it didn't take very long before his excuses and bluster had run out. He had sat and listened to Big Toni as he tore his story apart, questioning every excuse and reason, making it impossible for him to delay the inevitable outcome any longer. There had never been a search on the morning of April 26th. There had never been a genuine report. At least, not one made by Ken Toft at that time, as he had implied. He had submitted a report, one that failed to establish any hint that Caterina Marks might be present, but the timing of the supposed search didn't match to the time of day that Toft was there. It was fictitious. Bonner and Big Toni were sure that Toft visited the Nelson property but now they knew that it was not to conduct a proper search. *The search was compromised,* thought Bonner. Bonner knew that Betty had seen the van outside her house when she had looked out of the upstairs window, so he was convinced that he did attend. The more that Big Toni threw the difficult questions at Ken Toft, the more

Bonner wondered whether Wade Nelson might be the man with all the answers. No use now though.

Toft had explained, again, about the use of the acid to assist with the disposal of old Hastings, the Nelson family dog, and how the dog had been placed in the shed before going into the grave. That much was accepted to be true. But what else wasn't being said? What really happened that morning? *Where are you, Caterina?* thought Bonner.

Whilst Toft sat waiting in his van, Big Toni and Bonner were going over the story, trying to fill in the gaps from so long ago. If Wade Nelson really was involved, then they both knew that they may never find her or fully understand what had happened to her. He could have taken her anywhere. There were numerous wide-open spaces where he could have disposed of her. They both agreed that his suicide a few years after the event may have been directly connected to Caterina's disappearance, but they were clutching at straws. Bonner wondered whether Wade Nelson simply couldn't live with what he had done. As they talked, their opinions began to match up with regard to one aspect. Neither of them thought that Ken Toft had played a significant role in her disappearance, even if his actions with regard to the duplicitous report had made them wonder about his involvement. They felt that he was just a puppet in the deception, which again brought them back to Wade Nelson. When Big Toni had asked Toft what he was doing at the Nelson property, he had resorted to blaming Wade Nelson, and had said that he was the one who was adamant that he should be there. It was true that Nelson had contacted Toft and insisted that he came to the house and that although he had asked him to report that the girl was not there and insisted that he need not bring his dog, Toft didn't think any more of it. Wade Nelson had said that she wasn't there, so it was good enough for Toft. At that time Toft had an overwhelming admiration for Wade Nelson and trusted him implicitly, so much so that he hadn't thought for one moment to question why he had mentioned the girl hours before she was reported missing by Alexandria Org. There was no need for a search as far as he was concerned. Toft admitted to being foolish and accepted how this made it look for him, but he never stopped pleading that he was entirely innocent as far as the missing girl was concerned. He tried hard to convince Big Toni that he found Wade Nelson to be an overbearing and domineering man in an effort to exonerate himself from any sinister involvement. Bonner thought that his description of Wade Nelson fitted his character. Big Toni had just sat in silence, shaking his head slowly, and staring at Toft.

When Big Toni had finished his call to Deputy Chief Officer Jack Bolton, he looked at Toft and gave a very slight nod. Toft took this to mean that he was to follow his orders and remain close behind the patrol car as soon as it moved off. As he turned out from the sidewalk, his legs began to shake as his mind switched into gear and began to realise what this all meant for him. And as hard as he tried to convince himself that it would all be fine, he knew in his heart that it wouldn't. His days working with the Minnesota Search and Rescue Dogs Association were over for good. He wasn't even sure that he could avoid something far worse.

'Do you think we'll find her, Captain?' said Bonner, as soon as Big Toni had settled back behind the steering wheel of the patrol car.

'In all honesty, I don't know,' he replied.

'If Wade Nelson is the only one that knows where she is, then we could be looking forever.'

'Yeah. We'll let's hope that isn't the case then. According to the Deputy Chief, we don't have forever. He said that he will arrange for a team to meet us there, and that he was sticking his neck out on this one. He must have some faith in you, Bonner. Lord knows why.' said Big Toni.

'A team to dig?' said Bonner, hopefully.

'If necessary. Don't worry, you won't have to try to dig it yourself. He'll despatch a crew with a small excavator. It'll depend on how the dog behaves too. If what we know about how good these dogs are is true then, just maybe, we have a chance. But if the dog doesn't do his thing…well, that might be that, so you better keep your fingers crossed.'

Bonner's heart sunk a little at the thought of his search for Caterina coming to a fruitless end after all the numerous promises he had made to her, but he tried to remain hopeful. He knew that because of how Ken Toft's story had collapsed, that the location for a search was no longer restricted to any one specific area of the garden. If she was in the garden at all.

As Bonner sat staring out of the windshield, he began to imagine Caterina arriving at Betty's house, and tried to picture her with her white dress, pale blue cardigan and auburn hair. After just a few seconds he had the image in his mind. *Show me, Caterina.* He closed his eyes and could imagine her walking on the sidewalk, close to Betty's house. She was hurrying because Betty had been upset. At the last moment she saw Mr Nelson and sidestepped amongst the red Pines to avoid him. Caterina didn't like him much. She thought he was unkind to the girls. Then Bonner startled as he saw her face change. Her eyes opened wide, and her face went ghostly white. And then without warning the image vanished. As hard as he tried, he couldn't get it back.

'You ok, Bonner? Not falling asleep on me, are you?' asked Big Toni.

'No. I'm ok. Just thinking.'

'What about?'

'Caterina.'

'Look, don't get your hopes up too high. We don't know where she is. For all we know she could hundreds of miles away,' said Big Toni.

She's trying to show me. She will show me, thought Bonner.

Big Toni drove slowly away from 3452 Cardamon Avenue and checked his rear-view mirror to ensure that Ken Toft was doing as he was told. He was. There wasn't much likelihood of Toft changing the current course of events, and Bonner and Big Toni both knew that he had no way out of it now. His story had tied him in knots, and they knew that he would do anything they asked of him to try to save his skin.

Much to Bonner's delight, the snow had started to fall again, albeit lightly. As Big Toni cursed the weather, Bonner knew to keep his thoughts to himself. The last time the two men had been at the Nelson residence, Big Toni had fallen headfirst onto the frozen terra firma, much to his displeasure.

'How's your head now?' asked Big Toni, as the patrol car rumbled along.

'It's ok, thanks. I think all this has helped me to forget about it.'

'I should think so too.'

'Captain?' said Bonner.

'What?'

'I'm gonna miss you if you transfer,' he said.

Big Toni looked at Bonner and shook his head.

'Don't you go all soft on me, Bonner. I've spent years shouting at you and getting on your back about all sorts of things. Don't you make me like you now,' he said.

After a couple of seconds of silence, the two men turned to face each other. Big Toni cracked first. It wasn't so much of a smile as it was an awkward looking downturn at one corner of his mouth. Whatever it was, it was enough for Bonner to know that the Captain really did like him, despite his commanding presence. Bonner didn't speak. He just faced front and felt a glow inside him that he had secretly, always wanted to feel. *This is going to be a good day,* he thought.

SEVENTY-THREE

Interview Room 4.
Old Clapton Street Police Station.

DCI Cameron Blackery was upstairs in his office, accompanied by his precious but rather annoying carriage clock, compiling a report. He had, as the officer in charge, overseen the search of 38 Rodina Close, and worked in tandem with the Crime Scene Investigators. All of the probative property and evidence that may later be of use in court, had been correctly packaged and documented and was now safely and securely in the Evidence Room at Old Clapton Street, awaiting forensic analysis. The team at Rodina close had taken photographs and collected fingerprints and DNA, as well as bagged up and recorded all the relevant material that Carrie had so fortuitously stumbled upon. They had also spoken with several of the immediate neighbours and had extensive talks with Graham and Dorothy Walton who maintained that they were blissfully unaware of anything that might be considered suspicious with regard to Robin Greaves, other than that they both felt that he was 'a bit peculiar', as Dorothy had put it.

It was 18:05 when DI Marc Sutton and DS Carrie Linton walked into Interview Room 4 and closed the door. Both of them carried folders that contained the details of the murders of Haley Breen and Claudia De Luca as well as the whole of the Angelica Rowntree narrative. Everything that pertained to her disappearance was in it; statements, photographs, everything. Except the part that they wanted most, her present location. But finally, they both felt as if a huge corner had been turned, and that the discovery of Angelica Rowntree might not be far away. However, the full consequence of her disappearance was still in abeyance.

There were four people in Interview Room 4: Detective Inspector Marc Sutton, Detective Sergeant Carrie Linton, Police Constable Alex Tyler and Michael Abbot, aka Robin Greaves. For now, he was being referred to as Robin Greaves, as was his preference. PC Tyler, accompanied by PC Terry Rudge, had escorted Greaves, who had refused legal advice, stating that 'he didn't need it because he hadn't done anything,' from the holding cell and into the interview room ahead of Sutton and Carrie's arrival. He had been advised of his rights with regard to legal representation but had remained pertinacious. Once the detectives had arrived, PC Rudge had left the room to wait outside the door. At this moment in time Robin Greaves was under caution and required for questioning but had not been arrested in conjunction with the disappearance of Angelica Rowntree. So far, he had been acquiescent.

Interview Room 4 was bright and airy. There was a strong scent of furniture polish and air freshener, not dissimilar to freshly tapped maple. The carpeted flooring continued one metre up the walls and was of a soft lilac colour. An alarm strip ran along a piece of conduit which housed the electrical wiring and divided the lilac colour from the top section which was predominantly white. One large table and four chairs were situated to one side of the room. A wooden bench seat was affixed against the opposite wall. The table had four metal legs, painted black, and was topped with a teak surface. A tape recorder sat on it, close to the wall. The four chairs were of a similar design, each of which was bolted to the floor. There were no windows and yet it didn't feel overly enclosed.

Robin Greaves sat one of the chairs and looked across the table at his interviewers. He wore jeans and had a dark, lightweight waterproof coat on. He had met Carrie before and didn't dislike her but didn't know the other one. He glanced up at PC Tyler who remained focussed on the clock on the wall opposite her. Robin Greaves' attention then turned back to the folder that Sutton had placed in front of himself, and of which he was studiously turning the pages. Carrie too, opened a folder and then looked across the table at Greaves. It had been decided, between Sutton and Carrie, that she would take the lead during the questioning. They agreed that seeing as Greaves was known to be difficult to communicate with, it would be better if he was put at ease by talking to somebody that he had previously met.

Once Carrie had explained to Greaves that the interview was being recorded, she gave her name and rank and that of DI Sutton. She also mentioned that PC Tyler was in the room. The time, date and location of the interview was recorded as well as the caution that Greaves was under in order that he fully understood it. She also reiterated that he had been offered the option of having legal advice but that he had refused it. This was verbally confirmed by Greaves.

Carrie adopted a soft and gentle approach as she explained to Greaves why he was here and what the purpose of the interview was, as well as the basic outline of how it would be conducted. She told him that Sutton would be making notes but may also contribute to the questioning. Greaves said that he understood. It was also explained that they knew that Robin Greaves was not his birthname but that if he insisted on it being used, then this would be permitted for the sake of the interview. Greaves confirmed again that he preferred for it to be used. By the time that Carrie had finished with all the necessary preliminaries, it appeared that Greaves was content and understood everything that Carrie had carefully explained so far, including the part that related to him having the opportunity to explain whether he was directly involved with any of the aspects that Carrie was going to cover.

'As the interview proceeds, I may ask you about any other relevant issues that might help me to understand the facts. If you think of anything that is relevant, then please speak up and tell us. There is no rush. Take your time to answer. If there is anything that you don't understand then please tell me and I will explain it clearly for you,' she said.

Greaves nodded and Carrie stated his action for the sake of the recording.

'There are a number of things that I wish to ask you about but let's start with the items that were discovered at 38 Rodina Close. What can you tell me about them?' she asked.

'I can't say anything about them,' he said.

'Can't, Robin?' she said.

Greaves sat, making no further comment.

'Where did they come from?'

Greaves pondered the question. After what felt like a long a silent minute, Carrie prompted him.

'Are they yours, Robin?' she asked, softly.

Greaves looked like the proverbial 'rabbit in the headlights'. He sat with his lips closed tightly. After another few seconds his eyes shifted from Sutton to Carrie and then around the room. Sutton moved his hand across onto Carrie's folder and indicated at something.

'There was a camera found in a box on top of the wardrobe, quite a new one, is it yours?' she asked.

'I…yes.'

'Where do you go to take your photographs?' she asked.

'Nowhere, really.'

'The camera is one of those types that has a digital card, is that right?'

'I suppose so. I'm not very good with that sort of thing.'

'Well, fortunately, we are. The images can be downloaded onto a computer or laptop, can't they?'

'I don't know.'

'We have possession of your laptop now, so we'll know soon enough. Is there anything else you wish to add about the photographs that might help our investigation?'

'No.'

'Did you take the photographs that were found?' she asked.

'I have used it before,' he said.

'Did you take any of *these* photographs?' she said, as she turned her folder towards Greaves, allowing him to see the ones of the girls in the pub.

'I can't remember,' he said.

'I think you can, Robin. It could be very helpful if you could try to remember for me,' she said.

'I don't want to get into trouble. I didn't do anything,' he replied.

Carrie knew from previous brief chats with Robin Greaves that he wasn't the most forthcoming when it came to details and felt that she shouldn't put unnecessary pressure on him at such an early stage of the interview. She remembered only too well, how he had related his story of seeing a man talking to Angelica in Trenton Street and how he couldn't be certain whether it was a man or a woman. He was talking a little and she needed to encourage him, or he would probably clam up entirely.

'Dorothy Walton cleans for you, is that right?'

'Yes.'

'Does she do a good job?'

'Yes, I suppose so.'

'I guess it's a good job she doesn't have to do your washing too with all that dust on those boiler suits. Do you know how it got on there?' she asked.

'I work at the garage. I get dirty sometimes.'

'For the benefit of the tape, this is a reference to the garage in Trenton Street. Is that correct, Robin?' she said.

'Yes. I work there.'

'Angelica worked there too. Did you work with Angelica?'

'Sometimes,' he said.

'I've been to your garage. I didn't see any dust that was that colour. Did it come from somewhere else?' she asked.

'I don't know.'

'You must know how it got there,' she said.

Greaves said nothing.

Carrie knew that the answer would be available to them soon. The forensic report on everything that was removed from 38 Rodina Close would hopefully enable her and Sutton to fill in any unanswered questions.

'What about that mask, Robin? Is it yours?'

'No.'

'Who does it belong to?' she asked.

'Nobody. I mean I don't know,' he replied.

Carrie decided to come back to it later. She was sure that she would be revisiting several questions.

'So, let's just go over what we found at 38 Rodina Close. There was a camera, a box of photographs, a mask and dust that can't be explained. Remember, Robin, you are still under caution and if there is anything that you can help us with, you can just say.'

'I don't want to get into trouble,' he replied.

'Maybe, it would be better if you started to remember some of these things that I'm asking you about. If you don't own these things, then can you tell me who does?' she asked.

Carrie let Greaves sit for a moment and prepared to ask some of the more difficult questions that she wanted to cover. Greaves had remained fairly composed up to now but wasn't very keen to elaborate on his answers just yet. The interview hadn't been going for long, but Carrie thought it was time to up the ante and see what happened. A change of subject might spark him into life, after all.

'Do you remember Haley Breen?' she asked.

Greaves gave a worried look and flicked his eyes to Sutton and then back to Carrie. Carrie cocked her head slightly to one side and smiled, as she waited for an answer, but nothing came from Greaves.

'How about Claudia De Luca?'

'Who?' said Greaves.

'Surely, you must remember them. After all, there were two photographs of them in the box that was on top of the wardrobe.'

'I don't know about any photographs. I didn't do anything wrong.'

'Who took the photographs, Robin?'

'I don't know. Can I go now?'

'Not quite yet. I'll tell you when. Do you know who Emily Roache is?' she said with a smile.

'Who?' he said.

'Her name is Emily Roache,' said Carrie, showing Greaves the photograph of her, 'Was she one of the lucky ones?'

'I don't know what you mean,' he said.

Greaves began to fidget a lot more now and was beginning to show signs of being very uncomfortable. He was visibly sweating. Carrie decided to try to settle him down again.

'Robin, I need you to help me. I am trying to find out where Angelica is. Can you help?'

'I can't tell you anything,' he said.

'Can't? Do you think of Angelica as a friend?'

'I suppose so.'

'Don't you want to help to find her?'

'I can't. I don't want to get into trouble,' he said.

'Would you say that you liked her?'

'Yes, she was nice.'

'Were you the man who was talking to Angelica in Trenton Street?'

'No,' he said.

'Did you make the whole thing up?'

Greaves said nothing.

'Do you know where she is now?'

Greaves thought and shook his head. Carrie noticed how Greaves appeared to be at ease when he was talking about Angelica but less so when she referred to Haley Breen and Claudia De Luca. There wasn't any hint of concern in his face or in his voice but when she asked that last question, there was a definite pause before he answered. It was almost as if he was showing signs of discomfort for the first time. As if he knew more than he was letting on.

'Robin, do you understand how serious this is? These photographs are very serious. Two girls are already dead and now Angelica is missing. Right now, it looks as though you may have had something to do with these events. We will find out, so why don't you tell me what you know, so that we can find her and bring her to safety. You do you want Angelica to be safe, don't you?' she said.

He nodded and Carrie, once more, related his action for the benefit of the recording. Greaves clasped his hands together in front of him and stared at the floor. Carrie patiently waited until he looked up again. What she noticed was that his eyes were glazed. Not exactly tearful, but shiny. He was getting upset. Carrie was hoping that if he really cared about Angelica, that he might be able to help after all. Before she could speak, DI Sutton announced for the tape that he was now entering the proceedings.

'How many times had you met Haley Breen?' he asked.

'I don't know.'

'I think you do. It's a very simple question,' he said, and looked across at Greaves, waiting for his answer.

'A few times, but....'

'Did you like her?'

'She was alright, I didn't really know....'

'Where did you meet her?' said Sutton.

'I saw her in the pub a few times.'

'Did you used to talk to her in the Cactus and Coyote?'

'No. She was always with her friends, so…no.'

'But you said that you liked her. Did you like the other girls too? Is it right that you went there to be near her and the other girls?'

'No.'

'But you must have taken photographs of them. How come they were found in your bedroom if you didn't take them?' he asked.

Greaves looked away as if the question was too difficult and made him feel uncomfortable, but the next question shook him.

'Did you kill Haley Breen?' asked Sutton.

'What, no, no, I…' said Greaves.

'How about Claudia De Luca. Did you kill her too?'

'I don't know her. I didn't do anything wrong,' he said.

'Then tell me why we found photographs of these girls wrapped in a sheet, just the way they were when they were discovered?' asked Sutton.

'I don't know, I don't know, I don't know. I want to go,' Greaves shouted.

'Ok, Robin. I know you are trying to help, so just take a moment to think about the things we are asking you. Remember, as I said before, that if you had nothing to do with these murders or the disappearance of Angelica, then this is also your opportunity to explain this to us,' Carrie continued.

'Why did you leave Haley Breen at the bus depot?' said Sutton.

'What?' Greaves responded.

'Where did you keep her before you dumped her?'

'I didn't…'

'You left her to the rats, didn't you?'

'What, no.'

'Claudia De Luca hadn't been in this country for very long. Why did you choose her?' asked Sutton.

'I don't know her,' said Greaves, pitifully.

'You followed her to Brady's in York Street and then you watched her while she worked. We have a witness to this, so why don't you stop wasting everybody's time and tell us why you took her?' said Sutton.

It was clear to Carrie that Sutton had started to play 'good cop/bad cop' in an effort to break Greaves and get him to admit to the crimes. She could see that it was starting to make Greaves uneasy. She wasn't sure, yet, whether it would get them anywhere.

Greaves had gone quiet. He looked at Carrie as if he was pleading for her to make the questions stop. She returned his gaze without expression.

'You took her and then left her in the canal, didn't you? Was she already dead or did you allow her to drown, still restrained, just like Haley Breen was?' said Sutton.

Greaves' face was beginning to redden. He had a tear on his cheek, and a tremble in his voice when he spoke.

'I didn't kill anyone. I want to go now.'

'Did you take the sheets from your room?'

'What sheets?' replied Greaves.

'You know which sheets. The ones that you wrapped Haley Breen and Claudia De Luca in. Is this what you have done with Angelica too?'

'No.'

'Where have you put her?' said Sutton.

'I didn't take...'

'Just tell me where Angelica Rowntree is,'

'Stop it, stop it. I don't want to get in any trouble,' he said.

Just then, as Greaves sat with his arms folded, held tightly to his body, there was a knock on the interview room door. Carrie looked around at the glass panel and could see the face of PC Terry Rudge. She shook her head slightly expressing that she didn't want any interruptions, but Rudge obviously wanted to speak to Carrie. *What?* she mouthed, angrily. Rudge put his hand to his head and with his thumb and little finger extended, indicating that Carrie was wanted on the phone. *No*, she mouthed, and glared at him. Rudge nodded his head, and pointed a finger at Greaves, insisting that Carrie should take the call. Carrie's eyes flicked to Greaves and back to Rudge. *Yes,* he nodded. Sutton looked at Carrie. She let out a sigh and suggested that the interview was adjourned for a short period of approximately 10 minutes. Sutton didn't want to stop right now but conceded to Carrie's request. He then explained to Greaves that there was to be a short break and that he would be escorted to the holding cell where he was to remain until they returned. The interview was adjourned, and the recording device was switched off. Carrie and Sutton stood and left the room. PC Alex Tyler and another officer took Greaves back to the holding cell.

'What the bloody hell, Rudge?' said Carrie.

'I'm sorry. There was a phone call. Someone was asking for you…' he began.

'Not good enough. The last thing I want is interruptions,' she blurted.

'I know, I'm sorry,' said Rudge.

Carrie let out a half-stifled scream and Rudge inwardly shuddered.

'Well? This better be good,' she said.

'I took the call from a woman. She ended the call before I could get her number. She was insisting that she spoke to you straight away. Something about Greaves.'

'Woman? Is that it? Who?'

'Erm…' said Rudge, as he fumbled in his trouser pocket for the piece of paper that had her name on.

'Here,' he said, handing Carrie the folded note.

She took it and unfolded it. Carrie read the note.

Aimee Richards
Pavilion Care Home

SEVENTY-FOUR

The Riverside centre, Tilbury, East London.

The bleeding had stopped, and the man that Betty had been cradling, was in a far better condition than when she had first stumbled upon him as she stepped across the rain-soaked courtyard. She had virtually stood on him in the darkness by the time she realised that the crumpled heap was actually a person. His face was stained with dried blood and his shirt collar displayed a dark shade of red. He was fully conscious now and was listening intently to the conversation that was playing out in the Storeroom. He had shown Betty his warrant card that had informed her that he was a police officer. They had kept their exchange of words to an absolute minimum with nothing above the quietest of whispers. Very few words had been spoken besides a brief exchange of names. Kingham knew who the two men were but hadn't any idea about the woman prior to Betty whispering 'My sister.' As time went on, she was fast becoming what he might refer to as 'a person of interest'. They could both just see the shape of a man lying in the Storeroom with his face turned towards the floor, and although her view wasn't entirely clear, Betty could see enough of the bolt to know what had happened. At first, she thought it was the body of Karter Swann but to her relief she had established that it wasn't.

DC Steve Kingham had no idea where his mobile phone had ended up and through a series of hand signals had established that Betty's phone had left in her car. He was beginning to wish that he had called DI Sutton earlier and knew in his heart that he probably should have done. Too late now. He had a head wound to worry about that he assumed he had received from the close attention of Ray Keller, and a woman that he didn't know anything about, other than she was his helper's sister, and was very likely the reason that Ray Keller was lying prone in the gloom. Betty didn't want her police officer friend to interrupt the conversation, at least, not just yet. If Elisha stopped talking then Betty may never learn about this latest development with regard to what really happened between her and Karter. Up to now, she had heard enough to know that things were not quite as she had been led to believe.

'So, you mean the day that you tried to rape me?' said Elisha.

'You know that didn't happen,' he replied.

'It could have been so lovely, you know. Just like…'

'But that isn't the way it was, and you know it,' said Swann, angrily in an effort to avert any mention of the Travelodge.

'No, it wasn't,' she said.

Betty's interest increased immediately.

'You made Betty believe that you needed help with your car, otherwise I wouldn't have come.'

'I had to get you there somehow and it seemed plausible that I should ask Betty for your help. Her knight in shining armour. Anyway, you came because you wanted to.'

'Don't flatter yourself. I was only there because you lied to Betty. There was nothing wrong with your car, was there?' he said.

'Of course not, but it served a purpose, if you remember. It brought us together, darling Karter.'

'I remember how you came on to me, and I remember how I tried to leave the house. That's the truth isn't it, Elisha? I remember how you were dressed in next to nothing and tried to tease me into falling into your trap.'

'I thought you would like what you saw. I'm sure you did really. You could have done anything with me. Anything,' she said seductively.

'So why don't you tell me how you got those bruises. It was a bit of an extreme measure, wasn't it?' asked Swann.

'No more extreme than faking your own death.'

Kingham's ears pricked up.

Elisha pointed the crossbow at Swann's chest. Her eyes burned into his. Then she lowered the bow again. Another reprieve, but for how long? 'Ok. Have your last bit of fun if you like before Betty kills you in her fit of insane jealousy.'

'I'm waiting for my answer,' he said, hoping that Betty was too.

Elisha rested the butt of the Cobra RX on her lap as she perched on the beer barrel as if she was getting settled before she told him her story. The dangerous end of the bow remained aimed in his direction. Her finger never left the trigger, something that Swann was very aware of. Her face looked serious, and Swann thought that he shouldn't get her excessively wound up in case she gripped it just a little too firmly.

'It won't make any difference, but I'll tell you. It was never part of the plan, actually. Well, not entirely. I wanted you so much that day. I couldn't believe it when you turned me down. After you had gone, I sat and sobbed. I felt broken and angry. I was the one that had the sexiest looks and the gorgeous figure, not Betty. But for some reason, you still wanted her. After everything I dreamed about, I couldn't let you be with her. Most of all, I couldn't let *her* have *you*. She always got everything.

I was always the one that went without or had to settle for second best. But not this time. If I couldn't have you the way I wanted to, then I had to find another way. I knew I had to make Betty hate you, and what better way than an attempted rape on her loving sister. So, I had to make it look good, didn't I? Yeah, really good,' she said with a sneer, 'I imagined how you might act if you were trying to assault me, and I played it out. I banged my face against the door, but I didn't do it properly. So, I did it again. That really hurt, the second time. I checked in the mirror to make sure there was a mark, and there was. Then I picked up a book and hit myself with the spine of it. I wasn't so accurate that time. I meant to hit my chin, but I hit my lip instead. But when I looked, it was starting to drip with blood, so I squeezed it until it was on my top. I needed to make it look good, you see. I knew it would heal soon enough. I even pulled a couple of buttons off my pyjamas, but they went unnoticed. Actually, when dear, kind, pathetic Betty arrived in her panic, I forgot to mention that bit.'

'You bitch, you weren't even wearing pyjamas. You actually changed so that you could ruin everything between me and Betty, just because you couldn't get your own way,' he said.

'I had my own way,' she said.

Swann hoped, again, that he could avoid any reference to the Travelodge.

'I thought you said it was Betty that got her own way,' he said, trying to steer her back on track.

'Oh, she did. Daddy's precious little girl. Not like me. I was just 'the other one'. Mother loved us both, but not that bastard. I was glad when he was dead. He would have been dead sooner, but…Yeah, I had my own way in more than one way. Betty lost out big time. More than she knows.'

'What do you mean, more than one way?' said Swann.

'None of your business. You don't know the half of it, Kevin,' she said, scornfully.

'What do you mean by that?'

'Just keep your nose out of it. I've told you what you wanted to hear. I've kept my part of the bargain. Now keep yours. You can help me send Betty to prison for a very long time.'

Elisha glanced at the body of Ray Keller but didn't elaborate on her comment. She stood and pointed the crossbow directly at Swann again. He began to think that this was it and that it was going to really hurt, even if it wasn't for very long.

Swann desperately tried to buy some more time. He rolled to one side and shifted himself across the floor, trying to make Elisha lose sight of him. He just hoped that she would have to move around to the other side of the Storeroom to get him in her sights again. As he heard her step across, he kicked an empty beer barrel over, into her path, and then rolled back to the original spot. It gave him just enough time to stand, but not enough time to run. He was easier to hit now too.

'Betty would never do this. You won't get away with it, Elisha. Why do you think your plan will work?' he said, in desperation, praying that she would begin to answer him; anything for a bit more time.

'I've told you. It's all planned out. She stole my car. She bought the crossbow with her credit card. It's in her name, I told you this. It's over, Kevin. I loved you.'

'What about the photographs?' he said, in desperation.

Elisha appeared in front of Swann with the Cobra RX pointed at him. It was raised to her chest and pointing at his. She lifted it slowly so that her eyes stared straight down the sight. But her expression looked puzzled.

'What photographs?'

'I need to know if it was you that sent them. The ones of those girls. Did you take them? Is that what you've done, killed those girls and then tried to pin it on me?'

Did Swann really not know? thought Kingham.

'What girls, Karter?' she said, angrily.

'You sent them in white envelopes. Was it you?' he asked.

'I don't know what you're talking about. I haven't tried to pin anything on you.'

'What about the supermarket? Were you following me? I saw you there.'

'What? I don't have time for this *shit*, Kevin. Now it's time that Betty finished what she came here to do. If you had just played along, it could have been me and you all the way, darling.'

Kingham stood and leaned against the sliding door to get a better view of precisely where Elisha and Swann were, but as he did so, it shifted. The grit in the runners made a loud scraping noise. Elisha spun around, Cobra at the ready. Swann knew that this could be his chance. Elisha had caught sight of Kingham as he stumbled against the sliding door. She had her eyes on Swann too, rapidly switching her attention from one to the other with the Cobra changing its position as she did so. Swann knew that he couldn't move or somebody else was going to be the recipient of an unwanted bolt. Swann was fully aware that if the man tried to run, that Elisha would fire before he could get halfway across the courtyard. It was a stalemate. Swann had to hold his position. He had to keep the man and Betty safe.

As Swann looked towards the activity at the sliding door, he caught sight of Betty, just very briefly, but it gave him enough time to disguise a shake of his head so that she dipped her head out of view again. If Elisha knew that she was here, listening to all of this, he dreaded to think what would happen next. What did happen was that Swann saw the dishevelled shape of a man with dried blood on his face, wearing a blood-stained shirt walk into the Storeroom under the direction of Elisha's crossbow.

'Who's this Kevin?' she said.

'I don't know.'

'Really? You don't know?' she said.

Swann didn't know whether to make up a name or what to do for best. There was a man with a bolt in his throat and one with blood all over him and Swann didn't know what was going on. And to crown it all, Betty was still outside, sheltering out of Elisha's view. *How the bloody hell have I got in this mess,* he thought.

'So, who are you then?' she said, turning to the man and raising the Cobra.

Kingham tried to push the truth into the far reaches of his mind. Declaring that he was a Detective Constable was never going to end well in the circumstances.

'Ron,' said Kingham, using his father's name.

'And who's this?' she said, nodding her head towards the stricken Ray Keller.

'Ray,' said Kingham.

'Ron and Ray,' laughed Elisha, 'Are you some kind of double act?'

'Let him go, Elisha. It's not him you want,' said Swann.

'Oh, but it is now, Kevin. Betty is going to have to kill you all and I've got enough bolts for everyone.'

'You'll never get us both,' said Swann, edging slowly to the opposite side of the room from Kingham, creating a space between Elisha's targets.

'Do you know how fast I can reload this little darling of mine?'

About two seconds. Three to four, knowing how clumsy you are with a bow, thought Betty.

'I can reload it in a heartbeat, you'll both be dead before you know it,' she said with a smirk.

No, you can't, thought Betty.

Swann and Kingham locked eyes but neither appeared to have a workable plan that might be of use and avoid at least one of them being speared with a bolt. But luckily for them, Betty did. The only twist was that it involved Elisha firing the bolt.

SEVENTY-FIVE

Old Clapton Street Police Station.

'Where are you going now?' shouted Sutton.

Carrie scrunched the piece of paper in her fist that PC Rudge had given to her and hurried back to Sutton's office to make the call with less of an audience.

'Hang on a minute,' she shouted.

'Carrie, we don't have a minute,' said Sutton, as he quickly followed Carrie up the stairs towards his office.

'We have ten,' she called back.

Smart arse, Sutton thought, as he gave chase and bound up the stairs two steps at a time.

By the time Sutton got there, Carrie was already sitting at his desk and searching for the number for Pavilion Care Home in the contacts folder of her mobile phone. He could see that she was fully focussed. He had seen Carrie like this before and he instinctively knew that it would be pointless trying to interrupt her school of thought, but he tried anyway.

'Carrie, adjournment or not, we're in the middle of an interview,' he said, as if that wasn't obvious to them both.

'What? I know. I'm sorry, but she wouldn't call for no reason. There must be something that I need to hear, something about Greaves or Abbot, or whatever he wants to call himself.'

'Ok. Let's find out then,' he said with a sigh.

'It's ringing,' she said.

'Six minutes and I want you back in there, ok?'

'Hello, can I speak with Aimee Richards please, it's Detective Sergeant Linton from Old Clapton Street, I'm returning her call,' she said.

Sutton sat in the chair opposite Carrie, tapping his leg, and waited.

'They're calling her.'

From where he sat, he could see out into the corridor and across into DCI Blackery's office. He noticed Blackery's feet under his desk and stretched out a leg to toe the office door closed as quietly as he could manage. Sutton knew that unless Blackery leaned forward, he wouldn't notice any movement of the door and he assumed that he hadn't heard them scurry in and didn't want him asking why they were not downstairs doing what he expected them to be doing. Initially, Blackery had wanted to be a part of the interview, but Sutton had insisted that he take his Detective Sergeant instead because she had already made contact with the interviewee and was the best person to engage with him, considering his character. It was a worthwhile two minutes of Sutton's time.

'Aimee, it's Carrie. What's up?'

'Hi. I'm sorry to call you but I just thought I should. You said it would be ok, didn't you?'

'Of course. How can I help?' said Carrie, turning a new page in her notebook and holding her open hand out as she mouthed *pen*.

'There. In front of you,' he said, with a nod.

'Well, I've been talking with Margaret, Mrs Abbot, and I think we both got the wrong end of the stick when you were here last time. I'm sorry if I'm interfering.'

'No, it's fine. Go on. Take your time.'

No, don't take your time, thought Sutton, shaking his head and pointing to his watch. But Carrie wasn't looking.

'I don't know where to start. I've been trying to remember it all so that I could tell you,' said Aimee.

'Look, it's ok. If you think it's important, then just start at the beginning,' said Carrie.

Sutton saw Blackery's shadow pass the frosted window in his door and hoped that he wasn't on his way to Interview Room 4. If he was, Sutton would, no doubt, soon find out.

'Ok, I'll try. You remember when you were here last? Well, we talked to Margaret about the things that went on when she had her children all living at home.'

'Yes, I remember, go on.'

'Oh, I really hope I've got this right. I'm frightened to tell you something wrong, but I think I've got it.'

'Aimee, calm down and just go over it slowly. If it's important, I'll know,' said Carrie.

'Carrie, we don't have all day,' whispered Sutton, with growing impatience.

'I know, Marc, but I have to hear this,' Carrie replied as she cupped one hand over the phone.

'Hello?' said Aimee.

'I'm here, Aimee, carry on.'

'Ok, well, like I said I think we got a bit mixed up when we were talking to Margaret. I know it wasn't easy to follow, that's for sure, and she was upset and all, but I've been sitting with her today and we've had another good chat. You remember how it all got a bit confusing right before you had to leave?'

'I do.'

'Well, when I was talking to her today, she started to go over some of the same things again. I don't know why, I guess it was just whizzing around in her head, or something. Anyway, like I said, I'm sorry for interfering but, I think you ought to know a few things that she said. I think that they might help you understand what she really meant and get a clearer picture,' said Aimee.

'Aimee, please get to the point,' insisted Carrie.

'Sorry. Right. Here goes.'

Sutton held his watch so that Carrie could see it. She shrugged her shoulders as if to say *what do you want me to do about it?* Sutton held out his hand with his fingers spread. *Five minutes,* he mouthed.

Carrie nodded as she began writing down the story that was coming from Aimee Richards.

'I've made a note of the things that I thought you should know. After I spoke with Margaret, I had a break, so I got coffee and sat down in the staff canteen where it's usually pretty quiet. Luckily there were no other staff around so I had the place to myself, and I jotted things down so that you could...'

'Aimee. Please just tell me,' said Carrie, as gently as she could.

'Sorry. I'm just a bit on edge,' replied Aimee.

Sutton stood and told Carrie that he was going to extend the adjournment for another ten minutes. He also warned her that it wouldn't go on for any longer than that. She nodded again.

'The first point I've got is that I think we're wrong about the number of children. Well, not exactly wrong but it's not how it looks,' said Aimee, 'It was when Margaret said that they were hers. Do you remember when you confirmed with her that she had three girls and one boy, and she said that they were *hers*?'

'Go on,' said Carrie, struggling to remember that precise moment.

'Well, they *are* hers, but there's another one that *isn't* really hers,' said Aimee.

'Right, stop there,' said Carrie, 'Margaret had three girls, Jennifer, Joanna and Marion and one boy, who is Robin or Michael, in reality. Is that right so far?'

'Yes, but I think there's another one.'

'Another what? Girl or boy?' asked Carrie.

'Boy.'

'How have you arrived at this?'

'Well, it was when she said, 'they are mine', or actually it was the way she said it that puzzled me. I just thought that if she was making a point of them being hers, I wondered if there might be others that weren't hers, at least not biologically. So, I asked the question when she was talking about the girls and all the goings on at the house.'

'And?' said Carrie.

'And I think I'm right. There is another boy,' said Aimee.

'But not Margaret's?'

'That's right. It sounds to me as though there was a stepson, and it was him that Margaret was referring to when she kept saying 'him and he'. You remember when she said about the girls leaving the house after he came back? Well, I don't think she was talking about Robin. I think it was the other one, their stepbrother, that they were avoiding. And I hope I'm not imagining this, but I got the impression today that Margaret's daughters...I mean, Jennifer and Joanna...obviously not Marion...haven't told anyone where they live, even Robin, in case the other one finds out...I think.' she said.

'You don't sound very sure, Aimee.'

'I'm not, really, but this is just how it sounded to me,' she said.

'I thought Margaret said that they girls were in Bournemouth.'

'She did. At least she did when you were here. But today she didn't seem to know. I don't think that Margaret knows really. But they haven't visited for ages. It's like they are keeping a low profile so that they are not found,' said Aimee.

'Do you know their surnames?'

'No, sorry.'

'Ok. What else?' asked Carrie. *Five minutes more...Marc will understand,* she thought.

'I tried to be careful with the next bit, but Margaret seemed ok to talk about it...so...I don't think she was talking about Robin when she said about her husband hitting the boy in the family. I reckon it was the other one. He was not Margaret's. Not by birth, anyhow. I don't know why he was living there with the others, but I'm guessing the father sent him there or didn't want him with him or something. Either way it sounds as though it was him that was being ill-treated by Margaret's husband, not Robin. Margaret must have witnessed it at some point.'

'Ok, thanks, Aimee,' *Even if you are guessing!* thought Carrie.

'Wait, I've got a bit more to tell you before you go. Once I realised that each time Margaret mentioned 'him or he' that she could be talking about the other boy, I racked my brains to remember which parts of our conversation they referred to. In the end I had to ask

Margaret outright about a couple of things, you know, to clarify what she really meant. So…I took a chance and asked about the times when Robin was taken to the tip and left there and when he was under the water in the bath and, guess what?' said Aimee.

'It wasn't him?' said Carrie.

'Right. It was William. Although Margaret was a bit mixed, still. But that's how it came across to me.'

'William?' said Carrie.

'Yes. William Abbot. The stepbrother. That's his name. I'm sorry for over-stepping the mark but once I got this far into it with Margaret, I couldn't stop myself. I'm sorry but I also asked about Marion.'

'Oh! What did you say?' asked Carrie.

'I didn't know if I should, but I asked about when Marion fell down the stairs. I know I went too far but, it was that bit about how she said, 'he loved his sister'. With everything else unfolding I just had to ask. Of course, this time Margaret said 'stepsister'. That was when I knew that she was definitely talking about William and not Robin. You remember about the part when Margaret said that they blamed him for Marion's death. I think *they* were the girls and Robin. So…'

'They were talking about William. I don't know what happened that day and neither does Margaret, but I'd bet you that Robin does. He's just too scared to talk about it to anyone,' said Carrie.

'That's what I think too,' said Aimee.

'Aimee, you've been a star. I'm glad you called. You did the right thing.'

'There's one last thing,' she said.

'Yes,' said Carrie.

'I didn't get to ask Margaret anymore about this, but she said, 'he went to prison'. I couldn't get her to talk about that and I dare not upset her again, otherwise I could get in a lot of trouble.'

'I assume this relates to William too?' said Carrie.

'I guess so,' said Aimee.

'Right, well, you can leave that bit to me. Thanks again, Aimee.'

'Sorry if I overstepped the mark.'

'Don't worry, it's ok. Call me if there's anything else you think I should know. Thanks, bye for now.'

Carrie left Sutton's office and made her way back down to the corridor outside Interview Room 4. On her way she beckoned PC Rudge and asked him to check whether there is any record of a William Abbot having a criminal record, and if so, when. Carrie specifically asked Rudge to check on the dates and times and, of course, the nature of any crime.

'You, ok?' asked Sutton, looking at his watch.

'Yeah. That was interesting to say the least,' said Carrie.

'What's up,' said Sutton, noticing Carrie's strained expression.

'I don't think it's him,' she said.

'What? You don't think it's Greaves?'

'Well, if what I've just been listening to makes any sense, then we might not have the man we need to be talking to.'

'So, who do we need to be talking to?' asked Sutton.

'Somebody by the name of William Abbot.'

'Abbot? Do we know anything about him?'

'Yes. A stepbrother. I've asked Terry to check on whether he has a criminal record and he's going to let me know as soon as possible.'

'Well, it needs to be as soon as possible. We need to make sure we get our stories straight,' said Sutton.

Carrie leaned against the wall outside Interview Room 4. Sutton stood with his hands on his hips, waiting for a further explanation from Carrie.

'You'd better fill me in on all of this,' he said.

'Yes, of course. Aimee Richards is the name of the girl that I met at the Pavilion Care Home when I visited Mrs Greaves. Except we now know that she is actually Margaret Abbot, Robin's mother.'

'Michael's?' said Sutton, correcting her.

'Yes. Michael's. Anyway, when Aimee and I were talking to his mother, she told us about how difficult things were for her when the children were at home and relayed the story about Marion and…I did mention all that didn't I?' asked Carrie.

'Yes. You told me all about what happened to Marion, and you said about the teasing from his sisters and the treatment he used to get from his father too.'

'Right. So, the point is that Aimee has had another good chat with Margaret earlier and as she spoke to her, she started to get the impression that when Margaret was referring to her son, specifically *he* or *him*, that she wasn't talking about Robin aka Michael. Aimee found out that there is another son, actually a stepson, called William. The one I've asked Terry to check on. Thanks to Aimee, it appears that Margaret's account of the things that went on at the house were not specifically referring to Robin…Michael, but to William.'

'So, the events that you told me about regarding the boy that was left at the tip and the time when he was held under water in the bath…'

'Yes, William. Not Robin,' she said.

'Ok, but what about the stuff at Rodina Close? What about the photographs and the mask?'

'I don't know…unless.'

'Unless they really aren't anything to do with him. But why would they be there if…' said Sutton.

'Oh!,' said Carrie, raising a hand and interrupting.

'What?'

'The mattress beside the wardrobe. What if William stayed there too?' said Carrie.

'Possible, I suppose. Not that he'll be going anywhere near the place if he realises that we've been there. If he has a criminal record, then we should have his prints or something. It might account for why Greaves keeps insisting that he doesn't know anything about the photographs. Best we find out. Alex, tell Terry that I want that information yesterday and to knock as soon as he's got it. Then get Greaves and bring him in again,' said Sutton.

'Yes, Guv',' she said.

DI Sutton and DS Linton resumed their positions in Interview Room 4 and waited for the arrival of Robin Greaves aka Michael Abbot. They fished through the folders in front of them once again, jotted notes, and cross-examined the information they had, as they went along.

'So, which one of them has been seen wearing women's clothes,' asked Sutton.

'I don't know but the way this is switching around it could be William, I guess, or both,' she replied.

'So, maybe that is where the earring came from. Although we can't seem to find a match for it. But what about that bit you told me about the dust at the Care Home? How did it get there? Did Greaves wear his garage boots there as well as at work?'

'I'll ask if it comes up in conversation but with any luck, we'll establish enough about what has really been happening without that,' she said.

'Greaves' DNA is bound to be all over the things we retrieved from Rodina Close, but I wonder who else's we might find,' said Sutton.

'Yeah, me too.'

'Hopefully the blanket will be of use too, when we eventually get the results from it. But maybe he did just take it to work at the garage, after all,' said Sutton.

'Graham Walton, the Warden at Rodina Close, didn't seem to think so.'

'I hope your friend Aimee is right about all this. If not, we could be leading ourselves into a blind alley,' said Sutton.

'Me too. She wasn't totally sure of herself, but it does appear to make some sense of a confusing chat with Margaret Abbot, that's for sure,' Carrie replied.

'Oh, by the way, I had Steve Kingham's phoned tracked and he's in Tilbury.'

'What's he still doing in Tilbury?' she asked.

'The last we knew; he was following a lead to track down Karter Swann. You know what he's like. Loves to go it alone. If I don't hear anything soon I'll arrange the search party,' laughed Sutton.

'Fair enough, I'm sure he'll turn up.'

The pair of them sat in silence for a few moments while the new information sank in. Carrie had a clearer understanding of it all, having met Margaret Abbot and Aimee Richards in person, but Sutton wasn't far behind now. Even though his head was still spinning a little faster than Carrie's. As they sat patiently waiting for the door to open, Sutton began to recall some of the things that he had discussed with Patricia about how a person such as they are looking for, might have sustained physical trauma during their childhood which could have increased the chances of them committing violent acts in later life. Things were dropping into place in Sutton's mind.

When the door opened, PC Alex Tyler and PC Gavin Danvers walked in with Robin Greaves, aka Michael Abbot, and showed him to the chair opposite Sutton and Carrie. PC Danvers remained in the room.

Carrie reactivated the tape and made the necessary recording that stipulated the time and the names of precisely who was present. Once she had made it clear that the interview was back in session and that Robin aka Michael understood what was happening, she began.

'Robin, we are going to continue now. As before, if you have anything to say that may be useful to us in finding Angelica, please tell us,' she said, pausing to look across at him before continuing.

'Can you tell me about the mattress that was found in your bedroom?'

'It's just a mattress. What do want to know?' he said.

'Does anyone use it to sleep on?' she asked.

'No, I just have it as a spare.'

'Why do you need a spare if you have your own bed?'

'I just do,' he said, as he fiddled, child-like, with his hands.

'How many brothers and sisters do you have?' Carrie asked, rapidly changing the subject.

'What? I have two sisters,' he said.

'Any brothers?'

'No.'

'Where do they live?' she asked.

'I don't …they moved away.'

'When was the last time you saw your sisters, Robin?' she asked.

'Not seen them for ages. Can't remember,' he said, shaking his head.

'Surely, they must keep in touch with you, don't they?'

Greaves didn't answer.

'Does William keep in touch with you?' said Sutton.

Greaves looked at Sutton and then at Carrie. He looked as though he was in a state of panic.

'Does he come to stay with you?' said Carrie.

'Does he know where Angelica is?' asked Sutton.

'Did he kill those other girls, Robin?' said Carrie.

Greaves began to twitch and shake. He clasped his hands tightly in front of him and whimpered.

'Robin, does he hurt you?' asked Carrie, sympathetically.

'I don't know, I don't know,' he said.

At that point, PC Terry Rudge knocked on the door. Carrie rose from the table as Sutton announced that she had left the room. Outside, she spoke to Rudge.

'Found him,' he said.

'What have you got?' she said to Rudge.

Rudge handed Carrie a print-off that contained the details about William Abbot's criminal history. It showed that he had been arrested and charged in relation to an attack on a girl.

'As far as I can make out, the girl was walking along an unlit road with a couple of friends, and he grabbed at her. One of the girl's friends ran off but another witnessed it all. The unfortunate girl in question was struck across the back of her head. There were no serious injuries, just bumps and bruises and it went to Magistrates Court where he got 6 months. He served 3. The event took place almost three years ago, not long before Haley Breen was discovered,' he said.

'And I suppose no link was made between the two crimes?' she said.

'Apparently not,' said Rudge.

'How many girls were in the group?'

'Three, by all accounts.'

'Really. This might change things a bit. Thanks, Terry.'

Carrie went back into Interview Room 4 and sat down. Sutton announced her return for the tape.

'Why didn't you tell us about William before?' she asked Greaves.

Greaves didn't answer.

'Robin, we know about Marion,' she said, and waited for his reaction.

Greaves looked shell-shocked.

'You loved Marion, didn't you?'

'Yes,' he said, feebly.

'The girls didn't push her, did they?' she asked.

'No.'

'If you pushed her, Robin, you could be in a lot of trouble. You don't want that do you?'

Sutton kept his head down and pretended to be reading his folder. At this point he knew he was right to insist that he have Carrie in the interview and not DCI Blackery. His attitude would never have suited Greaves and he would have clammed up from the very start.

'I didn't do it. I don't want to get into any trouble,' he said.

'No. It wasn't you, was it?'

'No, I loved her,' he said again, shaking his head at Carrie.

'You know who it was don't you? You can tell me. He can't get to you in here, I won't let him,' Carrie said.

Greaves rubbed his face and wiped a tear away. He held his arms close to his chest, in a protective pose. For the first time he began to behave like a frightened child.

'It's ok, Robin. I'll protect you. Did William push Marion down the stairs?'

Greaves sat looking down at the table. Carrie wondered whether he would have the confidence to share the truth with her, but just as she drew breath to ask the same question another way, he answered.

'Yes. William did it.'

Carrie allowed Greaves to sit for a moment or two longer before she engaged with him again.

'Robin. Who put those things in your bedroom?' she asked.

'I don't want to get into any trouble,' said Greaves.

'If you help me find Angelica, I'll do everything I can to help you. Robin, we know that William went to prison for a little while, a few years ago, and we know that he used to live at home with you and your mother. I have spoken with your mother. She's a very nice lady. She told me about the time when William was left at the tip and when he was pushed under water in the bath. Do you remember that?' she asked.

'Yes.'

'Robin, when you visit your mother, you seem to leave behind a lot of dusty footprints. I think it's the same dust that we found on the boiler suit in the wardrobe. Is this right?' she said.

'They're not my boots,' he said.

'Why do you wear them?'

'I have to,' he said.

'Does William make you wear them when you visit your mother?'

'Yes.'

'I see. The dust doesn't come from the garage, does it?'

'No.'

'It's William that gets the dust on the boiler suit and on the boots, isn't it?'

Greaves looked down again but just as Carrie thought she had lost his attention, he looked up and spoke.

'He wants to get me into trouble. I didn't take those photos. I didn't hurt anyone,' he said in a rather stuttering way.

'Do you know what happened to Haley Breen?'

'Yes.'

'And do you know what happened to Claudia De Luca?'

'I think so.'

'Did William do these things?' said Carrie.

'Did he tell you anything else about what he did to the girls?' asked Sutton.

'Yes, he made a drawing on them,' said Greaves.

'What sort of drawing?' asked Sutton.

'It was like a heart.'

'Do you know why he did it?' said Carrie.

'He said he liked it,' said Greaves.

'Do you know why he chose that?' asked Carrie.

'The barman had one,' he said.

'Which barman?' asked Sutton.

'At the pub…where the girls went,' he said.

Carrie and Sutton exchanged a brief glance that indicated that they were both thinking of Swann.

Greaves had tears in his eyes now and was breathing deeply. There was a visible tremble in his hands. Momentarily, he broke into a cry and then stopped as if he was fighting the urge. Carrie and

Sutton watched him gradually crumbling in front of them. He put his finger in his mouth and bit down hard on it.

'I think he stays at your house sometimes and I think that he put those photographs in the box and placed it up on the top of the wardrobe. Did he tell you not to touch it?'

'Yes,' Greaves mumbled, almost incoherently.

'Did you say 'Yes', Robin?' Carrie asked.

'Yes!' he shouted, loudly.

When he released his finger, Sutton and Carrie could see the bite marks and the signs of blood in the indentations.

'It's ok. We're here to help you. You're doing really well. But I have to ask you something very important. Robin, do you know where Angelica is?' she asked.

Greaves nodded. Carrie announced this for the tape.

'I don't want to get into trouble,' he said.

'You help me, Robin, and I'll do everything I can to keep you out of trouble,' she said.

Greaves nodded.

'Now, let's talk about Angelica,' she said.

SEVENTY-SIX

Golden Valley, Minneapolis, Minnesota.

Ken Toft slowly drew his vehicle to a halt directly behind the patrol car of Captain Antonio Rodrigues. He had had plenty of thinking time on the journey and none of it had made him feel any better. He could sense that Leo was already on his feet in the rear. Leo always whined when Toft arrived at a search location. He always barked at least a couple of times too, and today was no different. Leo was primed for action, even if Toft wasn't. It was Toft that really wanted to just go home. He remembered the clear instructions that he had received from Big Toni; *when we get there, don't you move until I tell you to.*

The Captain had radioed to the Control Room, as per the request of Deputy Chief Jack Bolton, that he and Patrol Officer Gregory Bonner had arrived at the old Nelson residence. It was a matter of waiting for the digging machinery to arrive. Big Toni knew they wouldn't have long to wait because it had been mobilised from the moment that they left Toft's house in Eden Prairie. *Maybe another five or ten minutes, max,* he thought.

'You're awfully quiet, Bonner,' said Big Toni.

Bonner had been deep in thought as they rolled along into Golden Valley. He looked for the posters about Caterina that he had put up, but there were none left. He was a bit disappointed but somehow it didn't seem to matter so much to him today. Caterina was, once again, occupying his mind.

'Sorry, Captain. Just been letting my mind wander.'

'No prizes for guessing where it was wandering to then,' he said.

Bonner just nodded and gave a crooked smile.

'Shouldn't be too long with the digger now. The Deputy Chief has made all the necessary arrangements. In fact, I'd go as far as to say that he was positively enthused by the whole idea.'

'Presuming there is going to be a dig. It all rests with Leo,' said Bonner.

'The people in the house are expecting us, apparently.'

'Bet they were pleased.'

'Well, either way, it's happening. Good job the snow stopped ain't it?' said Big Toni.

'Yeah, I guess so,' answered Bonner, with an air of disappointment.

'So, where do you think we should start?' said Big Toni, as he peered out into the garden.

'Well, she came in from the corner of that line of trees so...'

'How do you know where she came in from, Bonner? You one of those clairvoyants?'

'No, Captain, I just...'

'What? You just know. Is that what you're trying to tell me now? You expect me to believe all that stuff, Bonner?' said Big Toni.

'No, Captain, I just...never mind.'

He thought about the time when he imagined her leaving her house and beginning her journey to Betty's on the day she went missing, and the times that he had sat talking to her in his den. Bonner could hardly explain his visions of Caterina to his Captain. He just sat quietly and waited. As the time went on, Bonner began to wonder whether she would appear to him again. He knew it wasn't any kind of spiritual experience but, then again, he didn't really have an answer as to what it was. *Maybe I'm making the whole thing up,* he thought, *maybe she's 500 miles away.*

Big Toni checked his rear-view mirror and watched Ken Toft sit in his van like a waxwork dummy, not moving, just as he had been told. He could see that Toft had realised that he had him in his sights and was eyeballing him. *After all these years, I'm gonna make you and that dog of yours do a proper job,* he thought.

'Captain,' said Bonner.

'What is it?'

'They're here.'

Big Toni looked down the street, ahead of him, and could see the truck that was carrying the small excavator. A row of lights on the cab roof flickered and flashed as it came into view. One patrol car was leading the way.

'Right then. You know what time it is now, don't you, Bonner?'

'Not really.'

'It's showtime, Bonner. Showtime.'

Bonner fastened his jacket and pulled his hat from the pocket, putting it on his head. Big Toni opened his door and stepped out of the patrol car. He immediately turned towards Ken Toft and pointed a finger at him, shouting 'Stay there until I want you.' Toft gave an obligatory nod.

Access to the garden wasn't a problem for the machinery as there was no fence or barrier to overcome. Bonner got out of the vehicle and watched as one of the two men that had arrived with the Officer in the patrol car stepped onto the small excavator and began to gently roll it off of the back of the low-loader. Big Toni was talking to the other of the operators, but Bonner was too excited about the prospect of a successful visit to listen properly. And then something dawned on him. *If we find her, it's over.* Bonner wasn't really referring to just the search, he was referring to the whole Caterina Marks mystery. Finally, he would have the answer that Alexandria Org had never known. Her daughter's location.

'Right, Bonner. We're going to get Toft and his dog ready soon. Just make sure he doesn't get in the way while we get the digger into position. I'm going to have it sit just here, on the edge of the grass. Then we'll get Toft and Lennie or whatever it's called to do what they do. I want you to watch that he does it properly this time. I don't want to hear any excuses from him about a compromised search or any other nonsense. Are you listening, Bonner?'

Bonner was in a daydream. *If we find her, then she's really dead.*

'BONNER!' shouted Big Toni.

'Yes, Captain.'

'Did you hear a word I just said?'

'Yeah, most of it,' said Bonner.

'Most of it? Sometimes, Bonner, I wonder about you.'

Why let today be any different, he thought.

The operator of the small excavator positioned it as per Big Toni's request and waited for further instructions. Bonner signalled to Toft for him to get Leo out of the van and get ready to start the search. He knew that these animals were pretty fantastic when it came to searching for people but in one way, he hoped that Leo didn't find her. Bonner remembered what he had learned at MinnSARDA about how the dogs could locate people that had been missing for years, even under water. This time, however, he had very mixed feelings about the outcome. In one way he wanted to find her. It was his promise to her, after all. But in another way, he hoped that she wasn't here, and maybe, just maybe, she never reached Betty's house, and maybe she is still alive somewhere. Perhaps she's living somewhere nice with a family all of her own. *Who knows where though? Oh, Caterina. Here we go.*

Leo barked loudly, expressing how keen he was to start work. Toft held him on the leash and looked at Big Toni, awaiting his signal. Bonner stood with his eyes closed, trying to imagine Caterina standing by the pine trees, the last place that he '*saw*' her in his strange vision.

'Bonner, you ready?' asked Big Toni.

'Yes, Captain.'

'Toft, you better do this properly or I'll have your guts for garters,' shouted Big Toni.

Toft didn't move or say anything. He just stared ahead at the garden with Leo beside him.

'Right then,' said the Captain, wondering what the correct command was for the beginning of a search. Ultimately, he chose 'Get on with it'. Toft and Leo began.

Toft led Leo up the line of Pines. Leo sniffed and ferreted about in and amongst the trees as Toft was being pulled along behind him.

'Toft. Let it off the leash. I don't want you telling it where to go,' called Big Toni.

Toft released Leo and slowly followed him along the tree line towards the rear aspect of the old Nelson property. The snowfall had been minimal in this area and the grass was mostly visible. Every so often a shower of fine snow fell from the branches of the trees and dusted the ground.

It's beginning to melt, thought Bonner as he looked around at the shrubs and bushes and hoped that Caterina would be there to help him find her. As daft as it seemed he found himself looking all around the garden for her. She had appeared in his mind's eye before, and he really needed her now. As Leo began to work his way along the rear fence, Toft positioned himself in the centre of the garden. Bonner wondered what was going through Toft's mind. *Did he want her to be found? Maybe, he didn't care either way as there were a lot more questions coming his way whatever the outcome.*

Big Toni sidled up beside Bonner and watched Leo. He was pleased about one thing. It was nowhere near as cold as it had been when the pair of them had attended the property a few years ago, when Wade Nelson had been discovered hanging, frozen solid, from the rear balcony. Big Toni scanned the garden and could recall explicitly, where he had fallen in the snow and hurt his shin. He was fairly certain that the unfortunate event had been a source of humour for Bonner over the years, but each time Big Toni had thought about it, his shin had hurt all over again.

Leo was scouring the grass in a kind of criss-cross pattern. Bonner didn't remember anything about this from his visit to Elk River, when he met Derek Grant. But then, at that time, he wasn't really interested in how they searched, he was more concerned with making his point about a possible error in the search for Caterina, much to the disgust of his host.

'He's going in circles now,' said Bonner.

'I can see that. I do hope this isn't going to be a waste of everyone's time,' said Big Toni.

Bonner looked behind him at the corner of the garden where the line of red Pines began.

'What're you looking for, now?' said Big Toni.

'Nothing, Captain.'

'Nothing? Well, don't look for nothing. Start looking at what Toft is doing.'

'Yes, Captain,' said Bonner.

Big Toni walked back to the edge of the property to speak with the crew that had arrived with the small excavator. Bonner studied Leo and watched as he sniffed purposefully at the ground. He wondered if Leo was going to indicate or just keep going around in circles. Bonner reflected that it was Gretel who was supposed to have been here all those years ago; Gretel that was supposed to have indicated close to the shed. He recalled where Toft had put the X on the map of the property that Bonner had taken with him to Toft's house and how it had taken him a long time to decide whereabouts it should go. Bonner didn't really know how long a search should take or, indeed, what he was going to do if Leo came up with no answers, but he knew that, at this moment, everything was out of his control. It made him smile to himself to think that it had all come down to the ability of a dog's nose. *A bit bloody late,* he thought.

He looked at the house, as his eyes followed the balcony that encircled the property, and remembered the girls, Betty and Elisha, and wondered what they were doing now. *Having a great time in London,* he thought. Bonner had no idea about what their life might be like nowadays, but he loved the Minnesota winters and could never imagine himself leaving them behind, even though he was a little envious. Perhaps he was more curious than anything else. Then as he looked up again, he recalled when he and Harry Bones had discovered Wade Nelson at the rear of the house and began to think about exactly what his part in Caterina's disappearance could be. Bonner wanted to know why Wade Nelson had forced Toft to give a false report. *What was he hiding? Did either of the girls actually know something after all?* Bonner doubted that the girls had any idea.

There was a shout. He looked up at Big Toni, who was pointing towards the main part of the garden. When Bonner followed the direction in which he was pointing, he saw Toft standing still in the centre of the grass, and Leo down on the ground a few yards ahead of where he stood. He was indicating. *Leo is indicating. This is it,* thought Bonner. His heart began to pound as he tried to establish precisely what Leo was indicating at. It looked like the shed.

Big Toni scampered across the grass and hurriedly made his way to join Bonner. The two of them stood together, anticipating that something crucial was about to happen. As Toft edged towards Leo, Big Toni yelled.

'Don't you touch that dog, Toft. Don't you dare go anywhere near it.'

Toft froze. Leo stayed down with his nose pointing in front of him. Big Toni and Bonner looked at each other. It was one of those surreal moments where everything seemed to be happening in slow motion. Bonner felt uneasy about the prospect of finding Caterina, even if it would only be a matter of finding a load of bones. Nobody had seen Caterina Marks for a very long time and Bonner tried to contemplate how this might make him feel.

'Is it the shed, Bonner?' asked Big Toni.

'Looks like it, Captain,' he replied.

'Right. Let's get Toft and Lennie back in the van. Then we can get on with it,' said Big Toni.

'Leo,' said Bonner.

'Who?' said Big Toni.

'Leo, the dog is called Leo.'

'Yeah, well…whatever. Get them both out of the way.'

Whilst Captain Antonio Rodrigues went to speak to the excavator operators, Bonner ushered Ken Toft and Leo back to their van, explaining that they were to stay there until such a time as they were needed, if indeed they were. Ken Toft opened up the rear doors to the van and Leo bounded in with one leap. Toft made his way to the front with Bonner in attendance.

'Is that it, then?' asked Toft.

'Guess we're gonna find out soon enough,' said Bonner.

As Bonner walked into the garden, he saw his Captain wandering in his direction. Bonner diverted towards him to meet him in the centre of the lawn.

'It looks to me as though the shed is sitting on a hard surface, so I'm wondering about getting the guys to jam the tip of the bucket under one end and see if it'll drag.'

'Ok, sounds reasonable,' said Bonner.

'You alright, Bonner?'

'Yeah, I'll be better when this is over with, Captain.'

'Look, I know she meant a lot to you. But if Lennie's nose is anything to go by, then maybe the mystery will be over soon. I'll make sure the guys are careful, Bonner.'

'Thanks, Captain.'

Big Toni strutted off to pass on his instructions, leaving Bonner to look around the garden for Caterina. He checked the Pine trees and swivelled around to look out into the street, but he didn't see her. All he saw was a small gathering of people on the opposite side of the street and the excavator rolling slowly up the garden towards the rear of the shed with Big Toni alongside it, pointing to precisely where he wanted it to be situated. When the machinery was in position, Big Toni said something to the operator and headed back to re-join Bonner who was still checking if she was going to appear to him again.

'They're going to drag it back slowly. Hopefully it won't fall to bits. Then I'll get the digger around the front of it, and they can do what they do. You can help me and the other guys set up the screens,' said Big Toni.

Bonner didn't respond. He couldn't believe that she had been under the shed for all this time without anybody knowing. The thought of her being alone there for so many years saddened him. He knew that he would have to find out if she was there and have to look at the evidence, but he wasn't looking forward to it. Big Toni waved a hand at the operator and the machinery revved its engine. Slowly, the tip of the bucket edged its way under the rear of the shed. There was a shudder and then the bucket began to lift ever so gently. Once it had raised the end of the shed up a few inches, the crunch of a reverse gear engaging was heard and the whole structure began to creep back. Bonner watched the underneath of the shed come into view. Two scrape marks, one at either side of the shed appeared like tramlines. He could see the hard standing that for years had supported the weight of the shed, and it was then that he began to doubt the whole scenario. *A concrete base,* he thought.

The excavator fell silent as the operator looked to Big Toni for his next instruction. There was an eerie mist of thick exhaust smoke wafting around the property and amongst the Pines in the cold air. Every other sound seemed to be deadened by the blanket of a thick dark cloud which formed a layer of insulation across the whole sky. For a few brief moments, the operation fell silent.

'Captain, it's a concrete base,' said Bonner.

'I can see that, Bonner.'

'Well, it's just that…well, if she is under there…when was the concrete mixed? Do you think that she was buried and then the shed was repositioned so that the concrete could set before it went back again? I don't remember the shed ever being anywhere other than where it is now, and I was around a lot in those days, especially after she went missing.'

'So maybe it always had a concrete base,' said Big Toni.

'Maybe, but…Well, if it did, how did she get under there? The shed was here first, Captain. It was always here as far as I can recall,' said Bonner.

Captain Antonio Rodrigues looked hard at his Trouper and then at the shed. His mind was trying to fathom a reasonable conclusion to Bonner's latest curveball. But he didn't have one. Big Toni waved his hand at the operator in a way that said *cut the engine*. The excavator puffed out a thick fog of dense and murky smoke which wafted towards the two police officers, as its engine sputtered to a stop. Both men turned their bodies away from the direction of the shed and lowered their heads until the stench had passed. Big Toni let out a cough.

'So, you're telling me that she isn't under the shed, Bonner?'

'I'm just saying that it always had a concrete base as far as I remember and that was way before Caterina went missing.'

Big Toni let out a big sigh. He stared at the shed and turned to ask Bonner what he thought they should do next, but Bonner wasn't listening. He was transfixed by the image he could see standing at the edge of the pathway opposite. And she wasn't alone.

SEVENTY-SEVEN

Ahuja Industries, East London.

It was 04:45. The light rain had subsided, as they sat in silence, quietly observing the darkest of the thin strips of purple/blue clouds as they drifted away to the east. Through a small gap in the undergrowth, they could see the ghostly image of the dusty site in Creekmouth, once a thriving industrial pocket of Barking, that is situated close to where the River Roding slowly discharges into the River Thames at Barking Point. It is approximately 10 miles from Old Clapton Street, in the heart of the River Road Industrial complex.

'Who came up with the name Operation Liberate?' said Carrie.

'Not me. I think the likely suspect might be sitting a few cars behind us though,' said Sutton.

'Hmm. Sounds about right.'

Sutton and Carrie were together in one car, DCI Blackery in another, and 4 more cars were parked out of sight behind them, further along Rose Lock Lane. Six armed officers waited in a black van at the rear of the convoy just ahead of an ambulance that was waiting to take Angelica straight to hospital for an assessment of her condition, which wasn't expected to be terribly good considering her traumatic experience. She would most likely be dehydrated and in dire need of a host of vitamins and supplements. Sutton had chosen this spot because it was completely shielded from Ahuja Industries by a number of silver birch trees and a thickly overgrown hedgerow. The entrance into Rose Lock Lane was also fully obscured from view by a row of large warehouses making it impossible to see from the old redundant site.

PC Alex Tyler sat in her car, on River Road, at the other side of the cement works, keeping a watchful eye for any activity at the main gates to the premise. From where she sat, she could see that, although the gates were loosely chained, the left hand one swung freely at the top of the gatepost permitting an easy access point to anyone who wanted to enter the derelict wasteland. William Abbot wouldn't need a key.

'Alex?' Sutton said into his radio.

'Here, Guv.'

'Anything?'

'Nothing, Guv.'

With the sky now mostly clear, the sunrise was just starting to become faintly evident as Sutton radioed to the second of the four cars and instructed the officers within it to make their way, with their breaking-in gear, along Rose Lock Lane to where the chain-link fence met the road. It was their job to first, make a large enough whole in the fencing for the team to gain easy access to the site, and then to check for an entry point at the rear of the main building, creating one if necessary.

'Do you reckon he'll show?' asked Carrie.

'Yeah, I reckon so. If what Greaves is telling us is right, then he'll be bringing Angelica her breakfast in a couple of hours. Except, with any luck, she won't be there to accept it,' said Sutton.

'We've got to find her first, and by the looks of the size of the place, that won't be easy,' said Carrie.

'Yeah, possibly.'

'He was really hard work tonight. For one minute I thought he was going to change his mind and just clam up on us,' she said.

'I know. It was strange how he went from talking about William to not wanting to give us the answers we needed about Angelica. It took hours to get it out of him,' said Sutton.

'Yeah, nightmare. I think he was afraid to let the cat out of the bag,' said Carrie.

'Probably.'

'We could pick Abbot up at the gates,' she said.

'We could, but I want him to show us exactly where he's been keeping her. That's if we don't find her first. And besides, there's that comment that Patricia made about letting him come to us. Greaves didn't seem to know where he is right now, and we could be chasing all over London, trying to locate him. So, if he's going to be here soon, I thought we may as well let him walk into our welcoming committee. Once he's this close, he'll have nowhere to run to, even if he did smell a rat when he finally turns up.'

Seconds later a group of officers carrying the prescribed breaking-in gear shuffled swiftly past Sutton's car. Four officers dressed in black coveralls moved into position at the chain-link fencing a few metres ahead of where Sutton had parked the car. Sutton and Carrie watched as they removed the bolt-cutters from a large black holdall and began to snip at the fence. Short work was made of the task and within a few minutes Sutton could see a gap in the fencing that was large enough to get everybody through.

'I hope we find her alive,' said Carrie, with a rather downcast expression.

Sutton looked at her but didn't respond.

'Right. C'mon. Let's get inside,' he said, into the radio that was clipped to his coat.

Carrie and Sutton left their vehicle and made their way to the newly created entrance into the perimeter of Ahuja Industries, followed by DCI Blackery and the rest of the team. They were as certain as they could be that Angelica was the only person in the building but had no idea exactly where to find her. Greaves had said that he had no knowledge of precisely where she was being kept and seeing as it was a substantial structure, they were unable to hone their search on any particular section of it.

The team with the breaking-in gear had side-winded their way down the damp and slippery grass bank that brought them to the rear aspect of the factory, avoiding rabbit holes as they carefully traversed the slope. From where Sutton was positioned at the bottom of the bank of grass, he could see a number of windows high up on the exterior wall, none of which were going to be of use to them. Not without a hydraulic platform and a head for heights, neither of which he had. He looked up at the rear façade of the cold steel monstrosity and wondered how she had survived her cruel confinement. At least, he hoped that she had.

'She could be anywhere,' said Carrie.

'Yep.'

The breaking-in team were busy trying to gain entry through any means that would permit them access to the menacing-looking construction. The first two doors that were tried appeared to have been welded in their closed position. Sutton wanted to gain access at the rear so as to keep his team entirely out of sight and avoid any possibility of alarming William Abbot as to their presence. He wanted the front of the building to look exactly as it always had. No suspicious vehicles, even if they were unmarked, or evidence of any form of attendance. He was happy that Alex Tyler would go unnoticed. He patiently watched the breaking-in team as they systematically worked their way along the building from left to right and knew that it wouldn't be long before he and Carrie were inside.

'For all we know, this place could have floors below ground,' said Carrie.

'It could, but let's take one thing at a time. Once were in, we can get a feel for the layout. Depending upon what we find, we'll start on the ground floor. The team can split up and report anything they find by radio,' replied Sutton.

'I bet he kept Haley and Claudia here too.'

'We might find out soon enough,' said Sutton.

'They're in,' said DCI Blackery.

Sutton looked to his right and could see one of the breaking-in team waving at him. The combination of the Halligan Tool and the sturdy Door Enforcer had finally been successful.

'Here we go,' he said to Carrie as they both began to run towards the open door.

The team waited for Sutton. It was his show and he wanted to be first through the door. As he stepped inside with Carrie and DCI Blackery close behind him, he could immediately smell the musty atmosphere. His first impression of the interior was one of how colourless and drab it was. A strange silence seemed to hang in the air like a dismal cloak of dread causing a chill to run through him at the thought of what they were going to find. Sutton began to organise his team and quickly set them to work. There were enough officers to spread out across the width of the factory in small groups and start their search for Angelica. As they dispersed, Sutton, Carrie and Blackery made their way down the centre of the ground floor. Even after years of it being in an unused and desolate state, the factory still managed to whip up a swirl of cement every so often, reminiscent of a previous practise.

As the three of them slowly walked along together, they could see the mountains of dust heaped up against the walls and the long-retired silos and conveyor belts, all of which had not witnessed any signs of activity for many years. Sutton's radio chirped into life every few minutes as the search teams reported back to him. None had any good news up to now.

'Angelica,' shouted DCI Blackery.

They listened in hope for a reply but there was none. The only sign of life came from a scurrying rat that shot across their path and out of sight underneath one of the conveyor belts. Sutton's teams could also be heard as their movements echoed around in the vacuous emptiness of life in the factory.

'Guv.'

It was PC Alex Tyler.

'Go ahead,' said Sutton.

'I've got a single male walking down the road behind me.'

'Any idea if it's him?'

'Not yet. It looks like he has a bag over his shoulder, but it could still be somebody on their way to work.'

'Has anyone else passed you up to now?' he asked.

'No. That's why I thought I'd let you know.'

'Ok. Keep an eye on him and let me know what he does.'

Sutton and Carrie had walked on ahead of DCI Blackery who was talking to one of the other teams. They had wandered into a part of the factory where the ceiling had opened up. They were able to see right up to the roof. They could see that there were railings on both sides of the building that stretched all the way to the other end. An occasional flutter of pigeons could be heard high above them. The sunlight was now beginning to pour into the higher reaches of the factory which helped their general view of the structure.

'Look, Marc,' said Carrie

'What have you found?'

Carrie walked over to one side of the ground floor and bent down to take a closer look at something. Sutton stood behind her, peering over her shoulder.

'Somebody has been here,' she said.

Sutton could see it now. There was a regular pattern in the dust. A sort of half circle of flattened cement dust. Trodden down over time.

'What do you think it is, Marc?'

Sutton studied the pattern of dust. He could see that there was no other signs of it anywhere else. Since they had gained entry, the layers of dust had been regular, like a carpet of fine powder. But this was different. Somebody had created this pattern. Both Sutton and Carrie knew that no amount of wind was likely to create such a particular shape in the dust. Carrie stood next to Sutton and almost simultaneously they both noticed a major difference in the dust in this particular area. They could tell that there had been a lot of disturbance to the point where the dust was noticeably thinner. It had been flattened out by somebody or something. Somebody had been in this area but apparently had not stood outside of the half circle. There was no noticeable evidence of any footsteps beyond the ridge of dust. At least none that would have survived the regular blasts of wind that carried through the factory every so often.

Sutton and Carrie stepped into the half circle. All they could see was a wall of brick that had been built at a right angle. *Probably, a machine had been sited here at some point and since removed,* he thought.

'Carrie,' said Sutton.

He was looking at a piece of metal that had been fixed into the wall, again, probably years ago. A chain, or part of one, that dangled to the floor, was attached to it. Carrie began to amble to one side of the area and was attracted by something on the floor that felt out of place. A food container. Similar to those that usually contain takeaway food.

'Marc,' she said.

Sutton let the chain drop and took a look at what Carrie was showing him.

'This could be hers,' she said.

'Anything in it?'

'No, it's clean. And I think I know why,' she said.

Sutton turned to look behind him to see what Carrie was looking at. There was Socks, as Angelica had named him. His eyes were staring at them both, inquisitive and yet annoyed that anyone was invading his territory.

'Marc, I think I there's a faint smell of the food that was in it.'

'It's not that old then. It must be hers.'

Sutton and Carrie began to call Angelica's name. The sound of their voices echoed around the factory. As they fell silent, so too did the factory. Sutton turned his attention back to the wall. He was looking at the marks on the brickwork. He crouched and noticed the brick dust on the floor, just below where the chain was affixed. It looked as if somebody had been striking the wall, perhaps to release themselves from the chain. Sutton looked around him for something that might have made the scars on the brickwork.

'Something made these marks,' he said to Carrie.

'How about this?'

Just at the edge of the half circle, tucked right up against the one of the walls, was a metal bar. Carrie put her foot on it and rolled it to Sutton.

'That would do it,' he said.

'This has to be where he kept her. If she was tied by that chain, then she wouldn't be able to go far.'

'It must have been just long enough for her to go out to the edge of that pattern in the dust,' he said.

'It looks like she's been here. The question is…'

'Yeah.' said Sutton. *Where are you, Angelica?*

As Sutton and Carrie stepped back outside of the half circle, she kicked an old hairbrush across the factory floor. She picked it up and studied it. Carrie could see that there were strands of dark hair in amongst the bristles. She held it up for Sutton to see.

'Could be,' he said, 'Make sure that's collected. We'll have it tested for DNA.'

SEVENTY-EIGHT

Angelica couldn't understand it. This had never happened before. *Why the hell?* She had her blankets, she had her disgusting bucket, she was tied as usual, but she couldn't understand why he had put a gag on her. The tape that was stuck fast across her mouth was pulling and pinching on her face every time she twitched. He had wrapped it all the way around her head so that it was stuck to her hair, and that was really grating on her nerves. She was also hoping that she didn't sneeze. *I'll tear my head off!* A little earlier, Angelica had been awakened by a sudden noise somewhere in the far reaches of the factory. She had no idea what it was, but it had been just loud enough to startle her. At first, she thought that she had imagined it, but then she heard something else, or thought she did. *Maybe it's that weird man again. The one I saw looking at me.*

She was sure about one thing though. She had definitely been dreaming. She heard her own name being called. Quietly, as if from a distance. She had thought that she had heard her Mum and Dad calling her, sometimes it was her friends. It had happened before. Angelica used to think that she was going mad but then again, she just accepted that she was bound to have these odd dreams and weird moments. *It was just my brain crying out for help and making sure that I didn't forget who I am.*

Angelica arched her back and caused it to crack. How she wished she was in her corner so that she could stand properly and walk to the edge of her world and back again. *When I get out of here, I'm going swimming and running...and I'm going down the pub,* she thought. These thoughts only served to upset her and remind her of the image of the girl that she saw being carried away. *Not my turn yet, I guess.*

Another noise. *Something is moving around down there. Must be the boys,* she thought. *I hope breakfast comes soon, I'm bloody starving. Then I can get this sodding tape off.*

One of Sutton's officers took photographs of the area that he and Carrie had been exploring whilst DCI Blackery began to check on another section of the building with a team of two. Stripe and Speckle had now joined Socks to watch the activities but kept their distance from the unexpected guests.

'Guv.'

'Yes, Alex.'

'That guy has walked on towards the south end of River Road. I expect he was just on his way to work.'

'Ok, thanks. Keep me posted,' said Sutton.

Sutton and Carrie had found no other signs that might suggest that Angelica might be nearby. Despite their calls, Angelica had not responded. From what they could see, it looked as though they had walked about halfway down the length of the ground floor. They checked every corner, behind each piece of machinery, and under each of the conveyor belts as they progressed. Some of the smaller silos had ladders fixed to the sides of them that Sutton and Carrie had ascended to peer inside, but they had not found any sign of Angelica. Sutton's radio had also piped up with regular updates from his team, but nobody had found anything of note. The search wasn't proving to be as straightforward as they had hoped.

I can hear someone. Or something. Can't be the boys this time. Maybe it's the weirdo. Or my breakfast at last. Angelica shifted her position as best she could and tried to see further along the factory. All she could see was the sidewall of one of the larger silos. She looked down to the ground towards the point where she had seen him coming before and checked to see if her breakfast was arriving…and then she had a thought.

I didn't hear the gate open. I always hear the gate scraping along the ground before he comes in. Why would he use a different way in? It can't be him. It must be the boys. Perhaps they're chasing a poor rabbit and making a noise. Hope it gets away. Sorry boys.

A set of stairs that led down into the dark, enticed Sutton and Carrie to take a look. The steps were shallow, and they were both glad of the handrail that was affixed to one side of the entrance, even though they didn't trust it entirely. As they descended, they listened for any sounds that might alert them to Angelica's presence. It was quiet, save for the sounds of their own footsteps on the gritty treads. At the bottom of the steps there was nothing more than a dead end and several more unfortunate creatures. A brick wall faced them and put an end to this particular aspect of the search.

'Oh, it's disgusting down here,' said Carrie.

'Well, that was a waste of time, then,' said Sutton.

'Yep.'

'Why have a stairway that leads nowhere?' he said.

'Beats me. Maybe once upon a time it did go somewhere and has been bricked up.'

'Seems so. At least we know she isn't down here.'

'I suppose that's something,' said Carrie.

They both turned to climb the stairs and resume their walk through the factory.

'The place seems to be filled with foxes. How many have you seen?' she asked.

'Only a few. I think I've seen more rats than anything. Most of them are dead though,' said Sutton.

'Maybe it's the same ones that I keep seeing. They're certainly inquisitive,' said Carrie.

'Don't suppose they get many visitors,' said Sutton.

Back at the top of the stairs, both of them walked on, checking and peering into silos, under conveyor belts, and around the discarded machinery. Sutton was aware that if they couldn't find Angelica and release her from wherever she was being held captive before William Abbot appeared, they may struggle to find her at all if he saw any of them. He didn't imagine that Abbot would be very helpful in disclosing her location. Sutton would need him to go to her to show them precisely where she was, which highlighted his other alternative of hiding out of sight and waiting for him to appear.

About 100 yards ahead of them stood the foxes. More of them this time. There appeared to be at least five. They stood in a group, almost as if they were waiting for Sutton and Carrie.

'There. That's another lot,' said Carrie.

'Same ones, I reckon,' answered Sutton.

'Hope they don't bite,' she said.

'Looks to me as though they do plenty of biting going by the number of carcasses that are strewn about the place. Bodies everywhere.'

'Yuk, Marc. Hope Grace hasn't got rabbit stew ready for later,' she said.

'Not a problem for you if she has, is it?' he said.

'It will be, I'm round at eight for dinner,' Carrie said.

Sutton looked at her, shook his head slightly, and inwardly sniggered.

As Sutton and Carrie approached, the foxes shuffled back a little. Now Sutton could see that there were two larger foxes and three that were presumably younger. Their coats appeared to gleam against their comparative drab surroundings.

'Looks like the whole family has turned out to greet us,' he said.

'They look lovely, but I don't think we should get too close,' replied Carrie.

'I expect they are more frightened of us than we are of them,' said Sutton.

'Don't bank on it.'

Sutton and Carrie walked slowly towards the foxes, looking around them for anything that might indicate Angelica's presence. They could hear the other teams a little way behind them, still checking in every nook and cranny as they went. Sutton's radio had currently fallen quiet.

As Sutton and Carrie got within a few yards of the foxes, they stopped, allowing the foxes the opportunity to wander off, but they stood their ground.

'I thought you said they were frightened of us,' said Carrie.

'I thought they were. Either way, it doesn't matter. We have to keep going,' he said.

'I don't like the way they are looking at us,' said Carrie.

'It'll be ok, or at least you will,' he said.

'How do you mean?'

'Well, you're the one that knows karate.'

'Yeah, maybe, but I've never had to fight 5 hungry foxes,' she said.

'Always a first time,' said Sutton.

'Cheers for that, Marc,' she said. 'And of course, I can rely on you for back up, I guess.'

'Keep guessing,' he said.

They walked on, skirting around the foxes, and continued to look everywhere and anywhere for Angelica. All they found was more of the same dusty surroundings amongst the graveyard of discarded metal. Sutton and Carrie kept looking back at the foxes, just to check on where they were, and found that the three smaller ones were not far behind them.

'I think we're being followed,' he said.

Carrie stopped and considered trying to shoo them but wasn't sure whether that would aggravate them. She thought they looked so nice and didn't want to frighten them. *Cute with teeth,* she thought. As long as they kept a reasonable distance, she decided that they were not actually much of a problem. Carrie walked on a few yards behind Sutton and found that she was glancing back over her shoulder at the foxes, aware that they were following slowly behind.

'Looks like we've acquired some friends,' she said.

Sutton turned to see what she meant and saw the group of smaller foxes were ahead of the other two, apparently following Carrie.

'Well, you certainly have.'

Carrie noticed that when she stopped, so did the foxes. She began to walk on, slowly, towards Sutton and watched as the whole troop followed. It was a little disconcerting and the more she thought about it, the more she felt as though she was being stalked. With one eye on the foxes, Carrie and Sutton walked on and continued to inspect in and under the disused machinery. By now their trousers were the same colour as just about everything around them. As they advanced along the factory, they both thought that they heard a noise. Something that resembled a clanging of metal. It wasn't loud, but in the relative silence, it pierced the air.

'Did you hear that?' said Sutton.

'Yeah. I think it came from further down.'

'Angelica,' shouted Sutton.

They stood motionless and listened but didn't hear a reply. As they began to walk on, there was a more distinctive sound.

'There,' said Sutton.

'I heard it,' said Carrie.

They carried on walking, and for the first time since entering into the factory, they had a glimmer of hope. The factory opened out a little more. It was more spacious but no less filled with clutter. The main difference was that the roof was higher. When they reached the middle of this section, they stopped and looked around them. They squatted down and peered underneath the two large hoppers just ahead of them. Carrie spotted something that caught her eye.

'What's that, Marc?' she said, pointing.

Sutton reached under the hopper, using a length of wood, and pulled the object towards him. He shook the object causing a cloud of dust to fill the air around him.

'Looks like an old blanket. Been half chewed too,' he said.

'I bet I know where it came from,' said Carrie.

Carrie turned her attention, once more, to the foxes. They were closer than she realised, and all appeared to be looking straight at her and Sutton.

'Marc. Why are they looking at us? It's almost as if they're all staring.'

'They do seem to be staring at us…or…or above us,' he said.

Sutton and Carrie turned around and looked behind them. All they saw was more cement, more machinery, and a set of stairs that led high up towards the roof. As they tried to focus on the walkways above them, the sun shone in through one of the broken windows and caused them to shield their eyes. The intensity of brilliant sunlight made them turn their heads back towards where the foxes stood. They hadn't budged an inch. They were still gazing up above Sutton and Carrie, as if they were concentrating on something specific. In an instant the clouds rolled across the sun and the factory returned back to its original dull and gloomy appearance, allowing Sutton and Carrie to refocus on the structure above them.

'Marc, what's that? Further down.'

'Where?'

'Up there. On that landing. Further down,' she said.

Sutton walked towards the area that Carrie was indicating at and stopped dead.

'Oh, my goodness! Carrie, we've found her. We've found her. She's here,' he said into his radio.

'Angelica,' screamed Carrie, as loud as she could.

Angelica tried to speak but ended up squealing behind her taped-up mouth. She was trying to shout 'Mum, Dad'. She began to wriggle and fight against her restraints but still couldn't move freely. Tears streamed down her face in a huge overflow of pent-up emotion and her whole body began to convulse. Sutton and Carrie could hear her indecipherable high-pitched shriek over the sound of Sutton's radio responding to his announcement and the sound of boots running down the factory to where Sutton and Carrie were. Before Sutton could say anything, Carrie was already almost at the top of the stairs. In the blink of an eye, she was running along the walkway towards Angelica. It was then that PC Alex Tyler spoke into Sutton's ear to tell him that they had a visitor approaching the factory gates.

SEVENTY-NINE

The Riverside Centre, Tilbury, East London.

Swann knew that Elisha was running out of patience and that before long she was going to resume her warped identity as a dark and sinister Betty, and perhaps carry out the deadly deed that she had planned for him. The sudden appearance of the man with the blood-stained face who called himself Ron, had further complicated an already confusing situation. It was bad enough finding Elisha behind him after all these years, but to witness her kill another stranger, whoever he was, was especially spine-chilling. Swann's head was spinning with all the bewildering events that had happened since he arrived for his evening shift behind the bar. He was so focussed on how he was going to get out of this, that he hadn't even given any real consideration to what on Earth Betty was doing here. If anyone was likely to want to kill him, he reckoned that it might be her. Although, having made the best use of his opportunity to expose Elisha, perhaps she might forgive him after all. Swann's heartrate had resumed a much more normal rhythm, but his head was swirling with unanswered questions. *Who was this Ron, anyway? Why is this man covered in blood? If it wasn't Elisha, then who sent me those photographs? Who was trying to blame me for those murders? Who was the woman that watched me at the Supermarket?*

In one way, Swann was pleased that Ray and Ron had provided a distraction. If they had not turned up, he might have already been dead. He didn't know whether he would ever get the answers he wanted and right now, he didn't really care. He tried to tie in where these two men fitted with Elisha, but none of it made any sense to him. She had killed Ray without as much as a second thought and yet, for some reason, Ron was still alive. That was about the extent of his understanding up to now. He wanted to try to get both him and Ron out of here unharmed but was struggling to see how he could achieve it. Elisha had had plenty of opportunity to kill Ron if she had wanted to, but so far, he had been spared. Although if her threats were anything to go by, this scenario would be likely to alter at some point. And it could be soon.

DC Steve Kingham had mostly forgotten about his head wound and the accompanying ache. He assumed that the unfortunate Ray Keller had been responsible for the number of stitches he was likely to require, and that Keller hadn't expected to run into a crazy woman with a crossbow. As Kingham had stood with his back against the wall, he had been allowing the information that he had gleaned from Elisha and Swann to sink in. Although the story of the so-called attempted rape was all very interesting, he was more concerned with the apparent fact that both Swann and Elisha seemed to be oblivious with regard to the murders of the girls and that neither of them could provide an answer as to why Swann had received the photographs he had mentioned. If Swann was being truthful about the murders, then it made some sense to Kingham that he was possibly being set up for a fall. He also wondered exactly what part in this Ray Keller might be playing, if any at all, and why he may have been here to harm Swann. Too many puzzles were yet to be solved, not least who was really behind the murders.

Kingham assumed that he must have had good reason to make himself scarce and that perhaps the details would come to light later. Although, right now, he didn't really know quite how this was going to unfold but if he got out of it alive, then he was going to be very interested in seeing the photographs. However, currently, there was a much more pressing conundrum to solve. Survival.

The man that he had followed to the Riverside Centre was laying in front of him with a bolt in his neck. Given Keller's actions, Kingham was fairly certain that his interest in Karter Swann was as sinister as that of the woman with the crossbow. He wondered whether George Sullivan might be able to shed some light on why Ray Keller was tracking Swann.

Betty remained crouched outside the Storeroom. She had listened hard and heard every word of Elisha's confession. She had had to bite her lip on more than one occasion for fear of releasing a scream of anger at some of things that Elisha had admitted to doing, not to mention the insults that were directed at her. As Elisha disclosed more and more of the facts about what really happened at her house, Betty reflected upon the number of times that she had offered help and support to her sister when they were younger and living with their father like nursing her when she was upset and always keeping watch when she was alone with him. It was galling for her to think of how she had allowed Elisha to take her clothes when their father had refused to buy the things she needed. She remembered the times when she had completed Elisha's college work to save her from her father's scolding tongue and the occasions upon when she had protected her from his abrupt tantrums if she was to as much as forget to release the safety catch before shooting her bow when they went out into the woods on a Saturday morning. As she listened to Elisha's brazen confession, she felt as though her kindness was being thrown back in her face.

It was hard, even now, for Betty to feel a sense of bitter indignation towards Elisha, but she could feel it brewing up inside her for the first time. After everything that had happened over the recent years, after having wrongfully developed a scathing hatred for the man she once loved, after thinking that he had ran from the murders of those girls, after falling for Elisha's scam, there was one thing that Betty knew.

She had not lost Karter Swann. She had lost her sister.

EIGHTY

Golden Valley, Minneapolis, Minnesota.

The temperature had risen considerably during the day and most of the garden was now just wet, rather than a crisp, thin carpet of freshly laid snow. The red Pines had all but lost the layers of frozen ice crystals that they had been carrying, and the impatient gathering of local people had mostly dispersed. Just a few hardened souls remained across the street in anticipation of seeing something exciting take place. But their hopes were waning with every minute of the unscheduled delay.

Half an hour had elapsed since Big Toni had temporarily halted proceedings at the Nelson residence. He and Bonner had retreated to their patrol car to warm up a little. Big Toni tried to formulate some kind of message to send to his Control Room. It wasn't easy. The reality of what had caused him to stop what they were doing simply wasn't going to sound good on the radio. So, he made something up.

'So let me get this straight Bonner. Are you telling me that you saw her?'

White dress.

'I guess so, Captain.'

'Is she still there?'

Pale blue cardigan.

'No, Captain.'

'And now you're telling me that you know where she is? Just like that?'

Auburn hair.

'Think so,' nodded Bonner.

And something else.

Bonner had run out of any kind of believable explanation in support of what he had told Big Toni, and he hadn't even got to the best bit. He didn't even know whether to believe it himself anymore. But there was an added extra piece of information that he simply didn't know how to describe to his Captain. Even to Bonner, it all seemed quite ridiculous. *I can't be seeing these things. Maybe I never saw any of it. Not in the street, not in my den. None of it.*

'So, how come you suddenly know where she is? Did she speak to you?' asked an exasperated Captain Rodrigues, in disbelief.

'Not exactly, Captain.'

'Well, what *exactly* Bonner?'

That was the difficult part for Patrol Officer Gregory Bonner. He was as certain as he could be that Big Toni wasn't going to accept his story, and yet he didn't have a more plausible one. *Why should he believe it? Why should I even believe it?*

As the smoke had slowly cleared, Bonner had looked across the street and seen her image standing a few yards away from the small crowd of people. There was no mistaking her beautiful face, her lovely kind eyes, and her gorgeous auburn hair. She was just as he had remembered her. She looked straight at him, almost through him. She wore the same slightly sorrowful expression that he seen so many times before. *Help me.* Even in the den, she never really smiled. *Perhaps that was because she was never really there,* he thought.

'Bonner, I can't wait around here all day for you to come up with some crazy story about seeing a dead girl. Look, I'm sorry, but you gotta give me something here. Otherwise, I'm going to start digging. The Deputy Chief isn't going to be overjoyed if I tell him that you saw a ghost and therefore, we stopped what we were doing, and all packed up and went home. You gotta appreciate that I'm sticking my neck on the block just supporting your idea that she's somewhere in this garden after all these years, and Deputy Chief Bolton will have to answer to those above him if he has to try to explain why we wasted so many resources on this wild goose chase. And then to top it all off, there's this fabrication from Ken Toft. Damn, Bonner, you do understand that don't you?'

'Hastings,' said Bonner.

'What?'

'Hastings,' he repeated, with a nod.

'The dog? What about it?' said Big Toni.

'He was next to her in the street.'

Big Toni looked around him, towards the other side of the street.

'They're gone,' said Bonner.

Big Toni looked at Bonner. His mind was churning but he couldn't see the connection.

'What? Have you finally cracked, Bonner?' he said.

'I think she was telling me where she is,' said Bonner, as he wiped a lone tear from his cheek.

'Bonner?'

'I think she's been buried with the dog,' he said.

A weird atmosphere filled the patrol car. Just as if a cloud of calmness had descended upon them. Big Toni had nothing to say for once, and Bonner simply had no more to add. In one respect he felt stupid, but yet in another, he felt as though he had found her. The two men allowed the bizarre moment to linger in the patrol car while they tried to decide what to do next. Big Toni thought hard about his next move. Whatever he chose to do, he knew that he would have to warrant his actions to the Deputy Chief. Bonner just sat in stunned silence. He could see that Big Toni was lightly tapping his fingers on the steering wheel as his options ran through his mind. In the end there was only one thing to do.

'Right,' said Big Toni, as if he had arrived at a decision.

Bonner looked at his Captain but didn't speak. He wasn't entirely sure what was coming next.

'OK. Let's do it, then. I've followed your daft ideas so far. No point stopping now,' he said.

Bonner gave a crooked smile and a tiny nod and hoped that his Captain wouldn't suddenly change his mind. *This is it,* he thought.

Big Toni was out of the car quickly and moving towards the excavator operators with their new instructions, as Bonner went to speak with Ken Toft to tell him that he wasn't going to be needed anymore and to remind him that he was to stay put until Captain Rodrigues told him otherwise.

Once the large white screens were erected around the area, obscuring the view from the street, Big Toni and Bonner reconvened at the site of Hastings' grave. Both men stood motionless as the excavator rumbled from behind the shed and into its new position, unseen from the street, much to the disappointment of those that had patiently waited.

'If we do find her, I'll send a message back to Control, then we'll get the whole team out here; Forensic Archaeologists and all. We can manage for now, but I promise you that if there is one bone that doesn't appear to belong to old Hastings, I'll stop everything and let the circus begin.' said Big Toni.

'Ok,' said Bonner, thinking that he knew what Big Toni meant by 'circus'.

'You ready, Bonner?'

'Yeah, I'm ready, Captain.'

Big Toni waved a hand and the excavator engine rumbled into action once more. Carefully, the small excavator removed small slices of earth. With each movement, Bonner and Big Toni stooped forwards and peered at the ground. They didn't expect the old dog to be too far down. Once the top layers of soil had been removed, Big Toni signalled to the operator to stop. From now on, it was to be a matter of digging by hand. With the firmest of the recently frozen soil gone, the earth beneath was expected to be much more workable. Using the trowels that had come with them, the excavator operators began to carefully scoop the soil as Big Toni and Bonner watched closely.

Bonner couldn't help himself from looking out towards the street, just in case, but she wasn't there. He actually had a feeling that he wasn't going to see her anymore, at least not in that form. He reckoned that there was probably no need for her to ever appear to him again. He had had his doubts about the images of Caterina but right now, given what he had thought that he had seen, he was inclined to believe that she really did come to him for help. *Maybe.*

The first signs of bones emerged within a few minutes. Big Toni paid close attention to the proceedings as old Hastings' remains saw the light of day for the first time since April 26th, 2010. Bonner was concentrating hard on the bones that had already been revealed. He didn't know quite what to expect. He imagined that the old bones would be white but considering the length of time that they had been in the ground, he thought they could be grey or even brown, altered by the soil and their own decomposition.

As more of the remains of old Hastings were exposed, Bonner began to wonder when he might actually see some evidence of Caterina. As far as he could tell, it looked as though there were enough bones on show to account for old Hastings already. *How far down could she be?*

Big Toni stopped the dig. The excavator operators stepped away from the scene, allowing him and Bonner to carry out a much closer inspection of what had been unearthed so far. They agreed that this did appear to be a host of old dog bones. None of them looked remotely large enough to be considered human. Bonner had no problem viewing the skull and the other larger pieces because he knew that they had not belonged to Caterina. He didn't need a background in archaeology to arrive at that conclusion. But this only meant one of two things. Either she was never here, or she really is somewhere underneath Hastings.

'We can't stop now, Captain. We have to check further down.'
'How far down do you think we need to go?'
'Far enough,' said Bonner.
I promised her. I can't let her down now.

'Yeah, ok, Bonner. A bit further, then I'm calling it off,' said Big Toni.

With the excavator team back to work, Big Toni and Bonner stood beside the old grave in anticipation. All they saw coming out of the grave was earth. Bonner wanted them to dig much further, until he was absolutely certain that she wasn't there, but he was beginning to feel as though this whole episode was going to end in disappointment. It wasn't as though they had gone very far down seeing as Hastings had been buried fairly close to the surface. If the top of the grave had been flush with the ground, then Big Toni would never have stumbled over it in the first place. *The snow was truly beautiful that night,* thought Bonner. He studied the depth of the grave and realised that most of the mound of soil was above ground level. *Why would anyone dig a hole and put the old dog on the top of it?* thought Bonner, as he watched his hopes of finding her diminish in front of him.

'There's nothing else here, Bonner. Just a load of old dog bones,' said Big Toni.

As Gregory Bonner stepped closer to the where the excavator team had been digging, something caught his eye. He reached down to pick up, what looked like a coin. He rubbed the soil off of it, and could see that it was a disc, similar to that found on a dog collar. He studied it and turned it over. It revealed the name *'Hastings'*.

Poor old Hastings, he thought. He had liked the old dog and had always made a fuss of him whenever he had visited the girls, always in hope that Caterina would be there to see Betty. Sometimes she was. Bonner recalled how he used to hang around, just to see her for a little while longer, in the hope that she would speak with him. He was pretty sure that Betty knew what he was doing, and pretty sure that Caterina didn't. He never plucked up the courage to ask her on a date though. That was his biggest regret.

'C'mon, Bonner. Time to wrap this up, and time for me to make up a good excuse to give to Deputy Chief Officer Bolton. Boy, he's gonna pull me to pieces over this.'

Bonner gave a final solemn gaze down into the hole. *Not deep enough.* As he began to extricate himself from the hole, he raised one foot onto the ledge that had been the original ground level and pushed himself up with his standing leg. As he did so, he felt a sort of springiness underfoot. He pushed again. *I definitely felt that.* Bonner stood fully into the hole with both feet on the exposed earth and tried to put some more weight onto the ground. His feet sprung a little again. *There's something under here.* He grabbed at one of the hand trowels that were lying on the grass next to the hole and began to scrape at the soil beneath where he had placed his feet. Bonner peered around the screen and saw that Big Toni was talking to the excavator operators near to the street. *Good,* he thought. He scraped away with an urgency that he didn't even know he possessed. All the time he was aware that Big Toni would soon notice that he wasn't out of there yet. He was bound to turn around, expecting to see Bonner behind him. Not in a hole, digging. Bonner kept on scraping and digging towards whatever it was that felt so odd beneath his feet. As he did so, he could see that Big Toni had registered his absence and was already making his way back into the garden and heading in his direction. *Can't stop now. I promised I would find you.* Bonner knew that his Captain had shouted something, but he was so focussed on his task that he didn't actually have any idea what he had said. He could probably guess, though.

Then he saw something that shook him rigidly. *More bone.* Momentarily, Bonner froze, but he knew that this wasn't the time to stop. He crouched down and placed the trowel on the ground beside him. He felt something rough, something with a sharp edge that reminded him of metal. *A metal sheet?* he thought. He placed his fingers under the edge of it and tried to prise it upwards. It moved. He was gradually bending one corner of it. Now he could see more of the bones. Same colouring, similar look to them but these were connected together differently, somehow, as if there was a familiarity to their shape. As he pulled hard, aware that the sharp edge might cut into his hand at any moment, the earth began to shift a little more.

'Bonner, for crying out loud. What do you think you're doing now?'

Keep going, keep going. As Big Toni approached, he could see that his Patrol Officer was slumped in the hole on his hands and knees. When Big Toni got up to the hole, he heard him. Bonner was sobbing his heart out. Big Toni stopped moving. His eyes bulged at the sight of his Patrol Officer in this state.

'Bonner? Are you ok?'

All Big Toni could hear were more cries, as Bonner held his head in his hands and fell sideways in the hole. Earth was caked on his trouser legs and his hands were filthy. When Bonner looked up at Big Toni, he had earth all over the front of him. His face was a mixture of dirt and tears that streamed like rivers down his cheeks.

'It's her. It's Caterina,' said Bonner.

'How can you be sure, Bonner? Could just be more of the dog's bones,' said Big Toni.

'There's something else,' said Bonner.

Big Toni watched as Bonner held out his hand so that his Captain could see. When he unfurled his fist, Big Toni realised what it was.

'I gave her this. It was the last time that I saw her. Not long before she went missing. I thought she had probably thrown it away. But she didn't. She wore it, Captain, she wore it,' said Bonner as the tears resumed their flow and he crumpled down again.

The ring that Big Toni held was still as beautiful as the day that Caterina had slipped it onto her finger. Bonner knew then that she had worn it for a least a few days before she went missing. She hadn't discarded it. She wore it. Caterina wore his ring, and he never knew. The whole discovery had pole-axed Gregory Bonner. The sadness at her disappearance revisited him and hit him like a train, once again. If there was any sort of small consolation, it was that he had found her, just like he had promised. Big Toni assisted Bonner out of the hole and held him in his strong arms. Bonner was crying like a baby.

'I'll send that message now,' he said.

Telling Alexandria Org of the recent discovery was never going to be easy but Bonner and Big Toni both agreed that it should come from them and not a total stranger. Bonner tidied himself up as much as he possibly could. He ended up wearing a pair of Big Toni's spare trousers that he had stashed in the trunk of his patrol car. It was a good job that there was a belt to hold them up. After a quick inspection both men decided that he was presentable enough and that nobody would notice, providing they didn't look too hard, and providing the belt didn't give way. A stiff brush had managed to remove almost all of the earth from his boots too. And so, after all these years, it was time to break the news.

Before Bonner and Big Toni left the scene securely in the hands of the local police, they sat in the car and pieced together all of the information they now had about Caterina's disappearance and how she had ended up in Wade Nelson's garden. They knew that some of the finer details might never surface but neither of them could get away from the fact that it looked as though it was Wade Nelson that had killed her and buried her, and that after all those years, he had finally hung himself, consumed with the guilt and tormented by the possibility of her being discovered. Both men decided that it all added up. As for why and what really happened, it might remain a mystery and die with Wade Nelson. From what they knew, there certainly didn't seem to be any reason to suspect anyone else in her killing. Unless any new information was uncovered by the Forensic Anthropologist. The chances of a witness suddenly appearing were extremely improbable, and Bonner was sure that the girls had no idea about the events of April 26th, 2010. It had appeared that she simply didn't reach the front door of the Nelson property and the only doubt as to why appeared to lie firmly with Wade Nelson.

On the way to the Org's property, somewhere that Bonner still thought of as Caterina's house, he and his Captain, having concluded the likeliest outcome of her disappearance, tried their best to prepare for the next chapter in this lengthy saga. The news that they were about to deliver weighed heavily upon them both. They needn't have worried.

'You've found her, haven't you?' said Alexandria Org.

As Big Toni and Bonner had reached the porch at the Org's front door, it had opened, and Alexandria had immediately spoken. She explained to the puzzled officers that she had seen their car pull up next to the sidewalk and watched them get out. It was in their faces, she explained, and the way they walked up the path. She knew instantly. She described how something in the pit of her stomach had churned even more than it had been doing for many years. Today wasn't all that different in the end. She had watched them get closer and closer to the front door and by the time she decided to open it, there were no doubts left in her mind as to the purpose of their visit. She knew from what the neighbours were saying that something was going on at the old Nelson house, but she was not inclined to go to see what it was all about. She didn't need to. She had even mentioned to her husband that this was their last chance at finding Caterina. It was the last place that Caterina was expected to have been. After the search and rescue report had revealed nothing, she had all but given up. If she wasn't there, then she could have been almost anywhere else in the State or even in the country, or perhaps in the World.

'It was that man, wasn't it? Wade Nelson,' she said.

'I can't confirm that for definite, Mrs Org, but it does appear to be one of the stronger possibilities at the moment. What I can say is that I promise to keep you updated,' answered Big Toni.

'Of course. Forgive me. My mind has been racing with all the questions that I would ask you and yet all of a sudden, the time doesn't feel right.'

Conner Org had appeared behind her and put his arms around her. His face was ashen. It was one of those moments that could not be erased from memory. Bonner had not been fully prepared for this and began to struggle to hold back the tears again. Big Toni noticed and gave him a nudge, but it didn't go unnoticed.

'It's ok. It really is. I know how much she meant to you, and you to her,' said Alexandria.

Bonner looked up at her, slightly confused. He wanted to ask but didn't think it was really the right time.

'She told me that she liked you. A lot, really. But she didn't tell Betty or Elisha and she made me promise not to say, so I didn't. I wanted to but I would never break her trust,' she said.

For a moment, the four of them looked at each other in a stony silence.

'We found a ring,' said Big Toni.

'Ah, was it the one that you gave her? I looked everywhere for it,' she said to Bonner, 'She so liked it. She came home that day like a lovesick schoolgirl. I suppose she was in fact. I told her not to wear it for college because somebody was bound to ask questions, but as soon as she got home, she would slip it on. Then she would take it off again before she went to see Betty. But I guess she must have forgotten that day, Betty being so upset and all.'

'I guess so, Ma'am,' said Big Toni.

'What am I thinking? I should invite you in.'

'There's no need, Ma'am. We're not exactly dressed to come inside. Perhaps another time,' said Big Toni.

'As you wish,' she said.

'Forgive us for knocking on your door like this but we felt that…we thought that…'

'You thought that I would want to know. Well, of course, you're right, and I thank you from the bottom of my heart for all your efforts. It can't have been easy after all this time,' she said.

'It wasn't,' said Bonner, feebly.

Alexandria Org looked at Bonner with kindness in her eyes and a smile that filled him with a strange ambivalence. It was at that moment that Bonner knew that he had fulfilled his promise to Caterina. He could almost see Caterina's eyes in her mother's. Bonner had no words. He had nothing that he could say. Big Toni put his arm around Bonner's shoulders and steered him away from the front door as he explained to the Orgs that he would be in touch with any information that may be divulged as the investigation unfolded. His Patrol Officer had legs like jelly.

'Yes, thank you. Thank you for everything you've done.'

As the two officers reached the Patrol car, Bonner glanced up and down the street. It was deserted but for a few parked cars. *Of course, she isn't here,* he thought.

EIGHTY-ONE

The Riverside Centre, Tilbury, East London.

There was only a feeble light coming from the Storeroom, coupled with a dim glow from the bar, that provided any degree of illumination. The rest of the courtyard was more or less in darkness. Betty Nelson knew that she couldn't just cower out of sight indefinitely, although up to now, she hadn't had any choice. If Elisha were to suddenly come striding out of the Storeroom, Betty would be directly in her line of fire. Elisha had Karter at her mercy, so she had to think of something, and soon. As for Ron, she knew that wasn't his real name. She had briefly noticed his name that appeared on his warrant card, when he showed her it. Steve Kingham. Of course, Betty was fully aware that he was a police officer and could understand why he had chosen to give Elisha a false name, although she wouldn't have known any different if he had said 'Steve'.

What worried her most right now, was that there was little if any conversation coming from the Storeroom. Whilst Elisha was telling her story, at least she wasn't putting people in her sights. Betty raised her head as much as she dared in order to take another peek through one of the windowpanes in the sliding door. She moved very slowly and carefully, ensuring that she made no sound. First, she saw the back of Elisha's head. Swann was standing to the left side of the room and Kingham to the right. However rapidly Elisha thought she could cock the Cobra RX, Betty knew that she couldn't possibly kill both of them. Obviously, the two men were not in any position to test the theory as one of them would end up with a bolt in them.

Whilst Elisha held all the cards, nothing was going to change. Swann had tried to talk her out of it by explaining how weak her plan was, but she was having none of it. The only way that Betty could see that Elisha could regain the situation was to kill Kingham. She didn't need him there. He was an added complication to her plan. If her threats were anything to go by, it was Swann that she wanted. Ray Keller was dead, but she had made things more difficult by not killing Kingham as soon as she saw him. One more death wouldn't really have worsened anything, and it would all be blamed on Betty, as far as Elisha was concerned. After all, what did she have to lose? She was already in deep.

Betty had considered a few options of how she could help but none of them were feasible while the bow was loaded. If she could somehow get Elisha to fire, without killing anyone else, then she might just have enough time to interrupt the stalemate and shift the advantage to Swann and Kingham. *Reload in a heartbeat, no way. You're an awkward sod. You have never once beaten me to the reload.*

------

8 minutes ago, two police cars had arrived at the Riverside Centre. The team of 4 that Sutton had sent to check on Kingham were now inside. They had seen the light coming from the upstairs windows and were currently making their way across the dancefloor towards the bar. In no time at all they would be on the staircase that led down to the courtyard. Then things would become very unpredictable and could be even more dangerous for everyone.

If I can make her fire, I can disable her. Then the boys can take it from there. But how?

Betty looked around her. She needed a distraction and yet, at the same time, she couldn't afford to make a noise or be seen. Elisha was like a loose cannon with the Cobra RX in her hands. Betty couldn't see her changing her mind regarding her intentions. If she had to kill Kingham as well, then she was sure that she would do.

Something caught her eye. A movement. A shadow that flickered across the courtyard. She looked back towards the staircase and saw the shape of a man descending it. A woman and two other men were behind him. *Police! Oh, please don't make a noise,* she thought. She knew that she had to warn them somehow. She fancied that she only had one shot at making them remain quiet. All she could think to do was to allow them to see her, and press her finger against her lips, and hope that they got the message. A torchlight beam shone up to the top floor of the building opposite her. *Please don't shine that thing down here.*

Betty had to make her move whether she liked it or not. She moved as quietly as possible towards the officers with her finger against her lips and let out the quietest *shhh* that she could muster and still be heard. Luckily the officers got the message. One by one, they slowly made their way to where Betty sat crouched outside the Storeroom once more. It was all down to hand signals and almost silent whispers now. Betty put her head to the ear of the first officer and whispered that Kingham was inside and that a woman was holding a loaded crossbow to him and another man. Another was already dead. As the message made its way down the line, the fourth officer quietly scurried away to the far end of the courtyard to use his radio. *Right. Now the cavalry are coming,* thought Betty. The other three had realised the gravity of the situation and turned their individual radios off.

Inside the Storeroom, Kingham had spotted the torchlight from where he was standing and knew precisely what it meant. A certain amount of relief ran through his body, but he was still very much trapped in a dangerous situation without an exit strategy.

Swann had managed to get Elisha talking again. From the little that Betty had just overheard it sounded as though he was trying to convince Elisha that she didn't have to carry this out and that they could be together after all. By this time in the proceedings, Betty knew that he was simply resorting to desperate measures, and by the sounds of it, it wasn't working. Elisha's tone sounded much more agitated, and Betty knew that when she got in this mood, she usually exploded into a fit of anger, and with a Cobra RX in her grasp, that really wasn't a good scenario.

Time is just about up, she thought. She knew that the police weren't about to rush in. The stakes were far too high, especially with Kingham in there, and that she couldn't show herself to her deranged sibling. *So, something else. But what?* Then she saw it. In a way it was not what she would have chosen, but she didn't have the luxury of choice right now. She knew how Elisha hated them too. Betty felt that it would provide the perfect disturbance and render her sister into a state of hysteria. Maybe that would provide enough time for her to disarm her. She reached out and took the rain-soaked, dead rat by its spindly tail. It hung in front of her. As repulsive as she found it, she felt as though this was her best option. Now to get the conversation guided onto the right path. Betty held the rat up at the window and hoped that Karter would be able to see it. Her eyes and Karter's met, and it appeared as far as she could tell that he got the message. She waited for a lull in the talking and hoped.

'There are hundreds of rats around here, Elisha.'

Bingo, thought Betty. Elisha began to instinctively look around her feet.

'If one comes near me, I'll kill it.'

'They often come in here at night. Sometimes I've seen ten or twenty of them,' said Swann.

'I've seen at least two since we've been here,' said Kingham.

Excellent. Now we're a team, thought Betty.

'Arghh! Disgusting things,' she said, looking around the room.

Swann and Kingham took turns to wind Elisha up about the rats and Betty waited for the right moment. That was the riskiest part because she had to be successful or who knows what might happen next. Betty gave a deft nod to her newest friends outside and prepared to make her move. The three officers closest to her were ready. She gave one quick look into the window to make absolutely sure of where Elisha was standing and then shifted herself towards the opening to the Storeroom. *Get this right. It must work.*

Betty swung the rat by its tail and let it fly. She wanted it to appear to fall from above Elisha so that she didn't have the opportunity to sidestep it. It would have lost its effect if it had missed, but her aim was true. The rat landed perfectly on top of the Cobra RX. It brushed Elisha's arm and chest as it fell onto the top of the bow and balanced momentarily on the flight groove, the track where the bolt rested. The ensuing scream told Betty that she had hit her target. Elisha stepped back into a beer barrel and in her panic, squeezed the trigger of the bow, sending a bolt thudding up into the rafters above her head. *You can't reload faster than I can run.*

Elisha was so preoccupied with reaching for the bow and worrying about the rat that she didn't even see Betty coming. What she felt next was an impact on the back of her legs as Betty threw herself into her from behind. Elisha fell backwards, landing on the top of the beer barrel and gave a cry of pain as the Cobra RX bounced harmlessly on the stone floor. Kingham was on top of them both in a flash. He jammed his knee into Elisha's back and pinned her to the cold, stone floor. Elisha screamed and swore and flailed her arms at anyone that she could hit but it was over. With Kingham's weight on her back and Betty laying across her legs, all Elisha could do was swear and thrash until she could move no longer. Had she checked the inside pocket of Kingham's jacket, she would have found the handcuffs that she was now wearing. Swann ran to Betty and helped her to her feet. As the police officers secured their arrest and radioed for assistance in order to get a van in which to house Elisha, Kingham thanked Betty for everything that she had done, not least, caring for him after he had become the victim of Ray Keller's assault. Betty just smiled and told him not to worry.

'Thanks, anyway. I'll leave you two to talk. From what I heard; you've got some catching up to do. And Swann, don't go too far. We haven't finished talking to you just yet.'

'I'm not going anywhere. I have everything I need right here,' he said, putting his arm around Betty and pulling her close to him.

EIGHTY-TWO

Ahuja Industries, East London.

DI Sutton had got everyone into position. DCI Blackery and half of the Operation Liberate team were hiding out of sight, crouching behind a large concrete storage bunker, while the rest of them had found a variety of nooks and crannies to hunker down in. Each of the armed officers had ensured a clear view of the entrance to this part of the factory. Sutton had Angelica hiding with him behind a portacabin not far from where he expected William Abbot to appear at any moment. Everywhere was silent. He looked around for Carrie but didn't see her immediately.

'Stay quiet,' he whispered to Angelica, now free of her annoying tape.

She nodded in response.

Stripes innocently wandered into the factory and sniffed around, followed by Socks and Speckle. Angelica wanted to go to them to tell them she was going to be ok, but obviously knew that that would be rather silly right now. *Boys, I love you,* she thought. Then the foxes startled as the scrape of the metal gate echoed in the factory. He was coming.

Sutton continued to look around to make sure that everyone was completely out of sight, and then he saw something move up above him, on the walkway where Angelica had been discovered. It was Carrie. The brief movement Sutton saw was Carrie, throwing Angelica's blanket over herself.

'Oh, for Christ's sake, Carrie,' he mumbled quietly to himself.

Sutton knew that it was too late to do anything about it now. Angelica pushed herself against Sutton and buried her head into his chest as William Abbot appeared and began to ascend the stairs. He was wearing a boiler suit and a mask, just like the ones found in the wardrobe in Greaves' bedroom. Sutton wondered where he had got those things from. He thought that everything had been removed from 38, Rodina Close when the search had been completed. *Obviously, there are others.*

Abbot trudged up the stairs to the walkway. He had a red and black rucksack over his left shoulder. Angelica was peeping. *Breakfast,* she thought, causing her stomach to rumble. Sutton watched Abbot as he walked slowly towards the heap of blankets and the ropes that were still attached to the pipework on the factory wall. What he didn't know was what Carrie's plan was. '*Let him come to you*', Patricia had said. Sutton was convinced that Carrie was unlikely to come to any harm, given that she had a host of armed officers a matter of a few yards away. If Abbot appeared to put Carrie into danger, even for a second, then one of the officers would floor him with one swift shot. Sutton knew that Abbot had several weapons pointed at him right now, so he wasn't unduly concerned. He also trusted that Carrie's karate expertise would serve its purpose if necessary. Abbot certainly wouldn't be prepared for that.

Abbot stopped about ten yards from Carrie and took the rucksack from his shoulder, placing it carefully down on the walkway. He knelt beside it and began to loosen the drawstring and pulled open the top of it. Although Carrie couldn't see precisely what he was doing, she was listening intently to every sound, gauging exactly how far away he was from where she huddled silently beneath the blanket. *Angelica must have been terrified,* she thought. Sutton and Angelica were both watching every move from their secluded position behind the portacabin. Angelica found it really strange to see him doing the things that he had done for her on so many occasions. It was like watching a film of her own experiences, unfolding right in front of her. She had seen him many times, even heard him say something weird occasionally, but she had never seen the face behind the mask. *When they get you, I want to know exactly who you are,* she thought. *I hope they let me punch you in the face.*

Carrie could hear him breathing heavily. *Obviously, not very fit,* she thought. As she lay silently under the blanket, she held a canister of pepper spray in her hand, just in case things became difficult. Whatever happened in the next few moments, Carrie was in no doubt that he had nowhere to run and that there was next to no chance of him escaping. She knew it was all over for William Abbot and that finally they had managed to ensnare their prey. As he took a paper bag out from the rucksack, Angelica's stomach rumbled again. She instinctively knew what was most likely to be in it. There had been very little variation since she had been incarcerated in the cold and damp atmosphere of the factory. She was lucky to find anything that she would consider substantial, unless it was Chinese but that was rare. The usual roll filled with something just about recognisable was about as good as it ever got. Each time it was accompanied by a bottle of water. Angelica often wondered where he got these things from but decided that she didn't really want to know. Certainly, they didn't come from one of the delicatessens that she used to frequent, but it was food and water, and it kept her alive.

Sutton looked across in the direction of the large concrete storage bunker, where DCI Blackery had been hiding from Abbot's view. He could just see his face peering out. There were two armed officers close to him, but Abbot was never going to spot them at this angle. Sutton was waiting for Carrie to make her move before he raised the order for the team to rush William Abbot. Initially the armed officers would make themselves known, followed by Sutton and Blackery and the rest of the team. He knew that Angelica was safe and would leave her behind the portacabin until the arrest was secured. *Come on Carrie, you're enjoying this far too much,* he thought. Sutton didn't mind giving Carrie the honour of the arrest as long as she was safe.

Angelica watched with interest as Abbot stepped closer to the heap of blankets and held the paper bag out in front of him.

That's odd! Why doesn't he just put it down, like he always does? He never used to hand it to me, she thought. As Carrie held a corner of the blanket in her grasp and prepared to whisk it off her to deliver her surprise, she heard him mumble something. Her eyes widened and she remained still. Carrie recognised what he had said but became confused by it. *That didn't make sense,* she thought.

'Did you hear that,' Angelica whispered to Sutton.

He shook his head and put his finger to his lips, encouraging her to keep quiet. Angelica's mind was now working overtime. She was remembering the few times when she had heard him speak, like the time when he was brushing her hair and when he scurried out of the factory, and she thought that he was crying. Also, the time when he had accidently trodden on her when he was about to leave. But although her recollection of these moments wasn't crystal clear, she felt that something was wrong with what she had just heard. *Something's different,* she thought.

Carrie knew that she couldn't wait there any longer. The team were in position, and she knew it would just be a matter of an arrest being affected. Abbot had walked into the trap and Angelica was finally safe... *So, what am I waiting for?* she thought. Carrie could feel that he had stepped even closer to her, and she was sure that he didn't have any sort of weapon in his possession because the team would have acted way before this if he had. It was time.

Sutton and Angelica watched as Carrie swiftly pulled the blanket off her.

'Hello, William,' she said.

'Hello,' he replied, as if it was the most normal thing in the world to say.

Angelica stared at the scene that had unfolded on the walkway above. *Wrong,* she thought. Carrie had rapidly got herself into a crouched position and driven the sole of her foot into the side of Abbot's knee. He crumbled with a yelp and landed heavily, dropping the breakfast bag over the side of the railing. She shoved him down onto the steel walkway and used her handcuffs to quickly secure his hands behind him. There was no resistance from Abbot. Sutton and Blackery were already on their way up towards the landing as the rest of the team hurried out from their respective concealed locations. All of sudden the silence in the factory was shattered by the echoes of stomping feet and raised voices, shouting instructions to one another. As Sutton made sure that Carrie was ok and ordered the team to remove Abbot from the factory, Angelica watched on. Once Abbot had been hauled down the staircase, she stepped out from behind the portacabin and moved to within touching distance of William Abbot as he was being man-handled towards her. Angelica couldn't just let him be taken away without having the opportunity to see what he looked like. She had waited long enough. She stood entirely in the way of the team as they frogmarched their captive towards the factory entrance. She wasn't scared any more, she had no real reason to be now. He was done for.

'Angelica. No,' shouted Sutton, as he and Carrie quickly descended the stairs.

'Show me,' she shouted, 'Show me his face.'

'Angelica,' shouted Carrie.

The officers that were holding Abbot tried to push passed her, but she refused to move. They had enough of a task holding onto Abbot without trying to push aside Angelica. Sutton and Carrie were running towards her, but it was too late. Angelica reached up with two hands and grabbed at the mask. She pulled it with such force that Abbot's head bowed down towards his waist. It was off. Angelica threw the mask to one side in anger. For the first time Angelica could see the face that she had wanted to see for so long. She stared at him with clenched fists, and he stared back. It was a surreal moment for Angelica. After countless days she was finally looking at the man that had taken her from her family and friends. His face looked expressionless and paler than she imagined it might be. Her eyes were filled with hatred but his looked empty. Worst of all, she didn't know him.

'Get him out of here,' ordered Sutton.

The officers all but dragged Abbot away as Carrie took Angelica's arm and asked if she was hurt at all.

'I'm fine,' she said.

'You shouldn't have done that. You might have been hurt,' said Carrie.

'I don't care. I had to see his face.'

'Do you know him?' asked Sutton.

Angelica shook her head.

'You're safe now, Angelica. Let's get you to the paramedics. They will need to check you over before we reunite you with your family,' said Carrie.

'There was another girl.'

'Another?' said Carrie.

'When?' said Sutton.

'Before. I don't know when. I heard her cry. I used a piece of broken mirror to see where she was. I never spoke to her, but I saw him with her. I saw what he was doing. He had her wrapped up in a white sheet and he carried her out. I'm sure I saw blood. Did you ever find her?'

Carrie and Sutton exchanged telling glances.

'Oh,' said Angelica.

Sutton called to one of the team to take Angelica out to the ambulance. He told her that they would talk again once she had been checked over. As she walked away, he turned to Carrie.

'What the hell do you think you were doing?'

'I didn't have time to get down,' she said.

'You had plenty of time. Angelica got down,' he reasoned.

'Yeah, well…'

'Sometimes you…' he began.

Sutton looked towards the factory entrance as he heard Angelica shouting.

Now what? he thought.

She was running back towards him and Carrie with a helpless officer in pursuit, saying something, but Sutton couldn't make it out. Before he and Carrie could move, she was back beside them.

'What did he say?' she said.

'What did who say?' asked Sutton.

'No, not you. I'm talking to her. What did he say to you?'

'He didn't say anything,' said Carrie.

'He did. When you were up there, he said something to you.'

'It was nothing. It wouldn't make any sense to you anyway,' she said.

'I want to know,' said Angelica, raising her voice again.

'He just said 'hello''.

'Well, that's not right for a start. He wouldn't say hello. But what else?'

'Wouldn't? I don't know what you mean,' said Carrie.

'He said something else, before you said hello.'

'He called me a name, that's all.'

'A name? What name?' asked Angelica.

'Yeah, what name?' said Sutton.

'Marion. It's nothing for you to worry about,' said Carrie.

'Marion? So that was it. Marion. Oh, for goodness sake, I'm so stupid,' said Angelica, spinning around on the spot with her hands on her head.

'What about it?' asked Sutton.

'I thought he was saying 'marry me',' said Angelica.

'Hold on. Did he say it to you often?' asked Sutton.

'A few times. I always thought it was really weird. As if I'd want to marry *him*.'

'How many times did he call you Marion?' asked Sutton.

'I don't know, maybe four or something. He nearly threw me off the top once too.'

'What, from up there?' asked Carrie.

'Yes. It was this one time when he came and I thought he was just bringing me my food, as usual, but he didn't give me any. Well, not straight away. It was really scary. He untied me and I wanted to run but I couldn't get past him, and then he pushed me back towards the edge of the landing. I couldn't do anything. Then he grabbed at me. I thought I was dead. I thought he was going to kill me. But he held me out over the edge. He was like a mad man. He was really strong. In the end, I fainted, but when I came to, I found myself on the landing and what was really nuts was my food was next to me, as if nothing had happened.'

'Where was he?' asked Carrie.

'He'd gone.'

Sutton and Carrie were thinking the same thing. They understood the association with the name Marion, and now there was a story of Angelica being threatened with a fall, potentially to her death. Just like Marion. Sutton ushered Angelica and the officer away to the waiting ambulance once more and turned to Carrie.

'Marion? What was that all about?' he asked her.

'It's got to be the association that Patricia was talking about. The fact that he sort of replaced his sisters with innocent victims.'

'Stepsisters,' said Sutton.

'What? Oh, yeah, whatever,' said Carrie.

'So, to him, Jennifer and Joanna were Haley and Claudia?' asked Sutton.

'And to him, Angelica was Marion, which is why she came to no actual harm. She was the one he loved.'

'I wonder how long he was going to keep her here?'

'Who knows?' said Carrie, looking back up to the landing.

'Right, come on, let's get back to…Oh, hell, now what?' said Sutton.

'I'll go,' said Carrie, as she began to run towards the commotion 100 yards further down the factory.

Sutton broke into a trot and followed her to where Angelica was kicking and screaming to get free from the officer who was doing his level best to get her to leave with him.

'I need to tell them,' said Angelica.

'Angelica, hold on. It's ok, I'm here,' said Carrie.

Angelica continued pulling away from her protector.

'It's ok, Bob, she'll be fine with me now.'

The officer let Angelica go and turned away.

'What's this about?' asked Carrie, as Sutton arrived next to her.

'He wouldn't let me go. I told him I had something to tell you, but he keep saying that I had to go to the ambulance and…'

'Angelica. Calm down. We're here now so what is it?' said Carrie.

'Look, since I've been here, I've had little else to do than cry and worry but then I started thinking about, what if I get out? What if I find myself free?'

'So?' said Sutton.

'So, I started to try to memorise some things about him in case I ever got the chance to describe him to…well you, the Police.'

'And?' said Carrie.

'There were certain things that he always did. Like he never spoke to me.'

'But you said that he called you Marion,' said Sutton.

'I know. I mean he never actually said anything else like in a direct way. He never said hello, like he did to you. Not once. I never had any sort of conversation with him. I tried once or twice but it didn't work,' explained Angelica.

'Go on,' said Carrie.

'Well, he also never taped my mouth. But last night he did. I couldn't understand why he did that. It wasn't how things usually played out. He was very much for a strict routine, but that was different.'

'Anything else?' said Sutton.

'Yeah. He's right-handed.'

'What about it?' asked Carrie.

'Well, you couldn't have seen because you were under that blanket, but he held the food out in his left hand. He just never did that, that's all. I just know, alright? And he used his right hand when he brushed my hair too.'

'That was something that Margaret said about. He was the only one that Marion would allow to brush her hair,' Carrie said to Sutton.

'Yeah, I remember reading that,' replied Sutton.

'So, what about the other thing then?' asked Angelica.

'What other thing?' said Carrie.

'That tape over my mouth. I heard you coming, you know. I didn't actually know it was you, I thought it was him, but I heard some crashing and banging going on. But I couldn't shout out if wanted to,' Angelica said.

'So, he never taped your mouth before last night?' asked Sutton.

'No. Maybe he didn't want me to shout out. I don't know. Bit weird,' said Angelica.

'But he didn't know we were coming,' said Carrie.

'*He* didn't,' said Sutton.

'What do you mean?' asked Carrie.

'Ask yourself who *did* know,' said Sutton.

'You mean…Greaves?'

'Greaves? Robin fucking Greaves? Oh, I'm sorry…,'said Angelica, cupping her hand over her mouth.

'Acceptable, in the circumstances,' said Carrie.

'Yes, yes. For God's sake, I'm so stupid,' said Angelica, putting her hands on top of her head again and doing another spin around.

'Why? What do you mean?' asked Sutton.

'He *did* speak to me. Once. It was when he stepped on my leg, by accident. That was when he actually spoke in a normal voice, but I didn't recognise it. I tried to think but it just didn't register with me. But that was it. That was it. That was Robin fucking Greaves. I'm such a twat.'

'Twit, perhaps,' said Carrie.

'I'm so sorry,' said Angelica.

'Right. Angelica, I want you to go to the paramedics now, and this time I mean it. We'll have plenty of opportunity to talk later after you've been reunited with your family. Now, go please, we'll both catch up with you shortly,' said Sutton.

Angelica turned away and skipped towards the awaiting group of paramedics with the sort of freedom of movement that she had dreamt about so many times. Once Sutton could see that she was definitely in their care at last, he and Carrie made their way back to his car. Once inside, they began to piece together their latest theory. Sutton began.

'Ok, so, why did he tape her mouth?'

'To stop her screaming out?' said Carrie.

'Yes, I know that, but why? According to her he had never done it before. There must have been a good reason this time. She said herself he was a creature of habit.'

'So, if she couldn't shout out, she would be harder to find? Maybe he was just trying to make it more difficult for us.'

'But what would be the point? He had already told us whereabouts she was being kept. It would only be a matter of time, anyway,' he said.

'But it would still take us longer than telling us exactly where she was.'

'So, was he playing a game…dragging it out as long as he could? What's the point in that?' said Sutton.

'I don't know,' she said.

'Was it a matter of time?' said Sutton.

'Or a matter of timing?' said Carrie.

'I don't get what you mean.'

'Well, if it was Greaves after all, then he would need to make sure that we arrest William for the whole thing by catching him red-handed. He would need to be sure that we caught him with Angelica.'

'Right, but he gave us everything we needed last night at the interview. We had the location and we had William on his way. William was the one that bullied Greaves and William was the one that killed Marion and then took out some weird revenge for the way his stepsisters treated him by murdering the other two. What was the point of taping Angelica's mouth this time?' he said.

'What if he hadn't?' she said.

'What if he hadn't what?' said Sutton.

'Taped her mouth,' said Carrie.

'Well, then…she could have shouted to us once she knew that it was us. But we'd have still found her eventually.'

'Yes, but we'd have found her sooner,' she said.

'So what?'

'So, William wouldn't have been there. At least if we had found Angelica, say, an hour earlier, the whole place would have been swarming with Police investigators and Forensics, etc, etc, and William would have scarpered at first sight of them. That wasn't enough for Greaves, I think he wanted William to be unable to wriggle out,' she said.

'So, by taping her mouth and keeping her relatively silent, he bought some more time. We would take longer to find her, and William would have enough time to get there to deliver her breakfast. Is that why he dragged out the interview? So that we wouldn't be out looking for her until the appropriate time of the morning, when he had William primed to take Angelica her breakfast? Do you think he had it planned down to the last detail? Surely that's a bit too much to expect.'

'He knew when William would be leaving and knew more or less when we would be on our way to the factory, so, ok, I agree with you that it was a bit of a shaky plan, but he would have had a pretty good idea of the timings. Not only that, but I also don't think William knew that he was taking the breakfast to Angelica. I think he thought that he was going to see Marion again. I think Greaves, or Michael Abbot was the manipulator in all this. He's not as daft as he appears. He used William as a scapegoat for a lot of it. He had him stay at his house on that mattress and he cruelly teased him by making him believe that Marion was still alive. As for who really pushed Marion down the stairs, I don't know but I reckon he planned it out,' she said.

'So, are you telling me that Greaves or whatever he calls himself is not the simpleton that he appears to be? That it's William?'

'Yep. Remember when Greaves said that he saw a man talking to Angelica in Trenton Street on the day she went missing?'

'William?'

'Yep, but she didn't recognise him today so maybe he was made to look different in some way. And when those photographs were found…I reckon he had William take the pictures. Also, I don't think that Aimee's story is totally wrong. It was difficult to rely on what Margaret, Mrs Abbot, said but I think a lot of it was true. It was just mixed up. Even Aimee thought that the stories related to William. Maybe Greaves had primed Margaret on the occasions that he visited.'

'What about William's arrest and time served for hitting that girl? That was real,' said Sutton.

'Yeah, well, doesn't mean he did it does it? I mean, at least not voluntarily. Maybe Greaves forced him to do it and knew that he would do as he was told and just take the punishment. Maybe he set him up to be the aggressor knowing full well that he planned to kill soon.'

'What was with the horrible tattoos that he scratched on the girls?' he said.

'Swann. At that time, he tried to pin the killings on Swann. He certainly had Blackery convinced. He must have had plenty of opportunity to get a good look at him at the pub when he got William to snap away with his camera. William was probably just a stooge for Greaves at that time.'

'But Swann disappeared, and so he needed a new culprit to condemn,' he said.

'At the time, I think Swann was the main scapegoat. Maybe Greaves didn't know whether he could fully trust William to do everything he wanted him to do and so he hedged his bets.'

'So, do you reckon that the performance he gave in the interview was purely an act? The frightened persona, the biting his finger, the fear of William?' he asked.

'Yep.'

'And the woman at the canal?'

'Probably William, but it could have been Greaves trying to throw us off the scent. Look, if we're right about the rest of it, then it could have been either of them. After all, Angelica said that he never taped her mouth before and that he never spoke to her, and he spoke to me as if it was the most normal thing to do. He didn't even seem surprised that I wasn't Angelica. Let's face it, if he had been the one that had Angelica tied up in there, wouldn't he have been at least a little bit shocked to see me peering out at him? And before I moved the blanket, he called me Marion. Thinking about it, his voice sounded a little excited. A bit like he was anticipating something. It was like William was doing this for the first time,' she said.

'And she also said that he was right-handed, and I guess she would know.'

'Yeah…and look at her reaction when I said Greaves' name. She about hit the roof.'

'Where's Greaves now?' asked Sutton.

'Well, we couldn't hold him. He wasn't under arrest. So, I think he went back to Rodina Close.'

EPILOGUE

*The Karter Swann story.
10 months later.*

The room felt welcoming as the sunlight shone in through one of the large windows, and the atmosphere in the building was calm and peaceful. Even the street outside was empty of any traffic noise and not a cloud obscured the sky. In fact, there was a tranquillity about the whole day that made him feel as though the majority, if not all of his troubles, were finally behind him. He sat alone at the end of a row of six chairs, looking down at the plush dark blue carpet, unconsciously staring at the numerous cream-coloured floral circles that were haphazardly dotted around in its pattern, allowing his mind to wander freely as he did so. As he sat in the peacefulness of the room, he began to reflect on what the weirdest part of his experiences since meeting Betty Nelson at the Cactus and Coyote were. Swann had puzzled with this a number of times in the past but found that there were just too many odd things for him to decide upon as to which was the strangest of all, although the revocation of his presumption of death certificate was right up there with the craziest of them all. He often felt as though he had lived three lives. Once as Karter Swann during his innocent childhood in Bonn, Germany, the next as Kevin Marshall and his journey as a secretive recluse in Crete, then the third as Karter Swann again, the man that he wanted to be. But this renewed Karter Swann carried the scars of life's experiences. Some of which had been indelibly impressed into his mind as well as creatively inked onto his arm.

From the moment that he fell for Betty's eyes of coal and chestnut hair, he was smitten. He smiled as he contemplated the days when they first engaged into a relationship, but each time that he considered this, he was plagued by the episode at the Travelodge. Every time that he thought about what happened, he felt a dark and sinister cloud of guilt engulf him like a recurring nightmare. He knew that he deserved it. It felt like a kind of repetitive punishment. Whichever way he tried to play it out in his mind, he just couldn't get away from the facts. It happened. Sometimes he even felt sorry for himself although that didn't tend to last very long. Mostly, he felt sorry for

Betty and although he had tried to pluck up the courage to explain the whole scenario to her, he had never managed to allow the words to seep out. She had lost her sister, and although she would say that she didn't care, he knew that the natural kindness in her would never permit this to be so. How could he tear her apart all over again? Elisha was out of both of their lives, so why let her create even more destruction than she had already done.

Meeting Betty had altered the path of his life, and it wasn't necessarily always for the better, although he could never know where he might have ended up had she not wandered into the pub. Before she walked into the Cactus and Coyote, he was just a barman, just like any other. The shifts were as regular and uneventful as they could be. He worked, he chatted up the local girls and he went home, usually alone. But then…then, it all changed.

It wasn't a matter of him having any regrets about their chance encounter, the opposite in fact. He loved her. Always had, right from that first meeting. Right from when she used to tease him about his lack of knowledge of the Minnesota Vikings or even that they existed. It was just that so much had taken place since. The period where Betty had believed Elisha's fabricated story was really hard. He guessed that he couldn't really expect it to be anything else. But even through that very difficult spell, he never really gave up entirely, even though there were occasions when he felt that the candle had blown out forever. Swann consoled his own misdemeanours and his unfaithful act by thinking of it as more of an entrapment. It was, in reality, just that. He asked himself why he didn't just get out of the shower and leave Room 8. But he knew the answer, and he knew that no amount of wishing would change a single thing. He had to acknowledge that Elisha's plan was a pretty good one. It certainly had him cornered and served to expose his inner frailty. The existence of Elisha Nelson had made so much difference to the last few years and yet, it wasn't even her idea for him to have the tattoo that caused him so much trouble, it was Betty's. He couldn't blame Elisha for that, and it was an innocent enough intention.

Until it changed everything…

He wasn't even sure who Haley Breen was at the time, but he certainly found himself learning fast. How he was so very glad that he had an alibi for the time of her murder. The signature tattoo might have created a whole host of other problems and led to a very different outcome otherwise. But the horror of that time didn't just go away when he employed the services of an Irish Army Reserve Medic. If he had known that Claudia De Luca was going to be another victim, he may well have stayed away for a lot longer. Another girl, another tattoo, another photograph. He would never forget the stomach-wrenching feeling when he discovered the first batch of grotesque photographs that had been sent to him at the pub. Unfortunately, it didn't stop there. But now, they were all in the possession of the police, and he didn't have to worry about them anymore. They were just a part of an investigation. He didn't have to worry about the tattoo either. It had taken four hours for it to be covered with a different and much larger design, but it was worth each and every rapid stab of the needle.

As for who the woman in the Supermarket was, he wasn't sure. He was almost certain that it wasn't Elisha after all, and he believed that she really didn't know about the photographs, since the police had explained where they thought they had come from. However, his demons had not all been buried out of sight. There was one more. A certain Odhran O'Connell. Swann knew that he would surface again at some point. He knew that O'Connell would bide his time and wait for the dust to settle. It was in his nature. He had to concede that O'Connell had done precisely what he had asked of him and that he owed him. He just didn't know what he owed him or how costly it might turn out to be. Knowing how O'Connell worked, it wouldn't be money. That's too final. A debt to Odhran O'Connell was a heavy burden to bear, and complete relaxation was a luxury that Swann could not afford to enjoy just yet. With Ray Keller dead, Swann figured that O'Connell would be back, looking for answers. It could yet turn out to be a rather complex conversation. But he would deal with it.

A door clicked behind him. He looked up to see Betty holding the door open. She was wearing a lemon lace bandeau dress with heels. Through the door opening, Swann could see that Detective Constable Steve Kingham and his wife, Lucy, were waiting in the hallway.

'That's my nervous wee out of the way,' she said, clutching a modest posy of yellow roses.

'Are you ready then?' asked Swann.

'Yep. Are you?'

'Yeah, I'm ready.'

They clasped hands, kissed each other, and walked back out of the room and across the hall to the Ceremony Room at Cobbe's Chapel, less than 100 feet from where Karter Swann's memorial service had taken place.

EPILOGUE

The Patrol Officer Gregory Bonner story.
One month after the discovery of Caterina Marks

There were a couple of significant things that had occurred in the life of Gregory Bonner in the recent few weeks, other than the obvious. One was that he had moved out of his old, rather dilapidated house and into another property on the edge of the city boundaries. The two-story house was set next to a parkland in Rosemount, a city in Dakota County, on the southern edge of the Twin Cities Metropolitan Area. It was only a stone's throw from Vermillion Highlands Nature Reserve where Bonner had become accustomed to taking walks on his days off. It was relaxing in the summertime, but Bonner was expectantly anticipating that the next winter might provide him with some snow-covered panorama's all of his own. His beloved old den, where he had spent several hours in his own company talking to Caterina, was a distant memory already. The new house had a bigger, better den and Bonner was in the process of installing his new computer. He had managed to trade in some of his old, outdated equipment in a deal with an old college friend who worked at Chieveley's Computers in downtown Minneapolis. It was one of those strokes of luck. Bonner just happened to wander in one day having had no previous knowledge that the man worked there and found himself in a position to fashion just the sort of deal that suited him. Initially, he had promised himself that he would keep all his records at home, but he knew that it was unlikely to work out that way, and providing he was discreet when he loaded up the Snow and Cold Index at the police station, he thought that he could just about get away with it.

The second piece of good fortune that had come his way was strictly work related. He hadn't quite been fully prepared for the sudden burst of delight that he felt, but when he learned, through the office grapevine, that Big Toni was not going to be leaving the department after all, he actually shed a tear. It had taken a number of years for Bonner to establish a better understanding of his Captain's mood swings but once he had realised that his apparent cantankerousness was no more than his natural way of getting things done, Bonner felt that he had established a much better connection with him. Especially since their combined involvement at the old Nelson property, which was a good job as it turned out, for the good news didn't stop there.

Four days after the Caterina Marks mystery had been resolved, Bonner and Big Toni were both summoned to Deputy Chief Jack Bolton's office. It wasn't unusual for Captain Rodrigues to step into the Deputy's lair, but it wasn't such a common occurrence for Bonner to get an invite, and the fact that they were going in together was particularly off-putting for Bonner, and a little confusing for Big Toni.

'You're going in too?' he asked.

'Yeah, I got an email this morning saying that I should be in his office at 13:00,' replied Bonner.

'Hope it's not about my report on the Caterina Marks case.'

'What report?' said Bonner, nervously.

'I just told you yesterday what report. Honestly, Bonner…'

Big Toni waved a dismissive hand and grumbled to himself as the two men walked side by side down the corridor, towards the red mahogany door at the end that clearly stated in bold brass lettering that it was the office of J. Bolton. Deputy Chief of Patrol. Once inside the two men were invited to sit.

'Thank you for coming, Gentlemen,' said the Deputy Chief, 'I expect you're both wondering why I've asked you to come.'

It was one of those statements that wasn't really a question but more of an opening comment. Big Toni and Bonner remained quiet and waited for whatever was going to follow.

'Well then. I'll tell you. Oh, and, by the way, thank you for your report, Captain.'

Big Toni mumbled a courteous 'Sir', no wiser as to whether it was going to receive any criticism. He figured that if there were any inadequacies that he would find out soon enough.

'I assume that the word is already out there, but I shall tell you both officially that, you Captain Rodrigues, will be staying in the department for the foreseeable future. How long that is, is something that we'll find out as we go along, but I wouldn't worry too much because it was my recommendation and so as long as I'm here, you will be too.'

'Thank you, sir,' said Big Toni, none too relieved but trying not to show it.

'I'm not in the custom of losing a good man if I can possibly avoid doing so.'

Bonner was happy to hear it from the Deputy Chief.

'That is only a part of the reason that I've asked you to come here today. I have to say that I didn't expect you both to find Miss Caterina Marks, but I'm exceptionally delighted that you did. At least in one way. As you both know, I was under a certain amount of pressure to do something about the seemingly endless list of missing persons that related to our department. Most of which will remain missing for all eternity, I shouldn't wonder. It wasn't until I learned that this unfortunate young lady was personally known to Mr Bonner, here, that I decided to allow him to pursue, what I originally considered to be, a hopeless case. Don't think that I was doubting your ability, Mr Bonner, but let's just say that these people so rarely turn up after such a lengthy period of time, if indeed they turn up at all.'

Bonner began to feel quite pleased with himself. At the same time, he wondered how the Deputy Chief had learned of his connection to Caterina.

'And, following the successful outcome, as much as it was ever likely to be, and since you both did such a good job of finding her, I have been talking to the Assistant Chief. Now, seeing as he was the instigator of this push to eliminate at least one person from the 'list of the lost', as he put it, he has instructed me to set you both another task. Another needle in a haystack, if you will. I have already accepted for you because you don't have any choice. It was also your success that enabled me to ensure that Captain Rodrigues didn't stray from the department prematurely. What do you say? By the way, at this point I should advise you that 'Yes' is the only option available to you both. So, that's it then,' said a buoyant Deputy Chief.

Big Toni and Bonner thanked the Deputy Chief and turned to leave the office.

'Oh! Sit, sit, sit. I nearly forgot the point of you both coming in here in the first place.'

Big Toni and Bonner exchanged confused glances and took their seats again.

'There's something else, sir?' said Big Toni.

'Yes, there is, Captain. Or should I say, Major?'

'Sir?' said Big Toni.

'Hold your horses, it isn't official just yet, but just give me a little more time and I'm pretty sure that it'll be coming your way fairly soon.'

'Sir, that's…I mean, thank you, sir,' said Big Toni.

'Great news,' said Bonner as he stood and stepped towards the door.

'And where do you think you're going Mr Bonner?' said the Deputy Chief.

'Err...nowhere, sir,' he said, clumsily resuming an awkward sitting position.

'Good, because I haven't quite finished with you either. Now then, I won't be offering you a promotion, like Captain Rodrigues, but I can tell you that I am going to nominate you for Trooper of the Year. Now, I'm not saying that you'll get it, but just to be nominated is still a remarkable achievement, so fingers crossed that something good comes from it.'

'Oh, that's amazing...I mean, thank you, sir,' said a delighted Bonner.

Finally, Big Toni and Bonner left the Deputy Chief's office and headed back to the main part of the department. Both were fairly overwhelmed with the recent unexpected events. Big Toni closed his office door and sat down, trying to come to terms with his own good news and Bonner made his way to his desk. Before he reached it, Rachel Ortiz shouted to him from behind her computer screen.

'Hey, Bonner. There's a note on your desk for you. Somebody wants you to call them.'

'How long ago?'

'Ten, maybe fifteen minutes. Not long,' she said.

Bonner thanked her and picked up the note. He read the message and picked up the phone. In a matter of only ten minutes, Bonner was in his car, heading for Golden Valley and the house of his old friend, Harry Bones.

When he arrived at Harry's house, he had no real idea of what the trouble was but there had been something in Harry's voice that bothered Bonner enough for him to come straight over. When Harry opened the door, Bonner was taken aback by his old friend's expression.

'Harry, are you feeling ok?'

'No, not really,' he said.

Bonner followed him into the back room and sat beside him on a dinning chair whilst Harry slumped into his favourite old leather chair.

'Are you in pain? I can put a call in if...'

'No, no. I'm not ill. I just need to talk to you, that's all,' he said.

'Ok,' said Bonner.

Harry looked as though he was trying to summon the courage to say something or trying to remember exactly what he wanted to say. Bonner wondered what his old friend was going to tell him.

'Harry, whatever it is, you can tell me.'

'I should have done that a very long time ago,' said Harry.

'Well, we're here now, Harry. So…'

Bonner waited patiently while Harry reached for his handkerchief and wiped his eyes. At this moment, Harry Bones really did look his age. Bonner had never seen him in such an apparently distressed state. He asked Harry, again, whether he needed any medical assistance, but Harry was adamant that he would be fine in a few more minutes. Bonner offered to make him some tea and Harry gratefully accepted. He said that it would help stop his mouth drying up. Bonner went into the kitchen, found two mugs, two tea bags and boiled the kettle.

'I'll have mine black. Put a little drop of water in it, will you, just to cool it a little. There's milk in the fridge if you want it,' called Harry.

As soon as the tea was prepared, Bonner returned to the back room and sat down beside Harry again. Harry carefully sipped his tea and put the mug down on a side table. He turned to Bonner.

'I'm sorry,' he said.

Bonner still didn't know what it was that Harry needed to be sorry for.

'It's ok, Harry.'

'No, no, it's not. I'm sorry that I didn't tell you long ago,' he said, as his voice began to crack and his old eyes glistened.

Bonner could see that Harry had a very serious look in his eyes. Something was troubling him, and Bonner could tell that whatever it was, it sounded as though Harry had carried this around with him for some time. He assumed, years. He was right. Whatever the burden was, Bonner was here to help his old friend share it, even though he was a little concerned as to where it might lead. Bonner decided that the best thing to do was to be as patient as possible and allow Harry to take as much time as he needed. Rushing anything wasn't an option.

'It's about that girl. Caterina Marks.'

Bonner's stomach knotted, but he tried hard not to show it.

'What about her?' he asked, tentatively.

Harry took a few breaths and got himself ready to speak. The room was eerily silent. Bonner felt a chill run through his body. All that could be heard outside was the birds that were squabbling over the scraps on the birdfeeder.

'Some years back, before the girls moved to England, I got a visit,' Harry began.

'You mean Betty and Elisha?' asked Bonner, more for confirmation than anything else.

'Yes, I do. I was here, at home, when I looked out and saw Betty's bike on the grass at the front of the house. Naturally, I thought she had come around, perhaps for some of my lemonade that she loved, but it wasn't her. It was Elisha. So, I let her in.'

Harry paused to take another couple of deep breaths as if he was controlling his breathing. Then he continued with his story.

'Anyway, we talked about her mother. You recall Penelope, don't you?'

'Yes, she was a lovely lady,' said Bonner.

'Yes, she was that alright. She was…very special to me. Anyway, I had seen things…at the house. Elisha had too. Wade Nelson was a cruel and evil man. He used to…hit Penelope. He used to make her sleep in the shed at night, you know that bit. So, as I said, we talked about her mother. Elisha wanted to know more about the things that I had seen, and she dragged it out of me,' said Harry.

'Yes, I recall you telling me about this before, Harry,' said Bonner.

'Ah, yes. So, we talked, and I described what I had seen, and Elisha told me about the parts that she was aware of at the time. It was a difficult conversation to have but she was so determined to know.'

Harry seemed to stop, abruptly. Bonner wondered if that was it. He waited for a few moments but before he could say anything, Harry began again.

'That was only part of it. I'm sorry that I haven't told you before, but I just couldn't. I swore that I would never tell anyone and as the time went by, I couldn't see how it could help anything. So, I just kept it to myself. I know that it was wrong, and I hope that you will forgive me,' said Harry.

'Look Harry, whatever happened to Mrs Nelson, all those years ago can't change anything now,' said Bonner.

'I know it can't but that's not why I asked you here. It's about the young girl that went missing.'

Bonner had been so horrified to think that Wade Nelson used to treat his wife so badly that he had almost forgotten Harry's reference to Caterina. Now he was getting concerned.

'I was there when you and the others were in the Nelson garden with that digging machine. You wouldn't have seen me because I kept to the back of the crowd and made sure nobody spotted me. But I was there. I stayed right until the end. Even after most of them had dispersed. I walked away and back again. You were too busy to notice me by then.'

'What were you doing?' asked Bonner.

'Watching. Waiting.'

'Waiting for what?'

'Waiting for you to find her,' said Harry.

Bonner looked into Harry's eyes.

'What?' he said.

'It was when Elisha came here, that day, before they moved away. She told me something.'

'I think you had better tell me, Harry,' said Bonner.

'I'm going to. That's why you're here. I can't carry this around any longer,' said Harry.

Harry paused again and wiped his eyes once more. Bonner didn't care if it took all night. He wasn't going to leave until he had heard everything that Harry had to say. Bonner's mind was racing now. *Wade Nelson did it,* he thought, *I knew it.*

'On the day that Caterina went missing, she was supposed to be seeing Betty, because she was upset about losing old Hastings. Elisha said that Betty had pleaded with her father not to put him down, but he wouldn't listen. The night before old Hastings died, Wade Nelson made the girls dig his grave. Like I said, he was a cruel man. In the morning, he made the girls watch as he shot Hastings with his crossbow. By this time Caterina was already on her way. It was just around breakfast time, I think. I don't know the exact timings, but I think that was about right. Anyway, Elisha said that her father fired a bolt from his bow into poor old Hastings. It must have been horrible for the girls to have to witness. Elisha said that Betty had already ran indoors, and that Wade Nelson shouted after her or something like that. He was really angry that she had gone inside. But Elisha was still outside in the garden.'

Harry's eyes filled with tears as he struggled to relay his story to Bonner.

'Take your time, Harry. If you need to take a break, it's ok,' said Bonner.

Harry sipped some more of his tea and composed himself. His hand was shaking as he put the mug down again.

'Hastings was dead. Wade Nelson made Elisha pick the old dog up and temporarily put him in the shed. She said she was covered in blood and dog hair. It must have been terrible for her. Anyway, then…'

'It's ok, Harry,' said Bonner.

'I wish it was, young man. I wish it was,' he cried.

Bonner told Harry that whatever it was that he needed to tell him, he would treat it with confidentiality. He told him that he had done this many times during his years as a Patrol Officer and that it was all part of his job.

'Making arrests is part of your job too, isn't it?' said Harry.

'Well, yes, but what's that got to do with this?' asked Bonner.

Harry sighed loudly and picked up his mug of tea, drinking down the rest of it. He placed the mug on the side table and announced to Bonner that he was going to tell him everything and try his best to be as accurate as possible. Bonner was beginning to feel very concerned that Harry had something alarming to say, but there was still a part of him that didn't believe that it could be that bad. *Arrests?*

'Ok, so,' began Harry, 'It was the day when old Hastings was put to death by that evil Wade Nelson. Betty was inside the house and Elisha was in the garden. Elisha said that she had to move old Hastings into the shed, and that her father was adamant that she should hurry up. She thought that maybe he didn't want the neighbours to see old Hastings there and especially not see how he had been so horribly killed. Elisha said that she put the dog in the shed and stepped back out. She felt dirty and was shaking. Wade Nelson had leaned the crossbow against the house and was fiddling around with a box of bolts, or something like that. For some reason, it was that moment that Elisha picked up the crossbow. She said that she was almost in some kind of trance, as if she was sleepwalking or something like that. She told me that she could feel the hatred building up inside her. Elisha had had a tough time growing up and had always been second best as far as *he* was concerned. I guess this must have festered inside her for a long time. Anyhow, Elisha said that she could see that the Serpent, I think she called it, had a bolt in the chamber. Not chamber…track, no. Groove. I think that's what she called it. Anyway, basically it was loaded. From here on in everything changed for Elisha. And eventually me too, I guess.'

'How, Harry?' asked Bonner.

'She raised the crossbow up and fired at her father. She said she wanted to kill him. She said that she had wanted to get the chance for a long time and that this wasn't the first time that she had thought about it. Even when the girls had been out hunting in the woods, Elisha had wondered whether it would look like an accident if she fired at him. But she had never done it because Betty was always there. She didn't care about hiding a secret like that if it was just hers to hide but she didn't want Betty to have to keep quiet about it. In case she spoke about it, as much as anything else, she said.'

'Did she hit him?'

'No. She missed. Elisha said he bent over at the wrong moment, apparently.'

'Wow. Lucky for him, and lucky for Elisha that she didn't commit murder,' said Bonner.

'Yeah, I guess. Unfortunately. It didn't end there. Elisha said that her father thought that she had fired it accidently, so he made her go to fetch the bolt. Elisha went to look for it and as she was delving around amongst the Pines, she found more than she bargained for.'

'No,' said Bonner.

'Yeah,' said Harry, 'She found Caterina Marks. She was dead. The bolt had hit her in the chest.'

'Oh, Christ, Harry,' said Bonner, holding his head in his hands.

Harry sat in stunned silence as the weight he had carried for so many years drained from him. He wept quietly. Bonner felt paralysed and couldn't move or speak for several minutes. Harry was talking but Bonner he could no longer comprehend any of what he said. It was as if the room had become a void where all the furniture had vanished and all that was left was Harry and Bonner, surrounded by absolutely nothing. It was Bonner who managed to speak first.

'She was in the ground.'

'Yes, I know. Elisha said that Wade Nelson dragged her across the lawn and straight into the hole that had been dug for the dog. Elisha said that he folded her legs around her so that she fitted and then the evil swine made Elisha cover her with earth. He didn't even help her with that. When she had been covered, he made Elisha get Hastings from the shed and place him on top. Then she had to fill in the rest. That's why the old dog was on a mound of earth. And you know the rest,' said Harry.

'So that's why Wade Nelson didn't want a proper search to be conducted and why he made good use of his friendship with Ken Toft.'

Harry nodded.

'And you've protected Elisha for all these years,' said Bonner.

Harry nodded again, empty of words.

'And Wade Nelson hung himself because of the memory of it all?' asked Bonner.

'I guess,' said Harry, quietly, not wanting to mention the letters that he wrote on behalf of his beloved Poppy.

'The bolt wasn't found,' said Bonner.

'I don't know about that. She never said.'

'It sounds too gruesome to even think about,' said Bonner.

'I'm so very sorry, young man,' said Harry.

EPILOGUE

The DI Sutton / DS Linton story.
Seven weeks later.

'Did you go to see Angelica again earlier, like you said you were going to?' Grace called from the kitchen.

'Yes, I did,' said Sutton, as he slouched on the sofa with one eye on the athletics meeting that was on the TV.

'And?'

'And she was fine.'

'Has she kept her appointments with the counsellor?'

'She has. She's been really good, according to her Mum.'

Grace was feeling particularly inquisitive, but she wasn't getting much back from Marc.

'Did you talk to her about that Abbot bloke? I thought you said she was fretting about him still being around the last time you saw her,' said Grace as she walked into the living room and handed him a plated sandwich and a cup of tea.

'Thanks. I did and she was, but she isn't now. I think she knows that it's pretty unlikely that he will show himself. Anyway, I'd be surprised if he was anywhere near.'

'Let's hope he doesn't,' said Grace as she sat herself down beside him.

'He won't,' he said.

'Athletics? Didn't know you liked that.'

'Yeah, I do. I don't put it on because I know you aren't keen.'

'Well, how considerate, but if you like it, then watch it. I can always find something else to do,' she said.

Sutton smiled and gave a half nod as he took a bite of the sandwich and resumed his concentration on the athletics.

'Got any idea where he is?' asked Grace.

'Who?'

'Abbot, obviously.'

'Sadly not. We've done all we can to make every Police Force in the country aware of what he looks like. With any luck we'll get some good news soon.'

'Proper gave you the slip, didn't he?' she said.

'Hmm…For now,' he said.

'Where's that other one? William.'

'Still living in that flat opposite the bakery in Abigail Street. We're keeping an eye on him, but I don't think he'll be a problem. It's not as though he was actually directly responsible for anything that happened to Angelica, and we've talked to him over and over, but he really isn't much help. All the answers are with Greaves. Or Abbot.'

'Yeah, but he did talk to her in Trenton Street before she went missing, and he pushed his sister, or step-sister, Marion, down the stairs and killed her, and he's got previous for hitting that girl.'

'Hold on, hold on,' said Sutton, 'Where did you get all this from?'

'Nowhere,' she said, defensively.

'Carrie?' he said.

'No, she wouldn't.'

'So, you just took a wild guess then?' said Sutton.

'Well, no but…. you told me most of it.'

'Yeah, well, don't go blabbing to anyone.'

'I won't. I never would.'

'Good. Anyway, we don't know who pushed Marion. The way things have turned out, I would imagine that William was either coerced or threatened into it. If indeed it was him. The last time we spoke to him, he changed his story again and said it was Michael that pushed her. And for the record, we are only surmising it was William that spoke to Angelica. Even she still isn't sure. All she can remember is that it was a man, but she hasn't definitely confirmed it was William. She said that he didn't look like that, but I can't imagine who else it could have been,' he said.

'Well, I bet it was him. It wasn't that Michael Greaves, or she would have said.'

'Michael Abbot. You're thinking of Robin Greaves.'

'Same thing,' said Grace.

Sutton just nodded and sipped his tea as the athletics continued in the background.

'Anyway, there's one thing I do know.'

'What's that?' he said.

'That Emily Roache was a lucky girl, especially as her photograph was in that collection. You could have been fishing her out of the canal.'

'Who says her photograph was in there?'

'No-one, really,' said Grace, sheepishly.

Sutton sat and shook his head slowly.

Sutton and Grace sat staring at the athletes as they assembled at the start line for the first heat of the Women's 5000m. Sutton knew a few of them and was trying to explain to Grace as to who the favourite was, but Grace was more interested in what they looked like.

'She's pretty. Oh, and she's got a nice smile,' she said.

'I don't think being pretty is going to help much in this,' said Sutton.

'Well, I'd let the pretty ones go first to give them a head start,' she said.

'You'd win hands down then,' he said and kissed her cheek.

As Sutton watched the athletes edge towards the start line in readiness for the start gun, the house phone began to ring. Grace got up immediately and made her way to the kitchen to answer it on the cordless extension phone.

'Are you expecting someone?' said Sutton.

'No, not really.'

Grace pulled the kitchen door closed behind her saying that she would keep the sound out so that he could watch the runners, without being disturbed. Sutton hadn't really heard what she had said.

'Hello.'

'Hi, it's me,' said Carrie.

'Hi, and no I haven't had a chance yet,' said Grace.

'You must have by now, what are you messing about at?' said Carrie.

'I'll tell him tonight, I promise.'

'Well, hurry up or I'm going to burst.'

'Don't you dare, Madam,' said Grace.

'I won't, I won't. Have you thought of any names yet? What if it's a boy?'

'Oh, I can't decide. I'm still getting used to the idea.'

'What about a girl?' said Carrie, impatiently.

'Well, I thought of Carrie-Jane.'

'Oh, Grace. Oh, I love you. Oh, I hope it's a girl.'

Paris, France.

The Galerie de Paléontologie et d'Anatomie comparée was due to close in approximately 15 minutes. It is also recognised as the Centre de Recherche en Paléontologie and is situated in Jardin Des Plantes, only a stone's throw from the River Seine. Fortunately, the purposefully chosen location of his accommodation for tonight meant that he would only have to endure a relatively short walk to the Hôtel Libertel Austerlitz on the Boulevard de l'Hôspital. Palaeontology had become a fascination of his ever since he had undertaken an online Palaeontology Diploma Course a few years ago. As with most of the enterprises he attempted, it didn't exceed beyond the first module. However, he was smitten, and had promised himself that he would visit this particular museum whenever the opportunity arose and as luck would have it, he needed to make himself scarce, and grasped the chance to come to Paris and finally spend some time in the company of like-minded individuals in the surroundings he had rapidly grown to love. The hours spent inside the spectacular building had accelerated by far too quickly, and soon it would already be time to move on.

He had remained in the Jardin Des Plantes for the majority of the day since his arrival at the Gard Du Nord on the northern side of the city, only exiting briefly, to buy some lunch. The early morning train from Strasbourg to Paris had been on time and had delivered him feeling refreshed and relaxed. It had been the perfect day. From where he presently sat, he watched the late afternoon shadows lengthen across the façade of the Musée histoire naturelle building. Rows of sweet smelling, colourful plants adorned the flower borders that attracted numerous visitors as well as numerous bees, but as the evening encroached, he knew that his initial encounter with the dinosaurs would have to be cut short. For now. But when the time was right, he would be back.

Back at the Hôtel Libertel Austerlitz he showered and then poured himself a Birra Moretti from the minibar in his room. The balcony at the rear of the hotel overlooked the Rue Buffon and beyond that, the Jardin Des Plantes. As he sat enjoying his beer, he could see the impressive roof structure of the museum as it dulled in the setting sun. As the shadows lengthened, and the tranquil hum of the traffic faded, the peacefulness of the early evening allowed him to reflect on the events that had led him to this moment. Once again, he had not an ounce of contrition for the crimes he had committed. Merely a sense of satisfaction. As hard as he had tried to locate the whereabouts of his sisters, Jennifer and Joanna, he had failed. But there had been plenty of substitutes to choose from, and it hadn't taken him too long to decide upon precisely which of them were going to become the perfect choices. He considered that the evenings spent at the Cactus and Coyote were no more than a necessity, all part of his search for the first of the girls. If he couldn't have his sisters, then he was going to have to replace them, one at a time. No rush. They had to have a similar look and similar hair; they were always extremely precious about their hair. It was imperative to him that they gave him the feeling that he was dealing with Jennifer and Joanna. By the time he disposed of them, he couldn't tell the difference, such was his warped mind.

Jennifer had abandoned him at the tip, so he dumped her on a rubbish pile. Joanna had held him down in the bath, so he discarded her body into the canal. The house, where they had all lived, was like an asylum. He would walk around at night and terrorise the twins. He would taunt them and play all manner of cruel tricks, just for fun. At least, he found it amusing. He never liked them, but Marion was different. Despite his behaviour, she always showed him love. She was special. But one day, after he had been relentlessly teasing William about her and coaxing him to push her down the stairs, the unthinkable happened. He didn't ever think that William would do it, but when he heard the crash, he came running out from his room, and there she was, at the foot of the stairs.

The twins hadn't seen it happen and he ensured that they would keep quiet about it. He found William to be an impressionable simpleton. He decided that he would deal with him later, whenever the opportunity arose. Embroiling him in the killings and the disappearance of Angelica Rowntree fitted fine with his objectives for William. His evil intention festered over a period of a few years but once he had made up his mind, he was determined to implicate William. After all, he had taken away his lovely Marion, and the immense pain of that had to be atoned for. He studied William hard and remembered his fascination for the tattoo that the barman exhibited to the impressionable young girls and how he used to revere him. He even drew it onto William's arm, piercing the skin under the pressure that he exerted, and told him how rugged he looked. Of course, William wasn't the deranged fool that scarred his victims and sent exhibits of his work to his hero, with baseless empty threats. He could hardly trust him with that part. 'Quite mad,' he sniggered.

The visits to see his mother at the Care Home had purpose too. He knew that the Police would end up talking to her one day, it seemed inevitable, so he did everything he could to muddy the waters and confuse her about the past and get her to think that William was at the heart of the events at the house. She was perplexed at the best of times anyway, so he didn't care if he added to her confusion just a little more. It was cruel but pivotal to the success of his ultimate objective of implicating his unwanted stepbrother. Killer of his beloved Marion. It would have been a lot easier to have killed her too but when he met Angelica at the garage, he saw something in her that was just too similar. She wasn't Marion but she was close enough. He decided that he would keep her safe. He would keep her warm. He would keep her alive. She would become Marion.

Back inside, he placed his travel bags onto the bed and pulled out the train tickets that would enable him to progress on his journey south in the morning. The ticket information showed that Doctor Jacob Crane would be heading to Marseille. The few days in Strasbourg had given him the time to come up with a name he liked. It would do for now. Sadly, his obsession with palaeontology would have to wait until another time. Now, it was time for dinner, and apparently the salmon was first class.

Milton Keynes UK
Ingram Content Group UK Ltd.
UKHW010749110923
428455UK00014B/795